Raves for Diana Ro...

"A nifty combination of police procedural and urban fantasy. Not too many detectives summon demons in their basement for the fun of it, but Kara Gillian is not your average law enforcement officer."

—Charlaine Harris, *New York Times* bestselling author

"Rowland's world of arcane magic and demons is fresh and original . . . [and her] characters are well-developed and distinct. . . . Dark, fast-paced, and gripping." —SciFiChick

"A fascinating mixture of a hard-boiled police procedural and gritty yet other-worldly urban fantasy. Diana Rowland's professional background as both a street cop and forensic assistant not only shows through but gives the book a realism sadly lacking in all too many urban fantasy 'crime' novels."

—L. E. Modesitt, Jr., author of the *Saga of Recluse*

"I was awestruck at the twists and turns and the, 'Oh man, why didn't I see that before!' . . . This series is top-notch in the genre."

—Felicia Day, author of
You're Never Weird on the Internet (Almost)

"Rowland once again writes the perfect blend of police procedural and paranormal fantasy." —Night Owl Paranormal

"Phenomenal world building, a tough yet vulnerable heroine, a captivating love triangle, and an increasingly compelling metanarrative that just gets juicier with each book. . . . Blows most other urban fantasies out of the park." —All Things Urban Fantasy

"I would say [the series] just keeps getting better—but it was already so good that I'm not sure that's even possible."

—Fangs for the Fantasy

"*Mark of the Demon* crosses police procedure with weird magic. Diana Rowland's background makes her an expert in the former, and her writing convinces me she's also an expert in the latter in this fast-paced story that ends with a bang."

—Carrie Vaughn, *New York Times* bestselling author

LEGACY OF THE
DEMON

DIANA ROWLAND

DAW BOOKS, INC.

DONALD A. WOLLHEIM, FOUNDER

375 Hudson Street, New York, NY 10014

**ELIZABETH R. WOLLHEIM
SHEILA E. GILBERT
PUBLISHERS**

www.dawbooks.com

First Printing, October 2016

1 2 3 4 5 6 7 8 9

To Anna. Duh.

ACKNOWLEDGMENTS

This is where I struggle to remember everyone who helped out with the book, whether by providing information or giving support of one type or another. This is also where I realize that I'm absolutely going to forget someone, and I rail at myself for not being more organized and not keeping a list of the people who helped me out during the writing process. Seriously. Every Single Book I tell myself, "This will be the book that I stay on top of all that stuff!" And yet here I am, Every Single Time, racking my brain to remember the people who made it possible for me to even *have* an "Acknowledgements" page.

So, I'm going to take the easy (wimpy) way out and give an open and heartfelt THANK YOU to everyone who helped me get this book into its final majestic form, as well as everyone who simply put up with me when I was tearing my hair out. And, of course, an even bigger THANKS BILLIONS to every one of my readers. Because, duh. Y'all are my kind of insane.

Chapter 1

"Volcanoes spew the devil's flame in our heartland. Fire rains from the sky. Sinkholes suck sinners into the bowels of hell, while rifts vomit a scourge of demons into the streets of our cities. These are the plagues of our times, the signs of God's fury at our wicked—"

The bellow of a *reyza* accompanied by the shriek of tearing metal cut off the rest of the protester's tirade. I threw myself to the asphalt as the demon whizzed a tank hatch cover in my direction. It careened off the Stryker Armored Personnel Carrier behind me and slammed edge first less than a foot from my head into the Piggly Wiggly parking lot.

"Gillian! Status!" That was the squad leader, Sergeant Debbie Roma.

"Five by five!" I shouted as soon as I found my voice—and after I made sure I was still in one piece. The red block letters on the quivering metal hatch seemed to mock me. *DIRT*— Demonic Incursion Retaliation and Tactics. Yeah, we were retaliating. Like kids throwing marshmallows at rabid dogs. "DIRT" was supposed to represent our willingness to fight hard and dirty, but ten minutes into the skirmish and we'd already lost one tank.

But no people, to my relief. Petrev and Hines had managed to scramble clear of the tank and take cover behind an abandoned Toyota. Both Strykers and the Light Armored Vehicle were still intact, as were all fifteen members of Alpha Squad— though at the moment we were pinned down while the demon threw chunks of metal and arcane shrapnel at us. A scant meter in front of me, a two-foot-long, frost-rimmed crevice rippled with magenta flames. So far, the demon had only flown reconnaissance passes over the small dimensional rift, but I knew perfectly well he hadn't made a trip from the main incursion rift a quarter mile away just to sightsee.

Demons had been coming through the rifts ever since the arcane valve explosion at the Beaulac Police Department two months ago, and I—along with every other DIRT arcane advisor—still had no flaming clue *why*. Rifts opened at unpredictable intervals all over the world, destroying anything or anyone in the location. An incursion of demons inevitably followed, during which they harassed and attacked nearby citizens while one or more of their number made enigmatic adjustments to the rifts. If I could figure out what their end goal was, humans could develop a counter strategy.

In the meantime, we fought back with what tools we had: guns and grit and graphene-composite nets.

The demon beat his wings and roared a challenge. He was, hands down, the biggest reyza I'd ever seen in all my years as a demon summoner. At least twelve feet tall, with a wingspan four times that—half again as big as Gestamar or Kehlirik. Needle-sharp black horns thrust from his head on either side of a thick ridge, and yellowed fangs curved from a mouth filled with flesh-rending teeth. Broad nostrils flared within a bestial face, and his thick, sinuous tail thrashed back and forth, a weapon as deadly as his claws. Scars crisscrossed his skin in patterns that spoke of claws and teeth and frequent battles—unlike any reyza I'd known before. And though I'd never heard of a demon wearing jewelry, there was no mistaking the gold that glinted from a half dozen thick hoops in his ears or the heavy bands that circled biceps and wrists.

"Two months now since Satan and his demons were hurled to Earth. Time is running out for you sinners to beg for salvation, lest you be thrown into the lake of fire with the idolaters, the vile, the unbelievers, the sports fans, the comic book freaks, the hypocrites." The protester ranted on from the "safe" distance of the far side of the highway, his voice amplified by speakers mounted in the bed of his pickup and punctuated with random squeals and shrieks from arcane interference. Half a dozen people mingled near him, carrying enormous signs that said, in a variety of ways, that everyone was going to burn in hell except them.

Above the protesters, the morning sky shimmered with orange and magenta, beautiful and hideous, painted by arcane flames. Two days ago, the Beaulac Country Club tennis courts had crumbled into the maw of a fifty-foot-long dimensional rift, the tenth to form in the area. Small wonder that Beaulac was practically a ghost town now. Everything within a half-mile radius of the valve blast had been quarantined and cordoned off, and anyone who could leave Beaulac did. These days, nowhere was truly safe, but anywhere was safer than here.

The rift at the tennis courts was a relatively small one, but it had disgorged a number of vicious demons over the past forty-eight hours. Dozens of *kzak, savik,* and *graa,* and less than an hour ago this big ass reyza who was determined to transform the Piggly Wiggly parking lot into his own demon playground. Not that it would hurt business. A good two-thirds of the grocery store had been destroyed last week by a tornado that appeared out of a sunny sky, tracked an arrow-straight line for a hundred yards, then disappeared. Sadly, that wasn't the weirdest disaster to hit the area since the valve explosion. Hell, that didn't even make the top five.

The reyza leaped into flight from the top of the tank.

"The skeeter's aloft!" Roma shouted. "Cover!"

Maroon-fatigued squad members moved, but though I kept my eye on the "skeeter" as he gained altitude, I stayed put. My arcane skills were still a long way from their previous full strength—before I was ambushed and my abilities nearly obliterated—but I'd managed to regain complete use of my *othersight.* That allowed me to assess the little rift and the demon's arcane tactics, and give my squad a snowball's chance of winning. However, there were moments—such as this one— where I felt the loss of my abilities keenly. Even though we had no way to close the rifts, it *was* possible to arcanely "lock" them to prevent them from expanding. A rift this small would take about ten minutes of uninterrupted focus to lock it, but unfortunately I couldn't shape the potency to do so on my own. Vince Pellini and I usually partnered up to set the locks, but I'd split off with Alpha Squad to chase the big reyza, and only realized the beastie had been heading toward this mini-rift when we damn near fell into it.

The reyza swooped past, and I shielded my head with my hands, expecting the whine of the stinging arcane scattershot he'd peppered us with a dozen times before. Instead, a heavy *thoop thoop thoop* signaled the demon equivalent of an arcane grenade launcher.

No time to run for cover. Shiiiiiit. Adrenaline spiking, I tucked into a tight ball in the hopes of reducing the size of the demon's target. It was a solid plan except for one tiny detail: the demon wasn't aiming for me. The salvo struck the crevice, sending up flashes of purple and green.

For a heartbeat, nothing changed, then the asphalt heaved and buckled. The ring of frost expanded from the now gaping crevice, raced toward me and past to cover the parking lot. Magenta flames shot high, and the fissure screamed like a tortured soul.

Dismay left me colder than the frosted ground. I pushed up to a crouch and called out to Roma. "Sarge! He's widening the rift!" There was ample room now for demons such as *luhrek* and immature *savik* to come through—no less dangerous despite their smaller size. Not good when our resources were already strained to the breaking point.

"SkeeterCheater!" At Roma's command, Petrev and Wohlreich scrambled to deploy the lightweight, graphene-enhanced net over the rift and anchor it deep into the asphalt. DIRT had developed the nets as a counter-incursion measure since the demons were a helluva lot easier to kill before they emerged. The nets weren't a perfect solution, especially for large rifts, but anything that delayed the demons gave us a bit more advantage.

The reyza let out a triumphant bellow as he landed atop a Buick sedan. The roof buckled under his weight, and the side windows cracked, then burst.

Breathing deeply in an effort to settle my racing pulse, I remained crouched as I studied him. He'd already dodged and deflected everything we'd thrown at him, but there were a few tricks left in our bag.

The reyza beat his wings once, then folded them close. He swiveled his head toward me and bared his teeth—his personal promise to give me the extra special painful death—then traced a swooping pattern on his chest with one claw. Potency the color of old blood flickered. Sigils flared on his torso and sent a shimmering web over his head, limbs, and wings. I grimaced. No wonder we hadn't touched him yet.

"*Triple* duty," I called out to Roma. Her sharp curse told me her opinion of *full* arcane armor on a demon this size. We'd learned the hard way that aiming center mass on any demon was a waste of ammo, but we also knew that limbs and wings usually weren't shielded as well—until this bad boy.

I'd become an expert at adapting tactics in order to defeat demons, and I had no moral dilemma about killing them. *They* were attacking *us*.

It was the brand new orders, handed down this morning, that I had qualms about: *Capture* as many demons as possible, with reyzas the highest priority targets.

"Kowal!" Roma's voice carried across the grocery store parking lot to the Stryker on the far side. "Shimmy that lizard before it finishes getting into its party gown!"

I couldn't help but smile. *Force the demon out of that position before it gets fully armored.* Radio comms were useless so close to a rift, which meant the majority of commands were shouted. But since the demons could hear every word, human soldiers used idioms and code phrases that would be tough for any non-native speaker to understand. It made for a glimmer of humor in an otherwise grim setting.

"On it!" A woman with messy red curls peeking from beneath her helmet swiveled the APC's grenade launcher toward the reyza. I tensed as she fired two grenades. With inhuman reflexes, the demon swatted the first in my direction while the other sailed into the vehicle under him. I scuttled away, but to my relief—and horror—the grenade bounced across the pavement, danced on the SkeeterCheater, then tumbled through and into the rift.

The ground shuddered, and a gout of magenta fire erupted from the rift even as a blast rocked the Buick. Flames leaped through the windows, and the reyza roared and took flight.

Roma barked orders, and squad members scrambled to new tactical positions. I took the opportunity to belly crawl behind an upthrust of asphalt then resumed my search for the demon's weak spots.

Roma remained crouched behind a pile of concrete rubble, skimming her gaze over the area as she checked on her people and considered options. At fifty-something, she wasn't quite as fast as the youngsters, but she had nerves of steel and a serious knack for close quarter tactics. Yet she and I both knew that, even with the new weapons and materials that had been developed in the past two months, it would be a stone bitch to take this demon out, much less capture it.

"Morons," I muttered, which was the kindest thing I could say about DIRT HQ at the moment. The order to capture demons was perfectly logical, especially when it came to reyzas. They did the most damage and were the hardest to kill. HQ and their researchers wanted to find out what made these creatures tick, what their strengths and vulnerabilities were. I understood it. I really did.

And I hated it. The demons were sentient, resourceful beings. I didn't have to stretch my brain very hard to come up with *how* the researchers would find the demons' weaknesses. It wouldn't involve a pleasant conversation, that much I knew. Yet . . . we were at war. And we sure as hell weren't winning.

It sucked from every possible direction.

The reyza settled in the bed of a big pickup truck near the shopping cart corral, amber eyes blazing with keen intelligence as it assessed us and the rift. It spread its wings as if taking a stretch, then threw its head back and sounded a deep note that shook the air and lifted the hair on my arms. Across the highway, the protesters' speakers crackled to life.

"These demons have been sent to test us and punish the sinful and the wicked. Fornicators and masturbators, drunks and porno freaks—"

"Hey, that's me!" Scott Glassman—my former coworker—called out with a laugh from the Stryker behind me.

"—you false soldiers defy God's law and embrace sin by employing evil witches and sorcerers to battle these demons."

"And that's me," I said with a snort. Yeah, well, the preacher could rant all he wanted about my evil nature but, as an Arcane Specialist, my "sorcery" was part of the reason the DIRT forces could mount any defense at all.

Like right now, as my othersight revealed a nasty orange glow forming on the demon's clawed left hand.

"—demons to punish the sinners and—"

"Yek ziy!" the demon bellowed. *To punish all.*

"Double-M left," I yelled, scrambling up to dive behind the thick tires of the Stryker. Hatches clanged shut, and "umbrellas" made of an arcane-resistant polymer *snicked* open as the troops without cover deployed shields.

The ground heaved with a concussion that set my ears ringing, followed an instant later by a blast of heat and shriek of metal. My pulse slammed in reaction. A reyza cast that? I'd only ever felt an arcane detonation that powerful from a demonic lord.

Fear seized me. "Oh no . . ." I surged out from behind the Stryker. The umbrella shields were arcane *resistant*, meant to deflect a typical demon strike—not a blitzkrieg.

My heart dropped to my toes. I barely registered that the SkeeterCheater lay intact but unanchored over a widened rift. My focus was locked a dozen yards beyond it, where two squad members crouched motionless, fatigues seared and smoking while around them the asphalt popped and boiled. Nothing remained of their shields but the twisted metal of the frames.

The reyza let out a roar of triumph and sprang into the air with powerful strokes of his wings.

"Glassman and Chu, keep eyes on that demon!" Roma shouted with just the barest hitch in her voice. "Landon and Abercrombie, status!"

For an endless second nothing happened. Then Landon lifted his head, working his jaw as if to pop his ears. A second later Abercrombie looked up, blinking, then patted out a patch of flame on Landon's shoulder. "Five by five," Landon croaked, echoed by Abercrombie.

"Stay put until the medics can extract you," I ordered, wobbly with relief. "Arcane injuries aren't always immediately apparent," I added to Roma to explain why I'd stepped on her authority. Technically speaking, I outranked her, but I wasn't stupid enough to override her on tactical or military matters. And her nod told me she wasn't stupid enough to dig her heels in on arcane matters. Then again, one of the reasons I'd requested her for my squad was because she cared more about her people and the mission than her ego.

As the medics hurried up, Roma turned away to marshal the rest of the squad to re-secure the SkeeterCheater and track the reyza. Alpha Squad was one of a dozen special units deployed around the world to areas with high rift activity, its members hand-picked and carefully screened. Most of the men and women in DIRT had police or military backgrounds—such as Roma, who'd been a retired Marine Master Sergeant. But there were plenty who'd earned spots by being excellent marksmen or just plain hard as nails, relentless, and unflinching. Slackers weren't tolerated, not with the world at stake.

I kept one eye on the circling demon as I harangued the medics into moving faster. Due to the weak potency on Earth, it usually took a reyza at least a minute to ready an arcane strike— or "magic missile," as the first DIRT fighters had dubbed them, hence the "Double-M"—but it was obvious this was no ordinary reyza.

"Only God's power can truly defeat these spawn of Satan.

The gates of hell have opened, and the righteous shall endure for all eternity."

A familiar ache tightened my chest. No, the gates were closed. Within a day of the PD valve explosion that started this whole nightmare, contact with the demon realm was cut off. No valve travel, no summonings. The rifts were the last remaining conduits between Earth and the demon realm, but the invading demons were the only ones who understood how to use them.

Then again, the incursions were how I knew the demon realm still existed at all.

"You false prophets and so-called soldiers hide in the shadows like the craven cowards that you are, cringing from the face of evil."

Outrage boiled through me. The courts had ruled that the picketers and protesters had the right to say their piece as long as they didn't get in our way. I agreed wholeheartedly with the country maintaining its freedoms no matter what disasters befell it, but I was also relieved and pleased when the courts decreed that if any of them got hurt while demonstrating near rifts, it was their own stinkin' fault.

To my twisted delight, the reyza swooped low over the picketers, obviously not giving a shit that they were supposedly at a safe distance. The lead protester dropped his mic and dove out of the truck. A few others broke and ran, but the rest hunched behind their eight-foot-tall signs as if cardboard and plastic would protect them.

But hey, for all I knew the protesters and preachers were right. Maybe this whole nightmare started because some god looked down and thought, "Ew, what a mess! Time to wipe the slate and start fresh." Made as much sense as anything else at the moment.

The medics carted Landon and Abercrombie off. The demon circled the protesters. "Yek ziy," he roared.

My twisted delight turned to horror as orange light blossomed in the demon's hand. I needed to distract him, break his concentration, or the protesters would get fried. I didn't like their "helpful" messages—or their foolishness for setting up so close to a rift—but they were human, and no way would I sit on my ass and let them die. But what to do? Shooting at him was a lousy option. The demon had arcane shielding, plus the distance increased the chance that we'd hit the civilians with friendly fire. The Light Armored Vehicle was closest to the highway, but even they couldn't—

"Chu!" I yelled at the top of my lungs. "Crowd control the demon. Now!" I wasn't concerned about the protesters getting accidentally tear-gassed. Helluva lot less lethal than an arcane strike, and maybe they'd be smart and run away.

Chu immediately swung the grenade launcher around, loaded up the needed grenades, then sighted and fired four times in quick succession. I held my breath as the grenades sailed toward their target, then watched in relief as the demon wheeled toward the incoming threats, the orange glow vanishing from his hand. He batted a tear gas grenade into the midst of the protesters, but the second and third bathed him in gas and smoke, and the fourth peppered him with rubber pellets. While the demon pivoted in an aerial dance of gas and pellet avoidance, the protesters—including Microphone Man—made their own escape, scuttling like roaches into the woods behind them.

But they were still far from safe, especially if the reyza decided to blast the woods where they were hiding. Drawing my Glock from my thigh holster, I marched to the rift and began firing into its depths. As I'd hoped, the reyza let out a cry of outrage, then he turned on a wing and headed toward us. Yet instead of going straight to the rift, he flew high and circled twice before descending to land atop what was left of the Piggly Wiggly.

He crouched and settled, a pose a reyza could hold for hours on end. It was clear he was waiting for something. Reinforcements? The puny humans to give up? Screw that.

I jogged to the Stryker and pounded a fist on the side. "I need the wizard staff," I said after Scott poked his head out of the hatch.

He chuckled and passed down a six-foot-long black pole. "Don't step on any hobbits."

"They're going to have to stay out of my way." I curled my hands around the smooth metal and thumbed the button. Electricity arced from the tip of the staff—which was little more than a cattle prod on steroids. Scott had dubbed it the "wizard staff" after the first time I used it to stun a demon, and the name had stuck.

Staff in hand, I jogged over to where Roma was making notations and drawing arrows on a sketched map of the Piggly Wiggly and surroundings.

"God, what I wouldn't give for internet," Roma muttered. "And radio comms." I made a sympathetic noise. The folks in R&D had worked up shielding that reduced the arcane interference on electronic devices, but we were too close to the rift for it to have any worthwhile effect.

I peered at the map and took careful note of her plan for netting this giant beastie. "This is good. I can lure him off the roof." I jerked my head toward the reyza. Wouldn't be the first time I'd played bait.

Roma gave a brisk nod and tapped the map. "Get it on the ground in that clear area by the handicapped spots. We'll net it there." She gave me a hard look. "And try not to get et."

"No chance of that," I said. "I'm too tough and stringy."

She let out a dry laugh. "Ready when you are."

With unhurried strides, I made my way up the raggedly striped rows toward the shattered Piggly Wiggly storefront. Atop the grocery store, sunlight sparkled on the reyza's gold jewelry as he tracked his gaze over the parking lot. His pose was casual, indolent even. I knew better. A demon this big was old, smart, and tough. And he wasn't going to give up.

On the other hand, I was young, moderately clever, and sick of this bullshit.

"APCs, move into fishing position," Roma shouted behind me. "LAV, cork the hole. Blauser and Hurley, Metallica that son of a bitch as soon as it lands! Ahmed, Petrev, Hines, grate the cheese the instant the plastic's off!"

In my periphery, I noted people and vehicles shifting position in a clever dance of subterfuge. No point making it obvious where we wanted the demon to go.

When I reached the handicapped spots, I planted the butt of my staff on the head of the wheelchair-bound stick figure, stood with my feet apart and my chin lifted, and challenged the reyza with a glare.

"Lahnk hremtehl si bahzat bukkai imhritak!" I shouted, which loosely translated as *Your mother is an asswipe.* Or it could have been *Your breath smells like fairy farts.* A good chunk of the demon language relied on telepathic signals to clarify the meaning beyond words, but I figured I was close enough.

The reyza ignored me. Hell, maybe he agreed with the sentiment. I tried another insult that mocked his prowess as a fighter, then one that belittled his tail as thin and weak. Those earned me a chunk of rubble slung in my direction, but otherwise he didn't budge. Crap. Though my time on the nexus in my back yard had improved my grasp of the demon language, it wasn't going to take long for me to run out of clever abuse.

"Lah zhet unkh sutiva!" I hollered. *You have shit wings.*

The demon curled his lip in a sneer, then focused his attention on the rift.

"Lahnk vahl mumfir nurat!" *Your head looks like cheese.* I mentally riffled through the vocabulary I knew. Yeah, I was scraping the barrel now.

"Grahl ptur . . . uh, ptur unkh qaztahl!" *You serve a shitty lord.*

The reyza leaped up with a bellow of fury, wings snapping open with a *crack*.

I blinked in surprise at the sudden vehemence. He had some serious fanatic devotion to his lord if *that* pathetic insult set him off. But which lord? The sly and devious Jesral? Hot-headed Amkir?

With an ear-splitting roar, the demon leaped off the building and toward me. I clamped down on a yelp and fled. *Okay, lured him off the roof. Now to get him on the ground.* My inner survivalist screamed for me to sprint like hell, but I stuck to the plan. I couldn't risk drawing him too far from the target zone. So what if I was one hundred percent certain he'd rip me to tiny pieces if he got hold of me.

Gripping the staff in both hands, I slid under the cart corral then rolled to a low crouch, facing the demon. He was more than strong enough to shred the aluminum bars that sheltered me, but he'd need to land first. I hoped. He might decide to tear the corral from the parking lot mid-swoop, but then he'd have to make a second pass to grab me. I crossed fingers and toes that he'd favor the more efficient route.

To my right, Blauser and Hurley ran up with a device that looked like a pregnant rocket launcher. *Sonic weapons, yeah!* The throaty growl of diesel engines sang a wicked harmony that told me the Strykers were maneuvering into position.

The demon hit the parking lot with a *thump* that I felt as much as heard. *Score one for efficiency!* I jammed the butt of the staff into the asphalt and pointed the nasty end toward him, praying that everyone had made it to where they needed to be. The demon's eyes blazed, legs coiled beneath him for another leap—one that would end with me impaled on his claws. Out of the corner of my eye I saw Blauser snap open a tripod mount on the sonic cannon, holding it steady while Hurley took aim and pulled the trigger.

A low throb of sound shook the air, and the reyza staggered as if an actual cannonball had plowed into his chest. I allowed myself a quick mental fist pump. The air throbbed again, sending the reyza to his knees. Elation sang through me as his arcane protections flickered.

"Wings and tail!" I hollered then scrambled for cover behind the mangled tank. The plastic was off. Now it was time to grate the cheese. Ahmed popped up from the other side of the tank, rifle at his shoulder. I hurried to shove earplugs into place as automatic gunfire sliced through the air. The reyza howled as the rounds ripped through the membranes of his wings and took chunks out of his tail. Hines, Roma, and Petrev joined in the shooting—all positioned so that no squad member could be caught in crossfire. Ahmed dropped an empty clip and slammed a fresh one into place with barely a pause in his firing. Behind the demon, chips of concrete flew from the rubble.

A dark arrow launched in a lazy arc from Kowal's Stryker: the new demon-snaring SkeeterCheater net, spreading as it flew to settle over the demon. Roma held up her fist, and the firing stopped.

"Crank it!" I yelled. If the reyza had been three feet shorter, it would have been perfect. But with the net only covering him from his horns to his knees, we had to take him down fast. The winch on the front of the Stryker screamed, winding in the cable to close the net around the thrashing reyza. I pulled the earplugs out and ran forward as he toppled. Razor sharp claws tore at the net, but his incredible strength wasn't enough to defeat the graphene strands.

A triumphant whoop went up from Alpha Squad. Mission accomplished. Our squad had scored the first demon capture, and a big ass one at that.

I was in no mood to cheer. DIRT HQ would swoop in and cart the demon off—for the good of Earth—and would then refuse to let me anywhere near him. After all, my job was complete, and there were too many agencies wanting a crack at him to waste time letting me keep a hand in. Maybe they'd find better ways to kill demons, but they'd never break him and learn the reason for the incursions—info that could give us a real edge and help end this nightmare.

Anger burned in my chest—at myself and HQ and the demons and the lords.

The winch went silent, cable taut and net tight. Breath hissed between fangs as the reyza struggled. Blood dripped from his shredded wings, staining the asphalt beneath him.

"Kho lahn ettik ai vihr?" I demanded. "What are you doing to the rifts?" At his glare, I jammed the business end of the staff against his side and thumbed the button, held it for the count of five as his body jerked. I pulled the staff away and repeated my question.

His breath rasped, but the hatred in his eyes merely shone hotter. "Our blood. Our breath." He let out a rage-filled bellow that made me wish I'd left the earplugs in. "Our world!"

Huh? What did that even mean? "What do the lords want?"

His pupils thinned to slits. "Mraz gah qaztahl." The growl turned into a roar. "Mraz. Gah. Qaztahl!"

Fuck the lords. The hell? My knowledge of the demon language was far from perfect, but I knew the important things—like how to curse. "Why?" I blurted.

"Asssssssk Xharbek." His lips pulled back to expose wicked teeth.

The name thundered through me. Xharbek—demahnk counselor and ptarl to the exiled demonic lord, Szerain. Xharbek, who'd masqueraded as Carl the morgue tech and my Aunt Tessa's boyfriend. I'd last seen him minutes after the valve explosion when he was gunning for Szerain and Zakaar—a.k.a Ryan Kristoff and Zack Garner. Even more unsettling was my suspicion that Xharbek was after Jill and Zack's newborn daughter, Ashava, as well.

The reyza continued to twist within the net, reaching toward his head with one clawed hand. My instant of distraction over Xharbek was all he needed. "Jontari!" he roared then sank sharp claws into his neck.

"No!" I drove the spear into his side and jammed my thumb onto the button, but it made no difference. While I watched in helpless disbelief, he jerked his hand closed and ripped out his own throat.

Blood sprayed, and his body spasmed. I stumbled back, dimly aware of shouts and curses from the squad. A nauseating gurgle came from what remained of the demon's neck as he thrashed. Then he went still, clawed fingers loosely curled around the chunk of gore.

Chapter 2

An instant of shocked quiet hung in the air as our quarry lay twitching, then curses and shouts of dismay rushed in. Light poured from a thousand fissures in his body, undeniable proof that the demon was discorporeating—to return to the demon realm or, if we were lucky, be lost in the void. I retreated another few feet, jaw clenched. The light flared, a *crack* rattled our eardrums, and the graphene net sagged and collapsed over a dark stain in the parking lot. And enough gold to buy a small tropical island.

But at the moment I didn't give two shits about left-behind demon jewelry. Cursing, I flung the staff aside, then sank into a crouch and gripped my head in my hands. Frustration hammered through me with every throb of my pulse, yet guilty relief rode hard on its heels. I hated that I was still without answers, but I was *glad* the demon had found a way to escape capture—and that felt ten kinds of wrong. Yes, this threat was eliminated. But what about the next incursion? And why the purple hells had the demon reacted so violently to the mention of the lords? Fuck the lords? I'd certainly said the same more than once—about a few of them, at least, and not in a friendly way—but I couldn't fathom why a *demon* would say so.

A hand rested on my shoulder. I looked up to see Roma, her face scrunched into a sympathetic grimace.

"Not your fault." She gave my shoulder a comforting squeeze then released it. "Never thought one of those things would be willing to go that far to keep from being taken prisoner."

"None of us did," Ahmed said, eyes weary over his magnificent beard. "Sarge is right. That beast was hard core. Next one we'll wrap up tight." Behind him, other members of Alpha Squad murmured similar sentiments.

"Thanks, y'all," I said, forcing a smile as I straightened and accepted various pats on the back and further gestures of comfort I didn't deserve. Their show of support wasn't helping my guilt, but I knew it was their own way of dealing with the disappointment. Not to mention, they were simply an awesome team—which made letting them down even harder. Why couldn't any of this shit be black and white?

Keeping a brave face, I congratulated each one on a job well done then dismissed them with our traditional "I hope I never see you again"—our mutual prayer for a time when the squad would no longer be needed to respond to rifts and incursions. The current Alpha Squad record for the longest time without getting called out was four days.

Scott Glassman stooped to pick up the staff as the squad filed away. "Don't worry. We'll all back you up in the debrief."

I groaned. I'd forgotten all about that special level of hell. "I'm not sure I can get through a debrief without ripping my *own* throat out." A typical debrief involved a bunch of pricks who never saw the front lines Monday-morning-quarterbacking every decision and move we'd made. I'd agreed to fight with DIRT—hell, I'd helped found the unit—because it was the best way to defend and protect Earth. I believed in the mission, and I believed that, for the most part, the worldwide organization was making a positive difference. But the FBI special task force, Homeland Security, and a host of other Feds could go jump in a rift, as far as I was concerned.

"You'd better give me that," I said with a scowl, gesturing to the staff. "I might need to give a few people an up close and personal demonstration of how it works."

"Wouldn't blame you one bit," Scott said, wisely not handing it over. "I was only detained for ten hours of questioning. You had what, five days?"

"Six." Sharp pain lanced through a molar, and I forced myself to relax my jaw. Six days of FBI detention after the valve explosion. Before then, I never in a million years would've thought I could ever find a trace of benefit from the torture ritual I endured at Rhyzkahl's hands. But after experiencing the worst torment a body and mind could survive, the task force's interrogation was downright friendly.

"Who's on call?" I asked. Not *everyone* on the task force was a dickface.

"Clint Gallagher."

Ugh. Gallagher was one of the Feds who deserved a rectal staff insertion. A hard core pain in my ass. My satellite phone buzzed in my tactical vest. "Shit. Probably Gallagher wanting to start his rant early." But my dread turned to relief when I checked the ID. "It's Cory." Cory Crawford, our former sergeant at the Beaulac PD who'd been seriously injured while trying to evacuate prisoners before the valve blew. "I'm supposed to go see him," I added in a fit of inspiration. I'd made no such arrangement, but the day was young and the Feds were on the way.

Amusement flashed in Scott's eyes. He wasn't fooled. "Sounds good to me. Tell him to stop milking his sick leave. He was only in a coma for a week."

"Right?" I scoffed. "And it's not like he lost *both* legs."

"'Zackly. He can still hop on his left." He winked and turned away to help with cleanup while I answered the phone.

"Hey, Cory," I said. "Scott says you're a lazy wimp." In fact, Cory had been the polar opposite of lazy, diving into physical therapy with a vengeance the instant he was cleared to do so, and he had graduated to home health care three weeks ago.

"Yeah, well I learned from watching him," Cory said, voice thin and stressed.

I frowned. "What's wrong? You don't sound good."

"I don't feel good. My head is killing me, and I keep getting chills." He sighed. "I'm sorry. I just need some pills for nausea, and I can't get hold of my aide. I shouldn't be bothering you, but—"

"Don't be silly," I interrupted. "I'll be right over."

"No, you don't have to drop everything just for me," he said, though he couldn't hide his relief. "I figured you might know someone less busy you could send."

"It's cool, I promise." His unintentional barb hit home. War didn't leave much time for social niceties, and Cory had been low on my priority list. He deserved a damn visit. Everything else could wait. "I just finished taking down a demon and can be there with meds in thirty."

He exhaled. "Thanks."

"Anytime, Sarge." As I hung up, a cluster of four wheelers rumbled into the parking lot with Vince Pellini in the lead. At the sight of me, he peeled off and headed my way. Italian features, dark hair, and a mustache that belonged in a cheap porno. Pellini was a big guy, though in the past two months of fighting demons he'd traded a fair amount of flab for muscle. I'd worked with Pellini for nearly three years in the Investigations Division of the Beaulac PD, and my opinion of him had been pretty lousy—he was lazy, obnoxious, sloppy, and generally unpleasant to be around. It was only a couple of weeks before the valve explosion that I learned his carefully guarded secret: he could see and use the arcane, trained as a youth by none other than Lord Kadir and his demons.

We'd quickly become unlikely allies, working closely as a solid team. My arcane abilities were currently limited to sensing potency with minimal capacity to utilize it. Pellini could manipulate potency just dandy, but he didn't have the training and experience to know what to do with it. Together we kicked ass at hot spots all over the world, tackling the tough shit that few other arcane users could hope to handle. Not that we had much competition, with only eleven summoners total on DIRT's roster. However, shortly after DIRT was formed, I'd spearheaded a recruitment effort and screening-training program, and now most units had at least one "talented" person who could reliably sense the arcane.

Pellini killed the engine of his four wheeler. "Three more graa and a kehza since the big reyza took off."

"Anyone hurt?"

"Sykes is going to need a couple dozen stitches on his arm, and Ferguson took a claw swipe to the gut. He's in critical condition, but they think he'll pull through." His face sagged, and I steeled myself. "Nate Rushton is gone. A goddamn savik got hold of his ankle and dragged him into the rift."

"Shit." The gut punch of losing one of our own never got easier, even after so many. "His wife just had a baby six weeks ago. They're up in Kentwood." My throat tightened. "Safer there."

We both fell silent for several seconds. *Safer.* Nowhere was safe.

Pellini scrubbed his hands over his face. "One bit of good news is that HQ finally came up with enough SkeeterCheater to cover the whole rift. The rift maintenance unit should be able to pick off new arrivals now." He swung off the four wheeler and swept a gaze over the parking lot. "No luck on capturing the big reyza, huh?" His expression remained bland, but I knew his feelings on the issue were in line with mine.

"Had him in the net," I said. "And then he ripped his own throat out."

Pellini's heavy brows drew together. "You're shitting me."

I shook my head. "Dude, I've never seen a reyza like this before." I gave him a quick and dirty description, then showed him the pile of gold jewelry—currently being photographed and guarded by Petrev and Hines.

Pellini let out a low whistle. "Nice of the demon to pay for damages."

The comment wrung a laugh out of me. "Yeah, the Feds might be able to buy us a new tank with it. Speaking of Feds, I'm bugging out of here as soon as you and I lock this rift and before the debrief. Cory called and isn't feeling great, so I'm going to swing by with some nausea meds."

"I'll drop in after I give my report to the relief sergeant," he said then grinned. "I can get away with a five minute verbal report since I'm a lowly Arcane Specialist and not the Arcane *Commander*." He slammed a fist to his chest in a mock salute.

I rolled my eyes. "I swear they picked that title just to fuck with me. C'mon, lowly one. Let's lock this thing."

We'd had far too many opportunities to perfect our method of rift-locking on active rifts, with me giving instructions and him placing the strands, but that wealth of experience meant we got this one set without a glitch.

I'd barely stepped clear of the rift when I felt a vibration beneath my feet that I knew wasn't just a heavy truck. Breathing a curse, I swung around in search of cracks in the earth or arcane flames—any sign of another forming rift.

"Relax, Kara," Pellini said gently. "It's just the Horsemen."

"Oh." I blew out a breath. "It's possible I'm wound a teensy bit too tightly."

"Can't imagine why." He gave my shoulder a light punch then turned as a dozen horses and riders accompanied by a massive bear-like dog came trotting around a bend in the road. The DIRT 1st Cavalry Unit, more commonly known as the Twelve Horsemen of the Apocalypse. Riding at the front of the formation was Marcel Boudreaux—a former coworker who used to be Pellini's partner in the Investigations Division. He and I had never much liked each other either, but his feelings had shifted to outright animosity around the same time Pellini and I found common ground. Boudreaux suspected I had something to do with the death of J.M. Farouche—a local businessman who'd been a major figure in his life since he was a kid.

Didn't help that he was right. Though I hadn't pulled the trigger on Farouche, I sure as hell didn't stop the guy who did. Nor would I have. Farouche needed to be taken down.

At the sight of me, Boudreaux barked out a command. The riders turned their horses our way. Though Boudreaux and I had our differences, I'd actually come to, if not *like*, respect him a great deal more. His dreams of being a champion jockey had been shattered in a terrible racing accident, and his hopes of making a difference as a cop had fared only slightly better. Yet a little over a month ago, he'd shown up at a mid-level rift with half a dozen other riders and announced that they were ready for action, insisting that the horses were highly trained and wouldn't spook. The regional commander wanted to send him on his way, but I intervened—without Boudreaux's knowledge. Boudreaux knew horses *and* police work, and we were in serious need of a mobile unit that could operate in woods and ruins and trails—places where even four wheelers couldn't go.

Since that first day, Boudreaux had added another six riders, including one who handled a Caucasian shepherd—two hundred pounds of demon-killing canine perfection. The cavalry unit had proved to be invaluable, both in hunting down flightless demons as well as patrolling evacuated areas for human looters and law-breakers.

Boudreaux brought his horse to a stop a dozen feet away then made a show of shading his eyes and looking over the parking lot. "I see a net," he finally said, brow furrowed in mock confusion. "But where's the enormous demon you were supposed to catch? Don't tell me that Kara the Great and Powerful let it slip through her magical fingers?"

A chuckle rippled through his unit, but I kept a pleasant smile on my face. "It self-terminated," I said with a shrug.

He smirked down at me. "Then it's a good thing we knew what we were doing." He gestured behind him then reined his horse to one side. A pair of riders moved up with a wiggling bundle slung between their horses. Flashes of sharp, bone-white teeth and midnight-black reptilian hide showed through the layers of graphene netting.

Pellini stiffened. "It's a kzak," he murmured under his breath. My heart sank. Pellini had close ties with a kzak named

Kuktok, though we didn't know if the demon was still alive. While I sincerely hoped that Kuktok was indeed alive and well, I mentally crossed fingers that this captive wasn't him. No way in hell would Pellini let Kuktok be taken off to be experimented on and worse.

I summoned a bright smile and an impressed expression. "Nice work!" I said then boldly marched forward to inspect the kzak. It snarled and thrashed within the netting, glowing red eyes giving me a pissed look as it gnawed at the graphene without effect.

Pellini moved up beside me, and his soft exhalation was all the answer I needed. It wasn't Kuktok. "Yeah, these things are fast," he said. "Y'all kicked ass."

I glanced over and saw the struggle on his face followed by the grim acceptance that he could do nothing for this particular kzak.

"Horsemen!" Boudreaux thrust a fist into the air. "Time for a . . ."

"BEER!" The riders shouted in enthusiastic unison.

"And a shower!" someone cheerfully called out.

Laughing, Boudreaux wheeled his horse. "Later, losers!" he called over his shoulder, and then he and the rest of the cavalry unit headed off with their prize.

Sighing, I scrubbed both hands over my face. "I'd better get going to see Cory before the Feds get here."

Pellini tore his gaze away from the Horsemen and echoed my sigh. "Yeah. I'll be by as soon as I finish up here." He climbed onto the four wheeler, cranked the ignition and began to head off.

"Pellini, wait!"

He stopped and frowned at me over his shoulder.

I jogged to catch up and gave him a hopeful grin. "Can you give me a ride to my vehicle?"

"Seriously? You can't walk a quarter mile?"

"I'm lazy."

He shrugged. "I can respect that. Get on."

Chapter 3

There weren't a lot of perks that came with being the DIRT Arcane Commander. Being A.C. meant a fuckton of headaches and responsibility, hectic travel in military aircraft, pitched battles against otherworldly creatures, and of course mountains upon mountains of paperwork. A reasonable person might have expected the rank to at least come with unlimited chocolate donuts, but sadly even those were a distant memory.

However, the one perk that almost made up for it all was my DIRT-issued vehicle: a brand spanking new Humvee. This wasn't the watered down SUV version that entitled yuppies drove, either. It was the real deal—fully loaded and armored and able to go through all sorts of muck and rubble as well as handle steep inclines and side-slopes. And yes, after I got it I might have gone off road a few times and roared up a levee or three even when there were perfectly fine roads available. After all, I needed to be sure it lived up to its reputation, right?

I leaned in and cranked the engine to get the air conditioning going, grabbed a bottle of water and took several long glugs, then spent the next several minutes peeling off my tactical armor. The gear was specially designed to protect against demon claws and teeth, and had saved me from serious injury more than once. I also didn't mind that it looked seriously badass, especially when I was all kitted out—full uniform, armor and helmet, with a Glock on each thigh, a combat knife in my boot and another on my hip, extra ammo, fingerless gloves, and military goggles. I looked like a video game character—except for the fact that I didn't have the double-D boobs required for that sort of thing.

I stowed my gear in the back seat, noting as I pulled off my gloves that my ring had worn a hole in the left fourth finger. I'd requested replacement gloves twice already for the same reason. Maybe I could requisition a bunch of left ones? I certainly wasn't going to stop wearing the ring. Yes, it was scorched and scratched, with empty, twisted prongs that I'd crimped down as much as possible then covered with electrical tape, but it had been a gift from the demonic lord Mzatal and was deeply precious to me, symbolic on numerous levels. The glove was just a damn glove.

And I needed to get my ass in gear. A half hour had already passed since Cory called. Fortunately, he lived only a few miles from the crumbling Piggly Wiggly, and the one drugstore still open for business in the Beaulac area was just a couple of blocks out of my way.

Two National Guardsmen stood near the drugstore entrance and gave me crisp salutes that I returned not quite as crisply as I dashed in. Three minutes later I dashed back out with the anti-nausea meds, beef jerky, and a lemon Hubig Pie of indeterminate age, then jumped into my Humvee and roared off. At least I didn't need to worry about traffic. Ninety percent of the civilian population within Beaulac city limits had left the area, abandoning homes and businesses, and hoping for the best elsewhere while writing off their losses here. Whole neighborhoods were deserted now, long since picked over by looters. Beyond the city limits, over a third of the residents had stayed, with some communities forming tight, well-armed enclaves to fight back against both looters and demons. And, of course, the insurance companies were refusing to pay out any claims yet for rift or demon-incurred damage. No doubt they were waffling over whether to use the "Act of God" or the "in time of war" clause to avoid cutting a check.

I scowled as I made the turn into Cory's subdivision—which was definitely *not* anything resembling an armed and organized enclave. For every occupied house, seven stood empty, with broken windows and overgrown lawns. Except on one street where there were six houses in a row that had the front lawns tilled under and turned into a vegetable garden. As I slowed to admire the work involved, I spied a shirtless man with a hoe in one hand and shotgun in the other. He stood by a row of beans, eyes hard on my vehicle, and caution in his stance. I lifted a hand. He responded with a slight nod but continued to watch the Humvee until I turned the corner. He'd most likely taken over the yards of his neighbors who'd left. Or maybe he'd never lived here at all, but at least he was doing something productive and positive. More power to him.

Cory lived on a side street of ten houses, of which all but his and the one across the street were abandoned. I pulled into the driveway, pleased to see that wards still shimmered all over his house and several feet around it. After Cory came home from the hospital—and without his knowledge—Pellini and I had carefully crafted protections to discourage looters or anyone else who might wish Cory or his belongings harm. With his less-than-welcoming attitude toward anything even remotely weird, it was better for all involved that he remained unaware that we'd covered his house in magic woowoo.

I opened Cory's front door and stepped in. "Hey, Cor—"

That was as far as I got before a godawful stench of Pine-Sol, barf, and decaying roses smacked me in the face. Eyes watering, I stumbled back outside then retreated farther as a cloud of fumes followed me. By the time I made it to the lawn, the stench dissipated enough to let me draw a somewhat clean breath, and I did so while I frowned at the open door. I'd been to plenty of crime scenes that had far worse odors. Hell, the bathroom after Pellini had been in there was nastier. But this stink had a special quality that went beyond the assault on my nasal passages. This made me want to get in my car and drive away. It felt almost like an aversion ward, though more subtle.

I'm imagining things. Or I'm dizzy from the fumes. I allowed myself a few more non-toxic breaths, then ducked inside. "Cory? Knock knock." I rubbed my arms against the chill of the air conditioning. The smell didn't seem *quite* as awful now. Maybe I was acclimating.

"Bedroom," he called out, voice hoarse.

Breathing shallowly, I made my way through the living room: a man cave of brown and khaki with a weak attempt at a color splurge in the form of dull olive sofa pillows. I'd known Cory long enough to be certain the man didn't own a single item or article of clothing that wasn't some shade of drab. I was tempted to scandalize him with a bright red office chair for his birthday.

His ham radio setup occupied the far corner—a tidy sprawl of transceivers, amplifiers, and a couple of computers, with a beat-up rolling stool shoved under the desk. An exercise mat and resistance bands lay neatly rolled by the coffee table, and there wasn't a cigarette or ashtray in sight. In many ways, Cory had never been healthier. He'd quit smoking and started eating more fruits and vegetables, and a week ago he'd proudly shown off by doing a dozen tricep dips between two chairs.

As I passed the bathroom, I discovered the primary source of the stench. An open gallon jug of Pine-Sol sat on the counter, and a scrunched towel by the toilet half-covered a failed effort to clean up a pool of vomit. I winced in sympathy—and held my breath—as I found and replaced the cap for the Pine-Sol. I'd take care of the mess once I checked on him.

Though the eye-watering fumes abated in the bedroom, the weirdly familiar decaying rose stink hung thick in the air, despite the complete lack of plants or old floral arrangements. Puzzled, I tried to place where I'd smelled this before, but the wisp of scent-triggered memory slipped away.

Cory lay on the bed with the stump of his right thigh on a towel and a cell phone in hand. His face had a sickly grey cast made more ominous by beads of sweat. He gave me a half-hearted smile. "Nausea seems to have settled, but now I have these awful muscle cramps all over. Must be the flu."

"This is why I'm not keen on you living here alone," I said, glowering. "What if you'd fallen in the bathroom? I know you want to stay here, but most of the neighborhood has evacuated, and your sister in Kentucky is willing to—"

"Take me in and micromanage my life. No thank you." He waggled the phone. "This nifty little invention does me just dandy. Got you over here, didn't it?"

"Yeah. This time."

"I have everything under control," he said. "Plus, I have to man the emergency radio."

It was clear I wouldn't win this fight, especially since he had a point about the radio. Ham radio operators worldwide had stepped up to provide a much-needed emergency information relay service that was far more reliable than most cell phones. "Fine. But that doesn't mean I'll stop worrying about you." I smiled. "Humor me and call your doc, just in case."

"Seriously. I'm feeling better."

"Right, Sarge." I folded my arms and pursed my lips. "That's why you're pouring sweat even though the thermostat is set to 'igloo'. Call your doctor. *Now*."

"Anyone ever tell you your bedside manner sucks?" He scrolled through contacts on his phone.

"Every day." I moved to the bed to tweak the bedspread straight, breath catching as the aversion superpower of the smell reasserted itself. My stomach roiled, and I had to actively suppress the unnatural desire to leave. No doubt about it now. It was arcane. I sought the source, but all I could see were flickers of potency that teased the edges of my vision. No sign of wards, aversion or otherwise. The arcane—and the rotting-rose stink— radiated from *Cory*.

"Hold off on calling the doc for a minute, okay?" I said, nice and calm. "I need to check something out."

Cory eyed me with suspicion. "What's wrong?"

"Well . . ." I suppressed a wince. "Conventional medicine might not be what you need."

His eyes widened in alarm, which didn't surprise me. When I was a detective, he'd grudgingly accepted that I dabbled in the weird and woowoo—even helped me out a time or two. However, the subject clearly made him uncomfortable, and he'd done his best to avoid direct conversation about it. "What sort of unconventional medicine do I need? Please tell me you mean something like acupuncture."

"Nah, no needles." I paused. "Pellini."

Cory blinked. "Pellini?" He'd disliked Pellini damn near as much as I had and considered him to be little more than an inept fuckup. My eyes narrowed as a faint glow of arcane shimmered over Cory's body like wind over wheat. He cleared his throat. "I know he's been working with you . . . but that doesn't mean he . . . *Pellini*?"

I suppressed a grin and instead gave Cory a reassuring smile. "Yep. Good ol' Vince is a card-carrying member of the weirdo club now. He never set the world on fire with amazing police work, but when it comes to the arcane, I trust him. Plus, I don't have enough arcane juju to find the source of the problem, so I need him."

Corey groaned. "You've got to be kidding me."

"Nope. I can't make this shit up." I shot Pellini a quick text. *<Something weird going on with Sarge. Need your special skillz. ETA?>*

His reply came a few seconds later: *<Two minutes.>*

"Kara," Cory slurred. "I don't feel so great."

I jerked my attention back to him then had to clamp down on a gasp of dismay. Where only a moment before there'd been sweat, luminescent red slime glistened on his face and oozed from his pores, plastering his t-shirt to his chest. "Oh fuck," I breathed. "I mean . . . um, just relax, Cory. Pellini's on his way, and we'll get you straightened out." As I spoke, the smell shifted to a weird hybrid of spice and burned hair. *Arcane disease?* If there was such a thing, it could possibly be contagious. I needed to quaran—

Cory grabbed my wrist. I instinctively recoiled, but he held fast. His eyes went wide. "Kara . . . I can't . . . what's happening to . . ."

"Cory, focus!" I wrenched free then retreated a step for good measure. "Do you have any gloves?"

His breath wheezed. "Bathroom."

"Hang tight!" I ran for the bathroom. I wanted gloves between me and that ooze, but even more than that, I needed to be *away*. Angry fingermarks were the only sign that he'd grabbed me, but I cranked on the hot water and scrubbed the hell out of my wrist anyway. The towel lay crumpled over puke, so I dried my hands as much as possible on my shirt. "Just one more minute, Cory," I called out.

I clawed an emergency kit out from under the sink and yanked on a pair of nitrile gloves. Or rather, one and a half gloves. My damp left hand got stuck part way in, giving me more of a nitrile mitten effect. I doubted that the gloves would be much protection against arcane slime, but it felt better than doing nothing. I shoved a pair in my pocket for Pellini, dug for a filter mask with no luck, then dashed to the bedroom. "Sorry. Just a precau—"

Cory stared blankly, head lolling to the side. Red covered every inch of him, giving the illusion he'd been flayed—except that the slime undulated like a living thing. I couldn't even tell whether or not he was breathing.

"Cory!" No response. I felt for a pulse, relieved to find it strong and steady. But what the hell was happening with him?

His body jerked, and he gasped a rattling breath. "Kara, nine one one . . . Kara . . . don't let me . . ." Gurgling drowned his words as slime filled his mouth.

Crisis training kicked in. *Get him on his side. Clear his airway. Call the paramedics.*

"Stay with me, Cory," I ordered. "You're going to be okay."

I gripped his shoulder and hip to roll him, and the slime writhed, hot and viscous beneath my gloves. An electric vibration shot up my arms, distracting me long enough for the mucus to surge, congeal, and lock itself around my hands.

"Shit!" I tried to yank free, but I might as well have been trapped in cement for all the good it did me. My right hand wouldn't budge from his shoulder at all, however the one on his hip gave a little, thanks to being only partially in the glove.

Without warning, Cory swung his fist toward my head. I jerked back enough for the blow to glance off my temple. "Stop fighting! I'm trying to help you." Before I could reposition, his other fist shot out and caught me square in the ribs.

I *oofed* out a breath and wrenched my hand out of the glove, barely in time to twist away from another head shot and catch his wrist. Slime-gel still sealed my other hand to his shoulder, but I managed to wrestle his arm above his head and pin it to the bed. At least whatever the fuck was screwing with him hadn't made him super strong.

But now what? With one hand trapped and the other holding his arm down, I was in the worst game of Superglue Twister ever.

Eyes wide, Cory thrashed wildly and let out an inhuman roar. Impossible, considering his mouth and nose were completely filled with yuck, but though the sound remained physically in-audible, it bombarded my brain from the inside out like a tele-pathic grenade.

Breathing hard, I mentally traced the *pygah* sigil for focus and managed to clear my mind. "Back off, alien slime shit," I growled, teeth bared. "Get out of my head and stay out!"

As if in reaction to the rebuff, Cory relaxed and his eyes fluttered closed.

"Yeah, damn straight," I said, voice quavering, then re-grouped and reassessed. I'd fended off the mental crap, but I remained stuck. And Cory wasn't breathing. "Cory?!"

No response, but the slow, steady beat of his pulse under my fingers gave me a whisper of reassurance. Not breathing—but not dead. *I'll take it.* The slime still held me fast, but the consistency had shifted to more like a rubbery gel with a bit of give to it.

Pellini skidded into the room. "What the—! Jesus! How long until EMS gets here?"

"I haven't called anyone yet," I snapped. "Maybe you could give me a hand here? I'm stuck. Gloves are in my side pocket."

Pellini took in the bizarre situation: Cory covered in a thick layer of red glowing gel and me sprawled half on top of him. A lesser man would have walked right back out. But not Pellini. The picture of calm, he retrieved the gloves from my pocket and tugged them on. "How are his vitals?"

"Heart rate sixtyish. Respirations *zero*. Gel from hell. Now please help me get loose."

Pellini gave a slow nod as he peered at my trapped hands. "I'll call dispatch as soon as you're—"

"No! What could they do? It's not like he ate a bad tuna sandwich or jabbed a screwdriver in his eye! He'll end up in a bureaucratic nightmare with people who have no clue what to do with this shit."

"And you do?" Pellini moved to the other side of the bed.

I glared at him. "Better than anyone else would."

He leaned forward to examine Cory, and I bit down on my lip to keep from shouting at him to hurry. His way of seeing the arcane was different than mine and, I hoped in this case, better.

"The slime-gel is all one piece," Pellini finally said. "A full-body mucus wetsuit. Both physical *and* arcane."

"I figured that much out when it grabbed me," I muttered. "Is there an origin point or source? Somewhere it's more concentrated?"

"Uh huh. Damn." He peered closer. "It's like someone shoved a radioactive arcane pool ball in his gut."

"A tumor?" That fit the arcane disease theory.

Pellini gave me a hell-if-I-know shrug. "It's solid. Dense. And spitting out god knows what."

With Pellini's guidance, I located the tumor with my other-sight, *felt* it as a low level ache behind my eyes. And, surprise surprise, it carried the same resonance as the brain roar. "Okay, first order of business is to get me free of this crap. Can you lay a few Pellini-pygahs around it? Maybe if this thing chills out a bit it'll loosen its hold."

Pellini moved his hands in simple patterns over Cory. "And if it doesn't?"

"Jeez, nice positive attitude. It'll work." The ache behind my eyes wavered as Pellini wove his sigils. I retraced my mental pygah and envisioned the tumor swaddled in a blanket of serenity. *Everything's cool*, I thought to it. *Nothing to worry about*. After a moment, the hell gel softened enough for me to wiggle my fingers, but I resisted the temptation to jerk away. Before, pulling had only made it tighten its grip like a Chinese finger trap.

The gel softened a bit more. "That's it, you vile little lump," I murmured. "Keep it up and you'll move off Santa's naughty list in no time."

Pellini added another sigil, and the ache behind my eyes dulled a notch. I eased out, millimeter by millimeter. The instant my knuckles cleared the gel, I yanked my hands free then shook them hard. "It *worked.*"

"That's why you make the big bucks," Pellini said, gaze still on Cory.

I flexed my fingers. My hands looked sunburned—including the palms—but seemed fine otherwise. The ache behind my eyes surged to its former strength as Pellini's sigils faded. Grimacing, I rubbed at my temples. "What do we do with Timmy the Tumor now?"

"It's physical," Pellini said, forehead creased. "A surgeon could cut it out of him. Nip it in the bud." Uncertainty colored his tone.

"Or possibly kill him outright." Instinct screamed that cutting into him was wrong. "No. We don't know anything about this except that it definitely has an arcane component. How's a surgeon supposed to deal with that? We can't risk it."

"What's your alternative?"

"Get him to the house. To the nexus." My hope was that the arcane focal point in my back yard would allow me to delve deeper into what was going on with Cory and give me the info I needed to sort this out. "Timmy's resonance reminds me of the arcane implants demonic lords stick in people for tracking or surveillance." I blew out a breath. "Except those aren't physical."

Pellini folded his arms over his chest and regarded me. "In other words, you got nothing."

"Well pardon me for not being the font of all arcane knowledge," I shot back, stung. "We need a lord's expertise, but unfortunately, with the world completely fucked up, I have no way to summon one."

His expression darkened. "You don't need to summon one. Rhyzkahl is right in your—"

"No! I'm not using Rhyzkahl as any kind of resource. That's

not an option." I took a deep breath. "We'll get Cory to the house," I continued in a calmer tone, "and I'll assess from there—*without* Rhyzkahl."

He opened his mouth to argue, but snapped it closed as Cory let out a low chuckle. My pulse lurched at the eerie sound. Pellini breathed a curse and shifted away from the bed.

"House," Cory said, voice slurred. "Why are we going to your house?" Though his mouth was free of slime, the red gel shimmered creepily above his soft, peaceful smile.

"Oh, hey, Cory," I said, doing my damndest to sound calm. "I have a diagnostic tool there that'll let me see what's going on with you."

"Everything's A-okay, Kara girl," he sing-songed. "Never better, Kara girl Kara girl Kara girl. Pretty pretty colors around Kara girl. Blue . . . purple . . . pink . . . greeeeeeeen . . ." He trailed off, and the gel closed over his mouth again.

Pellini shuddered. "Jesus Christ, I've got the fucking willies now. Let's move."

"I'm with you. I don't want to risk touching him again, so that bedspread is coming with us. If you can back your truck into the garage, we can load him up without the neighbors freaking."

"On it," he said and was gone.

I kept a wary eye on Cory while I made a call to security at the house, letting them know they needed to prep a quarantine area.

Pellini returned as I disconnected. "Can't back in. Bertha's in the garage."

"Crap. We'll have to—" I stopped and reconsidered. Bertha was Cory's 1976 Chevy Nova, decked out with radio equipment and an antenna farm. "Load him into Bertha. You drive it and him home, and we'll send someone for your truck and the rest of Cory's radio setup."

He didn't look at all happy about abandoning his truck but was smart enough to catch on. "Not only can we use the radios, it'll be good for Cory when he gets through, um, this."

"Exactly," I said then tensed at the sound of a car engine. A careful peek through the blinds revealed a government sedan blocking the driveway. "Sonofabitch. Feds."

Pellini groaned and smacked his forehead. "Gallagher texted he was coming after us for the Piggly Wiggly debrief. I forgot because of all this." He waved a hand at Cory.

"I'll deal with him. Lock the door behind me and don't let them in." I walked out of the stinky house and closed the door, relieved to hear the *snick* of the deadbolt. At the end of the driveway, Clint Gallagher stepped out of the sedan.

Damn, but I sure hoped I didn't smell as if I'd been dunked in a vat of Eau de Hell Gel.

Chapter 4

While the majority of the Feds assigned to this area opted to wear practical and comfortable fatigues, Clint Gallagher stuck with the men-in-black dark-suit-with-sunglasses look. He regarded me through those sunglasses now, mouth pursed in annoyance. I couldn't deny that he was a handsome man in an FBI-recruiting-poster sort of way. Square jaw, high cheekbones, fierce blue eyes, and even a frickin' cleft in his chin that I promised myself I'd someday get to punch.

Gallagher had been on Ryan and Zack's task force, but the combination of my snark and the stick up his ass meant we'd never hit it off. I considered giving him a bright smile as I strolled toward my vehicle, but opted instead for a surly glare. He'd know I was faking any hint of pleasure at the sight of him. Besides, I didn't want him to think I enjoyed his company and run the risk of having to be sociable.

My plan was simple: pacify Gallagher, send him on his way, and get Cory to the nexus. "You didn't have to chase me down."

He whipped off the sunglasses to better glower at me. "Is it in your job description to make my day harder than it already is?"

"It's in the fine print."

Gallagher looked past me toward the house. "How's Cory getting on?"

"Pretty good. He's wiped out from PT, so he's taking a nap." All I needed to make my day extra super special was for Gallagher to decide he wanted to visit the squishy-gooey Cory. "Pellini's making sure Cory has everything he needs, then we're out of here." I fished my keys from my pocket. "I need to get home and hook up with the Russian DIRT liaison. How about we get that debrief out of the way?"

"Deal." His mouth flattened into a thin smile. "I'll follow you over to the Federal Command Center."

I faked a wince. "Sorry. My schedule's too tight to hit good ol' Fed Central today. I'll give you a quick verbal report and email the full thing later."

"You had enough time to make a social call."

His tone put my back up. "A few minutes with Cory versus the hours that Fed Central would chew out of my day? No comparison. Not to mention, how I schedule my time is none of your goddamn business." I scowled. "Since when is face-to-face a requirement?"

"Since now." Gallagher jabbed his sunglasses at me. "Word has it we had a Class 1A demon down in the dirt, and *you* let it get away."

"*We* had it?" I narrowed my eyes. "When was the last time you got down and dirty with any demon, let alone a Class 1A?"

"That's not the point."

I took a step into his personal space and jerked my chin up. "We—the DIRT team—did indeed have the demon netted."

Jaw tight, he closed the distance until only half a foot separated us. "Exactly. Research shows that an LG4-621S stun net should be more than adequate to incapacitate a 1A demon."

"That's a nice theory," I said, planting my hands on my hips to help power my mega-glare. "Small technical difficulty, though. The stun feature doesn't work so great when the net is here and the power supply is snowed in at Memphis R&D. All I had was an untested, undersized, *unpowered* net, and the wizard staff."

He blinked and retreated a step. "I didn't get that in the briefing."

"I reported the missing power supply before we engaged the demon. If you'd stayed on top of it, maybe you wouldn't be badgering frontline people over bullshit."

"There's more on my plate than incursions," he said, exasperation in his tone. "I dropped everything when the 1A capture report—"

"Who classified the Piggly Wiggly demon as 1A anyway? No one asked my opinion."

"It looked like a 1A."

"And an alley cat looks kind of like a panther."

He shook his head as if he was struggling to keep up. "Are you saying it's a new breed?"

"I'll be sure to include everything in my *emailed* report to Command." I opened the Humvee door. "Are we done here?"

"No. Wait. You have to—" His phone rang with an annoying laser beam sound, and he snatched it from its holster. "Don't go anywhere."

"Wouldn't dream of it," I muttered as he turned away to answer. I cast a furtive look at Cory's bedroom window. Pellini would signal me if something had gone wrong—wronger— unless he was stuck like I'd been earlier. I sent a quick text. *<Status?>*

<Stiff as a board but stable. Bryce is sending a team to help.>

Good deal. House security was on the ball. Now I just needed to clear Gallagher's rigid ass out of here so we could get Cory to the nexus.

Gallagher cursed under his breath. "But she was holding her own a half hour ago," I heard him say as I oh-so-casually eavesdropped. "I thought the techs weren't going to—" He broke off and listened. "Jesus. How many more?" Pause. "Dammit. I'll be there in fifteen." He slammed the phone into its holster, but remained facing away from me for a good five seconds before turning. He rubbed his eyes with his thumb and forefinger, suddenly looking as weary as I felt. "Look, Gillian. You *need* to come to Fed Central."

Under normal circumstances I'd have told him where he could shove Fed Central, but the uncharacteristic hint of desperation in his voice capped my snark.

"Gallagher," I said then took a deep breath. "Clint. If you're like me, you haven't had a full night's sleep since the valve explosion. Why don't we call this a standoff and leave it at that. Command will get their report, just not in person."

"What if I swear you won't be tied up for more than a half hour?"

"I'd say you were a liar." I kept my tone light, but the worry on his face deepened. "What the hell is wrong with you, Gallagher? Is your ass on the line if you don't get me in there?" I didn't like that thought one little bit. "If that's the case, put me on the phone with your boss. We'll sort it out here and now."

"No. I'm the only one who wants you at Fed Central." He swept an oddly furtive glance around, as if he suspected ninjas might be hiding in the bushes.

I threw my hands up in the air. "Spit it out. I don't have time for—"

He stepped close. "A consult," he said, voice low. "I need an arcane consult."

"Great. Fine." Except that I *really* didn't have time for a consult. "I'll have DIRT expedite your request, and we'll get it scheduled."

"I can't put in a request." He did another wary check of the area. "But if you just happened to be at Fed Central . . ."

"Hold on. If you can't put in a request, that means your bosses haven't approved a consult." I folded my arms over my chest. "Or you've screwed up and need help covering your ass."

Frustration washed over his face. "I don't know why they won't call in an arcane specialist, but our orders are clear. No consults."

This kind of shit was *exactly* why I didn't want the Feds knowing about Cory. "Let me get this straight," I said with heat. "You want me to waltz into a hornet's nest, take a big stick and start swinging it around while I sing *Fuck the Feds*? Half an hour, my rosy red—."

"The task force has David Hawkins."

I blinked, nonplussed. David was a pleasant, unassuming man who'd spent his life savings to open Grounds for Arrest, the coffee shop across from the PD. The distress in Gallagher's tone made it sound as if David was next in line for execution.

Clearly I was missing a chunk of vital information. I counted to five in Portuguese and fought for patience. "What, pray tell, does the FBI Special Task Force want with the owner of a café?"

Gallagher scrubbed a hand over his face then blew out a breath as if resigned to being "that guy" who leaked classified information. "There's a . . . I guess you could say it's a plague. People are going into stasis in something like a cocoon. The CDC is all over it, but they don't know what they're doing. They've already managed to kill three plague victims. We still have two, including David, and four more were just brought in."

Shit. A cocoon? I restrained the urge to ask if it was gooey, red, and slimy. This "plague" had to be the same thing Cory was going through, but I wasn't convinced that a trip to Fed Central with Gallagher would be worthwhile, especially not if I ran the risk of getting detained because the higher-ups didn't want an arcane specialist nosing around. No, my best hope for getting useful information was to assess Cory on the nexus. I'd sort out the Fed mess afterward. "Whether they chose to call me in or not, I should have at least been notified," I said, more annoyed at being out of the loop than I'd realized. All these damn agencies were more concerned with hoarding secrets than cooperating on problem solving. "Who's blocking channels?"

Gallagher winced as if he had the mother of all headaches. "It's Garner's case. He hasn't been himself since he returned from leave. Maybe because Ryan still isn't back to work." His mouth pressed thin. "Or maybe power has gone to his head. He's the hot shit Division Chief of the new Arcane Investigations expanded task force."

Gallagher was still speaking, something about caseload and divisions and seniority, but I'd stopped listening. Garner. Zack Garner. Two months I'd been searching for him, his caretaker Sonny, Ryan, and Ashava: my "AWOL four", as I'd come to call them. And now Zack was doing his FBI thing as if nothing had happened?

I tuned back in to hear Gallagher finish with, "—and he's been on call twenty-four seven."

"Got it. No worries," I said. Gallagher needed an under the table, no strings attached consult. Meanwhile, I needed to pay a visit to Division Chief Zack Garner and, as a side bonus, I could check out the slime victims. "I'm starting to see the wisdom of going to Fed Central . . . to give my *report*." I stopped short of giving him an over-the-top sly wink. "Let's go. I'll follow you."

Chapter 5

Zack Garner was back. Without a word to me. No phone call, no email, nothing.

I followed Gallagher out of the near-deserted neighborhood, past shaggy yards and boarded up houses, while my confusion rose along with my anger. Clearly, Zack's return from his "leave of absence" hadn't been in just the last day or two. No, he'd been back at work long enough to be well-established at Fed Central. But what about the others? Szerain and Zack had taken Ashava then fled—with Xharbek in hot pursuit. Sonny Hernandez, Zack's caretaker, was also missing, and I could only assume that he'd gone with them. Yet if Zack had returned, did that mean the others were still in hiding? Or had something happened to them?

Not long after I met Zack, he and my best friend, Jill Faciane, became an item, and then he'd failed to tell her that he was a demon before he "accidentally" got her pregnant. And not just any old demon. Zakaar was one of only eleven demahnk: mind-reading, shape-shifting, power-wielding, secretive beings who were oathbound to the demonic lords—and, as I recently discovered, were the nonhuman "daddies" of the half-human lords. Which meant Jill's baby was a *demonic lord*.

But had Zack prepared any of us for that little surprise? Hell no. It didn't help that I had a really tough time believing he'd knocked up Jill by accident. I *wanted* to, but . . . damn, that dog just didn't hunt, especially since Jill had been using protection, and Zack was—to put it bluntly—a super-being. I also wanted oh-so-badly to believe that his original intentions were nice and benign and involved everyone being happy and in the know, and certainly not at all like the godawful shocking way we found out about Ashava's true nature. Jill had given birth to her mere minutes before the valve explosion. Except, instead of wasting time with actually getting born the old fashioned way, the kid had *teleported* herself out of Jill's body . . . in baby dragon form. Then again, Ashava had good reason to be in a hurry. It was her efforts that kept the valve explosion from being about a thousand times worse.

Yet after Ashava saved the world, Jill had barely a minute to hold her before Zakaar and Szerain appeared and stole her away—ostensibly to keep her from Xharbek. And I *wanted* to believe that stealing Ashava was in her best interest. But now Zack was out of hiding? Just like that?

Yeah, I had a few trust issues where the various demahnk were concerned. I *liked* Zack, but he and the other demahnk were playing deeper games, with rules and stakes they refused to share.

And we're all players—or pawns—whether we like it or not.

Adrenaline surged, and I slammed on the brakes, managing to avoid plowing the Humvee into Gallagher's car by at *least* a whole millimeter. When my brain caught up with my reflexes, I realized he'd stopped at the ID checkpoint into the restricted area. For security and public safety reasons, no unauthorized personnel were allowed within a two-mile radius of Beaulac's former police department building.

The guard scowled my way. I mouthed "sorry" as my heart lurched its way back to a semblance of a reasonable pace. After Gallagher was cleared through, I pulled up to the checkpoint and submitted to the ID/fingerprint scan/smile-for-surveillance routine.

A block away, the Federal Command Center loomed—formerly the top-ranked Southern States Heart Hospital. It had been a logical choice for the command center since a) no heart patient in their right mind wanted to be in a hospital that was a mile and a half from ground zero, and b) being in the restricted zone gave Fed Central yet another layer of security. The hospital building and grounds had been converted into a compound that served as local headquarters for several agencies, including DHS, NSA, CIA, and others, with the FBI task force supposedly taking the lead. Joint occupation of the building gave the illusion of hand-holding cooperation, but with each organization in its own wing, the reality fell short.

I passed through a second checkpoint at the facility's perimeter fence and into the shadow of the monstrosity that had once been a sleek, modern building. The ground level windows had been bricked over, with no consideration for aesthetics, and the upper level ones barred, giving the place an overall grim prison effect.

Gallagher parked and headed for the door with only the barest of glances my way. I parked a few spaces away then followed. I had no clue what his plan was to facilitate this unauthorized consult, but apparently he trusted me to follow his lead when the time came. Gallagher was sharp and dedicated. He'd never have been recruited into Zack and Ryan's task force otherwise. And though he and I butted heads constantly, I was confident he'd come up with a way to get me past the "no arcane specialists" order and into the medical wing.

Security had increased in the two weeks since I'd last been here. Substantially. Not only had two machine gun turrets been added on the mezzanine overlooking the entrance, but the checkpoint at the door included a blood test, for additional identification. In the lobby, a handful of agents and support personnel passed through as they went about their business. Gallagher was nowhere to be seen, but I figured he'd find me when the time came.

Since my cover purpose was to file my report on the Piggly Wiggly incident, I made my way down the corridor to the communication room. The computer station nearest the door was empty, so I snagged it, logged in, and pretended to be absorbed in the details of the morning. And waited. The wall clock—like all the Fed Central clocks—had a sharp and annoying *tick tick t-t-tock* at the top of every minute, emphasizing how much time I wasn't spending helping Cory. I had faith that Gallagher wouldn't leave me hanging, and he clearly had the same sort of faith in me, but it would've been nice to know the basics of his plan. Should I be bracing for a distraction? And if so, what? Fire alarm? Inexplicable swarm of ferrets?

Ten years later—or about five minutes, if the clock was to be believed—I heard Gallagher's voice down the hall, coming closer.

"We'll get the logistics sorted," he was saying. "Will allocation of another twelve rooms be adequate for today?"

A woman's voice replied. "I can only hope. We barely have the resources for the victims brought in this morning, let alone a dozen more cases. But best to have space ready."

"Medical personnel screenings for Level 1 clearance are underway," Gallagher said as he and a petite older woman wearing a white lab coat passed the doorway. "You'll have more support by tonight."

Good, no ferrets or fire alarms. High level security clearance for standard medical conditions wasn't the norm, which meant that was my cue. I stepped into the corridor behind them.

"Excuse me, y'all," I said amiably. When they turned, I smiled at the woman then peered at her name badge. "Dr. Patel is it? I'm Kara Gillian, Arcane Commander. I couldn't help but overhear you mention victims and Level 1 clearance in the same context?" I gave her the gently perplexed look of an authority figure who expects nothing short of a full explanation.

Dr. Patel's expression was one of surprise and, oddly, what seemed like awe. "Yes. But . . ." She glanced at Gallagher, then back to me.

"I had a busy morning at the rifts and haven't had time to check my interagency updates yet," I continued, trusting the grimy condition of my uniform fatigues to back me up. I made my smile friendly and full of understanding. "But for important matters like arcane medical conditions, I'd rather get the info firsthand."

Gallagher stepped forward. "Sorry, Gillian. You're not on the list for—"

My smile went to full glare at light speed. "Don't give me the bureaucratic bullshit runaround, Gallagher. I have clearance, and I'm not afraid to use it."

Dr. Patel shouldered past him with her hand extended and relief on her face. "Dr. Aja Patel. A *pleasure* to meet you."

I shook her hand, but she kept hold of it when I released my grip.

"I can't wait to tell my daughter I met *the* Kara Gillian," she gushed, eyes wide with unfeigned delight. "We read *every* blog post and article about you. I just love what you said about the ethical impact of demon incursions on civil rights. It was *so* insightful."

I managed to disengage from her hand without seeming rude. "As much as I'd like to take credit for an insightful comment, I'm afraid that one's not mine. Either someone misattributed it or made it up." I'd stopped trying to keep up with all of the crap about me on the Internet—love, hate, glory, blame. Who had time for that?

Her face fell. "I'm so sorry. I didn't mean to—"

"Oh, it's all right. It happens all the time." I added a warm chuckle since I didn't want to put her off. Gallagher had obviously known that her awe would work in my favor. "There's plenty of insightful and plain old brilliant stuff I've really said. You're probably thinking of the commentary I made about the efficacy of martial law and the need for compassionate population distribution."

That seemed to take the edge off of her embarrassment. "Yes! The *Arcane for Humanity* documentary was awesome. The way you dealt with those two kehza had me on the edge of my seat. And then you were so cool and calm afterward when you talked to the reporter!"

Right. I'd been calm because the sudden appearance of the demons had startled the shit out of me, and I'd done a triple pygah tracing so I could function at all. "Experience, I guess," I said with a smile. "And I very much appreciate the compliments." I straightened as if I suddenly had a great idea and pulled my phone from my pocket. "Would you mind if I took a picture with you? It's always a thrill to know that I have supporters." While Dr. Patel smiled in delight, I looped an arm around her and did a quick selfie. In my periphery I caught Gallagher's pained look. "After we get done with the briefing on the victims, I'd be happy to personalize a photo for your daughter," I added, tucking my phone away. "I mean, if you think she'd like that sort of thing."

"She'll be over the moon." Dr. Patel beamed. "We'll get that briefing taken care of in a snap. Right this way." She headed toward the elevator, bounce in her step.

"Dr. Patel," Gallagher said, expression back to stern. "This is highly irregular. I'll have to notify—"

"Do whatever you need to do to ease your conscience, Agent Gallagher," she announced without turning. "I'm doing what I must to ease mine."

A twinge of guilt plagued me as Gallagher and I followed her into the elevator. It didn't feel right for us to play her, but then again she seemed genuinely relieved that I was here. Everything balanced out. I hoped.

The elevator disgorged us onto the third and top level. Unlike the others, this floor remained very hospital-like, except for the agents—armed and in tactical gear—posted by the nursing station and corridor entrances.

A nurse in dark blue scrubs pulled Dr. Patel aside for a quiet but visibly urgent conversation.

Gallagher ushered me to the nursing station then folded his arms over his chest. "Sign in unless your high and mighty clearance can't handle the bureaucratic bullshit."

I smiled sweetly at him. "Aw, Gallagher, if you want my autograph, you only have to ask."

He growled something incoherent. I signed a messy scrawl that looked nothing like my actual signature. No sense making it obvious that I'd been here. "Does Zack have an office in this building?"

"Second floor. North wing."

"Cool," I said lightly. "I'll swing by and give him a wave before I leave." *And shake him until he tells me what the fuck is going on and where Szerain, Sonny, and Ashava are.*

Dr. Patel hurried over to us. "The good news is that the recent arrivals are stable. We learned from earlier patients not to disturb them." She shook her head. "The rest is a mystery. I need an arcane opinion."

So why hadn't Zack given her one? He was a demahnk, with more arcane knowledge at his disposal than I'd ever have. And sure, *Special Agent Zack Garner* wasn't supposed to have all the arcane skillz, but I found it hard to believe he'd let people die just to maintain his cover. "Show me."

She gave me the rundown as we walked to the far corridor. The first six cases had been brought in late last night: Three men disoriented and covered in red slime, one woman in stasis and coated in a rubbery gel, and two others who Dr. Patel said it would be easiest to just show me. The medical personnel attempted to wash the slime off one of the victims, but when he died screaming, that treatment plan was quickly abandoned. A second slime-victim died during the prep for surgery to remove a fist-sized growth in his abdomen. The third went from slimy to gel-covered in a matter of seconds and was currently in stasis. Less than an hour ago, a tech tried to collect a small sample of gel for analysis from the woman who'd arrived in stasis, and she died within minutes. Then four new cases were brought in, all in a gel-stasis condition.

No pathogens or toxins had been found, and there was still no known cause, but the common denominator was that all had been within a half mile of the PD when the valve blew.

And I'd been *literally* right on top of it. Lovely.

Dr. Patel stopped outside a room with a handwritten sign on

the door: *Chrysalis Project, Phase 3*. "This is one of last night's arrivals," she told me as we entered.

The instant I stepped into the room, a weird smell of spice and burned hair hit me. It was the same odor that came over Cory when he went all gummy, though much more bearable without the barf and Pine-Sol mixed in, and far less cloying than the decaying roses stench of the slime phase. Resting on the bed before me was a large red lump of smooth, dry gel shaped like a slightly flattened egg, completely unrecognizable as human. Lead wires for a heart monitor were stuck to it, looking as absurd as wires jammed into a tomato. Yet the screen showed a heart rate of twenty-four, so obviously something was going on in there.

Gallagher stopped a couple of feet into the room, face haunted. I realized with sick certainty that this patient was David Hawkins. But why wasn't everyone wearing oodles of hazmat gear? I'd always thought that was the protocol for unknown plagues.

Dr. Patel peered at the monitor. "I've observed several distinct phases so far. This patient was in Phase One when he came in last night—the red slime. He moved into Phase Two—gel-coated, but lying flat and rigid. This morning he curled into a fetal position, and the gel expanded to completely cocoon him: Phase Three." She looked at me with a mix of hope and desperation. "Have you ever seen anything like this?"

"No," I said. It wasn't a total lie since Cory had apparently only reached Phase Two. "If you don't know the cause, why aren't the patients in quarantine?"

"Word came down through Chief Garner that there's no need," she said as if that was explanation enough.

"Ah. Gotcha." I knew damn well that an ordinary FBI Division Chief would never be allowed to overrule CDC policy. However, Zack Garner was in no way ordinary, and clearly there was some demahnk-level mind manipulation going on. I had no clue what Zack was up to, but I had faith that propagating a plague wasn't part of it. He simply knew it wasn't contagious in the conventional sense and saw no point in making everyone go through the godawful hassle and headache and expense of quarantine procedures when there was no need for it.

"Give me a moment to assess," I said, easing closer to the gel-egg thing. The gel was completely opaque, giving no indication that a human lay curled inside. Though the physical surface appeared smooth, arcane patterns covered it in a thick layer of glimmering hexagonal cells reminiscent of a honeycomb. The resonance was similar to Cory's, but far more organized. In the center, a tumor the size of a basketball pulsed, with delicate tendrils of potency branching from it like blood vessels. Only their arcane network revealed the shape of the man it covered.

I met Dr. Patel's eyes. "I'm sorry. I don't know what's causing this other than it's definitely arcane. However, I can give you more than you'll get in a physical assessment. The tumor in the middle isn't draining him. It's *feeding* him."

She nodded with enthusiasm. "Considering the outcome, that makes perfect sense. I *knew* the transformation energy had to come from somewhere. How does—"

Dr. Patel to unit twelve, emergency, a voice announced from her pocket. *Dr. Patel. Unit twelve.*

She made a noise of frustration. "A.C. Gillian, I'll be right back. Agent Gallagher will continue your briefing while I'm gone." She burned a you'd-better-do-it-right glare in his direction then hustled from the room.

Damn it. What the hell had Patel meant by "outcome" and "transformation energy"?

Gallagher moved in close. "Can you do anything for Hawkins?"

"Nothing directly," I said with a sigh. "What's his prognosis? I mean if they manage not to kill him."

"We've observed two very different outcomes," he said, eyes dark and grim. "I'll show you."

I followed him out of the room but paused when he started down the corridor. "I need to make a pit stop first," I said. "Won't be a minute." I didn't wait for a response before ducking into the ladies' room and on into a stall. As quickly as my little thumbs could move, I texted Pellini: <*Move Cory to living room. Don't worry about quarantine. Don't disturb gel gummy stuff! Will kill Cory if it's messed up! Will tell you more as soon as I can.*> I shoved my phone into my pocket then flushed the toilet, washed my hands, and returned to the corridor.

Gallagher looked up from his own phone as I returned. "Got word of three new cases. Quebec, San Diego, and Boston. All are refugees from the Beaulac area, but haven't confirmed if they were here the day of the blast."

"I'll wager they were."

"I'm not taking that bet." He shook his head. "At least the media hasn't gotten hold of it yet."

"I'm surprised it hasn't already gone viral." I grimaced. "You said you were going to show me the outcomes. Is that the transformation Dr. Patel mentioned?"

He nodded and led the way down the corridor again. "Don't be shocked by what you see."

"I deal with demons, remember?" I wished I felt as confident as I sounded.

Gallagher *hmmfed* then ushered me into a room marked *Phase 4*. A woman rested peacefully on the bed with monitors attached and an IV in her arm.

I peered at her. "Yeah? She looks normal."

Gallagher lifted her hand and uncurled her fingers. Her nails curved abruptly beyond the tips of her fingers and terminated in wicked sharp points. And it didn't look like malformed human nails, either. More like unnaturally natural claws. "That's not so bad. It's weird as hell, but—"

He drew the sheet back from the woman's legs.

I let out a low whistle. Fur—orange, white, and black—covered her hips and thighs, and a fluffy tail lay alongside her leg. Yep, showing me was better than telling me that Cory was going to turn into a cat. A calico cat. Seriously? "That's . . . definitely bizarre. How is this happening?"

"We don't know. We've had," he glanced at the clock, "fourteen hours, and the only two patients we have in Phase Four arrived that way. We don't know how they transition or emerge from the jelly cocoon thing to become this." He waved a hand at the transformed woman. "Both fours seem stable, though. Robust, in fact."

"Is the other one a cat, too?"

A scream and metallic crash sounded down the corridor.

"Shit. That's the other Phase Four," Gallagher said. Together, we hurried toward the source of the fracas. "He was in the jail when it blew," he continued. "Nasty piece of work."

We swung through the open door to see Dr. Patel and two nurses wrestling with a naked man who was handcuffed and shackled to the bedrails. Metal clanged against metal as the man jerked at the cuffs. He screamed again, a deep, inhuman sound, reminiscent of the bellow of a reyza.

A bolt of surprise went through me at the sight of the man's face. I knew the guy—Earl Chris, a repeat offender who'd been in and out of jail over a dozen times for everything from drug possession to battery. Hell, I'd arrested him twice myself. But my shock went deeper than simple recognition. He'd always been a tough-looking guy, but now he had a mouth full of sharp teeth, and his skin from chest to toes was mottled like a mass of dark bruises. Yet at the same time it looked as tough as a rhino hide. And his hands—

"His left hand's out of the bag!" the nurse nearest me shouted.

The right hand remained bagged and cuffed, but stinger-tipped tentacles squirmed on the left where fingers should have been.

"Push another bolus of diazepam," Dr. Patel ordered. "Jacobs, get that bag!"

Jacobs had his hands full with the struggling patient. I slapped the call button then snatched the bag from the floor. But before I could jam it over the tentacles, Earl yanked on the left handcuff, breaking it.

Everything descended into chaos. Gallagher dove at Earl's now-free hand, then jerked back as all five stingers jabbed into his arm. The second nurse moved forward with a syringe, but Earl ripped free of the other handcuff and tossed him against the wall even as Gallagher slumped to the floor. *Shit. Venom in the tentacles.*

"Dr. Patel, get away from him!" I shouted, drawing my weapon. Where the hell was the backup?

Dr. Patel cried out in pain, gripping her stung hand as she stumbled back. Earl let out another horrible scream and ripped the leg shackles free.

"Stay back, Earl!" I brought my gun to bear on him. Out of the corner of my eye I saw the doctor stagger and slump. Everyone was down except me, with no sign of any backup. "These people are trying to help you!"

Earl wasn't listening. He scrambled off the bed and lunged toward me. I gritted my teeth and shot him point-blank in the chest.

But instead of staggering or falling, he *imploded*, sucking down to a single point before the gunshot finished echoing through the room.

A wave of arcane passed through me even as Earl poofed out of existence. I whirled to see Zack Garner standing behind me.

Blue eyes, tanned face, and sun-bleached hair—still looking more like a surfer than a federal agent, despite the suit and badge. Breaking the ptarl bond with Rhyzkahl had left him a shadow of his former self, and while part of me was thrilled to see him looking healthy and whole again, the rest was reeling from the last few minutes.

"What the fuck is this, Zack? Why didn't you do something sooner? All these people got hurt, and I had to kill the guy!"

He regarded me a moment then knelt beside Dr. Patel and laid his hand on her forehead. She stirred and sat up, a bewildered look on her face.

"It's all right, Aja," he said as he helped her to her feet. "Go get cleaned up. We'll chat soon."

" 'We'll chat soon?' " I sputtered. "That's *it*?" I caught Dr. Patel's arm as she moved for the door. "Are you okay?"

She gave me a serene smile that sent a chill down my spine. I released her then bit my tongue as Zack repeated the process with Gallagher and the two nurses. Better for them to be serene and out of harm's way when I had my *own* chat with Zack.

After the last nurse left, Zack lifted his hand, and the door swung closed. A twitch of his fingers set an aversion ward on it to keep people out. It was so subtle I could barely detect it, yet more powerful than any I'd felt before. And there was something indefinably *wrong* with it.

"Zack, what's going on?" I asked, perplexed. "Why are you here manipulating and vaporizing people?"

"Everything is going to be fine, Kara." He stepped toward me.

I took an equal step back. I wasn't about to let him touch my forehead. "Fine as in 'we'll chat soon'? No thanks, dude. I'm not into the serene-and-creepy thing." Then again I wasn't sure if he actually *needed* to make physical contact to manipulate me. My gun felt comfortable and heavy in my hand. "I thought we were beyond the lies and games. Where's Ashava?"

He regarded me coolly. "Safe in hiding."

I stared at him. "Zack, do you know what this is doing to Jill? Do you even care?"

His expression didn't change a whit. "She is a survivor."

That wasn't an answer I ever expected from Zack, but neither was this iceman act. Or maybe I was seeing the real Zack for the first time? An unfamiliar mental touch brushed my mind. I

tensed and bared my teeth. "Fuck you. If you're going to manipulate me and make me forget I saw you, go ahead and do it already. But tell me how Ashava is first."

"I'll know soon enough," he said with a faint smile that was
just . . . wrong. He dropped his head a fraction.

His answer made no sense, but I knew that in another few
seconds I wouldn't remember it anyway. *Fuck!* I didn't know if
it was possible to beat demahnk manipulation, but I was damn
well going to try. I glared at him and clung to the memory of his
face—Zack Garner, here at Fed Central. If I could hang on to
that one tiny fragment, I'd find him again. Asshole. I hated this.
Hated him.

His expression flickered in an instant of puzzlement.

And like looking at an optical illusion and seeing that the
duck could also be a rabbit, I suddenly saw everything that was
wrong. The wrongness of the ward. The unfamiliar touch. The
wrong smile. *Wrong* because I was expecting Zack's energy signature and Zack's smile. I didn't recognize the signature, but I
recognized that smile. Carl. No. *Xharbek.*

Even as the realization hit home, I leaped toward him,
slammed him against the wall and jammed the muzzle of my
gun up under his chin. That I could do so without him deflecting
me told me everything I needed to know. He couldn't read me.
Couldn't anticipate my moves. The real Zack Garner and Kadir's
estranged demahnk ptarl, Helori, must have implanted mental
protections in my head when they shielded other sensitive information.

"What happens to a non-corporeal being if I blow its corporeal head off?" I growled, finger on the trigger.

He didn't move—an eerie, unearthly stillness impossible for
a human. "You hold the means to find out, Kara Gillian."

"FUCK, you're annoying. I'm two pounds of pressure away
from scattering sparkly demahnk brains all over the ceiling, and
you're still playing the evil-Gandhi act and spouting vague bullshit." I held the means, all right. Maybe I couldn't actually kill
him, but either way I wasn't going to come away from this
empty-handed.

I drank in his signature, allowed its resonance to suffuse me.
At least once a day, I searched Earth's arcane flows for any hint
of my four AWOL people. Now I'd have a fifth signature in my
arsenal. This bastard didn't know where they were, but not

through lack of seeking. If he left even the slightest fart of a trail, I was going to sniff it out and use it to locate the others.

"You are not a murderer, Kara Gillian," he said and teleported away a microsecond before my bullet buried itself in the ceiling.

"Pussy!" I yelled into the emptiness.

Chapter 6

The morning after the Beaulac PD valve explosion two months ago, I woke up to the world in shock and the FBI at my door. Well, at the end of my driveway, since very powerful arcane protections kept them out. They needed to get my input, they'd said, since I was a consultant for the task force.

I, very stupidly, believed them.

On the sixth day of my detention as a suspected terrorist, Gallagher and two other agents barged into my cell and announced that my house and property had been seized by the U.S. government, and if I wished to spare myself the certainty of life in federal prison, I would cooperate and allow them to take possession. They assured me that it was only a matter of time before they broke through the arcane protections, and therefore I was merely delaying the inevitable and making my predicament much worse.

When they finished their little speech, I laughed and said, "Good luck with that."

At that point, they attempted to convince me that everyone who was currently holed up behind my fence would go to jail forever and then some if I didn't cooperate, but I could spare them that fate if I simply accompanied the agents to—

I stopped them and said, "Let's cut to the chase. You guys want to poke around my house and property because you have satellite imagery and probably drone video that shows something very interesting in my back yard. Only problem is that you can't get past the fence. Not one bloody inch. And anything aerial you send can't get within three hundred feet vertically. So how about we skip all the bullshit. I'll take you three agents—

and only you three—onto my property and give you the grand tour. You can even keep me cuffed and shackled and duct taped if it makes you feel safer."

Which they did. They had no doubt there was a catch of some sort, but they also knew they weren't getting past the fence without my cooperation. Within an hour we were in my driveway, which was when I discovered that my super cool and smart demonic lord boyfriend Mzatal had included a nifty feature on the new and improved back yard nexus—allowing me to tap it from anywhere on my property. It was a mere fraction of the power I could pull when standing on its surface, but it was all I needed.

Long story short, I gave the nice FBI agents an up close and personal demonstration of the power of the nexus, which included their very own aerial—though upside down—view of my house, and made it very clear that I could have easily squashed them flat if I'd wanted to. I then told them to stop fucking wasting my time and maybe now we could work together and do something about the rifts that had started opening up. Oh, and it looks like a rift is about to open up on the south end of Lake Pearl, so you jackholes might want to make sure that area is evacuated. I didn't tell them that I'd sensed the rift via the nexus, and they didn't push the issue of how I knew. It helped that I was right about the rift.

Needless to say, that was the end of my detention. It was also the beginning of DIRT, and how I became the Arcane Commander.

The protections that kept the agents and other official busybodies out were kickass, but Bryce Taggart—former hitman and my current security expert—informed me that, with the increased activity, we needed to add a few measures. He proceeded to hand me a breakdown of the expected costs, which included actual human security guards and improved surveillance and communication systems. I added the other costs of living that I expected to incur, as well as healthy salaries for all of us since why-the-hell-not and yes I was still mega-pissed about being detained for six days, then gave my funding request to the powers-that-be, told them it was what I needed in order to best do what needed to be done, and was utterly shocked when I got it.

The very next day, Bryce brought in portable buildings and handpicked security guards: people who he knew had excellent skills, experience, and reliability, but also wouldn't freak about any weird shit that might happen. We had Jordan Kellum, a former world-class powerlifter who was barely 5'4" but strong as an ox; Chet Watson, gunsmith and firearms expert; David Nguyen, an expert tree man—which was a seriously useful skill with the zillion pines I had on my property; Dennis Roper, a whiz at logistics and planning; Lilith Cantrell, our resident tech guru; Ronda Greitz, mechanic and engineer-type; Bubba Suarez, construction and all around handyman; Nils Engen, medic; Sharini Tandon, who had umpteen black belts and considerable military experience; and several others who didn't necessarily possess a definable specialty but were sharp and intuitive and darn good picks.

The guard shack at the end of my driveway was one of the many new additions. I stopped in front of the gate and rolled my window down. The guard on duty was Tandon—tall and lean, with ink-black hair pulled back into a tight coil at the nape of her neck. She gave me a smile but kept a hand on her sidearm and maintained a distance of no less than ten feet from my vehicle.

"Afternoon, Miss Kara," she said. "Any word on when football season might start up again?"

"Afternoon, Sharini. I figure the Saints will come marching in when the moon turns red with blood." A coded question and response that changed daily and would hopefully trip up a shapechanged demon attempting to infiltrate. It wouldn't stop Xharbek since he could simply read the answer from the guard's mind, but the protections that Zack laid around the perimeter would hopefully be more up to the challenge.

She nodded at my correct reply then hit the button to open the gate. I continued up the long winding driveway and to my lovely hundred-year-old Acadian style house—still in need of a paint job, a task that kept slipping lower and lower on my list of priorities. Fifty yards to the east of the house was a double-wide mobile home, current residence of my best friend, Jill Faciane. To the west, five short and squat trailers sat in a line at the edge of the woods—housing and office space for the security team. It truly was a compound now.

Cory's Bertha was parked near the front of my house. I pulled in beside it, and as I climbed out of the Humvee a flash of red hair drew my gaze to the woods beyond the house. Jill, running the obstacle course. Probably not the first time she'd gone through it today, either. Hardcore exercise was only one of the ways she'd been burning through her grief and anger over the kidnapping of Ashava.

Jill had been understandably devastated, but she wasn't the sort to wallow in misery. By the time the Feds sprang me from detention she was already working her ass off to get strong and tough. "I need to be ready to do whatever needs to be done to protect my daughter," she'd told me.

I had zero doubt she'd be ready for anything. A mama grizzly was a fluffy bunny compared to Killer Jill.

And yet . . . I knew Jill, and she wasn't fooling me. She was like a Prince Rupert's Drop, able to withstand hammer blows to its body but exploding into bits at the slightest flick to its tail. The more time that passed without word of her daughter, the longer that vulnerable tail grew. High on my mental to-do list was "Talk to Jill about Xharbek being Fake-Zack," but I was going to have to approach the issue carefully. I had no intention of keeping her in the dark, but the last thing I wanted was to get her hopes up about finding Ashava when nothing might result from it. I'd track her down after I finished assessing Cory. That would give me time to plan my approach.

She vaulted over a wall with an ease that showed her gymnastics background, did a diving roll under a log, then sprinted to the finish, face set in a snarl of determination. As she slowed, her expression shifted to a smile, and I realized Bryce was there, holding a stopwatch. I was too far away to hear what he said, but it made her laugh and smack his arm. A measure of my worry slipped away. Yep, Bryce was damn good for her.

Maybe one of these days he'd let Jill know how much he loved her.

No, he does that every day, I thought with a smile. But at the same time he never crossed the line. Though Zack was nowhere to be found, he was still a part of Jill's life, and out of respect for their relationship, Bryce remained an absolute rock of support for her without ever doing anything to make her feel uncomfortable or pressured. And, in turn, she'd been there for him when he needed it. Bryce shared an essence bond with demonic lord Seretis—a union of minds that went deeper than the closest friendship. After the valve explosion, not only had the ways closed between Earth and the demon realm, but his bond with Seretis had gone silent as well. Yet that silence was more than just a closed door. For Bryce, it was as if the room beyond it had been a favorite space, a treasured and safe retreat that was now an empty void.

Yep, Jill and Bryce were a good team, helping each other through loss and worry.

I grabbed my bag and headed toward the porch, reaching it as Pellini's chocolate Labrador trotted up the steps carrying a kitten by the scruff of its neck. Granger, by the look of it. One of the six kittens Fuzzykins had splorted out onto my bed around three months ago. They were more "catlets" than kittens now. Certainly a lot more rambunctious. To everyone's amusement, Sammy had become fiercely protective of the litter, even enduring swats and growls from Fuzzykins to be near them.

But two weeks ago, Sammy had saved Bumper from a red-tailed hawk, earning him belly rubs for life from every human in the compound. Even Fuzzykins stopped harassing him. Mostly. After that, Pellini and I fashioned an arcane perimeter around the house that had so far proved successful in containing the catlets, and kept hawks, owls, and other possible kitten snatchers out.

"You're fighting a losing battle, Sammy," I told him even as he set Granger safely on the porch. No sooner did Sammy release her than the fluffball raced to the stairs. Without slowing, she launched herself off the edge and into the grass where two of her brothers were busy attacking a vicious and dangerous leaf. Bewildered, but determined, Sammy bounded down the steps and after them.

Fuzzykins lay sprawled in front of the door, apparently content to let Sammy run himself ragged chasing after her wild brood. I stooped to give her a head scratch which she accepted with a soft *brrrmp*—a far cry from the hiss-growl-scratch she'd have granted me before Angus McDunn reversed his skill-enhancing talent and stripped my arcane abilities. For reasons unknown, cats—especially Fuzzykins—hated summoners. It remained to be seen whether she'd resume hating me as I grew stronger in the arcane.

I stepped over her and let myself in then closed the door gently behind me. Cory was laid out on the opened sofa bed. Pellini sat in the armchair near him, working on his computer.

"Any change?" I asked.

Pellini closed his laptop. "He's sleeping. I think. Otherwise, everything's the same. No respiration, but his heart is beating."

"We'll find an answer," I said with as much conviction as I could muster.

"You're goddamn right we will." Worry darkened Pellini's expression as he looked at Cory. "He's been through too much to end up as a fucking bug."

"Might end up as something else entirely," I said quickly. "The mutations seem to run the gamut of—" I grimaced and shook my head. "Sorry. That's not exactly reassuring."

"It's cool." He gave a soft snort. "I'll hold out hope that he turns into something kickass like a unicorn centaur."

"You want him to have a horn growing out of his forehead?"

Pellini let out a breathy chuckle. "That'd be funny as shit. But still better than being a bug."

I couldn't argue with that. "I'm going to grab a quick shower then get the nexus ready. Ten minutes, tops."

"I'll let security know."

I desperately wanted to let a blistering spray pound me for twenty minutes or so and maybe boil away some of my tension. Instead I settled for a mostly warm two-minute scrubdown that got the worst of the grime off. I hated to waste even that much time before starting my assessment of Cory, but physical impurities such as grime, sweat, and stench tended to interfere with tricky arcane processes, and I didn't know what I was up against.

As I toweled off, I scowled at my reflection out of habit. Eleven intricate scars covered nearly every inch of my torso—a sigil for each of the demonic lords, and souvenirs of Rhyzkahl's torture ritual. A twelfth sigil rested at the base of my spine, transformed by Szerain and his command of *rakkuhr* from an unfinished unifier scar into an enigmatic glyph, visible only to othersight. I still didn't know his purpose for creating it other than that it was connected to Ashava.

I yanked on clothing to cover the sigils and myself, then detoured through the kitchen, grabbed a protein shake and glugged it down. Movement caught my eye through the window, and I steadied my gaze on a shirtless Rhyzkahl tracing the sigils of the *shikvihr*. Crap. I didn't want him to know what was going on with Cory. I'd have to make sure the captive lord was in no position to watch us.

My back yard had changed significantly in the past two months. Mzatal had transformed the nexus slab from ordinary concrete into an obsidian-black, diamond-hard surface that shimmered with intricate patterns of silvery threads. A five-foot-wide swath of grass ringed the nexus, and beyond it was another five-foot-wide ring, where little grass remained. That outer ring was Rhyzkahl's prison, where wards and protections—brilliantly crafted by Mzatal—kept him in place, like a planet that could neither approach nor retreat from the sun.

Though Mzatal was judge, jury, and jailer, I was the warden—not that I'd been given a choice in the matter. Still, I did my best to be fair and considerate. I'd even arranged to have a narrow house built for Rhyzkahl, one that fit perfectly along the curve of the circle, with doors at both ends to allow him to pass right through. While the center of his orbit was packed dirt, small gardens dotted the circumference, coiling vines of pumpkins and runner beans alongside neat clusters of beets and chard and tomatoes, with interspersed pockets of marigolds and cosmos, zinnias and celosia—all grown from seeds and soil that Rhyzkahl had requested. His activity fit with what I knew of the lords. They weren't averse to hard work nor did they feel themselves too good to pitch in as needed. They had demons to help with household tasks but didn't treat them like servants. Plus, the lords worked their asses off to keep their planet's potency from going out of whack. Rhyzkahl would probably go stir crazy if he couldn't keep busy.

Gardening. Occupational therapy for a caged demon.

Purple irises flourished on both sides of his house, encouraged to bloom out of season by what little potency he could muster within the prison. On the roof lay yet another granted request: a coil of leather straps and a pile of sandbags that he used to work out.

I didn't grant all his requests. I was proud of myself that I no longer laughed in his face when he demanded to be released.

Rhyzkahl paused between one sigil and the next, flexed his right hand several times before continuing. A deep scar crossed his palm, a remnant of the searing hilt of his essence blade, Xhan, when Mzatal struck through it in order to free me from Rhyzkahl's torture ritual. It was a vicious wound that never fully healed, but I couldn't muster up much sympathy—not when that ritual had left me covered in scars.

I chucked the empty shake bottle into the trash then stepped out the back door. Rhyzkahl immediately stopped the shikvihr and turned to face me, proud and aloof. Sweat glistened on his skin, but his white-blond hair flowed in glowing perfection past his shoulders, seemingly untouched by Louisiana humidity. Mzatal had left him a thread of potency—enough that he could heal himself and even regrow his hair. Now Rhyzkahl once again looked every inch the demonic lord, a far cry from the pale and stumbling figure who'd been cast out of the demon realm.

Only the incessant twitch in his scarred right hand betrayed the profound damage that wasn't so easily healed. Each of the demonic lords had a ptarl, a demahnk advisor with whom they shared a deep bond that was both arcane and emotional. And unknown to the lords, their ptarl was also their parent. The lords relied on their ptarls for counsel, support, and focus. Yet during the battle at the Farouche Plantation, Zack/Zakaar—Rhyzkahl's ptarl—made a radical, terrible, and necessary decision to sever the three thousand-year-old bond, an act that left them both shattered.

I stopped just beyond his orbit and met his ice blue gaze. "I need you to go into your house, please."

He turned his back on me and began the shikvihr again.

Tension stiffened my spine. An overtired toddler would be easier to manage. Taking a deep breath, I mentally traced the calming *pygah* sigil. Nope, didn't help. "Go to your house, Rhyzkahl," I said, without adding any number of curse words that leaped to mind.

He moved with inhuman grace through the practice of the intricate potency-augmenting ritual. "It worries you that, each time you have made this demand, it has been more difficult to force it." As if for emphasis, he ignited a sigil.

I managed to contain my jolt of surprise to a mere twitch. The glowing loops of the arcane symbol hung in the air, the first he'd been able to ignite since being placed in my tender, loving care. Stark evidence that he was regaining control and command of his abilities.

He's still locked out of the flows, I reassured myself, yet a whisper of doubt clung close. No way would I admit it to this asshole, though. Fortunately, his prison prevented him from reading minds, plus I had the extra mental protections implanted by Zack and Helori.

"You think I'm worried?" I let out a soft chuckle and deliberately stepped onto the packed dirt of his orbit. "Your little rebellion is no match for what Mzatal has wrought here. If I feel anything, it's *disappointment* that your best effort at defiance is little more than a tantrum."

He finished the shikvihr, and the sigil dimmed as he drew on its weak augmentation to potency-evaporate his sweat. "It pleases me that I cause you to feel something."

"Yeah, I *feel* like I'm dealing with a spoiled brat." I marched across his orbit and stepped onto the nexus. Power embraced me and escalated to a deep thrum as I stopped at the center of the slab. Beneath my feet, a thousand silvery repetitions of a sigil—*my* sigil—formed the shape of a woman with her arms extended, much like Da Vinci's Vitruvian Man. A gift from Mzatal, and my focal point of power. Like Bryce and Seretis, Mzatal and I shared an essence bond. Yet ours had gone silent for a different reason than the closing of the ways between the worlds. At my urging, Mzatal had walled himself off, mentally and emotionally, and taken up his essence blade in order to maintain the undivided focus necessary to save his world.

I could no longer feel him, but I didn't need to. I *knew*, and that was enough.

Tipping my head back, I inhaled deeply and let the power fill my entire being until every cell tingled. This was a lord's power: Rhyzkahl's. Mzatal had plugged him into the infrastructure of the nexus like a lordly battery. Here on the slab I was a demigod.

Or more like a semi-demigod since I didn't know how to do most of what was surely possible. Though the nexus hadn't come with an instruction manual, I'd puzzled out enough on my own to allow me to do my part to help both Earth and the demon realm. But, most importantly, the nexus gave me full access to the arcane and had become my therapy of choice to "rehab" my own damaged abilities.

Rhyzkahl continued to eye me from the middle of his swath, his arms folded and feet planted.

"Go into your house," I snapped. "I don't have time for this today." To emphasize my point, I raised a strand of potency behind him and gave him a rat tail flick across the back of his legs.

Ignoring the swat, he lifted his chin in challenge. His scarred hand twitched hard at his side, but he lifted his other and gave me a bring-it-on gesture.

He might as well have given me the middle finger. Anger swelled as the mounting worries crashed down on me, as if summoned by that stupid gesture. Cory and the others who were mutating. Xharbek. The Feds. Everything. I was sick to death of this game, sick of having this hated creature in my back yard and in my personal space.

"I don't have time for this shit!" Teeth bared, I flung my arms out, snaking a dozen bands of potency around Rhyzkahl to push-drag him to his stupid house. For a heartbeat he held firm against my efforts. Doubt flickered ever so briefly within me as he resisted. An invalid no longer, he was most assuredly regaining his strength.

But without Zakaar he couldn't hold the focus. A cry of frustration burst from him as he staggered back and fell through the open door of his house. Right before I slammed the door closed with a burst of potency, I caught a glimpse of his liquid expression. In it was triumph for holding out at all underscored with bleak despair at his failure, along with a shimmer of fear that he might never regain the powerful focus necessary to manage the arcane flows of an entire world, might never truly be a lord again.

Shaken, I dropped to a crouch. I hated this. Hated Rhyzkahl. Hated everything about this entire situation. Hated that I knew the taste of that fear—the gut deep terror that I might never truly be a summoner again. And I especially hated that I'd lost my temper and given him an opportunity to defy me.

Why why *why* did Mzatal have to send him *here*? Having my tormentor as my prisoner sounded fine and dandy, but it sure could suck hard. Resentment rose in a choking wave—partly toward Rhyzkahl, but also toward Mzatal for placing this burden on me. Like I needed even more shit to worry about and deal with and be responsible for. Because I *was* responsible for Rhyzkahl. I was his warden and his caretaker, which fucking *sucked*. And what was I supposed to do when the day came that Rhyzkahl managed to scavenge or hoard enough potency from the trickle allowed to him that he could, in fact, fully defy me?

What was I supposed to do with any of this mess I was in?

Well, you sure as hell don't give up, I thought savagely. I'd take what I'd been given and use Rhyzkahl-the-battery for the good of humanity. I swiped at my damp eyes then straightened and meticulously cleared all stray potency from the slab. By the time I completed the process, my head was as clear as the nexus, and I felt ready to take on the Cory situation.

Chapter 7

Not that it made a difference. With the help of two security guards, Pellini and I carried Cory out to the nexus where I was able to get a nice clear view of Timmy the Tumor with my borrowed lord-sight. A filament of potency finer than spider silk led from the tumor down into the ground. It moved with him, and every effort to track its end—or origin—was met with a potency resonance I couldn't penetrate. After an exhaustive examination, I couldn't find a single thing to explain Cory's condition or hint at either a cause or solution.

"He's still alive," I said to Pellini. "That's about all I'm sure of." I sat back on my heels and rubbed my face with both hands. "Shit. He's going to mutate, and I only know that much from seeing the victims at Fed Central."

"He and the others must've been exposed to something at ground zero," Pellini said. "If so, there's no unexposing them at this point. We can't stop it."

We fell silent, and I didn't have to be a mind reader to know we had the same question rattling through our heads.

"So are we next in line to be slimed?" I finally said.

Pellini blew out a heavy breath. "If it came out of the valve, we were exposed. Moreso than anyone else." He turned his hands over and peered at them. "But no red slime yet."

"Yet," I murmured. But why not? Did our arcane ability protect us? Or Ashava's shielding? Or did some other factor give us immunity. Or perhaps we *were* affected, but the slime was incubating.

With that last joyous thought echoing through my skull, I called for the security dudes to help Pellini get Cory back inside.

I remained on the nexus, feeling like a tiny fish in an unknown ocean full of sharks. Crouching, I placed my palm flat on the cool black surface, spread my fingers over my silvery sigils and let their potency tingle through me. Mzatal trusted me to not only swim with the sharks and avoid being eaten, but to beat them at their own deadly game. "I could've used a rule book, *zharkat*," I murmured, "but I'm figuring it out bit by bit. Rak-kuhr. Demahnk. Lords. Demons. I'll do whatever it takes to keep Earth from getting wrecked." Deep resolve welled in me. "Whatever it takes."

Straightening, I released the potency lock on Rhyzkahl's door then headed for the house, refocused, recentered, recommitted, and ready to tackle the next crisis.

The basement door was ajar when I came in, which told me Jill was most likely working. Maybe it would be better not to disturb her?

No, that was me being a chickenshit. She needed to know about Xharbek impersonating Zack, and with the Cory emergency in a lull, I had no valid reason to avoid it any longer.

I helped settle Cory on the sofa bed then made my way downstairs. My basement had undergone darn near as much change as the rest of my property. All told it was about the size of the entire ground floor of my house, which had made it the perfect spot for a summoning chamber. Though the middle third of the basement remained clear for potential arcane work, Ryan had built out the south end months ago as an extra bedroom. Before the valve explosion, Idris Palatino had bunked down here, but he'd been gone for well over a month. When we began assigning arcane specialists to DIRT units, he'd requested Sector 5—South and Southeast Asia.

Idris was an insanely gifted arcane user and summoner, and I hated to see him go. But I also completely understood why he wanted to be far from here. Rhyzkahl was an ever-present reminder of the Mraztur—the demonic lords Rhyzkahl, Jesral, Amkir, and Kadir—whose atrocities included the brutal murder of his sister. Unbeknownst to Rhyzkahl, Idris was his son and despised the shared blood. If Idris stuck around, an ugly confrontation was inevitable. And while that kind of showdown had the potential to be highly entertaining in its own twisted way, none of us had the time or energy for it or the potential fallout. Besides, popcorn was hard to come by these days.

At the north end of the basement, bookshelves covered the walls, crammed with the entire contents of my Aunt Tessa's arcane library. I'd taken every last scrap from her house, right after I learned that she'd been lying to me for years, deliberately sabotaging my education as a summoner, and even collaborating with Master Summoner Katashi to have my arcane abilities stripped. She wanted to fuck me over? Fine. I'd use her own resources against her.

Not only was Tessa without her library, but she didn't have Katashi's support anymore either. We'd captured him shortly after the valve exploded in the Beaulac PD parking lot, but unfortunately he was savvy enough to know that our demonic lord allies would strip his mind bare of every detail of the Mraztur's plans. He goaded poor Idris into attacking him, and in a haze of fury, Idris slashed the old summoner's throat.

And that's when things got weird. Katashi did the expected bleed-choke-gurgle-die thing, but then he *discorporated*, just like a demon. We eventually decided that he must have, in fact, been a demon—most likely a syraza, since they could shapechange. But of course that only left us with even more questions, such as who, when, why, and what-the-actual-fuck.

The library in Tessa's house had been a nightmare of piles and clutter and complete lack of anything resembling organization, much less a filing system. But not here. Not after Jill took over. The library became another outlet for her, and now every book, scroll, tome, page, or scrap of parchment was neatly shelved, and steadily being catalogued with ruthless efficiency. Moreover, a couple of weeks earlier, Jill had put out a call through DIRT and civilian channels worldwide asking for scanned copies of any documents, ancient or modern, that might have bearing on the arcane, demons, rifts, or anything else related to our current situation. Even better, several mega-PhD librarian types stepped up to filter, sort, classify, and database every scrap of info that came in. It was no doubt a fraction of what existed—collectors might be loath to reveal that they owned missing or stolen manuscripts, and there were countries who hoarded their secrets in case it proved valuable later—but every little bit helped.

Jill sat at a long table in the middle of the library area, typing away on a laptop and occasionally glancing at a legal pad beside the computer. Her short red hair was damp from a shower and neatly combed, and she'd changed into jeans and a lace-edged, black tank top that showed the definition in her shoulders and arms.

She looked up when I reached the bottom of the steps. "Hey, chick. Find out what's going on with Cory?"

"No." I slumped into a chair at the head of the table. "I hate this. Even using the nexus, I found absolutely zip that could help me help him. The only thing I know is that Cory isn't the only one." I went on to tell her what I'd seen and learned about the "plague" at Fed Central.

Jill's eyebrows drew together in a frown. "I haven't run across anything like that in what I've catalogued so far, but I've only scratched the surface. I'll drop a note to the librarians to keep their eyes peeled."

"Anything you can find will help us get a clearer picture."

She scribbled a note on the legal pad beside her. "I'll start focusing on references to red slime or cocoons or mutations." A grimace twisted her mouth. "Unfortunately, only about a third of the materials are in English, but I'll skim for drawings."

"If it's a language that's still in use anywhere, I can absorb enough understanding via the nexus to read it." I'd discovered by accident that tapping into the arcane flows for a particular area was like plugging into a database of the culture, language, and customs.

Jill smacked her forehead with an open palm. "I forgot about your nexus trick!" She smiled. "How many languages are you fluent in now?"

I grinned. "I'm not *fluent* in anything but English unless I'm still connected to the flows for that region. But apparently enough sticks to the walls of my brain after I unplug that I can *almost* make myself understood in Spanish, Portuguese, Mandarin, Farsi, Punjabi, and Zulu."

"Zulu? Seriously?"

"Yeah, though I have a tough time getting my tongue around the consonants." I reluctantly dragged the subject back on track. "Jill, I ran into Xharbek at Fed Central."

She drew a sharp breath . "I have every law enforcement agency on the lookout for Carl! Is he still there?"

"I don't know. But he wasn't using the Carl, er, shape." Disguise? Outfit? Skin? Was there a correct terminology?

Her forehead creased. "Then how did you know it was him?"

"Because he was . . . Zack Garner."

"Does that mean Xharbek found them?" Jill seized my hand

in a painful grip. "Does he have my daughter?" She couldn't bear to say it, but her eyes shrieked, *Has he killed her?*

"No, I'm positive he doesn't have them." Though not for lack of trying. "Xharbek is taking advantage of Zack's absence, using his Special Agent Garner persona to infiltrate and commandeer the FBI's arcane division and influence everyone at Fed Central."

Anger flashed in her eyes. "I don't understand. You were right in front of him and you didn't do anything?" The chair skittered back as she pushed to her feet. "How could you just let him go? Are you too fucking high and mighty to get your hands dirty?"

I slowly stood, remaining silent while she continued to rage. She needed to get this out of her system.

"Goddammit, Kara! I got to hold my daughter for one whole fucking minute! You know what kind of hell I'm going through here, and you didn't do *shit!*" She seized the legal pad and flung it away. No doubt she'd intended for it to smack impressively into a bookcase, but instead it coughed out a few papers during a short and wobbly course before flopping to the floor in a sad heap. A single piece of paper floated down in lovely back and forth swoops, finally settling gently to the table.

"Well, shit," she said. "So much for my grand tantrum."

I scooped up the paper and skimmed it, then gave her a horrified look. "Jill, this is awful!"

"What?" She started toward me, worry filling her eyes. "What is it?"

"Oregano. Macaroni. Sardines. Peanuts." I backed away as she tried to snatch the paper from me. "These will be *horrible* cookies!"

"Oh! You!" She grabbed the shopping list then seized me in a hug. "I'm sorry. I'm so so so sorry."

I wrapped my arms around her. "You should be. Sardines in cookies? What kind of monster are you?"

Jill hiccupped a laugh then released me and wiped her eyes. "You are such a dork." She took a deep breath and blew it out. "Okay, Xharbek is impersonating Zack, and you didn't grab him because, duh, you're not a demigod and you don't have a death wish."

"Actually, I did grab him. But, yeah, demigod." I made a face. "I hate to say it, but taking Zack's place is a pretty smart move on his part. Not to mention, an added *Fuck You* to Zakaar."

Jill dropped back into her chair with a sigh. "Yeah. He's smart."

"Hey now, our AWOL four are smart, too," I said. "Smart and sharp enough to have hidden from Xharbek all this time." I mentally crossed fingers that Xharbek's energy signature would give me an edge in locating them. "They're going to be all right," I insisted. "No getting bummed out now."

She remained silent and still for close to half a minute before she finally spoke. "There are days when this library seems to mock me with how much I don't know, but then I realize that I know things it doesn't, and I can learn, and conjecture, or have faith that something is true." She spread her hands flat on the table. "I know that my daughter is special. *Very* special. I've learned that the man I knew as FBI Agent Ryan Kristoff is actually Szerain, an exiled demonic lord, and I learned that the man I fell in love with, the father of my child, isn't a man at all, but a beautiful and powerful creature who's lived longer than humans have walked on Earth." Her eyes lifted to mine. "I've conjectured that if Xharbek gets his hands on my daughter, I will never see or touch her again." Her breath shuddered. "But I have faith . . ." She shook her head. "I *have* to believe that Zack would never hurt our child and would never separate us unless he felt the need was truly desperate." Her hands tightened into fists. "Yet at the same time, I'm absolutely certain that he was *wrong* to take her away from me. I'm her mother. I should be with her."

"You'll get her back," I said fiercely. "We'll fix everything and take down Xharbek, and you'll get her back."

Jill squared her shoulders, pulling her composure together to give me a nod. "I have faith in you most of all."

"You fucking bitch," I muttered as my eyes filled with tears. Sniffling, I blotted them with my sleeve. "That was really low."

She laughed. "Well, I do. You're Kara Gillian, the Supreme Arcane Commander, Mistress of the Nexus." Her eyes danced. "And of a certain demonic lord."

"You did *not* just go there."

"I'm sorry, how long have you known me?"

"Not nearly long enough."

Chapter 8

Rhyzkahl was still in his house with the door closed when I returned to the nexus. Fine with me. The less distraction, the better.

Though I'd spent countless hours searching for Ashava and the others, this time a flutter of anticipation accompanied me as I stepped onto the slab. I had Xharbek's energy signature now, as well as my suspicion that he'd narrowed down where they were. If I could find where his nasty self had left the most footprints, I could focus my own search.

I danced the shikvihr, tracing the swoops and arcs of the luminescent sigils with practiced grace until seventy-seven of them floated around me—seven full rings, bright and potent thanks to the augmentation and lord-like focus of the nexus. Though I was able to create floating sigils here on the nexus, mastery of all eleven rings would give me the ability to do so everywhere else on Earth. Floaters offered a huge advantage in speed and intensity over chalk diagrams or glyphs traced without substance in the air. Moreover, each completed ring came with an increase in power. Unfortunately, my training with Mzatal had come to a screeching halt after the battle at the Farouche Plantation, and I had zero idea when it might resume, if ever. With Mzatal closed off and the worlds at war, it was all too possible he might never train me again. And the only other available lord was not someone I wished to train with.

My gaze slid to the little house in Rhyzkahl's orbit. No fucking way did I want him training me, but there was more than one way to skin a cat. Part of the upgraded security system included surveillance cameras that monitored every inch of the nexus and

Rhyzkahl's prison. And he practiced the shikvihr for hours every day.

A smile stretched my mouth. Learning the sigils from security videos was far from ideal, but it was better than the nothing I had otherwise. Time to take matters into my own hands. After all, no way would I settle for less than the complete ritual.

In the meantime, even a partial shikvihr augmented my arcane skills. Every day I repeated the ritual, using the borrowed power of the nexus like a robotic suit to move my arcanely paralyzed body. Sigil by sigil, I re-carved the mental pathways that made me a summoner, and sigil by sigil, I reminded my essence of who and what I truly was.

Angus McDunn had left a seed of my talent behind when he'd stripped the rest. The nexus and my work with the shikvihr were its fertilizer and super-grow lights, allowing me to regain in weeks what might have otherwise taken years.

With a sweep of my arm, I ignited the rings and drank in the power. They flared then settled into a slow spin around me, seven concentric rings. Using my lord-sight perspective, the flows of Earth potency leaped into a colorful other-worldly hologram around me. Here on the nexus, I sensed them like a network of luminous arteries that spanned the globe. I was able to easily decipher their pulses, detect and smooth turbulence, and identify affected locations. Off the nexus, I could barely even grasp the concept—clear evidence of the vast difference between humans and the demonic lords. Though the lords were half human, their other half came from the nearly godlike demahnk.

Now that I was connected to the flows, I recalled the feel of Xharbek, used it as a focus and methodically eliminated areas where I sensed nothing of his signature, like crossing off states on a map. I continued to painstakingly exclude sections of flows until I was left with perhaps a dozen possibilities, places that flickered with Xharbek's arcane footprint. Faint, but there.

So far so good. Now to search within those areas. Though Ashava and Zack had strong arcane signatures, I limited my search to Szerain's since I knew his best of all. Made no difference that he'd been suppressed as Ryan during most of my time with him. The signature was the same. Szerain was Ryan. Ryan was Szerain.

Deepening my concentration, I called up memories to augment my search. Laughing with him while watching his sci-fi

TV shows. Arguing over waffles. Promising I wouldn't forget him when he faced being submerged again. A parting kiss. Hours of . . .

Like an electric shock, resonance of Szerain's signature shuddered through me. Yet in the next instant it slipped away. Pulse racing, I expanded my senses and traced the energy—right to Beaulac. Beaulac? No way. Had Szerain seriously been hiding under our noses this entire time? I zoomed in on the echo then screeched to a figurative halt.

"The hell?" I muttered. A dome of potency shimmered like an iridescent soap bubble over a ten-mile-wide circle, with downtown Beaulac smack dab in the center. I *knew* that dome hadn't been there the day before. Moreover, Szerain's signature echoed from somewhere within it, fading with each second that passed.

Baffled and worried, I probed the dome then, emboldened, sent my consciousness through its outer layer.

Xharbek. I felt his undeniable stamp on the dome like a prickle at the nape of my neck. But no hint of the AWOL four. I tried to push farther in, but my progress slowed, as if I was slogging through honey. *It's a shield*, I realized in annoyance, yet with a hint of triumph as well. Xharbek must have constructed this after our encounter, which told me he'd narrowed down his quarry's location to this ten-mile area and didn't want me snooping around.

This was cause for a little mental boogie. My missing people were still missing, but this was the first definable *progress* I'd made toward tracking them down. Plus, if the shield was here to keep them from getting out and finding a new hiding place—like putting a cup over a spider—maybe I could figure out a way to pry up the edge, or at least peek in.

I pushed deeper, but had to stop almost immediately as a tangle of detached potency strands blocked the way. Usually this sort of worm knot writhed and disrupted the flows around it, but this one was stuck tight to the shield-dome and still as stone. Strange, but I figured that meant it should be simple enough to bypass. Yet when I attempted to skirt it, I received a mind-numbing jolt of *badness* that left me trembling, both physically and mentally, for half a dozen heartbeats.

Fine. I'd take the time to unravel it. No problem. I'd untangled dozens of potency knots over the last two months, and those were the thrashing, squirming kind. This would be a breeze.

A minute into the process, it kicked into life and began to wriggle, but I already had control of it. Plus, now I had no trouble seeing which strand I needed to pull to undo the knot. I gave it a tug, then watched with satisfaction as the tangle writhed like flailing worms. In a few seconds it would slither apart and settle into a nice, uncomplicated state, allowing me to continue on my merry way.

It began to expand—unusual, though most likely the precursor to separating out. But all thoughts of worm knots fled my mind at a feather touch. Exultation rose as I felt my AWOL four like an echoed whisper—Zakaar, Szerain, Ashava, and Sonny. The contact lasted only the barest of instants, but it was enough. *They're alive. And I know where they are.* Well, almost. Still, "somewhere in the Beaulac area" was a tetch more precise than "somewhere in the universe or possibly on another plane of existence."

Brimming with confidence, I returned my attention to the knot, startled to see that it had expanded even more. And the number of strands had at least *doubled*. My confidence melted into unease then shifted to outright dread as the knot began to pulse in a heavy, ominous rhythm that sent shudders of discord through the shield-dome and adjacent potency flows.

Great. Wonderful. I'd gone and taken a stable construct and made it awful. Not only that, but it was my mess to clean up since it was Earthside. No chance that one of the lords in the demon realm would see the issue and fix it for me. I groaned. There was only one lord on Earth and available to possibly help me out. Crapsticks.

"Rhyzkahl," I called out, hating it with every fiber of my being.

He didn't emerge for nearly half a minute, long enough for me to wonder if he was doing another stand-and-defy-me. I really didn't want to drag him out, since that would be a lousy preface to asking for his help. I was just starting to get antsy when he finally stalk-sauntered out. His expression announced *I could not care less what you think or want to do*, but a hitch in his bearing made me wonder if perhaps he'd chosen not to defy me this time because he didn't have the confidence to test his power so soon after his last defeat.

I shoved down the flicker of sympathy. No time for that shit right now. "I need your help," I said, not bothering to hide my worry. "Or advice, or whatever you can offer. There's a really weird knot in the flows."

Rhyzkahl crouched to inspect the irises beside his door. He cradled a rich purple bloom against his palm, caressed a petal with his thumb. "What can I do from within this prison?"

Aggravation swelled at his bullshit antics, but I managed to keep it from my voice. "You can tell me what to do."

"What did you tamper with to cause such an issue?" he asked, tone smooth and snide. He shifted to pull a weed from a row of beets.

I scowled. "There was a worm knot over Beaulac. I've unkinked dozens of those with no problem, but this time it—" I broke off in horror as the blob pulsed, and flows from Greenland to Brazil flickered and dimmed. "Shit. Shit. The knot expanded and went crazy. It's causing potency fluctuations all over the world." I swallowed, mouth dry. "Rhyzkahl, I need help. Your help."

He went stone still, hand an inch away from a plant, then stood in a fluid move. "Release me."

My glare could have melted steel. "You know I can't do that!"

"Then this issue must not be of grave importance to you."

Before I could snarl a reply, a sudden gust of wind whipped my hair into my face, and a shadow fell over the nexus. Cursing, I shoved my hair out of my eyes only to see Rhyzkahl staring past me in open-mouthed shock. Expecting a threat, I whirled. Then stared.

A massive tree speared into the sky above us, with a trunk that spanned the five-foot gap from the inner edge of Rhyzkahl's orbit to the lip of the nexus. A tree with a smooth, white trunk and leaves the color of emerald and amethyst, that towered over even the tallest pines on my property.

This was a demon realm *grove* tree.

My mind flopped and fumbled uselessly. I couldn't even begin to comprehend the significance of a grove tree insta-sprouting on Earth, much less in my back yard. Yet I had no time to speculate. I reestablished my lord-view of the flows, heart sinking as I assessed. The knot was over ten times its original size, and a half dozen major flows were dull grey and stagnant. "It's sucking the life out of the other flows," I said in a voice that cracked and shook. "I think it's going to burst!"

Rhyzkahl tore his eyes from the tree and gave me his full attention, arrogance and swagger gone. "Show me."

"How?" I demanded. "How am I supposed to show you?"

"Find a way or open my prison." His gaze lifted over my head and tracked down to me even as I felt a feather light touch on my shoulder.

A jewel-tone leaf shimmered against the maroon of my shirt. I reverently grasped the stem, and pins and needles prickled in my fingers as if they were waking up. I'd never held a leaf from a grove tree before. As far as I knew, no one had. Leaves didn't *fall* from grove trees.

Except for this one.

The tingle swept up my arm and through my head. "Weave it," I murmured. Holding the brilliant purple and green leaf in my left hand, I spun out glowing strands of potency with my right, shaping them into an arcane macramé sculpture in the likeness of the aneurysm knot. "There," I said to Rhyzkahl. "It looks like that."

He paled. "It is the precursor to an anomaly, Kara Gillian."

Dread snaked ice-cold tendrils through my gut. An anomaly was a destructive—potentially catastrophic—breach in the dimensional fabric. Not long ago I'd watched via dream link as a gigantic anomaly spawned in Rhyzkahl's realm, spewing fire rain and triggering catastrophic degeneration that undermined the integrity of both the physical world and the arcane. It had taken the combined efforts of the demahnk and every available lord to bring it under control, and all had suffered injuries during the protracted battle.

We both looked up as the sky shimmered then settled into a darker shade of blue. Rhyzkahl stepped as close to the nexus as his prison would allow, his jaw set in determination. "You must release me, or you doom both our worlds."

When was he going to get it through his thick skull that I *couldn't* fucking let him go, and wouldn't if I could? It was clear he didn't think I could do what needed to be done, even if he decided to unbend enough to tell me. But who else was there? Xharbek? Sure, he might defuse the pre-anomaly . . . or he might rip it wide open and be done with the whole mess. Even if I had a way to reach him in time, I couldn't risk it.

Flows from Beijing to Honolulu dimmed. *It's on me to fix this.* "Can I bleed off the pressure behind it?"

"It cannot be bled into either realm," he said, urgency in his stance and tone. "How can this be here?"

"What difference does it make? Focus on the problem! Tell me how to fix it!"

"It . . ." He cursed and clenched his right hand to control the shaking. "You . . . you must . . ."

"Can it be bled elsewhere? Maybe into the valve system?" I shot an uneasy look up at the sky, now a weird shade of indigo.

"No! To the—" He said a demon word that I knew referred to the interdimensional space. Even balled into a fist, his hand shook. "I can repair this, but I cannot tell you how to do so. *Release me.*"

The back door banged open. Pellini glanced up then over at me, startling at the sight of the gigantic tree. "Weird shit's going on all over the place, Kara!" he called out. "But I'm thinking you already know that."

"I sure do," I shouted. "Trying to deal with it. Keep monitoring reports and let me know if anything's about to hit here!" *Can't save the world if a tornado sucks me up.* To my relief, Pellini simply nodded and returned inside. Either he had faith in me or he figured we were all going to die and there was no point getting worked up about it. I yanked my attention to Rhyzkahl. "Tell me what to do!"

A sheen of sweat glistened on his forehead. "You must . . ." He swallowed, gaze skittering around him as if seeking a lifeline. Panic filled his eyes, and his mouth worked soundlessly.

The leaf tingled warm in my hand, and realization struck home. Rhyzkahl wasn't being defiant. He literally *couldn't* tell me what to do, didn't have the focus to break things down and explain them. He'd lived with the support and influence of Zakaar for three thousand years, and his brain wasn't going to rewire itself to stand on its own overnight.

"Zakaar isn't here, but I am. You know what to do. I have no doubt about that." Behind me, the leaves of the grove tree rustled like a whispering voice. "Don't think of everything that needs to be done. Step by step. Tell me the first thing I need to do. Nothing else."

Some of the panic melted from Rhyzkahl's expression. "Find . . . the strand with the least energy in it."

Progress at last. "Right. I can do that."

Except I couldn't. It wasn't a dozen tangled threads anymore. Hundreds, *thousands* of strands teamed like eels on meth. *I'm going to fail.* The thought sliced through my skull with blades of despair. What the hell was I thinking? Anomalies were battled by demahnk and lords—teams of them. Not one human quasi-summoner.

Chest tight, I tore my gaze from our impending doom. Below me, the silvery patterns glistened in the black stone of the nexus.

The despair vanished. I knew exactly what I needed.

With zero grace, I flopped onto my back atop the pattern of silvery sigils, then relaxed and allowed its potency to embrace me. In lord-sight, the Earth flows surrounded me as if I lay in the center of a spherical planetarium.

No. Too much input. Too much for my human mind to process even with the nexus boost. With deep, slow breaths, I calmed my racing pulse and refined my focus. Thousands upon thousands of meth-addled eels writhed and pulsed. *Closer. Focus on the problem.* I blocked out the rest of the flows, pulled in on the pre-anomaly until it occupied the entire sky above me, like zooming in on a touchscreen. Amongst the flailing eels, one strand twitched, curled and grey.

"I found the weak strand," I said. "Now what?"

"If it is retroflexed, do not touch it."

"Can't you just say 'bent backwards'? It's curled. Is that what you mean?"

"English is inadequate."

Despite our desperate situation, I grinned. "Then tell me in demon."

If he was surprised that I'd tapped into the language, he didn't waste time showing it. Step by tedious step, he gave me detailed instructions that I carefully followed to unite or disentangle or destroy. The demon language flowed through me, rich with telepathic nuances unavailable in English.

Hours later—or at least that's how it felt—I'd resolved the knot from millions of strands to a single bulging balloon with two outlets. Even though I'd been lying down the whole time, my entire body ached, muscles quivering at the end of their endurance.

Rhyzkahl gave me the final steps. I simultaneously activated the refeed to Earth's flows and the pressure release to interdimensional space. For a moment, nothing happened, then the pre-anomaly shrank and vanished with a *pop* that seemed to echo throughout the universe.

A weak chuckle rasped out of me. "We're still here, so I guess it worked." The world flows seemed intact and had regained much of their previous luster, but the number of interdimensional rifts had increased. Damn it. At least no anomalies. I reassessed Xharbek's shield-dome of potency over Beaulac.

Now it quivered like fluorescent lime Jell-O rather than the surface of a bubble, but it appeared stable enough.

Zoop. Sha.

I sat bolt upright. "What the hell?" The sound was the dimensional fabric opening and resealing, which told me something had come through. But I had no idea *what*, and my attempts to track it yielded zilch.

Zoop. Sha.

This time, I caught an echo. Whatever-it-was had passed through somewhere to the south. Within seconds, the Beaulac shield-dome flattened as if an invisible weight slowly pressed down on it.

Zoooooooop. Splort. Sha.

I couldn't have missed that one if I tried. A compact ball of bluish potency flashed and rotated about ten miles away, even as the shield-dome re-expanded. Narrowing my eyes, I focused in on that area. The parking lot of Ruthie's Smoothies—a known hot spot that now had a brand new irregularity. "Gotcha, you little bitch." As soon as I finished dealing with this crap, I could go investigate the—

The Earth flows winked out. My heart lurched in shock, but a heartbeat later they flickered back to life in sections, like power returning to a city, grid by grid. I blinked, then blinked again and shook my head. Something was different. The flows *felt* the same, but the color seemed off.

My head throbbed with the effort of holding the lord-sight for so long, which was probably why the flows looked odd. I released it then gasped with relief under a perfectly normal blue sky and a perfectly un-normal demon tree. *We're still here. The world is still here.* Good enough.

I staggered to my feet with *Thank you for your help* on my tongue, but the words crumbled beneath sudden revulsion. Tendrils of red potency crept along the ground and wound through the trees like arcane kudzu. *Everywhere.*

Rhyzkahl startled, recoiling from the strands nearest him before steadying. "Rakkuhr," he murmured, eyes alight with victory at odds with the dismay in his voice. "They succeeded."

Aghast, I took in the sight and feel of the sinister alien potency of the demon realm. Terrible comprehension hit me like a hammer between the eyes. The rakkuhr hadn't popped into existence when the flows went dark. It had already been here. Undoing the tangle of the pre-anomaly had somehow opened a pathway that made it visible to othersight.

"How can it be here?" I sputtered. "It's not native to Earth. How did it . . . ?" I yanked my gaze to the flows as my dread flared into pure, unadulterated horror. Not only was the rakkuhr on Earth, but it permeated the flows as well. Throughout the world, rakkuhr seeped from every rift. And there, at the rubble of the Beaulac Police Department, a.k.a. ground zero, rakkuhr streamed from the demon realm to Earth.

Nauseated, I pulled away from the flows. "What did you mean, 'they succeeded?' Was this the Mraztur plan? Flood Earth with rakkuhr?"

Rhyzkahl surveyed the coils of rakkuhr, brow furrowed. "Not this soon," he said as if to himself. "Not this much."

All that rakkuhr at ground zero . . . I sucked in a sharp breath and pressed a hand to my stomach. "Cory. Is the rakkuhr the reason why he and the others are changing?"

"Changing? How?"

I narrowed my eyes. "Red gel pod and metamorphosis."

As if I'd thrown a switch, Rhyzkahl regained his composure and put on a neutral mask.

Well, that answered my question. "You're attacking Earth," I said, anger rising. "Why would you maniacs do that?"

Rhyzkahl gestured toward his orbit. "I am attacking nothing."

Hands clenched, I fought the urge to pound him flat with the potency at my disposal. But through my haze of rage, I mentally replayed the last few seconds. He'd been shocked and damn near appalled by the amount of rakkuhr, right up until the moment I mentioned people changing. Then he became all lordly.

I carefully banked my fury and stepped off the nexus, walked up to him and folded my arms over my chest. "People are changing. That didn't surprise you, which tells me you were expecting it." I lifted my chin. "Is that your goal? Mutate everyone?"

Rhyzkahl met my gaze levelly. "With so much rakkuhr, such is always possible." An unpleasant smile curved his mouth though a glimmer of fear haunted his eyes. "Have you never wondered why the *nyssor* and *mehnta* resemble humans so closely?"

He could have slapped me with a fish, and I wouldn't have been as shocked. Nyssor were demons who looked like adorable human children, except for eyes with sideways-slit pupils, and a mouth full of hundreds of needle-sharp teeth. And mehnta looked like human women, except for the wings beneath a hard, shiny green carapace on their back, and a dozen or so tentacles in place of a mouth. And sure, I'd wondered why those two species resembled humans, but I'd chalked it up as yet one more weird thing about the demon realm.

But humans mutated by rakkuhr made perfect and horrible sense. Of course, it also confirmed Rhyzkahl had known the rakkuhr influx would happen, and that people would be mutated by it.

"This is an attack, and you were a part of it," I said with sad weariness. "Part of the Mraztur's plan to send rakkuhr pouring through to Earth." I shook my head, feeling numb and sick. "Even after how you betrayed me, I never expected your end goal to be the destruction of my world." I sighed. "You really are a piece of filth."

"It was *not* my goal," he replied, lip curling. "Your *chekkunden* lover destroyed the last chance of a gentler solution."

"Chekkunden" roughly translated to "honorless scum." Damn, was I ever tempted to smack him into a different kind of orbit. "That's hysterical," I said. "Mzatal's the only lover I've had who *isn't* chekkunden. Meanwhile, *you* lead the pack when it comes to my asshole exes." I narrowed my eyes. "And what did Mzatal do to fuck up your so-called gentler solution? And solution to what?"

His scarred right hand twitched, and he clenched it. "He disrupted our ritual. Stole you away."

Stole you away. Time slowed to a crawl, and I went completely and utterly still. Mzatal had indeed stolen me away—from the ritual in which Rhyzkahl had tortured me, bringing pain upon pain as he carved sigils into my flesh with his essence blade and rakkuhr. Had Mzatal failed, I would have lost my *self* and become Rowan, a weaponized summoner for the Mraztur.

"*That* was your gentler solution?" My voice was soft with rage. "Torturing me? Destroying me? Turning me into a thrall?"

Rhyzkahl's gaze bored into mine. "Gentler for Earth," he said. "Gentler for humans."

Every beat of my heart seemed to shake the air. I didn't want to ask the question, didn't want to know the answer. Didn't want to know if perhaps it had been wrong to survive the torment.

"And what, pray tell," I managed, "is the problem that requires such a *gentle* solution?"

His face remained impassive. "The impending destruction of the demon realm and, subsequently, Earth."

Bullshit. I didn't trust him. Couldn't trust him. And I certainly couldn't believe that anything was as cut and dried as "had to sacrifice you or we all die." Asshole.

"Then I guess I need to get my ass in gear so I can save the world." I gestured grandly to the arcane tendrils of red and shadow. "Enjoy your rakkuhr." And with that I turned my back on him and headed to the house.

Chapter 9

Pellini came out onto the back porch as I reached the steps. "I'm going to go out on a limb and say that this is bad. Right?" He swept a worried look over the tendrils of rakkuhr.

"Extremely," I said, "and it'll only get worse." A low headache took up residence at the base of my skull. "Is Jill inside? I'll fill everyone in about all this crap, but I need to talk to her first."

"She's in the war room."

I thanked him and headed to what used to be my dining room. Now maps covered three walls, and dominating the fourth was a giant flatscreen TV permanently tuned to the recently created Demon News Network. Despite the silly name, DNN really did maintain the best and most up-to-date coverage of arcane-related world events. Jill sat at the far end of a long table littered with papers, and weapons. A thick, leather-bound book lay open in front of her, and a plate of chocolate chip cookies remained untouched atop a pile of reports.

She frowned when I entered. "You look stressed. Eat a cookie."

"I am, and I will," I said, "but before I tell everyone the bad news, I have a bit of good news for you." Jill straightened. I took a deep breath and bulled on. "Even though things went to shit out on the nexus, I got a signature hit on the AWOL four."

She dropped her hands to her lap. I didn't need to see to know she was clenching them together. "What does that mean in people-speak?" she asked quietly.

"That they're alive for sure. And on Earth . . . sort of."

"Where?" Her eyes narrowed. "And what does 'sort of' mean?"

I probably could have left off that last part. "I know they're within a five mile radius of downtown Beaulac, but the arcane signatures phase in and out. Like they're here then they're not, but . . . more here than not." I winced. "I wish I could explain it better."

Jill sat in silence for a moment. "You'll tell me when you have more specifics." It was an order backed by a scary undercurrent of intensity.

"The instant I know."

She nodded, quick and firm. "I'll call Bryce and Pellini in so you can give us the bad news."

After the two arrived, I briefed everyone on the unfolding rakkuhr disaster. Pellini monitored our DIRT feed on the laptop, face going stony as I spoke.

"Are we all going to mutate?" Bryce asked when I finished. "I'll put in my order for wings now."

"I'll make a note of it," I said, grateful for the attempt at humor in a terrible situation.

"Is the new landscaping part of this?" Jill asked.

It took me a second to figure out what she meant. "Oh, the tree! No, it's a demon realm grove tree. As weird as it sounds, it's more than just a tree. It's, er, an ally." I spread my hands. "Sorry. It was freaky for it to appear out of nowhere. And no, I have no idea how or why it did."

Jill rolled her eyes. "I've seen weirder things. At least it hasn't tried to eat anyone. Yet."

"I think we're safe from being eaten," I assured her.

"Can you draw on grove power now that it's here?" Pellini asked.

"No, it won't work quite like that," I said, knowing without even needing to try. "This tree is just a satellite branch of the demon realm groves." I managed an innocent look as a collective groan rose at the pun.

"So what's our next move with the evil red magic?" Bryce asked.

"I don't know how to stop the flow of rakkuhr," I said, "but there has to be a way, and we're going to damn well find it."

"Well, duh." Jill flexed her biceps. "Saving the world is what we do."

I chuckled. "Yeah, I guess it kind of is." But my good cheer quickly drained away under the weight of everything else. "Speaking of, how's the rest of the world?" Maybe we'd be lucky and the only fallout from the worm-knot-pre-anomaly-crap would be a few minutes of oddly colored skies around the world.

Pellini's grim expression gutted that hope. "Earthquake in Kansas. Fire rain in Buenos Aires. Tornados in Manhattan and Fairbanks. Over a dozen simultaneous rifts, including a hundred-footer down in New Orleans." He turned the laptop so I could see the DIRT command reports updating like crazy on the screen. I'd be up to my eyeballs in calls soon. No rest for the—

A flurry of action on the TV caught my eye. "Someone unmute that!"

DNN coverage showed a jagged crevice running several hundred yards down a traffic-clogged street in India. A thick layer of ice rimmed its edges—a sure sign of a sizable interdimensional rift below. Within the fissure, garish magenta flames roiled and lit the night. The ticker at the bottom of the screen read "Hundreds feared injured and dead in Mumbai" between insets of chaos at two other sites. I watched in sick horror as a black and yellow auto-rickshaw teetered on the brink then tumbled into the abyss. I didn't want to think how many vehicles and people had been swallowed when the thing opened.

Pellini hit the remote just as DNN anchorman Nigel Crowe turned the audio over to their man in the field. Screams, shouts, and honking horns backed the reporter's frenzied commentary.

"That's the biggest rift yet," Bryce said. "It'll be a bitch to contain."

"No demons yet, though," Pellini said. "Maybe we'll luck out."

"That's like hoping for no mosquitos in the swamp." I slouched into my seat but straightened again as the camera panned to the arrival of DIRT helicopters. With nowhere to land, the choppers hovered while armed team members rappelled to car roofs. Idris Palatino was the first down, expression deadly serious.

"Thank god Idris was close enough to respond," Bryce said.

"Blind luck," I said. "That team was on twenty-four hour R&R in Mumbai before heading to Kolkata." With the super-fast response time and Idris's skill, there was a slim chance he could slap an arcane Band-Aid on the rift before any demons came through and complicated matters. It wouldn't stop them, but it would at least keep the rift from expanding long enough for the DIRT team to get into position.

"He's looking pretty buff," Jill said. The cameraman seemed to agree since he stayed on him. Idris swept an appraising gaze over the scene then began to dance the shikvihr atop a van while the rest of the team deployed SkeeterCheater over the far end of the rift. No way would they have enough of the graphene-composite netting to cover a fissure this big, but they might manage to tangle a few demons.

As if the bastards heard my thoughts, at least a dozen kehza swarmed from the rift, gaining altitude fast. Crocodile-like savik clung to the walls just below the lip, working their claws to weave potency in ways that could only mean bad news for Earth.

Idris sealed the second ring of his shikvihr, then scanned the area to assess the demon activity. He unslung something from a shoulder strap and fished a golf ball-sized glass sphere from a belt pouch.

Bryce leaned closer to the TV. "Is that a *slingshot*?"

As the world watched, Idris wiggled his fingers over the sphere, then loaded the slingshot and fired at the nearest kehza. The cameraman zoomed on the demon in time to capture the sphere bouncing off an invisible shield a few inches from the demon's hide. Idris raised his hand to signal his team, and an instant later bullets tore into the demon's midsection. Shrieking, it tumbled to the ground.

"Oh snap!" I cried out in delight. "He used an arcane grenade to disrupt the kehza's shielding!" It didn't matter that the arcane wasn't visible on TV. I could infer what he'd done. About a year ago I'd fallen victim to an arcane "grenade." When I told Idris about how it had dampened the arcane in its area of effect, he'd been fascinated by the concept. I wasn't at all surprised that he'd figured out a way to replicate it. He must have made several in advance and infused them with potency right before firing them.

For the next minute or so Idris "charged" and shot more spheres. To my surprise, he had a Glock and was helping take down the demons as soon as they lost their shielding.

His gun jammed, and we all held our breaths as a kehza wheeled toward him. But without an instant of hesitation, Idris went straight into the slap-rack-ready procedure to clear the jam then fired on the kehza, taking the demon out before it could dive.

Pellini let out a whoop. "I taught him that! Did you see how smoothly he cleared that jam? And look at that perfect shooting form."

"Your training just saved his life," I said with a warm smile. "You have a right to be proud."

I looked back at the TV in time to see a kehza with a wing-span of at least twenty feet swoop toward the camera, a single gold loop glinting in the demon's ear. The jaws of its Chinese dragon-like head stretched wide in an all too familiar ululating war cry. The camera swung away and tumbled before it cut out, but the audio continued for another disturbing second.

Pellini jumped to his feet. "Jesus fuck!"

I hit the mute button as the coverage switched to a smaller scale incursion in Jakarta, where the Indonesian Army with no DIRT backup fired grenades to try to dislodge savik from the fissure. "Shit! Bryce, contact DIRT HQ and tell them to get word to Jakarta to stop firing grenades into the rift." The locals were doing what made sense to them, but they were only going to make the rifts bigger. We needed liaisons in all the local militaries, but there was never enough personnel, never enough training, never enough time.

Bryce retreated to the living room to make the call. I sagged back into my chair. "At least we still *have* a world." I sighed. "Even if it is getting demon smacked."

"We're going to need a lot more cookies," Pellini muttered.

As I snorted in amusement, my phone rang. Detective Marco Knight of the NOPD. So much for the rift in New Orleans being just a rift.

"Hey, Marco," I said. "Lemme guess, you have a bunch of demonic arrivals?"

"Huh? No. No demons. At least not with me." The connection hissed and crackled from the ever-present arcane interference. "I, uh, had a feeling I needed to go out to Audubon Park."

"No kidding?" I kept my tone light. Knight got hunches about stuff that usually turned out to be important, but he seldom enjoyed the results of his talent. "Did you find a pot of gold?"

"No gold, but about a minute after I got here, a guy appeared out of thin air. He's stretched out on the grass naked as a jaybird. White male, olive complexion, black hair, dark eyes. Looks like he's in his twenties."

I massaged my temples. When it rained it poured. "Has he said anything to you? Like where he came from and how he got there?"

"Yeah, he muttered something I couldn't understand except for *Kara* clear as day, then he passed out. Hang on, I'm sending you a pic of his face." He made a frustrated noise. "I know I should call it in to NOPD dispatch and Fed Central, but I just . . ."

"No, I get it," I said. He'd had a feeling. And I'd learned to trust Marco's feelings. I peered at the picture, but nothing clicked. Hard to tell much with the potency distortion. "I hate to do this, but is there any way you can bring him here?"

"I was afraid you'd say that." He let out a sigh. "Sure, I'll do that. DIRT has the roads blocked off between here and the station anyway."

"Thanks. I'll save some cookies for you."

"That's more like it."

Chapter 10

I wanted to nap. Holy cripes, did I ever want to nap, especially considering that I'd been called out at around five a.m. this morning. But there was shit I needed to do before I could rest. Hell, there was always shit that I needed to do, but some needed doing more than others.

A call to Idris went to his voicemail, which I totally expected considering I'd just watched him battle demons live. I left a quick message on the order of, "Saw you on TV. Looking sharp, and I want to know how you did that thing with the slingshot. Pellini cheered when you cleared the gun jam. Bad news is that rakkuhr is leaking through ground zero and the rifts, and it might be causing mutations. Call me when you get a chance."

That done, I called DIRT HQ to report the locations of the various new rifts I'd spotted from the nexus. I was often able to give DIRT a head start by seeing disturbances in the flows before a rift actually formed, but this time, it was too little, too late. After that, I sent an email to the other DIRT arcane specialists telling them about the rakkuhr. Though I didn't want to cause a panic by letting the general populace find out about an invisible magic mist that could mutate them, keeping this all to myself was impossible since the arcane users would see the rakkuhr for themselves. Besides, I wasn't the only arcane user in the world who might be able to come up with an answer. Of course that meant I had to officially include the Feds in the loop, since I had absolutely zero doubt they were monitoring all of my communications. I therefore shot off a carefully worded email to the various powers-that-be to whom I supposedly reported.

My final task was to call Dr. Patel and the CDC to let them

know what I'd discovered. Or I thought it was my final task. The instant I hung up, my phone rang from a number that had only called me twice before.

Gulping, I answered, "Good afternoon, Madam President," and then spent a solid quarter hour telling the President of the frickin' United States what I knew and didn't know, and yes ma'am I completely agree that this would cause a huge panic if it got out, etc.

By the time I hung up I was so exhausted and wrung out that it took me several seconds to realize Jill was speaking to me in her mother hen naggy tone.

I blinked at her. "Huh?"

"Eat something that's not cookie-shaped before you fall over," she ordered, pushing me to sit at the kitchen table. In front of me was a bowl of gumbo. I didn't think I had enough energy to even pick up the spoon, but after the first few bites, my body agreed that the whole fueling up thing was a darn good idea, and by the bottom of the bowl I had my second wind.

Good timing, since the gate guard radioed to let me know Knight had arrived with the mystery dude.

His car crunched to a stop in front of the house a minute later. I went out onto the porch and gave him a weary smile as he got out. He'd suffered a nasty ankle break in the valve explosion, so I was pleased to see that he'd graduated to an air cast.

"Thanks for doing this, Marco," I said as I came down the steps. "Is he conscious?"

"No, thank god," he said fervently. "The whole way here I kept muttering *don't wake up, don't wake up*. I could picture him coming to and freaking out, and then I'd get busted for not reporting it."

Knight was risking his career by not following proper procedure—possibly even risking his freedom, given the current state of affairs. I owed him. "If this guy was saying my name, I don't want Xharbek getting his hands on him." I filled Knight in about my encounter with fake-Zack at the command center, then added a quick rundown on Cory's situation and the plague victims.

"This is all so crazy. But for what it's worth, I got nothing as far as intuition about my passenger." His expression briefly shadowed. He didn't like talking about his clairvoyance. "Anyway, come see your boy."

Lying across the backseat was an unconscious man wrapped

in a blanket, belted down with all three sets of seatbelts. I leaned in to take a look at his face then jerked back so quickly I cracked my head on the edge of the door frame. "Shit!" Heart pounding, I rubbed my head while I struggled to comprehend what I'd seen.

"You okay, Kara? Do you know him?"

Cautious, I peered at the man's face again. "Sort of," I said, mouth dry. "But he's supposed to be dead. I mean, everyone thinks he died."

"Huh? Who is he?"

I looked at Knight. "An artist. Giovanni Racchelli, and he supposedly died in the seventeenth century."

It was a good thing I'd included "lots of really weird shit happens" in the job description for the security personnel, because once again I needed help moving an unconscious man. Fortunately, Giovanni weighed a lot less than giant gummy bear Cory, and the strong and burly Jordan Kellum scooped him up with ease and got him settled in the guest room. And, to my relief, scrounged a t-shirt and shorts and dressed him.

After Kellum left, I adjusted the blanket over Giovanni then flopped into the recliner beside the bed. In the kitchen, the microwave dinged—Knight heating a well-earned bowl of gumbo. I nestled into the cushions and told myself I could sit without moving for five whole minutes. Surely I deserved that much. I needed to let Idris know about Giovanni, but that wasn't mega-urgent. He had enough on his plate already. Besides, it was, what? Three in the morning or something in Mumbai? I tried to do the mental math to figure out the time difference, but my tired brain shot me the finger and refused to cough up anything useful.

As crazy as things were two months ago, they'd still been kind of normal. But now Cory lay encased in arcane rubbery goop in the living room, and Giovanni slept like the dead a few feet away. Would the world *ever* feel normal again? I let my head drop back and closed my eyes. Five minutes. I could pretend the world was fine and dandy for five minutes . . .

Warm comfort, nestled close to his side. His arm around me, my head on his shoulder. The scent of flowers is like the breath of heaven.

"Elinor! Wake up! There are stars to count."

I smile, only pretending to sleep. "And if I am weary of counting cakes and tunjen fruit and stars? What say you?"

"That you are the most contrary of all women." Giovanni laughs, and I laugh with him. How can I not?

The grass cushions us amidst the flowers of Lord Szerain's plexus garden. I open my eyes to the canopy of endless stars in the moonless night.

"Uno. Due. Tre," Giovanni says.

"Quattro. Cinque. Sei," I continue. "You have taught me the numbers to one thousand. Let us not fritter away this night counting. What other game shall we play?"

"Whatever we can imagine." He tightens his arm around me. My breath catches. "I have a rich imagination."

"What is it you imagine in this moment?"

I pull away and leap to my feet. In a heartbeat, I kick free of my slippers and take hold of my skirts. "That when I flee, you will pursue," I shout and dash for the grove.

"Always," he calls out.

Laughing, I run, the grass softer on my feet than the finest carpet. Starlight yields to the gentle amaranthine glow of my beloved grove. I pass into the tunnel of trees that leads to the heart. The leaves murmur, and I feel as if I could fly, as if Giovanni could dance among the stars with me.

He catches my arm in the central clearing, draws me around to face him. His smile is brighter than a night full of stars. "And in this moment, what shall we play?"

"A game." Heat spreads through me. Has his voice ever sounded so rough, so beautiful? "One where you strive to touch your lips to mine."

He bends close. "And should I win this game, what then is my prize?"

The heat turns to fire, and I can barely manage the words. "Then, you may kiss me."

He smiles and nuzzles my cheek. "This game is much to my liking."

"Of course it will then be my turn to play."

Giovanni brushes my lips with his, softly. Invitingly.

I shiver, pulse thrumming. "Ah . . . you play this game well."

"I would play it with no other, my precious Elinor," he murmurs against my lips then kisses me.

I moan as I sink into the kiss. He deepens it, and I lose myself for an eternity.

He breaks the kiss and caresses my hair. "Now it is your turn."

My breath shudders. "I should do well after experiencing your masterful play." I nuzzle him, almost touching my lips to his, teasing. He tries to capture them, and I evade but care not to resist longer. I entwine my fingers in his hair and pull him into my kiss.

He wraps me in his arms and kisses me as never before, then pulls back to gaze into my eyes. "You are my lifeblood and my laughter."

This is, in truth, heaven. I sigh and rest my head on his shoulder. "You are my light and my heart."

"As the stars and the grove are my witness, I will never leave you. I swear to you upon my essence. Never."

"Nor I, you," I murmur. "I love you, Giovanni."

"And I love you, Elinor." He holds me close, nuzzles the top of my head. "You are such a silly girl. What will I do with you?"

I smile against the demon-silk of his shirt. "You shall grow old with me and sit by the fire as we watch our grandchildren play."

A hissing growl from the direction of the tree tunnel stills his response. "Come, summoner."

Giovanni tenses. I try to turn, to face Lord Szerain's essence-bound demon, but Giovanni holds me fast. "Who bids this, Turek?" he asks.

"I do," Lord Szerain says.

Giovanni loosens his hold such that I may turn, but does not release me.

Turek crouches, toothy and fearsome, beside my lord. Xharbek, behind them, his iridescent wings folded close. My heart seeks escape from the confines of my breast. What dire need brings all three?

"What do you require of her?" Giovanni demands, his voice unwavering.

"The time for the ritual is upon us."

"But, my lord," I say, "it is not meant to be for a fortnight."

Lord Szerain extends his hand toward me, waiting. "The plans have changed, my dear."

"Szerain," Giovanni says, "she is not ready."

"I am!" I say. "I . . . have worked hard. Studied. Practiced."

Lord Szerain steps closer. "You have indeed. You are ready. Trust me."

Giovanni tightens his arm around me. "Elinor," he murmurs, "tell him no. Not tonight."

I twist to look into his face. "How can I deny him?"

He moves in front of me. "My lord, grant us until the sun rises. I beseech you."

Lord Szerain hesitates. Xharbek lays a hand upon his shoulder, and the lord draws a deep breath. "I cannot risk Rhyzkahl's interference. It must be tonight. It must be now."

I trust Lord Szerain with my life. Though ice fills my core, I incline my head to him. Trembling, I turn and lay my hands on each side of Giovanni's face. "When this is done, we shall watch the sunrise from atop the eastern tower."

"Elinor. Beloved. I will join you there anon," my love says with such tender earnest that my heart breaks to leave him thus.

Before I can tell him to be at peace, Lord Szerain loops his arm around my waist and propels me down the tree tunnel.

"Elinor!" Giovanni calls after me. "Elinor!"

Kara.

"Kara!"

I startled awake to Knight shaking my shoulder. In the bed, Giovanni murmured in his sleep, *"Elinor . . . Elinor,"* then fell silent again.

I grabbed Knight's wrist. "She went with him. She's going to die!"

"Who?" Knight said. His eyebrows drew together in question, yet his tone remained calm. "Was it a dream? Or a vision? It took a whole minute to wake you."

I gripped my head and stared at Giovanni. "A dream. I don't know. It was so real."

"A nightmare?"

"No. Just a dream. It was like I was experiencing Elinor's memory." At his puzzled look, I lifted my chin toward the bed. "His girlfriend. She died in the demon realm, and I have a glob of her essence hitchhiking on mine. Don't ask me how."

He peered at me with interest. "Could you control the dream?"

"I didn't even try. I was just there. I was *her*." I sorted through the experience. "I've had memory flashes from her before, but never this vivid. I felt what she felt." I managed a weak snort. "And trust me, it wasn't anything like what I'd've felt in the same situation. She was timid, without a shred of snark. Afraid. Trusting. But at the same time, strong."

"I get it." A note of excitement crept into his voice. "I really get it. You were seeing through her eyes, but was there more? Was there another perspective?"

"No." Gooseflesh crawled over me as the images whispered. "Maybe. It's weird. The dream was through her eyes, but now I can also see it as if from a camera nearby. How is that possible? I don't . . ." And then it was gone, leaving me with memory of only her perspective.

Knight grinned and slapped me on the back, startling me with both. "That's a dream-vision, Kara! That camera view will be there during the dream, too, but it takes practice to separate enough from the subject—Elinor in this case—to fly with the camera."

"Fly?" I'd had plenty of dream experiences thanks to the dream links Rhyzkahl had forged with me. Some were fully lucid, with others like flashes of memory. I'd even had Elinor dreams, but never where I'd *been* her while also having a separate perspective. Knight lived with visions and "feelings," so I had no reason to doubt him. Yet I also wasn't sure his experience applied to me.

"Flying is what I call it," he said. "Once I learned to separate from the person, I was able to use that camera view to fly around and get more information. Stuff they couldn't see or hear."

"You're telling me that I could have moved behind Szerain, or up above the trees?"

"It works that way for me, but I can't say for sure it would be the same for you," he said. "It sounds crazy, but that's how . . ." He hunched his shoulders, enthusiasm gone like a pricked soap bubble.

"How what?"

He shook his head. "It's probably nothing like your dream. Forget I said anything."

"Marco, if there's a chance there's more I can do in these dream-visions, I need to know. If you could teach me how to be a flying camera, it might come in handy if this ever happens again." When he fidgeted and glanced toward the door, I put the pieces together. "You've never talked to anyone about this before."

He shook his head but didn't volunteer more.

"It's cool. You don't have to spill your guts." I gave him an understanding smile. "Trust me, I've seen and done things I have no desire to share."

"Not like me," he murmured.

I shrugged. "You have visions." And occasional prophetic moments, but he didn't seem to remember those. "You know things about people, and yeah, it makes them uncomfortable, but that's their problem."

"It's all the time, Kara. *All* the time." He shoved his hands in his pockets. "I can't help it. I can't unsee or unhear it. I can't shut it out. I know more than I have a right to know. Especially . . . especially about emotional moments." His gaze cut toward me then skittered away.

"Have you ever seen *me*?" The instant the question left my mouth I realized how stupid it was. He'd just told me he saw stuff *all* the time.

Knight flushed. "I'm late for a detective meeting," he said and hurried from the room.

Crap. Did he see something bad? Or just really personal? "Marco, it's cool," I called after him. "I'm used to having no privacy." Shit. Wrong thing to say.

The front door opened and closed.

"Nice job, Kara," I muttered. The guy already lived an isolated personal life because of his "gift." He didn't need me to go all passive-aggressive on him. I debated buzzing gate security to stop him but realized that would probably only make matters worse. I'd call him later—after he had a chance to chill out. Or after he decided he'd never tell me anything again, *ever*.

Maybe I wasn't as used to having no privacy as I believed. Before Zack and Helori implanted their mental shielding, the demonic lords and their demahnk ptarl could read my every thought, whether they wanted to or not. I'd stopped being pissy about it some time ago since there was nothing they or I could do about it, and staying mad about unintentional voyeurism seemed like a huge waste of mental energy. But clearly, "not being mad" wasn't the same as "being totally okay with it," and in my overtired state I'd slapped out at a stressed and exhausted Marco.

I'd already known he had visions, but I hadn't realized they happened all the time. Or perhaps that was a recent development? I couldn't imagine how he'd remained a cop for so many years if he was constantly seeing and feeling things about perps and victims and even other cops. Was it getting worse for him? And if so, how long before he cracked?

"Crap," I sighed. My insensitivity had also lost me the opportunity to learn the flying camera trick. At least that was a low priority. I'd apologize to him later, when we weren't both so exhausted. *Ha!* Like that would happen anytime soon.

I pushed to my feet and stretched the worst of the kinks out of my back then checked on Giovanni. He still rested peacefully as if in natural sleep, and so I trudged on to the kitchen. "C'mon, Pellini. Let's go to the ice cream shop."

He gave me a narrow look over his laptop screen. "There's no ice cream at the ice cream shop."

"I know, and it's criminal. But there are big shiny crystals there along with a new irregularity that spawned while I was on the nexus."

Grumbling, he shut the computer. "Fine. But after we save the world again, I want some ice cream."

"And I want the cats to stop shredding the curtains. I guess we're both fucked."

Chapter 11

Though Pellini was right about the dearth of frozen delectables at the ice cream shop, there was something else almost as appealing. Mere minutes after the valve explosion, two six-foot-wide, fifteen-foot-high crystalline shards had materialized in the parking lot in front of Ruthie's Smoothies. The media had coined the name "Spires" for them, even though in my opinion they were more like Stumps, since they were about fifty feet too short for true spire-ness. But nobody bothered to ask me. Their official DIRT designation was Incursion Zone 212 or IZ-212 for short. Nobody asked me about that either, but at least "IZ-212" was merely boring and forgettable instead of inaccurate.

It was no secret that the Spires were arcane. Anyone with a hint of sensitivity could feel that the crystalline structures carried unearthly resonance. However, it *was* a secret to everyone except Pellini, Idris, and myself that the Spires were infused with the potency signature of demonic lord Kadir—a.k.a. Creepshow. That wouldn't mean squat to those new to the concept of demons and lords, but it would to the other DIRT summoners. Since I still had no idea if the Kadir association with the Spires was good or bad, I'd elected not to share that detail with them.

No unauthorized personnel were allowed within a quarter mile of the Spires. A high fence topped with barbed wire marked the boundary of the secure area. Stern-faced soldiers manned the gate and patrolled the perimeter with orders to use extreme prejudice when dealing with anyone foolish enough to ignore the prominent "Restricted Area" signs.

As I pulled up to the gate, a soldier with a rifle slung at his side stepped out of a guard shack and glowered until we came to a full stop. Pellini and I dutifully handed our IDs over. With meticulous care, the soldier compared our faces to our ID photos then scanned our thumbs on a handheld fingerprint reader. Didn't matter that we were well known to the local DIRT personnel. These guys didn't take any shortcuts.

At long last the soldier appeared satisfied that we weren't doppelgängers and called for the gate to be opened. Pellini cursed under his breath as we passed into the IZ-212 compound, and I echoed his sentiments. A couple of months ago, this little strip mall had been a slice of normal, with its karate studio, dry cleaners, and smoothie shop. Now the shops served as headquarters and barracks for the compound, stripped of their non-useful content. The signs were all that remained—a sad reminder of what was lost.

I parked in my designated spot in front of large block letters that announced "3 shirts cleaned for price of 2!" Pellini and I checked that our weapons were locked and loaded, then we climbed out and approached the giant crystal shards. Clear as glass, they each had eleven sides and stood about fifteen feet apart. They also had intrinsic arcane protections with a strong aversion and amnesiac effect. Anyone who got within arm's length would wander off in the opposite direction without a clue where they'd been going in the first place.

Except for Pellini and me. So far it seemed that we were the only people who could touch the things, and I suspected it was because we each had a unique connection to the strange and creepy Lord Kadir.

Needless to say, the powers-that-be had tried their damndest to find a way around the protections, using everything from drugs to hypnosis in their attempts to subvert the mental effects, with zero success. Even robots and drones proved useless, since their inner workings went up in sparks within about ten feet of the shards, no matter how much arcane shielding they had.

"The crystals are still humming," Pellini said once we were out of earshot of any of the soldiers. "But can you hear the chimes? That's new. Except it's not sound."

I moved to the nearest Spire then held my hand an inch from the surface, assessing. "It's like it's in a register that doesn't actually exist."

Pellini frowned. "Kara, look."

I followed his gaze to the tops of the Spires where rippling patterns flickered like a net of pale blue lightning. "Whoa." I pulled my hand away from the crystal and retreated a step. "Something woke up."

"A strategic retreat would be a pretty smart move right about now," Pellini said, watching as the flickering net spread downward to cover the Spires.

"Sure would be," I murmured as the rippling increased. Neither of us budged. Shouts of alarm told us the light show wasn't going unnoticed. "Screw it," I growled and pressed my hand to the surface an instant before Pellini did the same.

My awareness spread into the shard and beyond, to a space that was neither Earth nor the demon realm. There, potency rotated like an eleven-sided glass planet. At its core, ugly, tangled energy strands writhed. "Sonofabitch."

"It's awake, all right," Pellini said, "but its wires are all crossed up. Maybe we can untangle that—"

"No!" The word burst from me before my brain could engage. "I mean . . . wait." I licked dry lips. Even when I'd had the nexus resources at my disposal to help me untangle the preanomaly, I screwed it up. If not for Rhyzkahl's guidance, I'd have caused a planet-wide cataclysm on Earth. Here at the Spires, I had only my othersight and my shaky arcane skills.

I shifted my stance and felt the weight of the sidearms that were strapped to each thigh. A faint smile pulled at my mouth. *Silly woman.* My *resources* went far beyond my abilities. Bryce had helped me find the best tactical holsters to fit my needs. I'd asked for his help because he knew all about that shit. He was a resource. Right now I had Pellini, along with the crystals and their inherent potency. This tangle *probably* wasn't a preanomaly, so I could stop freaking out about destroying the world. A little.

That said, even if it wasn't as nasty as a pre-anomaly, I had a gut feeling it would wreck the crystals if it broke loose. However, my options were to trust myself and Pellini, or risk losing the opportunity to figure out the purpose of the Spires.

With any luck, they weren't a doomsday device that would vaporize the Earth once activated. That would kind of suck.

"That loop needs to be untangled without disturbing the glassy planet thing," I said, "but don't tug on any of the pulsing strands. I made that mistake once already."

Pellini's eyes unfocused as he pressed both hands to the shard surface. "Gotcha. Pull from the middle then?"

"Sort of." Pellini and I had worked together enough that I

trusted him to understand my directions. I hoped. "Need to find the strands with the least amount of energy and then shunt power to them from the pulsing strands."

He mulled that over for several seconds. "So I'm making a new connection to bleed off power, and that will make it a cinch to untangle?"

I breathed a sigh of relief that he'd grasped it so easily. "Exactly."

For the next ten minutes, I located suitable strands while Pellini did the shunting and power-bleeding. With every success, the tangle loosened.

"Okay, last one, you little fucker," Pellini growled. "Not you, Kara. I mean, not at this moment."

"Har har," I said with a grin. "C'mon, get it done."

Pellini pulled the final strand into place. The loop resolved into a perfect chartreuse Möbius band sigil with a pinpoint streak of potency running along it in a never ending circuit. Before I had time to gawk at its beauty, it expanded to fill the confines of the rotating glass planet. Power thrummed through the crystals, shaking my bones.

"Is that good or bad?" Pellini said through gritted teeth. "It doesn't feel good."

"Hold on." Arms numb to the shoulder, I splayed my hands and pressed harder. "There's something else. I can almost sense it. Just on the verge of . . ." A whisper like wind through leaves passed through me, and a feather touch fluttered across my lower back. I laughed as I realized the simple clarity of it. "I see it! It has eleven. Needs to be twelve."

"I can't hold this much longer! What has eleven? Twelve what?"

Eleven lords plus one. It was so obvious. "Faces. On the glass planet thing. It has eleven. Need to merge it with the loop to make a twelfth face."

"Got it." Pellini cocooned the polyhedron with a blanket of potency, then drew the loop outward to meld with it. Power flashed white hot, and we both yanked our hands away and retreated. The Spires flickered with lightning as their tones rose to a crescendo, then they went silent and dark.

Panting, I bent to brace my hands on my thighs. "Well, we didn't destroy the world," I said once I'd caught my breath. "But I still don't understand what it . . ." I trailed off and straightened.

Standing between the Spires was a wide-eyed young man—
Hispanic, with a slight build, and dressed in demon realm clothing.

"Paul?!" Paul Ortiz was an incredibly gifted hacker who'd
nearly died from accidental arcane damage inflicted by Mzatal
during the Farouche Plantation conflict. It was only through
Kadir's efforts that Paul survived.

Paul spun toward me, confusion melting into relief. "Kara!"
He started my way then stopped at shouts from the barricade,
smile vanishing. I turned to see half a dozen soldiers running up,
weapons trained on Paul. Beyond them, the compound seethed
like a stirred-up anthill.

Shouted commands rattled the air. "Get on the ground!"
"Keep your hands where we can see them!" "Get down NOW!"

"Stand down!" I yelled at the soldiers, pissed when they
completely ignored me and continued to fling orders at Paul. He
stood frozen in place, face paling. I jumped in front of him,
spread my arms and glared at the weapons pointed my way.
"He's a friendly! Stand the fuck down!"

I might as well have been speaking Greek for all the good it
did me. Pellini gave the soldiers a black scowl and joined my
human shield. Paul shamelessly huddled behind us while the
soldiers kept their weapons trained in his direction as if we
weren't even there.

"Great to see you, Paul," I murmured over my shoulder, "but
how the hell are you here?"

"Accident," he replied in a hoarse whisper. "I was at the gate
in Kadir's realm when it activated just a minute ago."

The squad leader barked into his radio, "We have a confirmed
intruder at location alpha niner."

"Hold that thought," I said to Paul then turned my best com-
manding look on the squad leader. "Sergeant White, I outrank
you, and I'm ordering you and your men to stand down!"

"With all due respect, ma'am, my orders come from General
Starr. All intruders are to be taken into immediate custody, and
any resistance is cause for—"

"He's not resisting," I snapped. "I am! I suggest you take a
fucking pause and let your higher-ups know that this man is
under my protection."

White's glare could have burned a hole through the Spires,
but he gritted out an order that had the soldiers easing fingers off

triggers, though they kept weapons aimed at us. White pulled out an arcane-shielded satellite phone, probably to call someone who could give him the okay to shoot my annoying ass.

That settled for the moment, I shifted to look at Paul. "A *gate*? Like, a way to travel between the realms? *That's* what these crystals are?"

He flashed a nervous smile. "Considering I was in the demon realm a few minutes ago, I'd say yes." He looked up at the two crystalline shards with naked awe. "This is one of the Earthgates from the first age."

The first age of the demonic lords, over twenty-five hundred years ago, when there were open pathways to the demon realm. Before summoning was necessary.

I flicked a quick glance at the soldiers. They were still merely aiming at us, but I noted that all the military personnel in the area were on high alert, with weapons in hand and ready. The ones wearing rank were on phones or radios. Trusting that Pellini would warn me of any status changes, I returned my full attention to Paul. "But weren't there more Earthgates?"

"One for each lord," he said with a nod. "Though they've all been dormant for thousands of years."

That took a few seconds to process. "So how did this one wake up?"

"There's a pair of crystals in Kadir's realm that look *exactly* like these." He traced his fingers over a zigzag ridge on the shard. "Back when the valve exploded, they appeared and started humming. Lord Kadir stabilized them, and since then I've spent a lot of time in their potency flows." A smile lit his face. "My god, you should have seen the arcane polyhedron awesomeness between the columns. For a month, there were two cubes, then those merged and morphed into a hendecahedron with primeval strands inside."

Pellini and I exchanged a glance.

"It was the most incredible thing I've ever felt," Paul continued, oblivious. "You know how the effulgent binaries usually have opposite rotation to their associated quaternaries? These were—"

I held up my hand. "I want to hear all about it, but for now, you'd better skip to what happened today, before these guys crash our party." I jerked my head toward the soldiers.

Paul flushed. "Oh. Right. Sorry. A few hours ago, the hum

changed to this awful clanging. Kadir balanced the potency and harmonized the tones, but as soon as he did, the strands in the center tangled and started pulsing. Before Kadir could sort them out, a huge anomaly formed over the valve crater in Rhyzkahl's realm, and he had to go deal with it. I stayed behind to monitor the gate."

Pellini frowned. "A few hours ago?" At Paul's nod he turned the frown on me. "That's when you were doing the nexus shit."

"That's not a coincidence," I said with a wince. "Neither is the giant demon realm anomaly." My actions with the pre-anomaly on the nexus had obviously bled over to the demon realm and caused big problems. I quickly explained to Paul about the pre-anomaly and the various Earthside fallout. By the time I finished, Paul looked as if he'd eaten bad shrimp.

"God, Kara," he said with a shudder. "That could have gone really badly."

"Yeah, thanks for the reminder," I said with a snort. "Lucky for everyone I managed to avoid destroying the known universe, *and* I even hit the 'on' button for an interdimensional gate. And here I thought this was a regular old Monday." I cocked my head. "Let me guess the next bit. About five minutes ago, the tangle turned into a pretty Möbius band, expanded as if it was going to explode, then merged with the eleven-sided shape and turned it into a twelve-sided shape."

Paul's eyes widened. "Yes! Then the gate glowed, and bam, I was here. How did you know?"

"Pellini and I sort of, uh, fixed that hendeca-doohicky problem from this side. Had no clue about this being a gate, though." I gave Paul a careful once-over. "You seem to have made it in one piece. Did it hurt? Summonings sure do. Feels like being dragged over broken glass."

"Didn't feel a thing except cold and an odd spinning." He darted a distressed gaze around. "The lords and demahnk haven't sealed that anomaly yet. I need to go back. I should be there in case Lord Ka—"

"Stand down," a gruff voice ordered. The soldiers lowered their weapons as a man in captain's bars strode up. His pressed fatigues bore the nametag "Hornak." I wasn't looking down a rifle barrel anymore, but I knew we weren't out of the woods yet.

Captain Hornak gave me a thin smile as he approached. I

didn't recognize him, which meant he must have been assigned here within the past week, but I had little doubt he knew exactly who I was.

"Arcane Commander Gillian, I hope you have an explanation for what just happened and can tell us who this intruder is." His sharp eyes flicked to the Spires, to Paul and his unusual clothing, then to Pellini and me. "Because it sure looked as if this fellow appeared out of thin air."

"He's not an intruder." I gave Paul's shoulder a firm squeeze, surprised to feel him trembling. Face pale, he continued to scan almost desperately, like a kid searching for his lost dog. "He's an ally," I continued, "and we're still not exactly sure how he got here." I kept my hand on Paul, not only for reassurance, but also in case he tried to make a dash through the gate.

Captain Hornak eyed me as he tapped something on his phone then lifted it toward me. Out of its speakers came a voice, distorted by the arcane, but definitely mine. *"A gate? Like, a way to travel between the realms? That's what these crystals are?"*

Shit. I kept my face as composed as humanly possible and tried my best to look as if I had not, in fact, just been totally busted. I knew the area was under twenty-four seven surveillance, but I hadn't known there was audio, or that it could be sensitive enough to pick up a whispered conversation. "Yeah, well," I said, lifting my chin, "I'm *not* exactly sure how he got here."

The captain's lips pressed tight. "A.C. Gillian, if you think I'm in the mood to play games, you're sadly mistaken. Your *ally* will be taken into custody for a debrief, after which it will be decided whether he is indeed an ally or an enemy to the people of Earth."

An angry retort built in my chest, but I swallowed it as Paul let out a low hiss and jerked from my grasp. His scan turned frantic, as if—

As if he's missing a piece of himself, I realized in a light bulb moment. I'd known that Paul and Kadir had developed a strange yet close relationship after the lord took him to his realm to heal. But I was starting to understand it was more than that. My guess was that somewhere along the way they'd formed an essence bond—a bond that Paul couldn't feel now that he was on Earth.

Paul edged toward the space between the crystals. "I'm not

going *anywhere* with you," he told Hornak, voice defiant yet shaking.

"Son, take another step, and it'll be your last," Captain Hornak growled as, with drill team precision, every weapon in a hundred-foot radius was trained on Paul. "I only need to say one word."

Paul froze, but I felt him considering a dive through the gate.

"I don't think you want to do that," I told Captain Hornak—and Paul. I slipped my hand beneath my shirt and pressed it over Kadir's sigil scar on my side.

"You're in no position to make threats, A.C. Gillian," Hornak replied, but his gaze had turned to the Spires. "A gate to the demon realm, eh? About damn time we have a way to reconnoiter and get some worthwhile intel on the ugly sons of bitches."

"We don't know if the gate works both ways yet." I casually set my free hand against the nearest crystal spire. "There's research that needs to be done first." Before Hornak had a chance to realize I was stalling, I tapped into Kadir's ubiquitous potency signature in the gate. With every bit of focus I could muster, I concentrated on touching Kadir through both the sigil scar and the crystals with a simple message: *Paul needs you. Gate. Earth.*

I edge close enough to Lord Szerain's library window to glimpse the lords gathered in the courtyard below during a recess of the Conclave. Uno, due, tre, quattro . . . only ten. I bite my lip.

Tick. Tick. Tick. Tick. Not as pleasant as grandfather's bracket clock. Yet there is no clock here in the library. Daft I am. *Tick. Tick. Tick.*

The malaise of a thousand plagues descends upon me. Dread sucks the strength from my body. I cannot breathe. Cannot move. *He* is behind me.

He wraps his arm around my waist, pulls me back against him. Were it not for his hold, I would surely collapse.

"Elinor." His breath is hot against my ear. I dare not recoil lest he take offense.

"L-lord Kadir," I whisper.

He inhales deeply, close to my neck. "I know your scent, *baztakh*."

Tick. Tick. Tick.

My knees fail. My senses flee.

Kara!

Get a medic over here.

No! She'll be all right. Give us some room.

"Buhllini," I mumbled. "What're you doing in the demon realm?"

"You gotta get up, Kara. C'mon." Strong hands dragged me to my feet, out of Kadir's grasp.

No. Only a dream-vision of Kadir. I slammed into full awareness. "I'm okay. Rebound potency knocked me silly."

Pellini had a firm grip on one of my arms and stood with his free hand extended protectively in front of us. To my dismay, Paul struggled facedown on the asphalt in the midst of a knot of soldiers, his hands cuffed behind him. An abrasion marred one cheek, but he appeared to be free of bullet holes, at least. And, other than tingling all over, I didn't seem to have sustained any lasting damage. "How long?"

"Thirty seconds."

And no sign of Kadir.

Captain Hairball turned from Paul to face us with an annoying gleam of triumph in his eyes. I glared at him. "You need to let him go. Don't make me put on my I-outrank-you-on-arcane-decisions hat."

His gaze narrowed. "What the fuck is going on, Gillian? I need an explanation yesterday."

I proceeded to spew a ridiculous mass of arcane terminology to rival Paul's technobabble, real and fabricated. After half a minute he held up his hand, clearly unimpressed.

"You're coming to DIRT HQ with us where you can discuss your 'hat' wardrobe with the General." He flicked his hand, and two soldiers hauled Paul to his feet. "What we have here is an intruder who needs to be locked down until he's been fully debriefed and cleared, and a couple of DIRT specialists who need checkups."

Shit. There was no denying Hornak had the manpower to "escort" us in. Short of trying to dive through the gate, I was out of options.

Pellini shifted his weight beside me. "They aren't backing down," he murmured.

My breath caught as pins and needles prickled through Kadir's sigil scar. A grim smile curved my mouth. "Neither are we."

The web of lightning flared over the Spires, and a single tone sounded, long and low. Heart in my throat, I watched the space between the crystals. *C'mon c'mon c'mon, you creepy weirdo. Don't you dare let Paul down.*

As if in answer to my summons, demonic Lord Kadir stepped out of thin air and into the realm of humans.

Chapter 12

An unearthly wind whipped pale blond hair around androgynous features as Kadir's icy-as-death aura inundated us like an arctic tsunami. Fresh burns marked his exposed skin and peeked from beneath fire-rain-shredded clothing—evidence of his engagement with the anomaly in Rhyzkahl's realm. Tendrils of rakkuhr slithered to him and writhed over his boots. Though it had been my bright idea to call him, doubt gripped me.

"My lord!" Paul cried out. I dragged my gaze from Kadir, fully expecting to see a compound in full freakout and all weapons turned on the newcomer. But no one moved. With the exception of Pellini, Paul, and myself, every single person in sight was eerily still, with only their frantic eye movements confirming they were alive. Captain Hornak stood motionless with his hand inches from his sidearm, face locked in a scowl. His eyes followed Kadir as the lord strode toward Paul.

"He's here," Pellini said, voice filled with awe.

"Yep," I murmured. "And for the record, I've never seen a lord do this living statue trick."

Kadir flicked his fingers. Paul's handcuffs disintegrated into black dust. He quickly wriggled free of the two soldier-statues who held him then fell to his knees. "I'm okay," he said, eyes locked on Kadir's face. I could almost feel him trying to convey that he wasn't hurt and to please not kill anyone.

Any doubts about the essence bond between the two evaporated when Kadir crouched in front of Paul and healed the abrasion on his cheek with a pass of his hand.

Pellini nudged me. "You think they're . . ."

"Beats the hell out of me." At this point, I figured anything was possible—even the unsettling lord having . . .

I shuddered. Nope. Couldn't make my brain accept any thought that combined *Kadir* and *Sex*. Some things went far beyond the realm of human comprehension, and I was okay with that.

Kadir stood and paced a slow circle around Captain Hornak then sauntered toward a squad frozen with their rifles partly raised.

I nudged Pellini. "I'll keep an eye on Kadir. See if you can find a way to reverse the gate, to suck him back through in case he does something Not Good." That was the only possible option at hand if things went to shit. I couldn't go head to head with a demigod, and I doubted verbal negotiation would get me very far.

"That's one hell of a long shot," he muttered, "but I'll see what I can do."

I hurried to Paul as he clambered to his feet. "What's he doing?" I asked with a tilt of my head toward Kadir.

Paul's gaze followed him. Kadir wove between the squad members, pausing to trace the line of one poor soldier's jaw with a graceful index finger. "Acclimating. Getting a sense of Earth and the situation."

My eyes narrowed. "And then what?"

"I don't know," Paul said. "He's been itching to experience what it was like to pass through the gate, but beyond that—"

"Wait, what?" I put a hand to my head in confusion. "I thought this was *his* gate. Hasn't he been through it before?"

"Yes, it's his, but it was only usable by humans. The lords themselves couldn't travel through any of the gates. But ever since this one woke up, Lord Kadir has been working to change that."

"Looks like he succeeded," I murmured, regarding Kadir as he leaned close to the soldier and sniffed. A glance at Pellini showed him running his hands over the nearest crystal in search of a miracle.

I had a feeling we were going to need one. The premeditation behind Kadir's arrival left a nasty taste in my mouth. Even if his plans didn't fully align with the Mraztur's, he itched for unrestricted access to Earth—and I highly doubted it was so he could kick back by a campfire under the stars of our world and sing

Kumbaya with his new human buddies. "Does Kadir have anything to do with the rifts and the demons and *rakkuhr* coming through?"

"Absolutely not," Paul said without hesitation. "In fact, it's ticking him off. The flows are getting screwed up, and there's nothing he can do about it. The demons creating the rifts are in the Jagged Peaks region, and it's off limits."

I gave him a sharp look. "Off limits?"

"Something to do with oaths and agreements. That's all I know."

"Damn demon oaths have gotten in my way more than a few times."

He grimaced. "I wouldn't have known even that much except Lord Kadir got zapped when he probed the off limits area from his plexus. He was out cold for a whole day."

Interesting. I rather doubted that the demons had the kind of protections that could lay out a lord. Seemed far more likely that Kadir got zapped by the oh-so-sweet-and-loving Demahnk Council for poking his nose where they didn't want it poked. Considering that they'd submerged and exiled Szerain to Earth, I had no doubt they'd slap down a lord who broke rules. "Was it worth it? Did he find out anything?"

"No!" Paul folded his arms over his chest and glowered. "He was just trying to figure out why the demons weren't making it through the void alive after getting killed on Earth."

"Maybe it hasn't been long enough," I suggested. "After I died in the demon realm, it took me two weeks to return here. And I think it was about that long before Eilahn made it back after she was shot on Earth. Or maybe the demons who didn't make it back had died here once before?" A first death for a demon on Earth or a human in the demon realm often meant a return to the home world safe and sound. A second death usually meant death for realsies.

Paul shook his head. "That's not it. They're coming through without a mark on them, but eight out of ten are dead, as if the bodies got remade but didn't get turned back on. It's been like that ever since the valve explosion back-blasted into the demon realm. A syraza showed up on the clifftop in Mzatal's realm a few days later, dead as a doornail."

I sucked in a breath. "Katashi!" I exclaimed. "I *knew* he had to be a demon. Am I right?"

"Got it in one," he said, smiling at my excitement. "Lord

Kadir believes the syraza took over the life of the real Katashi nearly forty years ago, after a decade of preparation." His attention drifted back to Kadir who strolled toward a knot of soldiers and auxiliary personnel in front of the old smoothie shop.

I managed to catch Pellini's eye then sighed when he gave me a "still no luck" glower. Crapsticks. "So fake Katashi is *dead* dead." At least I could be hugely relieved on that count. Scratching even one name off the My Nemeses list was a huge deal. Though I sorely wanted this news to exonerate Tessa, the unpleasant truth was that the Katashi she'd known and revered for the past thirty years had been the fake-Katashi. Hell, she might have even known he was a demon. "Whose puppet was he? Jesral's?" That made the most sense considering one of Katashi's key summoners, Tsuneo, had a tattoo of the slimy lord's sigil.

"Nope," Paul said, to my surprise. "All the lords seemed truly shocked that he was a demon. They—" He broke off, tensing as Kadir stopped in front of a burly soldier.

"What is it?" I frowned in Kadir's direction but couldn't see anything different in his terrorize-all-the-humans behavior. "Paul, what's wrong?"

The words were barely out of my mouth when Kadir's aura shifted from ice-cold scary to trapped-in-a-room-with-one-hundred-serial-killers scary. Paul started toward Kadir but halted when the lord glanced at him over his shoulder.

Paul retreated to me, pale and tense. "It's . . . okay," he told me. "He's not going to hurt the guy."

The burly soldier unfroze and dug in his pockets. A moment later he came out with a pen and what looked like a paper napkin and began to write.

"What on earth is Kadir doing?" I asked, frustration and bafflement rising. "Getting the dude's phone number?"

Paul didn't answer. Kadir left the soldier to his writing then strolled toward us, his aura engulfing me like a tidal wave of eel-filled slime. Palms sweating, I squelched my survival instinct to get the hell away. Along my ribs, Kadir's sigil scar itched.

He stopped before me with an enigmatic smile that sent chills up my spine. "No need to fret thus, Kara Gillian. I depart."

"Wait," I said and forced myself to stand taller and lift my chin. "We have common ground. You don't like the flow disruption caused by the rifts. We don't like *anything* about them. What can we do Earthside to counter the damn things?"

Kadir studied me for several heartbeats, ice-cold gaze intensifying. "Use the rakkuhr as the demons do. Tame it. Shape it to your will."

Gooseflesh swept over my skin at the mere thought of handling the vile shit, but I gave a nod of acknowledgement. "Show me how."

He hissed out a breath. "I do not touch it. It is insidious."

Interesting. Kadir and Mzatal vehemently reviled rakkuhr. Rhyzkahl and the other Mraztur used it, though I had the sense it held them in a stranglehold grip. Not so for Szerain. He *commanded* it. That was likely at least part of why he'd been exiled to Earth. "Then how can Szerain manipulate it unscathed?"

Kadir leaned close until his face was only inches from mine. "*Szerain* is dangerous."

"That's why I need him." Szerain was dangerous because he'd broken the rules, pissed off the Demahnk Council. That alone earned him a gold star in my book. And with rakkuhr screwing up Earth, I needed him more than ever.

Kadir straightened, his eyes narrowed. "You dabble in destruction, Kara Gillian."

I bared my teeth. "I *dabble* in survival."

Kadir laughed, a sound that lifted the hair on the back of my neck. "As do I." He glided toward the Spires with Paul in his wake. "In the end, we shall see whose dabbling leads to survival."

"Working together to save both our worlds would be a nice change," I called after him.

Pellini dropped his hands from the crystal and wisely shifted well away from the gate-gap, clearly uninterested in a surprise vacation to the demon realm. Kadir paused and regarded him, dangerous expression warming ever so slightly, then he placed his hand on Paul's shoulder and stepped into the gap between the crystals. The gateway flickered, and Paul gave me an encouraging smile an instant before he and Kadir vanished.

Pellini and I exchanged a what-the-fuck look.

"Did they—" He clamped down on the rest, but it was obvious we were both wondering the same thing. Despite the gate's showy flickering, neither of us had felt it activate. Did that mean Kadir had found a means to teleport like the demahnk? It was certainly possible. The lords were all half demahnk, and Kadir had previously demonstrated the ability to surf interdimensional flows in a way no other lords could. But if Kadir *had* teleported rather than use the gate, then I had an uneasy feeling that he was still on Earth—with Paul, who could tap into computer networks as effortlessly as a lord tapped into potency flows.

"Whew!" I said, eyes on Pellini. "I'm glad they've gone back to the demon realm."

"Yeah, no kidding!" He blew out an exaggerated breath. "That was intense."

As if some deity had thrown a switch, the statue-people staggered free of their invisible bonds. Hornak barked shaky orders for status updates and surveillance footage, but my eyes went to the burly soldier as he looked around furtively and shoved the pen and napkin in his pocket. Crap. What had Kadir done to the poor guy? I headed his way as Hornak cursed about hazy memories and nothing but fuzz and static on the camera feeds. At least the consensus seemed to be that Paul and Kadir had, indeed, returned to the demon realm.

I glanced at the soldier's name tag and gave him a kind smile. "Corporal Frazier? Are you all right?"

Sweat beaded on his forehead and dark splodges marked his maroon shirt under his arms. "Yes, ma'am. Just shaken."

"That's understandable. Lord Kadir has that effect on pretty much everyone." I gestured toward his pocket. "What did you write on the napkin?"

He paled and took a half-step back. "It's . . ." The word came out in a strangled croak, as if he'd tried to hold it in and failed.

"Corporal? It's important for me to know." Even more so now that it seemed Kadir had put some sort of compulsion on him.

Frazier fought his hand as it moved toward his pocket, while I watched in growing confusion. Tense and shaking, he withdrew the napkin and offered it to me. "My . . ." he said through gritted teeth. "My . . . confession."

Confession? What the hell? I took the napkin, one corner tearing where he held it in a vise grip. The instant I had it in my hand, Frazier stiffened and shouted, "I did it. I kidnapped Tommy Lochlan."

I stared in utter shock as I struggled to place the teasingly familiar name.

"Are you shitting me?!" Pellini roared, startling me out of my daze. "That was my case!" He barreled toward Frazier, fists cocked and murder in his eyes. "What the fuck did you do to him, you fucking piece of shit? I held his mom while she fucking cried her eyes out!"

Oh, shit. Now I remembered the name. "Pellini, no!" I jumped in front of him and prayed he wouldn't simply sweep me aside. Tommy Lochlan was a Beaulac kid who'd disappeared during a third grade field trip a year or so back. Despite intensive searches and a media blitz funded by the Child Find League, no clues to the boy's disappearance ever turned up.

Pellini stopped, eyes blazing in fury as the MPs seized an unresisting Frazier. "What'd you do to him, you shitstain? Where is he now?"

The terrible, nauseating details poured out of Frazier as everyone in the compound looked on in stricken silence. He concluded by choking out, "F-false wall in my closet. Still th-there. Alive."

Curses and exclamations of shock erupted throughout the compound. The blubbering Frazier got hauled off while Pellini made urgent calls to scramble a team to recover Tommy.

I tuned out the noise and commotion while I tried to sort through the entire turn of events. Kadir had compelled this teddy bear of a guy to confess to kidnapping and heinous child abuse. But *why*? Kadir seemed to delight in tormenting people. Was his purpose simply to break Frazier and make him suffer? Yet, his aura had gone to hell-frozen-over pissed when he confronted Frazier—as if it was the idea of the kid locked in the closet that affected the ice king. None of it fit my mental image of Kadir's style. Weird.

Once Pellini finished his calls, we returned to the Spires. The number of security personnel around it had tripled in the last two minutes, though the invisible barrier that kept people from getting close remained in full effect.

"We need to take the fight to them," a young private announced as we drew near, face flushed with the excitement of the recent events. "Go through the gate with a few tons of C-4. That'll shake 'em up!"

I drew breath to rip him a new asshole, but Pellini beat me to it. "What a great idea! Except for the fact that you can't get near the gate, and even if you could, you'd end up in Lord Kadir's lap." The soldier swallowed, wide-eyed, but Pellini was already wound up over the Frazier incident and on a roll. "But sure, maybe we could all go through the rifts instead. I'm assuming you somehow know where the rifts come out in the demon realm? Because a rift a hundred feet in the air is no problem for winged demons, but you and your precious C-4 might have a hard time flying. Or maybe the rift will open up in the middle of a demon encampment. But, hey, you'll have a few tons of C-4, so you'll be fine. If C-4 even works there, that is, which none of us know for sure." His smile grew fierce as the young man's expression went sullen. "And it's a good thing you have other-sight so you can see the arcane traps and wards. Oh, wait, you can't see the arcane."

Pellini lifted his hands and spun out a sweet little coil of potency. I had to bite the side of my cheek to keep from smiling. He'd been practicing. A lot. The kid couldn't see the odd, Kadir-style aversion sigil, but it was clear he felt it as Pellini advanced on him. His face paled, and he stumbled back.

"Y'think you can remember to stay tough when you're pissing yourself?" Pellini said through clenched teeth.

"Pellini," I murmured and took hold of his forearm. "Stand down."

He stabbed a glance my way then exhaled and dispelled the sigil. Immediately the private straightened, gulping as he tried to regain his tough-guy composure.

"Remember that sensation," I said, voice hard. "That was one variety of an aversion, and Pellini snapped it out in a matter of seconds. Now think about being faced with large numbers of creatures who've lived and breathed the arcane for their entire existence—and I'm talking hundreds or *thousands* of years." I paused to let that sink in, pleased to see that I had the attention of everyone in the area, even Captain Hornak. "Whether it's a rift or a gate, we can't go in blind. Remember the Dirty Thirty? They were brave and ready for anything, just like you." A week after the incursions began, DIRT Command—against my advice—sent thirty volunteers through the New York rift. A few days later, demons were taken down wearing weapon harnesses made from their uniforms and skin and teeth. "You want your mama to bury a hunk of your skin, private?"

He quickly shook his head. "No, ma'am."

"Good. Because I don't want to tell her that's all we could find." I turned my back on the private then stalked toward Captain Hornak with Pellini beside me. Hornak frowned at us as if we were the root of all his problems and drew breath to speak, but I beat him to the punch.

"Get me a secure line to General Starr," I snapped out. I knew he wanted to order us both to come to HQ with him, but I had zero time for bureaucratic games.

A muscle in his jaw twitched, but Hornak didn't have an argument for my request. A few minutes later I was tucked in the back office with Pellini and a video conference connection to a harried General Starr. Behind him, a wall screen showed a world map practically glowing with rift activity.

I gave the general a full report, including several details the statuefied people likely weren't too clear on, and made sure to point out that Pellini and I were still the only ones who could get near the gate. Hopefully, that would quash any ideas of sending troops through. I also emphasized that Kadir had departed peacefully and of his own accord, but left out my suspicion that he might still be on Earth since there was nothing to be done about it at the moment.

When I finished, the general grimaced and scratched a hand over his stubbled scalp. "Thank god you were there to keep the situation from going batshit crazy." He hooked his thumb toward the screen behind him. "A crisis at the Spires on top of all the new rifts would've screwed us royally. We're down to raw recruits and shitty equipment already. Don't have even half enough SkeeterCheaters to do the job."

I straightened in surprise. "I thought production was on track?"

"A rift in New Mexico took out a train carrying critical components. Whole goddamn train is gone." General Starr scowled. "I don't know if the demons knew about the cargo or just got lucky, but either way it set us back months. Those nets might as well be made from Elvis Presley's hair for what they're worth now." He shook his head. "We'll have to figure out another way to deal with the fuckers. When you get a chance, write up your report on this incident and then one with projections for anticipated SkeeterCheater need and possible alternatives."

"Yes, sir," I said with a confident nod while I sent up a silent wail of despair.

"Good deal. Get on that." With that he clicked off.

Pellini snorted. "I am so incredibly glad I'm not the Arcane Commander."

"Paperwork." I sighed. "Can't I just go through a rift with some C-4?"

Chapter 13

The house was quiet when we returned, and the mouth-watering aroma of lasagna filled the air—reminding me that I had no idea when I'd last eaten. A cookie in the war room? And that was hours ago.

Cory lay on the fold-out sofa and had progressed from merely hell-gel-covered to the Phase Three red-egg state. Giovanni still slept peacefully, and Bryce and Sharini Tandon huddled in the war room, reviewing our surveillance camera footage. At the kitchen table, Jill perused a fat tome from the basement library, while two huge pans of lasagna sat atop the stove.

She glanced up. "I just took them out of the oven. They need to cool down about ten minutes before you cut them."

"I wish everything else would cool down so easily. Now we have even more weirdness." As I hunted up a cold drink, I filled her in on the gate and Kadir situation.

"Huh. That's interesting." Jill gave me a speculative look. "About an hour ago Bryce told me he could feel Seretis again through the bond—just barely enough to know that he's alive. I wonder if there's any connection to what happened with the Spires?"

"I don't know, but that's fantastic news. How is Bryce handling it?"

Pleased affection lit her eyes. "It's like a thousand pounds lifted off his shoulders. Nice to have some good news." She closed the tome. "I'm glad you got to talk to Paul, too. Plus now we know the hostile demons aren't the only ones still in existence in the demon realm. I'm not thrilled your Lord Creepy Psycho is on the loose, though."

As she straightened papers, I glanced out the kitchen window to see Rhyzkahl doing pushups on the roof of his house. "Fuck the lords," I murmured.

"Not *that* one, I hope!"

I snorted. "Don't worry, that one is never getting 'twixt my nethers again." I turned away from the window. " 'Fuck the lords' is what that big demon said a few seconds before he ripped out his own throat and dropped a buttload of gold in the Piggly Wiggly parking lot."

Jill pursed her lips. "Was it a Jontari warlord?"

"It was a reyza, the biggest . . ." I fumbled to a stop. "Wait. A whatsit whosit?"

"I'm probably pronouncing it all wrong," she said with a little shake of her head. "I was guessing based on the gold, but you'd know better than I."

"I've never seen a demon wear gold before, but the Piggly Wiggly demon shouted 'Jontari' before he died. What do you know about it?"

"Oh! Not a lot. I came across a reference to warlords wearing gold. Armbands. Wing, ear, tail, and nose jewelry. That sort of thing."

"Back up." I felt as if I'd stumbled into deep water while wading in a familiar pool. "I've never heard of demon warlords either."

Jill looked puzzled. "They're the leaders of the major Jontari clans." At my baffled expression, she narrowed her eyes. "Are you messing with me?"

"I swear, I'm not."

She didn't seem convinced but carried on. "Jontari are the demons *not* associated with the lords. Like, ninety-nine percent of the demon population."

"That's impossible." But even as I said it, doubt crept in. Though I'd lived in the demon realm for months, I'd only seen relatively small numbers of demons in the various lords' realms. A couple of hundred total at the most. "No, I guess it's not impossible. I've been finding gaps in my knowledge big enough to drive a planet through. This could be yet another sizable hole."

She tapped her chin in thought. "Maybe it's not an accident. Between the library here and the database the librarians are maintaining, I only found one sketch, one memoir, and three partial sentences in as many different books—with adjacent pages torn out."

I tensed. "As if someone was trying to erase knowledge of them?"

"Could be," she said. "The sketch looked a bit like a graa and had text beside it in Aramaic, but there was a margin note that said 'Jontari.' I only noticed it because that was the only word on the page written in the Roman alphabet. The memoir was uncensored, probably because it was wedged inside a book of insect drawings and got overlooked. It has a story about the summoning of a Jontari ruling warlord. An imperator." She made a face. "Before the summoner could finish feeding blood to the demon, it ripped him in half and ate his guts as he died."

A shudder went through me. I'd been eviscerated by a demon, though not during a summoning. And what was the deal with *feeding* it blood? The blood I spilled during summonings was to add strength and power to the diagram. "Was there anything else?"

"That's all I remember. It's in your great great great grandmother's memoir from the eighteen hundreds."

"Hang on. That doesn't fly. The ways were closed after the cataclysm in the late sixteen hundreds, up until 1908. Summonings weren't possible."

Jill nodded sagely. "The summoning was by *her* great great great great great *great* grandfather. She'd translated his memoir into a more readable modern English, preserving what had been passed down to her." She stood and headed for the basement. "Be right back. You'll probably get more out of the memoir than I did."

"Yeah, I need to see it," I said absently as I mulled over the implications. The Jontari bombshell made sense once I got past the shock of it. My awesome syraza bodyguard, Eilahn, had mentioned demon cities, though I'd assumed she meant within the realms of the lords. An uneasy knot formed in my belly. Why hadn't anyone told me about the Jontari? Helori had taken me on an extended tour of the demon realm but had apparently bypassed cities and clans and warlords—including the Jagged Peaks, homeland of the rift-creating demons. And what about Mzatal? Had he kept me in the dark on purpose? It didn't feel right, but the silence of the lords, demons, and demahnk, coupled with relevant pages missing from books, hinted at a colossal conspiracy.

Because apparently we didn't have enough conspiracy and intrigue bullshit going on already.

Jill returned and set a battered, leather-bound book on the table. "I'm off to do the evening perimeter check with Bryce. I'll be back in a couple of hours. Text if you need me."

"Mosquitos are out. Don't forget the repellent."

She snagged the bottle from the counter and headed out the back door. I dished up a plate of lasagna and plunked into a chair to eat and peruse the memoir. The relevant entry sprawled in a thin, spidery hand over ten ink-splattered pages, and dove straight into the gory details of the summoning and aftermath. With every sentence, my grip on what I thought I knew about summoning slipped. Bindings and protections four times the number I'd been taught to lay. Several sigil configurations I'd never heard of. The Jontari reyza guzzling the summoner's blood sacrifice from a bowl before the demon exploited a flawed potency anchor and shredded the bindings. The lengthy torment of the summoner before the demon killed him. The crippling of the witness—the summoner's daughter—and the slaughter of dozens in the household.

The story ended with the warning: *When conjuring Dekkak, secure the perimeter with thirty binding layers lest the beast break free and strike you down.*

It went on to say that for most Jontari, twenty bindings would do. That told me they were summoned frequently enough to have a protocol. I read the half page of general information then closed the book, cold. My training had been full of warnings of how dangerous the demons were and how it was vital to make satisfactory offerings in order to avoid horrific death by teeth and claws. But the truth was, I'd never been in real danger from any demon I'd summoned. Sure, the ritual itself could kill you if the diagram was chalked wrong or the potency not anchored, but the demons themselves had been . . . accommodating. Lord-affiliated demons. Not Jontari. I'd paid them with popcorn and books and bacon, not blood.

I felt as if Idris and Tessa and I had been playing at summoning. And I had a feeling the rest of the modern summoners were in the same boat, since no one had ever sent one of those badass warlords after me, even in the worst of times. We were being played, but why? And by whom? And how exactly did "fuck the lords" fit into it all?

The weight of the day settled heavily upon me. It was still

light out, but it didn't matter. I needed a reprieve from world chaos and screwy demon conspiracies—and sleep was the only way to get it. I texted Bryce and Pellini to monitor DIRT calls then shambled to my room.

Bumper, Fillion, and Squig squinted at me with sleepy eyes from the foot of the bed. I stripped off my uniform and dropped it in a crumpled heap on the floor. Yawning, I stepped over it to snag a clean t-shirt, then stopped and stared at the pile. *The grove tree leaf!* "Oh, no," I moaned, heart sinking at the thought of it crushed and forgotten. I scrabbled through the pants pockets to find it but, to my amazed relief, not only was it undamaged, it gave off a soft glow, emerald on one side and amethyst on the other.

Clearly, I needed a better way to carry it. I placed it on the nightstand and dug an old cord necklace out of the bottom of my jewelry box. Maybe I could wrap embroidery floss around the stem and tie it to the cord? But not now. Wrapping and tying would have to be a tomorrow project. I flopped into bed and turned out the light.

The leaf glimmered in the darkness. I peered at it then sat up, delighted and astonished. What had been a single solid stem now formed an unbroken natural loop around the cord. A laugh welled up inside me as I slipped the necklace over my head.

I needed a little inexplicable magic in my life.

Beyond the balcony, demons wheeled and dived in an intricate aerial dance. The waterfall below cascaded to its distant pool with a comforting hiss as the sea reflected rich orange and purples of the setting sun.

Mzatal draped his arm over my shoulders and drew me to his side. "Would that we could be here now, beloved."

I snuggled close, cradled in the luxurious warmth of his aura. "We *are* here, zharkat," I said with a smile. "At least, I'm sure I am."

"I defer to your assessment." He laughed, a rich sound that twined around my heart and set me laughing with him. I gripped his thick braid of obsidian-black hair and tugged hard. He rewarded me with a groan that thrummed in his chest, then he caught me up in his arms. I wrapped my legs around his waist, cradled his face between my hands and kissed him in the light of the dying sun. My hips rocked against his as he deepened the kiss.

A demon bellowed.

A strangely familiar woman yanked my shoulder, her eyes wide with fear.

I tumbled from Mzatal's arms and over the balcony wall, plummeted toward rocks and sea while Elinor's scream drowned out the roar of wind.

Heart pounding, I jerked awake. Dust motes floated lazily in early morning light that seeped around the edges of my curtains. A squirrel fussed in the tree outside my window, and the air held a whisper of coffee and biscuits.

Eerie remnants of the dream lingered. I hurried to flick on the lamp. Mzatal's aura immersed me still, but darker, more—

I flung off the covers, grabbed shorts from the floor and yanked them on then sprinted down the hall to the kitchen window.

Mzatal was *here*, crouched in the center of the nexus. I ran out the door, pulse hammering with a rush of elation and apprehension, then stopped on the bottom step to drink in the sight of him.

Moisture from a humid Louisiana morning clung to the grass and slicked the porch rails, yet the surface of the nexus remained dry and unaffected. Mzatal looked dressed for battle, in close-fitting pants and shirt in a color somewhere between black and dried blood. A cord of the same color bound the thick braid that hung down his back.

On the far side of the nexus, Rhyzkahl paced a short arc, eyes trained on Mzatal, and jaw set in anger.

With the deadly grace of a lion, Mzatal stood and drew his essence blade, Khatur, from a sheath at his side.

Worry punched through me. I'd *never* known him to carry Khatur in a sheath. He'd always sent it away to whatever dimensional pocket of space-time the essence blades went when not in use. Had he become so dependent upon the knife that he wouldn't let it out of his sight?

He turned toward me. Eyes locked on mine, he drew the blade across his left palm. An unwholesome hiss of satisfaction whispered through my mind like the breath of an alien wind: the nightmarish sentiments of Khatur. My uneasiness spiraled higher.

Mzatal flicked his hand, spattering blood onto the nexus. It sizzled when it struck the black surface, and a white hot glow raced through the delicate silver tracings.

My sigil.

Heat blossomed in my head like reverse brain freeze. I grabbed the porch railing to keep from losing my balance.

The glow on the nexus crept outward as Mzatal continued to bleed. Warmth spread from the top of my head through my neck and into my chest. Beyond Mzatal's aura of power, I felt *him*, felt his intensity. Pulse thrumming, I crossed the grass to the outer edge of Rhyzkahl's prison.

Rhyzkahl strode toward me. "What is he doing?" he asked, voice edged with frustration.

"He'll tell you if he wants you to know," I said archly. I wasn't about to admit I had the same question. Rhyzkahl growled and turned his back on me.

Blood disappeared from the surface of the knife as if sucked into the metal. Mzatal sheathed Khatur and held up his left hand. A different essence blade coalesced against his palm, and cold slid through me. *Xhan.*

Rhyzkahl staggered as if struck, naked shock flashing over his face before he regained composure. Xhan was Rhyzkahl's blade. The one he'd used to carve the sigils into my flesh. He'd lost the knife at the plantation battle after Zakaar severed their bond. I'd last seen it when Jesral picked it up—or tried to, and had been forced to wrap it in a cloth. I wasn't at all surprised that Mzatal took it from Jesral, yet I'd never in a million years expected him to actually *wield* it. And, clearly, neither had Rhyzkahl. He stepped to the inner boundary of his prison, eyes on his blade and hands fisted white at his sides.

Thorns burst from Xhan's hilt, writhing as they sought to entrap Mzatal's fingers. Sweat broke on his brow, and I felt the depth of his battle of wills with the knife. Mouth tight as if steeling himself, Mzatal set the knife against his bleeding palm and closed his fingers around it. Blood hissed and sizzled on the blade as he slowly drew it from his fist. He held it at arm's length, his body taut and teeth bared while his free hand dripped blood onto the nexus.

Xhan's voice whispered in my head. *You are mine. You are mine.*

"No," I breathed. "What the ever living fuck is he doing?!"

Rhyzkahl's attention remained riveted on Mzatal and Xhan. "He is not strong enough," he murmured. "The fool will doom us all."

I shot Rhyzkahl a scathing look then crossed to the nexus.

Warding shimmered around the perimeter, but my experience and instinct told me none of it targeted me. I stepped onto the stone then staggered, throwing my arms wide for balance as potency unlike anything I'd ever felt seared through my bones and threatened to rip me apart cell by cell.

Drawing demigod-like power and focus from the nexus, I centered and stabilized. I was still in one piece, but I needed to adapt to the frequency if I wanted to stay that way. As soon as I felt balanced, I moved behind Mzatal and wrapped my arms around him. He tensed as I made contact but didn't hesitate to tap into the support. We'd worked as one more times than I could count, and even though we no longer had an open connection, I knew him and he knew me.

He drew a deep breath, and I *felt* him intensify his efforts to subdue the blade. I joined the battle, using all of my nexus-derived ability to concentrate on beating Xhan into submission. My scars flared with burning pain, real and remembered. I clung to the sensation, used it as focal point to overpower the very knife that had carved the sigils.

Treacherous. Traitor. The words slammed through me like a scream. *Vile oppressor.*

Teeth clenched, I willed the blade to shut the fuck up and settle.

As each drop of Mzatal's blood struck the nexus, potency pounded from my feet to my head. Mzatal entwined his aura with mine, and our power increased tenfold. Unintelligible words screamed through me as Mzatal wrested control from the blade and sent it away. Arcane silence filled the void it had left. Mzatal shook from the effort, his breath labored. Sweat soaked his shirt, and mine as well where I embraced him, but I didn't care.

Rhyzkahl looked on with an expression of grudging awe tinged with envy.

I held my beloved for a few heartbeats longer, then reluctantly released him and stepped back. I'd intruded upon his self-imposed isolation for long enough, though I didn't regret a single second of it.

Mzatal lifted his bloodied hand high and tightened it into a fist. When he opened it again, the wicked slice was healed. In a fluid motion, he turned to me, stripped off his sweaty shirt and cast it aside.

I stared at his chest, where a new, intricately beautiful pattern of raised scars formed a sigil, much like the ones that covered my torso. Yet while my sigil scars represented each of the eleven demonic lords, the sigil over his heart was mine. *My* sigil. Tears spilled over as I lifted my eyes and found his gaze upon me, if only for a heartbeat.

When he began to dance the shikvihr ritual, tracing and igniting the sigils of the first ring with fluid grace, I danced my own right along with him. We moved in harmony, each creating our own shikvihr. Trace, ignite. Trace, ignite.

Ring after ring of sigils flowed from us until we reached my skill limit at the culmination of the seventh. Without missing a beat, Mzatal ignited my shikvihr before continuing on with his. Joy and power and exhilaration surged through me as he danced the eighth ring around me. I stood motionless, adapting to the energies.

Mzatal completed the eleventh sigil of the eleventh ring and ignited his shikvihr. We stood at the center of a vortex of potency like nothing I'd ever felt before. The full power of Mzatal. The full power of me.

But he wasn't finished.

With delicate movements, he drew spider-silk strands of potency between his shikvihr sigils and mine in an act of unspeakable intimacy. I turned as he turned, watching every movement, feeling them as a caress on my essence. Now I understood why he bore my sigil. Closed off and merged with his essence blade, Mzatal was ruthless and formidable. He commanded unmatchable resolve and focus that allowed him to stay a thousand moves ahead of his opponents, and see and anticipate distant potentials. He'd been closed off once before—a solitude that lasted two thousand years, with all distractions shut out and full focus on his goals.

But this time one of his goals included me. He'd carved the sigil as a lifeline, to maintain a connection despite the barriers. A hope for a life beyond his self-made prison.

Together we can do anything. Even if we aren't together.

He finished the intricate weave of our potency. "Remove your shirt," he said, voice uncompromising. I tore my gaze from the connected sigils. His face was as hard and intense as ever, an unreadable mask of stone. But his eyes . . . I drew a steadying breath. His eyes held the emotions he dared not otherwise reveal.

I stripped off my shirt and tossed it aside. He moved the leaf from where it lay over my heart to rest on my shoulder, then he placed his palm over his sigil scar in the center of my chest. "Damaged."

"Only the sigil," I said, mouth dry. Curves and patterns severed when Szerain had thrust his essence blade into my heart in order to save my life.

Without a word, Mzatal began to slowly trace the loops of his sigil on my skin, his touch sensuous, light, and undeniably powerful. Where the lines were broken, he repaired them, and with a final touch ignited the sigil with searing fire that faded to comforting warmth in a heartbeat.

He replaced the leaf atop it and covered both with his hand. "It is of better use whole."

I spread my hand over the sigil on his chest. "*We* are better whole."

Rhyzkahl gave a rude snort.

Without taking his eyes from mine, Mzatal sent a shrieking bolt of lightning from his free hand to strike Rhyzkahl square in the chest. While Rhyzkahl writhed among the zucchini, Mzatal moved behind me and set his hands on my shoulders. As he slid them down my arms, the strands between our sigils flickered with golden light to match the morning sky. He covered the backs of my hands with his, laced his fingers between mine as the strands glowed strong and steady.

Moving as one, hands united and arms sweeping in graceful arcs, we called forth the full union of our shikvihr. When our dance was done, a new construct surrounded us. Not a pair of eleven-ringed shikvihr entwined, but a thrumming single circle of potency that flowed like liquid light in an endless loop. Beautiful, with a purpose and function that shone with dazzling clarity. Two months ago, Mzatal had gifted me the power of a lord via the nexus and Rhyzkahl, but this addition, this *super-shikvihr* would remain in place and allow me to tap into that power even away from my property.

I leaned back against him, enjoying the contact, the *touch* I knew we might never share again. Fingers still joined with mine, Mzatal wrapped his arms around me and crossed our wrists over my heart. After a moment, he shuddered then stepped back, breaking away before his will crumbled.

As I turned to face him, he caught my left hand and stripped the stoneless ring from my finger. While I watched, baffled, he placed it in my palm and folded my fingers over it, then clasped my hand between his. Heat flashed within my fist, gone before it could register as pain. Mzatal released me, wheeled away and strode from the nexus. The demahnk Helori appeared in human form beside him, and then they were gone.

I let out a shaky breath and opened my hand. Mzatal had given me this ring last Christmas, and the stone was broken not long after during a terrible argument. I'd kept the ring as a reminder of that schism—one we never wished to repeat. Later, Rowan had destroyed the stone, but after Szerain ripped her away from my *Self*, I'd stubbornly continued to wear the twisted ring. Now it lay on my palm as a raw lump of gold and silver alloy.

"I can work with this," I murmured. Mzatal hadn't destroyed the broken ring. Instead he'd made it ready to be created anew. A fresh start. Drawing potency from the super-shikvihr loop, I reshaped the lump into two slender rings, gleaming and unadorned. The smaller one I slipped onto my finger. The other, I threaded through the cord that held the grove leaf, keeping it safe until the ring's rightful owner could bear it.

A laugh bubbled up. "My preccccioooouuussss," I whispered. Grinning, I pulled my shirt on and headed inside, while Rhyzkahl twitched in an inglorious heap.

Chapter 14

Pellini handed me a cup of coffee when I stepped into the kitchen. "I was about to call for security until I realized it was Mzatal out there with you."

I smiled and took a sip, pleased to find it perfectly over-sugared and mega-creamed. "Guess you saw my topless act."

His mouth twitched in amusement. "Nothing I haven't seen before."

"It has to be getting old by now," I said. A couple of years back, Pellini had been among the Beaulac PD personnel who saw me appear naked in the station break room after I died in the demon realm and returned to Earth. And, after Angus McDunn stripped my abilities, Pellini had busted into the bathroom to drag me from the tub and my spiral of despair.

"Looking at boobs *never* gets old," he said with a grin.

Laughing, I rolled my eyes then moved to the kitchen window. Rhyzkahl had stopped twitching and dragged himself up to a sitting position. "Can you see the changes in the nexus?" I asked Pellini.

He squinted out the window. "I saw the sigils when y'all were laying them, but now there's only a shimmer, like heat waves. I feel like there's more, but when I try to *see*, it slips away."

"It's plain as day to me. Mzatal created—" I stopped and shook my head. "No, *we* created this super-shikvihr loop that extends my range. It'll be a game changer for me."

Pellini frowned. "What exactly is he doing on Earth?"

"I don't know specifics, but I have no doubt it involves countering the Mraztur, and that has to be good."

"Uh huh." He made no attempt to hide his dubious tone. "I'll add him to the DIRT Alpha-level watch list."

I bristled, but I made myself take a sip of coffee before speaking. "You mean the list that has Kadir, Angus McDunn, Tessa, and Katashi's people on it?"

Pellini's gaze remained steady on me. "That's the one." Though he didn't say it, I clearly heard the added *Do you have a problem with that?*

And my initial gut reaction was, *Yes, I have a huge problem with lumping Mzatal in with confirmed assholes.* But I forced myself past the knee-jerk loyalty to consider where Pellini was coming from. It wasn't doubt in Mzatal, but a perfectly sensible caution where any of the lords were concerned. To Pellini, the lords were guilty until proven innocent, and he intended to remain alert and suspicious of everything they did. I couldn't find it in myself to blame him, especially in light of how the plans and actions of the lords had fucked up Earth. In fact, I held the same attitude, except about Mzatal, of course. He'd already proven himself in my eyes.

I took a deep breath and nodded. "Personal bias aside, it sounds reasonable to me."

Pellini's shoulders relaxed.

"But," I added and hid a smile as he tensed again. "If Mzatal takes his shirt off anywhere on this planet, I want a priority rush on that footage to my inbox."

Pellini let out a strangled laugh. "God almighty. I don't know whether to be thrilled or terrified that you're in charge of defending the planet." Shaking his head, he retreated to the war room.

"I can save the world *and* enjoy sexy pics of my hot hunny!" I called after him.

"Earth is fucked," he shouted back.

Still smiling, I returned my attention to the nexus in time to see Rhyzkahl pull himself to his feet and stagger around his circuit. My amusement drained away, and I took a long drink of coffee to cover my twinge of guilt that I'd enjoyed seeing him put in his place.

He collapsed to sit with his back against the grove tree, head lowered. My guilt gave way to sympathy. Mzatal hadn't shown mercy with that blast. Then again, it was possible the blast had given Rhyzkahl an attitude adjustment. And I had questions that he might only answer in a weakened state.

We didn't have tunjen fruit on Earth to make the demon

realm restorative drink, but I created the best equivalent possible with what I had available—a concoction of lemon, orange, and carrot juices. Glass in hand, I headed out back with my bribe.

Rhyzkahl didn't lift his head as I stepped into the deep shade of the tree.

"Have you come to gloat?" he asked, voice ragged and face hidden by his hair.

"I've already done that," I said. "But I'm trying to not be cruel. You let Amkir zap me back when I was at your palace, so I know how much it sucks. I'm sure a Mzatal lightning bolt is a hundred times worse." I crouched and held out the glass. "Here, I brought you some juice."

For an instant I thought he'd play the stubborn lord and refuse, but he finally lifted his head and took the juice with a trembling hand. "Mzatal proved himself to be a true chekkunden," he said, then drained the glass.

My eyebrows lifted. "Because he slapped you down for being a dick?"

"For drawing you into his game."

I gave a harsh laugh. "Are you kidding me? First off, there's no game between us, and he hasn't drawn me anywhere I wasn't willing to go—though that's probably impossible for your devious little mind to understand. And second, if he's a chekkunden for loving me, empowering me, and treating me like an equal, what does that make you?" I cocked my head. "What's the demon word for lying scheming treacherous back-stabbing asshole son-of-a-bitch motherfucking deceiver?"

"Qaztahl."

"Give me a break. You expect me to buy that all the lords are shitstains like you? Seretis? *Elofir*?"

He leaned his head back against the white bark of the tree. "Believe what you will."

"Certainly nothing *you* say."

"You did not come to me simply to provide sustenance." He tapped his finger against the empty glass. "What is it you want?"

"You're right. Comforting you isn't on the top of my to-do list." The voice of the essence blade echoed in my mind. "Who is the vile oppressor?"

He flexed his scarred hand. "You will believe nothing I say."

"Humor me. Who is the vile oppressor?"

Rhyzkahl regarded me with contempt. "You. Mzatal. It is difficult to choose which to name."

I threw up my hands. "You're a captive because of *your* actions."

"And you are an oppressor because of yours."

"Serving justice doesn't make me an oppressor!" I caught myself before I blurted out further defensive justification. The asshole was baiting me. I stood and folded my arms. "Let me clarify. Xhan said, 'Treacherous. Traitor. Vile oppressor.' What did it mean?"

His gaze narrowed on me. "Tell me how Mzatal came to be on Earth."

Aha! It wasn't Rhyzkahl's weakness from the lightning strike that would dredge answers from him. It was his craving for information from beyond the confines of his prison. "I'll answer that one. Then you answer mine."

"On my honor."

I snorted. I'd been taught that demons held honor above all else, but Rhyzkahl and company had clearly demonstrated how much steaming bullshit that was. "You'll probably just lie, but I'm in a good mood." I shrugged. "I'll play along."

"Agreed."

This would be interesting. "An Earthgate from the first age is open. Mzatal came through it."

"An Earthgate? Where?" He staggered to his feet. *"How?"*

"Sorry, dude. One question. One answer." I spread my hands. "Your turn. Who is the vile oppressor?"

He ground his teeth and gave a grunt of frustration. "The one who held Xhan."

"Do you mean today? Mzatal? Or you, before?"

"One question. One answer."

"One *clear* answer," I said.

"It is clear to me. Clarity for you was not specified in the agreement."

"Fine." I *clearly* showed him my middle finger. "The gate is about thirty miles from here"—I pointed in a vague southerly direction—"that way."

He went lord-still. "Crystals?"

"Uh huh. Big and shiny. I gave you where and what. That's two answers." He couldn't do anything with the information, so there was no harm in throwing him a few crumbs—extra incentive for him to answer my questions. "Now, tell me *clearly*, using a name I know, who your blade meant by 'vile oppressor'."

"Mzatal."

"You owe me another one."

"I owe you nothing. You volunteered a second answer." He leaned close. "But I will tell you what I have told you before. Your lover's hands are not clean. Do you abide slavery?"

Cold rage filled my veins. "You're trying to implicate *Mzatal* in slavery? You who had your Earth flunkies kidnap innocent women to use as sex-slave currency for demonic lords?"

He gave me a smug look. "You know nothing of it."

I swayed, dizzy.

Sunlight streams through the library window, but it cannot compete with his radiance.

Breath catching, I step closer. "I know my heart, my lord Rhyzkahl."

His hand rests on the frame of my portrait. I seem so young, captured on canvas by Lord Szerain. Could it truly have been only a year past?

"Elinor, it is my will that you abide here."

"Do you always get what you want?"

He lowers his head, eyes on mine. So beautiful. "Yes."

Tick. Tick. Tick.

The sound teases my consciousness. My *consciousness. Kara. This is a vision. I need to follow the ticking. Marco Knight told me I can camera-fly, but how? Looks like I'll learn by trying. I reimmerse in Elinor's experience, aware this time.*

I conjure Giovanni's face in my mind to give me courage, and I pray my voice does not tremble when I speak. "Forgive me, my lord. It is no longer my desire to abide."

No, damn it, I'm still in Elinor's perspective. I need to escape it. I'll fly my camera-view up there, to the top of the bookshelf. I can do this. Uno. Due. Tre . . .

The world shatters and reforms.

One. Two. Three.

Moonlight floods the library. Rhyzkahl's back is to me.

A different time, but not the bookcase camera-view I was trying for. It doesn't feel like Elinor's perspective either. Did I screw something up?

His hands grip the frame of Elinor's portrait, and he drops his head. He heaves out a deep sigh and pushes from the wall. He gazes long at her image then drapes it in deep red silk.

Not Elinor's perspective. I'm me. Of course I'm me.

I sneer. "Did you fuck her over as badly as you did me?"

He turns on me, and his face twists in fury. "What are you doing? You should not be here!"

"I can be wherever I damn well please." I lift my chin. Why wouldn't I be here? "You burned all of your tell-Kara-what-to-do privileges."

He advances on me, grips my shoulders. Shakes me hard enough to make my teeth clack together. "Depart. *Now*."

This is no meek Elinor he's dealing with. I snag a book from the nearest shelf—War and Peace, hardback—and whack him on the side of the head. For good measure, I drive my knee into his groin, delighted at his grunt of pain.

He releases me and staggers back, overturns a bookshelf. I sidestep, but he recovers in a heartbeat. Lunges. Grabs my hair at the scalp. Drags me. "Kara, go *home*."

"Fuck off!" I slap my hands over his to hold them close to my head, twist my body in a move that should break his wrist.

He pivots with me, snakes an arm around my neck and gets me in a headlock. "Kara, stop! You need to remember—"

The world tilts. Shade and sunlight beyond. The nexus. Dizzy, I claw at the arm around my throat. The world tips back, wobbles drunkenly. The library and moonlight.

Rhyzkahl's hold is like iron. I kick and struggle to no avail. "Let me go!" The Nexus. War and Peace. Light. Darkness. What is he doing to me?

"You don't belong here, Kara." Dappled shade. Red silk.

"No!" I fight down the panic and call up my rage instead, lash out with the one weapon I have in my grasp. "It's you lords who don't belong here! You don't even know where you came from!" Vicious mind control by the demahnk prevents the lords from even considering certain topics. I seize onto the deepest secret I know and wield it as a white hot spear of hatred. "What's your real connection to Earth? You and all you lordly types."

Grass and flowers. The world stabilized. Heat. Humidity. *Home*.

No dream-vision, yet Rhyzkahl still held me. Breathing hard, I scrabbled at his arm. "How'd y'all come to be so high and mighty in the demon realm, huh? Where's your mama? Who's your daddy?"

Rhyzkahl released the headlock. I whirled, fists raised and ready to slug him, but he staggered back against the tree trunk and stared at me in open shock. His mouth worked, but nothing came out but an inarticulate gurgle. The leaves of the grove tree rustled as if stirred by a wind I couldn't feel. Sinking to his knees, he gripped his head and moaned in agony.

The sound ripped through me like a horrific wake-up call. *What have I done?* He'd dragged me out of the Elinor vision after I screwed up the attempt to camera-fly, and I'd repaid him with crushing pain. My stomach clenched, and I tasted acid. Sure, I'd been disoriented, but I'd *wanted* to hurt him, to pay him back for the pain he'd inflicted on me. I'd overreacted, and now I had no idea how to fix this. Usually the demahnk intervened to ease the excruciating headache, or sometimes a sufficient distraction could pull a lord from the mind-loop of agony. But I'd unloaded on Rhyzkahl with the heaviest weapon in my artillery.

"I'm sorry," I choked out, even as he curled into a fetal position against the trunk of the tree. The leaves murmured. I lifted my eyes to the brilliant canopy. "I swear I didn't mean to hurt him this badly."

The shade around him flickered with emerald and sapphire sparkles as if the sun shone through gem stones. I didn't know if the tree was telling me to go the fuck away since I'd done enough damage, or saying *It's okay, I'll help him.*

It was beautiful, and I felt like shit.

Tears stung my eyes. I spun away and fast-walked to the house. The headaches encouraged the lords to forget the thoughts that triggered them. Maybe this one would also erase that I was a cruel bitch.

But even if Rhyzkahl didn't remember what I'd done, I would.

Chapter 15

I slumped to sit at the kitchen table. Fillion mewed fiercely, then climbed up a chair and onto the table, trotted over to me and jammed his head into my chin.

"You just want a treat," I said but accepted the nuzzle. And of course gave him a treat. Cats were pretty cool for cheering a body up.

Ooh! I pushed up from the table and ran to my bedroom where Squig was curled into a tight ball of fur on my pillow. I carefully scooped her up then hurried out back as quickly as I could without jostling her fully awake.

Rhyzkahl still lay huddled at the base of the tree, eyes squeezed shut and face etched in pain. As gently as possible, I settled Squig into the crook of his neck. Neither kitten nor lord opened their eyes, but Rhyzkahl shifted one hand to cup the kitten closer and murmured a word that didn't sound like demon and definitely wasn't English. Squig yawned mightily then revved up a loud purr. The lines of pain in Rhyzkahl's face eased a bit.

Exhaling in relief, I slipped away and returned inside, then snuck a peek out the window. Rhyzkahl was stroking the kitten with gentle fingers. Good. We both felt better now.

My phone buzzed with a message from Idris. *<Video chat in five?>*

I texted back confirmation then headed to the war room with its video conferencing setup. At precisely five minutes after his text, his call came in, and the wall screen lit up with his image. He sat at a table in a mobile camp, camouflage net overhead and DIRT personnel bustling in the background. Sweat-streaked soot and grime covered his face, and one sleeve of his maroon fatigues hung in tatters. A heavy bandage was visible on his forearm.

"Looking good out there, Idris," I said. "How bad is the arm?"

He shrugged. "Only fifteen stitches. I'd just sling-shotted a reyza when a savik decided that getting its claws on me was more important than anchoring the rift."

"Ouch. Glad you're still in one piece," I said. "Would you mind writing up how you do those arcane shield busters?"

"Sure can. I'm in touch with a guy who wants to design a gun for arcane specialists—combination mini-grenade launcher, super-Taser, and rifle. He says he can build it where it'll fire a disruptor sphere that can be followed with bullets."

"Dude, my squad would pee themselves if I handed them a weapon like that," I said. "If you think your guy is legit, tell him to work up a prototype. I'll make sure it's seen by the right people."

"Awesome. From your message, it sounds like I have a lot to catch up on."

"Uh-huh, and there's more since I called." I proceeded to brief him on the pre-anomaly tangle and the situation with the rakkuhr and the mutations. I gave him a moment to curse his demonic lord-father's part in it before I moved on to Giovanni's arrival. After that, I texted copies of the Jontari memoir, and we spent a good five minutes hashing over possible reasons for why we'd been kept in the dark, and by whom. Even though we didn't come up with definitive answers, it felt good to talk it out with another summoner who shared the same confusion and outrage.

I went on to describe my discovery of the AWOL four in the Beaulac area. "It was odd. Like they're here but not."

"You could check out places that've had arcane activity in the past to narrow down where they might be holed up."

"Good idea. I'll do that." I scrawled a note to myself. "Now for the other big news. Fixing the pre-anomaly powered up the Spires, and Pellini and I kind of finished switching them on. Turns out they're a gate that's been dormant for thousands of years. Kadir's Earthgate. It's working."

His face lit up, then he let out a whoop and leaped up to punch the air. "A gate! That's incredible!" He dropped back into the chair, grinning. I found myself grinning as well. I hadn't seen him *enthused* since before the Mraztur captured him.

"That must mean the ways are open," he continued. "Summonings might be possible again."

"Right, though I wonder how having a gate will affect the need to summon." I tugged a hand through my hair. "I don't know if the demons can use it. Lords can come through. Kadir is on Earth . . . somewhere. And Mzatal is working rifts with Helori for transport. You've probably seen him mentioned in DIRT reports from China, Nigeria, and Australia."

I might as well have thrown a wet blanket over his joy-fire. "I thought you'd found a way to bring him through," he said then slammed his fist against the table. "So, just like that, the qaztahl have access to Earth with *Kadir* as the gatekeeper. After all we went through."

"At least it *has* a gatekeeper. I don't know what the hell Kadir is up to, but we need Mzatal's help, and he's dominating the other lords right now."

Idris blew out a breath. "You're right. It's just one more level of complexity to keep up with. It'd be nice to have a chance to come up for air once in a while." He looked down and fiddled with his bandage. "I don't think it's in the cards for me, though. I saw *her* today. At least I think I did."

I took in his demeanor and tone. "*Tessa*?! Where? What happened?"

"She was on the roof of a building overlooking the rift. As soon as I spotted her, she ducked down. By the time the incursion was settled enough for us to check it out, there was no trace of her and no clue of what she was up to."

A pang of sympathy went through me. Idris was Tessa's son, but he'd never had a chance to know her—or know what she felt toward him, if anything. Hell, we weren't even sure if she had any clue she was his mother. I had no doubt that, where she was concerned, his emotions were a messy soup of longing, confusion, and anger, along with an aching need to *know* the true story.

I tilted my head. "I'm thinking of having her house painted black," I said. "And I'm stealing her rosebushes. I'll probably end up killing them, but I'm feeling kind of immature and petty."

"And take that stupid Welcome sign, too."

"Ha! I'm burning that thing."

A whisper of amusement crossed his face, then he nodded to someone off camera before looking back at me. "I need to get going. Rift burped." He smiled. "It was good talking to you, Kara."

"Ditto. You take care of yourself."

The screen went blank.

"Kara?" Pellini called from the front room. "You need to come here."

My heart skipped a beat. "Cory?" I shoved up from the chair and broke into a run. "Is he okay?"

"Honestly, I have no idea," Pellini said.

I slid to a stop then could only stare. The red rubbery egg was gone, and the sofa bed had buckled under the weight of a four-foot-wide sphere of what looked like polished obsidian laced with pulsing luminescent red veins.

I finally found my voice. "That's him?"

Pellini gave me a *look*. "Unless someone snuck in, kidnapped Cory, and left a small asteroid behind, I'm thinking that odds are it is indeed him."

I moved close and peered at the surface in amazement. "The arcane is active all over it, so I'm going to assume Cory is still alive and well in there."

"If the egg was Phase Three, and the final mutated form is Phase Four, then what is this?" Pellini asked.

"Phase three and a half, I guess," I said with a shrug. "The Feds didn't have anyone in a 'meteor' phase. They'd concluded that the Fours were emerging changed from the red jelly egg— the chrysalis, according to their terminology." So was *this* the last phase before the mutation? Worry resurfaced. What would Cory *be* when he emerged?

"I'm betting this is the actual chrysalis," Pellini said then leaned close and squinted at the sphere. "How long do you think this phase lasts?"

"I have no idea, but my oh-so-accurate guess is not too long. They had a couple of people who'd already been transformed and who weren't discovered in this chrysalis stage." I shook my head. "My tongue keeps wanting to say 'crystal-fitz.' Let's keep it simple. Pod."

I regarded the pod and my poor, smushed sofa bed. "I'd love to try and roll him into the corner to clear space, but I don't dare. Not after people died when the gel-stuff was disturbed."

"Yeah, well, you can't anyway." When I shot him a perplexed look, he continued, "Squig and Cake were chasing Sammy through the living room as I came in, and when I tried to avoid stepping on a kitten, I lost my balance and fell against the pod. Hard. That sucker didn't move a millimeter."

"Weird." I cautiously placed my hand on the surface. "It doesn't look big enough to be that heavy."

"I'm not sure it's an issue of weight, per se." Pellini spread his arms and nodded down at his bulk. "I ain't exactly a little guy, and it felt like falling into a building."

Curious, I gave an experimental push, then a harder one. The thing might as well have been Thor's hammer.

"Y'know, I think Cory can stay right where he is," I said, earning me a bark of laughter from Pellini. My phone rang, a welcome distraction from Cory's predicament, even with the caller ID showing Knight. I headed out to the porch before answering. "Hey, Marco."

"Kara," he said, voice strained. "I'm sorry about yesterday."

"No, I'm the one who owes you an apology. I was being bitchy, and you didn't deserve to have me take it out on you." But surely my bitchiness wasn't enough to warrant the undercurrent of anxiety in his tone. "Is everything okay?"

"Not really."

My heart sank. "Shit. Did you get in trouble over not reporting Giovanni?"

"No." He paused. "I'm . . . sweating. A lot. It's red."

My heart finished dropping all the way down to my toes. "Are you able to drive?" I even managed to keep my voice mostly calm.

"Yeah. I think so."

"Can you make it here?"

He exhaled. "I'll make it."

"If at any point you feel like you might not be able to keep driving, you fucking call, got it? We'll come get you."

"I will. Thanks."

"Marco, no matter what happens, I promise we'll take good care of you."

He hung up without replying. My anxiety had retreated, but dread took its place. I returned inside and filled Pellini in.

"Huh." He frowned. "Does that kill your theory that having arcane abilities is a protection?"

I massaged the back of my neck. "I don't know. I'm not sure if Knight's abilities are arcane or something else."

Pellini's mouth twisted. "Don't know about you, but I sure hope they're something else."

A cry of alarm from the guest room cut our discussion short.

"Shit!" I dashed down the hall and careened into the room.

On the bed, a disoriented Giovanni clawed from beneath the blanket, eyes wild with confusion.

"Giovanni." I grabbed his shoulders. "You're safe. It's okay."

A small measure of the panic left his eyes as he took in the sight of me, though the confusion remained.

"I'm Kara. Kara Gillian." I released him and eased back.

A frown puckered his forehead. "Sì, Kara." Except he pronounced it Kah-rah. He muttered something in Italian, gaze darting around the room, then switched to English. "You cannot be here. Where is Elinor? Elinor!"

At least I was pretty sure that's what he said. I hadn't counted on a language barrier since I knew he spoke English, but apparently the seventeenth-century version had evolved in accent and pronunciation and inflection in the past three hundred plus years.

"I can help you understand me better," I said, slowly and distinctly. "But you need to come with me." I added gestures to get my point across.

He scrambled up and backpedaled shakily toward the window, rattling off a stream of Italian that included my name, Elinor, and Szerain. I had no clue about the rest. My smattering of nexus-imbued Italian was useless, since mine was the current-day version.

"Pellini, a little help!" I advanced on Giovanni and threw an arm around him as his legs gave way. The sight of Pellini sent him into more of a panic, but he weakened as he struggled against me and passed out when Pellini reached him.

Pellini looped one arm around Giovanni's waist and drew his arm over his own neck. Giovanni topped me by only a few inches but was solid enough that I was glad to relinquish him.

"To the nexus," I told Pellini. "I'm hoping that if I can connect him to modern Earth flows, we'll be able to update his language and orient him."

"Makes as much sense as anything else," Pellini said with a shrug. "What about your other guest?"

I thought about it for less than a heartbeat. "I don't have the time or energy to deal with Rhyzkahl or his bullshit." Or the stomach to force him into his house so soon after the headache incident. "Let him see. Let him wonder. There's nothing he can do about it, and he'll find out eventually."

Pellini chuckled under his breath and helped me get the unconscious Giovanni out the back door and across the porch. Rhyzkahl sat against the tree with Squig beside him. He didn't look at me with malice, which told me he didn't remember my Cruella de Kara act. But shock registered on his face as he recognized the supposedly long-dead Giovanni, and his gaze remained locked on us until we made it onto the nexus and I raised a curtain of potency as a privacy screen. We could see out, but he couldn't see in.

Pellini laid Giovanni at the center of the slab then retreated to the grass. "Can you keep him calm while you're doing the language trick?"

"I can get him nice and chill." I crouched beside Giovanni and tapped in to the super-shikvihr that flowed around us then traced four floating pygah sigils over Giovanni. Envisioning calm clarity for him, I placed one each on his forehead, throat, chest, and abdomen. His aura shimmered over his body like a layer of azure fog and, with slow precision, I selected delicate strands of local potency and attached them to it, then more and more until I had five times the number I would have needed for myself.

I closed my eyes to shut out all visual stimuli. The strand colors intensified in my mind's eye, displaying subtle differences in hue. I expanded into clear intention beyond thought, called in conversations and culture and images and objects. As those flowed—"downloaded"—I overlaid impressions of the environment: Rhyzkahl and his prison, the grove tree, Sammy, the kittens, security, warding, personnel, the house layout.

More and more, until his aura crackled with sparks like static electricity. Enough. Deep in the flows, I moved, reluctant to release the luscious connection, yet aware of my purpose. One by one, I disconnected the strands and merged them back into the flows.

At long last I looked up at Pellini. "I'm going to try to wake him. Stand by in case he freaks." I traced a fifth pygah for good measure then called potency up from the nexus in gradually intensifying waves like a giant sensory alarm clock.

He groaned and threw an arm over his eyes to shield them from the midmorning sun. "A smith pounds his anvil within my skull."

"Giovanni," I said, "do you know where you are?"

"Earth. Louwheezy . . . Louisiana." The words came out slowly, but clearly. "On the nexus?" He pushed up to sit cross-legged, squinting in the bright sunlight.

"That's right. And if I told you I needed to drive my car to the gas station, would that make sense to you?"

He tilted his head up at me and frowned. "A mechanical wagon." He spoke carefully as if choosing from a selection of words. "The car requires gas as the hearth fire requires wood. I understand this."

I breathed a sigh of relief. I wouldn't have to explain every technological advance made in the last three centuries. Sometimes this magic shit could be really handy.

Giovanni put a hand to his head. "There is much else I do not understand." His forehead puckered. "And I know you, though we have never met."

"That's right, we've never met," I said. "I think we need to continue this inside, where there's food. And coffee."

Pellini muttered agreement, and together we hauled up an unresisting Giovanni and marched him back across the yard.

"Giovanni Racchelli," Rhyzkahl said in a clear voice when we were still a dozen feet from the porch steps. He stood, eyes intense on us as he drew breath to say more.

I started singing at the top of my lungs, drowning out whatever Rhyzkahl was trying to say. "*Do your balls hang low, do they wobble to and fro.*" Pellini grinned and joined in, deep baritone belting out the silly lyrics with me. "*Can you tie them in a knot, can you tie them in a bow.*" We hauled Giovanni up the steps and across the porch. "*Can you throw them over your shoulder like a continental soldier, do your balls hang low!*"

We slammed the door behind us.

Chapter 16

Somehow, I resisted the urge to flip Rhyzkahl off through the window, and instead helped get Giovanni into a chair. Pellini set two ibuprofen and a glass of juice in front of him, while I loaded up a plate with various pastries, bread, cheese, and fruit. If the dude had been dead for three hundred years, he was probably hungry.

"Would you please give Bryce an update?" I asked Pellini. "We're going to need a *companion* for our guest." I dropped into the chair across from Giovanni and gave him my best friendly smile. "Go ahead and eat. I'll answer your questions."

He didn't argue and tucked in like a starving man. "This is Earth, yes? But it is slip timed." He shook his head. "Out of time."

"Yes, time has passed since you were last in the demon realm."

"You must send me back."

"I can't. I didn't summon you."

"I *must* return. Elinor needs—" He broke off, face paling by degrees. "Elinor." His hand flew to his throat, and his eyes grew distant. "Call her," he murmured.

"Giovanni," I said gently, "she's—"

Through bared teeth, he snarled a word. "*Szerain.*" He shot to his feet, chest heaving. "Szerain bade me call her only to bury his essence blade in her breast. Serpent! Betrayer! Most accursed of all of the qaztahl!"

"I'm sorry." I kept my voice pitched low and even as I did my best to project calm.

Giovanni leveled his gaze my way as if seeing me for the first

time. "Kara Gillian. What have you to do with this tragic tale?"
He sank into the chair. "Call her. Call . . . you."

"I heard you call," I offered cautiously. "I thought it was only
a dream memory of Elinor's."

"A nightmare." He shook his head slowly, eyes unfocused.
"And I am yet impaled upon its bloody claws."

"Giovanni, what do you remember?"

Confusion knitted his brow. "How much time has fled since
Elinor . . ." His eyes stretched wide in realization. "Since *I* . . ."

I took a deep breath before assailing him with the lovely
news. "Over three hundred years."

He sagged, squeezing his eyes shut as my words hit home.
"Three centuries."

"I'm sorry," I said. "I can't even imagine how much of a
shock this is."

"Elinor," he murmured, voice shaking.

He thinks her dead all this time, I thought. That was no doubt
kinder than the truth: trapped in Szerain's essence blade for centuries. "What do you remember," I asked again, "of what happened to her . . . and you?"

Giovanni raised his eyes to mine but didn't speak for several
seconds, as if gathering pieces of the nightmare. "Elinor danced
a ritual with Szerain in his summoning chamber. It was sooner
than planned. She was not ready, but neither she nor Szerain
could be dissuaded. I waited in the antechamber for her to finish,
but . . ." He pressed his fingers to his eyes. "The ritual shattered.
I felt it. Heard it. The palace shook, and the air shrieked. I should
not have been able to enter the chamber, but the door lay askew,
wrenched from its hinges."

I'd felt Elinor's terror and panic, seen glimpses through her
eyes of the ritual spiraling out of control, but now I wanted his
perspective. "What did you see?"

"A vision of hell," he said, staring at nothing. "Violence and
chaos. A wailing vortex of corpse-livid hues. Elinor . . ." His
voice caught. "My Elinor in the center of it all, eyes glowing,
fierce and terrible. And terrified. Though I have but small ability
to see the arcane, the power burning through her . . . coming
from her . . . near blinded me. Yet I could think of nothing but to
reach her side and save her from the madness." Grief and helplessness swam in his eyes. "But it was Szerain who stood behind
her, holding her upright with his arm tight around her waist as if
in a grotesque dance. He looked at me over her head and

shouted, 'Call her.' " Giovanni tensed, and one hand curled into a fist on the table. "I did. I called her name, screamed it through the gale that sought to tear me away. Szerain raised Vsuhl, and it shrieked louder than the vortex." His jaw clenched. I waited on tenterhooks for him to continue, even though I knew what happened next.

"I trusted him, *believed* with all my soul that he would protect her, save her." Anger darkened his face. "But no. He drove that accursed blade into her heart." The anger melted into distress. "I fought to reach them, to drive him away from her, but for naught. He bore her to the stone as the blade consumed her soul, and he commanded me, 'Call her. Do not cease calling.' " A shudder went through Giovanni. "I called her. I have never stopped calling her. I . . ." His voice broke. "Elinor."

Holy shit. I sat back and struggled to process everything—not only his account of events but also the unbelievable determination of this young man to keep calling to the woman he loved for over three *hundred* years. Not to mention, Giovanni's version of events shone a slightly different light on Szerain's actions. Yes, he'd killed Elinor and trapped her in the blade, but what was Giovanni's role? Had Szerain held hope for her recovery down the road? Why else order him to keep calling her?

But not centuries down the road, I thought with a pang of sadness for Giovanni. All that remained of Elinor existed in the fragment of essence attached to mine. "*Slew Elinor. Created you*," Szerain had once told me. Why? How?

"You called to me," I said gently.

"In the darkness," he murmured.

"Yes, you helped save me." He'd kept me from losing my Self. Kept me from becoming Rowan, thrall to the Mraztur. "How did you know to call me? How did you know my name?"

"A whisper in the darkness," he muttered, eyes growing haunted. "Like leaves in the wind, but there was no wind. There was nothing."

The darkness of the void? A chill walked down my back. I had shadowy memories of my own trip through the void, yet mine had only lasted a couple of weeks.

I leaned forward. "Do you remember what happened to you? How you died?"

He blinked and seemed to come back to himself. He looked briefly perplexed at my question, as if still unable to believe that he could have *died*—which I figured was perfectly reasonable.

"Szerain came to me. Bade me to continue calling Elinor." He frowned. "I remember nothing more."

With the world falling apart around him, there were any number of ways he could have bought the farm. I banked my frustration and changed tack. "What about the ritual? Do you know what it was for?"

His expression cleared. "To awaken Szerain's Earthgate." He hesitated and gave me a hopeful look. "Did it succeed?"

"No, it didn't," I said, then watched him deflate. Great, I couldn't even tell him his girlfriend's death had actually been for a good cause. And here I was about to make it worse. "It wreaked a terrible cataclysm upon the demon realm, and the ways between Earth and the demon realm slammed closed. That's why it took you so long to return." Yet now Kadir's gate was awake. Could the others be far behind?

Giovanni remained silent for close to a minute as he struggled to reconcile this new and unpleasant information. "I *must* return to the demon realm," he finally said with intense determination.

Damn, it was Kara-disappoints-Giovanni-at-every-turn day. "You can't," I said. "Not right now. I'm sorry. There's too much upheaval both here and there."

He stood, eyes blazing as he clenched and unclenched his hands. "I must see Szerain," he said through his teeth.

Yeah, he was a tetch upset. I couldn't imagine what he'd be like without the five nexus pygahs. I leaned back in my chair. "He's not in the demon realm. He's in hiding on Earth now." Of that I was *mostly* sure. I paused as a spasm of grief tightened my chest. "He was my friend." Or rather, Ryan was my friend. But Ryan was gone and had never even been real. I barely knew who Szerain was.

Giovanni's shoulders sagged. "He was mine as well. And he . . ."

"He killed the woman you loved." I let out a low sigh. "I'm sorry. I wish there was more I could do for you."

"I need solitude," he said, voice hollow.

"Of course," I said without hesitation. Pellini stepped in from the war room right on cue, followed by Sharini Tandon. "You can go anywhere you want," I continued to Giovanni, "but for your own safety, we're assigning you a bodyguard. Her name is Sharini, and I promise she'll keep her distance unless there's reason to do otherwise. For now, I'm asking you to stay within the fence line. It's not safe beyond it." I had no intention of letting him leave—at least not yet—but it would be a lot easier if he remained here willingly. "If there's anything you need, you have only to ask."

Tandon stepped up. "Signor Racchelli, it's my pleasure to serve as your security detail. If you're looking for a quiet place, there's a nice little shady spot where Miss Jill put a couple of benches." She smiled. "How about I show you the way, then I'll leave you be."

Giovanni mutely pushed up and allowed himself to be escorted out. As soon as the front door closed, I dropped my head to the table and groaned.

"When this is over, I want to spend a month in Tahiti." I looked up at Pellini. "Tahiti still exists, right?"

"Far as I know."

The walkie-talkie on the counter buzzed. I snagged it and pressed the button. "Go ahead."

"Detective Knight is at the front gate." A pause. "He doesn't look good."

"Copy that," I said. "Clear him through. We're ready for him."

Knight was indeed covered in a hideously familiar red, viscous sweat. We wasted no time and got him settled on a futon mattress on the living room floor—well out of the way of foot traffic, since we knew about Pod Phase this time.

I crouched beside him. "I know it doesn't feel like it," I said, "but you're going to be okay. We'll take care of you."

He gave me a wan smile. "Thanks." His smile faded, and his throat worked as he swallowed. "I guess whatever I end up as can't be worse than what I am right now."

My heart squeezed at the depth of emotion in his voice. "You're magnificent now, and you'll still be magnificent when you come out of this."

His breath shuddered from him. "I never told you how to camera-fly in the dream-visions. It's not hard—just a different way of looking at things."

The red sweat thickened to mucus consistency and oozed to form an ever-thickening layer. "Just rest. You don't have to—"

"I do!" he said, eyes wide. "Gotta have something good come out of this." A shiver wracked him. "You're not you. You're not the dream person. You're a drone controlled by you.

Separate. From everything. God that description sucks. Float up. But keep connected. Like a balloon on a string. You'll be able—"

The slime swept over his face, swallowing his last words. I quickly straightened and backed away, unwilling to repeat my experience with Cory, but to my relief the slime undulated for several seconds then seemed to settle.

And now we hoped for the best. "Make sure no one goes near him," I told Pellini.

"Already put the word out." He cracked his neck then exhaled gustily. "I'm heading into town to check the rifts and make a supply run. Need anything?"

"Chocolate donuts."

"I *might* be able to scare up white bread and chocolate syrup."

"I'll take it."

Chapter 17

I spent the next hour working on the reports for General Starr and had just hit "send" when my phone rang. No number I recognized, but I was used to that. "This is A.C. Gillian."

"I need you."

My heart skipped a beat. Mzatal, his voice like cold steel. In the background, I heard shouts and screams.

"Where?"

"Siberia. Ust-Ilimsk. Helori will—" The line went dead.

That was all I needed to know. "Jill! I'm going to Siberia! Ust-Ilimsk. How cold is it there right now?" I ran for the closet, pulled out my rucksack and quickly checked weapons and ammo. I'd learned from hard experience to always have a bag packed and ready to go with necessary items for a variety of scenarios: flashlight, first aid kit, crowd control devices, toiletries, clean underwear and socks, and even a small packet of coffee.

"Off the top of my head, I'd say it's really, really cold." Jill stepped out of the dining room, already busy pulling info up on her phone. "Okay, got it. Temp is minus twelve. Ugh. Strip down while I grab your cold weather gear." She sprinted to my room while I groaned. "How long before the helicopter gets here?"

"No chopper," I said as I shucked off my jeans and t-shirt. "The demahnk Helori is coming to get me." At least, I assumed that's what Mzatal was going to say. "Crap. I'll have to send him back here to pick up Pellini." I'd be handicapped without him there to shape the arcane for me. "Isn't Ust-Ilimsk somewhere near the 1908 Tunguska event?"

"About two hundred miles south of it" she called out from

the bedroom. "But it looks like that's the closest population center of any decent size." She returned with a bundle under one arm and her eyes still on her phone. "Oh, wait, that minus twelve is Celsius." She tossed me silk thermals and dumped a clean DIRT uniform at my feet. "It's ten Fahrenheit."

"Above zero?" I shimmied into the thermals then yanked on the fatigues.

"Yep, but they're thirteen hours ahead, so it's full night. And it's snowing. I'll get Pellini's gear together. He should be back in about ten minutes. Wear the insulated boots and change your socks. I pulled out the good wool ones for you."

I obeyed then looked up to see her holding my tactical vest in one hand and my super-sleek mega-insulated coat in the other. "Gloves and balaclava are in the bottom zipped pockets," she told me. "Headlamp and light sticks in the arm pockets."

"Thanks. You're my hero."

"How bad is it?"

I shook my head as I shrugged into the vest and strapped on my weapons. "Dunno. I heard people yelling and screaming, but all Mzatal said was 'I need you.'"

She winced. "I'd make a snarky joke about that, but if it's so bad he needs your help . . ."

"Yeah, my thoughts exactly." I took the coat and slung the rucksack over one shoulder. "I'm heading to the nexus to familiarize myself with the area. Hopefully Helori will meet me there."

"Stay safe," she ordered.

"Always, ma'am." I gave her a quick hug then dashed out the back.

Rhyzkahl glanced my way as I ran across the yard and leaped onto the slab. He wisely remained silent while I dropped the rucksack and coat at my feet and called up the flows. He knew by now that if I was geared up, shit was going down somewhere, and I was in absolutely zero mood to play games.

Thankfully, the day was still mild, saving me from instantly passing out from heatstroke in the thermal clothing. I found the flows for Ust-Ilimsk, Siberia, "plugged in," then closed my eyes and let the culture and language of the region seep in, like water filling a sponge. I was getting to be an old hand at this kind of download. It wasn't my first time learning Russian—though my previous trip had been to Moscow in late August, with temps in the seventies and a rift in Red Square—but right now I was more interested in gaining a superficial knowledge of the city layout and a familiarity with the region.

A change in air pressure prompted me to open my eyes. Helori stood beside me in his human form—tall, lean, and lithe, with a multi-ethnic look that allowed him to blend in anywhere. At first glance he appeared as calm and collected as ever, but his eyes, typically so full of life, were dull and bloodshot. He looked weary and harried, I realized with a twinge of dismay. Though I was only up to "somewhat conversational" in my super-speedy Russian course, I swallowed back a request for a few more minutes. I had enough to get by.

"Pellini will be back in about five. Can you come back for him?" I pulled on the coat and rucksack then took the hand he held out for me. It trembled ever so faintly in mine.

"Only your presence is needed," he said with a smile.

I gave his hand a light squeeze and pushed down the flutter of nerves. "Got that covered."

The nexus and my back yard blinked out. Demahnk travel was usually as effortless as stepping from one room to another, but this was a way rougher ride. My stomach did a couple of unpleasant flip-flops during the heartbeat or so it took for the world to reappear.

I flinched as noise assaulted my eardrums. Screams of fear and pain, shouts and sirens, the crackle and snap of flames, and an earsplitting roar from a holy shit massive reyza.

Helori disappeared, leaving me in the middle of a snow-covered four-lane street. Fifty yards away, a rift spanned from curb to curb, casting malevolent patterns of orange and magenta and red onto the dull grey buildings that stretched along both sides of the roadway. At the edge of the rift, Lord Elofir worked complex weaves of potency as arcane flames leaped around him. And a dozen feet beyond the rift, Mzatal wielded both essence blades in a pitched battle with the gigantic scar-covered reyza. A Jontari. No doubt about it.

I broke into a run toward them, yanking on gloves and bala-clava and cursing the ice and snow that made footing treacherous. Dark patches dotted the street, and it took me a moment to realize they marked where demons had been killed—the snow melting beneath the discorporeation and then refreezing. The bitter cold air seared my lungs, but I was pleased to note distant barricades and flashing lights forming a half mile perimeter around the incursion. The local first responders seemed to be on the ball, which would make my life easier. Even better, I noted that Elofir and Mzatal were drawing potency directly from the rift. Not only did that explain how Mzatal was able to maintain a fight against such a powerful demon, but it meant I didn't have to worry about either lord depleting their reserves and collapsing.

Coils of rakkuhr wound lazily atop the snow and flowed around abandoned cars. Around the rift, the gouts of magenta and red lowered, like a gas burner turned from high to medium. Elofir sent out an intricate web of green potency to further contain the wild energies, at the same time keeping one eye on Mzatal and the demon. I suspected he wouldn't involve himself in the fight unless the situation turned absolutely critical. He had a reputation for non-violence, and even his aura radiated gentleness that spoke of a deep reluctance to do harm.

The reyza deflected a lightning bolt then snapped his wings out, buffeting Mzatal with great strokes of what had to be damn near a hundred-foot wingspan. *Holy Christmas.* And here I'd thought the demon at the Piggly Wiggly was big. This one looked to be at least two stories tall—well over twice the size of Gestamar.

Maybe that can be our new measurement system, I thought with a touch of hysteria. *Yes, General, the class 1A demon was a 2.4 on the Gestamar scale.*

Teeth bared, Mzatal braced himself with a wide stance and sent an arcing strike into the reyza's midsection. The demon grunted and staggered a step but the flicker of arcane shielding told me he hadn't taken any real damage. Mzatal slashed out with power to shred the shielding, but the reyza reacted with blinding speed to deflect the attack. His tail whipped around, and my heart spasmed in dread as it caught Mzatal solidly in the chest and sent him flying a good fifty feet, over the sidewalk and into a scraggly stand of trees.

My feet skidded on a killed-demon ice patch, and only the wild flailing of my arms saved me from falling on my ass. When I looked up again, Mzatal was climbing to his feet with slow, murderous purpose. Snow clung to him, hissing into steam as he straightened. Behind him, the trees burst into flame. Holy fucking shit, he was primed for dealing out a world of hurt. But it meant nothing if he couldn't get past the shields. *And I can't shape the sigils for a shield buster unless I'm on or near the nexus.* The brand spanking new super-shikvihr loop on my nexus was supposed to give me a boost when I was away from home, but I was on the other side of the friggin' world. How the hell was I supposed to help Mzatal?

Adrenaline slammed through me as a child screamed somewhere to my left. I whirled, shocked to see a half dozen people huddled beneath a walkway, among them a wide-eyed man with a frightened little girl in his arms. So much for the local police making my life easier. *"Evacuate the area means evacuate the area,"* I grumbled to myself as I jogged toward them. None of them looked hurt, but they might not stay that way unless I got them to a safe place. And soon.

I spared a glance at Mzatal, in time to see him hammer the reyza with a potency strike that knocked the demon on his ass. With a mental cheer for my badass sweetie, I swung my attention to the cluster of people, poised to shout for them to come out and make a dash for the barricade.

My words died in my throat as the reason for the girl's scream moved into sight. A second reyza prowled the raised walkway above. Though not as large as the other, it was still at least as big as the Piggly Wiggly demon. *Only one point five Gestamars,* I thought, pulse quickening. *A mere sprout.* But this mere sprout had the people trapped, and I had zero doubt he intended to do more than scare them.

"Elofir!" I shouted, pulling both of my guns as I ran. "People!"

He jerked his head my way. At the sight of Sprout, he tied off the potency in moves too fast to follow then sprinted toward the huddled people, reaching them the same time I did.

The reyza let out a shriek of fury and launched himself into the air. I jerked my guns up but immediately lowered them, frustration clawing at the sight of the demon's arcane shielding.

Sprout pivoted mid-air and flung a ball of red-orange potency at us. With a sweep of his hand, Elofir raised a shimmering green barrier in time to scatter the blast, but the demon continued to lob volley after volley. Though the barrier held, we were trapped behind it. In the street, falling snow flashed with lightning and potency as Mzatal and the big reyza fought.

"Why is this guy bothering with us when he could be helping his buddy out there?" I shouted at Elofir over the crackling din of the strikes. Not that I wanted a second demon attacking

Mzatal, but at least I wouldn't have to stay and protect these people and could instead help him out. Somehow.

"Demon honor," Elofir replied through gritted teeth. "Bikturk chooses to engage Mzatal alone."

Bikturk? *Ha! More like Big Turd.* With Sprout unlikely to abandon his attack to fly off and help Big Turd, taking him out of action became a priority. However, I knew better than to ask pacifist Elofir to zap him. "Can you wrap this asshole up in bindings?"

We flinched at a hard strike that shattered like bloody stars against the barrier. Behind us, the girl whimpered.

Elofir staggered and struggled to reinforce. "His protections are such that I would have to drop this barrier in order to craft effective bindings," he said. "I would require no more than three heartbeats, but in that time the reyza would have ample opportunity to cause great injury or worse."

Double shit. I missed my arcane abilities now more than ever. Back at home, it would take me less than a minute to make shield busters. Too bad I was *really* far from home right now.

But did that matter? What if "other side of the world" wasn't too far for the super-shikvihr boost?

Silently chanting *please work please work please work,* I mentally *reached* for my nexus, then jerked in surprise and relief as power leaped into my control. It wasn't as god-like as when I stood upon the nexus—more like what I'd had before my abilities were stripped from me. I could make floaters though, and that was all that mattered.

I dropped to a crouch, hit the mag release on my Glock and thumbed the first five rounds into my palm. According to Idris, metal would only hold a fraction of the charge that the quartz spheres could. That would be a serious problem if I was on my own, but not so much when paired with a demonic lord who only needed a point of entry. "If you can hold this barrier another minute, I'll punch a hole in his shielding." I hoped.

An almost-smile touched Elofir's face. "That would simplify matters greatly."

Across the street, Big Turd took flight, landed atop a battered five-story building then rained arcane shrapnel onto Mzatal. I yanked my right glove off with my teeth and concentrated on weaving the sigils to turn the bullets into shield busters.

Sprout let out a roar and dropped to the ground near the curb, lips pulling back from his fangs as he assessed Elofir's barrier.

Between his clawed hands, roiling potency gathered, seething with the red and black of *rakkuhr*.

"Almost done," I muttered, blowing on my fingers to warm them before sketching the final patterns. In my periphery, I saw Mzatal leap a zigzag course from balcony to balcony, like a parkour god, evading Big Turd's strikes to reach the roof and engage in furious battle.

Sprout let out a piercing war cry and hurled the *rakkuhr* at the barrier. It impacted and spread like a glop of jam then snaked dark tendrils over the barrier's surface.

Elofir hissed through his teeth as he fought to counter the insidious *rakkuhr*. "Ten heartbeats, Kara. No more."

"Got it." Fingers numb, I wove the last sigil on the bullets, reloaded the mag, slammed it home, and chambered a round. "Now!"

As the barrier dropped, I brought the gun up, sighted and squeezed off two rounds that struck Sprout dead center mass. In the blink of an eye, Elofir sent a spike of potency through the opening. It spiderwebbed on the inside of the demon's shield, destroying it before constricting to envelop Sprout in a tight potency net.

The demon squawked and flopped into the snow. I grabbed my glove and sprang up, sprinted past him and toward the Mzatal vs. Big Turd main event. Their battle flowed along the rooftop, brutal and beautiful like a perfectly choreographed dance of death between equal opponents. Bloody gashes marked the reyza, and Mzatal's face was a mask of red, likely from a scalp wound. Big Turd moved with a grace and speed in stark contrast to his size, using wings and tail, claws and teeth to hammer Mzatal with blows, both arcane and physical. Mzatal ducked and leaped, slashed and struck with both essence blades. It would only take one slip, one misjudged strike to tip the balance. How long could Mzatal hold so much power?

I slid to a stop in the middle of the street, dropped to my butt and tugged on my glove, then pulled my right knee up to use as a base to steady my aim. *Forty yard shot, minimum,* I thought as I settled into position. *Three shield piercers left.* I'd been an average marksman at best when I was a cop, and that was with a max target distance of twenty-five yards. But I'd gone through twice as many rounds in these past two months than in my entire police career. *I can do this.*

My finger rested lightly on the trigger as I sighted down the barrel and watched for an opening. The reyza was a whole lot larger than a paper target, but he and Mzatal were in constant motion, shifting position with inhuman speed. "Let's not shoot the wrong one, okay?" I murmured. Even though I knew our bond lay cold and silent, I *reached* to the core of Mzatal's essence, opened my mind so that he could feel my intent.

And hopefully get the hell out of the way of a bullet.

I pygahed and slowed my breathing. Mzatal took what had to be an intentional misstep, giving me what I needed. Big Turd lunged into the opening, and I squeezed the trigger.

The demon let out a roar that shook the earth and shattered windows even as the next two rounds found their mark. Mzatal drove lightning spikes into the punctures, and the shielding burst like shattered glass. Big Turd snapped out his wings and surged into the air, but Mzatal had clearly anticipated the retreat and leaped after the demon.

He sank one blade then the other into Big Turd's lower back. The demon bellowed and twisted in flight, clawing at his attacker in mounting desperation as, hand over hand, Mzatal used the knives like cruel climbing pitons to scale him. High between the shoulder blades, he buried Xhan in the muscle of the right wing then wrenched the knife, slashing flesh and membrane. Blood showered the snow as the demon faltered then careened toward the ground in a poorly controlled descent.

My breath caught as Mzatal reversed his grip on Khatur and ran the point alongside the demon's spine. *He's positioning for a heart-strike*, I thought with a mix of relief and horror. *He's going to kill him with an essence blade.* Even as the realization hit, Mzatal plunged Khatur between ribs and into the reyza's heart.

Bikturk howled like a tortured beast, head thrown back and limbs stiffening in rigid spasms. The terrible howl trailed off into a strangled croak followed by awful silence as he went limp and plummeted toward the street.

I hurried to back away, nearly tripping on the curb. With seconds to impact, Mzatal wrenched Khatur free and jumped clear. For an instant, he seemed to fly, then he landed in an effortless crouch that sent smoking cracks radiating across the pavement. The massive Jontari crashed behind him, the great wings collapsing last, perfectly framing Mzatal for a split second before they settled gently to the snow.

A ragged cheer rose from the people behind me, but it

quickly died away to uneasy murmurs as Mzatal straightened. Blood flowed over his face from a laceration along his hairline. His black gaze took in the bound reyza and the huddled humans, and his lips pulled back from his teeth in a silent snarl. He advanced, malevolent aura rolling before him in a smothering wave like heat before lava, Khatur and Xhan still gripped in each hand.

No, it was the blades that had *him* in *their* grip.

Throat tight, I pivoted to Elofir. "I need you to get these people to safety."

He looked at Mzatal with naked grief before giving me a weary nod. "Save him," he said quietly.

Death and destruction roiled in Mzatal's eyes. For several nerve-wracking heartbeats, he watched Elofir shepherd the group up the street, but then he focused on the demon bound in Elofir's potency net.

Sprout let out a piercing whistle like I'd never heard from any reyza ever, and it took me a moment to realize it was a squeal of terror.

Because he knows he's about to be killed with an essence blade, I realized. Death by essence blade meant death for real, with no chance of passing through the void. But the badass Jontari demon was all but pissing himself in fear, struggling violently against Elofir's bindings. I couldn't imagine a war-focused demon like Sprout fearing death—not after witnessing the suicide of the Piggly Wiggly reyza. Plus, I'd killed Pyrenth with Szerain's blade, and the reyza had shown no fear. A hideous realization slid icy fingers through my chest. Sprout wasn't afraid of death by the essence blades. He was terrified of a fate far worse than the mere cessation of life: whatever hellish doom he faced with those same knives in the hands of a nightmare Mzatal.

I put myself between the lord and the demon. "Mzatal," I said in a loud, clear voice, mentally calling to the very core of his *essence*. "Is the rift secure?"

His only response was to call potency to him—both native and *rakkuhr*—until the air around him rippled. Out of the corner of my eye, I saw Elofir carrying the little girl while he and the humans ran for the barrier. They were out of danger—for the moment—but I had a sinking feeling that if Mzatal succeeded in blading Sprout, he would turn on them next. No one would be safe.

"Mzatal!" Pulse pounding, I closed the distance between us and seized his bloody face in my hands. "Mzatal, leave the demon be." My eyes sought his. He ripped his gaze from the reyza and looked down at me as *rakkuhr* rippled over him.

"I'll take care of the demon," I said. "That's why you sent for me—to take care of . . . the situation." *To take care of you*, I silently added. *That* was why he'd said he needed me. With two of the domineering essence blades in full use, he'd known he would need me to bring him back to himself.

Red flickered deep in his eyes. I kept my hands on his face. "I'm here to take care of things," I said. "I'm here for you. You sent for me."

His breathing quickened, and a deep shudder went through him. The knives spoke to him in ceaseless, insidious whispers. Xhan, possessive and demanding. Khatur, silky and persuasive. But Mzatal had sent for me to be the third voice, and now he had my words to listen to as well.

He spoke through clenched teeth. "I . . . need. You."

"Yes. You need me. That's why I'm here. For you." I stroked my thumb over the ridge of his cheekbone. "You can do this. I'll help you."

Eyes never leaving mine, he sheathed Khatur at his waist then used the free hand to seize the hair at the back of my head in an iron grip. With the other, he lifted Xhan. *Rakkuhr* flickered over the blade as he brought it close to my face.

I didn't shrink from it. "I've felt the kiss of that blade before, zharkat," I murmured. "I'll suffer it again if it calls you back to me, but I prefer *your* kiss."

Mzatal remained utterly still for half a dozen heartbeats then crushed his lips to mine, grip still fierce against my scalp. I tasted blood. His. Mine. It didn't matter. I returned the kiss just as hard and wrapped my arms around his neck. My hand found his braid and gave it a sharp tug.

A shiver went through him, and beyond the kiss I was distantly aware of him drawing Xhan across his thigh. *Blooding it*. Distracting it enough to allow Mzatal to send it away.

The knife vanished. He wrapped an arm around me, holding me hard against him even as he tightened the grip in my hair. Relief and a zillion other emotions surged through me as I clung to him. "I have you," I breathed. "I have you now."

He potency-burned away the blood from his face, then simply kissed me again, hard and deep. I responded in kind, not giving a shit that we were in the middle of a rift-broken street in Russia.

I sketch hurriedly in my journal under warm amber sigil-light. If only I can remember this last portion of the trancer glyph before the Conclave ends, Lord Szerain will—

"Elinor."

Lord Mzatal! He will flay me while I yet breathe. I shove the journal closed, heart fluttering in my breast.

He grasps my shoulders and calls me a name I do not know. The world tips.

Cold. Snow. Rift-light.

Mzatal held me, grip hard and eyes narrowed. There was no need to tell him this wasn't the first time an Elinor dream had blindsided me. Though the demahnk and other lords were blocked from reading me, my mind and heart and essence were ever open to him.

He slowly relaxed his grip as if prying himself free then released me. To my relief, his eyes were his again, but a sliver of dread persisted at the sight of Khatur sheathed at his side rather than sent away.

"Elinor's journal," I said, annoyed at how thin my voice sounded. "Do you know where it is?"

He regarded me for an oddly long moment before his head dipped in a slow nod. "The black enamel chest in the solarium."

I had more questions, but the appearance of Helori stilled them.

"You are needed," the demahnk said to Mzatal.

Mzatal reluctantly tore his gaze from me. Then, with a casual flick of his fingers, discharged a bolt that atomized Sprout. As the reyza bits discorporeated, Mzatal extended his hand to Helori, and then they were gone.

Chapter 18

With Mzatal's departure, a blanket of silence seemed to drop over everything. It hadn't, of course. There was still plenty of noise. Cries of pain, sirens, the crackle of fire, shouted orders. But it felt as if a vital part of me had left.

Sappy much? There was no time for that kind of handwringing. Besides, I couldn't be sad after getting to share that moment with him, after being here to help him withstand the influence of the two blades. I couldn't even imagine what Mzatal would be like with all three blades. Never thought I'd be glad that Vsuhl was safe and sound with Szerain.

Vsuhl is with Szerain. Duh. Maybe I could find Szerain and the others by first finding his blade? I'd been its bearer for a short time, which meant I stood a chance of touching it and following the connection to Szerain.

The rift vomited a gout of flame, and I was relieved to see Elofir sprinting back from the barricade. Between us, the corpse of the massive Jontari lay crumpled in the street. This was only the second dead demon I'd ever seen, since on Earth they usually discorporated—except when they were killed by an essence blade, as I'd done to the reyza Pyrenth at the Farouche Plantation. I hadn't known the knife would kill him dead, and it was the first time I'd ever killed a sentient creature. It was only a tiny consolation that Pyrenth had died on Earth before, so *any* death here would have probably been a true death. Still, I'd been the one to end him, and even though it had been in pure self-defense and as justified as a killing could get, I knew I would never forget that sick feeling, never lose that tiny pit of grief. Not that I should ever lose it or forget. The day

I could take a life without regret would be the day that I became a monster.

I shook my head to dispel the grim thoughts and considered the dead Jontari. Though I continued to have qualms about capturing a live demon, a dead one was fair game. With luck, an examination of the corpse might reveal a vulnerability that could perhaps even the odds.

I turned away and called DIRT HQ. I had no suggestions for their query of how to pack up the humongous corpse, except that they needed to bring something big enough to—

Heat washed across my back. I spun then had to throw up an arm to shield my eyes from the glare of arcane flames roiling over the Jontari.

"No . . . No!" I looked around in shock for some explanation. My gaze froze on Elofir a dozen paces away. "Elofir, stop!" I cried out in dismay. "Don't destroy it!"

"It is done, Kara Gillian," he said, quiet voice somehow cutting through the noise. "Leaving it intact would threaten all demonkind."

My dismay shifted to *pissed*. I yanked the phone to my ear. "Belay that pickup request," I snapped at the DIRT person, jammed my finger on the disconnect button then advanced on Elofir. "My fucking world is getting torn to bits because of these demons," I shouted. "We have to find ways to defend ourselves! And if that means the 'good' demons can't roam free on Earth because they might get hurt, that's better than humans being sitting ducks for the Jontari!"

"I seek to preserve both worlds."

"You think I don't?" I shot back, voice shaking. "I've been busting my ass—and getting it busted—to help save your world." Blood pounded in my ears. "We *need* an edge, any advantage. Anything!"

"Not like that." He exhaled softly and shook his head. "There is too much risk to the demons—"

"I'm the best fucking advocate the demons have! But in the meantime, Earth is getting fucked because you lords couldn't clean up your own goddamn mess!"

He stiffened. "We render aid now."

"Yeah, for this rift. Gold star for the lords. What about all the incursions during the past two months? What about the ones tomorrow and the next day? Are you going to fight every demon that comes through *before* they can kill more people?"

Grief flashed across his face, and guilt speared through me in response. But though I felt bad for trampling on his sensibilities, I wasn't sorry. "You want to be a pacifist? Then don't get in my way when I'm trying to save human lives. Standing by and cockblocking our efforts isn't preserving peace. That's condoning genocide."

He jerked as if I'd slapped him then went lord-still, expression smooth as marble. In the next instant Helori blinked in between us. Whether by chance or design, I didn't know, but it broke the tableau.

Helori looked from me to the burning Jontari then to Elofir. His face betrayed nothing.

"If there is time," Elofir said, voice unspeakably weary, "I will remain to seal the rift while you take her home."

Without a word, Helori extended his hand to me. At least he wasn't giving me the finger. I knew damn well he'd read the gory details of what had just happened, if not from me, then from Elofir. I took his hand, and a heartbeat later the sights and sounds and smells of Siberia disappeared to be replaced by those of my back yard. The pleasant fall air felt like a furnace after the frigid temps of Ust-Ilimsk.

I expected Helori to release me and go, but instead he shifted to take my other hand as well.

"Yaghir vahn," he murmured. *Forgive us all.* With that, he kissed me lightly on the forehead and vanished.

Rhyzkahl strode to the edge of his circuit, face twisted with frustration. "What is happening? Where did Helori take you?"

"Your buddies Jesral and Amkir aren't on Earth." I shed my coat, gloves, and rucksack, then stepped up onto the nexus and gave him a cool look. "Which means you know as much as you would if you were free of my tender loving care."

He scowled and turned away. Score one for Kara.

Within the super-shikvihr loop, I began my own shikvihr. I didn't bother putting up a shield of potency or telling Rhyzkahl to go to his house. I didn't care if he knew what I was doing, with this or anything else, as long as he didn't interfere. I finished my seventh ring and ignited the series.

"A pity Mzatal cannot spare the time to grant you the eighth," Rhyzkahl said, not sounding the least bit upset on my behalf.

"Yeah, it's almost as if he's been occupied cleaning up after you," I shot back then forced myself to pretend Rhyzkahl wasn't there. I had more important things to focus on. The shikvihr was a foundation and only the beginning. To have any chance of touching Szerain's blade, I'd need to do more than simply holler for it. I needed to have some *oomph* to my call.

I'd called Vsuhl once before. I still remembered the ritual that Mzatal and Idris and I used to gain the blade, and it was those sigils that I traced now to hang in the air. When I ignited the new pattern, a subtle energy shimmered through me like an echo of electric current, its potential harnessed and ready to be unleashed.

Visualizing the essence blade, I recalled every nuance of its form and feel. Though I held no illusions of wresting Vsuhl away from Szerain, there was no wiggle room in the ritual for wishy-washy thinking. The call had to be a pure laser beam of intention to summon the blade. All I needed was a touch, an opening to find the knife—and by extension, Szerain.

As my breathing deepened, I tapped into the ritual and thrust my hand into the air, willing Vsuhl to me. At the edge of my awareness, I heard Rhyzkahl shout something—disparaging or warning, I didn't know. Didn't care. I shut him out. Shut out the world and focused on the blade.

Familiar power, a furnace of potency, teased at the edges of my senses.

"Vsuhl!"

A whisper of a touch. An acknowledgment. It knew me, remembered me, and its power vibrated my bones like the buzz of a thousand angry bees. And there, beyond the blade, Szerain—turmoil beneath a calm exterior. Surprise, wariness. A hint of Zack and even Sonny. And, like a white hot sun, Ashava. I trembled with the effort of maintaining the tenuous connection, even as an exultant grin stretched across my face. *More*, I thought, drawing potency through the ritual to widen the channel. They were on Earth, in the Beaulac area, but—

I throw out my hands for balance as the summoning chamber shakes. The ritual has become a maelstrom, and I cannot stop it. Potencies flash red and purple as fire races through my veins. My lord, help me!

In Lord Szerain's hand, Vsuhl flashes with the energies of the vortex. A savage wind tears at my robes, snatches the scream from my lips and hurls it into to void. My lord steps behind me and wraps his arm around my waist, steadying me against the breaking of the world. He will save me.

The fire fills my eyes, and through the flames I see my love, my Giovanni, waiting for me.

"Call her!" Lord Szerain's words reverberate through my essence and beyond the world.

The walls crack. The sound drives through my existence.

Pain sears my chest.

Crack.

A dark-haired woman in white robes frowns down at me.

"Elinor!"

"Call her!"

A bald man in blue.

Blinding light.

Crack. C-c-crack.

"Do not stop calling!"

A blond man smiles. "Everything is going to be fine."

"Nobody knows who she is?"

"Elinor!"

The man in blue grips my wrist.

Tick. Tick. Tick.

"Kara!"

My entire body jerked as awareness slammed into me. Blinking, I struggled to orient myself as my breath burned my lungs, and my heart hammered. The stone of the summoning chamber cooled my cheek. No, the nexus. I was crumpled on my side on the slab. Shit.

I pressed up to sit, gritting my teeth against the low throb of a headache.

"Kara."

Rhyzkahl stood at the inner edge of his orbit, eyes narrowed at me. He'd called me out of the dream, I realized. Again. Even after what I'd done to him.

"Thanks," I said in nearly a growl and climbed to my feet. *Elinor, you're starting to be a real pain in my ass.*

The ritual sigils tumbled in place, dark and fractured, and I dispelled them with annoyed sweeps of my hands. Lousy timing for that fucking dream-vision. I'd been a hair's breadth away from truly connecting with Vsuhl and . . .

My annoyance abruptly shifted to outrage. No, it wasn't lousy timing. Elinor—meek, sweet little Elinor—had purposely interrupted my attempt to reach Vsuhl. Because of her own fear of it? I could totally relate to having an aversion to the knife that had been shoved into your chest. Really, I could. What I couldn't tolerate were hissy fits that fucked up important and possibly unrepeatable work.

Scowling, I stepped off the nexus then paused. I was missing something.

The tree whispered beside me, leaves rustling like a hundred voices. The leaf warmed between my breasts.

The dream. Setting my hand on the smooth white bark, I closed my eyes and murmured, "Clarity. I need clarity." My palm tingled, and a hypnotic vibration like a distant heartbeat pulsed through me. I immersed in the dream. Not the ritual and Elinor's death. What came after.

The dark-haired woman. White robes and pale walls. Bright light.

No. Disengage. Fly. Be the drone camera.

A beige-walled room. The dark-haired woman. Not white robes. A white coat. Beyond her, a wall clock ticks.

Fly back more.

The bald man is wearing blue scrubs and stands beside a bed. He shines a light into the patient's eyes. Takes her wrist to check the pulse.

He looks up as a blond man opens the door. "Nobody knows who she is?"

Tick. Tick. T-t-t-tock.

The blond man.

Zoom in on him. Zoom in on the blond man. Easy smile. Tanned face.

Zack. No, not Zack.

Xharbek.

I opened my eyes and gazed up at the purple and green canopy of the grove tree. "Thanks." I smiled as the leaves rustled an answering song. Mind clear, I headed inside.

The kitchen was empty, but a brief search turned up an odd party in the war room. Giovanni sat sketching at one end of the table, while Jill slowly flipped through a thick and ancient book and took pictures of the pages with her archive camera. Between them, Pellini and Bryce cleaned guns.

Pellini glanced up. "How was Siberia?"

"Siberious," I said. "But I was just on the nexus and discovered two things." I had everyone's attention now. "First off, Szerain, Zack, Ashava, and Sonny are definitely alive and on Earth. And, second, so is Elinor."

Chapter 19

"Elinor!" Giovanni shot to his feet at my little bombshell. "Is she—" He abruptly clamped his mouth shut and looked to the other end of the table.

As far as I knew, Jill had no arcane abilities or extra-human powers. She hadn't moved a muscle or said a word, but everyone in the room *knew* they needed to shut the fuck up and give her the floor.

Her eyes bored into mine. "Tell me," she said in a soft command that even Mzatal himself would hesitate to disobey.

"I don't know much," I said as I took an empty chair. "But I felt Ashava, clear and strong. She's alive and, as far as I can tell, safe."

Jill's tension melted away, and the spell was broken. "Is she scared?" she asked then let out a small laugh. "No, of course she isn't scared. She's tough, and she has her sire with her."

I held back a smile at her use of "sire." She'd been spending way too much time in ancient tomes. "I only had a sense of her for a second, but she didn't seem distressed."

Giovanni flicked his eyes toward Jill—checking whether it was safe to speak—before locking his intense gaze on me. "You are saying that Elinor is on Earth because Szerain is here, and she is entrapped in Vsuhl?"

"No, I'm saying she's here in an actual body." I held up my hand as exultant joy flooded Giovanni's face. "That's the good news," I said. "But there's bad news, too—namely that she's in the high security medical ward at the Federal Command Center. Xharbek's turf. I have no idea how she escaped Szerain's essence blade, but I suspect she came through at the same time you did. Xharbek must have sensed when she appeared on Earth and scooped her right up."

"Pawn or hostage?" Bryce asked.

"Could be either. Or both," I said. "Or Xharbek might want her for something else entirely." I took a deep breath. "On the plus side, I don't think he knows that I know he has her." A razor-slim advantage, but I'd take it.

Giovanni was ready to charge to her rescue on the power of his undying love—which, I had to admit, had served him pretty well so far. Yet as I detailed the levels of security that stood in his way, he sank back into his seat.

"I will not abandon her to leeches and blackguards!" he insisted.

"I couldn't agree more, and we *will* find a way to rescue her." I paused. "But I have to warn you, I don't know what condition she's in."

"She is alive. It is enough."

"Yes, but that doesn't mean she's . . ." Crap. I didn't want to crush the poor dude's spirits by telling him flat out that she might not be mentally whole. But the truth was, her essence had been trapped in an arcane knife for a few hundred years, not to mention having a chunk of it stuck onto mine. There was no telling what mental or emotional condition she'd be in.

"I understand," he said quietly. "She may not be the same Elinor I knew before. But she will ever be my Elinor, and I will do all I can to bring her home to me."

"As will we. Plus, as much as I want to reunite you two, I have a personal stake in this. I'm hoping that, once she's physically here, I can find a way to stop the waking dreams." I gave the group a brief recap of the last few dreams, including the most recent one where Elinor interrupted my attempt to reach Szerain through Vsuhl. "She's interfering when I encounter people or situations that trigger her."

Pellini glowered. "It's getting worse. And more dangerous."

Bryce tapped the table. "Do you have any thoughts on how to spring her from Fed Central?"

"Possibly," I said. "Dr. Patel is the head of the medical ward *and* a hardcore A.C. Gillian fan. She might give me access." But then I cursed under my breath. "No, that won't work. I guarantee Xharbek has manipulated the staff to keep me out and/or to alert him. And even if Dr. Patel *could* get me past the multiple levels of security, that doesn't help me steal Elinor out from under Xharbek's nose."

"We'll need to take a less subtle approach," Pellini said then flicked a glance at Bryce. "Would a frontal assault stand a chance?"

Bryce stood and moved behind his chair. "To get through the Feds' security without inflicting significant casualties—while going up against highly trained agents who would *not* be averse to inflicting casualties—we'd need a crack team of a dozen or more operatives, all of whom would have to be willing to risk federal prison or worse."

I raked a hand through my hair. "Yeah, I don't see us assembling a hotshot team to storm the place."

"Mzatal is badass," Jill said. "Could he pull it off?"

"If Xharbek wasn't Elinor's captor, I'd say yes," I said. "But he and the other demahnk control the lords with those spiking headaches that zap them for simply *thinking* about taboo subjects. I'm sure that asshole wouldn't hesitate to use pain to stop Mzatal."

Bryce pulled up recent DIRT updates. "Doesn't mean you can't consult him. I'll find his last location."

"Do that," I said. "I also might be able to pass a message via Mzatal to Helori and see if he'd be willing to simply teleport her out of there." I frowned. "Only problem is that I don't know if Helori would act so directly against another demahnk." My gut told me No, but it was still worth pursuing.

"What about summoning one of the reyzas you know?" Pellini suggested. "Aerial assault, arcane ability, and pretty damn strong."

I shook my head. "Too much risk of the reyza getting killed, and with only twenty percent of Earth-killed demons returning *alive* to the demon realm, dying could well be permanent." I exhaled. "Besides, I'm not sure even Gestamar would be able to get through all the security . . ." I trailed off, pulse thumping erratically. "Is there any footage online of the Siberia incursion?"

Pellini pulled his laptop to him. "There isn't much. Civilian video from a distance. Let me see if I can—" His eyes widened. "Sweet Jesus. That's not a demon. That's a goddamn T-rex!" He stared at me in shock. "Hang on, are you thinking of summoning *that?*"

"Not that particular one," I said. "Mzatal dispatched him with an essence blade, which means he's dead-dead. He didn't discorporeate, so he can't possibly return. But there's got to be more like him back home."

"Don't you need to know a demon's name for a summoning?" Pellini asked.

"Fair point." I thought furiously for several seconds. "Crap. The only Jontari demon name I know is Dekkak. But demons live a hella long time, which means he might still be around."

Jill stabbed a finger at me. "Stop right there, chick. I read that memoir, too. You do remember that bit about how insanely hard it is to summon a Jontari—*especially* Dekkak? Not to mention that little snafu with the gut eating and mass slaughter."

I winced. "Yes, I know, but it's worth exploring as a possible option."

Giovanni smacked his hands on the table. "You can do this binding," he announced with fierce confidence. "You are the sorceress Kara Gillian!"

Jill folded her arms over her chest and glared, first at Giovanni then at me. "Don't take this the wrong way, *Sorceress,* but do you even know how to do that kind of summoning?"

"No, I don't," I said. "A Jontari binding ritual is completely new to me. The only type of bindings I've done have been to enable the demon to stay on Earth, not to actually subdue it." I certainly wasn't stupid enough to think I could just wing it, especially with a demon that was sure to be at least the size of Big Turd. "It's true that with the nexus I'd have the necessary foundation and power to manage it, but successful summonings aren't just about having enough strength. They require skill, finesse, and a knowledge of the right protections and rituals. Brute force alone won't cut it." And if, by some miracle, I did succeed and survive, what then? I shivered as an image filled my mind of Big Turd rampaging through a hospital. How many people would end up hurt or killed during the rescue?

"It doesn't matter anyway," I said with a shake of my head. "Even if I was an expert at those bindings, summoning Dekkak— or any Jontari strong enough for our needs—would still be an absolute last resort. We simply can't justify the risk of casualties." I held up a finger to forestall Giovanni's protest. "We'll find a way," I told him. "From what I saw, Elinor is being cared for and is in no immediate danger. I can cope with her interruptions until we come up with a workable plan." I hoped. Until we retrieved her, I'd be rolling the dice that Elinor wouldn't disrupt anything critical.

"Well, I for one thank you for not leaping headlong into suicide," Jill said then gave a humorless laugh. "Maybe all the information about summoning Jontari was suppressed because too many summoners were being killed off."

I chuckled. "There had to have been *some* successful imperator summonings, or the memoir wouldn't have warned to build the perimeter with thirty bindings 'lest the beast break free.'" Yet even as I said it, my humor faded to a frown. "Thing is, nothing about suppressing that knowledge makes sense. We *know* that summonings were possible. Even of Dekkak. So why scrub that info along with all references to the Jontari?" I shook my head. "I can't help but think the *why* matters somehow."

"I'll keep delving for answers in the library," Jill said, gaze sharp and steady on mine. "But you're hoping I'll find info on how to summon one of those things, aren't you."

"No!" I snapped. "I mean . . . shit." I gripped my hair. "Believe me, I do *not* want to summon some humongous, brutal demon, because, fuck, I'm happier when I haven't been torn in half. Summoning Dekkak is a last resort, but even a last resort might come into play." I let my hands fall to my lap. "So, yes, I *am* hoping you'll dig up a copy of 'Jontari Summoning for Dummies', and I want you to start looking now so that if the worst case scenario happens, I won't get caught with my pants down and have to scramble for answers at the last second."

She flushed, abashed. "Sorry. I can't help but worry."

I sighed. "I'm sorry, too. And you're right to worry. I'm grasping at straws here." I was all too aware that the chances were slim to none of finding nice, clear, step-by-step instructions for how to summon a Jontari imperator, especially since the books had obviously been censored to quash that knowledge. At best we might find bits and pieces, faded with age or in barely legible cramped handwriting.

"Then you need all the help you can get," Jill said with a lift of her chin. "The memoir I gave you is the most extensive reference there is on the Jontari. I have a pile of fragments downstairs, though not everything's in English. I've held the admittedly weak hope that we might be able to find someone to translate the languages that are too archaic for you to obtain via the nexus flows."

"I read many languages." Giovanni announced with zeal. "French, Latin, Greek—"

"Aramaic?" Jill all but pounced on him. "Can you read Classical Aramaic?"

"A smattering," he said with a note of hesitation.

"Can you read it well enough to tell whether it's about the Jontari?"

His zeal faded to uncertainty. "It is not my best language."

"Wait a sec," she said. "Remember that Jontari sketch I found? I archived the bit of text beside it." She popped the SD card out of her camera and fiddled with the computer. The wall screen lit up with an image of a ripped and badly faded manuscript page, but after a few clicks, the barely visible smudges resolved into actual letters.

Giovanni's brow furrowed as he puzzled through the remnant of text. "Jontari, yes. Warnings of the physical and magical power of the great beasts. And how it is, ah,"—he cleared his throat—"idiotic for a sorcerer to attempt to bind a Jontari warlord without a . . ." He frowned. "Without a *gimkrah*? I do not know this word."

"Wait. A what?" I peered at the screen as if I could discern the meaning of the word through force of will. "What else does it say?"

"Only a few words. Without the influence of a full moon, the ritual is doomed to failure, and the sorcerer to death." Giovanni shook his head. "The remainder is missing. There is nothing more regarding the gimkrah."

"Huh." I steepled my hands in front of my face. "Huh," I said again. "Can we Google that word?"

"Sure, but we run the risk of tipping off anyone who might be monitoring our internet," Pellini said.

"It's a risk-benefit scenario." I drummed my fingers on the table then shrugged. "Eh, I'm the Arcane Commander. Why wouldn't I be looking for ways to deal with the invaders? But it can't hurt to muddy the waters. Do a search on a bunch of different weird made-up words and throw gimkrah into the bunch."

"On it."

"Giovanni, you're hired as a translator," Jill announced then turned to me with a fierce smile. "I have books in all sorts of dead languages that I haven't even touched yet, but the pictures make me think they have stuff about summoning."

"And if they're that old, there's a chance it'll pertain to the Jontari," I said.

Jill beckoned imperiously to Giovanni. "Let's get started. I've been through too much with this woman to see her get eaten by a demon now."

They headed for the basement, each on the same crusade albeit with different motivations.

"Two hits on gimkrah," Pellini said, eyes on his screen. "But nothing worth a shit. The first is some dude's dwarf character in an online role-playing game, and the other is part of the name of a company in Eastern Europe that makes plastic piping. However, I did learn that, according to the Urban Dictionary, a 'gimk' is a cross between a geek and a gimp."

My lips twitched. "I am indeed the richer for that bit of knowledge."

Bryce looked up from his laptop. "No reports of Mzatal since Siberia."

"Damn." I pulled a face. "I assumed Helori took him to another rift. Then again, Mzatal had some injuries, so maybe Helori made him take a break instead." I pinched the bridge of my nose. "Oh. Hang on. I'll try calling the number he called me from."

Six rings later, a generic DIRT voicemail told me to leave a message. "Mzatal, call me," I said. For good measure, I added, "If you're not Mzatal, please tell him to call A.C. Gillian ASAP." I disconnected and shoved the phone in my pocket. "Crap. I *need* expert input on both the Jontari and the Elinor situation."

Pellini gave me a long look. "You know what I'm about to say, don't you?"

"Yes, I do." I sighed. "And yes, I'll ask Rhyzkahl."

Pellini gave a firm nod. "Good. That saves me the trouble of kicking your ass."

Chapter 20

I stepped outside in time to see Rhyzkahl hurl something across the yard. My stomach lurched as a thousand possibilities crowded in. *He found a way to break free. He hoarded enough arcane power to make a weapon. He's testing . . .*

My thoughts stuttered to a halt as Sammy tore across the grass, seized up a ball, and raced back. He dropped his prize and looked up expectantly. Rhyzkahl glanced my way then scooped up the ball and chucked it away again.

Dumbass. He's playing with the damn dog.

Wearing my best I'm-not-at-all surprised expression, I crossed the yard and reached Rhyzkahl's orbit just as the dog returned once again with the slobbery tennis ball.

Rhyzkahl gave Sammy's head a good solid scratch, which of course only encouraged the silly dog to flop onto his back in hopes of getting a belly rub. I watched, bemused, as Rhyzkahl crouched to provide it.

"I have a question for you," I said before I could get too distracted with this heretofore unknown facet of Rhyzkahl.

"I have little doubt every moment of your existence is filled with questions for your betters."

Nice jab. But hard to get pissy at him when Sammy was wiggling in delight beneath his hand. Fine, I'd cut to the chase. "How do I summon a Jontari?"

He stood abruptly, leaving Sammy to look up at him with a bewildered expression. "You do not," Rhyzkahl said in a voice that invited zero argument. "You know nothing of the Jontari."

I folded my arms over my chest. "Tell that to the ones I've killed."

He stepped so close to the arcane wall of his prison that it crackled with azure sparks. "Where have you killed Jontari? When?"

Well, that got his attention nicely. The dampening effect of Mzatal's warding prevented him from sensing the state of the world—apart from the pervasive rakkuhr—and I'd made damn sure no one shared information with him. The less he knew about the his cohorts' progress, the better. But since I wanted to pump him for information, this was the time to drop a few key details. "*Where* is right here on Earth, and *when* is these past two months—sometimes on a daily basis. Your Jontari invasion strategy is in full swing."

He recoiled as if stung, lordly aplomb forgotten for the moment. "Kara, tell me what has happened."

I offered a nonchalant shrug. "Oh, nothing too special. Just that ever since Katashi blew a hole in the dimensions, demons have been coming through rifts all over the world."

A vein throbbed at his temple. "The Jontari are not my allies."

"Oh, whew!" I said, dragging a hand across my forehead in mock relief. Did he really expect me to believe that the demon incursions *weren't* part of the Mraztur's plan to take over Earth? "That is *such* a load off my mind. I'm so glad you set the record straight!" I allowed myself a moment of grim amusement at the petulant scowl that crossed his face. "Now that we've established that you're oh-so-very innocent, we can move on to the good stuff: How do I summon a Jontari imperator?"

Composure regained, he eyed me as if I'd asked him how to drain the sea. "An imperator? Impossible."

"No, it's not," I replied. "It's been done before, and I may opt to go for it in the near future." Time to play my trump card. "Elinor is on Earth, locked away by Xharbek in a secure facility." I didn't miss his twitch of reaction. "An imperator is one possible means of recovering her."

"Elinor is on Earth," he echoed. "Alive and whole, else you would have no need to retrieve her." His words were measured and even, a little too controlled. He'd been fond of her—as much as he was capable. Nearly a year ago, I'd learned through one of Elinor's dreams that Rhyzkahl had popped her cherry, and it was only yesterday that I experienced a dream-glimpse of his melancholy when he lost her.

"I don't know what condition she's in," I said.

The leap of a muscle in his jaw was the only sign that my words affected him. "You are correct in your assumption that a qaztahl-bound reyza would be unable to accomplish the task. Their talents lie elsewhere."

"Yeah, I've realized that Gestamar and Kehlirik are essentially giant winged nerds."

A whisper of amusement flitted across his face before vanishing beneath a mask of scorn. "You have never performed a dangerous summoning," he stated, "nor been in true jeopardy from any demon summoned. Even had one made an earnest effort to break your bindings—which they never have—you would have survived the experience." He lowered his head, eyes hard on mine. "I am the only one who chose to break your pathetic bindings, and I did so with ease—for my amusement. A Jontari would do the same. But instead of granting you the carnal pleasure you craved, he would slaughter you and all those in this compound"—he sneered—"whom you hold so dear."

"I know it's possible to summon one and survive," I said. "I've learned a few things since that night in my basement."

"I am certain Mzatal has trained you well to service a cock."

No way was I going to rise to his bait. "I know far more about the arcane and summoning now," I said, holding onto calm. "Let's try this again. How do I summon an imperator?"

"Your chekkunden lover refused to offer aid?"

"This has nothing to do with Mzatal. I'm asking *you*. I'm open to any advice you're willing to give." But even as the words left my mouth, I shook my head. "Who am I kidding? You won't help me. This is the part where you demand release, and then I tell you I can't. All right, go ahead. Let's get that over with."

"I will not demand release," he growled. "Nor will I aid you in this mad undertaking. You have not the means to control an imperator."

I regarded him for a thoughtful moment. "What if I had a gimkrah?"

He visibly startled. "How do you know of such?"

My pulse quickened. Score! "I read a lot. Well? How does a gimkrah help, and where can I get one?"

It was at least a dozen heartbeats before he finally spoke. "They were artifacts created to subdue Jontari. But the two held by Earth summoners are long lost." He waved a hand. "Kara Gillian, this is folly. You must seek another way to retrieve Elinor."

"I'm open to suggestions," I snapped. "Let me know if you decide you really *do* want to help her." I turned away to stalk back to the house, but he spoke before I took two steps.

"Mzatal possessed the master gimkrah."

I spun on my heel. "Does he still have it?"

Rhyzkahl's mouth twisted. "He is unlikely to have rid himself of it. Such an artifact will be well hidden and protected." He met my eyes. "Even with a gimkrah, you have not the strength, skill, or experience to craft bindings strong enough to contain an imperator."

Annoyance prickled. "Gee, maybe because there's a conspiracy to hide information about the Jontari from us puny humans?"

"Be that as it may, you are not equipped," he said, tone imperious. "You *will* die in the attempt. Seek a different means."

Though I knew all too well that Rhyzkahl was an excellent liar, I felt certain he was telling it to me straight—not for my sake, but for Elinor's.

Fine. I didn't have the know-how to create the right bindings. But I did have the sudden spark of a potentially clever idea.

"What if we cheat?" I spread my hands. "We use graphene-enhanced nets on the demons that come through the rifts. So far, they can't break them. Add an electric charge from a power supply, and we can incapacitate the demons as well."

Rhyzkahl stared at me with a *You can do that?* expression. "Physical restraint has never been successfully employed in summonings."

"That's because the physical means were crap back in the good ol' days. We have science on our side now." I hid my amusement as Rhyzkahl adjusted to this new paradigm.

"*If* you are able to locate the master gimkrah," he said reluctantly, "and *if* this netting works as you claim, there is a remote possibility you might survive the summoning of a Jontari imperator."

"I'm not afraid of the odds," I lied. "What does the gimkrah look like?"

"An orb of crystal"—he held his hands apart as if gripping a cantaloupe—"with a heart of blood, bound with *makkas*."

Makkas. The pinkish demon realm metal that dampened the arcane. Made sense that it would be used in a tool meant to control an arcane being. "Thank you." I paused. "I'll get her back, one way or another."

Uncertainty flickered in his eyes. "Kara, there are yet perils to summoning a Jontari."

"There are perils to everything," I said. "But I have to start somewhere."

I left Rhyzkahl's charming company and headed toward the war room, but Bryce intercepted me in the kitchen.

"A letter came for you," he said, face in neutral mode.

"Seriously? Who sends snail mail these days?" The U.S. Postal Service managed to forge through snow and rain and heat and gloom of night, but "demon pestilence" cramped their style a bit. Especially in the Beaulac area. "And what warrants hand delivery by the head of security?"

Without comment, he held the envelope out to me. As I took it, the handwriting on the front answered my question. *Tessa.*

My chest constricted with fury. "Why the fuck is she—" I clamped down on the internal volcano of anger, frustration, confusion, and loss. No good careening down an ugly, dead road while important shit needed to be dealt with. That was probably the whole reason she'd sent it—to rattle me and screw with my head. *If I ever find that woman—*

Bryce placed a hand on my shoulder and squeezed.

"Thanks. For this." I held up the envelope and smiled brightly, well aware that I wasn't fooling him one bit. Before I could derail again, I shoved the envelope deep into my pocket where I wouldn't have to think about it for a few minutes. "As of yesterday, there was a SkeeterCheater with power supply snowed in at the Memphis supply facility," I said in a sharp change of subject. "I'd like it in our arsenal as a just-in-case, but I don't want to go through any official channels." Not only would official channels mean lots of questions that I had no desire to answer, but I knew for a fact that, with the shortage, their reply would be *Fuck no, are you fucking nuts?*

Bryce gave me a mock-puzzled look. "And you're telling me this because I'm such a good listener?"

"Sure," I said then quirked a smile. "That and your experience with organized crime."

He exhaled a tragic sigh. "I really need to edit my résumé." His brow creased as he considered the problem.

"I know this isn't your typical under-the-table deal," I said, grimacing. "We're talking theft of critical military equipment, which means there are a shitload of risks associated with it."

"You're right about that." He rubbed the back of his neck. "It'll be pricey, I'm warning you now, but I'll see what I can find out."

"Awesome. Once we know more, we can decide if it's worth it or not."

That done, we headed to the war room, where Pellini had moved on from cleaning guns to working on DIRT reports.

"I know our AWOL four are in the Beaulac area," I said, "and for a host of reasons, it's past time that we drag their asses home and spoil Xharbek's plans."

Pellini looked up from the computer. "Have you narrowed their location down to something more precise than 'all of Beaulac'?"

"No, but earlier today Idris suggested checking places where there's been arcane activity."

He *hmmfed* through his mustache. "Not sure how much that narrows it down. Around here, that's like searching a swamp for places that are wet." He did some computer magic and pulled up a satellite map of Beaulac on the wall screen. "You've got the usual suspects—the Spires, the police department. Maybe other places with valves?"

Bryce peered at the map. "Kara, what about the warehouse where you and I first met?"

"That definitely counts as having arcane activity, especially with the valve node in it." I moved around the table and tapped the spot on the screen. "Plus, Ryan and Zack have both been there." A little red X appeared over the warehouse, and I shot Pellini a grateful look. "I can't see them hiding out anywhere near the Spires since there's so much military activity there, and the area around the PD is a mess and under crazy tight guard. I suppose it's possible that they're camping out by another valve, but right now the warehouse is high on the list . . ." My stomach did a little flip, and I pointed to an area on the outskirts of town. "As is the community outreach center."

"Where you died," Jill said from the doorway. Her face was calm, but worry and hope shadowed her eyes.

I gave her a slow nod. Technically, I'd died in the demon realm, but I'd received my mortal injury at the outreach center. "I don't intend to repeat the experience," I said. "As for the other valves, the nature center is the most likely campout spot."

"Where Angus McDunn stripped your abilities," Jill added helpfully.

"I've left pieces of me all over town." I smiled wryly. "And yes, you're absolutely on the away team for this venture."

She pursed her lips. "As if you could keep me off it."

"The force of your personality *might* have factored into the decision," I said. "Okay, we have three strong location contenders, and Szerain and Zack are familiar with each of them."

"I'll stay here and keep an eye on Giovanni," Bryce said. "Plus, I need to make some calls."

I nodded. "Pellini? You in?"

"Only if I get to drive the Humvee."

"Works for me. That way I can nap." I shifted and felt the letter crinkle in my pocket. "Let's get geared up and plan to leave in fifteen." Without waiting for an answer, I went to my bedroom, locked the door, then pulled out the letter.

The envelope was battered and filthy, and bore a Royal Mail stamp with a Cardiff postmark from almost five weeks ago. No return information, but my name and address were in Tessa's neat and distinctive handwriting. Bryce must have recognized it from when we cleared out her library. I had no idea what her evil-aunt masterplan was, now that fake-Katashi was out of the picture. She could be with his other summoners or even with the remnants of Farouche's organization. Angus McDunn had been Farouche's second in command and was currently in the wind. She'd avoided Idris when he spotted her at the rift in India. All I knew for sure was that, in over two months, this was her first attempt to contact me.

I glared at the envelope for a moment while anxiety and ire played leapfrog in my chest. Finally, I flipped it over, pulled my combat knife from my boot, and slowly ran the tip of the blade under the flap, checking every millimeter for signs of arcane nasties. After finding none, I slid the letter out and unfolded it. It was handwritten on simple white printer paper, smudged with sooty fingerprints and a brownish streak that looked like blood.

"Nice play for sympathy, Tessa," I muttered. "Will you also have the ink trailing off the page at the end as if you were being attacked?"

I read, all the while imagining her lying mouth speaking the words.

Kara,

A letter is the only way I have to reach you without interference, and even then, it's only a slim chance. I wasn't a good surrogate for your mother, I know, but I did the best I could given the circumstances at the time.

I shook the paper. "You have the gall to bring up my mom in the same sentence as your own two-faced mothering? And what 'circumstances'? The ones that had you grooming me for sacrifice so you could stay in good graces with Katashi and the Mraztur? What kind of person *does* that? You never gave a shit about me!"

I'm sorry. I did what I thought was right. In hindsight, maybe there was a better way, but you have to believe me, I couldn't see it then.

"I've already wasted enough of my life believing you," I growled. "And gee, I can't see beyond Fuck You."

Everything has changed.

"Yeah. Because Katashi blew a hole in our world. Can't be his lapdog now that he's dead, huh. Sucks for you."

There is so much I want to tell you, but I can't like this.

"Of course not."

I don't expect you to forgive me, but maybe we can come to an understanding.

"You got the first part right."

I'll be at Lee Circle in New Orleans at 11pm on September 30. Please be there, sweetling. I need you. Tessa.

"Seriously? You are *so* full of shit. Even if your dumb letter hadn't arrived a week after the meeting, you think I'd've fallen for whatever game you're playing?" Scowling, I stuffed the letter and envelope into my dresser drawer. "Fool me once, shame on you. Fool me twice, shame on me. And all that." I slammed the drawer shut. "And I'm not your damn sweetling!"

"You okay in there?" Jill asked through the door.

Stupid tears stung my eyes, and I swiped them away. "Yep!" I chirped. "Just getting my gear together."

"Uh huh. We're ready when you are."

"Two minutes." I quickly changed out of my DIRT uniform and into plain black fatigues. I got both tactical holsters strapped on but froze with one bootlace half tied. Katashi was dead, but his little empire wasn't. If all the lords had, indeed, been truly shocked to learn that an as-yet-unknown syraza had taken over Katashi's identity, that meant someone besides a lord had trained the demon. That someone *had* to be a demahnk, and I had more than a sneaking suspicion that the culprit was none other than the Emperor of All Assholes, Xharbek.

Frowning, I finished tying my bootlace. Xharbek had masqueraded as Carl, Tessa's boyfriend. Though she wasn't

Katashi's lapdog anymore, she might very well be the new Empress.

I holstered my weapons then stepped out of my room with a bright smile for Jill.

She gave me a cool, knowing look in return. "You want to talk about it?"

Damn it. "Bryce told you."

"Uh huh, but I'd have known anyway," she said. "You only get that look on your face when it has to do with *her*." With that, she gently but firmly pushed me back into the bedroom, closed the door then held out her hand, palm up. With a sigh, I retrieved the letter and handed it over.

She read it, lips pursed. "Well, I can see why you're upset."

"Duh! Tessa stabbed me in the back, and now she wants to *justify* it to me."

Jill skimmed the letter once more before she passed it back. "She hamstrung you."

"Huh?"

"Hamstrung. Crippled." She angled her head. "Tessa told you she'd advocated for having your abilities stripped. She didn't want to kill you."

It took me several seconds to find my voice. "Are you *defending* her?" I finally sputtered.

"No," Jill said sharply. "I'm defining the parameters of the situation."

"Fine." I gritted out. "She hamstrung me, and she *claims* it was to keep them from killing me. But I think it's because she—they—wanted me alive for some future plan. Either way, it was a fucking betrayal!"

Her expression gentled. "And it broke your heart." She moved to the bed and sat. "Tessa hurt you far more than Rhyzkahl did."

My throat tightened. Jill was right. I'd endured unspeakable agony at Rhyzkahl's hands, but it couldn't hold a candle to the pain Tessa had caused.

Jill patted the comforter beside her, and I obediently sat.

"You were just a kid when your mom died," she said quietly, slipping an arm around me.

"Eight." My voice cracked as I leaned into her. "I was eight. And I was eleven when my dad was killed."

"And then Tessa raised you."

"If you can call it that," I said bitterly.

Jill exhaled a slow breath. "Your parents got you through the walking and talking stage and taught you all about manners and morals, but it was Tessa who was with you through the really tough times—growing up and puberty and being a teen and becoming an adult. She had no small part in you turning into the smart, kind, kickass chick you are now."

I glared at her. "You think I should just welcome her back with open arms?"

"Don't be silly," she replied, tone mild but with steel at its core. "I'm simply pointing out how important she is to you."

"Again, duh!" I waved the letter. "Why do you think this has me so twisted up?"

"You're twisted up because you don't know *why* she did what she did." Jill gave me a squeeze, or maybe she was simply tightening her hold to keep me from bolting. "Tessa acted against you for a reason. Her reason may *suck*, but I don't think you'll be able to move past this until you know the truth."

I scowled. "Except I can't trust her to tell me the truth."

"Maybe listening to her explanation wouldn't change anything," Jill said with a shrug, "or maybe it would."

"Or maybe Tessa doesn't want to explain shit, and this gag-me fake contrition was just another ploy to lure me into a trap so she and her cronies could *hamstring* me even more, especially since my abilities are coming back."

"Sure. But if and when the opportunity arises again, you'll be braced for it, and her actions will tell you all you need to know, don't you think?"

"I'll know there isn't any hope for us!" I snapped. My breath caught an instant later. "Oh. That's it, isn't it?" I looked over to see Jill wearing a faint smile. "I'm still clinging to the hope that this is all some big misunderstanding. I haven't given up yet because I don't understand why she betrayed me. I just don't fucking get it, so I keep walking on the same broken glass over and over, looking for a pattern that probably isn't even there." I shook my head. "It doesn't help that I'm not sure I can trust my own judgment anymore. I mean, I never saw it coming."

Jill made an exasperated noise. "How could you? Good grief, Tessa has been the most important person in your life for *twenty years*. Not to mention, you're so fiercely loyal you could teach seeing eye dogs a thing or two about unswerving support and trust. That's *not* a bad thing."

I glowered. "Don't know if I agree with you. Being loyal

seems to have a habit of biting me in the ass. First Rhyzkahl, now Tessa."

"Oh, *please*. Being loyal is why you have so many people ready to ride into battle with you." She squeezed me again. "Look, Tessa may never tell you why she betrayed you. But you're Kara Fucking Gillian. You're tenacious and stubborn, and you won't be satisfied until you dig up the truth. It's what made you such a good cop."

I sniffled and hugged her back. "If I'm so awesome and loyal, I think I deserve chocolate donuts."

She laughed. "Yes you do, and since there are none to be bought, I'll hunt down a recipe. But, in the meantime, at least you have kittens."

"Demonic battle kittens."

"Those are the best kind."

Chapter 21

It had been nearly a year since the summoner Tracy Gordon attempted to create a permanent gate to the demon realm, using me as the sacrificial focus. That was also when Mzatal and Idris finally succeeded in summoning me—a turn of events that ended up being both life-changing and eye-opening, to put it mildly.

The warehouse where Tracy tried to end my awesome life was in a crummy industrial park that had been deserted long before the demonic incursions began. Oddly enough, now that the rest of Beaulac resembled a ghost town, the industrial park didn't seem anywhere near as creepy as it once did. But creepy or not, one of its warehouses harbored an arcane valve node.

The façade of the warehouse in question was the same dull grey as I remembered, but the double glass doors were smashed. Since we'd seen similar damage on every other building in the park, we felt safe enough chalking it up to the work of vandals or looters.

Within, we found rakkuhr seeping from the node, but no sign of vandals, Szerain, or anyone else. After a thorough search, we left for the outreach center, which was several miles from downtown Beaulac and well away from Lake Pearl or any of the tourist spots. Or rather, former tourist spots. The lake was now home to a sucking whirlpool at one end and a thirty-foot geyser at the other, and toy boats sent through the former came out the latter crushed and iridescent. Moreover, an active fifty-meter rift sliced through the ball fields, the sand at the public beach was a sickly green, and trees in the surrounding woods had an annoying tendency to burst into flame for no discernible reason.

Hunting season was open, but the only game anyone cared about now was demons. No license required and no bag limit.

I'd first visited the outreach center during my search for the Symbol Man serial killer. Not long after, said serial killer lured me there as an intended sacrifice for a ritual to summon and bind Rhyzkahl, and I'd ended up eviscerated by the reyza Sehkeril. Fun times.

The neighborhood had been crappy back then and was currently well into majorly shitty. Abandoned cars huddled along the curb, stripped of tires and engine parts. At the end of the block, the burned husk of a pickup lay on its side. Every building bore a variety of spray-painted opinions and pictorial suggestions. The doors of the center were boarded up and chained shut, but similar security efforts on the other buildings hadn't made a difference. Splintered plywood lay scattered under the broken windows and smashed door of the café across the street. In front of the dry cleaners further down, clothing lay strewn amidst broken glass on the sidewalk.

As I swept my gaze over the street, my cop-sense gave a little tingle. "Every building has been broken into but this one."

"The vandals might've busted in from the back," Pellini said, but he didn't sound convinced. "Or maybe word spread that the chief of police got his head ripped off in here."

"Dude, the *morgue* got looted. I'm not so sure these assholes would be scared of a crime scene over a year old." There were no aversions or other protections on the doors that I could see, but when I rested my hand on the plywood, I felt a faint and familiar touch, an odd arcane whisper like a lingering scent. Though it dissipated even as I tried to focus on it, it was enough. *Szerain.*

"Bingo," I breathed.

"Well?" Jill demanded.

"I sensed Szerain," I said. "Just a whiff, but it was him." I glanced at her. "I don't know what to expect in there, so we need to stay on our toes. For all I know, Xharbek has demons prowling around while our people are holed up in an office."

Jill drew her gun and flashlight, expression fierce. "I'm ready."

With bolt cutters and a crowbar, we made short work of the chains and boards. Pellini and I pulled the doors open and, by unspoken agreement, let Jill go in first. She entered, gun at the ready and flashlight sweeping the interior, while I followed an instant behind. Shotgun in hand, Pellini came in last, pausing only long enough to put a small aversion by the door to keep anyone from wandering in after us.

We passed through the foyer and a common room, our breath pluming in unnaturally frigid air—a possible indicator of arcane activity. Or yet another weird weather quirk of the rift-riddled area.

In the main meeting hall, light streamed through chinks in boarded up windows, revealing card tables, folding chairs, and a pair of worn sofas shoved to the walls. In the center of the cement floor, faded chalked sigils and cold puddles of melted wax from long-dead candles marked the outline of a large ritual diagram about the size of my nexus.

Jill moved around the perimeter of the room, panning her flashlight over every nook and cranny and crouching to peer beneath furniture. I did the same, though I doubted our people were hiding under the pool table. Still, there was a lot of building left to cover, and my instinct continued to swear this was the right place.

"Jesus," Pellini muttered. "I remember coming in here after all that shit went down. Blood *everywhere*, and the Chief of Police lying right there with his head ripped off. I couldn't believe he was the Symbol Man."

"The decapitation was Rhyzkahl's doing," I said. "Twisted Peter Cerise's head right off with his bare hands." All that remained of the blood was a few stains in the concrete. "Can't say I disagreed with the move, considering the number of people Cerise killed."

Working quickly but thoroughly, we finished searching the downstairs then made our way to the second floor. The first two offices were unremarkable—bare wooden doors, serviceable desks and chairs, unexciting paperwork. But pasted haphazardly on the third door were pencil sketches of people and demons.

"Are these Szerain's?" Jill asked, an edge of excitement in her voice. "Isn't he an artist?"

"No. I mean, yes, he's an artist." I blew out a breath. "But these were drawn by Greg Cerise, the Symbol Man's son." I'd last seen him alive here in this office a few days before he became yet another victim of his serial killer father. I pushed the door open to reveal a tiny office with barely enough room for two chairs and a desk. A portable drawing table rested on the latter, bearing an unfinished sketch of a mermaid fleeing a sea creature. More sketches and drawings were taped to nicotine-stained walls.

"Damn," Pellini murmured as he took in the various pieces of art. "He was good."

"That he was." I started to pull the door closed then stopped at the sight of a drawing on the floor under the desk. With one finger, I slid the paper out, heart hammering like a college drumline.

"Huh," Jill said, peering over my shoulder. "It's you. You made an impression on Greg."

"No," I managed to say. Back at the house, I had one of Greg's sketches: me, dressed in metal and leather bikini-armor, and holding sword and dagger as I faced down a reyza. The drawing I held now showed me in full space-cowboy attire—flowing brown coat, dark red shirt with leather suspenders, and a pistol in my hand. Leaves swirled at my feet, and two moons hung in the sky behind me, shining down on a spaceship that looked just a bit like a chicken. The whole thing was nothing more than colored pencil and paper, but it was so real I could practically see the movement of the leaves and the coat. Greg's chain-mail-Kara drawing was awesome and showed the depth of his skill, but it couldn't hold a candle to this.

Szerain did this. He drew me, I thought, stunned. And not only that, it was a nerdy-geeky picture, the sort of thing Ryan was into. But he wasn't Ryan anymore. What did it all mean?

I looked up at Jill. "This isn't Greg's. It's Szerain's."

"Are you sure?!" She reached to snatch the paper from me but stopped before tearing it from my hand.

"I'm sure," I said. "We're in the right place."

Exultant hope lit her eyes. "Then let's keep moving. Time to bring all the chicks back to the nest."

But with every subsequent office we cleared, my uncertainty grew, as did Jill's tension. And after the last room failed to turn up anything but a nest of mice, I made my way downstairs in a cloud of bafflement. Jill jammed her gun into its holster and stalked behind me.

"Now what do we do?" she asked in a tight and brittle voice then nearly ran into me when I stopped in the center of the common room.

"I don't understand," I said, frustrated and perplexed. "I know he's here. This *feels* right." Didn't it? Maybe I wanted them to be here so badly I'd imagined it?

No, I was missing something. The echo of Szerain I'd felt on the door nagged me with a familiarity I couldn't place. Perhaps there was a clue there? I closed my eyes, remembered the feel, and sought the connection. The memory of my attempt to touch Szerain's essence blade from the nexus came to mind, and I sank into it. I'd called to Vsuhl—most likely in the dimensional pocket where it was stored when not in use. Right before Elinor interrupted, I'd felt it, and—

Crap. That was it. The whiff of Szerain had the same quality as Vsuhl in storage.

"I wasn't wrong." I pinched the bridge of my nose. "They're here but not *here.*"

Jill rounded on me. "What the hell does that even mean?" She flung an arm out. "There's no one here but rats and roaches!"

Before she could retreat or resist, I closed the distance and threw my arms around her. In my periphery, I saw Pellini step discreetly away to give us space. "They're hiding in a dimensional pocket," I said and felt a tremble go through her. "It's where the essence blades go when they're sent away. They slide into a little pocket of universe that folds around them, and that's exactly what Zack and Szerain did to make a secure hiding place. They're safe. I promise." Only problem was that I had no idea how to reach a *person* in wherever-it-was. Damn it, I hated this, hated with every fiber of my being that I couldn't do more, couldn't reunite her with her daughter *now.*

Jill's shoulders slumped. "I don't even know what color her hair is," she said softly, but in the next breath she gave a strained laugh. "With Zack's shapeshifting genes, I guess it's any color she wants it to be."

"Darn it, and I was going to give her hair chalk for Christmas." My attempt at a joke trailed off to a sigh. "I'm so sorry, Jill. I swear I'll figure out how to get them out of their little bubble."

She echoed my sigh. "Red. She has red hair like her mom."

I laughed and gave her a squeeze. "I'm sure I saw red peach fuzz on her little noggin."

A wan smile touched her mouth then slipped away. "I feel like I'm in a holding pattern. I can't grieve because she's not dead. Even though I've lost her for now, I haven't lost her forever." Her hand trembled as the unspoken *I hope* hung in the air.

"You *can* grieve," I said. "You haven't lost her forever, but you did lose this time with your baby, and you lost any feeling of security, and you lost the chance to be there for her now. You can grieve and cry and throw things because holy fuck, woman, you've certainly earned it."

She hiccupped a tiny laugh and brushed tears off her cheeks. "I guess I have. And I do believe I'll get her back. My beautiful, brilliant, special baby girl." She looked up at me, eyes shimmering with sadness and uncertainty. "What if she's so . . . so like a demonic lord that she doesn't want or need her mother?"

"Ashava will *always* want and need her mother," I said with such intensity that Jill twitched in surprise. "She's half human, and that half is irrepressible. That's an absolute fact. Look at the demonic lords. It's been three thousand years, but they *still* grope for that aspect, even though they don't know why." The manipulation and mind control of the lords hadn't stamped out their yearning.

I looped my arm through hers. "Let's get out of here. I have a few ideas crawling around in my head, and I'm pretty sure they need to be lured out with cookies."

"Sardine cookies," she said, managing a faint smile.

I shuddered. "If you kill me, the ideas die, too."

Chapter 22

Back at the house, Jill returned to the basement to continue her Jontari research while Pellini and I headed for the nexus.

"That whiff I caught at the outreach center of Szerain and the dimensional pocket is still fresh in my senses," I told him. "I want to take full advantage of it to track down the AWOL four."

"Pursue every lead," he said with a sage nod. "It's the only way to determine which one is right."

"Unless all of them are wrong, of course."

Rhyzkahl's gaze followed us as we stepped onto the nexus. I gave him a bland look then swept my arm in a broad arc to raise a shimmering privacy veil around the slab. The last thing I needed right now was a nosy neighbor.

Pellini moved beyond the super-shikvihr to his usual position. "Need me to do anything special?"

"Stay close and keep your eyes peeled for weird stuff." I stepped through the ring of undulating colors to the center of the nexus.

He let out a bark of laughter. "In other words, you're making it up as you go."

"I'm deeply offended at the insinuation that I don't always know precisely what I'm doing." I grinned as he rolled his eyes. "For your information, I have an actual plan. Now that I know Szerain and company are in the dimensional vicinity of the outreach center, I can use the nexus to do a more meticulous search."

"Gotcha. Like how, once you know your evidence is in a specific room, it's feasible to get down on the floor with a magnifying glass."

"You nailed it." Time to make the magnifying glass—or rather, a Szerain-finding Dimensional Pocket Detector.

After a brief moment to acclimate to the upward swirling power vortex, I dropped to one knee and pressed my palms against the familiar stone. Beneath them, the silvery inlay of my personal sigils brightened as if welcoming me, and an instant later, raw power engulfed my hands like hot wax.

I commanded more to me, drawing it from the combined reservoir of the nexus, super-shikvihr, and Rhyzkahl. It answered in an electric blue surge of heat and pressure that shoved my hands upward. Tense and focused, I shaped the potency, tamed it until I held a scintillating globe the size of a basketball between my hands. So far, so good. I stood and transferred it fully to my left hand. Now to—

Crimson flashed beyond the edge of the nexus as a whip-thin tentacle of rakkuhr snapped toward the globe. I threw up my free hand to ward it off, but the vile strand wrapped my wrist like a tether ball around a pole. A racking shudder raced up to my shoulder, and I yelped, flapping my hand in the universal gesture of *get it off me get it off me get it off me!* To my surprise and relief, it uncoiled and withdrew, leaving me gasping in reaction.

"You okay?" Pellini said.

"Yeah." I gulped. "Got a little distracted, but I'm good." The potency globe began to hiss and shudder, and I hurried to cradle it between both hands and stabilize it. But my gut clenched as I saw strands of rakkuhr merging and snaking on the grass beyond Rhyzkahl's orbit. The globe. The rakkuhr was attracted to it. Cold sweat broke out beneath my arms as old terror whispered of hideous pain.

No! I pushed down the irrational fear. There was no sentience or malevolent purpose at work here. The rakkuhr moved mindlessly—one form of energy attracted to another. It was *Rhyzkahl's* will and purpose that had delivered agony to me through his rakkuhr-enhanced essence blade. Screw him. I wasn't going to let the Ghost of Torture Past ruin my work.

"Pellini, can you put a simple shielding veil around the nexus?"

"Sure thing," he said and did so. "It won't last long against the rakkuhr, though. It'll weaken every time the stuff brushes it."

"It'll last long enough." The potency tingled against my palms. I recalled the feel of Szerain and the dimensional pocket, amplified and focused it into the globe. My nexus-boosted senses kicked in to give me a lord's eye view of the potency flows in the vicinity of the outreach center, and with the resonance of the globe acting as magnifying glass and Szerain-detector, I began a meticulous search of the arcane landscape.

After a few minutes, the globe began to vibrate and buzz like a balloon full of angry wasps. Where the common room would be, potency bubbled up like dry ice in water, creating clouds of luminous fog that hugged the ground and coalesced to feed surrounding flows.

I stared, dumbfounded. Why in blazes hadn't Pellini or I seen or sensed *that* when we were there? A second later I gave myself a mental forehead smack. Duh. Same reason I couldn't see ultraviolet or radiation or x-rays. That potency fountain was in a different "spectrum," one that my lordy supertastic nexus vision allowed me to see.

Around the potency fountain, rakkuhr oozed and pooled like coruscating ruby syrup. *Beautiful in its own way,* I thought then gave a mental shudder. Lava could be beautiful, but that didn't mean I should go swimming in it.

But no resonance match to Szerain or his dimensional pocket. I scrutinized the area to no avail. Three times I conducted a painstaking scan. Nothing. Frustrated, I centered the globe on the focal point of the bubbling potency and stared at the mesmerizing fluctuations. I'd been so sure I could locate him, that this would be the plan that worked. I was getting sick and tired of starting over at square one.

As I stewed in my annoyance, a pattern emerged. Each bubble carried a spark of resonance like a red-ringed speck of crystalline glitter on the surface of distortion.

"I found them!" I shouted in elation. "They're using the turbulence of a potency spring along with a touch of rakkuhr to mask their location."

"Great!" Pellini said. "Now what?"

I thought quickly. "I'm betting Szerain and Zack shift things up regularly, like changing the combination on a lock. That's what I'd do in their place. But it means the feeling I picked up earlier will likely be obsolete soon." A decision solidified. "I'm going to try to reach them. Maybe even bring them home."

"Excellent," he said. "Tell me what to do."

As if I was unwinding a ball of yarn, I extruded a strand of potency from the globe and passed the end to him. "Hang on tight to this. It may take both of us to pull them through." I continued to unwind the potency until the globe was no larger than an orange. "Oh, and save my ass if I get in trouble."

He snorted. "That's item one in my job description."

"Har har." I reassessed the bubbling potency spring then hurled the ball and its trailing potency strand toward it, as if casting a fishing line into the perfect spot beneath an overhang. Once it settled, I'd send a signal down the line.

With zero warning or the slightest nibble, the line jerked with enough force to send me sprawling. "Hold onto it!" I yelled to Pellini then scrambled up to one knee, wrapped the strand in both fists, and braced against the pull. Szerain's signature resonated through the connection, though with no hint of the others. Breath hissing through my teeth, I tapped the nexus resources and drew the strand toward me, hand over hand. It thinned to little more than a glowing thread yet held strong. Szerain's presence intensified. I almost had—

The balance tipped. I let out a shocked *urk!* as Szerain's aura enveloped me, dragging me forward.

"Kara!" Pellini yelled.

This was *so* not part of the plan. I fought to hold on, invoked the nexus, and anchored strands, all to no avail. This had the feel of an attack. What the hell was Szerain doing? Did he not want to be rescued? Had I been wrong about him this whole time?

Szerain yanked me through what felt like viscous snot loaded with razor blades. Before I could form a mental scream, I collapsed face down on a cool, glassy surface. Blinding golden light flared, seeming to penetrate all the way to my bones before settling into a soft glow. Twinges of pain skittered through my limbs like electrified fleas on speed. I tried to scramble to my feet, but my muscles didn't want to cooperate.

Strong hands gripped my upper arms and hauled me up. Szerain.

While my body refused to obey my orders to struggle, he crushed me in an embrace and hugged my head to his shoulder. "You foolish, headstrong, insane, brilliant woman."

Whew. Not an attack. Still a good guy. "You forgot pushy bitch," I croaked. The pain eased, either through Szerain's doing or on its own. I still fell like a ragdoll, though. "Something went wrong. I thought I had you, but—"

"Kara, you did. I mean, you would have if I'd wanted to come through." He pushed me out to arm's length and eyed me critically. His features were Szerain's, and the gold-flecked green eyes were the same as Ryan's, though somehow they held more vitality despite the dark circles beneath them. "I reversed your hook and dragged you here."

"Here" was a golden bubble surrounded by darkness and not much larger than a stall in a public restroom. A dimensional pocket, I assumed.

"But why?" I asked, perplexed. "Don't you want to be rescued?"

"Not without preparation on both ends. We'd be sitting ducks for Xharbek." He released my shoulders, but kept a supporting hand on my arm.

"No, see, Mzatal turned my nexus into—"

"I know about your nexus," he said. "We felt it when Mzatal created the link to Rhyzkahl. But it's not enough."

I sighed as my plan crumbled. "Where are the others?"

"Still in our stronghold. It was safer for Ashava if I came out and met you."

"How is she?" I gave him a worried look. "Jill is going crazy."

His eyes lit up as he smiled. "She thrives. She's strong and clever. Smarter than me, I'm certain."

"Well, so is Fuzzykins."

Szerain laughed. "All right. Smarter than *Mzatal.*"

"That's pretty smart." A pang went through me at how much I'd missed this kind of back-and-forth. "What about the others? Is Sonny doing okay? Has Zack recovered at all?"

"Sonny is coping with the situation as well as can be expected, and he dotes on Ashava. They're good for each other. Zakaar . . ." Deep worry shadowed his eyes. "Zakaar continues to fade." Grief tinged his voice. "We're on alert twenty-four seven, which means he's had no recovery time."

His bleak expression shouted what he hadn't said: Even spending weeks lounging stress-free in Tahiti wouldn't be enough to save Zack. He needed more than mere time. For the fifteen years of Szerain's submersion as Ryan, Zack had not only been his guard and guardian, but his lifeline to sanity in the inhumane prison. And now it tore at Szerain that he couldn't do a damn thing to save him.

"I'm so sorry." Without thinking, I pulled him into a hug, same as I'd do for any other friend going through a hard time. And, like any other friend, Szerain accepted the comfort and returned the embrace. "Let's bring him home," I said. I didn't add an empty promise that we'd find a way to help him. I held on to hope, but that wasn't the same. "What preparations do I need to make on my end?"

Szerain briefly tightened his embrace then released me. "I can't determine the timing and nuances until I have a update on everything that's happened since Katashi blew the PD valve. However, I can start laying out the basics." He lifted his hand, and a spiral notepad and pencil appeared in it out of thin air—or, rather, out of a handy dimensional storage pocket.

"You should teach me that trick," I said. "I need a place to store my summer clothes, plus I could finally clear out the shed in my back yard."

His mouth quirked into a sly smile. "How can I amaze and mystify if I give away my secrets?" He flipped to a blank page and began to sketch interlocking sigils. "You'll need to create a matching trio of diagrams on your nexus then reach for us, as you did just now, and pull us through. The nexus setup will act as a temporary bunker until we can raise the needed protections to keep Xharbek at bay." He paused and met my eyes. "In the meantime, Zakaar, Ashava, and I have much planning to do."

Ashava, planning? I had a sudden mental image of a baby wearing an Army general's uniform, moving miniature tanks and soldiers around a map.

On the other hand, the kid had only been a few minutes old when she kicked serious ass at the Beaulac PD and prevented the valve explosion from being exponentially worse. Maybe Ashava's involvement in the planning wasn't so ludicrous after all.

However, getting him caught up wasn't going to be easy. "You missed a lot of stuff after you and Zack vanished with Ashava," I said. "For starters, Idris killed Katashi. Except it wasn't really Katashi. A syraza was masquerading as Katashi for who the hell knows how long. And the syraza ended up dead-dead because about eighty percent of the killed demons aren't making it through the void. Right after the blast, an Earthgate popped up in the Ruthie's Smoothies parking lot. Kadir came through it yesterday, but we don't know where he is now. Rifts have been opening—" I stopped, frustrated. Every event intersected with a buttload of other important points without respect to chronology. "This isn't working. There's no way I can give you a coherent and comprehensive summary before we both die of starvation. Just read it from me."

Szerain tore out the page of diagram sketches, stuffed it into my hand then sent the notebook back to its interdimensional hidey-hole. "I can't," he said matter-of-factly. "You've shielded yourself."

"Shielded *myself*? No, Zack and Helori did it to protect sensitive info."

"Yes, but it's more than just demahnk tampering." His eyes went distant as he seemed to ponder the concept, then they flashed with fierce amusement. "I bet it chaps Xharbek's ass that he can't read you."

I grinned at the very Ryan-like remark. I couldn't imagine ever hearing those words from Rhyzkahl or Mzatal. "My shielding definitely frustrated the hell out of Xharbek at Fed Central when—" I shook my head as his gaze sharpened on me. "See? There's way too much to tell. Can't I let you in somehow?"

"Possibly, if you open to me. It's worth a try." He placed his hands on each side of my head and leaned down to touch his forehead to mine. "Xharbek can't read me either. None of the demahnk can without my consent. I chose submersion and exile to Earth rather than put myself at their mercy again."

Great. He'd dropped yet another snippet of info, but I was still missing the meat of the story. "Why can't you go ahead and tell me everything?" I asked somewhat petulantly. "If I can't be read, then you don't have to worry about the demahnk finding sensitive info in my brain."

Szerain lifted his head and blinked at me. "That actually makes an enormous amount of sense." The golden light dimmed like a flashlight with a weak battery. He cursed under his breath. "We don't have much time. We're well shielded, but Xharbek is seeking."

"Then hurry up and find out what you need to know." Fortunately, I had plenty of experience with mental touch through my connection with Mzatal, and I drew on that familiarity to relax and open. Ghost images of rifts and demons, DIRT teams, giant crystals, Pellini, and more flashed in my mind as Szerain scanned months in a moment. Sudden worry hit me. What if he discovered something that triggered a lord headache?

"No need to fret," he said. "I'm free of those fucking headaches." He paused. "And I already know my parentage."

I exhaled in relief, but then I winced. His own father was after him. That had to suck.

"No, Xharbek isn't my—" His grip spasmed tight on my

head. "Elinor! Xharbek has her." He staggered back, eyes wide with shock.

"See, I knew I'd forget to tell you important shit! Yeah, she's on Earth and so is Giovanni. Trust me, I was just as shocked, but we're already working on rescue plans." So what if they were all shitty. "Maybe Zack could teleport you in as soon as we get y'all home? Snatch her and poof—" I shook my head. "No, forget I said that. Zack's probably too weak to do any teleporting."

"You're right. It would destroy him." Szerain's forehead creased as he stared off over my head. "Even so, we can't return to Earth while Xharbek has Elinor."

"Why? What difference does that make?"

"She has a strong connection to me. He'll use that like a tracking device, with an alarm set to go off the moment I leave interdimensional space." The weariness in his face deepened. "He'd be on us—on Ashava—the instant we arrived on the nexus."

"Why does he want Ashava so badly?"

"She's a free demahnk-human hybrid, and he *can't* allow her to remain free." He shook his head. "It has something to do with the demahnk codes of conduct."

"Why didn't he just teleport in and kidnap Jill when she was pregnant?" But then I scowled. "Wait. He *tried* but had flunkies attempt to nab her rather than doing it himself."

"He couldn't intervene directly," Szerain said with a nod. "Not until after Ashava was born."

"Zack tiptoed around ancient oaths and agreements made with entities he referred to as 'the others.'" I made a face. "They sounded more like 'the enforcers,' to me."

"The demahnk constraints are a mystery to me, but I do know Xharbek is the least restricted of their kind." He drew a deep breath and focused on me. "One step at a time. You must get Elinor. What are your rescue plans?"

I made a face. "Nothing workable yet. See for yourself." I gestured toward my head.

A tremor shook the bubble, and the golden light flickered. Szerain scanned the darkness surrounding us then seized my head and dove into my mind with no subtlety. "Mzatal. No. Helori, definitely no. Conventional assault. No no *no*." He went still. "Dekkak. With the gimkrah and a graphene net? Yes!" He released me. "Kara, that's genius. And the full moon is only—"

"Whoa whoa whoa." I stabbed him with a glare. "There's the

teensy issue of me having to learn the lost art of summoning a Jontari imperator—in a matter of *days*—without instructions."

"You can't *learn* the summoning in such a short time," he said. "Not even with months of training. But with your innate gifts *and* the gimkrah *and* the nexus at your disposal, you have what's needed to *know* it."

"Know it," I echoed, then peered at him. "Do you have any idea how much sense you're not making?"

"Be lordy," he said as if that answered all. "*Be* the summoning."

I made a strangled noise. "That didn't help! What the fuck does that even mean?"

"You'll understand," he said with annoying calm. "I have the utmost faith in you."

"Fine. Whatever." My frustration made way for more sobering concerns. "Let's assume I can be all lordy and bring Dekkak through. There's collateral damage to consider. Innocent people will get hurt or killed. We need to get Elinor *and* you guys, but there has to be better way."

Szerain gently took my hands. "I know it would pierce you to your very essence to be the instrument of tragedy, even if indirectly. However, there's no faster or more certain means to recover Elinor, and the damage in Dekkak's wake would be as *nothing* compared to what will come if Xharbek restores Elinor."

"Why would he want to . . ." The answer hit me with a frisson of primal terror. "Because he and the Mraztur still want a weaponized summoner. Rhyzkahl failed to turn me into Rowan, but with Elinor, they have the original."

Szerain nodded once, a simple movement laden with centuries of anguish. "If Xharbek restores Elinor, he'll give the Mraztur a tool capable of destroying Earth."

"But how could he possibly hope to restore her if the majority of her essence is safely trapped in Vsuhl?"

His eyes met mine. "Because it's not. You have it all."

I stared at him in horror. "Wait. *What?*"

"It had stayed far too long in Vsuhl's possession and was beginning to degenerate." A bleak note shadowed his voice. "I risked losing it altogether, and I'd long given up hope of Elinor herself returning."

Sympathy chased away my unease. "It was a way to preserve it."

He nodded. "And, in theory, a way to tap its—her—potential, if encapsulated and fused to a host rather than simply merging essences."

"Sort of like how if someone's hand gets chopped off doctors might sew it to their ankle to keep it alive until it can be reattached?"

He gave me a long look before laughing under his breath. "God, you're weird," he said and wrapped me in a hug.

Lord Szerain. Elinor clawed into my consciousness. *Not to be trusted. Not to be trusted!*

Panic rose. My muscles tensed and twitched as adrenaline raced through my system. Heart pounding, I pushed away and staggered back, torn between fleeing and lashing out.

I settled on a third option: putting a stop to this bullshit. Distracting-Memory Elinor was one thing, but Body-Take-Over Elinor was *oh, hell no.* Teeth clenched, I planted my feet and willed the completely inappropriate panic to retreat. I felt Szerain grab my head, and I spared just enough focus to let him read me and see how Elinor was entwined. The rest I used to painstakingly remove her control of my body, like removing burrs from socks.

Soon enough I had my limbs under my own power, and my breathing and pulse to normal rates. I gently eased Elinor back to her usual "place," sending thoughts of understanding and calm encouragement toward her the whole time.

"She doesn't like you very much," I said once Elinor was fully settled.

"Understandable, considering her end," he said, voice thick with sorrow. "I tweaked the attachment so she can't mess with you physically again."

"Thanks. That's the first time she's ever taken over like that, and I'm happy for it to be the last." The mental invasions were bad enough. "Once we rescue her, can you unhook her essence from me and restore her?"

"If all goes as planned, yes."

"Good. We'll beat Xharbek to the punch." Then I frowned. "But how can Xharbek hope to restore her if I have her essence?"

Szerain's face could have been carved from a block of ice. "As soon as he devises the means, he'll rip it from you like a scab from a wound and leave your essence to bleed out."

Shock wiped out my power of speech for several seconds.

"The *fuck?*" I finally sputtered. "Are you absolutely shitting me? I'm only now finding out that this whole time I've been living with a motherfucking heartplug that Xharbek could've popped free on a fucking drive-by—"

"Kara, stop it!" Szerain snapped.

I cut off my spew of vitriolic what-the-fuck but kept my glare at full power.

"Xharbek is not going to snatch the piece of essence in a drive-by," he said with exaggerated calm. "He *can't*. One aspect of the demahnk constraints, their very *nature* prevents them from bringing direct harm to the demahnk-human hybrids or their descendants—no matter how distant the relationship. And summoners are in the lineage of the lords."

I all but pounced on him. "They are? Hot damn! I had a suspicion, but— Do you know who I'm descended from? Oh, hell, please don't say Mzatal."

"Amkir would make the most sense."

I stared at him in horror. "Amkir? Why would that make sense?"

"Well, you both have quite the temper—ow!" Szerain laughed and ducked a second demonstration of that temper. "All right, all right. I don't think you're descended from either Amkir or Mzatal."

I put my hands on my hips and narrowed my eyes. "What about the headaches and stripping memories and whatever other control the demahnk have over the lords? How does that not count as direct harm?"

Szerain lifted his shoulders in a shrug. "Zack is too weak to challenge the constraints and give me the details of demahnk's cryptic moral code."

The light dimmed several more degrees, and I held back a nervous shudder. "Tell me about the Dekkak summoning before this dimensional bubble thing pops. I need to get the gimkrah, but what then? You said to be lordy, but how do I—"

Szerain jerked his hand up to cut me off, tilting his head as if listening to a distant sound. "*Fuuuuuck.* Elinor's earlier freakout attracted Xharbek's attention."

A shiver ran down my back. I suddenly felt like a glowing fishy trying to hide from invisible sharks, all too vulnerable in the sea of darkness. "You need to get back to your stronghold."

"I will, once you're back on Earth." Szerain flicked his fingers and set a whirlwind of crimson rakkuhr sparks dancing over our heads. "This will give him pause," he said with calm certainty. "Go home. *Now*."

How the hell was I supposed to do that? Yet even as the thought surfaced, I instinctively called up the sight and sound and *feel* of the nexus and the super-shikvihr, the scent of pines and damp grass, the familiarity of Pellini's resonance and his gruff laugh.

Szerain scattered the sparks. The glow of the dimensional pocket shifted to bloody red, save for a rapidly diminishing patch of golden light. My way out.

I dove for it, reached for home and the strand of potency that would show me the way. Nexus. The tree. Pellini's aftershave. The screech of blue jays. Kittens chasing a butterfly through the grass.

An arcane shove from Szerain propelled me onward into razor-filled snot.

"Dekkak on the full." Szerain's voice echoed distantly, fading. "Elinor. Bunker diagrams. Reach for us exactly two . . ."

Two what?

I crashed onto the nexus and tumble-slid from the center to the edge. Ears ringing, I flopped to my back and stared up into grove tree leaves alight in green and purple jeweled splendor by the late afternoon sun.

"Kara!" Pellini dropped to his knees beside me. "Jesus fuck, I'm glad to see you. Are you all right? You scared the crap out of me."

I gave him a shaky thumbs up.

"Thank god," he breathed. "I damn near had a heart attack when you disappeared, but I kept hold of the strand. I could feel you, but that's it."

"You did good," I said as I heaved up onto my elbows.

He blew out a breath and shifted to sit. "I knew if I lost you Jill would never let me hear the end of it." He crooked a weak smile as I laughed. "So, did it work? Or have you been bobbing around in the ether examining your life choices this whole time?"

"I already know my life choices are questionable," I said with a grin. "But yes, it worked. I met with Szerain."

Chapter 23

I filled Pellini in on the stuff he needed to know and left out everything else—an editing of events that he was totally fine with. Like everyone else in the compound, he knew we had mind-reading enemies and didn't expect, or want, to be privy to the more sensitive info. Once that was taken care of, Pellini headed to the war room while I hurried to the basement to give yet another censored briefing—though with a far different tone.

Jill looked up as I clattered down the stairs, a whisper of annoyance on her face at the noise.

"I just talked to Szerain," I announced and leaped down the last few steps. "And Ashava's doing great!"

"What did he say?" She shoved up from the chair like a starving tiger lunging at a hunk of prime rib. "Where are they? Tell me everything!"

"We didn't have a lot of time," I said. "But Szerain said she's healthy and smart and strong-minded." I grinned. "Ashava keeps them on their toes."

"She's such a little thing." Jill sank to sit again, face full of relief and wonder and worry. "It's hard to think of a baby as strong-minded, but I know she's . . . different."

I quickly recounted what I could of my meeting with Szerain, taking care to emphasize anything that was even remotely related to Ashava. As I spoke, the stark lines of tension in Jill's face eased. Her daughter was not only alive, but *thriving*, and that knowledge melted away a generous portion of her fear and distress like a flamethrower on a snow bank.

A measure of the worry returned when I explained that the

imperator summoning was now our only viable option. Jill wasn't at all happy with the new development, but she didn't waste time snarling about it. After giving me a bone-cracking hug, she dove right back into her research.

A call to Idris was next on my agenda. There was nothing in the rule book that said I had to do the summoning on my lonesome, but even if he couldn't break free of his DIRT duties, I figured it would be useful to get his input and bounce ideas off him. It didn't seem possible that our last conversation had been only this morning, considering how much had happened since then.

A quick check of the DIRT status board showed me that it was early morning in Pohang, South Korea, where he and his team were currently deployed. I hated to risk waking him, but with sleep being a whenever-you-can-grab-it luxury, now was as good a time as any to call.

I plopped down at the kitchen table and dialed his number, relieved when he picked up on the third ring.

"Hey, Kara. Everything cool?"

"Would I be calling if it was?" I asked and received a dry chuckle in return. Good, he sounded awake, though tired. "Got a few minutes?"

"Not really, but for you, I'll pretend I do."

Using vague terms, nicknames, and the occasional demon word to throw off anyone who might be listening in, I gave Idris a "Previously on Kara's Kompound" recap of the day's events: Knight and Cory changing from gummy bears to mega-heavy pods, my going to Siberia to help Mzatal fight the Jontari, my subsequent attempt to contact Szerain through Vsuhl, Elinor's interruption and my realization that she was on Earth and in Xharbek's control and, finally, the censored rundown of what transpired in the dimensional pocket with Szerain, including the decision to summon Dekkak to rescue Elinor.

"Holy shit," he breathed. "You've had one hell of a day. And you'll be doing the first Jontari summoning in *centuries*." His voice held awe, dread, and more than a touch of envy. At least he wasn't telling me I was insane to even consider such a dangerous summoning.

"I have a few tricks up my sleeve. In fact, I'll tell you all about them if you happen to swing by the ol' homestead, say, day after tomorrow. I could really use your help."

"I'll do my best," he said fervently. "This seafloor rift is kick-

ing my ass, so I can't promise anything, but wow. An imperator!"

"You don't want to miss it," I assured him then grimaced.
"Rhyzkahl will be there. I can't do anything about that."

"I haven't forgotten about *him*," he said, voice abruptly a
hundred degrees colder and razor-edged.

"Look, I know how you feel about—"

"Really?" he snarled. "You know what it feels like to have a
lying, evil piece of shit for a father? To see him smirk? To know
that he's getting stronger every day after everything he's done?
You know what it's like to have a mother who slept with the
asshole and doesn't give a rat's ass about you?"

My calm sympathy snapped in the face of his rant. "Oh, give
me a *fucking* break, Idris! Look, I love you. You're family. But
sometimes family gets to tell you when you're full of shit. You
have Rhyzkahl's and Tessa's DNA. So fucking what? Rhyzkahl
doesn't even know he's your dad, and you sure as shit can't
blame *him* for that lack of knowledge. And we still *don't know*
whether Tessa has any idea you're her son. Yes, you have every
right to be upset and bitter that your biological parents are assholes, but you've taken righteous indignation to a whole new
level of crazy. If you're waiting for either of them to crawl to
you and beg for forgiveness for *having sex and making a baby*,
then you're going to be a long time waiting. You need to move
on from this shit, and no one can do that for you. You're the only
one who can decide when it's time to stop beating up yourself
and everyone around you."

Silence.

A loooong silence.

Shit. "Idris, I—"

"You've made your point," he said, voice stiff. "I have to go.
The rift is belching demon sea monsters."

The connection went dead.

I set the phone down and pressed the heels of my palms
against my eyes. "Wow, Kara, you really have a way with people. You couldn't have given him an 'Oh, you poor baby' just
this once? No, you had to let him have it with both barrels."

So much for having another summoner to back me up. But
hey, maybe between now and the full moon, the sea rift would
calm down, Idris's curiosity and sense of duty would override
his anger at me as well as his less than loving feelings toward

his father, he'd show up in time to help, and everything would go perfectly.

Uh huh. Right. And maybe the invading Jontari will develop an allergy to Earth smog and slink back home.

To add insult to injury, with the way the conversation had gone pear-shaped, I couldn't even enjoy the absurdity of demon sea monsters.

Enough wallowing. Time to deal with all the other crap on my to-worry-about list.

After grabbing a quick, oh-so-healthy snack of cookies, I joined the others in the war room. Bryce sat at the table with a phone to his ear, while across from him Giovanni sketched in a spiral-bound pad. At the far end, Pellini scowled at his laptop screen as his meaty fingers flew over the keyboard.

Bryce growled an ultimatum about a delayed shipment of bricks and hung up, then stood and handed me a slip of paper. "That's the best deal I could make on the graphene net. But it's a big one. Almost twice the size of the prototype. No luck with a power supply, though." He paused. Grimaced. "The Memphis contact is solid, but he's risking his career as well as his freedom to make that net disappear from DIRT inventory."

"I'm not thrilled about putting that burden on anyone, but there's been a development. I had contact with Szerain. It's critical to rescue Elinor ASAP, so we have no choice but to move forward with the Jontari summoning." I frowned at the paper and then at him. "Fifty pounds? Of what? I'm guessing this doesn't mean British money."

"Ah, no." He winced. "See, cash isn't as welcome what with the world falling apart and all. That's how much *gold* he wants."

I goggled and sputtered. "Are you shitting me?"

"Wish I was. Also, it's fifty pounds of pure gold, not fifty pounds of fourteen karat stuff. However, if we come up with enough of any quality, it'll be no problem for me to get the equipment to melt, purify, and cast it into bars."

"That's a real big if!" I threw my hands up. "Where the hell are we going to get that much gold?"

Pellini's brows pulled together. "How much gold did the Piggly Wiggly demon have on him?"

"Nowhere near enough." Glowering, I flopped into a chair. "Ten pounds, maybe. Besides, DIRT scooped it up."

Bryce gestured to the corner of the wall screen where a timer unobtrusively counted down. "We have until midnight tomorrow to get the gold to the contact or the deal's off. No compromise on that."

"Great. Just great." I dropped my head back. "I guess that's all the time we have anyway. The full moon is day after tomorrow which means that's when I have to do the summoning. Net or no net." *Working without a net.* Fuck. The damn thing was both literal and figurative. Without it, I'd be like a trapeze artist who'd never performed a flip before, hurtling through the air over razor sharp rocks and hoping to hell that I could catch the other swing.

Yet the outcome would be far worse if I didn't make the attempt. Xharbek would have Elinor, and it would be only a matter of time before he found a way to rip her essence from me and created an Elinor-Death-Star capable of wiping out Earth.

"What about going through official channels?" Bryce asked. "Can you—as Arcane Commander—requisition gold for some bogus purpose? It's a fortune for an individual, but nothing for the government."

"Con the government in order to pay off a government employee to steal government property." I let the idea percolate. I didn't much like playing the bad guy in order to be the good guy, but I'd already started down that rabbit hole when I decided to steal the net.

"It's a big risk," Pellini said. "You'd need a convincing story *and* tangible results within twenty-four hours, all while preparing for the summoning of a lifetime."

Frustration rose. "If you have a better idea, by all means, spill it."

"Loot one of the wealthy neighborhoods?" Bryce offered.

"The rich folks who stayed are armed to the teeth and way too trigger-happy," I pointed out. "And museums nationwide have been hiding their valuable stuff away. Pawn shops and jewelry stores are also a no-go since pretty much every non-essential retail business within a hundred miles has closed up shop."

Giovanni cleared his throat softly. "There is gold to be had."

We all turned to look at him.

"Excuse me?" I said.

"Szerain's palace." He opened his hands and shrugged. "Statuary gold. Cast figures large and small."

My brain fumbled for a few seconds. "Let me make sure I

have this right. You're suggesting we steal and melt Szerain's *art*?"

Giovanni crossed his arms over his chest. "He stole far more than mere gold from Elinor."

Ouch. "Okay, that's a valid point." I considered this new development. "Y'know, I think this gold acquisition scheme could work." I'd find a way to make it up to Szerain later. Preferably from a distance. "I need to go to the demon realm anyway to get the gimkrah."

"Do you know where it is?" Pellini asked.

"Not yet, but I'm going to call Mzatal and ask."

"I assume you're planning to use the Spires to get to the demon realm?"

"Not sure we have any other options for interdimensional transport," I said. "Of course, we don't know if the Earthgate is an option at all. Just because we can touch it doesn't mean we can use it."

"I can," Pellini said quietly.

"What? How?"

He gave a self-conscious shrug. "When Kadir came through the gate, I got a glimpse of the other side. I could feel it." He shook his head. "Look, I don't know what to say other than I'm sure I can get us through."

"Then that's good enough for me," I assured him. Looked like Pellini's connection to Kadir might actually pay off. "Giovanni, where do we find the gold?"

He lifted his chin. "I will show you."

"Not sure that's a good idea," I said with a wince. "The demon realm is a dangerous mess right now."

"It matters not," he announced fiercely. "I do that which brings Elinor closer."

I tapped the table in front of him. "As long as you understand it's not going to be a walk in the park, I won't stand in your way."

Pellini's heavy brows drew together. "Kara, I don't know that he *can* come with us."

"Huh? Why couldn't he—? Oh." Damn. Pellini and I were the only ones who could get near the crystals. "Do we know for a fact that no one else can approach, even if they're with us?"

"I tried it with Idris, and he still couldn't get close." Pellini leaned back in his chair. "But since that's the only attempt, I'd say that we don't know for sure."

"And that was two months ago, right after the Earthgate appeared," I said. "Kadir has tinkered with the crystals since then. I'm going to cross fingers and think super positively that he tweaked settings in our favor, since you're his protégé. Plus, they've activated."

"I'm happy to give it a try," Pellini said, "but we still need the location of the gold in case I can't get Giovanni through."

"The west tower," Giovanni said. "In the gallery below Szerain's bed chamber."

My heart sank to my toes. "A chasm swallowed that tower nearly a year ago." *When I almost caused a second cataclysm during the ritual to retrieve Vsuhl.*

The color drained from Giovanni's face. "His studio? The galleries? It cannot be so."

"I'm sorry," I said with a sigh. "The whole tower is gone."

Pellini cursed under his breath. "So much for that plan."

"No, there are others," Giovanni's voice wavered then steadied. "In the west wing. Smaller pieces, yet there should be enough."

"All right, that works. Even though Giovanni's info is a few centuries old, and stuff might have been moved, Turek will know where things are." I smacked my forehead. "Holy shit! We'll bring Turek back with us. And Michael, too! They can help me communicate with Szerain."

"Who in god's name are Turek and Michael?" Pellini growled.

I grinned. "Sorry. Turek is an ancient savik who's essence-bound to Szerain. He'll do whatever is needed to help Szerain. And Michael Moran is the brother of deceased rock singer Lida Moran, and can sometimes 'see' where the lords are at any given time."

He straightened. "I remember that case. Your report said Lida coerced Michael into murder, then she killed him but his body was never found. Didn't he have something wrong upstairs?" Pellini tapped the side of his head.

"Michael suffered a head injury when he was twelve," I said. "His condition made it easy for his piece of shit sister to exploit him. She used his talent for making earth golems to get rid of anyone in her way."

"Huh. And so you shipped him off to the demon realm." Pellini stroked his mustache. "But if we already know where Szerain is, why do we need someone who can see him?"

"We know he's in a dimensional pocket that's tied to the out-reach center and that he needs help making a move soon after the summoning. Unfortunately, we weren't able to finalize plans, which means I have to improvise a way to communicate. I think that *how* Michael sees the lords can give me an arcane road map." I pointed at the security monitor. "For example, how do we see the guard at the front gate?"

"Combination of wired and wireless signals." Pellini frowned at the screen. "I think I understand. When Michael sees Szerain, you'll use arcane tracers to home in on whatever signal he's receiving."

"Right. Then I'll create a conduit to follow that frequency, giving Turek a pathway to telepathically reach Szerain. That's my theory, anyway." It was equally possible that Michael wouldn't be able to see Szerain at all in the dimensional pocket, in which case he'd at least get the chance to play with fluffy kittens before he returned to the demon realm.

"There's certainly enough to justify making the trip," Pellini said. "The gold, the gimkrah, and getting a message to Szerain."

"I'm going to ignore your weak-ass alliteration attempt, because this trip keeps getting better and better. I can grab Elinor's journal, plus we can finally bring back that poor woman Farouche kidnapped last year and who Rhyzkahl enslaved." I snapped my fingers as I dredged the name from my memory. "Janice. Yeah, that's it. She's been under Mzatal's protection ever since right before the valve went kablooey."

"I bet she'll be glad to see us," Pellini said.

I swung toward Giovanni. "Since we're not sure if we can get you through the gate, and I don't want to be caught with my pants down if we can't find Turek, I need you to write down every place in the west wing where the gold statues could be."

He gave a resolute nod. "I will scribe that which you require. Should calamity befall and the fates bar my participation in this quest, you will yet succeed."

"That'd be great," I said, "but trust me, I'm hoping we can pull this off and get you through. After all, we need to grab fifty pounds worth. And Pellini can only carry so much." I ducked as Pellini winged a pen at me.

"I'll carry your ass to the curb," he said with a mock snarl.

"I have no doubt," I said. "In the meantime, let's get the logistics for this trip hammered out then grab a few hours of sleep. Tomorrow's going to be a busy day."

Chapter 24

With the clock ticking for the gold delivery, four hours was the most we could spare for sleep. Though, considering the stressed and frenetic pace of the past two months, four uninterrupted hours felt positively decadent.

Pellini and I were old hands at going to strange and distant locations at the drop of a hat, which meant gearing up went quickly. Our rucksacks each had enough room for twenty to thirty pounds of gold, but in a burst of optimism that we'd get Giovanni through the gate, we found a rucksack for him as well. Carrying fifty pounds would be a lot easier if divided three ways.

"I assume you have a fallback plan in case we can't get the gold at Szerain's?" Pellini asked as he packed the luggage scale we planned to use for weighing the gold.

"I do," I said, checking off items on the must-bring list. "Rhyzkahl has all sorts of gold crap in his throne room and on decorative panels throughout his palace. It's nowhere near as easy to remove as statues and art, but we can hack off enough hunks to hit our quota." I smiled. "That's why I stuck a camping hatchet in your pack."

"Yeah, saw that. Somehow I accidentally dropped it into Giovanni's. Dude could stand to put some muscle on his bones."

"Aw, cut the guy some slack," I said with a laugh. "He's been dead for three hundred years."

"Sounds like a pathetic excuse to me." Pellini smiled. "Is there a Plan C?"

I made a face. "More like a Plan F, since it's a last resort. The summoning antechamber in Mzatal's palace has gold all over it, but it's leaf."

"And it would take serious time and effort to collect the amount we needed."

"Exactly," I said. "But between those three options, I'm positive we can get the gold we need, one way or the other." I zipped my rucksack closed. "And now it's time for me to lay down some smooth-talk bullshit on General Starr so we can actually *get* to the demon realm."

That was my next hurdle: obtaining official clearance to use the Earthgate to travel to the demon realm. Sure, we could likely get to the crystals and make the transfer before anyone stopped us, but we'd have a world of trouble waiting for us upon our return and would likely never get near them again. Therefore, before I called General Starr, I prepped a solid and compelling argument for why Pellini and I needed to reconnoiter the other side of the gate, as well as why we needed to use our own "expert consultant" to test whether we could bring other people through.

But General Starr readily agreed, expounding with great exuberance on the tactical benefits of direct reconnaissance. In fact, while we were still on the phone, he passed along an order to allow us and one civilian unrestricted access to the Spires. The only hitch was that the general wanted us to each wear a body camera at all times—a completely valid request since we were supposedly doing recon. However, I shot that idea down nice and quick by oh-so-regretfully telling him there was simply too much arcane activity in the demon realm to make pictures or video even remotely possible. I didn't need DIRT spying on our business, plus I had zero intention of feeding their invasion cravings by giving them the layout of the demon realm.

My next call was to Mzatal. I clung to the hope that he could tell me where I could lay hands on his master gimkrah—while I crossed fingers he wouldn't react as Rhyzkahl had and tell me I was insane to even consider it. He hadn't returned my previous call, but there was a chance he hadn't checked messages.

After four rings, the DIRT voicemail picked up, but I'd prepped for this, too. Never knew who was listening in on my calls, and I didn't want to drop any more info than was absolutely necessary.

"Mzatal, it's Kara. A student of yours from a long time ago is here, and she's having a really hard time getting home. I need to get the help of someone related to that big guy you were dancing with last time I saw you. Word is you have a gizmo that can help me out with that, and if you could let me know where to find it at your crib, that would be righteous."

I hung up, pleased with my subterfuge, only to see Jill biting back a laugh. Behind her, Giovanni simply looked perplexed.

"You're the dorkiest sorceress ever," she said with a grin.

"I'd rather be called the dorkiest sorceress than supreme arcane commander."

"Well, D.S. Gillian, Giovanni found another reference to the master gimkrah. I'll warn you now, it's a bit vague."

"I'll take anything you can throw at me."

Giovanni handed me a sheet of loose-leaf paper. "Parts of the original are smudged and unreadable." He winced. "And the rest is in a poetic style that is not conducive to the most accurate translation. I have scribed my best interpretation."

I murmured a thanks, already reading.

creatures of night and blood
hold back the claws and teeth
make gentle the beast summoned to serve lest it serve honor
with pain and death
master and slave of torment and treachery
the gimkrah lies in wait
surrounded by emptiness
deep in the heart of darkness.

"That is indeed annoyingly vague and flowery," I said. "Plus, now I have 'Deep in the Heart of Texas' stuck in my head except with *deep in the heart of darkness.*"

Jill made a noise in the back of her throat. "Great. Now I do, too!"

"Glad I could share." I read through it again. The last part sounded like Mzatal during his millennia of walled-off isolation. Alone, with a ruthless heart. "Maybe something will pop for me when I get to Mzatal's palace." I folded the paper and stuck it in my front pocket. "Still way more than we had before. Thanks, Giovanni. We're hoping to leave in twenty minutes, so if you need to do anything before we go, now's the time."

He nodded and hurried off to the guest room.

Jill gave me a worried smile. "Be careful and come back in one piece."

I gave her a cheeky grin. "Will you have macadamia white chocolate chip cookies waiting for me?"

She snorted. "Sure. As soon as you get me macadamia nuts and white chocolate."

"Damn. How about sugar cookies?"

"You got it. And I won't even add sardines."

As soon as Pellini and I finished double-checking weapons and gear, we bundled Giovanni into the Humvee and headed to the Earthgate. Tandon and Kellum followed us over and went through the security checkpoints with us, then settled in to wait. If it turned out that Giovanni was unable to pass the arcane perimeter around the crystals, my two security guards were ready to scoop him up and get him the hell out of there, hopefully before any DIRT personnel decided to scrutinize our "expert consultant."

Captain Hornak looked as if he'd rather chew glass than have anything to do with us, but he remained professional and made no attempt to interfere with or question our mission. Hell, maybe he was hoping this jaunt of ours would rid him of a Kara-sized thorn in his side once and for all. Niceties taken care of, my trio proceeded toward the crystal gateway and the invisible arcane barrier that, thus far, very effectively blocked everyone but Pellini and me.

"I propose we each take one of Giovanni's hands," I told Pellini as we neared the barrier, "and think super hard about how much we want him to come with us."

Pellini nodded slowly. "When I was a kid, Kadir showed me how to 'slide' through matter in the sparkly dimension. It wasn't so much about *thinking* as *believing* it had already happened. Since this barrier is Kadir's, his believing method just might work on it." He took one of Giovanni's hands, and I took the other. "Maybe do your pygah, and we'll cruise on through."

"That's probably better than my plan of running at it full-tilt while praying for the best, like Platform Nine and Three Quarters." I grinned as Giovanni gave me a perplexed look. Apparently his download from the current-day flows didn't include finer details such as Harry Potter. "After this is over, we'll get you caught up on the current cultural icons," I promised him.

"Here goes," Pellini said.

I blew out a breath and reminded myself that Pellini had a close tie with Kadir and was practiced in the *believing* technique. Tightening my grip on Giovanni's hand, I relaxed into a pygah and imagined all of us smiling between the crystals. A casual stroll forward . . .

And then we were through the barrier and at the base of the

Spires. We cautiously released Giovanni then breathed mutual sighs of relief when he stayed right beside us, clearly unaffected by any aversions or compulsions to leave.

"So far so good," I said. "Now for the fun part." Right. Fun. I wiped sweaty palms on my pants. Nothing set a mood quite like the total uncertainty of using an alien teleport gate. I was pretty sure it would take us to Kadir's realm, but for all I knew we might end up in a galaxy far far away. Or simply disintegrate. "Let's see if we can fire this puppy up."

"You have any idea how to work it?" Pellini asked as we stepped between the Spires.

"Nope. I'm implementing Standard Operating Procedure Alpha."

His mouth twitched. "So we're winging it."

"Pretty much." I set a hand on the crystal to my right. Pellini did the same to the other one.

"I hope I never have to find out what Standard Operating Procedure Beta is," he muttered.

I laughed, clinging to humor to combat the *ohfuckohfuckwhatthefuckamIdoing* sproinging around my gut. "Stop your whining and focus," I ordered with an oh-so-stern glare.

"Yeah, you'll look like an idiot if you can't make it work," Pellini said. "In front of Captain Hardass, no less."

"Me? What about you? You're the Kadir expert."

"I'm just following orders, Arcane Commander Gillian."

I snorted. "Then I *order* you to do expert shit."

"I'll get right on it, ma'am!" he said with a smartass grin edged with tension. He splayed both hands on the crystal and closed his eyes in concentration. For a good thirty seconds nothing changed, then a throbbing hum rose from the Spires, so powerful it set me swaying.

I grabbed Giovanni's shoulder with my free hand. "Stay close—"

The muggy parking lot disappeared, and we dropped into a sickening freefall through pitch black, bitterly cold nothingness. No air. No breath. Panic squeezed me. *I'll lose my Self again.*

No! Not this time. Pellini's words ghosted through my flailing thoughts. *Believe it has already happened.* That was it. *Believe I'm already there.* I floundered for an image of what "there" would be like, then remembered it wasn't about thinking. *Believe.* The feel of solid ground beneath my feet. A breeze. A deep lungful of air. Gravity.

Nothingness gave way to blinding sun and arid heat. I staggered into Pellini and gasped a grateful breath. Giovanni lay sprawled at our feet, wide-eyed and hyperventilating. A pair of crystals towered over us, identical to the ones on Earth, just as Paul had said.

"Ow," I said and took another deep breath, pulse still in sprint-from-imminent-death mode. "Somehow I don't think it's supposed to be that hard."

Pellini shrugged, looking none the worse for wear. "Seemed okay to me."

"That's because you were driving," I retorted, resisting the urge to sprawl in the sand beside Giovanni. "Wasn't much fun in the back seat."

"Sorry. No instruction manual." Pellini gave Giovanni a hand up. "We made it, didn't we?"

"Fair point." I took stock of our surroundings, shading my eyes with a hand as I gazed out at what seemed an endless stretch of rolling dunes of white sand. "We're in the middle of a friggin' desert!" And on top of that, it felt as if my skin wanted to crawl right off my body. Ugh. Kadir's realm was "out of phase" with the rest of the demon realm, like a radio tuned to a different frequency. It obviously suited him—and Paul as well now—but the other lords and most demons avoided the place.

Giovanni tapped my shoulder. "Oasis."

I spun to see shimmering mirages and, beyond them, a sparkling pool of what appeared to be real water. Surrounding it, like broken and blackened teeth, were remnants of what might have once been trees. Beside the water crouched a simple whitewashed structure, no bigger than a middle class family home and with a flavor of adobe meets Mediterranean. It was austere yet appealing, and by far the least palace-like of any of the lord's dwellings I'd seen.

Past it, emerald and amethyst shimmered. "There's his grove," I said with undisguised relief. The feel of it enveloped me, like sliding into a warm pool after being forced to wade in the shallows. The planetary network of groves were like teleport stations between the lords' domains, and this one would be our transport to Szerain's realm. "Let's move."

Only half a mile lay between the gate and the oasis, but the sand shifted and slid beneath us, and it took at least triple the usual time to cover the distance. The first few steps on solid ground felt as odd as if we'd been on a rocking boat, but we made better time once we found our gait again. Surrounding the pool were over a hundred charred, waist-high tree trunks, yet the ground was free of ash, as if wind and sand had scoured it clean. Sturdy tufts of grass struggled to make a comeback, but the water that had looked so inviting from a distance was a murky brown with an oily sheen on the surface.

"What happened here?" Pellini asked, brow furrowed.

"An anomaly with fire rain hit a couple of months ago," I said, unsettled and saddened by the destruction. "Elofir helped Kadir, but I guess they couldn't protect the oasis." I had no trouble picturing what the area had looked like before. Lush and lovely. An oasis of calm for body and mind. For the first time, I found myself glad that Paul was with Kadir—a sentiment that took me by surprise. Paul certainly seemed content with the odd lord, and perhaps he helped Kadir find a measure of peace in the chaos of his internal world.

There was no sign of Kadir and Paul, which only added weight to my suspicion that they were still on Earth. However, the oasis was by no means deserted. A half dozen still and silent shapes crouched on the roof, watching us with gleaming eyes. One hulking shadow spread his wings and issued an ugly hissing growl.

Pellini cursed. "Wouldn't mind having Sehkeril here as a little friendly backup."

I had a very different feeling about that particular reyza, considering he'd ripped my bowels from my belly during the Symbol Man's ritual. But the nasty fucker had been one of Pellini's mentors, and so I kept my opinion of him to myself. "I think it's best that we don't stop to sightsee," I said in a low voice, quickening my pace.

"Right," Pellini muttered as he and Giovanni hurried along with me. "I keep telling myself that if we go straight to the grove we'll be fine. I don't want to find out what'll happen if I'm wrong."

Fortunately, it took only a few more minutes to reach the entrance to the grove. White trunks lined each side of a broad, grassy passage beneath the sheltering canopy of the trees. I sighed in relief as we stepped into the tree tunnel, feeling as if a blanket of menace had dropped away. Beside me, Giovanni breathed something in Italian that was probably on the order of "fucking glad that's over."

Sweet birdsong accompanied us down the avenue of trees

and to a clearing ringed by white trunks. I stopped in the center of the heart of the grove and gazed up at the shimmering violet and green leaves.

Leaves that never fell.

Warmth spread over my sternum, and I pressed my hand over the leaf that rested there. The familiar grove-sentience embraced me even as the branches stirred and the leaves whispered. But there was no wind. There were no words.

We didn't need words.

The warmth spread from my chest up through my head, along my arms, and down my legs. I closed my eyes, sank into the *feel* of the grove as I had so many times before, a delicious drifting meditation. Except this time awareness and understanding inundated me, a tidal wave of images and emotions and perceptions that saturated my entire being and rolled on. As it receded, I drifted.

Warmth prickled through me, and I slowly opened my eyes.

Pellini and Giovanni sat cross-legged with their backs against a tree, water bottles in hand.

"How long was I out?" I asked.

Pellini shoved his bottle into his rucksack and stood. "Only about ten minutes. I'd have shaken you out of it after thirty seconds if this one hadn't reined me in." He nodded toward Giovanni.

"Elinor would spend time thus," Giovanni said as he scrambled to his feet. "And I would rather wake a sleeping dragon than disturb her in the grove."

"Smart man," I said with a smile. Though I couldn't recall the specifics of my communion with the grove, it didn't matter. Not yet. I turned a slow circle, taking in the trees and the peace and birdsong. I understood so much more now. I'd assumed—and even been told—that the grove was a semi-sentient organic network, cultivated by the lords for instantaneous travel. But this wasn't just a bunch of magic trees who were all connected like a colony of aspens. The trees here and in the groves all over the planet were extensions of one *fully* sentient being. Even the tree in my back yard—an extension of the grove entity that I now understood had been sent to me with purpose.

Rho. The entity's name was Rho. Peace. Harmony. Wisdom. With the worlds as screwed up as they were, I could do worse for an ally.

"Let's go, y'all," I said. "Meditation break's over."

Rho picked up my intended destination, and the grove shifted around us. A softer light, a different arrangement of white trunks, a whisper of breeze. I stood quietly for a moment, thanking Rho, then smiled to the others. "C'mon, let's go burgle the palace!"

Chapter 25

I practically skipped up the tree tunnel, but once outside, I stumbled to a shocked halt. To the distant east, the chasm that had opened centuries ago during Elinor's cataclysm belched greasy smoke to form a gloomy pall over the entire landscape. Szerain's palace rose before us, not even a hundred yards away from the low valley that cradled the grove. But one entire side of the palace was now a crumbled heap, and the surrounding woods that only months before had been thick and verdant, now stood bare and burned like blackened spikes. I turned a slow circle, shuddering with grief as I took in the devastation wreaked by fire rain. Though the grove remained untouched, every other living thing in sight had been reduced to char, from the palace all the way over the rolling hills and up into the once-forested mountains.

Yet at the edge of the mountains, the pale columns of an Ekiri pavilion shimmered amidst the destruction, visible now that the shrouding forest was gone. And between the grove and the palace, a small but lofty building of honey-colored stone stood undamaged, bounded by a swath of bright green grass dotted with the blue and gold of wildflowers. A tiny measure of relief stole through me. That stone building was Szerain's plexus, and the powerful arcane protections encompassing it meant the ancient savik, Turek, was still alive and guarding it.

A low moan of horror came from behind me. I spun to see Giovanni sink to his knees, distress carved into his face. Though, I'd warned him about the unpleasant changes to the palace, nothing could have prepared him for the scene that lay before us.

"I'm so sorry. The fire rain . . . ." My throat tightened, and I couldn't continue.

Giovanni's mouth worked, eyes swimming with devastation and shock as he lifted a trembling hand. "The . . . west wing?" he finally managed.

My stomach dropped as my gaze settled on the rubble. Sonofabitch. "W-we can search the rest of the palace. C'mon, we need to get moving."

Pellini took hold of Giovanni's arm and hauled him to his feet, then we all quick-marched up the char-covered path to the palace, every step stirring fine soot that scraped at the backs of our throats. Yet when we reached the broad doors, powerful warding barred our entry.

Dismay rose as I skimmed the complex sigils. "Maybe we can get in through the broken walls."

Pellini thumped me on the arm. "Kara, look."

I followed his gaze, appalled to see a luminescent puke-green cloud forming above the chasm and expanding our way. "Fire rain," I breathed, pulse slamming. I instinctively swung my attention to the palace doors in case the wards had somehow magically disappeared, then scanned the vicinity for the closest shelter. No way could we make it back to the grove in time, especially with the horrific cloud doubling in size every few seconds and racing our way as if drawn.

"The plexus!" I choked out then spurred the others into a run toward the structure. As we ran, I risked a look over my shoulder. Yellow-green fire rain hissed down, sizzling as it struck. Ahead of me, Pellini kept a good pace, surprisingly less winded than Giovanni.

"Turek!" I shouted as we neared. The plexus was heavily warded, and it would suck rotten demon guts to end up trapped outside. "Turek! It's Kara."

From within the plexus, a lithe, seven-foot-tall reptilian demon leaped through the doorway to land on the path in front of the steps. Turek—six-limbed and upright, resembling a black-skinned, emerald-scaled crocodile with a splash of wolf thrown in. Between us shimmered a veil of wards that might as well have been a titanium wall.

"Turek! Let us in!" I grabbed Giovanni's arm and dragged him faster, yet Turek didn't move. A scant dozen feet behind us, the ground smoked and popped as the caustic rain struck. We stumbled to a stop before the veil, breathing hard. A furnace of heat swept over my back. "Turek, we're out of time here!"

The ancient savik's purple eyes rested on each of us for a heartbeat then fixed on Giovanni. Before I could blink, the veil parted, and Turek seized him by the throat and drag-carried him toward the structure.

"No!" I leaped after them with Pellini on my heels, even as a droplets of molten death burned through the air inches behind us. The veil snapped into place with a whoosh, shielding us from the fire rain.

With two of his four hands, Turek pinned Giovanni to the plexus wall and leaned in close, saliva dripping from his toothy, elongated jaw. Carved sigils flickered to life in the honey-gold stone. Giovanni cried out in shock as Turek dug the claws of a third hand into his belly, hard enough to draw blood.

My overstressed brain finally clicked into gear. Turek had no reason to think this could be the real Giovanni. "He's not an imposter!" I put a hand on Turek's arm, though I knew better than to waste energy trying to pull him away. "This *is* Giovanni, I swear it."

"Dahn," Turek growled. "Giovanni Racchelli died in the cataclysm." He spoke with a prominent guttural click-pause of his hard 'c' and 'k' sounds, giving his speech a cadence that made his English sound alien.

"She speaks truth," Giovanni croaked through the grip on his throat. "Remember . . . remember the spring when you helped me find the midnight sparkler flowers for Elinor?"

"I forget nothing." Turek flicked out his tongue, pitch black and sinuous, and licked Giovanni's cheek in what I hoped was a demon version of a DNA test. "What came to pass when you gifted Elinor the blooms?"

A weak smile struggled across Giovanni's face. "She began to sneeze and could not stop until I removed all trace of the flower and Lord Szerain attended her."

"The ways were sealed after the cataclysm," Turek said in a thoughtful rumble. The glow in the wall-sigils faded, and he eased his grip to release the pale and shaken Giovanni. "Hundreds of your kind died and discorporeated. Yet as there was no conduit for them to pass through to Earth, all were thus consumed by the void."

"Except Giovanni, who had good reason to hold on for centuries," I said quietly. "Elinor."

Turek dipped his head in a nod then murmured to himself in demon, *And now I understand so much more.* He remained still for several heartbeats then abruptly swept Giovanni off his feet and into a four-armed hug. "It pleases me that you are whole and well," he said, "though I see you are still bony and weak."

Giovanni wheezed a laugh, feet dangling as he returned the embrace. "I am whole, apart from the pinpricks left upon my person by your feeble attempt to disembowel me."

Turek hissed with amusement and set Giovanni carefully down. "And why have you come to this beleaguered realm?" His keen eyes fixed on me.

"Because Elinor is alive, too." I proceeded to give him the quick and dirty rundown of that whole situation, including the business with the Elinor dreams and her current location in lockdown at Fed Central in Xharbek's tender loving care. I finished by telling him of my decision to summon a Jontari warlord, fully expecting Turek to echo the other "are you nuts?" reactions. But when I explained the incredible strength of the graphene net, and my idea to use one in addition to arcane bindings, he let out a hissing snort.

"No Jontari will expect physical restraint."

I smiled, relieved. "My thoughts exactly. It should give me the advantage I need." My gaze flicked toward the palace, and I winced. "Only problem is, we need gold to trade for the net. Since the west tower is gone, can you tell us where we can borrow some statues or other art?"

"There are none in the palace that would serve your need, Kara Gillian," he said, shaking his wide head. "Statuary, yes. But none of gold."

My heart sank. "What about silver? Or platinum?"

"Dahn. Sesekur dih lahn. There is but stone and wood."

Shit. I plunked to sit on the steps. Fire rain splattered and hissed against Turek's dome of protective warding with no sign of abating. "I guess we'll have to implement Plan B and loot gold décor from Rhyzkahl's palace."

Turek growled. "The Jontari Sky Reaper clans overran the demesne of the shamed one a mere eight thousand two hundred and thirty-three heartbeats after Mzatal departed for Earth. It is inaccessible."

I gave my head a sharp shake as if I could dispel this unpleasant situation. "Eight thousand two hundred . . ."

"A little under two and a half hours," Pellini said quietly.

I blinked at him, briefly distracted from my disappointment by how fast he'd whipped out the conversion. "Um, thanks." Mzatal had been on my nexus yesterday morning. "Shit. That means they've had plenty of time to get settled. No way could we get in and survive, and they've probably looted the gold for themselves already. Guess we're stuck with Plan F. Great. Looks like we're going to scrape gold off Mzatal's walls."

"Fifty pounds worth." Pellini shuddered. "Man, that gold leaf shit is like tissue paper. That'll be a long, miserable job."

"Doesn't look as if we have a choice," I said, throat tight with frustration. "Fuck. It was Plan *F* because it was the absolute last resort. Even with arcane help from demons, we'll be hard pressed to get it done and make it back in time for Bryce to finalize the deal tonight."

Giovanni touched my arm tentatively. "Szerain . . . has other gold," he said in a strangled voice, expression agonized. Turek let out a strange whine, as if he knew what Giovanni referred to.

"Where?" I asked.

His throat worked. "Long, long ago, he created eleven discs of gold. Nearly pure. Each disc is embossed with exquisite imagery, the fruit of a century of labor . . . and his genius." His shoulders sagged. "They are deeply precious to him."

I took a moment to process the stark difference in the young artist's demeanor from the anger that had driven him up until this point. Though Giovanni was furious with Szerain, he wouldn't callously destroy Szerain's most precious work.

"We'll think of something else," I said, but I couldn't hide my uncertainty. "Maybe one of the other lords can help. Seretis, maybe. Or Elofir."

Turek huffed. "Only Rhyzkahl and Szerain amass gold. Szerain for art, and Rhyzkahl to feed his lust for opulence."

Giovanni's expression turned bleak. "It seems the discs are the only hope for Elinor." He scrubbed his hands over his face. "Please . . ."

"Then I guess we'll have to use the discs," I said with a tight, forced smile. "Isn't that peachy. I get to be the chick who melts down the Ark of the Covenant."

"Dahn!" Turek roared. He stretched to his full height, clawed hands crooked as if poised to rip flesh apart. "This iniquity shall *not* come to pass." With each word, the protective dome flickered.

I scrambled to my feet and fought the instinctive urge to get

the hell away from him. Instead, I jerked my chin up and planted
my hands on my hips. "Fuck your iniquity!" I yelled back, channeling my frustration and desperation. Turek hissed menacingly,
but I barreled on before he could do more than roar at me.
"You're essence bound to Szerain, right? Well, your bro is in
deep shit. He's hiding from Xharbek in a dimensional pocket,
and it's only a matter of time before Xharbek locates him, breaks
through, and has him in his grasp." My blood pounded in my
ears. "I can help Szerain. I truly believe that. Except that I *can't*
because I keep getting blindsided by dream-visions of Elinor's
life, thanks to Szerain sticking her essence onto mine. In order
to have any hope of rescuing Szerain, I need to shut Elinor up,
which means I need to rescue her first, which means I need to
summon a Jontari imperator, which means I need a graphene
net, which means I need fifty pounds of motherfucking pure
gold *now*!"

Turek very slowly lowered his hands but remained silent,
eyes on me in a manner that seemed both disapproving and ag-
gressively reproachful.

"Oh, and, um." I cleared my throat, feeling abruptly self-
conscious after my impassioned tirade. "I was also hoping you'd
come back with us and help make contact with Szerain."

The demon didn't speak for another dozen heartbeats then
finally rumbled a low, "Kri."

"Er. 'Kri'? Yes?" My brow furrowed. "To which part?"

"I will grant you the discs, Kara Gillian," he said. "And I will
go to Earth to seek Szerain."

My knees wobbled in relief. "Really? Oh man, thanks. You
have no idea—" I stopped at Turek's *hsst*—a sound that meant
stop talking in every language ever.

The savik eyed me for a moment more, then he lifted all four
hands before him, as if in supplication. The air above his palms
shimmered and coalesced into three gold discs in each hand.
Twelve discs, not eleven. *Called from a dimensional pocket*, I
realized. Stored in the same manner as the essence blades. They
remained ever so slightly transparent, as if Turek hadn't *quite*
called them fully in. Each was about the size of a CD, but nearly
a half inch thick. Delicate runes I didn't recognize adorned the
edges, and the sculpted face of a different lord gazed from each
of eleven discs, so exquisite I wouldn't have been at all surprised
to hear one speak. The face on the twelfth was unfinished, with
ghostly hints of features waiting to be born.

Giovanni lifted his hand toward them. "They . . . have changed. He has breathed life into them."

"They're incredible," I murmured. How the hell could I even think of melting these down?

"Szerain must be freed, Kara Gillian," Turek said, voice low and adamant, as if he could divine the direction of my thoughts.

I sighed out a breath and nodded. "Right. Priority one."

Giovanni gazed at the discs, his face drawn down in an expression of misery. Pellini leaned in for a closer look. "Maybe we should weigh them to make sure there's enough."

Turek slammed both pairs of hands together, and the discs vanished. "The quantity is sufficient, disciple of Kadir," he hissed. "I will not call forth the twelve again until the time comes to relinquish them for the net."

Unabashed, Pellini let out a dramatic sigh of relief. "Thank *god*. Now I don't have to carry that crap home!"

Chapter 26

We stepped out of the tree tunnel into bright sunlight reflecting off brilliant green-blue sea—and into a gag-inducing stench of rotten fish and seaweed.

Giovanni clapped a hand over his mouth and stumbled a few feet off the path before puking. Pellini cursed long and colorfully, as if foul language could drive the stink away. I settled for holding my nose and breathing shallowly while I got my bearings.

Behind the grove rose a steep mountainside covered in fire-damaged forest. A hundred feet before us, a cliff dropped to wet sand dotted with tide pools and blanketed with thousands upon thousands of dead fish and sea creatures. A natural stone arch connected the mainland mountain to a massive sea stack, on top of which rested the palace of Seretis and Rayst—though "villa" was a far better description for their residence.

It was clear a major storm had recently swept through. Trees were snapped, and detritus lay tumbled among the rotting fish. Whole sections of the villa terraces had collapsed, and the roof of the seaside wing was missing. The stone arch, however, still appeared intact and sturdy, and the shimmer of arcane reinforcements provided an extra measure of reassurance.

"Hurricane," I said as we started across the arch. "Or demon realm equivalent. I've been through enough big storms to recognize the aftermath, but I've never heard of one causing a fish kill this large."

Atop the villa, a cluster of syraza perched, tissue-thin wings spread to catch the sun. As we reached the middle of the arch, one vaulted into the air and arrowed toward us. My hand went to my gun, and I noted that Pellini already had his out and trained on the demon. Logic railed at me to draw mine, but I hesitated for reasons I couldn't name. Turek remained quiescent, yet he might have been poised to spring into action, for all I knew.

The syraza landed and pushed off in a graceful bound toward us. Recognition finally clicked in.

"Eilahn!" I squealed, racing forward to throw my arms around her. She gave a trilling cry, sweeping me into her arms and enfolding me in her wings.

"You're not mad at me?" I asked. I still felt guilty for having Idris dismiss her back to the demon realm without her consent.

"No," she replied in a voice chiming with crystalline tones. "Had our positions been reversed, I would have done the same to protect you." She finally eased her embrace enough to gaze down at me with wide violet eyes. "And the timing was fortuitous. I am needed here to aid with the anomalies. Oh, but it is good to see that you are well."

We hugged again, like best friends reuniting after decades apart, then turned to the others to make introductions. Pellini knew Eilahn already, and apparently she and Turek were well acquainted to judge by their exchange of comfortable greetings.

"Giovanni, this is Eilahn," I said. "She was my guardian on Earth for quite some time. Eilahn, this is—"

"I know Giovanni Racchelli," Eilahn said. "Returned from death. Fair greetings, *kibit*."

I blinked in surprise, not only because I'd never considered the possibility that the two had met, but also because Giovanni was blushing furiously. Did it have something to do with Eilahn calling him "little snake?"

I cleared my throat and regarded them. "Anything y'all want to share?"

Eilahn bared her teeth in a syraza smile, obviously highly amused by whatever was embarrassing Giovanni. "It is nothing of import," she said, eyes flashing with humor. "What brings you to Seretis's realm?"

Now I was even more determined to find the truth about Giovanni "Little Snake" Racchelli—but it was going to have to wait until I took care of the more pressing business. Damn it. "Earth's a mess," I said and gave her the quick and dirty recap. "Michael may be able to help, so I need to speak to Seretis or Rayst."

"An as-yet-unmanageable anomaly manifested over the southern pole two days past," she said. "All available lords work a grueling rotation to counter it. Rayst is there now, but Seretis rests on the east terrace. Cheytok will lead you to him." She gestured toward a streak of blue rushing in our direction from the villa. "I will find you when your business is complete." Her wings vibrated and her eyes glittered with excitement. "I have a surprise for you!" She gave me a quick embrace then flew off before I could respond.

"Alrighty then," I said, amused, then continued on toward the villa. Near the end of the arch, the faas Cheytok met us, looking for all the world like a furry, six-legged lizard.

"Come come come come come!" it said in a way that reminded me of a fussing squirrel. "Way to palace is this. Way to Seretis is this." The faas scurried off ahead, its rich blue fur glistening in the sun. "Come come come come!"

Pellini snorted. "Impatient little bastard."

"The faas tend to be *very* eager," I said, smiling.

We followed Cheytok through a trellised garden that had no doubt been breathtakingly beautiful at one time. Now dead vines covered the frameworks, and rock and leaf debris littered the ground and path. The villa itself hugged the contours of the sea stack, giving the impression that it was a natural part of the landscape. The structure would have been stunning were it not for the damage wrought by storms and the neglect that resulted from everyone being otherwise busy dealing with near cataclysmic world events.

As we walked, I kept a sharp lookout for Seretis's ptarl, Lannist. I'd only seen him from a distance a few times and preferred to keep it that way. Bryce had told me how the demahnk dislodged a massive chunk of masonry to distract Seretis from forming the essence bond with Bryce. The ploy had ultimately failed, but the act placed Lannist high on my do-not-trust list.

Cheytok chittered continual disapproval at our human pace but faithfully led us to the east terrace, one of the few that remained intact. Seretis sat on a demon realm equivalent of a fainting couch, though I had a feeling he'd been reclining moments before.

He stood as we approached. "Kara Gillian," he said in warm greeting, then he took my hands and kissed my cheek. "Eilahn informed me of your arrival. You and your associates are most welcome." He smiled to the others and gave them a make-yourself-at-home gesture toward couches and cushions.

"You look like hell, Seretis," I said, returning the cheek kiss.

No point in pretending I didn't notice the bags under his blood-shot eyes, the lines of exhaustion in his face, or the droop in his bearing.

He chuckled. "And here I had convinced myself that I am yet as handsome as ever."

"You'll always be that," I reassured him then grinned. "I have absolute faith in your power of sexiness."

This time he laughed, full and genuine, and a touch of the grim despondency left his face.

"Your presence is a treasure, but what brings you to my realm during such upheaval?"

"Szerain is fully himself again," I said in a low voice, "He's in hiding, hunted by Xharbek."

His mouth tightened, and he traced a glowing pygah above himself, followed by an anti-eavesdropping sigil. Calm and privacy.

I placed my hand on his arm. "I sure wish the weather would cool off back home," I offered as a change of subject. "Still hot as hell some days." It was a bit dicey telling Seretis about Xharbek and his perfidy, since the truth about him and the other ten demahnk was one of the verboten topics that could trigger the lords' vicious headaches.

But Seretis showed no sign of pain, only focused control. "I have been practicing," he said softly.

Relieved, I nodded. I knew exactly what he meant. Practicing to mentally dip briefly into a taboo topic while channeling his thoughts in the "acceptable" areas so as to avoid the headache. I suspected the support from his essence bond with Bryce gave him the stability, insight, and edge he needed to practice—even with the screwed up ways between the dimensions preventing direct telepathic contact.

I gave his arm a squeeze and then, for what seemed like the millionth time, told the tale of the past two months, especially the part about the rakkuhr, the rifts, and the Jontari. I wrapped up with a reminder about Szerain's plight, while skirting the Xharbek part, then I moved on to my primary business. "Here's the thing," I said. "I think Michael and his talent of seeing the lords could be a huge help in locating—"

Seretis held up a hand, stopping me. "I understand your dilemma, and while I agree that Michael's talents could prove useful, I cannot allow him to return to Earth with you. I swore to keep him safe."

"And you've done that. Now let me take care of him for a while."

"I cannot allow it," Seretis said firmly. "He is under my protection."

"I don't need care sitters," a baritone voice said. "I want to go."

I turned to see a strapping young man barely into his twenties standing in the doorway. Michael Moran.

"Michael," Seretis began gently, but Michael stepped onto the terrace, jaw set.

"I *want* to go, Seretis," he said, voice clear and strong. "You worry about me, but I'm lots and lots better now, and I want to help Earth."

He *was* better, I realized. Even more so than when I'd seen him a year ago. Back on Earth, his childhood head injury had left him able to understand simple instructions and situations, and not much more. The lords' healing and a caring environment had made all the difference in the world.

Seretis moved to him. "There is great peril there."

"There's big peril here, too! All the fish ran smack dab into peril." Michael sighed. "You've been real nice to me, but I did some bad bad stuff. Maybe helping out is how I'm supposed to make up for the bad."

"Hang on, Michael," I said. "You were used by your sister, no ifs ands or buts. You have absolutely nothing to atone for."

"See? You're nice, too," he said with a sweet smile. "But both of you listen up, and I'll explain it so you can understand." He crouched and traced a finger across the tile. "Snails make a shiny trail behind them, y'know? They don't clean it up, 'cause they don't know any better. They're snails." He drew another line with his finger. "I made a trail behind me, too, but it's real ugly, and people got dead." He looked up, first to Seretis then to me. "I *gotta* help clean up, 'cause I'm not a snail."

"Because you know better," I murmured.

Though Seretis tried to look serious, his lips twitched. "How am I meant to counter the snail argument?"

"You're not!" Michael said. "It's the best."

Seretis gave him a fond smile. "And if I were to forbid your departure, I would be making you more a pet than a companion."

Michael grinned and leaped to his feet. "You'd need a *big* litter box!"

Seretis tipped back his head and roared in laughter then pulled Michael close in a fierce hug. "My realm is ever open to you, *ghastuk*."

"I'll come back 'cause this is my home, and you're my friend," Michael promised. "But I gotta help save the world first."

"I understand completely, and you have my eternal support," Seretis said warmly. "Cheytok, will you please help Michael pack a travel bag?"

Cheytok trilled an assent and scurried off with Michael right behind him.

"I can't get over how much he's improved," I said. The Mraztur could learn a thing or two from Michael.

"Incredible, is it not?" Seretis said. "He has far exceeded all expectations, though it is unlikely he will ever be as he would have been had the accident never occurred. But I believe that neither would his gifts have manifested."

"Really?" I cocked my head. "Talent can be, er, knocked into place like that?"

"It can be awakened." Seretis spread his hands. "Humans have fascinating innate abilities—though in most cases they are forgotten, dormant, or suppressed. In Michael the talent was always there, but his injury allowed it to blossom unhindered, given the favorable conditions."

Like the gradual increase in potency on Earth over the past few years, I mused. I was positive that particular favorable condition had also led to the expression of talents in others, such as Bryce's intuition, and Paul's computer flow connection. But before I could press Seretis for more details, Eilahn swooped in and landed on the terrace, a shoebox-sized bundle of shimmering, deep orange cloth in her hands.

"I crafted these so that you might properly decorate your abode." She thrust the bundle at me, violet eyes sparkling, and wingtips quivering. "I am truly pleased that I am able to gift them to you in time for the festival of All Hallows' Eve!"

"I'm not sure I could ever hope to match your decorating enthusiasm and skill," I said, carefully unwrapping the demon silk. "But I'm sure this is—Whoa!" Tucked within the folds of silk was a delicate silver chain, and upon it hung dozens and dozens of exquisitely crafted crystalline miniature skulls and carvings of what I could only assume were species native to the demon realm. "Holy shit, Eilahn, these are incredible!" I gingerly lifted a length of chain to appreciative *oohs* and *aahs* from Pellini and Giovanni. Sunlight caught the crystal and sent flecks of colored light dancing over the terrace.

"I believe there is sufficient length to drape your front doorway," Eilahn said. "I apologize if the figurines are not sufficiently terrifying for the hordes of children who will descend upon your house to demand sweets."

"I don't think we're going to get too many children this year," I said absently as I continued to marvel at the artistry.

"No children?" Eilahn said in the same horrified tone a child might say *No Santa?*

"Oh, but it's all right!" I hurried to reassure her. "Er, because . . . all of the security guards will trick-or-treat. And I'll, uh, pass out cookies to my squad."

She trilled in relief. "That is very good. Remember to teach Fuzzykins how to assume the correct arched back posture, and she then will teach Fillion and Bumper and Cake and Squig and Granger and Dire."

"I'll get right on that as soon as I'm home," I said with what I hoped sounded like conviction. My breath caught. I'd almost forgotten. "Steeev. Eilahn, did Steeev make it back?" Steeev was the syraza who'd agreed to be Jill's guardian. Not long before the valve explosion, he'd died on Earth after being shot by a sniper.

Her smile dimmed. "He returned alive," she said. "But the ways closed while he was still in passage through the void. He remains yet in stasis."

"Will he recover?"

"There is great hope yet," she said to my relief. "He is under the care of the syraza matriarchs." She embraced me again, enfolding me in her wings. "You are to stay safe throughout these troubles."

Tears pricked my eyes as I hugged her back. "I will. And you'd better do the same."

"Tah agahl lahn," she said. It meant *I love you*, with the kind of deep and eternal love that went beyond family or lovers.

"Tah agahl lahn," I echoed.

She thrummed deep in her chest then reluctantly released me. "Michael awaits you by the arch."

We said our goodbyes to Seretis with the promise to give Bryce a full update, then my little troop headed out to make the trek to the grove.

As we passed into the sadly neglected garden, a cool breeze

spun a vortex around me then died to stillness. A subtle fresh-
ness replaced the fish rot stench, and the sound of waves and
demons and life faded to silence.

The hair on the back of my neck lifted. Unsettled, I turned to
find Pellini, Giovanni, and Turek frozen mid-stride, much as the
soldiers had been at the Spires when Kadir arrived. Except not
even their eyes moved. A bubble of golden light formed around
us while the outside world darkened, as if a dimmer switch was
being turned down. A dimensional pocket, like the one Szerain
had pulled me into.

I startled as a man appeared beside Pellini, fine featured with
rich brown skin touched with bronze. Bare-legged and bare-
footed, he wore a simple mid-thigh tunic of saffron-yellow silk.
Seretis's ptarl, Lannist, in human form. And, if my theories were
correct, his father as well.

The blackness of the void closed in beyond the bubble, trap-
ping us together. In one stroke, Lannist had eliminated the possibility of interruptions—or my departure. My stomach
clenched, but I forced myself to cling to annoyance at the universe for throwing one more shittastic thing my way. And right
now it was a lot better to be ticked than terrified.

I affected a bored expression and folded my arms over my
chest. "Nice mannequin trick with my boys," I said, nudging my
chin toward Pellini and the others. "But this conference room of
yours could use some furniture." I glared at him. "What do you
want?"

"It is you who sought me, Kara Gillian." His voice flowed
over me like soft rain.

I graced Lannist with a tight, cold smile. "There's a big difference in watching for a snake in the grass and going out
searching for one."

His brow furrowed gently above liquid brown eyes. "Is that
what I am to you? A serpent?"

"You've kept your distance from me, so I only know you by
your masonry-shoving reputation." A chunk the size of a Volks-
wagen, according to Bryce. "In my book, that's edging toward
the slithering reptile category, though I might be unfairly ma-
ligning snakes."

"Much has changed since that moment, Kara Gillian." He
stepped to within arm's length of me.

I resisted the impulse to back away. "Gee, I hadn't noticed,
what with Earth being invaded and all."

Lovely regret fluttered over his face. "The incursions were never intended."

"Funny, that sounds like what Rhyzkahl said about the flood of rakkuhr. 'Not this soon. Not this much.'" I stabbed a finger at him. "*Someone's* grand scheme went tits up, but no one gives enough of a shit to fix it. Meanwhile, we're the ones getting screwed by rakkuhr and Jontari incursions. What the hell did y'all do in your last Demahnk Council meeting? Scratch Earth off the list then move on to who had to bring the donuts next time?"

He shook his head, the simple move fraught with grace. "You do not understand. We—"

"Like hell I don't!" I bit back my tirade and pygahed. Venting my spleen on him might make me feel better, but it wouldn't help shake loose information. "You're right," I said with a touch more calm, "I don't understand. Enlighten me."

"We strove—strive—to preserve both worlds." He spread his hands, as if in supplication. "We have failed."

My eyebrows winged up. "Ya think? Y'all blew it on a whole bunch of levels. Like how you keep the lords—your *sons,* for fuck's sake—ignorant of their heritage by controlling them with pain so they can't even think about it."

Lannist remained silent and aloof for a moment then lowered his head. "Yes. We failed them as well."

The admission of failing the lords took me aback, but I seized the opening. "Why? Why is it so important for the lords to have no clue of their parentage and origin? And what else have y'all done to fuck them over?" I scowled as he remained silent. "You want me to *understand*, but I'm stuck in the middle of someone else's game without a playbook. I'm forced to operate on what info I've pieced together through observation and the bits I've pried from others."

His lips parted as if he was about to speak, then he shuddered. For an instant it looked as if he went a little see-through around the edges, but the illusion was gone before I could be certain. Surely my mention of the lords' parentage wasn't taboo enough to affect him so?

"Lannist? You okay?" Uneasy, I strained my physical and arcane senses for sign of any other possible influence, but there was only nothingness beyond our bubble of light.

His gaze dropped to where the grove leaf lay cool against my sternum. I covered it with my hand. "Why did you want to talk to me?" I asked, eyes narrowed.

He jerked rigid as if touched by a live wire, and his eyes went wide. "Out of . . . time."

"What's happening?" I demanded. "Time for what?"

"Heed Rho." Lannist spoke the words as if each one cost a piece of his soul. "Eighteenth convergence factor less nine ascen—" His body went semi-transparent, and his chest filled with amorphous prismatic light—the true form of the demahnk. I'd seen Zack shift shape before, but it had been beautiful. This was *wrong*. Was this punishment control like the headaches that plagued the lords? But if so, from who?

"Lannist!" I watched in mounting distress as the light roiled within him. "How can I help you? What can I do?"

He fixed wide eyes on mine, gripped my shoulders with hands that had little substance, as if nothing remained but an outer membrane of energy. "Consent . . . to accept my final . . . service." His voice skittered away like shattered glass. In the span of a heartbeat, fine strands of potency like molten diamond appeared around the light in his chest, a viciously beautiful web that encased the shifting colors of his essence and constricted.

Lannist threw his head back and screamed, an inhuman sound of agony. I caught him as he sagged, his body light as tissue paper in my arms.

"No no no." Heart pounding, I knelt and took his head between my hands, pressed my forehead to his and willed him strength to counter whatever was trying to silence him. "I consent. I accept!"

"Trask." The name of Rayst's ptarl arrowed through my consciousness. "Ilana." Mzatal's ptarl. More followed that I couldn't comprehend, cut off by a searing blast of suffocating pain, gone in an instant. The last vestiges of Lannist's physical form faded, leaving only his light—compacted by the web into a white-hot sun. It hung motionless for a silent heartbeat then burst into a billion flickering particles that swirled around our bubble like glitter in a snow globe. They passed over and through me, bombarding me with images and sounds then dimming as they imparted their gifts.

A boy with raven-black hair stands naked atop a mountain, arms stretched wide and head tipped back to catch the sun. Mzatal.

A youthful priest sits upon the steps of a graceful temple, three shining pyramids beyond him in the distance. Vahl.

A white-blond man in a grain field drops his scythe to scoop up tow-headed twins who run laughing to him. Rhyzkahl.

A great wolf with fur the color of pale beach sand bounds through a highland meadow.

I jerked in shock. That was Rhyzkahl as well. I *knew*.

The wolf stops, gazes up expectantly.

A dragon with scales like flakes of obsidian and eyes of molten gold circles down to land in the grass.

Chills swept over me. Mzatal—terrible and beautiful.

A willowy being with captivating dual-pupiled eyes stands atop a shining pavilion of pale stone columns.

Image after image. Hundreds. Too many to process, but each indelibly burned into my essence. Amkir. Seretis. Rayst. Elofir. Szerain. Vrizzar. Jesral. Kadir. Dozens of wondrous creatures of legend. The lords not only had human mothers, but all save Kadir had lived on Earth for a time, in full control of their paternal shape-shifting abilities. Happy. Free.

One last particle struck me between the eyes. It carried no image or sound, only the feel of Lannist and the immersive plea of *save them*.

And then all trace of him was gone.

I remained on my knees, hugging myself. Grief for the lords clogged my throat, and sobs racked my chest. Even quick-tempered Amkir—who I utterly despised—had once been soft-hearted enough to jump into an icy river to save a stray dog. These rich and full lives of the lords had been stolen, but *why?* What possible reason could exist to commit such an atrocity? And now Lannist was dead because he'd exposed it.

Zack had spoken obliquely of the Demahnk Council and the "others," the enforcers who held him and the rest of the demahnk accountable through ancient agreements, oaths, and decrees. One of Lannist's images was of an unfamiliar creature on an Ekiri pavilion. And I'd seen dual-pupiled eyes like that before—carved in bas relief in the anteroom of Szerain's summoning chamber. Had Lannist been trying to impart that the enforcers were, in fact, the Ekiri? Yet, according to the reyza Kehlirik, the Ekiri had left for a new world millennia ago.

Whoever these enforcers were, I had a sick feeling Lannist had purposely defied them in order to give me information—and paid dearly. The entire incident was a glimpse into the high-stakes game played by the demahnk, and a terrifying demonstration of the power and reach of what I was up against.

Eighteenth convergence factor less nine . . . ascendants? As-

cending? It didn't make any sense to me, but clearly it was important. *Heed Rho.* That one was easy. But what about *Ilana* and *Trask*? Was Lannist telling me to heed the ptarls of Mzatal and Rayst? Or was he warning me against them?

And what would happen to Seretis now? This ugly turn of events with Lannist was sure to affect him. Rhyzkahl had been shattered when Zack broke their ptarl bond. Would the death of a ptarl have the same effect?

Still raw from the visions and feeling three sizes too big for my skin, I staggered to my feet and took stock of the situation. It didn't take long: the situation sucked ass. The dimensional pocket remained intact, and Pellini, Giovanni, and Turek were still statuefied.

"This is lovely," I muttered. I couldn't see or sense anything beyond the bubble of light, and reaching into the darkness was like pushing my hand into liquid mercury. We were stuck in here.

Cold tendrils of fear wound through me. Fighting for control, I sought to distract myself by clinically memorizing every sensation of the bubble and filing them away for future reference. After all, soon enough I'd be reaching for Szerain and company in their dimensional pocket stronghold. Knowledge was power, right?

Yeah, well, that power wasn't doing me any good right here and now. I needed to get us out of this thing. But *how?* A demahnk had created it. Even at my best I couldn't match their abilities, and I didn't have a strand of potency to follow out this time. Hell, I couldn't even shape basic sigils without the help of the nexus, and I felt absolutely nothing of it here, no matter how hard I tried. Meanwhile, Pellini and the others appeared to be in some sort of stasis, while I continued to breathe and have normal metabolic functions. Would they remain frozen in place long after I died of dehydration? Or would I suffocate instead?

Or maybe I'm not completely out of options, I thought as I slapped my hand over the leaf and called to Rho. Though I couldn't sense even the faintest whisper of the grove, I envisioned the one in Seretis's realm as a distress beacon beaming an urgent, repeating S.O.S.

Nothing. I pygahed and focused, intensified my distress call. Minutes ticked by.

More than a quarter of an hour later, the normal world supplanted the void. The stench of rotting fish flooded in, accompanied by a wash of sound: waves, the calls of demons, wind through trees. Pellini crashed into me where I stood gasping in relief.

"Jeez, Kara." He grabbed my arms to steady me as I staggered. "Didn't see you stop. Sorry."

"Uh, no prob," I said, trying to get my heart rate under control. Apparently time didn't pass for statues. I considered telling the others what I'd learned and what befell Lannist, but immediately realized how dangerous that could be. I had shielding from the mindreading lords and demahnk, but the others didn't. Lannist had sacrificed himself to pass on the information, and I intended to keep it safe.

Pellini's gaze focused beyond me. "We have company."

I turned to see a demahnk a dozen feet away, pearlescent wings glimmering in the sunlight. Trask. My distress call through Rho had brought in the one-demahnk cavalry to pop the dimension bubble, but I had no idea if he was ally or enemy. "Hey, Trask." I gave a casual wave and smile. "How's things?"

"Grievous, with the calamitous southern anomaly, Kara Gillian," he said, his voice like soothing chimes. "Seretis is needed." He remained cool as ever, giving no hint that anything was amiss, even though he'd just released me from the bubble and had to know by now that one of his fellow demahnk was gone. According to Zack, the demahnk lived in constant telepathic connection. Was Trask maintaining an implacable demeanor in order to protect enemy interests, or save his own skin, or snub me, or all of the above? Even a brief knowing look would have taken the edge off my unease.

Instead, my worry escalated. With Lannist out of the picture, how could Seretis possibly cope with day to day pressures, much less hidden enemies?

"I am ready." Seretis stood at the garden entrance, one hand on the stone arch as if for support. A droplet of sweat trickled down the side of a face rigid with a megadose of focused control.

He fixed haunted eyes on mine. "I am ready."

Those three little words told me everything I needed to know. Though the unthinkable loss of Lannist wasn't as overtly devastating as a broken bond, it still struck Seretis to the core. Yet he wasn't going to show any vulnerability. Not now. He was undeniably the most "human" of the lords I knew, but maybe that aspect contributed to his immense strength in the face of adversity. Other lords considered Seretis a minor player. Kadir dismissed him as weak. They were wrong.

I gave him a nod. "Yeah, I guess you are."

He approached, briefly placed a trembling hand on my shoulder, then continued past to Trask. A second later, they vanished.

"What got into him?" Pellini asked.

A vision rose of a distraught Seretis singing to soothe a panicked infant Kadir. "He's exhausted," I said. "And he has no choice but to keep on fighting." I blinked back tears and started toward the grove. "Let's pick up Michael and get out of here."

Chapter 27

Cool sea air touched with the scent of conifers welcomed us upon our arrival in Mzatal's grove. I caught myself smiling as we trekked up the tree tunnel toward late afternoon sunlight. I'd missed this place more than I realized. "Pellini and I will go for Elinor's journal and search the upper levels . . ."

The rest of my words lodged in my throat as I stepped out of the grove. I was vaguely aware of Pellini catching my elbow to steady me. My chest squeezed tight, and a weird numbness crept through my whole body. Mzatal's palace still occupied the top of the sea cliff ahead, but it was all *wrong*. The balconies he loved and *needed* as a refuge from the confines of indoors had been sheered away, lost to the sea far below. The demon-glass that had given an all-window effect to the entire structure was gone as if blasted away from the inside out, leaving a stark skeleton of wood and basalt held together by arcane reinforcement. Where the waterfall should have cascaded from the midst of the palace to tumble to the sea pool far below, a sickly trickle of brown sludge stained the cliff face.

Someone was talking to me. Pellini. I felt his arm around my waist, supporting me.

"We can sit for a few," he said gently. "Take it nice and slow."

I wanted to collapse right there, sob my heart out and wallow in the bullshit unfairness of it all. But I couldn't. I *wouldn't*. Mzatal didn't have that luxury, and neither did I. Not as long as we still held hope for our worlds. I disengaged from Pellini, squared my shoulders, and swallowed the pain. "Better get moving," I said, voice thick, and started down the basalt steps toward the palace.

Pellini didn't say a word as he followed, but I felt his eyes on my back.

"This place is a big ol' mess," Michael said.

I glanced at him over my shoulder and plastered on a smile. "No worse than other places. And see? Mzatal has fixed it up a little with potency."

"Mzatal's sad," he said as we reached the bottom of the ravine and started the climb to the entrance.

"I'm sure he is." I fought to keep my tone light. "It had to be hard to see his home destroyed."

"I mean now, silly."

I whirled. "You see him?"

He nodded earnestly. "Uh huh, but I dunno *where* he is."

"What does it look like?" I resisted the urge to shake the details from him. "What's he doing?"

"He's smack dab in the middle of a big, black circle, sitting on one knee." Michael squinched his eyes as if trying to see better. "There's a blue house and grass. He's going like this on the black part." He wiggled and waved his fingers.

Emotion squeezed my chest. "That's my house." Mzatal was on the nexus, in contact with my sigils. "Can you see anything else?"

"Nope, that's it. All gone now!" He continued past me up the steps.

I followed. "How do you know he was sad?"

"I just know," he said, as if it was the most natural thing in the world.

Why was he sad? My worry ratcheted up a few more notches. We needed to finish up here and get the hell back to Earth ASAP.

A bellow came from off to our right. I looked to see a reyza swoop toward us from atop the column, the basalt pillar Mzatal used for arcane training.

"Incoming," Pellini said, hand on his weapon.

"And it's not large enough to be Gestamar," I said, shading my eyes.

"Summoner," the reyza boomed as he overflew us.

"Kehlirik?" I called back in surprise. "What are you doing here?" Kehlirik was one of Rhyzkahl's demons, and the first reyza I'd ever summoned. With his amiable personality and passion for popcorn and Earth novels, he'd become my favorite demon to summon. Despite his ties to Rhyzkahl, I considered him as close to a friend as any demon, apart from Eilahn. In fact, not long after Rhyzkahl betrayed me, he'd offered me subtle help during an ugly battle with the Mraztur.

"We good?" Pellini asked.

"I think so," I said.

Kehlirik landed nearby, on an outcropping beside the palace entrance. "After the Sky Reaper clans overtook Rhyzkahl's realm, Gestamar and Ilana gave sanctuary to many of his sworn demons."

I grimaced. "It sucks that you were driven out."

"It is done. It is past." He shook out his wings then folded them close. "We are here."

"I'm glad to see you safe and unharmed." I scanned the cliff and sky and palace roof. Not another demon to be seen. That was unusual. "Where are the others?"

"Ilana is at the southern pole with the anomaly, and all others are on patrol," Kehlirik said. "I watch here. Mzatal's realm is well protected by arcane means, but he is away, and the Jontari are relentless."

"I am grateful for your service, honored one," I said. "I will see you again when we leave."

Kehlirik gave a soft whistle of acknowledgement and took flight, buffeting us with his powerful upstroke.

"Let's get this done so we can go home," I said to the others.

We continued through the open doorway of the palace and stopped in the central atrium. With all the windows gone, the floors abruptly ended in open space eighty stories above the rocky sea shore. Not a place to be wandering around at night without a flashlight. "Turek, Giovanni, and Michael. I need you to stay here, please."

"I'll guard," Michael said. "Don't worry."

"Good deal," I said with a smile. "Make sure no one gets too close to the edge. Turek, could I speak to you for a moment?" The demon dipped his head in assent, and we stepped away from the others. "Rhyzkahl gave me a description of the gimkrah, but I don't trust him. Do you know what it looks like?"

Turek let out a low hiss. "A transparent sphere with a nucleus of pulsing crimson, caged with bands of makkas."

Huh. Rhyzkahl hadn't lied—about that much, at least. "Thanks. Pellini and I will be back soon."

"Kara Gilliannnn!"

A faas streaked across the room to excitedly twine around

and through my legs like an oversized meth-crazed cat, sending us both into a chaotic tumble of limbs and blue fur.

"Jekki!" I squeezed him in a hug as he snuffled my face in greeting. "I didn't expect to see you here. Kehlirik told me all the demons were gone."

Jekki snapped upright, quivering in outrage. "Dahn dahn dahn! Protect allllll inside. Tend Mzatal. Tend Janice Massi!"

Grinning, I clambered to my feet. "She's very lucky to have you taking care of her, but I bet she's ready to get home." Even though Earth was a mess, I doubted the demon realm held fond memories for her.

Jekki cocked his head. "Is home here!"

"And a lovely home it is," I said with a serious nod. "Can you take us to her?"

Chittering happily, Jekki sped down the broad spiral staircase, while Pellini and I followed at a more reasonable pace. I expected Jekki to stop on the next floor, since that's where the guest rooms were, but to my surprise the faas descended one more level.

"That's odd," I said as Jekki darted down the corridor. "The practice summoning chamber is on this floor."

Pellini gave me a sharp look. "Why would Mzatal have her here? Unless she's a summoner?"

"That's what I'm wondering." I cleared my throat. "Hey, Jekki?" I waited for the faas to race back to us. "Is Janice a summoner?"

His sinuous tail thrashed. "No summon!"

"Okay, can she use the arcane?"

"Dahn, no sigils! No arcane! Other skills!" With that he turned on his tail and dashed to the broad doors of the practice chamber.

Pellini snorted. "Yeah, I'll *bet* she has other skills."

I elbowed him in the side. "Hush."

He chuckled under his breath. "You were thinking it, too."

"Shut up." For good measure, I elbowed him again. Didn't help that he was right.

Bouncing eagerly, Jekki pulled the door open. Beyond him, a dark-haired woman crouched near the center of the room, head bent in obvious concentration as she tightened a screw on a contraption of wood and wires.

As I stepped in, she straightened and turned to face me with narrowed eyes. Her ethnicity seemed to be a mix of middle-eastern and African, but where I'd been expecting a stunning young beauty of some variety—or at least a lush body—this woman was nothing of the sort. Not only was she easily in her late forties, she looked, well, ordinary. Normal. She wasn't unattractive, yet she didn't *quite* make it to pretty. And her figure was average as well. Not particularly buxom or slender or even curvy. She was the kind of woman I saw a hundred times a day. Not at all the physical type I imagined would be hand-picked for sex trafficking to the demon realm.

"Janice?" I asked, just to be sure.

"Yes, I'm Janice Massi." Her wary gaze flicked to Pellini then returned to me.

"I'm Kara Gillian, and this is—"

"I know who you are." Her tone held zero friendliness.

I kept the smile on my face. I completely understood donning prickly armor as a means to cope with trauma. She'd probably heard of me through Rhyzkahl or Mzatal. "Then that saves us from a boring round of introductions. Anyway, we're here to take you back to Earth." I winced. "If you want, that is. Things are pretty hairy back there."

Janice glanced at her contraption then turned that penetrating gaze on me again. "Rhyzkahl." She lifted her chin, expression fierce. "He's with you on Earth?"

"Yes, but don't worry. You won't have to see him."

"I *will* see him," she said, voice intense.

"Fair enough." At least he hadn't broken her spirit. She deserved the chance to give him a piece of her mind if she wanted—and I'd sure as hell grab any chance to eavesdrop on that particular exchange. "We'll be leaving soon," I said. "Hopefully, no longer than an hour."

"I'll be ready," she snapped then stalked to the door, bumping my shoulder with hers on the way out.

Pellini and I watched her go.

"She's going to need a *lot* of therapy," I said with a sigh.

"With any luck it'll be right after she rips Rhyzkahl's balls off," Pellini muttered.

"Can't say I'd blame her if she did." I crouched before Jekki and did my best imitation of a faas chitter-click to get his full attention. "Jekki, this is really important. Do you know where Mzatal keeps the master gimkrah?"

He cocked his head. "Dahn. Secret for Mzatal. Mzatal keep safe!"

"Thanks, Jekki," I said with a pained smile. "Good to know it's nice and safe." Jekki was utterly loyal, damn it. Any attempt to wheedle, cajole, or force one of Mzatal's secrets out of him would be a waste of time and breath. I scritched the top of his head and straightened.

"At least it's not gone," Pellini said. His expression turned puzzled as he examined Janice's contraption. "Is this a *seismograph*?"

"Huh?" I moved closer to peer at it. A flat base supported an upright piece of wood, from which jutted another, longer arm of wood. A pen at the end of the arm drew a wavy line on a roll of paper, and closer inspection revealed a clever little bit of arcane that unwound the roll at a slow and steady rate. The whole thing was about the size of a carry-on suitcase. "I think you're right." I reached toward the paper then yanked my hand back at Jekki's screech.

"No touch!" The tip of his tail vibrated. "Janice Massi every day watches! Much every day! Watches all!"

"All what?" I asked.

"All!" He waggled his four hands at the device. "All ga-jits! All places!"

"Gadgets? What are they for?"

"To seeeeeeee moves." With that, Jekki zipped off, apparently confident that he'd explained sufficiently.

Pellini let out a low whistle. "It *is* a seismograph."

"Go figure. We can find out what the deal is from Janice." I grimaced. "If she'll even talk to me. At least I know where Elinor's journal is. Let's get that out of the way, then we can tackle the gimkrah problem."

We made our way upstairs to the hazy arcane veil that marked the arch entrance to Mzatal's personal floor.

Pellini shook his head. "I should probably wait downstairs while you look for the stuff," he said, turning to head back the way we came. "I can check on Michael and the others, too."

"Are you kidding?" I stared at his retreating back. "No! It'll take twice as long to search on my own. Plus, I'll need your input if I run into anything arcane." I sucked in a breath. "Crap! Pellini, wait! It's Mzatal's aversions. They're affecting you." This area was heavily warded, albeit "tuned" to allow me full access. I was so used to the veil and the wards that crawled over the arch that I hadn't paid any attention to them.

Pellini stopped then pivoted, face set in a grimace of will-power as he made his way back to me. "Wonderful," he grumbled. "Even if I could push past the aversions, I'd get zapped hard."

"Killed," I corrected. "So, not the best plan. But it's cool. I have 'admin access' and can alter the wards enough to get you in . . . Shit." My throat tightened. "Except I can't manipulate the arcane." I was worlds away from the super-shikvihr on my home nexus, which meant I couldn't tap into the potency. And since these wards were attuned to *me*, Pellini couldn't act as my proxy.

"Damn," Pellini said with a sigh. "This'll really slow us down. Sorry, Kara."

The wards shimmered, bright and tantalizing. It was so stupid and frustrating. I could *see* exactly what needed to be done, which loops to adjust, what aspects to shift, where to add Pellini's resonance.

The coil of an aversion twitched. "Hang on," I said. It might have been coincidence or . . .

I envisioned a change in the outer loop of the aversion ward then reached, physically and mentally.

The loop shifted.

"Holy shit!" Pulse thrumming, I tried again. The loop bent to my will and reshaped into the new configuration. A cry of pure joy escaped me.

Beside me, Pellini gave a fist pump. "Fuck yeah, Kara! You show that ward who's boss!"

Laughing, I dashed tears from my eyes and continued to re-structure the wards. I had no doubt the demon realm potency gave me a boost, but there was more to it than that. The nexus and the super-shikvihr and Pellini had all been vital to my recovery process, but perhaps I'd become too dependent on them.

I finished the adjustments then added the sigil that integrated Pellini's resonance.

"You did it!" His whoop echoed up and down the stairs. I staggered as he pounded me on the back then yelped when he lifted me in a giant bear hug.

"Erp," I croaked.

Grinning, he set me on my feet. "Always knew you'd get it back."

He meant it, I realized. He'd never once wavered in his faith in me. I sniffled and gave him a watery smile. "Thanks. Now let's find the stuff."

We proceeded through the arch and into the corridor—without any zaps to Pellini. Here on the top floor, the damage was most evident. A foot-wide crack ran the length of the basalt corridor that had once been covered in sumptuous blue carpet. Thick timber beams reinforced with potency shored up the ceiling, and all traces of home and comfort had been stripped.

But I couldn't let emotion overcome our mission. Chest tight, I led Pellini to the solarium. It had become an oversized open air balcony, with nothing but sky at the ragged outer edge.

Pellini gulped and stuck close to the back wall. "Jesus Christ. I'm not usually afraid of heights, but this is fucking unnerving."

"I loved this room." My voice quavered. "I wish you could have seen it before all the glass was destroyed." Grief squeezed at my heart. Mzatal had loved it, too—the spaciousness of the glass ceiling and wall, and the . . .

A wry laugh escaped me. "Oh man," I said. "I just realized that Mzatal would *love* how it is now."

"Are you serious?"

"As a heart attack. He hates to be enclosed. This," I spread my arms to indicate the extra-airy floor plan, "would be right up his alley." I couldn't count the number of times I'd walked in to find him with the glass wall open to the elements, or out on the balcony—as if his essence was too powerful to be contained. I moved to within a couple of meters from the drop-off, where arcane reinforcements and shielding glimmered. "He has it warded so you can't fall off, even if you try." A tremor rumbled through the palace and shook the cliff. I retreated, *quickly*, from the edge. "But let's not push our luck."

Pellini shuddered. "I'm with you there. You said the journal's in a black enamel chest?"

"That's what Mzatal told me." I knew which chest he meant, but it wasn't in its usual spot. I had a moment of panic that it had tumbled over the edge and into the sea then spied it shoved into a corner behind a cabinet and piled chairs.

Pellini helped me pull the furniture out of the way. Sigils danced over the shiny black surface of the chest, but I had my confidence back now, and it took me less than a minute to deactivate the protections.

The drawer whispered open beneath my touch to reveal a journal bound in indigo leather embossed with the purple flow-

ers I called demon roses. Familiarity whispered through me as I
lifted it.

*The heady fragrance fills my senses. I stretch in the tangled
sheets.*

*Lord Rhyzkahl props on his elbow beside me. "Another
bloom for you, dear one."*

*Petals caress my cheek, raise gooseflesh as he draws the rose
down my throat, between my breasts. He lowers his head to kiss
me. I bury my hands in the fine silk of his hair even as he buries
himself in me.*

The journal tingled in my grasp. Elinor's memory, but I had
lived it. Even now I felt the velvet touch of the flower like the
breath of a ghost, the ripple of his muscles, the sensation of him
filling me. I remained still and allowed her experience to unfold.

*I writhe in pleasure, lost. Gasp for breath. Cry out as I pulse
around him.*

He wraps me in his arms, presses deep, groans.

We lie entwined, his hair covering us like a veil.

He murmurs in my ear. "Tah zhar lahn, zharkat."

*Cold fills my belly, and I bury my face against his neck. "For-
give me, my lord. I . . ."*

He cradles my head, silent.

My heart flutters like a caged bird.

*He kisses my forehead. Disentangles. "I will make the ar-
rangements you desire."*

Then he is gone.

In his place, amaranthine petals lie crushed upon the sheet.

The memory faded, and I drew a slow steadying breath.
Rhyzkahl *had* loved her. And he'd let her go. The arrangements
had been for her to reside at Szerain's where her art could flourish and where her new friend Giovanni lived. Rhyzkahl could
have kept her. She knew it. "But he didn't," I murmured.

"Who didn't what?" Pellini asked.

"Oh. Nothing. Sorry." I used the feel of the journal in my
hands to shake off the spell of the memory. "This is the right
journal."

Wards shimmered over its cover—not only to protect it from
the ravages of time, but also to discourage prying eyes. Yet the
protections were far too elegant and sophisticated for Elinor to
have placed them. Plus, I had admin access to these, just like all
the other wards here. Mzatal's work. Interesting and puzzling
that he would bother to ward it.

I slipped the volume into a thigh pocket of my fatigues. "All right, let's find the gimkrah. Makes sense that it would be up on this level, in his rooms."

Pellini nodded. "If you don't mind, I'm going to let you search through Mzatal's skivvies."

I gave him a bland look. "What skivvies?"

He groaned. "Okay, I did *not* need to know that the badass demonic lord goes commando."

Laughing, I began my gimkrah-hunt. Yet a thorough search of the solarium and Mzatal's rooms turned up absolutely nothing. Frustrated, I went through the plexus then back downstairs to the summoning chamber, finally returning upstairs to go through his rooms one more time.

No gimkrah.

Now what?

Chapter 28

At a loss, I sent Pellini downstairs to confer with Turek while I retreated to the rooftop terrace to consider my options.

Though the terrace itself remained intact, the parapet was gone, and no warding had been added to prevent an inadvertent plunge. There was no trace of the glass conservatory or potted plants, and the area had been swept clear of debris. I felt as if I was standing on a giant's table under the open sky.

To the west, the sea sparkled in the late afternoon sun, giving the illusion that all was right with the world. I eased to the terrace edge and peered over. Far below, waves rolled onto the tumbled basalt and black sand of the beach, nearly reaching the stone circle of Mzatal's nexus. I moved to the opposite edge and surveyed the forested hills to the east. For a mile, the trees were vibrant, safe within Mzatal's protections. Beyond that, a patchwork of unhealthy green and ashy black marked the ravages of fire, storms, and other unknown cataclysmic hazards.

Below, a shadow coiled and uncoiled at the base of the basalt training column. A demon—one of the *ilius* who kept company with Mzatal, though I couldn't tell which. From this height, the flat top of the column was clearly visible: dark grey stone surrounding a circle of utter blackness.

My stomach flip-flopped. I'd only been to the top once, but that was enough to last a lifetime. After I'd crawled my ass off the column, Mzatal told me that the dark core could consume the resolve of even the most stalwart, and hoo boy did I ever believe him. That inky nothingness hungered for life force. Being absurdly stingy, I preferred to keep my essence all to myself.

Too bad I'd eventually have to test my resolve again. The final trial for the full eleven-ring shikvihr required that it be danced around that life-sucking hole. Even though I told myself today wasn't that day, cold sweat still trickled down my sides.

I dragged my gaze away from the column and shook off its unsettling feel. Great, I'd successfully checked out the view from the roof. Why had I bothered to come up here? It wasn't as if admiring the scenery was going to find the stupid gimkrah. "Damn it, Mzatal," I muttered. "Where did you hide it?"

For the thousandth time, I mulled over the clue Giovanni found. *The gimkrah lies in wait, surrounded by emptiness, deep in the heart of darkness.* I'd originally assumed that the emptiness and heart of darkness were metaphorical references to Mzatal, but what if I'd gone completely off the rails and the clue really did describe the location? Then again, it was possible whoever wrote that passage hadn't known shit or, even if they had, their info was obsolete by now. Maybe it had never been meant to be a clue at all and was simply a poetic attempt to capture both the literal and the figurative.

That was a useless line of thought. Stumped as I was, it couldn't hurt to focus on literal locations, places surrounded by dark emptiness—

I smacked my forehead. Duh! I'd been in a place surrounded by dark emptiness twice already. A dimensional pocket. Mzatal had created pockets to safely store the three essence blades. It made total sense that he would also hide the gimkrah in one.

My exultation was short-lived. How was I supposed to find that particular pocket? After Szerain hid his essence blade, Mzatal and I spent a whole month preparing a ritual to locate it. I didn't have the skill or the time for that.

Except I was looking for *Mzatal's* dimensional hidey-hole. I'd successfully tracked Szerain to his stronghold with only a trace of its arcane scent, and I had an even better chance of connecting with Mzatal's signature since it was a part of me. I could use his nexus as a starting point for the search. As much as I dreaded a trek down—and back up—the bazillion cliff steps, it was my next logical move.

Movement caught my eye as the ilius scaled the column in a fluid motion that was little more than flashes of color in camouflaging smoke. At the top, it turned my way and stretched itself tall and straight, reminiscent of a meerkat. A greeting posture. I waved and suppressed the urge to holler at it to be careful so close to that horrible darkness.

Darkness.

Deep in the heart of darkness. Deep in the void-core of the column?

I did a fist pump and ran downstairs.

Turek, Michael, and Giovanni went to round up Janice, while Pellini and I exited and made our way around the palace.

"You're sure about this?" Pellini asked as we followed the path along the ravine's lip, away from the cliff and sea.

I winced. "I can't be positive the column is the key to finding the gimkrah, but it fits the clue, and it fits Mzatal."

His dark eyes narrowed. "You don't know what you're getting into."

"I'm not getting *into* anything," I retorted then took a deep breath. "If I'm right, I should be able to sense the gimkrah from up there. I won't do anything stupid."

"Not on purpose," Pellini grumbled. "But you getting sucked into a soul-hungry void could put a hitch in our plans."

Scowling, I stuffed my fists into my pockets then had to unstuff them to clamber over a boulder. "We need the gimkrah."

"Yeah, I guess," he muttered.

"What's gotten into you?" I shot him a disparaging look. "If you don't want to back me up, don't."

"It's not that," he snapped.

We hiked up the hill to the base of the column in silence. At the top, I turned to him and folded my arms. "What is it then?"

He looked away. "I have a bad feeling."

"Can you elaborate?"

"Not with anything substantial." He pulled out a camo bandana and mopped his face. "Sorry, Kara. I know we need the gimkrah. I just can't shake this feeling of a crap storm on the horizon."

I exhaled. "Fair enough. I'm the last person to dismiss a bad feeling as bullshit. All I can do is promise to be quick and doubly careful." I offered him a reassuring smile. "Trust me. I don't want to be up there any longer than necessary."

"I'll be here," he said, folding his arms over his broad chest.

I ran my hands over the basalt of the column, murmured to it. In answer, the stone flowed and morphed, creating narrow stairs that wound up around the thirty-foot column. As I climbed, I kept my eyes on the steps ahead of me. The last time I'd made this ascent, falling was my only worry. This time I knew what awaited me at the top, and a misstep seemed a minor concern.

But knowing what to expect meant I could prepare, and by the time I reached the top I had four pyghahs drifting around my head like a glowing special effects crown of chill-out. Calm and cool. That was me.

I eased off the steps and onto the foot and a half wide circle of stone that surrounded the void hole. The blackness pulled at me with invisible fingers that promised eternal un-life in death. Breath shuddering, I added a fifth pygah sigil to the others. Better. Somewhat. At least I could concentrate without imagining the Icy Claw of Doom reaching for me out of the depths.

Faint traces of arcane flickered around the edge of the hole—not that I was even sure it *was* a hole. Not a bit of light penetrated, which made it appear less like a shadowy well and more like a two-dimensional circle of unrelieved black. I knelt to get a better look, absurdly pleased that I did so by choice rather than because my legs buckled in fear—like the last time I was up here. Thousands of teensy sigils no larger than sugar ants formed a barely detectable band around the perimeter. Mzatal's work, and I marveled that he could create so many so small. I peered closer then straightened. *Pellini was right. It's stupid for me to risk myself up here. We should go home.*

No. I caught myself before I stood. Aversion wards, and seriously powerful ones at that. Fortunately, as with all of Mzatal's wards, they were attuned to me. Yet even so, they emitted a muted aversion—the cumulative effect of their sheer numbers, I suspected.

Interesting. This was clearly Mzatal's next layer of protection in case anyone got past the initial fear of the void itself. I sat back on my heels, daring to hope. With a security system this meticulous, he had to be protecting something, and that something just might be the gimkrah.

Now to tap into the core and see what I could find. I pushed down the incessant gnaw of the aversions and focused on the center of the darkness, visualizing and feeling everything I could remember of Lannist's dimensional pocket. A whisper of familiarity brushed my senses. Encouraged, I closed my eyes and recalled the description of the gimkrah, creating my best-guess vision of it in my mind's eye. First, a ball of crystal. Then pulsing red at its center. So far so good. I had a nice, clear image. The last part was to form a cage around it with bands of pinkish metal. How many bands though?

Eleven, I thought on wild impulse. The lords' magic number. I mentally added eleven bands to my structure.

I startled as the image snapped into 3D crystal clarity. The red deepened to a maroon shot with flickers of crimson lightning. Unfamiliar runes marked the bands like etchings made with ink born of the void. Okay, I had my gimkrah. Concentrating, I called in the feel of a dimensional pocket around it. A bubble of golden light in utter darkness.

The gimkrah hovered in that bubble, so real I felt sure I could reach out and simply take it. Was it possible I'd somehow called it to me? I didn't want to open my eyes and break whatever mojo I had going. I tried reaching for it, but it lay inches beyond my fingertips. I stretched farther. Just a little more, and . . . I'd . . . have it.

My eyes flew open as I tipped forward. I scrabbled at the lip of the hole, but it might as well have been greased ice. Before I could draw breath to cry out, the darkness swallowed me.

Nothingness. No sense of my body. No sense of falling.

Silence.

Every thought an eternity.

Shit.

Voices whisper. Thousands upon thousands. A few that I recognize surface in the sea of murmurs.

"Zharkat." Mzatal.

"This is not as it should be. What is happening?" Elinor.

"There must be another way." Rhyzkahl.

"You wouldn't do it unless you were confident of success." Jill.

"Kara! Get your shoes on. Time to go!" My mom.

"Believe that you're already there." Pellini.

"Sweetling, pay attention." Tessa.

Somewhere in my nothingness, I remember anger.

I'm not your sweetling! I'm not—

I remember myself.

I am. I am here. I am Kara Gillian.

And I had no intention of becoming the late Kara Gillian.

Pay attention. I opened my non-physical senses and reminded myself what it felt like to have a body, to breathe, to see. Reminded myself of the feel of stone beneath me.

The stone of the column. I'd been on top reaching for the gimkrah and lost my balance . . .

Realization slammed home. The vision of the gimkrah had lured me closer—and straight into a trap. Like the opposite of an aversion ward. Mzatal's third layer of protection? But it had been so powerful, as if intended for me rather than attuned to me. Whatever it was, I had no intention of waiting around to die like a mouse on a glue board. Screw that.

I *believed* I was on solid ground, and stone chilled my palms and knees. *I am here.* My breath hissed through clenched teeth. Shadows flickered. Where there were shadows, there was light. I commanded the light to intensify, and it obeyed.

There was still blackness everywhere, but instead of the void's nothingness, it was that of a dimly lit obsidian chamber no larger than my living room. A scattering of blue-white sigils twinkled on the high ceiling, giving an impression of the openness of a night sky. The only furnishing was a black glass pedestal topped by a matching basin. Mzatal's signature frequency permeated everything, like a familiar and comforting scent.

"Well, aren't you a clever girl." Zack.

Except I knew it wasn't Zack.

I scrambled to my feet and peered into the gloom for Xharbek. "Can't you come up with your own persona?"

"Is this more to your liking?" A lanky man with short, nearly colorless hair appeared beside the basin. Carl the morgue tech.

"Not really," I said. "But it might look better if you were a few billion miles from here. Let's try it and see."

He laughed—a disturbing sound, especially coming from the customarily dour Carl. "I wouldn't want to miss the entertainment." He passed his hand over the basin, and an image of the gimkrah appeared above it.

"*You* lured me into the trap," I said.

"I only tweaked Mzatal's wards. You were the one who reached."

For the bait Xharbek had dangled, damn it. "Fine. Whatever. All my fault. Why the trap?"

He waved away the gimkrah hologram. "It seemed the easiest solution."

"It must really burn your bacon that you have to resort to a namby-pamby void trap." I made a *tsking* sound. "Here you are, a big bad demahnk, desperate to take me out of the game, but your demahnk constraints prevent you from acting directly unless you want to end up shredded into a billion sparkly bits."

He rewarded me with delicate applause. "Bravissima. Molto bene."

"So instead you whisper poison, influence people, and let them do your dirty work for you." I gave him a look of unreserved disgust. "And now, here we are. What's your next move, hot shot?"

"A sincere offer of peace between us."

Sincere, my ass. "Unless it involves Szerain, Zack, Ashava, and Sonny safe and sound and free, you're wasting your breath."

"They have chosen their path and will drag you down with them if you are naïve enough to allow it."

"Ashava didn't choose shit," I said with heat. "She was born into this crap situation. And for the record, I'd rather go down whatever path Zack's on than follow your twisted lead."

"Ashava chooses her path even now." He flicked his hand as if shooing a fly. "Lamentably, it is the path to her destruction rather than to the salvation of all."

"You're trying to tell me that if Ashava was with you, everything would be A-okay?" I asked, incredulous. "Good thing I don't believe anything that comes out of your lying mouth. Remember, I know all about your underhanded ways." I held up my index finger. "*You* posed as a morgue tech and weaseled your way into my life and Tessa's bed. *You*—"

"Is this offense worse than Zakaar posing as a human, seducing your dearest friend, and getting a child upon her?"

"It wasn't like that," I snarled, though I couldn't deny that the same worry had crossed my mind more than once. I lowered my index finger and lifted the middle. "*You* groomed a syraza to take over as Isumo Katashi to influence summoners and spread your diseased agenda on Earth. Did you kill the real Katashi?"

"*I* did not." He leaned toward me. "A tragic outcome too often follows an attempt to summon beyond one's skill and knowledge."

"I wonder who gave him the idea he could do it."

"Not I," he said, amusement in his eyes.

Sick bastard. Had the real Katashi—Mzatal's sworn summoner—proved to be an obstacle in Xharbek's plans? Dread settled in my chest. Xharbek knew I was here for the gimkrah, which most likely meant he knew of my intention to summon an imperator. An imperator who could remove me from the game with a *tragic outcome*—while putting Elinor's essence in his hands to give him the ultimate weaponized summoner. Devious. "*You* used your puppet Katashi to set an arcane bomb and lay the groundwork for the Mraztur to . . ."

I dropped my hand, silent for a moment as puzzle pieces rearranged themselves. This asshole had been playing hardball for a long time. When I'd asked the Piggly Wiggly Jontari reyza what the lords wanted, he'd said *fuck the lords* and *ask Xharbek*. Rhyzkahl had been surprised by the amount of rakkuhr that flooded Earth, and when he denied alliance with the Jontari, I hadn't believed him. But I was starting to change my mind.

"No," I said softly, "it's *you* behind all of it. You aren't helping the Mraztur along with their plans. They're just as much your tools as fake-Katashi, blind to it because you feed their own interests. Nice and indirect. What I don't get is why."

His lips formed an infuriatingly enigmatic smile. "For the game to be won, it is best the pawns not know the designs of the king."

"Seriously? King? That's the lamest super-villain goal *ever*."

Xharbek's expression hardened. "You understand nothing of my goals, but it matters not." He waved his hand over the basin. Above it, an image appeared of a half dozen reyza flying over a rift in a city street. "Too much is in motion for you to stop what is coming to pass. The Jontari have their own agenda."

"Aided and abetted by a deceptive shithole of a demahnk with *his* own agenda."

"Go home," he said, expression compassionate but eyes dead and flat. "Help Earth adjust."

"That's your idea of peace? Go belly up to the enemy and accept invasion?" I snorted. "For all your posing, you don't know jack shit about humans."

He regarded me as if I was an insect that needed crushing. "Take what you came for, Kara Gillian, but tread softly. Yours is a fool's errand."

"Bite me." My tactical gear made mooning him impossible, so I settled for a two-handed crotch grab followed by a double bird-flip.

He swept the basin from the pedestal to shatter on the floor and was gone.

"Loser," I yelled into the empty air. Wonderful. Now I was stuck in a black box. So much for going home.

Shards of glass from the basin crunched under my boots as I explored the perimeter of the chamber. Eleven sides, each faintly reflecting my image like a dark mirror. No obvious doors, but since Mzatal obviously frequented this place, there had to be a way out.

I placed my palm against the nearest wall, and Mzatal's resonance hummed through me. Around my fingers, the stone took on a golden glow that diffused across the surface, creating what seemed to be a shadowy window. To my delight, I could see the shimmer of a dimensional pocket through it. Empty, but this was progress. Encouraged, I moved to the next section and repeated the process with the same result. The third wall revealed yet another pocket, but this one wasn't empty. In what appeared to be a luxurious bedchamber, a woman dressed in voluminous sea green silk stood in the middle of a single shikvihr ring. Silver-white hair flowed unbound around her lined face as she traced and dispelled the beginning sigil of the second ring over and over. Practicing. Rasha Hassan Jalal al-Khouri, the elderly summoner who'd chosen to work with Mzatal. When I'd last seen her, her hands were crippled by arthritis, but now they swooped with grace as she finished the sigil and, finally appearing satisfied, continued to the second sigil. Mzatal must have tucked her into this pocket to keep her safe while he was away on Earth. A skilled summoner left unprotected in the demon realm was a treasure an enemy lord might dare attempt to steal. Apparently, this chamber was Mzatal's surveillance room where he could check in on his various pockets.

Though I felt as if I could step right into Rasha's pocket if I wanted, I pulled my hand away. My time was short. Plus I didn't want to risk disturbing the protections.

My pulse leaped as the view into the next pocket crystallized. Resting on a three-foot high podium was the gimkrah, exactly as it had appeared in Xharbek's trap vision. On the floor lay manacles large enough to fit around my waist along with a heap of chain with massive links, all forged of the same pinkish arcane-dampening metal that banded the gimkrah. *Makkas.* Goosebumps swept over my skin. Those were chains for a huge demon. But why?

I pushed aside the disconcerting questions and focused on my goal: Get the gimkrah, Get out, Get home. Only one problem: I was fairly certain I could enter, but what about exiting? The last thing I wanted was to trap myself in a dimensional pocket. Mzatal was able to pass in and out at will, but he was a lord, and I was me.

His resonance whispered through me, and I steadied. We were as one, with everything attuned to me. If I had the ability to enter the pocket unaided, I'd have the ability to exit. Besides, I was too close to the gimkrah to wimp out now.

Decision made, I let my hand sink into the wall, then I was inside the pocket with only the barest sensation of movement. A shiver ran through me, and not only because the air was as cold as a meat-locker. Though I was several feet from the chains, their effect smothered my arcane senses like a thick blanket of wet cotton.

After taking careful note of precisely where I'd entered, I approached the podium. The core of the crystal globe had been dull brownish red when I arrived, but as I neared it flashed with scarlet lightning, giving the unsettling impression it was snapping at me. I unslung my backpack and pulled out a fleece jacket. I couldn't risk direct contact with the makkas bands on the gimkrah, and who knew what the runes on them might do. Using the jacket like oven mitts, I lifted the globe from the podium and stuffed into the backpack. Mission accomplished.

To my relief, the return to the main chamber proved as simple I'd hoped. But how was I supposed to get out of the column? The room had a serious lack of glowing EXIT signs.

"Doesn't Mzatal know about fire codes?" I muttered. Sign or not, a way out existed. All I had to do was find it.

I checked each wall in turn but found only more dimensional pockets—some empty, some like arcane attics filled with stored furniture and miscellaneous objects, but none with another living being. My gaze fell on the pedestal. Could it be that simple? As I placed my hands on the cool stone, a mild sensation of being inside an upward swirling vortex permeated me. This was it. I closed my eyes and envisioned the top of the column then let the vortex lift me.

Chapter 29

"You all right?" Pellini called out from below.

I gave him a thumbs up then scuttled down the column steps. When I reached the grass, I kept going and beckoned him to hurry away with me. "I got the gimkrah, but Xharbek was there," I panted. "That asswipe is the puppet master behind everything." As we hustled down to the ravine path, I briefed him on the highlights. "I'm sure he wants me to get shredded in the summoning, but he practically gave the gimkrah to me, which makes me suspicious as all hell. I just want to be home. Now."

"You won't get any argument from me."

To my relief, our little group and Janice were waiting across the ravine on the path to the grove. Michael grinned and waved, but Turek let out a furious roar. Alarm swept over Michael's face as he pointed above my head. Hand on my Glock, I spun to see four reyza hurtle from a rift high in the sky. The instant they were clear, the rift snapped closed behind them.

"Pellini, incoming!" I shouted, drawing my weapon. Gold adorned one of the demons. Jontari.

"Sonofabitch," he growled, already sighting on the approaching threat. "Not a single goddamn place to take cover."

And no way in hell could we make it to the palace before they were on us. "Then we stand and fight," I said, copying his stance.

As I sighted on the lead demon, an arc of lightning incinerated it. A killing ward of Mzatal's. No time to celebrate, though. The other three reyza shot through the dispersing ash-cloud of their dead brother, taking full advantage of his sacrifice and the brief hole in the defenses.

Kehlirik let out a fierce scream of defiance as he arrowed toward us from atop the palace. That evened the odds a bit, though it would be a race to see if he could reach us before the Jontari. A dozen feet ahead, the earth heaved upward and resolved into a hulking humanoid shape. One of Michael's golems. I breathed a *thank you,* hope for survival rising as Pellini and I ducked behind its bulk for cover.

"This is going to be brutal," Pellini muttered, eyeing the quickly approaching Jontari.

"Good thing we're awesome." Working the arcane at turbo-speed, I prepped six makeshift shield-busters. The quartz spheres that Idris used held the potency better than brass and lead, but my buster-bullets had done the trick against Big Turd in Siberia. I gave Pellini three, and we each loaded them into our respective magazines and chambered a round.

Peeking from behind the cover of the golem, I fired twice at the closest reyza then cursed as the rounds flashed and pinged off his shielding. "No good!" I said. "The demons can tap full potency here for shields."

And then we were out of time. The reyza dove at us and raked claws over the golem, scattering dirt, but the golem snatched it out of the air, giant earthen hands twisting to break one wing. Demon and dirt limbs flailed as the two skirmished. Pellini and I scrambled away, and the other two attackers took immediate advantage of our loss of cover. A scarred yet agile reyza hit Pellini like an airborne freight train, sending both of them tumbling over the edge of the ravine.

"Pellini!" I cried out, running toward where they'd disappeared. I'd barely closed half the distance when the demon rose into view then swooped on me. I dodged and rolled, but he caught me with pathetic ease then tossed me in the air like a rag doll before slamming me face down on the grass.

My breath whooshed out with the impact, and my gun tumbled from my grasp. I struggled to fill my lungs then wheezed out a scream as the demon gripped my calf and wrenched, sending pain exploding through my knee. I scrabbled for my gun, but he pinned me down with a foot across the back of my thighs then ripped the backpack from me. With a scream of triumph, he pressed down harder on my legs. Heart racing, I steeled myself for the downward slash of claws that would finish me.

Kehlirik bellowed in fury. The weight on me disappeared, and the sting of arcane fallout rippled over me. *He just saved my ass.* I lifted my head to see my attacker fend off Kehlirik with a vicious claw kick and tail lash then leap into the air with my backpack in hand. The other Jontari sent an arcane blast sizzling over me to strike Kehlirik, then both climbed high, wings beating hard.

Dazed, I flopped onto my back and sucked in precious air. Twenty yards away, Kehlirik struggled to get to his feet while ugly red arcane flickered over him. Nearby, the broken-winged demon thrashed out from beneath a pile of dirt, but Turek streaked toward it and swept two sets of claws out to lay open its throat. High above, a new rift swallowed the two departing Jontari then closed after them.

Despair squeezed my chest. In mere seconds, a single Jontari had not only dispatched Pellini and me with ease, but stolen the gimkrah as well. Bam, bam, bam.

Pellini! I pushed up and limped to the ravine edge, knee threatening to give way with every step. He lay at the bottom of the ravine, crumpled on his side. It was clear he was hurt, but I couldn't tell how badly. His legs jerked, and he had his arms clutched around his middle. But he was alive.

"Pellini!" Gritting my teeth against the pain, I clambered over the edge and slid-staggered down to him. "Hey, man, did you break something?"

He rolled to his back, breath coming in short, agonized rasps. For an instant I thought he was cradling a small, bloody creature—a mishmash of lumpy dark yellow and rust brown and whitish-pink coils.

"Oh fuck," I breathed. Abdominal fat and liver and intestines. A vicious gaping wound ran from just below his right ribcage to his left hip. Several feet of intestine lay in the dirt beside him.

He focused on me with effort, eyes glazed and shocky. "Kara," he wheezed. "I think this is bad."

"We'll help you," I told him in a shaky voice then screamed, "Turek!" Dropping awkwardly to my uninjured knee, I ripped my jacket off and tried to cover the gash. Blood pooled and spilled over my hands. "Pellini, it's going to be okay."

Turek leaped down and landed beside me. He took a fraction of a heartbeat to assess, shouldered me aside, then sunk four sets of claws into the edges of the horrible wound to pull it as closed as possible. Pellini was still conscious, but there was too much blood.

And dying in the demon realm probably won't save his life

like it did mine, I thought with numb dread. With the ways between the worlds so screwed up now, dead was dead at least eighty percent of the time.

Janice scrambled down the ravine. "Is he—oh, Jesus."

I fully expected her to turn away and puke, but to my surprise she ran to Pellini's other side, yanked her own jacket off and wedged it under his neck to open his airway. His awful wheezing eased a bit, and I spared her a brief nod of gratitude. Still, Pellini had minutes, at most. "Turek, can we get him to the grove?" Even if Rho couldn't help, perhaps it could at least get us to the realm of a friendly lord. Except that all the lords and demahnk were likely either battling the big southern anomaly or on Earth.

Turek growled. "Moving him would but hasten his demise."

Pellini's hands went slack and slipped to the ground.

Fear clawed at my chest. "Shit! Pellini, don't you dare die on me!" I mentally reached for Mzatal in the desperate hope that my need could penetrate both the screwed up interdimensions and the walls between us. But I might as well have been shouting into the void. I fumbled a shaking hand beneath my shirt and pressed it over his sigil on my chest, tried again.

Nothing.

Blood burbled from Pellini's mouth. Cursing, I shifted my hand to cover Kadir's sigil scar. Pellini was his protégé, and I knew damn well the clever lord had learned to teleport. He had the best chance of getting here in time.

I focused on Kadir—the feel of his aura, the sound of his voice, the violet of his eyes—and sent out a call through the sigil. Nothing. Not the slightest tingle. I grabbed Pellini's hand, pressed it to the sigil, and willed the lord here. More nothing. "I . . . I'll go to Kadir's realm and run to the gate. I can call Kadir from there."

Before I could get to my feet, Pellini jerked beneath our hands then went limp.

"He's not breathing," Janice said.

"CPR," I managed to fumble out. I moved into position and began compressions. Buying time at the most. *One, two, three, four, five.*

Janice grabbed my elbow. "Kara, it's just making it worse."

"No. That can't be right." I pushed again to prove it then saw the pressure forcing blood from the wound. Horrified, I yanked my hands back and looked from Turek to Janice for a solution.

Her eyes swam with sympathy. "He's lost too much blood. I'm sorry."

Turek released his hold and edged back.

I can't save him. The thought careened through my skull. Even if I ran flat out, I couldn't possibly get to Kadir's gate to call him before Pellini finished dying and discorporated. Utter helplessness threatened to drown me.

"You stupid fucking asshole," I croaked. "You weren't supposed to fucking get killed here. That wasn't part of the plan." Any second now the light would start to consume him, and he'd be gone. In a week or two he'd reappear on Earth. His body would, at least. But not his essence, unless he was very lucky. "I need you. Don't you know that? You're—"

Janice let out a shriek. I jerked my head up to see Kadir standing only a couple of feet away with Paul beside him.

"Save him," I gasped out, scrambling back to give the lord room. "Please." I turned an imploring look on Paul. "Please."

Kadir regarded me, his head tilted and lips parted slightly, as if I were a perplexing problem.

"Lord Kadir," I said, doing my best to keep my voice strong and steady. "We need your help. He's dying."

His laugh sent a chill through my bones. He sidled close, nostrils flaring as he took in my scent. "Dead."

"No," I said with conviction. "You wouldn't have come here for a dead man."

He traced the line of my jaw with his index finger. "I tend my children."

With that, he went to one knee beside Pellini and placed a pale hand on the exposed liver. Paul knelt by Kadir's side, then both went stone still. I realized with a start that Kadir wore Earth jeans and a polo shirt, and his golden-blond hair was woven into a braid.

Seconds ticked by while nothing happened. At least nothing I could see. Pellini hadn't discorporated yet, which I hoped was a good sign. But he wasn't breathing, either.

The seconds stretched to minutes, and I clamped down on my urge to demand an update. I pressed my fist to my mouth, unable to tear my eyes away from Pellini.

After several agonizing minutes, Paul lifted his head and met my eyes. "I need you to do the shikvihr with me."

"Huh?" I said, caught off guard by the nature of the request. Do the shikvihr with Paul? He had the ability to interpret and subtly influence energy flows, including potency, but his skills weren't the "make sigils and wards" kind.

"I need you to do the shikvihr with me," he repeated. "To support Kadir. Please."

Okay, so I hadn't misheard him. "Yeah," I said, shaking off my surprise. I staggered to my feet, nearly going down again when my knee gave way. "Hang on." I quickly wove a binding that had a secondary property of radiating cold and placed it on my knee, then I wrapped a band of potency around the whole thing. It was a sucky brace, but better than nothing. "How do you want me to do this shikvihr?"

"Dance it like normal." He positioned himself beside me so that only a few feet separated us. "I'll do the rest."

More questions crowded in, but I shoved them aside. I took a few seconds to pygah to help mask the distraction of the knee pain, then I began tracing the glowing curves of the first sigil in the air. I faltered as Paul joined me, matching my movements as if he'd danced the shikvihr a thousand times before. Quickly regaining my focus, I moved on to the next sigil. Though Paul danced the ring precisely, he wasn't forming actual sigils—which baffled me. What was the point? My sigils tingled in my awareness like mini-beacons of various frequencies, but I sensed nothing from his efforts.

Of course it wasn't as if I had anything better to do at the moment, and I'd provided support diagrams for lords before, just not through a shikvihr.

I completed the first four rings, igniting each in turn. On the fifth ring, a whisper-touch of Kadir resonated in the pattern. Paul's expression—lips parted and head tilted—reminded me more than a little of the lord.

They're using their essence bond, I realized. Mzatal and I had worked together countless times, each an extension of the other, to create an outcome greater than combined individual efforts. It was how we'd created the super-shikvihr. Paul didn't have the ability to trace sigils but, through the union of minds and beyond, Kadir guided his movements and used him as a proxy. In a way, it was like how I'd been using Pellini as an arcane proxy for the past two months, talking him through needed arcane manipulations. Yet these two didn't need words.

Kadir's resonance in the ritual increased with each new sigil I traced, though there was something different about the feel of it that I couldn't quantify. It wasn't until I ignited the fifth ring that comprehension hit me. *His resonance doesn't make my skin crawl as much as usual,* I thought in amazement. That was Paul's doing. He influenced potency flows as easily as breathing, and in ways that differed from how lords or summoners worked. Right now, not only was Paul acting as a shikvihr proxy, but he was also modulating the resonance of my rings so that out-of-phase Kadir could draw from them. Freaking awesome teamwork.

And together, we'll save Pellini, I thought fiercely. Already the lord worked to close the last of the horrific wound.

Halfway through the seventh ring, a faint echo of Pellini filtered through Kadir's resonance. I finished the ring and ignited it then gasped as the sigils pulsed in time with Pellini's heartbeat. Hope lifting, I started toward him, but Paul took my arm.

"Wait," he said. "Kadir needs more."

My heart sank. "I can't. I don't know the eighth ring." Sure, I'd watched surveillance video of Rhyzkahl practicing, and even followed along, but while that gave me a head start on the broader strokes, it was useless for finer movements.

"It's all right," Paul said with an encouraging smile. "Just follow my lead." With that he began to dance the eighth ring, oh-so-slowly.

You can do this, Kara. Focusing, I copied his every movement, from the angle of his feet and tilt of his wrists all the way down to the subtle movements of his fingers. Kadir's resonance enveloped me like icy snot, charging my hands with the esoteric energy I hadn't yet mastered.

Though Paul's tracings left only empty air, mine formed shimmering sigils. Twice he had me dispel a sigil, patiently repeating the movements until I got it right, but at long last I completed the very last sigil of the eighth ring.

"I can't ignite it," I said, panting as if I'd just finished a marathon. Not only did a lord have to culminate a newly learned ring, but I'd first have to dance it on my own and with no assistance. Still, even an unculminated ring gave the shikvihr more oomph.

"Pretend like you can," Paul said.

Pretend? Then again it couldn't get much more bizarre than it already was. With a mental shrug, I went through the physical and arcane motions for igniting a ring, oddly unsurprised when it flared bright, igniting to pulse in blazing glory with the other seven.

The sigils dimmed as Kadir tapped their power. I scrambled to fuel them with redirected flows. Pellini sucked in a labored breath, and though I wanted to rush to his side, the ritual needed constant tending.

Kadir formed a gelatinous globe of scum-green potency between his hands and dropped it onto Pellini's chest. The blob shuddered then broke into a billion chartreuse fragments that crawled over Pellini like neon maggots and burrowed into him—his joints, his gut, his throat, his eyes. *Everywhere.* Though Pellini didn't appear to be conscious, he writhed as if being eaten alive.

I turned my worried gaze on Paul.

He met my eyes, his face serene. "It's part of the process."

Fine. Weird lord. Weird healing.

But no way was Kadir doing this out of the goodness of his heart. What price would he exact for bringing Pellini back from the dead?

Kadir continued to draw potency from the shikvihr, his long-fingered hands flowing in an intricate dance over Pellini. He brought his palms together, and potency maggots flooded from Pellini's nose and mouth to gather on his chest in a seething mass. Kadir hummed tunelessly and stroked the pile of maggots. The shikvihr whined like an engine pushed too far then faded to a ghostly grey.

Pellini's eyes flew open. His back arched, and he let out a scream that went right through my essence. The shikvihr shattered, echoing the sound.

"No!" I hobbled toward them. "What are you doing!?"

Without a glance my way, Kadir lifted his hand in a gesture that could only mean halt. "Interfere, and I will rip out his heart and feed it to you."

Breath seizing, I stumbled to a stop. I had no doubt he would do just that.

Pellini thrashed, and Kadir immobilized him with bands of potency. I looked on in helpless horror as the maggots spread and began to form a pattern on Pellini's chest. He wasn't screaming anymore, but his eyes were wide and locked on Kadir.

The maggots jostled one another as if seeking precise positions until a recognizable pattern emerged—Kadir's sigil laid out in neon chartreuse potency bugs. Kadir placed his hand upon them, his face a rictus of anticipation.

For a moment nothing happened, then Pellini's mouth opened

in a soundless scream that made the audible one seem subdued. Smoke rose from his chest along with the stench of burned flesh even as the maggots vanished. Kadir leaned in closer. I could *feel* his sick fascination like a river of toxic sludge in his aura.

Paul placed a hand on Kadir's shoulder and murmured something I couldn't hear. Kadir went still for a heartbeat then touched Pellini's forehead with his fingertips. Pellini sucked in a breath as all indication of pain faded from his face. The potency bindings dissolved, and he lay breathing hard, whole and seemingly uninjured, other than a sigil scar the size of my splayed hand in the center of his chest.

With a flash of potency, Kadir burned away all traces of blood from Pellini, the ground, and himself, then stood smoothly. He was paler than usual, though. The healing—and the hurting—had clearly taken a toll on him.

Paul remained kneeling and rested his head against Kadir's thigh. The lord stroked Paul's hair, a gesture that still unsettled me. But I couldn't deny the look of peace on Paul's face and the diminished chaos in Kadir's aura. They were one hell of an odd pair, yet they seemed to complement each other perfectly in some mystifying, mutually beneficial way.

Kadir gestured for Pellini to get up. Pellini clambered to his feet, grinning despite his ordeal. Before I could sort out whether I needed to yell at Kadir or thank him, he and Paul were gone.

I rushed to Pellini and threw my arms around him. "You scared me," I said, voice only quavering a tiny bit.

He returned the embrace. "Yeah, well, this manly chest *is* pretty intimidating. Especially now."

That wrung a weak laugh from me. I gave him a squeeze then pulled back to look him over. "Are you . . . okay?"

He pulled the tatters of his shirt around him. "Yeah," he said softly.

Worry stole through me, but it was evident he needed some time to process everything. I summoned what I hoped was a reassuring smile. "You'll be in a nice hot shower before you know it."

"Yeah." He looked around at the others then back to me. "We're done here, aren't we?"

"We're done here," I said. There was no getting the gimkrah back, but at least I hadn't lost Pellini. "Let's go home."

"Home." A faint smile touched his mouth. "That's your best idea yet."

Chapter 30

With Turek supporting me, we gathered up the various members of our party, along with a cask of tunjen juice Jekki brought for us, then got our butts to the grove. Rho's presence was more tangible than ever, and I let myself sink into it for a precious moment as we made the transfer to Kadir's realm.

Our subsequent trek to the gate stayed blessedly uneventful. I took advantage of the conflict-free moments to prepare for what was sure to be a battle royal when we came through the gate on Earth. No way would Captain Hardnose take kindly to us arriving with two strange humans *and* a big scary demon. I'd have to utilize my full ninja powers of bullshit and persuasion to keep the newcomers—and the rest of us—out of a holding cell.

Once we made it across the sand to the gate, I gathered everyone into a tight group between the two crystalline spires. "There's a military detachment on the other side of the gate," I said, wrinkling my nose. "Since I don't want anyone getting hurt by accident, I'd like Turek to get between Pellini and me."

The demon hissed but complied.

"When we go through the gate," I continued, "it's going to feel really strange for a few seconds." I paused. "*Really* strange."

Pre-flight instructions complete, I nodded to Pellini. We both placed a hand on the crystal nearest us, focused and . . .

This time I was ready for the disorienting free fall through cold, black nothingness. I firmly reminded myself to *Believe!* and fixed in my mind the image and feel of the parking lot and the DIRT units and air and gravity with all of us through, safe and sound.

The frigid dark shifted to cool breeze and the soft light of dusk. My head spun as if I'd been twirling, but I wasn't nearly as disoriented as the last time. Within a few seconds, I was clear-headed enough to take stock of our group. Janice looked a bit green, as did Giovanni, but Michael had a broad grin on his face and was looking around in utter delight. Reassured that everyone had made it through safe and sound, I turned to confront the more pressing threat of trigger-happy DIRT personnel.

As if on cue, an alarm blared, and a voice rumbled through the PA. "Remain where you are and keep your hands in plain sight."

"Stay on your toes," I muttered to the others, making sure everyone had their hands and claws in the open.

A squad in riot gear trained their weapons on us, while another half dozen soldiers hurried toward the gate, demeanor downright unfriendly. Off to our left, Captain Hornak exited the command center and jogged our way. *Now* we'd get the "detain them all and let god sort them out" treatment. I struggled to scrape together an oh-so-compelling argument for why we all needed to remain free to go. Maybe I could threaten to call the President? Of course, there was always the chance that she'd agree with Hornak. Crap. This was going to be a mess.

"Welcome back!" Captain Hornak cried out with a broad smile, pairing it with a cheery wave. He stopped just beyond the arcane protections that surrounded the gate then leveled a scowl at the soldiers. "Stand down! That's no way to greet returning heroes."

The confused soldiers lowered their weapons. I slid a perplexed glance at Pellini. The fuck?

He returned a baffled shrug. "We're in the goddam twilight zone," he muttered.

Before I could offer agreement, Hornak gave a little fist pump of victory. "I can't tell you how thrilled I am that you made it back safe and sound." Impossibly, his grin widened. "And you brought some friends with you. Welcome to Earth!"

I gaped at his downright creepy enthusiasm but finally recovered enough to whisper to Pellini, "What the fuck is going on? I didn't think his face could *make* a smile. It's got to be a trick of some sort to get us out of the protected area."

"If so, it's the weirdest tactic I've ever seen."

Captain Hornak bounced on his toes, looking as excited as a tween at a boy band concert. "When I heard that you had extra people and a demon with you, I arranged for an Armored Personnel Carrier. It should be ready any second now." A neon maggot wriggled up his neck and disappeared into his ear. "That way you can get everyone back to your headquarters without having to squeeze into your Humvee."

I cleared my throat softly and glanced Pellini's way. "I think Kadir must have, ah, smoothed the way for us."

His bafflement vanished. "Of course." He snorted and tapped his scarred chest. "Kadir wanted to make sure his handiwork stayed in one piece."

Strangely enough, the idea of Kadir manipulating the captain was a lot less creepy than Hornak suddenly being *nice* on his own. Not that I was thrilled with the prospect of Kadir on Earth influencing people at will—which probably tied into why he'd been dressed like an Abercrombie & Fitch model.

While Hornak busied himself shouting orders at the bewildered soldiers, we hustled our group into the waiting APC. It would have been a tight squeeze getting Turek into the Humvee, even without the human passengers. After a quick game of rock-paper-scissors to see who got to drive the APC, I hauled myself into the driver's seat, Pellini retrieved the Humvee, and we all got the hell out of there.

As soon as I felt confident that we wouldn't be chased down by soldiers who realized Hornak was off his rocker, I called Bryce and told him that we had the gold and were on our way home. I almost told him to go ahead and fire up the smelter, but caught myself just in time. Turek was sitting only a few feet behind me, and I didn't want to remind him that we intended to destroy unspeakably priceless artifacts and risk him changing his mind. Besides, Bryce was smart and knew we were in a time crunch.

I also told Bryce that we didn't have the gimkrah, but to my relief he didn't press for details. He could probably tell from my tone that it was a sore subject and best discussed later, preferably with alcohol in hand.

The roads were empty enough that after I hung up I could zone out a bit. By the time we rolled into my driveway, I had my second wind. Or fourth. I'd lost count.

Pellini parked the Humvee beside me, sketched a small wave in my direction then headed straight inside. To his room, I assumed, for some alone time. Janice seemed pensive as everyone else unloaded from the APC. While she looked around and got her bearings, I sent a quick text to Jill, asking her to please turn off the TV in the war room. I needed a place to stash Janice until I was ready chaperone her reunion with Rhyzkahl—however entertaining that might be—but I didn't have the time or energy to go into why there was a TV channel called Demon News Network, much less explain whatever godawful horrific scene might be showing. To my relief, Janice made no argument when I asked her to give me a few minutes to take care of other pressing business, and she allowed Giovanni to escort her inside, Michael tagging behind.

With the humans settled for the moment, it was time to focus on the gold situation. Damn it.

I inclined my head to Turek. "Would you please come with me?" At his low hiss of assent, I limped around the side of the house to where Bryce, clad in a heavy apron, waited in a floodlit space halfway between the house and Jill's trailer. Beside him was what looked like a bright blue refrigerator but, I assumed, was the electric furnace. A stainless steel table held a scale, tongs, welding gloves, and molds for ingots, and all of it stood in the middle of a wide circle of sand. Good. Maybe we wouldn't end up burning the woods down.

Bryce frowned as we approached. "Where's the gold? We're cutting it close on time."

"Turek has it," I said, briefly amused by the deepening confusion on Bryce's face. But my humor faded quickly beneath the weight of what we were about to do. I looked up at the demon. "Honored one, will you please recall the discs for us?"

The savik bared his teeth then lifted all four hands. The air shimmered, and eleven gold discs coalesced into his palms.

Bryce's eyes widened as he took in the brilliant engraving and details, but he quickly schooled his expression to the impassive mask that had served him so well during his years as a hit man.

"What about the twelfth disc?" I asked. I couldn't tell which one was missing.

Turek snapped his teeth together inches from my face. "Eleven are adequate for the barter."

Bryce eyed the demon, no doubt assessing the threat level. "Kara, are you sure about this plan?"

"I had the gimkrah then lost it," I said around a thick knot in my throat. "Without it, we have no choice but to get the net. It's our only advantage now."

Turek hissed as he placed the discs on the table. "Szerain *must* be freed."

Bryce tugged a hand through his hair. "Guess I'd better get to it then."

Grief swelled within me as Bryce picked up the first disc and placed it on the scale. "I have to take care of some things," I blurted. It was totally chickenshit, but I simply could *not* stay and watch the destruction of the discs. "Just . . . do what you have to do."

Bryce's eyes were full of understanding. "I'll handle it," he said gently. "Kellum and I will head out to finish the deal as soon as the bars are ready to transport."

Eyes already filling with tears, I nodded then hurried to the house as fast as my knee allowed. I had to stop on the porch to catch my breath from the pain, and I hazarded a look back. Bryce was cradling one of the disks between his hands, head lowered. Memorizing its beauty before he destroyed it?

I continued straight to my bedroom, aching at the suckiness of the whole situation. As soon as I closed the door, I flung myself on the bed, buried my face in a pillow and let myself have a full minute of good solid bawling. Everything was fucked up. Except for the gold, the trip to the demon realm had been a nightmarish waste of time. Lannist was dead, Pellini almost died, my knee was wrecked, and I'd managed to lose the master gimkrah. The need for the summoning hadn't budged, but what if the graphene net wasn't enough to hold a Jontari imperator? Had I ordered the destruction of unspeakably priceless artifacts only to end up as meat confetti at the claws of a demon?

Sitting up, I scrubbed at my face then checked my reflection in the dresser mirror. Yup, puffy eyes, red nose. A real vision. My eyes fell on Szerain's drawing that I'd brought back from the outreach center. Me in the tight pants and flowing brown coat with a spaceship in the background. That Kara didn't look like a frazzled, exhausted wreck. She was cool and confident and tough as nails, ready to stand firm against her enemies.

A faint smile struggled into place. Had Szerain seen that in me?

"Oh, Kara," I breathed, "you can be a doofus sometimes." We'd lost the gimkrah but brought back more than gold. We also had Turek and Michael which meant my chances of contacting Szerain were drastically improved. And if I could pull it off sooner rather than later—like in the next few hours—Szerain and I could hash out the no-gimkrah problem.

I did a mental fist pump. Maybe we wouldn't need the net. Maybe we wouldn't need to destroy the discs.

I was almost to the bedroom door on my way to stop Bryce when the ugly truth slid home. The deal for the net was due to go down in mere hours, and it wasn't the kind of thing that could be rescheduled for my convenience. Not when the people getting us the net and risking major jail time had set a hard deadline. I had at best a fifty-fifty shot of communicating with Szerain before the full moon, and even *if* I made it past that hurdle, there was only a slim chance that we'd come up with a solution that didn't require the net. But if we missed this window for making the deal, we'd lose *all* chance of getting the net. No net plus no alternate solution equaled screwed for the summoning, screwed for Elinor, screwed for everything.

I muttered a variety of curses at the universe in general. There were too many variables in play for me to gamble the lives of not only everyone I loved but possibly all of humanity on an emotional decision to save *things*—even exquisite, irreplaceable things. Worst case scenario, I'd fail to reach Szerain before the summoning, and we'd be back to square one. But by that time, Bryce would have the net, the moon would be full, and I could re-evaluate my summoning plan.

I returned to the mirror and met my own eyes. *This* was the Kara from Szerain's drawing, the one who could make the hard decisions and stand firm. The one he trusted to "be lordy." My dark mood lifted a little. Things weren't so bad after all.

And they'd only get better if I could watch Janice give Rhyzkahl a healthy piece of her mind.

Humming in anticipation, I dabbed concealer over the worst of the cry-face then headed to the war room.

Chapter 31

Janice was kicked back in a chair when I entered, but the jiggling of her foot betrayed her tension.

"I'm sorry that took so long," I said. "I'll take you to see Rhyzkahl now if you want."

She nodded stiffly and got to her feet. "I do."

"Just so you know, there are protections set up." Mzatal's, of course, which meant they were oh-so-very effective. "If you try to hurt him in any way, you'll get zapped."

"So noted," she replied, words clipped.

I'd warned her. Whatever happened now, I was off the hook. One of our first security guards had snapped when Rhyzkahl taunted him, and unloaded a half dozen rounds at the lord before a flash of light from the slab dropped the guard like a stone. Rhyzkahl remained unharmed, but the guard was out cold. He woke up a day later with zero memory of anything after being hired, and with an inexplicable desire to leave security work altogether and take up cheese making.

I led Janice through the kitchen and out to the porch then gestured toward where Rhyzkahl was dancing the shikvihr. "As promised, one Rhyzkahl."

She ignored my feeble attempt at humor and moved to the top of the steps. At the sight of her, Rhyzkahl stopped. He dissipated the thready sigils then stood motionless, face a cool mask.

I glanced at her, expecting to see a good dose of anger or possibly a flicker of fear. Anything but the smile that dawned on her face. My bafflement rose as she leaped off the steps and ran toward Rhyzkahl. Was she trying to get a running start so she could pile drive him? Cursing, I started after her. Hadn't she heard my warning about the protections?

Rhyzkahl remained still until she was a dozen feet away then held his hands out. I stopped and stared in shock as she threw her arms around him in a hug. He pulled her close, his shoulders relaxing as if she brought a fragment of peace with her.

What the actual fuck?

A heartbeat later, he took her hand and started to lead her to his house.

"Oh, *hell* no," I announced as I hobbled forward. "You want to speak to her, you can do it out here."

Janice gave me a startled look, but Rhyzkahl ignored me and continued walking.

Anger swept through me. Baring my teeth, I called up a strand of potency and slammed the house door before he could reach it. "I said *no!*"

Rhyzkahl turned then stepped between Janice and me. "Leave us."

"Not a chance." I gave him a tight smile. "Think of me as your chaperone. I'm not about to give you any opportunity to hurt her." Beyond him, I saw Janice taking in her surroundings: the circle of trampled grass, the odd dimensions of the little house, the black slab at the center of it all. Her expression shifted to a scowl, and I could only assume she was pissed about the state of his prison. Great. I knew she wasn't manipulated, but that didn't rule out Stockholm Syndrome.

"Why did you bring her here?" Rhyzkahl demanded, anger coloring his words.

"She asked to see you," I said, taking a small pleasure in the frustration that tightened his face. Thanks to the arcane constraints and my shielding, he couldn't read me or her, which had to be driving him nuts.

Janice stepped forward. "Yes, I did. And would prefer to do so without a chaperone. Rhyzkahl won't hurt me."

"Yes, because the protections Mzatal set won't allow him to. Physically, at least. But I don't want him to say anything that'll twist you up inside either."

A muscle twitched in Rhyzkahl's jaw. "I am caged. She is free. Do you choose to oppress her as well?"

"I'm not trying to oppress her!" I narrowed my eyes at him. "I'm trying to protect her from you, because I know what you're capable of."

Janice threw her hands up in the air. "I don't need your protection."

I cursed under my breath. "Look, Janice," I said as calmly as I could manage, "I'm not the enemy here, though I'm sure it must seem that way. Traumatic experiences can really tangle loyalties. I know you've been through a lot of terrible shit, and I'm sorry any of it happened to you. I'm just doing my best to get everyone who was kidnapped and trafficked in the demon realm released and given whatever help they need to deal with what happened."

Her mouth dropped open in a silent O, then she turned toward Rhyzkahl with a look I couldn't interpret at all.

"Go," he told her, curt and short. "Address this matter that we may be done with it."

"Gladly," she muttered then stalked toward me. "Let's take this inside," she said, passing me on her way to the house.

Gee, this day was turning out super extra peachy.

She rounded on me the instant I stepped into the kitchen. "What kind of messed up 'prison' is that?" She flung an arm in the direction of the back yard. "Murderers on death row have more room to move than he does! And where in heaven's name did you get the idea I was some sort of sex slave? Just who do you think you are to be—"

"*Sit down and shut up!*" I roared, backing it with just a touch of potency.

She closed her mouth with a snap and flung herself into a chair, gaze murderous.

"Do you remember that young man with Lord Kadir?" I didn't wait for an acknowledgement before storming on. "That's Paul Ortiz. He was a gifted programmer and hacker, living in Albuquerque until the day that a businessman by the name of James Macklin Farouche had him kidnapped so that he could exploit Paul's talents. Amber Palatino Galvan was a beautiful young woman who was kidnapped by Farouche's people and then raped, tortured and murdered as part of a ritual meant to target me—one that was orchestrated by your boyfriend out there." I let out a humorless bark of laughter. "We won't even get into what he did to *me*. But as for J.M. Farouche, he had business competitors assassinated, and disloyal employees tortured and killed. A number of people besides yourself were kidnapped by his underlings and delivered to Rhyzkahl to be taken to the demon realm. But you're right, I had no business whatsoever to try to free women who I truly believe are—at best—being held against their will and—at worst—trafficked as sex slaves." I tossed my hands up. "What the *hell* was I thinking!"

Her defiance had drained away during my speech to the point that she now seemed cowed. I lowered myself into the chair across from her and eased my aching leg. "Sorry," I said. "It's been a shitty couple of months."

She exhaled softly. "I was wrong to jump down your throat. Of course it would look like sex trafficking to an outside observer. Before I left Earth, I certainly thought that's what I'd fallen into."

"But you *were* kidnapped, right?"

She lifted her eyes to mine. "Yes, we were all kidnapped, but none of us are being held against our will, and we certainly aren't being used as sex slaves."

I shook my head in the vain hope it would help everything make sense. "Then why were y'all snatched?"

A faint smile touched her mouth. "The lords wanted . . . companions. Conversation. Human interaction. All of us who were brought to the demon realm are sharp cookies. Not a dummy among us."

"Huh," I said while I tried to rejigger my entire outlook. A piece clicked into place. Around a year ago or so, I'd questioned demonic lord Vahl about his relationship with Michelle Cleland, who Rhyzkahl had taken to the demon realm after the Symbol Man offered her as a sacrifice. Vahl had said the lords all missed humans, though some wouldn't admit it. Michelle now lived quite happily with Elofir, and definitely wasn't forced or manipulated. "Huh," I said again then frowned. "Hang on. Seretis told me that the captives were being held against their will."

Janice rolled her eyes. "Seretis doesn't know anything. He's not an ally of Rhyzkahl's, so he was kept in the dark about the real deal."

And was probably fed misinformation as well, I mused. Seretis had negotiated with Amkir to obtain Michael, fearing that the young man might be mistreated. Of course Amkir would encourage that assumption to get more out of the deal.

But I had a feeling Seretis had gained far more than he'd lost.

On the other hand, even though Janice hadn't been manipulated, she might not have had full disclosure on the other abductees. She hadn't mentioned the two men who Seretis reported as killed by Kadir. I couldn't take her belief at face value until I confirmed it with Mzatal, or saw for myself.

"So you haven't slept with Rhyzkahl?" I asked.

She chuckled low. "I never said that. But there was no coercion. Or manipulation."

And Mzatal would have confirmed that.

Her expression sobered. "I had congestive heart failure. A year or two left to live at most. Couldn't walk up a flight of stairs. Could barely walk to my car, for that matter. Rhyzkahl healed me, gave me back a life worth living. But that's not why I stayed." She shrugged. "Okay, maybe that was part of it. But, honestly, I liked my life in the demon realm."

"Were the others sick, too?"

"Not everyone was terminal, but all had issues or diseases that drastically affected quality of life." She took a deep breath. "We were told that if, at the end of two months, we wished to return to Earth, we could, with memory of the demon realm erased. None of us wanted to go. Whatever screening Farouche did to pick us was solid. No attachments, open-minded, intelligent, and living crippled lives."

"Sorry," I said. "I'm having to readjust everything I've been thinking for the past half a year." I couldn't think of how they'd been screened so well, unless maybe demahnk help had been involved? My thoughts turned to poor Amaryllis Castlebrook who I'd impersonated in order to save her from being kidnapped as well as to infiltrate the Farouche Plantation. Though my intentions were solid, had I inadvertently kept her from getting help she needed? I made a mental note to track her down and check on her. Assuming she was still alive.

Janice was silent, probably readjusting a few opinions of her own as well. At least I hoped so. After a moment, she drew a deeper breath and smiled. "Teri Abraham didn't graduate from high school due to paralyzing social anxiety and panic attacks, but she must have an IQ out in the stratosphere. Lightning quick and witty to boot. She's blossomed with Amkir."

I gaped in surprise. Amkir? Try as I might, I couldn't imagine that harsh lord nurturing anything or anyone. Yet an instant later, memory flashed, as clear as if it was happening right here and now, of Amkir rescuing the stray dog from the river. Back when he'd been more than he was now, before the volatile anger.

"And me?" she continued, oblivious to my shock. "I was a

geophysicist in a dead end job and staring death in the face. I got the chance to live again, to make a difference. My seismologic research in the demon realm is helping the lords predict problem areas. In fact, while I'm on Earth I want to pick up equipment to take back."

"You really *do* like it there," I said.

"I do," she said fervently. "It's different with Mzatal, but he respects my work." Her gaze went out the window. "He didn't tell me why he exiled Rhyzkahl."

"I think there were several reasons for it," I said. "But one was that Rhyzkahl was so out of whack after losing his ptarl bond with Zakaar that his presence in the demon realm was causing a potency imbalance and messing things up there."

Her lips pursed. "And I'm sure there was a strategic aspect as well as far as getting him out of the game." She winced. "Not that Rhyzkahl was able to do much after he lost Zakaar."

"Agreed, on both counts." Other than the part about *losing* Zakaar. Rhyzkahl was given every opportunity to salvage the relationship and spurned them all. "I also suspect that part of why Mzatal locked him down here was to let Rhyzkahl rehab himself—physically, mentally, and arcanely. The demon realm can't afford to be short a lord right now. Any lord. Not with so many anomalies along with the screwed up potency balance." I shook my head. "Covering for Rhyzkahl takes a toll on all of them."

Her gaze sharpened on me. "But why is he here with you? Don't take this the wrong way, but it's clear you hate his guts."

I let out a breathless laugh. "Funny thing is, I don't. Not anymore, I mean, though I certainly have every reason to." I sobered and met her eyes. "But I don't trust him. I can't ever trust him again." I sighed. "I won't lie. There are times when it's really hard to deal with him."

"What the hell did he do to you?"

He used me, preyed upon my vulnerabilities, and tortured me, I thought, yet I suddenly had no desire to launch into the ugly details. I'd lived through them. I'd relived them a thousand times in my dreams. I was done rekindling their power through retelling the story. Screw that. "He betrayed me," I said. "And he tried to destroy Kara Gillian."

Questions furrowed her brow at my phrasing, but I spoke before she could voice them. "Now that we've straightened out the misunderstandings, I won't keep you from your reunion with

Rhyzkahl any longer." I gave her a smile. "He seemed happy to see you, and I'm sure you both have catching up to do. That cask on the counter is tunjen juice. I bet he'd appreciate some. Glasses are in the cupboard over the coffeemaker. Feel free to get one for yourself, too."

Janice blinked then stood. "Right. Um, thanks. For the talk and the tunjen."

"Anytime."

She found two glasses and filled them from the cask then headed out the back door. Though full night had descended during our chat, the security lights on the house gave plenty of illumination for me to see her cross to Rhyzkahl. She handed him the glass of tunjen and said something that made him laugh, then he took a drink, draped his arm around her shoulders, and headed with her toward his house.

I wiped the smile off my face. Damn, I was getting soft in my old age.

Now that I had a quiet moment alone, I pulled Elinor's journal from my pocket. I couldn't articulate why I'd felt it was so important to retrieve it—whether due to Elinor's influence or my cop sense—but there was no denying my relief that I had it. I opened it now and began to page through it almost reverently. The text had seventeenth century style and spelling, but fortunately Elinor's essence allowed me to read it with ease.

To my surprise, for every page of text, there were at least five containing finely rendered sketches of demon realm flora and fauna, as exquisite as any naturalist could desire. Curiously, the inside of the back cover held a mix of letters and numbers that seemed to be arranged in words and sentences, though "H4rq9pr" looked more like a never-to-be-remembered computer password than a language. A personal code, perhaps? Yet I didn't see it used anywhere else in the journal.

After a quick and fruitless check for anything in the various drawings that might help in my current situation—such as pictures of Jontari or sigils for binding—I moved on to skim her written entries.

They began with her arrival in the demon realm and befriending Giovanni, touched lightly on her training with Mzatal, then changed in tone, with coy references to a *Him* that I knew was Rhyzkahl. The entries stopped for several months then picked up again, though less frequently than before, with her in Szerain's realm. Far more talk of Giovanni, and dozens of sketches of him. Sketches of Szerain as well, along with a variety of demons and one demahnk that I recognized as Xharbek.

But nothing of the ritual that killed her and caused the cataclysm.

I stroked my fingers down the spine of the journal, thoughtful. I clearly remembered an Elinor-dream in which Mzatal took the journal from her because she was doodling instead of studying. That was right before he sent her away to train with Szerain, but obviously she got the journal back somehow. Most likely, Mzatal returned it later on—since it seemed more than a little cruel to flat out *steal* a girl's diary. The real mystery was how it ended up in his possession again, stored away in his solarium.

Yet another question to ask the next time I saw him.

Jill came up from the basement, summoned by my shamelessly pleading text, since no way did I want to navigate the basement stairs with my wonky knee. After I filled her in on the events of our demon realm trip, I handed Elinor's journal over to her with the request that it be photo-archived.

"I'll get right on it," she said. "You go get that knee checked out."

"As soon as I look in on Pellini," I promised.

"Fair enough." With a crisp parting nod, she returned to the basement.

Pellini's door was ajar, and a peek inside showed him sitting on the end of the bed, looking out the window. His hair was damp, which told me he'd caught a quick shower while I was involved with all the other shit.

I tapped lightly on the door frame. "Mind a little company?"

"Nah, come on in." He gave me a slight smile. "Found out Kuktok made it through okay."

"Dude, that's fantastic!" I plopped into the chair beside the bed and cut right to the chase. "How do you feel?"

"Kind of tired but, overall, better than I've felt in decades." Pellini snorted. "Kadir fixed me right up. I mean, everything. Knees, back, all the little aches and pains from being overweight. And . . . well, I already knew I wasn't in the best of health, what with my high blood pressure and diabetes, but Kadir showed me that, even if the demon hadn't ripped into me, I was going to bite it within a year or two."

I raised my eyebrows at that. "How come?"

"I had a couple of blockages in my heart, plus a little cluster of cells in my liver that were ready to join the cancer club. Would've been a tight race to see which took me out first." His words were light, but the catch in his voice revealed how freaked out he was. His gaze drifted out the window again to where the nearly full moon hung above the tree line. "Kadir took me . . . elsewhere," he continued more quietly. "It was like the dream-space but less shifty colors and more solid. And he wasn't Mr. Sparkly. Just himself. Normal. I mean, as normal as he can be." He drew a deeper breath as if amazed he could still do so. "He told me I was dead. *Dead*. Asked me if I wanted to stay or go, live or move on to whatever comes after."

"That's a hell of a thing," I murmured.

His hand crept up to touch the sigil scar through his shirt. "Kara, there was a big part of me that was ready to let go. Like, everything would be *lighter*. No more pain or bullshit. And, hell, a few months ago I would have just . . . gone." He jerked his hand down and tucked it under his thigh, as if he'd only just realized he'd been tracing the scar.

"I'm glad you didn't."

He gave a slow nod, brow furrowed. "When he asked me the live or die question, my first thought was of all the shit we're doing to try and put both worlds right, and all the people who need my help."

"We *do* need your help," I said.

"Yeah. Go figure." He grimaced. "I didn't become a cop for any noble purpose. I had everything going for me coming out of college. My big plan was to work my ass off for a couple of years to squirrel away some cash for law school. But when Kadir abandoned me, and my mom passed away, I turned into a surly bastard. Ran my fiancée off within a month." Old grief shimmered in his eyes. "That was the last straw. I didn't give a shit about anything or anyone—especially myself—but I needed a job and thought being a cop would be cool, a way to get re-spect and have people look up to me. Of course the whole in-stant respect thing didn't happen, because that kind of shit has to be earned. And my attitude was so lousy it only pissed me off when people weren't falling all over themselves to kiss my feet." He gave me a crooked smile. "Man, I was livid when you got promoted to detective. Here you were, young and sharp and get-ting all the attention I never got. Took me a while to figure out you were getting it because you fucking did your job and took pride in it." His posture straightened subtly. "But I'm finally getting my act together and doing something right again. And when Kadir asked me to choose, I realized it'd be stupid to check out now when I have a chance to make a real difference."

"If you keep this up, I'm going to start crying all over again," I said. "I mean, not that I cried or anything when I thought you were dead."

He chuckled then took my hand. "Kara, the other thing that tipped me to the 'stay' side was that I realized there were some people who would miss me. People like you who are apparently dumb or desperate enough to let me matter to them."

I slugged him in his thigh even as my tears spilled over.

He gave a soft grunt, squeezed my hand before releasing it. "These past couple months have been fucked up in a lot of ways, but they've also been some of the best times of my life."

"I never thought I'd have to be grateful to Kadir," I said, "but I sure am now."

A wince shadowed over Pellini's face. "Yeah, well, he didn't do it to be Mr. Nice Guy Humanitarian."

I straightened. "He asked for something in exchange?"

"Not until he was certain I wanted to live." Pellini's eyes met mine. "The bastard was slick. He steered clear of deals he knew I'd turn down, even if it meant dying, and managed to nail one right on my moral line without going over."

"It has to do with the sigil, right?"

"It's tied to him, yeah." He tapped his chest. "Kadir said something about you being the inspiration."

My brows drew together. "I used his sigil scar to call him for Paul at the Spires and then again to get help for you."

"Apparently you made an impression." A barely perceptible shudder went through him. "He can, um, summon me to him."

I sat up straighter. "You mean he snaps his fingers and, poof, you're wherever he's at?"

"I guess. I'm not really sure."

That sounded weirdly like the strange bond Rhyzkahl had forged with me after my very first summoning of him where I only needed to call him with strong intent to bring him to me. "Just once or whenever?"

"I don't know that either."

"Being able to summon you to him isn't exactly insignificant," I said slowly. "But it also isn't as if you agreed to slaughter all the youngling Jedi."

Pellini nodded. "In the end, I think I made the right choice. For the sake of humanity, I mean."

I laughed. "Don't get too full of yourself, or I'll have to find you a bigger room."

"Nah, you got it all wrong. This is about you."

"How the hell is it about me?"

"See, if I died, you'd be so prostrate with grief that Xharbek would win without breaking a sweat," Pellini said, smiling. "So, y'know, I *had* to make a pact with the devil in order to save the world. If it wasn't for you, I'd be kicked back on some fluffy cloud right now tuning my harp and eating grapes."

"I don't have grapes, but I could probably scrounge up some old raisins. And I think I still know how to put together a guitar out of a shoebox and yarn."

"Yeah?" Pellini grinned. "But what about the fluffy cloud?"

I tapped my chin, considering. "How about a leaf pile? Complete with a goofy dog and a bunch of kittens."

"Now *that* sounds like heaven."

Chapter 32

Once I had Pellini all tucked in, I made a quick trip to see Nils Engen, our resident medic, who delivered the very scientific diagnosis of "Yeah, your knee is pretty messed up." Fortunately, he also gave me a proper knee brace, though it came with orders to rest, ice, elevate, and ibuprofen the offending body part. With the knee braced and ibuprofen speeding through my system, I returned to the war room where, for the next two hours, I did my best to follow Engen's orders while on conference call after conference call—catching up on DIRT business, being debriefed, and hunting down updates on rift activity.

Or rather, the complete lack of rift activity. Not one single demon had come through any rift worldwide since midday. The previous record for no demons had been seventeen minutes. Ten hours made me edgy. It felt too much like the calm before the storm. Moreover, I had to wonder if events in the demon realm had triggered this lull. Lannist's demise? The Jontari theft of the gimkrah? Unfortunately, I'd barely glanced at my watch while we were hopping from realm to realm, so I couldn't be sure of the timing.

After I finally disconnected from a conference call with the Joint Chiefs of Staff, I got as far as swinging my braced leg out from beneath the table before the security switchboard patched through yet another call: Lieutenant Garvey, the officer on duty at the Spires.

"Good evening, ma'am," he said. "As per your standing order, I'm calling to notify you of activity at IZ-212 that occurred at eighteen-oh-three."

"Right. That's when we pulled out of there." I winced at the unintended annoyance in my voice. It was possible Garvey had only recently come on duty and didn't know we'd been at the Spires. I forced a smile that I hoped carried through into my tone. "Anything after that?"

"No, ma'am. That's—"

"Alrighty then. Have a good night, Lieutenant."

"Do you want me to email the full report?"

"What report?"

"Of the eighteen-oh-three activity, ma'am."

"I was *there*. I don't need it."

"No, ma'am, you weren't. Your group left at seventeen fifty-nine."

I pounded my fist against my forehead. "You said there wasn't activity after I left."

"No, ma'am. Let me clear up the confusion." He spoke with the unruffled patience of a math tutor explaining fractions. "Your group left the area at seventeen-fifty-nine. At eighteen-oh-three, the Demon Lord Muzztol appeared out of nowhere on the road outside the compound, near the security checkpoint."

The fog of exhaustion burned away, and I sat up straight. "And then?"

"The guard on duty opened the gate for him, at which time Lord Muzztol proceeded on foot to a point between the two Spires and disappeared, presumably transporting out."

Huh. Mzatal had arrived at the Spires only four minutes after we left. My instinct told me the timing was significant, but more telling was the part where he appeared out of nowhere. It was possible the lords had the teleportation aptitude of their daddies, but if so it was dormant—with the exception of Kadir. "I trust you have surveillance footage of the incident?"

"Yes, ma'am. I have it ready to send over on the secure network."

"Do that. And thank you for being patient with my confusion."

"It was my pleasure ma'am." His voice held a smile.

I punched the end call button on the war room phone then retrieved my cell phone from where it was charging on the side table. I had over half a dozen unread messages, but none of them were as important as the one voicemail that Mzatal had left at 17:55, mere minutes before our departure from the Spires.

The solution for this student does not lie with what you seek, nor with kin of my partner in dance. Do not act. I will come to you in an hour's time.

He'd responded in code based on my original message. I mentally translated. *The solution for Elinor's predicament isn't the gimkrah or the Jontari. Sit tight and wait for a face-to-face discussion in an hour.*

Except he hadn't come to me or called again. Instead, he returned to the demon realm minutes later without calling me back.

Maybe the surveillance video could tell me why? I switched the wall screen over to DIRT Secure and clicked on the file from Lieutenant Garvey. Distortion lines waved through the video images but, sure enough, Mzatal magically appeared about ten feet from the guard shack, strode unchallenged into the compound and to the Spires, then vanished.

Huh. I seriously doubted Mzatal had teleported himself there. Far more likely that Helori blinked him in and departed in the same instant, too quickly to spot. I watched it several more times in an effort to confirm my suspicion, but it wasn't until I ran the arrival clip at quarter speed that I saw the ghostly image beside Mzatal. Pleased, I isolated the frame and enlarged it.

Except it wasn't Helori. It was *Ilana*, Mzatal's ptarl. But why drop him off outside the gate? I fiddled with the enhancement adjustments in an effort to get a clearer picture then gave up and called for Lilith Cantrell, our resident double-duty security guard and tech specialist. While I waited for her, I tried to make sense of it all. There were any number of reasons to explain why Ilana came for him, especially with the rifts quiet on Earth. Perhaps a worsening of the southern anomaly in the demon realm. Or fallout from the Jontari after the gimkrah incident. Maybe a potency imbalance emergency.

I drummed my fingers on the table in a tense staccato. Despite all the perfectly logical reasons, a thorn of worry dug into me. It didn't feel right. Even if Mzatal was needed in the demon realm, why the odd subterfuge? And why in *that* moment, a scant four minutes after I left? It didn't help my uncertainty that Lannist had named both Ilana and Trask before he died. Unfortunately, I had no idea whether he'd been warning me about them or telling me they were allies.

Lilith sauntered in, a laptop case in one hand and a cup of coffee in the other. "Whatcha got, boss lady?" she asked, smile and tone bright.

"Technical ineptitude," I said with a self-deprecating snort. Fortunately, once I showed Lilith what I wanted, it took her no time at all to enhance the image enough to let me see Ilana's position better.

The demahnk had her fingertips on Mzatal's forehead—the ideal position for manipulation.

I thanked Lilith then waited until she departed before letting my fury boil up. That fucking demahnk bitch Ilana thought she could fuck with *my* man?

My anger cooled to icy calm. Ilana had done something to Mzatal, and though I didn't know what or why, my gut told me it was far from benign. Good thing I wasn't as oblivious or helpless as she thought. And, best of all, I had resources she didn't know about.

I found Michael sitting on the front porch steps, throwing a tennis ball for Sammy while two kittens played hide and pounce between the porch railings.

"Hey there, Michael," I said. "I really need your help."

His face lit up. "I got ways to help."

"I know you do, and I have a couple of important jobs for you." I sat beside him on the steps. "First, I'm a little worried about Mzatal. Could you please check and make sure he's okay?"

He grinned wide. "That's easy 'cause I just saw him before I ate cookies. Makes it speeeedy to see him again fast." He went still, eyes unfocusing, but a heartbeat later his smile turned into a deep frown. "There he is." His brow wrinkled.

"What's he doing?"

"I'll show you." He sprang up and crossed the porch to sit with his back to the house. "Not done yet," he cautioned then drew his knees up and rested his forearms on top of them, tipped his head back against the wall and let his face go slack, eyes staring. A few seconds later the life returned to his expression. "He's like that," Michael said. "Just sitting and looking."

A chill walked down my back. "Where is he?"

"I dunno. It's a hallway. Kinda dark with light way down at the end. Ilana's there, too. She's talking to a man. I dunno who he is."

"What's she saying?"

"I can't *hear*, silly."

"Right. Sorry." A man who Michael didn't know. There weren't a whole lot of those in the demon realm. He would recognize all the lords and the human forms of their ptarls. Maybe it was an enemy summoner?

Or a certain asshole ptarl who only recently came out of hiding. "Does the man have really light hair?" I asked. "And is he tall and slender?"

"Yep." He gave me a hopeful smile. "Can you see him, too?"

"No. Just a guess." Xharbek in Carl form. My worry became a physical ache. Mzatal craved wide open spaces, the freedom of the air and wind. He despised being confined and would never in a million years go sit in a closed-in, dark place like some emo-lord. Ilana had done something to throttle him back.

Lannist had specifically named both Ilana and Trask. With Ilana now firmly in the Enemy column, it was safe to assume that Trask could join her there.

"Whoops. They're gone. Mzatal's still sitting in that hallway, though." Michael returned to sit on the steps. "Okay. That's all I can see for now."

"That was a lot," I said warmly. "Was he sitting like that when you saw him before you ate cookies?"

Michael scooped up the ball and chucked it for the dog. "Nope. He was in a funny place with black all around it. There was a stump in the middle and big ol' chains on the floor."

The gimkrah's dimensional pocket and the podium. "What was he doing?"

"He banged his hand down on top of the stump. BAM!" Michael slammed a fist into the palm of his other hand. "And two more times. Bam bam. Broke the stump all to pieces. Blood came out of his fingers. Then Ilana came and made it all better and took him away." Michael dropped his hands. "That's all I saw."

Dread pooled in my belly. What did the loss of the gimkrah mean to Mzatal? And what had Ilana done to him after that to cause him to sit and stare in a darkened hall when worlds were at stake?

Oh shit. Xharbek. He'd dangled the gimkrah image to make sure I entered the column then, after I managed to escape the void trap, he left the way open for me to get the gimkrah. He'd *wanted* me to take it. I already knew he was in league with the Jontari on the invasion. It was no coincidence that those reyza picked that precise moment to risk an incursion into Mzatal's realm to steal my backpack—and the gimkrah.

"You okay?" Michael asked, his face lined with distress. "I'm sorry I did it wrong."

"No! You didn't do anything wrong. You were absolutely

perfect." I threw an arm around his shoulders and gave him a hug, glad to see him brighten. "I have one more very important job for you. Szerain is lost. Can you see him?"

"Nope. He's gone since the bad day when Earth went kablooey."

The day the PD valve blew—when Szerain went into hiding from Xharbek. "I know it's getting late, but maybe you could do some super-secret looking for him."

"I can stay up and be a spy."

"Good deal. I'm going to talk to Turek about it, but don't tell anyone else, okay?"

"Secret agents don't tell," Michael said, low and serious.

"Jill left more cookies in the kitchen if you need a spying boost," I said, though I wasn't sure he'd heard me since he already had the distant look in his eye.

I found Turek crouched in the spray of a lawn sprinkler at the side of the house, oblivious to the chill in the air. I quickly filled him in on Michael's quest then explained that I intended to contact Szerain in a few hours and would need his help. Turek, of course, offered his support without hesitation, which meant I could now focus my remaining energies on Mzatal's plight.

I limped to my room and crawled into bed, propped my leg on a pillow and pulled the comforter over me. After setting my phone alarm for two a.m., I closed my eyes and focused on my breath, slow and easy, then sent a silent appeal to Rho, asking for any assistance the grove might offer.

I visualized my sigil scar on Mzatal's chest while I held the leaf and ring against his sigil scar on mine. I reached mentally for Mzatal, through the silence of our connection and to the isolating walls he'd raised around himself. It was those walls that allowed him to maintain the will, focus, and control needed to marshal the lords through this crisis—and to wield the power of the essence blades.

Our connection was silent because of those walls. But it wasn't dead.

And I had a plan. As their creator, Mzatal had a connection to all three essence blades—and I intended to use them as a backdoor, bypassing his stupid walls altogether.

When I'd last seen him, he carried both his own blade, Khatur, and Rhyzkahl's Xhan—and I had zero reason to believe he'd set either knife aside. Khatur was familiar to me, but Xhan . . . I knew Xhan with hideous intimacy, thanks to Rhyzkahl's torture.

Now I needed to get its attention.

The scars covering my torso were a constant reminder of Xhan's vile resonance and touch. I reached for that resonance, sent out a mental spear of mocking disdain and contempt followed by as many insults as I could think of to use against a semi-sentient knife. *Useless, weak, and pathetic. You're a tool, with no power of your own.* Keeping my mental voice filled with sneering derision, I continued in that vein. *I look forward to the day I can melt you down into hair clips.*

Over and over, I stabbed into the silence.

No response.

Are you stupid, too? Do you even understand how pathetic you are? Oh, you talk tough enough when a lord is holding you, but once they send you away, you're stuck there in the dark. You're nothing more than a glorified letter opener, imprisoned in a desk drawer.

Heat flickered through my scars. My mouth stretched into a feral smile. "I feel you, you obsolete shard of cheap tin," I murmured. *Aww, it's like a warm hug. Is that the best you can do? A butter knife made out of cardboard could do better.*

The heat wavered and shifted, scars prickling now with the faint resonance of Xhan like an assassin's whisper. Without hesitation, I sent out another hate spear, seeking the pathway Xhan had used to reach me, and tracing it back toward its source.

While I maintained a barrage of taunts as a distraction, I worked my true purpose under their cover. The prickling flared, and I pressed my palm against my chest. *Mzatal*, I called.

Though he didn't answer, I sensed him, like feeling the *presence* of someone in the room with you, even though they remain silent and out of sight. Yet my elation faded within the span of a heartbeat. It was Mzatal, but not as I'd ever felt him before. Subdued. Watery rather than molten earth fiery.

It was an abomination. Ilana. Ilana had reduced him to this, dimmed the light of his essence. My rage could have scorched the seas, but that wasn't what I needed. Instead I poured my love and my heart into the thread of connection.

Mzatal. You are Mzatal. I am here. We will not let those bastards win.

I repeated it over and over as a mantra of will and truth, all the while taunting Xhan in order to keep the channel open and alive.

Hundreds or thousands of iterations in, the ghost-touch of

Mzatal fluttered through my consciousness. His touch faded within a heartbeat, but one word remained.

Zharkat.

One word, one concept, one truth that none could strip from us. One word that told me he'd received and embraced my message.

A mantle of peace settled over me like a soft fall of leaves, and I drifted into sleep.

Chapter 33

My alarm dutifully went off at two a.m., and I forced myself out of bed before I could even consider the merits of more sleep. In a perfect world I'd have grabbed a quick shower to finish waking up, but I settled for dunking my face in a sink full of cold water. Same effect in a fraction of the time.

Pellini was already awake when I went to rouse him, and agreed to meet me at the nexus in ten minutes. After a brief search, I found Michael dozing on the back porch swing with Turek laid out at his feet like a giant six-legged alligator. I felt a brief stab of guilt that Michael wasn't in a proper bedroom, then I saw the blanket tucked around him and realized there was absolutely no way my security people would have allowed him to sleep outside unless he'd expressly wished to do so. Besides, it was a lovely cool night, and he had Turek watching over him.

I crouched by the demon. "Any news?" I asked quietly.

He lifted his head, eyes luminescent violet in the shadows. "Michael glimpsed Szerain, but dwelt not long in the vision. We await your direction."

"Will you be able to contact Szerain once we pinpoint his location?"

"Our essence bond is strong," he hissed. "I will reach him."

"Dak lahn, honored one." A knot of tension unwound. "If you could wake Michael and bring him to the nexus in the next few minutes, we'll begin."

"It shall be done, summoner." Turek's manner and tone left no doubt that it would, indeed, be done.

With my compatriots awake and making ready, I limped across Rhyzkahl's orbit. He sat with his back against the grove tree, eyes closed, and softly dappled with moonlight filtered through the leaves. The effect softened his features, making him look less imposing and more approachable. Though he didn't so much as twitch when I stepped onto the nexus, I didn't assume for an instant that he was asleep.

The super-shikvihr undulated with softly shifting colors around the center of the nexus, reassuring in its steady strength. I moved to the opposite side of the tree from Rhyzkahl and placed both hands on its trunk. The other times I'd come to the tree, I simply basked in the grove aura to absorb the subtle energy and often intangible benefits. My approach this time was far more direct.

Rho, honored grove, I need your support to reach Szerain. Whatever aid you offer, I receive with gratitude.

Warmth flooded my hands, flowed up my arms and through my body, driving off the slight chill. The pain in my knee eased from barely tolerable to nonexistent, and an unequivocal sense of support suffused me. With a wordless expression of gratitude, I stepped back, surprised to see that Rhyzkahl had retreated to the patch of irises near his house, and Pellini, Michael, and Turek were standing in the grassy ring beside the nexus, obviously waiting for me to be ready.

I grimaced. "How long was I standing here?"

"It's been three days," Pellini said. "We were getting hungry."

I laughed and gestured toward the sky. "I call bullshit. The moon phase hasn't shifted one tiny bit."

He shrugged. "Well, I *am* getting hungry."

"We'll have a pancake party for breakfast," I said with a grin then passed through the shikvihr ring to the center of the nexus. Within the vortex of power, the pull of the moon became tangible, like a gentle updraft. I motioned the others to me and circled up with them in the midst of the power. The demon stood tall with both pairs of hands locked together before him while Pellini looked as relaxed and easy-going as if this was a daily occurrence. Michael fidgeted, eager and excited.

"Okay, let's get this ball rolling," I said, clapping my hands together. "Pellini, you do whatever it is we pay you to do." I paused briefly at his amused snort then continued, "Michael, you look for Szerain. Turek, I'll arcanely follow Michael's gaze and create and hold open a conduit for you to communicate." Easy, right? "I'll get the—"

"I see him!" Michael shouted.

Crapsticks. I wasn't even close to being ready.

"He's all lonely walking back and forth with dark all around," Michael went on. "He looks like he needs a nap."

My knee-jerk reaction was to hurry and lay the conduit before Michael lost the vision, but my inner Responsible Summoner pointed out that forging ahead without the proper groundwork was not only a way to guarantee failure but dangerous to everyone involved. "Don't focus too hard," I said, keeping my voice calm and reassuring as I worked the needed preparations. "I need you to keep seeing him for about a minute more, okay?"

"I'm trying, but it's all wiggly with stars and hard to look at long."

"Hold steady for as long as you can." My original plan to form a conduit relied on Michael maintaining a stable and reliable vision for several minutes. Gut instinct told me that wasn't going to happen, which meant it was time for a change of plan. "Pellini, follow my lead and reinforce." Working as quickly as I dared, I placed knots of potency along Michael's line of sight, like tying string around trees to mark a path through the woods.

"I can't do it anymore, Kara!" Michael's voice quavered with distress.

"It's okay, you can let it go now." I gave him a warm smile. "You did great!"

Michael sagged as the pathway shut down, and Pellini lowered him to sit. My focus stayed locked onto the potency knots. As I'd hoped, they remained as a faint but perceptible trail, and I proceeded to run threads of potency from knot to knot, until I had an arcane strand that ran from the center of the nexus to where Michael had seen Szerain.

"All right, that part's done," I said. "Turek, can you feel him through the strand?"

The demon lowered his head. "I have reached him, but his response is dampened to impressions only."

Right. Because a nice, easy, two-way communication was obviously too much to ask for. I mentally flipped the universe a middle finger. "That's okay," I said as if I believed it. "We can make this work. Tell Szerain I'm set to do the Dekkak summoning at the height of the full, at 11:23 p.m. tonight. But I don't have the gimkrah. Does that change anything?" *Like, has he come up with a plan that doesn't involve me dancing with an ancient killer demon?*

Turek's nostrils flared. "The impression I sense is to ask all and tell all with haste, then wait."

In other words, we didn't have time for a leisurely back-and-forth. "Did he get stuck away from the others? Is the plan still on for me to set the bunker diagrams and bring everyone home once I have Elinor? How soon? The Jontari have the master gimkrah. Lannist is dead. I have Elinor's journal. Ilana has manipulated and suppressed Mzatal. Xharbek knows about the summoning, and I'm sure he wants me to do it and die. Should I proceed with the summoning or not? I'll hold this connection open and wait for an answer." I bit down on the urge to ask Turek if he'd gotten all of that.

The demon went still while I fed potency into the strand to maintain contact. A good thirty seconds later, he lifted his head. "I have transmitted the information, but know not if it was received in full."

"It's a darn good start." I tried to sound cheerful and upbeat even though my nerves jangled. I hadn't realized until now just how badly I wanted Szerain's reassurance that we were on the right track and good to go with what little plan we had.

The strand of potency abruptly flared then burned away like a fuse on dynamite. Aghast, I swung my full attention to the demon. "Did you get an answer?" My voice shook. "Anything at all?"

"Secrets," Turek hissed. "Nothing more."

I shook my head in confusion. "Secrets? That doesn't make any sense." Frustration and despair rose in a choking wave. All of this effort for one cryptic word? No answers. No advice. Just *secrets.*

Pellini softly cleared his throat. "Did y'all have a secret hideout or handshake or something? Maybe it's a clue."

A caustic retort boiled up, but I choked it back as his words triggered a memory.

A spiral notebook appearing out of thin air.

"You need to teach me that trick some day."

"How can I amaze and mystify if I give away my secrets?"

My pulse pounded with relief and excitement. "Secret hideout is right. Pellini, you just earned your pancake party."

"Glad to hear it," he said with a chuckle. "So, where is the hideout?"

"Right here," I replied, spreading my hands. "He's using a dimensional storage pocket as a drop site. For a reply to my questions, I hope."

"Do you know how to get into one of those things?"

"Umm, I'm working on that part." I chewed my lower lip as I considered. The situation felt like the kind of trick questions where the answer was obvious to everyone but me. Except Szerain *knew* me. No way would he use a drop site I couldn't access, which meant he felt certain that I'd figure out how to reach into the dimensional pocket.

Relaxing, I called to mind the familiarity of Szerain. Of Ryan. A smile tugged at my mouth. He'd probably store his secret messages in something silly and nerdy, like a Star Wars lunchbox.

Exactly. Okay, not exactly. But the image carried the perfect Szerain-Ryan-secret-hiding-place resonance I needed as a focal point.

I fixed the concept of a Star Wars lunchbox in my head, Darth Vader on the front and Princess Leia on the side, blaster at the ready. My hand reached into that lunchbox.

And closed on something solid. "Holy shit," I breathed, staring at the notebook in my grasp. "I did it."

"Holy shit," Pellini echoed with a laugh. "So you did."

The notebook was plain, blue, and spiral-bound—and sealed with a ward woven from rakkuhr. Bracing myself against the odd feel of the potency, I unwound and dissipated the seal then opened the notebook.

The first thirty or so pages were taken up with sketches, but I forced myself to flip past them. A few pages from the back, I found Szerain's answers to my questions written in an exquisite cursive.

I couldn't return to the others without risking them.

Trust yourself. You have all that you need for the summoning. You have the use of a lord's power. Be lordy.

I will attempt to distract Xharbek during the time of the summoning in order to draw his attention from you.

After the summoning, and once you have Elinor, cleanse the nexus and set the three bunker diagrams. Keep Elinor on the nexus and within the diagrams. Reach for us precisely two hours after the peak of the full moon. We will be ready.

Be wary of all the demahnk, save perhaps Helori. Zakaar is cut off and cannot track their current agendas.

Activate and memorize this:

A delicate arrow pointed to an odd little knot of rakkuhr attached to the paper right below "memorize."

Use it if—when—you want Dekkak to pay close attention to what you're saying.

All right, I could follow directions. I activated the knot of rakkuhr, watched as the potency resolved into a three-dimensional hologram-type thing. As far as I could tell it was a depiction of interlocking loops of pygah. As I carefully memorized it, I expected to understand something of its purpose, as was the norm with the mental tracing of any other arcane construct, but I gleaned absolutely nothing. Not the slightest hint of what this thing was or how it was meant to get Dekkak's attention. Hell, it could be a clown with a water pistol for all I knew.

Still, I mentally filed it away, confident that Szerain wouldn't have wasted time on it unless it could somehow prove useful.

"This is what I needed," I said, looking up at the others with gratitude. "I can't thank you enough for all of your help."

Turek hissed acknowledgment before leaping off the nexus and into the shadows of the woods. Pellini helped Michael to his feet then clapped me on the back.

"I haven't forgotten the pancake party," he said, "but the circles under your eyes are darker than the slab. I'll get Michael settled. You go back to bed."

I shook my head. "I need to find Jill first."

"She went with Bryce to make the exchange for the net." Pellini glowered, as if daring me to come up with another stupid excuse.

As if I'd waste a Kara Gillian Clever Retort on him. And totally not because I was so wiped out I couldn't think of a single thing to say that wasn't "Oh, okay." I finally settled on a very smart and witty nod, then I marched off the nexus and to my bed.

Though fatigue had a firm grip on my eyelids, I took a moment to look through Szerain's sketches. As I paged through the notebook, tears filled my eyes. Dozens upon dozens of sketches of Ashava, documenting her life—and growth—over the past two months.

Szerain gave me these on purpose, I realized, throat tight with emotion. He could have easily torn out and passed just the one page that held his notes and the rakkuhr knot, but he'd captured these moments and delivered the entire notebook so that Jill could have a badly needed glimpse of her daughter.

Damn. I wanted to show these to her in person, but she wouldn't be back for several hours yet. And it didn't feel right to just leave them out for her to find when she got home. No, as soon as I woke up, I'd hunt her down.

I turned the page for the next sketch then stared. Instead of Ashava, it was Elinor, smiling and full of life. But what sent my heart thumping was the note below it in Szerain's hand.

Kara, Elinor is my daughter.

"Are you shitting me?!" I fumbled the page over to see if there was more but found only blank space. The Elinor sketch was the last one.

I'm going to punch him, I mused in quiet shock. *I'll rescue everyone from their stronghold and then,* kapow, *I'll deck Szerain right there on the nexus.* The jerk had time enough in the dimensional pocket to mess with me about an Amkir ancestry, but he couldn't tell me this?

Elinor smiled up at me. My outrage drained away. In his place, I'd have done the same—tossed a note and ran, rather than open a fifty-five gallon drum of worms. He'd killed her. *Bladed* her. Had he known of their relationship at the time? Either way, it was a subject fraught with too many emotions to name.

With the utmost care, I tore out that page and the one with the answers to my question, set the notebook on the nightstand and slipped the two pages into the drawer.

As I reached to turn off the lamp, I saw the voicemail light blinking on my phone. Idris had called at 2:13 a.m., right when I was getting started on the nexus.

"Hey, Kara. Guess you're either asleep or busy. I'm really sorry I lost it the other day. I was out of line." He sighed. "And what's worse is that I don't know if I'm going to make it to Louisiana in time to help you." His voice held true regret and worry. "Things are quiet in the seafloor rift, but a couple of massive Class 2C demons came through right before the lull. We kept them contained for the better part of the day, but about fifteen minutes ago they broke through my warding, and now they're swimming toward the Sea of Japan, I think to take out a container ship that's carrying critical equipment. My chopper's leaving in just a few minutes. Best estimate is that it'll take us close to four hours to intercept the demons."

Well, that sucked. Eight hours there and back, and demon sea battles were notorious for lasting the better part of a day. Plus, it was a *minimum* of twelve hours travel time from Korea to Louisiana—and that was if he could jump right onto a fast military transport heading straight here.

"On a related note, I called in a few favors, and I'm sending you pics of some old documents that were found near Puryong. I didn't have much time to look over them, and they're not in English, but I think they might pertain to your current project. The encryption keys are the tower with the cracks and the scumbag whose balls you crushed near there."

I grinned. Trust Idris to remember that.

"Be careful, Kara. You're special to me. I'll be there as soon as I can."

"You're special to me, too," I murmured.

After I dried my eyes, I pulled up his email. The south tower of Szerain's palace held a room with eleven strange cracks. And it was Amkir whose nuts I'd crushed during the battle to get the essence blade, Vsuhl.

"Nice going, Idris," I breathed as I scanned the pictures. The documents were old, faded, and in a language I couldn't read, but several of the drawings were almost certainly binding sigils. Every bit of ammo helped.

I forwarded the pics to Jill for possible translation then killed the light, closed my eyes, and dropped right off to sleep.

Chapter 34

My gaze skimmed the tops of dark green waves as I swiveled the periscope. Pellini came into view, wearing a Speedo and surfing on the back of a bright purple whale. The sigil on his chest glowed neon green. I scowled. Why the hell wasn't he wearing a life jacket?

Weeeeeeeeeeee clatterclatterclatter chunkchunkchunk wrrr-rrrrrrrr

I frowned at my submarine crew. "What was that?"

The crewmembers waved tentacles and clattered wings in reply. My first mate blew out a stream of bubbles, and I hurried to pop them to hear her words. "He lost the petunias, Admiral Commander. Now the prisoners know too much."

"What prisoners?"

"The ones in the prison, Admiral."

CLUNK whooosh clatter.

"Fuck!"

The dream popped and vanished like one of the first mate's speech bubbles. Prying my eyes open, I struggled to place the weird sounds that had woken me.

"No, you need to repressurize the air canister to—don't tangle that cable! C'mon, we don't have all day to be fiddle-fucking around with this. Kellum, hold that steady while Greitz resets the motor."

That was Bryce, sounding mega-stressed. *The net*, I realized. The noise was him test-firing it. Because today was Summoning Day. Whether I was ready or not.

"Like Christmas, but with more bloodshed," I muttered.

Be lordy. Right.

Groaning, I flopped onto my back and stared up at the ceiling. It was made of dozens and dozens of narrow boards that were all meticulously linked with tongue and groove joints. Every wall and ceiling in my house was like that. Hell, the whole house was a marvelous example of construction done right, with every section planned in detail and built with care and precision by my grandfather. One of our security guards, Bubba Suarez, had an extensive background in construction. He'd once spent the better part of a rare morning off going through the house, from attic to basement, making manly noises of appreciation for details I'd been blissfully unaware of but apparently made an enormous difference in the structural integrity of the house.

"You got yerself a mighty fine place here, Miss Kara," Suarez had announced. "Keep up the maintenance, and this beauty'll last 'til the Mississippi dries up, s'long as a twister don't hit it dead on." And then he went to gaze adoringly at the brickwork in the fireplace.

Experience told me that my summoning diagram needed to be as solid and precise as this house. Every piece doing its part and working together as a perfect whole for maximum strength and stability. Easy. Except that I had only a handful of scattered and incomplete references that could tell me *how* to create it. Szerain expected me to do the most difficult and dangerous summoning of my life without any sort of blueprint. Me, who'd only ever summoned "tame" non-Jontari demons. It would be like trying to build a mansion, sans instructions, after only building doghouses.

The one thing that kept me from descending into full-blown panic was the essence-deep knowledge that Szerain believed I could pull it off. Since I couldn't possibly learn it in time, I needed to *know* it.

I struggled to wrap my brain around knowing the entirety of a major and unfamiliar summoning but gave up when my eyes began to cross. All right, what if I broke it down into its components? That was much less head-hurty.

I *knew* how to open a portal. That was the same no matter what kind of creature was being summoned. Same with the call, the command to appear, though this one would require way more *oomph*—like fishing with braided monofilament instead of dinky ten pound test. However, the nexus would provide all the power I needed.

It was the bindings that stopped me dead and left me cold. When push came to shove, I had to admit that I'd never done real ones before. The protections I'd always laid were sturdy enough to hold a weak demon, but for any creature with more than a smattering of arcane skill, they'd be about as effective as chains made of construction paper. I needed to *know* how to contain a Jontari imperator, but I had no foundation to draw on. I was expected to chain the beast with only the barest knowledge of metal.

No, it was even simpler than that. I was trying to make electricity without knowing to wrap a copper wire around a magnet. Once I grasped that missing core aspect, that spark, I felt certain that my experience would fill in the rest. If I could just find *one* complete drawing or description of a full old-school diagram with protections designed to contain a mega-powerful creature, then I—

I jerked upright. The outreach center! Peter Cerise built a diagram there to summon and bind Rhyzkahl, who certainly counted as a mega-powerful creature. Even when Cerise was bleeding me, I couldn't help but admire the exquisite brilliance of what he'd created, unlike anything I'd seen before. Too bad I'd been a bit preoccupied and unable to give it a close examination.

Crime scene photos would show the diagram, I thought then immediately abandoned that idea. The Crime Lab had been reduced to rubble when the PD valve blew.

My smile grew. But Peter Cerise had used my blood to paint the sigils. With the right equipment, I should be able to see every single one.

"Oh, Kara, you so awesoooooome," I sang. With any luck, I'd find that core nugget of info I needed to summon the big bad demon and rescue Elinor.

After coffee, of course.

I tugged on a sweatshirt and shorts, dragged fingers through my hair then shuffled to the kitchen. Janice sat at the table, coffee in hand as she watched news footage on a tablet. She had on black fatigue pants and a green, long-sleeved shirt that bore a computer company logo and looked exactly like a shirt our tech whiz Lilith Cantrell owned.

"Crap," I said as my brain finished waking up. "Forgot to make arrangements for clothes for you. Sorry." Or any other arrangements, for that matter.

"No worries." She shut off the tablet and gave me a light

smile. "You have a good crew here. They made sure I knew the drill and had what I needed." She lifted her chin toward the stove. "There's bacon and biscuits if you want them."

Relieved, I continued to the coffeemaker where a sticky note from Jill told me to check my email. Definitely the best place to leave me a note and guarantee that I'd see it. "We're lucky to have so many solid people working with us." I filled and doctored a cup then took a long sip. Go, caffeine, go!

After a few more gulps to finish waking up, I pulled up my email on my phone and found a message from Jill with a time-stamp of five a.m. In other words, after she returned from getting the net with Bryce, she'd stayed up to work on the Korean document. I wanted to show her the sketchbook, but I'd wait another hour or so before waking her.

Hey K—

Between the power of the internet and Giovanni's awesome brain, we translated that doc. Quick summary: There's a Korean artifact—a stone turtle—that's actually filled with makkas.

Since I figured that might prove useful, I searched online with the description from the text, and I'm pretty sure I found it. Even better, it's currently part of an exhibit at the National Art Center in Tokyo. I've attached a picture and a copy of the translated documents.

J

Hot damn. Even though there was no possible way to get our hands on it in time for the summoning, I liked the idea of having a stash of the arcane dampening material as a just-in-case. Idris could swing through Japan and scoop it up. Of course, I had zero idea what was involved in "borrowing" part of a museum exhibit, but I had friends in high places—Hello, Madam President—who could pull the right strings.

And when she inevitably asked why I needed an ancient stone turtle, I'd do what I always did: make up something clever and confusing.

Pleased, I sent the necessary emails winging their way through the internet then topped off my coffee. As I spooned in more sugar, clanging from the back yard drew my attention out the window to where Bryce and three security guards laboriously rolled up a huge SkeeterCheater net. Its launcher squatted on the far side of the nexus, about a dozen feet beyond Rhyzkahl's orbit. Our mechanic, Ronda Greitz, hunched over the launcher as she tinkered with its inner workings.

●

"I just have one question," Janice said, having politely waited until I wasn't so obviously busy.

"Only one?" I smiled, appreciating her courtesy.

She chuckled. "Okay, I have thousands, but the most burning one is, why do you have two giant boulders in your living room? And what on earth are they made of? It's no mineral or substance I've ever seen."

Exhaling, I took a seat across from her. "Each one has a person inside of it," I said then went on to give her a quick rundown of the "plague" and its phases, as well as its connection to the rakkuhr that was pouring through the valves.

Janice sobered. "I watched TV for a bit last night and this morning. Mzatal had told me there were rifts opening up on Earth and that Jontari were coming through, but I had no idea there'd been so much or so many." Her dark eyes filled with worry.

"It's bad," I agreed, "but humans are stubborn assholes, and we still have an ace or two in the hole."

One side of her mouth curved up. "We're pursuit predators." At my blank look, she went on, "Humans have survived and evolved and prevailed by letting our prey wear itself out. That nice juicy antelope might be fast, but the human hunter simply follows its tracks and keeps going, keeps following until the antelope can't run anymore. We're pretty tenacious."

"The demons aren't running away from us," I pointed out. "And they have claws and teeth, and are dangerous and deadly."

Janice leaned forward. "But they're *completely* dependent on the arcane."

"You're right about that." It was one of the reasons summoned demons couldn't remain long on Earth without some sort of link that would give them arcane support. Eilahn had been able to stay with me because Rhyzkahl had been her link, her lifeline to the arcane. Before the PD incident triggered the flood of potency—and rakkuhr—to Earth, even the lords were limited on the time they could spend away from the demon realm. "Unfortunately, the invading Jontari can draw all the arcane they need from the rifts, not to mention the rakkuhr that's coming through."

She made a face and sat back. "Darn. And here I thought I'd solved all of our problems."

"Well, you're right about us not giving up," I said with a smile. My coffee cup was empty, so I stood to get a refill. "And on that note, I need to move my ass and start chewing away at my to-do list. Is there anything you need? Didn't you say you wanted to bring equipment back to the demon realm?"

Her eyes lit up. "I did. I need computer equipment and solar charging—" She stopped at my wince.

"Potency levels in the demon realm are hell on electronics," I said. "However, DIRT has some shielding cases that might help. Give Pellini the list of what you need. If it can be had, he'll know where to find it."

Her smile turned brilliant. "Terrific. I'll work on that while I have breakfast with Rhyzkahl."

Carefully withholding comment, I watched in bemusement as she loaded a plate with biscuits and bacon then headed to the back yard. With only a teensy bit of shame, I moved to the kitchen window and watched her settle under the tree where Rhyzkahl stood amid a weak circle of sigils. In his hand was one of his purple irises, and at first I thought he was going to give it to her as a barf-worthy too-sweet gesture of affection. Instead, he dispelled the sigils and laid the flower at the base of the tree, and only then did he turn and welcome Janice with a smile. He seemed happier with her here, but even though I had zero doubt she'd spent the night with him in his little house, it was clear their relationship wasn't a romantic one. They *enjoyed* each other. They were friends.

It was curious and unexpected. But nice.

Purple flower. A shiver ran through me. Rhyzkahl had once placed a violet bloom on my pillow, the same type of flower that was carved in stone at a shrine to Elinor in Rhyzkahl's garden. The same kind he'd used to caress her in the memory-vision, when he called her zharkat and she denied him.

My gaze swung to the sea of rich purple irises near his house. *He still loves her.*

CLUNK whoooosh

Janice startled as the net shot from the launcher. Fortunately, she and Rhyzkahl were sheltered by the grove tree trunk and safe from getting accidentally netted. Unfortunately, it looked as if a just-summoned demon would be equally safe. The net opened in a beautiful spread then sailed down in a perfect arc to cover a spot a few feet beyond and to the right of the nexus.

Bryce threw down his work gloves. "FUCK!"

An exasperated look swept over Janice's face. "You're going to kill yourself trying to sight it in through trial and error!" She pushed up and jogged over to Bryce and the crew. Though I couldn't hear what she said, her gestures led me to believe she was talking angles and force and other physics-mathy stuff that was way beyond my pay grade.

Good. She was smart and blunt and would get that shit straightened out. Which meant I didn't have to deal with it.

I rinsed out my mug then climbed up to the attic to tackle the next item on my to-do list. The bulb remained stubbornly dead when I tugged on the string, but enough light shone up from the laundry room below to let me move around without breaking my neck. Luckily, I didn't have to go far. On the third shelf of a battered metal cabinet, tucked between a stack of old board games and a broken clock, rested the wooden cigar box that held my summoning implements. I'd retired them after Angus Mc-Dunn decimated my abilities, and putting the box away had been symbolic for me. Not because I was convinced my days as a summoner were over, but because I'd realized that I was *more* than just a summoner.

My breath shuddered out of me. *And now I'm a summoner again.* Along with everything else that was Kara Gillian. My arcane ability was only one facet of my identity, but I was stronger for it.

"Time to come out of retirement, y'all," I murmured, blinking back silly, emotional tears. I slid the box off the shelf then blew across the top of it, hoping for a cool cloud of dust like in the movies. But clearly two months in a closed attic was insufficient for any sort of decent dust gathering, and the only thing my breath dislodged was a dead mosquito.

"Eh, it'll do," I said with a shrug then tucked the box under my arm and returned downstairs.

Pellini was at the kitchen table making notes on a yellow pad and munching bacon. As I set the cigar box on the counter, my gaze went to the left side of his face.

"Who gave you a black eye?"

"It's not a black eye," Pellini insisted. "It's a small bruise beneath my eyebrow, and Jill gave it to me when we were sparring this morning." He scowled. "Damn, that bitch is fast and flexible. She did this with a *kick* while I was standing up straight."

"She's sneaky," I said, not hiding my amusement. Pellini wasn't a short guy, but Jill was a former world class gymnast. And I'd been wrong about her going to bed after finishing the translation. "After she finished kicking your butt, did she finally go get some sleep?"

"She claims she slept in the truck, then said that once the sun came up she had too much on her mind to sleep. About half an hour ago she headed into town on a supply run with Suarez."

"Hope Superwoman gets more eggs," I said.

"Even better, she's getting chickens."

I did a double-take. "Seriously?"

"Apparently so." Pellini spread his hands. "She said that with everything in turmoil and prices going up and all these mouths to feed, it was high time we got as self-sustaining as possible."

"Huh." I gave a slow nod. "I haven't had a spare second to think about any of that, but she's right."

His mouth twitched. "She did all sorts of research on how to take care of chickens, had Suarez build a coop and enclosure behind the barracks, and made arrangements to purchase a passel of poultry." He paused to sip his coffee. "Plus, she's looking into the feasibility and cost-benefit of maintaining other livestock."

"Hang on, you mean like cows and pigs and stuff?"

"Milk goats, cattle, pigs, and a couple of horses are all on her wish list."

I shook my head. "Where does she expect to put them?" Sure, I had ten acres of property, but most of it was woods. Even if we cut down several acres of trees—a thought that sent a pang of grief through me—surely cows would need actual pasture with grass and stuff?

"Jill's already considered all of that," he said. "Turns out that the property behind yours is up for sale, dirt cheap. Forty acres. Sadly, no mule."

"Tell me again why we don't simply have her run the world?"

"She'd get everything straightened out, that's for sure. Oh, almost forgot." He set his cup down and reached into his backpack. "Those Jontari pricks got the gimkrah, but they didn't get this."

My breath caught as he placed a bundle of orange demon silk on the table. "Eilahn's Halloween decorations!" Tears of relief stung my eyes. "I forgot that we traded backpacks before I went up the column." I unwrapped the silk from the exquisite garlands. "I need to hang these up before things get too crazy."

"I'll give you a hand with that," Pellini said. "Are those little figures all demons?"

"Since technically any resident of the demon realm counts as a demon, then probably so," I said. "All of the commonly summoned types are here—except ilius, of course." Even Eilahn would have a tough time carving a figurine of the barely corporeal demon. "But there are a half dozen or so that have me stumped. I've never seen or heard of anything like that bird-snake one or the mushroom-head dude."

"That slug-squid-octopus-tentacle thing looks . . . interesting."

"Maybe Sammy wants a playmate."

"Or Fuzzykins."

"Ha! Fuzzykins would eat that thing for breakfast. She loves seafood." I carefully gathered up the garlands. "Let's get these hung up. I have places to go and demons to summon."

"Ah, the never-ending refrain of the modern woman."

Chapter 35

Though the air held a distinctly chilly bite, it was an absolutely gorgeous day, with bright blue skies and a scattering of happy puffy clouds. By the time Pellini and I had the garlands artistically draped around the front door, the net launcher had been properly sighted in, and Bryce's mood was drastically improved. Now that I knew I wasn't risking getting my head bitten off, I pulled Bryce aside to go over what to do with the various Kara's Kompound residents and working personnel during the summoning.

Bryce scrutinized the duty roster on the whiteboard. "As far as my security people go, we absolutely need to have a reserve force off-premises in case the worst happens." He frowned. "I sure as hell don't want everyone standing in a cluster on the big X when the bomb drops. Not a single one of them will want to leave, but that's too bad."

"Maybe they can draw straws," I said with a wry smile.

"That's exactly what they'll do," he replied, utterly serious. "The losers will have to ship out."

"At least they'll have company. Not only do I want Janice, Michael, and Jill out of here, but I want the dog, cat, and kittens safe as well."

Bryce laughed. "That'll make the losers happier. Kittens make everything better. I'll send everyone to Jill's house in town, unless you have an objection."

"That's perfect. It's already warded to the teeth with Zack's protections." I knew this was one decision Jill would be on board with, especially when she had a daughter out there who needed her alive and well.

"Good deal," Bryce said. "I'll get all of that rolling."

With that settled, it was time to deal with the rest of my pre-summoning must-do list.

As soon as I was showered, dressed, and armed, I stuffed Elinor's journal and Szerain's notebook into my bag then arranged for the security guard on standby, Dennis Roper, to follow my Humvee in a separate vehicle. Solo excursions were a big security no-no, and I heartily approved of our two-people-per-vehicle protocol. But at the moment, even the silent and stoic Roper was more company than I wanted.

After a quick stop for supplies at the temporary building that housed the Beaulac PD crime lab, I continued on to the outreach center.

My heart skittered when I turned onto the street and spied a military light utility vehicle parked out front. *One of ours,* I realized an instant later, recognizing the long dent on the right rear bumper. As we neared, security specialist Bubba Suarez stepped out of the vehicle with his weapon at the ready. The instant he saw it was me, profound relief flowed over his wide face.

"I'm sure glad it's you, ma'am," he said after I parked and hurried up to him.

"Is Jill inside?"

"Yes, ma'am. She was dead set on coming here. Told me she had special business. We did a sweep of the building for threats, then she asked me real nice to wait outside for a bit while she took care of something." He shifted his feet, grimacing. "I done texted her twice for status checks, and each time she says she's fine, but it's been almost a half hour now. I was just about to go on in when y'all came 'round the corner." He turned his head and spat a stream of tobacco juice into the street. "We still ain't got the chickens, dangit."

"I'll check on her."

I told Roper to wait with Suarez, then I pushed open the front door of the center and stepped in.

"Jill?"

A few seconds of silence then, "In here."

My footsteps echoed as I moved through the foyer and into the common room. Jill sat slumped on a dusty chair by a scarred metal desk. Shafts of light speared through the gloom around her.

"I thought that maybe if I came here I could feel something of my daughter, like how you felt Szerain," she said, voice cracking. "But it's just a smelly, dirty room." She let out a brittle laugh. "I guess I've finally gone off the deep end."

"Shallow end is for people who refuse to take risks." I brushed the worst of the grime off a second chair and pulled it over by her. "You're not crazy, Jill. Coming here wasn't crazy. Honestly, when I think about everything you've been through in the last year, I'm stunned you haven't started painting the walls with your own poop."

She blinked at me. "That's . . . completely disgusting."

"See? You're still a long way from totally losing it." I gave her a warm smile. "I was looking for you at home because I have an update for you."

Her expression turned guarded. "Spill it."

"After you left with Bryce last night, I tried to confirm arrangements with Szerain. We didn't get to chat this time, but he gave me written, final instructions. The plan is still on for bringing them home."

"It can't come soon enough." She closed her eyes and let out a long sigh. "I need to hold my baby girl."

"I have something to show you." I pulled Szerain's notebook out of my bag, placed it on the desk between us and opened it to the first drawing. A baby looked up from a tumbled blanket, eyes bright, and mouth open in an expression of delight.

"Oh my god. It's her." Jill's eyes went to a sketch in the corner, a small dragon with its eyes closed and its head tipped up to the sun. "And . . . that's her, too," she said with a note of amazement in her voice.

"Jill, she's growing up fast." I waited for her to tear her eyes from the sketch. "Maturing *really* fast because of her demahnk half."

"How fast?" The question came out in a strained croak.

"Fast." I flipped to a page with Ashava in human form—a little girl of nine or ten, eyes sparkling with humor above a mischievous smile. "This is her now."

Jill reached toward the page, hand trembling. "Oh my god. She's *beautiful*." Tears spilled onto her cheeks. "Look at her."

I waggled my fingers at the notebook. "There are more. *Lots* more."

She started at the beginning and paged through slowly, studying each drawing with reverent intensity as if absorbing every minute detail. Her gaze lingered on the last one. "I missed all of this. I missed her growing up."

"I'm so sorry," I said. "She still has plenty of growing up left to do, though. And it seems Szerain did his best to chronicle her life."

"Yes, he did." Her eyes met mine. "He did that for me." Jill sniffled and wiped the tears away. "It's settled then. He gets cookies for life."

I laughed. "Sounds more than fair."

"Do you feel ready to do the summoning tonight?" she asked, a steely glint in her eye.

"With luck, I will very soon." I patted my bag. "The Symbol Man painted his sigils with blood, and I have plenty of luminol right here."

Comprehension lit her face. "He was trying to summon Rhyzkahl." She laughed softly. "And now you're going to plagiarize his work."

"Exactly! Seems only fair he should help me out now, considering everything he did."

"You're looking for the glyphs from the big circle on the meeting room floor, right?"

"Those are the ones."

"I'd better give you a hand," she said, getting to her feet. "I think I have a bit more experience with luminol than you."

"You do." I grinned. "I've never used it. I always waited for the crime lab to do all that stuff." I dug the spray bottle and nitrile gloves out of my bag. "With two of us, it shouldn't take long."

I ducked outside to let Roper and Suarez know what we were doing, then Jill and I went to the meeting room and got down to business. The first task was to block as much light as possible from the chinks between the boards covering the windows, but the plunder of some old sofa cushions dealt with that issue. Once the room was nice and dark, I shone my flashlight on a place where I *knew* there'd been sigils.

Jill spritzed the spot. I turned off my flashlight. The sigils glowed.

"It's working!" I jumped up and down a few times and did a quick happy dance. "Hot damn!"

"So copy them down, you big weirdo," Jill said with a touch of her old asperity. I seized her in a hug then got to work sketching the sigils and their placement. We quickly fell into a pattern of shine-spritz-draw, sidestepping our way around the large circle. But we'd barely made it halfway around when the shine-spritz produced a large solid glow instead of sigils.

"Crap," I muttered.

"This is where the decapitated victim bled out," Jill said. "His blood obscured the sigils."

That victim was the summoner who'd caused all the trouble. Peter Cerise, whose head Rhyzkahl had twisted off. I peered at the area but couldn't make out a thing.

Jill took another two steps and spritzed. "It should clear up right about here." Light blood spatter glowed, but I could make out the sigils.

"Looks like that big blood spot obliterated close to a dozen sigils," I said. And there wasn't a thing I could do about it but keep going. Kind of like life in general.

To my relief, we didn't run into any other ruined areas, and we eventually shined, spritzed, and drew our way back to where we'd started.

I shone the light on the floor nearby, outside the ritual diagram. "Try here."

"Kara . . ."

"Just do it. Please."

With a resigned sigh, she spritzed the spot. I flicked off the light and crouched beside the glowing patch. *My* blood, where the reyza Sehkeril had hooked his claws in my belly and left me to die in a pool of blood and viscera. I drew my gloved fingers across the luminescence. "It seems like an eternity ago. I was so . . ." I couldn't find the word.

"Innocent? Naïve? You were played by a player and had been kept in the dark about *everything*. Considering what and who you were up against, you kicked ass."

My gaze drifted to the luminol glow in the shape of a boot print. Rhyzkahl's, where he'd tracked my blood after nudging my intestines with his toe. I let out a long breath that felt like the purging of toxic sludge, then stood. "I still don't know all of what we're up against, but the past is ancient history. I'm not that naïve woman anymore."

"You got that right, chick. You went through the fires of hell and came out fighting."

"I plan to kick a lot more ass," I said with a smile. "Starting with a Jontari imperator tonight."

Jill laughed. "Slow down there, partner. Start off light with subduing him and bending him to your will." She pulled a cushion from the window to let in shafts of sunlight. "Did you get enough of the sigils copied? I mean, considering about ten percent were ruined."

"I think it'll be enough," I said, looking down at my diagram sketch, easily picking out which aspects pertained to bindings and protections. The missing spark wasn't jumping out at me, but I strangled the worry before it could take up residence. As soon as I made it back to the house, I'd go through it sigil by sigil and figure it out. Somehow. "I have a hundred times more info than when I got here. I'd call that a win."

Jill peered at a pair of sigils on the outer edge then pointed at my sketch. "Those two aren't right. There's supposed to be a long curved part that goes from the top of one to the middle of the other."

"Damn, you're right. I forgot to put in the joining link." I quickly penciled in the correction then looked up at her with a frown. "How'd you pick out such a tiny discrepancy?"

She shrugged. "I have a good memory."

"A really good memory," I said, impressed. The diagram had hundreds of sigils in it. As I skimmed my eyes over it again, my breath caught. With those two sigils corrected, everything else took on a new pattern, and now the diagram practically glowed with a life of its own.

"Maybe I should learn what some of these things mean," Jill said. She gestured at the sigils. "Might come in handy with being mother to a qaztehl."

"That's not a bad idea," I said, closing my notebook to protect the diagram sketch. "There are a number of standard ones that you could learn to recognize."

"She's freaked out," Jill murmured.

I gave her a perplexed look. "Who? Ashava?"

Jill nodded. "Everything's scarier with Szerain gone and Zack still weak. She doesn't know what's going to happen next."

Holy crap. Szerain wasn't with the others in the dimensional pocket because he was still in the bubble. But I hadn't told Jill anything about that. She had no possible way to know where Szerain was or wasn't. Or Zack's condition, for that matter. But Ashava knew. Jill was feeling *Ashava's* worry and fear.

Suddenly, other little snippets of conversation made more sense, such as Jill referring to Zack as Ashava's sire and her certainty that her daughter had red hair. And now, correcting those sigils in my sketch.

Ashava, you clever little minx, I thought with glee. She'd maintained a thread of contact with her mommy. Not only had she just helped me out, but the sadness no longer haunted Jill's eyes. Ashava had reached out for reassurance and given it at the same time.

I opened my mouth to tell Jill then closed it. What if her knowing about the connection made it tougher for Ashava to get through? Maybe the kid needed Jill to be mentally relaxed so that she could slip in unnoticed? I wasn't sure how it worked, and I definitely didn't want to jinx it. Probably best to wait and ask Szerain before saying anything.

"I'll tell you what'll happen next," I said brightly. "I'm going to make sure Elinor gets rescued, then we'll follow through with the plan to get Szerain, Ashava, Zack, and Sonny back with us where they belong."

"That's exactly right." Jill gave a fierce nod. "Now get your ass home so you can summon a big bad demon."

"And you're going to get chickens?"

"Yup. Nowhere near as cool as a demon, but not all of us can be Kara Gillian."

"The world would run out of coffee within a week if everyone was Kara Gillian."

"Three days at best." Jill strode to the door with a lilt in her step. "Then it would be every Kara Gillian for herself."

A world without coffee? I shuddered and followed her out.

Chapter 36

Back at the house, I started chewing my way through my pre-summoning to-do list, adding items and tasks as they occurred to me, and doing my best to not fret about the *Be lordy???* at the very bottom of the page. Within the first hour, the list doubled in size, at which time I realized that I was *possibly* delving into minutiae in order to avoid dealing with that last item on the list. I therefore began a regime of merciless prioritization and delegation because, for fuck's sake, Kara. No, I didn't need to break out the weed-whacker and trim the grass around the nexus. I was summoning a demon, not the President. Nor did I personally need to change the burned out floodlight at the northwest corner of the house when I had any number of people who would gladly do it for me. In similar fashion, I delegated filling a sports bottle with tunjen, and crossed out *Clean oven* and *Fold laundry*. Seriously, what was I thinking?

"Lunch," Pellini said as I sat hunched over my list at the kitchen table.

I obediently wrote down *Lunch*. "Can you take care of getting my wizard staff from DIRT?" The six-foot long turbo-charged cattle prod was deliciously effective against most demons and would be awfully nice to have on hand.

"Sure thing, but only after you stop and eat your goddamn lunch."

I lifted my head, surprised to see a plate bearing a grilled-cheese sandwich, a generous handful of figs, and several strips of bacon. "Oh. Where'd that come from?"

He cast his eyes heavenward. "I fucking cooked it while you

sat there and muttered to yourself. Now eat it before I hold you down and force-feed you."

I snatched up the sandwich and took a hasty bite. Pellini was the sort to carry out a threat like that. "Thanks," I mumbled around bread and cheese. My appetite woke up as sandwich met stomach, and I tore through the rest of the food.

"That's better," Pellini said with a satisfied nod.

"Yeah, I *feel* better." I leaned back and rubbed my happy belly. "Did Jill find an open farmer's market?"

He gave me a curious look. "No. Why?"

"The figs," I said, gesturing to the remnants on the plate. "Where'd they come from?"

"Seriously? From the fig trees on your property."

I blinked. "Wait. I have fig trees?"

Pellini tossed his hands up. "Jesus. You have about half a dozen along the east fence line."

"Huh. That's cool. I love figs."

He shook his head, laughing softly. "I'm gonna go see about getting the wizard staff."

"Thanks for lunch," I said. "You take pretty good care of me."

He snorted and drew breath to make what I was certain would be a snarky reply, but instead he let it out and gave me a crooked smile. "Anytime, Kara," he said then strode off toward the war room.

Feeling restored in body and mind, I skimmed the rest of my list, pleased to see that the major tasks had all been taken care of—with the exception of the Be Lordy crap. Maybe being lordy was about being super confident? Lifting my chin, I filled my brain with positive thoughts. *Tonight, I will successfully summon a Jontari Imperator, survive the experience, and send him to Fed Central to snatch Elinor from Xharbek's clutches!*

Crap. Unless Xharbek had moved her. That was a very nonpositive thought, but a darn timely one. It would suck major ass to make it through the summoning only to send Dekkak to the wrong place.

After a moment of consideration, I pulled out my phone and called Agent Clint Gallagher. It was a total long shot, but if he was keeping tabs on the plague victims, he might know something about a non-plague patient.

"It's Kara Gillian," I said when he answered. "Do you know anything about patients brought to Fed Central since my last visit?"

"No, because there haven't been any," he replied gruffly.

"Wait," I said. "*No* new patients? There've been no more plague victims?"

"That's right. Guess there wasn't much of whatever infected them." He paused. "David Hawkins has been in a giant black sphere since a few hours after you saw him."

A pod. "Has Dr. Patel said anything about his potential outcome?"

He made a noise of frustration. "Not a word. Have you figured anything out on your end?"

"Nothing useful," I said honestly enough.

"All right," he said, voice thick with disappointment. "Why did you want to know about new patients?"

"Just checking on the status of the plague," I lied. "I'll be sure to keep you in the loop if I find out anything," I lied some more.

"Do that."

I disconnected and scowled at my phone. So much for my long shot. I was running out of time and options for nailing down Elinor's location.

"Kara, you dumbass," I muttered with a smile. I had an Elinor-sensor right inside me.

Relaxing, I closed my eyes and let myself sink into her awareness.

Bright light and pale walls. A man in blue scrubs.

That could be anywhere, damn it.

Tick. Tick. T-t-t-tock.

But *that* was Fed Central.

I opened my eyes, wrote *Find Elinor* on my to-do list, then drew a nice thick line through it. That was satisfying, but now I had no choice but to deal with the final item.

Scowling, I wadded up the list and chucked it in the trash, then I went down to the basement and made a pile of every bit of Jontari info we'd scraped up. To that I added Szerain's notes, Elinor's journal, and my own notebook, then I lugged it all out to the nexus, plopped down to sit on the slab beneath the grove tree, and tried to figure out what the hell to do next. Because I honestly had no idea.

All I knew was that this very evening I'd be calling Dekkak

to this gleaming black and silver surface—after spilling blood. Or maybe the blood part came after the demon was here. I didn't know when or even how much. But there would be blood. Mine.

Fuck. Me.

Instinct and habit yammered at me to prepare and make ready, but refused to give me any specifics on how or what to do. None of my usual habits or personal rituals were needed for this summoning. Well, except for the shower I always took before a summoning, this time as a courtesy to anyone standing beside me, but I wouldn't be doing that until later this evening.

At a loss, I attempted to diligently pore over the materials I'd brought with me but gave up after only a few minutes. There was nothing I needed to memorize. No sigils to double-check for what to use and in what order for my diagram.

Because I wouldn't be using a diagram.

Nearly twelve years of being a summoner. Twelve months in a year. At least one summoning every full moon. Okay, so I'd only performed a handful in the past year, but even so, I'd drawn out well over a hundred and fifty summoning diagrams in chalk and blood during my summoning career. That didn't even count the several hundred in chalk alone that I'd drawn just for practice.

Simple, low-level summoning diagrams could be sketched out in about an hour. For my first reyza summoning—Kehlirik—I'd spent nearly five hours on the diagram, checking and re-checking every aspect.

The summoning of Dekkak would be the biggest I'd ever done in my life—and I wouldn't draw a single sigil. Not the slightest dust of chalk. And that was freaking me out.

Be lordy. Yeah, right. Beeeeee the ritual. Beeeeee the summoning.

Beeeeee scared out of my mind.

Ugh. Stop being such a ninny.

I rested my head against the smooth bark of the tree. The leaves rustled high above. My fear retreated, and calm clarity took its place.

All right, so I'd never realized before how much the creation of a summoning diagram calmed and focused me. Chalking sigils required me to scrutinize every detail, every nuance, every fragment of the whole. The process embedded the many aspects of the ritual in my consciousness in a way rote study could never accomplish. It gave me an intrinsic and nearly instinctive awareness of how all the pieces fit together. The ritual diagram was more than a complicated picture. It was a set of instructions, a recipe. An incredibly complex program.

Want to summon a demon? There's an app for that. I thought with a quiet giggle. And the nexus was one hell of a supercomputer.

But how was I supposed to hold the entire program in my head? How was I supposed to *know* what to do?

A breeze stirred the branches, vibrating the trunk pleasantly against my back. Iridescent shadows rippled and danced over the grass and my legs, like a mystical alphabet holding the secrets to the universe.

Ohhhhhhh.

For a human summoner, the sigils were important, whether floaters or chalk-sketched. They were human-comprehension-sized building blocks that defined and specified the parameters and the limits of the conglomerate summoning blueprint. No ordinary human summoner could hold the complete essence of a ritual in their head, which is why the preparation of the diagram—using discrete units—was so important.

But at the end of the day it wasn't the loops and swirls and curlicues that mattered. It was what they conveyed. Just as black marks on pulped wood were only significant because they could form words that conveyed ideas and meaning.

My problem was that I'd been struggling to understand how I could *be* the ritual with my puny little human brain. I'd forgotten that the nexus not only allowed me to draw on Rhyzkahl's power, but also to tap his demi-god-like resources to *know* the ritual in full then shape and control the potency accordingly.

Relieved, I sent a wordless thanks to Rho for nudging my thoughts in the right direction. I let my attention drift to where Mr. Lordy himself was pulling cucumber vines and tossing them into a pile a beyond his orbit.

With Idris arriving in the next day or so, it was time to break the news to Rhyzkahl that he was a daddy. I briefly considered ordering him over to me, then decided I was feeling too good to be confrontational. Instead, I stood and made my way to the heap of plant detritus.

"Why are you destroying your cucumbers?"

"They have ceased producing," Rhyzkahl said as he chucked another clump of vines onto the pile. Dirt scattered onto my feet, which was no doubt by intent. "As they have outlived their usefulness, they must be removed and the soil replenished so that others may thrive."

"Uh huh. Are we still talking about cucumbers?"

He straightened, dusting dirt from his hands as he glowered at me. "Do you yet insist on engaging in this folly?"

It took me a second to realize he meant the impending summoning. "Unless you have a brilliant idea for some other way to rescue Elinor, yes."

"And so, without the gimkrah, you seek to summon an imperator." He spat the word. "Your imprudence will cost you your life, Kara Gillian."

"Nah, I think I got this shit," I said cheerfully. "Though, I gotta say, it wasn't easy digging up information about the Jontari." I cocked my head. "Don't suppose you happen to know why it was censored?"

"For a multitude of reasons that remain valid to this day," he growled.

"Aw, c'mon. Throw me a bone here. If I'm going to risk dying beneath the claws of one of their ilk, I'd sure like to know what the deal is." I eyed him. "Surely it isn't because the Jontari were killing all the summoners?"

Rhyzkahl gave a derisive snort. "The summoners who perished were either careless and lost control of the vortex and bindings, or were reckless enough to summon a creature far beyond their abilities to control." He eyed me right back. "Such as an imperator."

"Subtle."

He crouched and resumed pulling up vines. His face was a cool mask, but he flung the vines away with more force.

"You didn't answer my question."

"Quite perceptive of you."

"Fine. Keep your little secrets." I didn't mind him having that little win since it was a warmup to my real purpose. I folded into a cross-legged sit—away from any not-so-accidental dirt spatters. "I like Janice," I said casually. "She's smart and open-minded and doesn't take shit."

The tension cording his shoulders eased slightly. "I enjoy her company."

"And she clearly enjoys yours, too." I plucked a blade of grass and wound it between my fingers. "I can't imagine how lonely you lords must have been when the ways were closed during those years after the cataclysm."

"Centuries," he said, and only the barest hitch in his voice revealed that I'd brushed a nerve. He shifted to the inner circumference of his orbit and began pinching dead blooms from clumps of yellow flowers. "It is no secret that we qaztahl enjoy the . . . endlessly entertaining presence of humans in the demon realm." His tone became lofty, as if to imply human company was akin to watching kittens play. "Your species' antics are an interesting diversion."

Smartass replies crowded forward, but rising to his bait wouldn't serve my purpose. "Would it really be so terrible to admit that you've occasionally had feelings for a human?"

He fell silent for several heartbeats, though his deft fingers continued to remove spent blooms. "There have been humans whose company I enjoyed more than others," he said. Grudgingly.

I suppressed a grin of victory.

But Rhyzkahl shocked me by adding, "Elinor was dear to me." He turned and met my eyes. "But this you know already."

A flush crept up my neck, even though I hadn't spied on his intimate moments with Elinor on purpose.

"Through the millennia, I have held fondness for others as well," he said.

"What about Tessa?" I asked with a bared-teeth smile. "Were you fond of her, or was she just a casual fuck?"

Rhyzkahl went still.

"Surely you remember my *aunt*," I growled. "Yeah, I know you slept with her a couple of decades before you seduced, used, and tortured me." Damn it. I clamped my mouth shut and slammed a lid on the flood of condemnation that threatened to escape. "What's done is done. Just tell me. What was she to you?"

Rhyzkahl returned to culling flowers. "I was fond of Tessa Pazhel—as a student and a bedmate." A smile briefly touched his eyes. "At times Janice reminds me of her, with her spirited conversation and equally spirited bedding." He frowned and flicked a bug from a leaf. "My realm grew lonelier when Tessa chose to return to Earth and . . ." His frown deepened.

Aha! I leaned forward. "Why did she leave?"

His shoulders lifted in a careless shrug. "To return to Earth," he repeated.

A pat and simple reply. And too much like the programmed responses given by people who'd been manipulated.

"But why?" I pressed. "What was her explanation?"

"She decided—" Uncertainty flitted across his face. "No, she . . ." Still crouched, he jerked around to face me, muscles rigid. He'd surely manipulated enough humans to know what it meant when there was a wrinkle in an otherwise smooth memory. A glitch in the matrix.

He didn't speak a word, but I felt him pleading, urging me to tell him.

What to say? I did *not* want to cause another vicious headache. The last one had been triggered by Rhyzkahl's thoughts of his own parentage. I had to assume the info about the lords' own kids would be protected as well. "Too much sun will give you a headache." I nudged my head toward the grove tree. "How about taking a break in the shade?"

Without a word, Rhyzkahl stood, strode to the tree, and rested his back against it. I followed at a more leisurely pace to give time for the tree-calm to take effect. By the time I reached him, his features were relaxed, and the tension gone from his stance.

"She returned to Earth because she was pregnant," I said. "Tessa told me that she was living in Japan and had a fling with some American guy and that the baby was stillborn." I paused. "But it wasn't."

Comprehension flared in Rhyzkahl's eyes. He pushed off the tree trunk, expression a mix of shock and naked *hope*. "Idris," he choked out. "It is Idris, is it not?"

"Yeah," I said, more than a little off-balance by this startlingly human reaction. "Idris is, um, your son."

For the tiniest fraction of a second, Rhyzkahl's aura blazed as if he burned with elation. Then the mask dropped back into place, his features smoothed, and his lordly bearing returned. Damn, he had impressive control.

"My *son*," he said slowly, as if tasting the word. "He despises me." His brow creased ever so slightly, as if he was trying to determine if that should matter to him.

"Well, you do have a bit of a reputation."

He didn't reply or react save to turn away from me and begin to slowly pace the perimeter of his prison. Processing this new paradigm, I figured, and the implications. Rhyzkahl now held the forbidden knowledge that the lords could father children—and from there he could surmise that they had likely done so many times over the last few millennia. No doubt he was considering how this new information affected various plots and plans. And, surely, wondering why the knowledge had been suppressed and the children hidden.

I thought of Rhyzkahl's face shining oh-so-briefly after learning Idris was his son. I'd seen that look before, on fathers holding their newborn child for the first time.

Maybe that was why the demahnk didn't want the lords to know.

Maybe it risked making them too human.

Jill returned mid-afternoon with a truckload of supplies and groceries. But no chickens.

"I bought chickens," she assured me when I came out to help her unload. "They're being delivered tomorrow." Then she shrugged. "That is, assuming you haven't been eaten."

"Your faith in me warms the cockles of my heart. Admit it. You didn't want to bring chickens home today for fear that Dekkak would eat them all."

"It would be a terrible waste of money," she said with a tragic air, then her breath caught as she pulled me into a hug. "Bryce wants me and the pets and the civilians out of here in the next ten minutes. Stay in one piece, damn it. Call me the instant you know anything."

"I will, and I will," I said and hugged her back just as hard.

I released her as furious yowling heralded the arrival of Lilith Cantrell with a cat carrier in each hand. Behind her, Sammy bounced eagerly on a leash held by the stocky Kellum, with Janice and Michael bringing up the rear.

"Jill," Bryce roared from the door of the security outbuilding. *"Get your shit packed and your ass out of here."*

Jill shot him an affectionate middle finger then leveled a fierce look at me. "Remember: Don't die. I love you."

"I love you, too. Now go away."

She smiled and dashed to her trailer while I headed into the house to take the most important shower of my life.

Chapter 37

Okay, Kara, I told myself as I stepped onto the nexus, *we've been busting our asses for two days, planning and preparing for this damn thing.* I paused my silent lecture for a dramatic three heartbeats. *Don't. Fuck. Up.*

I positioned myself with the grove tree behind me, a pace from the edge of the slab. I'd given up wearing formal summoning garb not long after I started training in the demon realm. In its place I'd usually opted for whatever felt comfortable. But today, everyone here had on the full kit usually reserved for incursion response—combat fatigues, boots, body armor, guns, knives, you name it. For this summoning, I was happy to trade a bit of mobility for protection. Except for my feet, which were bare to allow me to better feel every shift and nuance of the nexus.

At those same feet, my blood bowl and ritual knife lay ready. Light from the full moon pierced the leaf canopy, patterning the area with misty color while, around me, woven strands of potency thrummed, ready for the summoning call. The supershikvihr undulated in scintillating electric blue waves and, directly beyond it, the amber glow of over a hundred floating sigils marked the Dekkak binding zone—an oval-shaped area nearly twenty feet wide and extending all the way to the vinyl exterior of Rhyzkahl's house.

Potency from both the prepared ritual and the nexus saturated me to the point that I no longer felt limited to flesh and bone and skin. My brain told me to use my eyes to confirm all my people were ready and in place, but my lord-sense *knew* before I looked. Each person shone with their own unique energy signature. Pellini, armed with the borrowed wizard staff, just off the nexus to my left. Rhyzkahl near the tree trunk behind me. Turek tucked in close to the house and, beside him, Giovanni within a circle of protective wards. Bryce and Suarez by the launcher, ready to deploy the graphene net upon Dekkak's arrival. Roper and Tandon hunkered down half a dozen feet into the woods as a last resort backup, both with weapons loaded with shieldbuster rounds.

"Status," I murmured, for the sake of everyone who didn't have the nifty lord-sense. A series of crisp affirmatives came through my earpiece. "Ready here, too. Time to boogie."

The moonlight abruptly brightened, and I looked up in surprise to see that the tree had withdrawn its branches from over the nexus. I grinned in gratitude and relief. Now I wouldn't have to worry about either demon or net getting tangled up in it.

As I'd done hundreds of times before, I began the familiar chant that would unite the energies and open the interdimensional portal. Yet the words jangled off my tongue, and the ritual was sluggish to respond. It felt *wrong*. Too structured. Harsh rather than harmonious.

Be lordy. Be the summoning.

All right. Time to let go of my preconceptions of what the chant should be and freestyle this thing. Starting anew, I allowed sound to flow—unfamiliar though melodic, but oh-so-right. In confirmation, the sigils flared, and a frigid arcane wind swirled around me.

I am lordy.

The guided potency of the ritual slammed against the dimensional fabric, but the portal itself was stubborn, like trying to open a door against a gale. I'd successfully opened hundreds of portals, but never with so much power at my disposal. It should have been easier, not harder. I was trying my best to *be* the damn summoning. What the hell was wrong?

I sought the calm center in the midst of frustration. Szerain had told me to be lordy and be the summoning. That instruction had brought me this far, but clearly, I was missing something.

Kadir's advice to Pellini whispered through my mind. *Believe it has already happened.*

Understanding crystallized. This was different, not harder. It wasn't all about control and rules like in a regular summoning. It was about creating. It was the difference between painting by numbers and translating an artistic vision to a canvas. Using a boxed mix to make a cake versus creating a breathtaking dessert from scratch.

Here and now, I was the artist. I breathed in the arcane wind, mingled it with my own potency then exhaled it, all while envisioning a pinprick of dimension-piercing light within the perimeter of the binding sigils. The vision became reality as the light expanded into a portal vortex. With it came a roaring rumble like boulders crashing down a mountainside.

I gathered the prepared potency strands, made the call in a voice that was mine but so much more. "Dekkak!"

The wind picked up the name, howled it through the roar and ensnared the demon on the far side of the portal. I braced against the tension on the strands and *pulllllled*.

For several tension-wracked heartbeats, nothing budged, then all hell broke loose as the demon fought the call. I thought I'd performed tough summonings before, but this was like trying to pull a pissed-off grizzly bear through a porthole using a bungee cord in the middle of a hurricane.

It took every bit of standard training and lordy experience to keep my wits and my hold, but I had the sucker, and I wasn't about to let go. Dekkak's shadow choked the portal, and with one final yank he was through and on my nexus.

He stood taller and broader than the Piggly Wiggly reyza—and wore ten times more gold—but to my surprise was nowhere near the size of Big Turd. Rakkuhr flames crawled over his blood-red hide and rose, smoking, from wicked double-curved horns. A thick, barbed tail twitched like an angry snake, and the stench of sulfur rolled from him in a noxious wave.

Fire and brimstone. A living hellish nightmare.

Not my *nightmare, damn it*. I fed potency into the bindings, imbuing them with his name—*Dekkak*.

His head swiveled toward Pellini, even as a lightning-fast whip of his barbed tail caved in half of Rhyzkahl's house. Pellini raised the staff, but the demon was already in motion, lunging toward him. I tightened the bindings, but to my horror they slipped from the demon like greased spaghetti. Out of the corner of my eye, I caught the recoil of the net launcher, its sound drowned out by the fading roar of the of the closing portal.

Dekkak ripped the staff away with one clawed hand and sent it skittering across the nexus then seized Pellini in a demonic bear-hug and launched into flight.

Heart in my throat, I gathered and checked the bindings,

watching with one eye as the net sailed through the air toward the target area. All the demon needed was another solid beat of his wings, and he'd be clear.

The net won—barely—fouling Dekkak's wings. Shrieking with fury, he crashed down, lower body and tail hitting the nexus, and upper torso slamming into the grass. Pellini let out a wheezed curse and scrabbled against the demon's hold.

Bryce and Suarez ran toward the netted demon and Pellini while I anchored the useless bindings and dove for the staff. Dekkak thrashed on his back, bellowing a deep scream full of rage and the promise of death. In a few more seconds he'd be free of the net.

With a fierce pull of nexus power, I focused a blast of potency at one of Dekkak's massive arms, burning through the rakkuhr shielding and biting into flesh. He jerked, loosening his grip. Without hesitation, Pellini shoved a flare of Kadir-chartreuse potency against Dekkak's chest.

The demon howled and pulled one hand free of Pellini to scrabble at the weirdly clinging glow. Leaping forward, I drove the wizard staff hard against the demon's side, thumb already mashing the button. His body spasmed as electricity found its mark, but I could already tell it wasn't enough to incapacitate him for long. "Get Pellini out," I hollered to Bryce and Suarez then sucked in a breath of shock as rakkuhr flames wreathed the staff and crawled toward my hands. "Hurry!" Part of me was impressed and fascinated by this utterly cool and badass use of rakkuhr as both defense and offense, but the rest of me did *not* want a personal introduction.

The guys moved fast to drag Pellini free then raced to secure the net. They got as far as pulling it around Dekkak's upper torso before I shouted for them to get clear and had to backpedal to avoid the rakkuhr.

The demon snarled and clawed at the net. The graphene-enhanced strands held firm, but it was clear we had minutes at most before he struggled out of it.

Rhyzkahl's voice cut through the final rumbles of the summoning and my own pounding heartbeat. "Kara! Bind with yulz. *Yulz.*"

What the hell was yulz? I wracked my brain futilely for a sigil or protection called yulz before his meaning hit me. Not what. *Who.*

"Keep him occupied." I shoved the staff into Bryce's hands

then dashed back to the Dekkak-attuned binding strands. No
wonder they'd failed. I'd sure enough lassoed a Jontari warlord,
maybe even an imperator, but it wasn't Dekkak. Baffling, but no
time to figure out how and why that happened. I recharged the
bindings with the name and energy signature of Yulz then sent
them to snake around the downed demon. With a triumphant
jerk of my fist, I tightened the hold.

Yulz hissed, unable to do more than wriggle within the confines of the physical net and arcane bindings. The rakkuhr
flames slithered from him and dissipated.

I bent forward and rested my hands on my thighs while I
caught my breath. Yulz wasn't the demon I'd intended to summon, but he was still one seriously potent motherfucker. We'd
have been dead meat without the net—or Rhyzkahl's well-timed
help.

Straightening, I gave Rhyzkahl a grateful nod and a mouthed
Thanks. "Status!" I called out then began to meticulously anchor
the bindings. No way did I want to risk releasing the demon
prematurely.

"Five by five," said Bryce and Suarez in unison, standing
tense and wary beside the demon. Suarez had a bloody nose, but
seemed okay otherwise. Bryce held the staff at the ready.

Pellini lay sprawled on the grass, breathing hard and staring
at the sky.

"You still with me, hoss?" I asked.

"Miffed that you wouldn't let me go flying with our new
friend, but except for that, I'm dandy." He shoved up to sit. "Are
we where we need to be with this?"

"I believe so," I said then gestured gracefully toward the demon. "Everyone, meet Yulz. Not exactly who we expected, but
he's badass. We'll make this work." As soon as I caught my
second wind, I'd figure out how to bind Mr. Yulz to the task of
fetching Elinor. The hard part was over, at least. Once Elinor
was successfully rescued and the demon dismissed, I'd spare a
minute to try and figure out why the hell Yulz came through instead of the demon I'd actually called. But for now, it was time
to get down to business.

My ears popped at a sudden change in air pressure, and the
scent of ozone engulfed me. "Stay on your toes!" I shouted as I
tried to figure out what the fuck was happening. It wasn't coming from the nexus or the demon, but beyond that I had no clue.

The slab shuddered beneath me, and an awful metallic tearing sound filled the air, like two eighteen-wheelers being scraped together by a giant. The remains of Rhyzkahl's house sank a foot, then plunged into the maw of an opening rift.

Oh shiiiiiiiiiiiiiiiiiit.

I flinched and threw a hand up to shield my eyes as light flared like an exploding transformer from the grass on either side of the rift. Lightning flashed at the outer edge of Rhyzkahl's orbit then streaked around the perimeter, jumping the rift gap and continuing in a blinding race for several heartbeats before ceasing in an instant.

Blinking spots out of my eyes, I made a hurried check to make sure everyone was clear and okay.

No, Rhyzkahl was lying crumpled on his side, stricken by the disruption of the prison warding.

"Turek, get Rhyzkahl to the tree!" I shouted then added, "Please," since I didn't know how he felt about the lord. "Pellini, scramble Alpha Squad. Bryce, give Suarez the staff and get someone on the hose in case the grass catches fire."

The tearing sound died away to the unpleasantly familiar hiss of a new rift. I allowed myself a few seconds to stare at it in horror and disbelief. Seriously? Of all the shitty timing, a rift had to choose *now* to appear and *here* by my nexus?

The lovely new addition to my back yard landscaping ran from the edge of the nexus to twenty feet beyond the outer edge of Rhyzkahl's orbit. Gouts of magenta flame erupted from its depths, and lining the rim were complex braids of rakkuhr, unlike anything I'd ever seen before. Ice spread across the ground, leaving only the nexus itself untouched. At least that was intact.

The netted demon began to laugh, deep and slow—a fiendish sound I hoped to never hear again, and a hundred times worse than any movie special effect.

A sick dread filled me along with the unpleasant feeling that this rift was no coincidence. I dashed to the center of the super-shikvihr, double-checked and reinforced the bindings on Yulz, then cleared away every speck of residual energy from the summoning.

Magenta flames leaped in the rift, casting an ominous light across the slab and highlighting the desperate circumstances. Around the nexus, chaos was held at bay by training, discipline, and loyalty. Roper had the hose pulled out and was wetting down the grass. Turek crouched in a protective stance beside

Rhyzkahl at the base of the tree. Bryce now had a shotgun slung over one shoulder and hustled to get as much heavy weaponry as we possessed to the security guards.

Everyone was doing what they needed to do, which left me free to figure out the rest. Anything that Yulz found amusing was surely bad news for me, but no matter how much I extended my demi-godlike senses, I couldn't get the slightest whiff of what to expect. Demons, no doubt, but how many? What kind?

I wove potency strands for ready use while I ransacked my brain for a solution to the dilemma. The only SkeeterCheater we had was wrapped around Yulz. I could banish him then use the net to cover the rift and slow down invaders, but I'd also lose the chance to get Elinor. That would suck, but so would dying in a hail of demon droppings. Then again, the fastest recorded time for demons to start coming through a newly opened rift was eleven minutes, with an average of eighteen. If I could get Yulz bound in agreement and on the task quickly enough, we might be able to salvage both the net and the mission.

That was a big *if*. And I needed to make a decision. Banish or bind?

The magenta flames abruptly snuffed out, and the hiss went silent. I froze, eyeing the suddenly quiescent rift warily, potency strands partially woven in my hands. In my peripheral vision I saw everyone else in similar attitudes of waiting for the other shoe to drop. Even Roper had abandoned the hose and backed slowly away as he unslung his rifle.

Rakkuhr fog mushroomed upward and spread with the speed of a tidal wave. My bad feeling quintupled. I'd dealt with hundreds of rifts and never seen anything like this before. The fog rolled toward me. I sucked in a breath and held it as everything was blanketed in uniformly opaque red.

Fuck this shit. I tapped into the vortex of potency at the heart of the nexus, drew out thick strands and set them swirling around me. Blind me with an arcane fog? I'd blow that crap away with an arcane fan.

At least I hoped it would work like that. I heard Bryce's murmured voice in my earpiece, telling everyone to stay calm and on their toes. Then, "Whatever you're doing, Kara, keep doing it." Relieved, I drew more potency, fed it into my whirlpool-fan-thing, and set it flying faster and faster.

The fog thinned then dissipated completely, revealing a naked man standing beside the rift. One eye was swollen shut, and crusted blood clung to his face. Pale gold potency ringed his neck and trailed into the rift like a collar and leash.

I heard Bryce suck in a breath, and a second later recognition punched me in the gut. "*Seretis*?" I started forward but stopped when he held a hand up in warning.

"Dekkak is coming through," he croaked.

I breathed out a curse as all the pieces fell into place. It was a setup. The whole thing. Xharbek was probably chortling right about now. All he had to do was tip Dekkak off about the summoning and let the imperator take care of the Kara problem. *Innards everywhere.*

Dekkak had sent Yulz through to let him spring the trap and take a hostage. That was why he grabbed Pellini. At least one thing had gone our way.

With the nexus, I had sufficient power at my disposal to bind Dekkak—except I had no idea how to bind a demon coming through a rift instead of a summoning portal. And with an open rift, Dekkak probably wasn't coming alone.

I pulled potency and started fashioning bindings. This would take being lordy to a whole new level.

Pellini hollered, "Alpha Squad's a good twenty minutes out!"

Great. Looked like we were going to be on our own for the worst incursion ever. Everyone here was armed to the teeth, but Pellini and I were the only ones with relevant experience. Maybe I could somehow use the nexus as a shieldbuster?

Bryce stood tense and motionless, eyes riveted on the lord. Seretis took a stumbling step away from the rift, gaze settling on his bond-brother. "This is for the best." He gave Bryce a flickering smile, then returned his attention to me. "I hope."

My apprehension skyrocketed. In the entire history of the universe, *This is for the best* almost always went hand in hand with, *This really hurts.* "Seretis, what have you done?"

He lifted his shoulders in a despondent shrug, demeanor an odd mix of weariness and sanguine anticipation. "Struck a bargain."

"With an imperator?" I asked in disbelief. "For what? Why?" Whatever the reason, it looked like he'd gotten the short end of the deal.

Seretis gave me a barely perceptible head shake then glanced at Bryce. As I watched, Bryce's face went from still as stone to alight with comprehension. They were communicating through the essence bond, I realized. Most likely relaying whatever Seretis didn't want to say aloud.

Dekkak wouldn't know about their bond, I thought and crossed mental fingers that Seretis was taking full advantage of Dekkak's ignorance.

"Desperate measures in desperate times, Kara Gillian," Seretis said. "You cannot blame me."

My lips pressed thin. "I'll decide who to blame when I have all the details."

Bryce's voice crackled brisk and urgent in my earpiece. "After you left the demon realm, Seretis started picking up some of my thoughts. He doesn't know why it started happening again. He got the drift of our plans that way and found out that the Jontari have the master gimkrah."

Seretis flinched as the rift burped a gout of magenta. "She is coming."

Wait. *She*? Dekkak was a . . . *girl* demon?

Bryce cut through my momentary stupefaction. "Jesral met secretly with Rayst."

Yikes. Poor Seretis. His life partner was hobnobbing with the smarmy head honcho of the Mraztur. And he had no Lannist for support.

"Seretis saw the writing on the wall," Bryce went on, "what with that crap on his homefront, his ptarl gone, our plans in motion, and the transfer of the gimkrah. So he messaged Dekkak with a proposal." Bryce paused. "One he hopes you'll turn in our favor, but if not, he's . . . sorry. That's all I know."

I kept my expression blank, but inside I moaned *fuuuuck*. Okay, so Seretis had been faced with dire circumstances and took action. Except he wasn't like Mzatal, who saw move upon move in advance. He was underestimated, sure. More empathetic than the other lords, yeah. But a strategic mastermind? Probably not.

The only possible upside was that, if Seretis thought there was a chance to turn whatever his proposal was in our favor, it meant Dekkak might not be in instant kill mode when he—*she*—arrived. Unless Seretis was playing us, but I found that tough to believe. Even though I couldn't be absolutely sure of his intentions, I had faith in the sanctity of his essence bond with Bryce.

Either way, I was stuck without a rule book in the middle of a game to decide the fate of two worlds. And, more urgently, the fate of me and everyone I cared about.

I briefly considered banishing Yulz then decided against it. One SkeeterCheater wasn't going to make a difference, and there was a chance I could use him as a bargaining chip. A very slim chance, but at this point I was simply trying to keep from sliding off a tilting chessboard.

Huge clawed hands reached upward from the rift and grasped its lip. Every joint of the scaly, blood-red fingers sported a gold ring etched with blocky symbols.

Heeeeeeere's Dekkak, I thought with just the right amount of hysteria.

With an agile move as if shrugging off the earth itself, Dekkak pulled herself up through the rift. She was bigger than Yulz—close to the two-story height of Big Turd and equally broad. Moonlight glinted off rugged scales that began at the top of her head and swept down to cover her back and shoulders. As far as I could tell, the scales were the only obvious physical feature that differed from a male, yet there existed an intangible quality about her that proclaimed her as powerfully *female*.

"Hold your fire," I murmured into the headset. "For now." She hadn't ripped anyone in half yet, and there was no guarantee we could take her down even if we dumped our entire arsenal on her at once. We needed to pacify her, cleverly work whatever bargain Seretis had cooked up, until Alpha Squad got here. Then we stood a fighting chance. Maybe.

Fucking hell, but this bitch was intimidating.

There was no hint of the rakkuhr flame-shielding, but potency radiated from her—different, but no less impressive than the aura of a lord. It penetrated me, setting my bones buzzing and my teeth on edge. Gold glittered on her hands and horns, but otherwise, she wore no adornments except . . .

Shit. On her left ear, a Beretta 92 dangled from a slim iron hoop.

Dekkak was scary enough with claws and teeth and size, but it was that relatively subtle detail that described the scope of what we were up against here. Whether that gun was a trophy from the Dirty Thirty—the DIRT team who'd gone through a rift to take the fight to the demons—or merely an amusing-to-her trinket, the gun-turned-bauble symbolized the vast power gap between Dekkak and my people.

Though my heart hammered, I willed my face to stone. I'd learned long ago to never reveal my internal battles during a summoning, even for the weakest of the relatively tame lord-bound demons. Mr. Poker Face Mzatal was the ultimate example of the impassive exterior, whether fighting for his life or deciding between tea and tunjen. I strove now to emulate him.

Dekkak's nostrils flared, and in a tiny corner of my mind I knew she smelled my fear. Yet her gaze swept over me and halted on the netted Yulz. Sucked to be him, but I was more than happy to be the unnoticed insect. Every second she spent focused on Netboy meant no one here died, and Alpha Squad was a second closer.

"Warlord," Dekkak said in demon, her voice rumbly, rich, and *loud*. "You failed your imperator."

Straight to the point. No abuse. No name calling. No nonsense. Which somehow made the castigation all the scarier. *Note to self: be nice and direct when chastising underlings.*

Dekkak moved with a speed at complete odds with her size, and in a single bound had Yulz pinned beneath one clawed foot. She crouched low and hissed into his face, baring gleaming white fangs that tapered to needle sharp points. I wouldn't have blamed big badass Yulz one bit if he'd peed himself, but he simply went stone still.

In a savage move that was almost too swift to follow, Dekkak hooked a claw through the three gold rings in his right ear and ripped them free, splattering the grass with blood. "These honors will abide on this crippled world where you disgraced yourself," she snarled and flung the adornments into the darkness.

Okay, maybe a little abuse. *Note to self: let's not take management lessons from Jontari imperators.* Though I supposed there were worse possible fates for a demonic employee who failed to meet goals. While the scary-as-fuck imperator was momentarily distracted, I edged my way to the center of the nexus, within the comforting bounds of the super-shikvihr and in easy reach of gobs of nexus power.

Dekkak stepped off Yulz then stretched her great wings wide, nearly spanning the entire distance between my porch and the edge of the woods. The internal vibration in my bones increased to barely tolerable discomfort, as if she'd fired up a potency generator. With a groan, Seretis dropped to one knee beside her, overwhelmed by her presence rather than as a gesture of homage.

My simmering dread cranked up several degrees. Alpha Squad was at least fifteen minutes away. If Dekkak decided to take flight and wreak havoc elsewhere, I had no sure way to stop her. A potency blast from the nexus was unlikely to take her out completely—even if I diverted power from the bindings on Yulz—and Dekkak's retaliation was certain to be swift and merciless. Except for the purported bargain, she had no known reason to stay. I needed to keep her here until the squad arrived.

"Dekkak!" I called out, amplifying my voice with potency.

I could have whispered for all the difference it made. Clearly the demon queen wasn't going to give the locals the time of day, and she sure as shit wouldn't be called to heel, no matter how loudly I shouted.

Instead, she let out an almighty roar followed by a bellowed "RHYZKAHL!" as she reached for him.

With zero hesitation, I released my gathered potency and sent it surging into the perimeter of Rhyzkahl's prison. I didn't know how much Mzatal's built-in protections were affected by the rift, or how they'd hold up against an imperator, but I was damn well going to do what I could to keep them working. I was the warden, and I intended to do everything possible to keep Rhyzkahl safe.

Violet lightning arced from the ground and struck Dekkak's outstretched hand. She jerked back, palm smoking. Residual arcane crackled over her arm.

Get away from him, you bitch! I silently jeered. This was one lord she wouldn't be adding to her collection.

"MZATAL!" she screamed, fangs bared. Rakkuhr flame-shielding blossomed over her like a manifestation of fiery hatred. Her tail slashed through the air, forcing me into a desperate leap and dive to avoid getting smacked.

I skidded to a stop at the edge of the nexus, already pulling potency as I scrambled to my feet. Through the headset, I heard Bryce snapping orders, but I didn't have the spare bandwidth to pay attention.

Dekkak rounded on me, powerful legs flexed as if poised to spring. "And *you*," she growled in heavily accented English. "*Kara Gillian.*"

NOW, she acknowledges my presence. I darted back to the center of the nexus and readied a shield of potency, though I doubted it would be enough to keep Dekkak from squashing me like a bug. Not with most of my available power tied up in the bindings on Yulz and the summoning in general.

Except that she could have squashed me at any point since

coming through and hadn't. I flicked a quick glance at Seretis, more curious than ever about the nature of the bargain he'd made with the imperator. Yet even naked, bloodied, and kneeling in the grass, he maintained an expression as impassive as any lord could hope for.

Dekkak's knees were at my eye level, forcing me to crane my neck in order to look at her face. "Dekkak," I said. "I am pleased to finally meet you, honored one. You are clearly more than worthy of your formidable reputation." The acrid stench of burned demon flesh stung my nose.

Dekkak sank into a deep crouch, shifting close enough that her rakkuhr shielding reached acid fingers toward my skin. But I wasn't about to step back and give her the satisfaction. Besides, it was just chest puffing. A true power play would have had me retreating out of a desire to keep my flesh attached to my bones.

She scraped the claws of her uninjured hand across the nexus, sending up a screeching nails-on-chalkboard sound. "Your human swarm, your *DIRT*, arrives here. Soon." Her eyes glowed red and gold as they rested upon me. "Our interplay begins. Now."

Could she sense the approaching team? Or was she making an assumption based on previous DIRT responses to rifts? Not that it mattered. DIRT was coming. She knew. Bad shit would happen.

I folded my arms and affected a casual stance to show how very not scared of her I was. "What *interplay* is that, Dekkak?" No, really. Not scared. Nope, not me.

Instead of answering, she extended a hand toward the rift and spoke in demon. "Emerge, my honored ones. The diminished Earth awaits you."

Since I didn't want to reveal that I understood her, I schooled my expression to "slightly befuddled." But on the inside I did a full body flail while shouting: *Oh, come ON! More demons?* Not quite the interplay I had in mind.

I pretended shock when the rift vomited a buttload of demons, but the dismay on my face was real enough. Four reyza and a Chinese-dragon-faced kehza took flight and scattered in all directions. A shadowy zhurn with burning red eyes followed, melting into the night as if it had never been there.

In my earpiece, I heard Bryce warn all personnel of demons on the property, and to shoot only if attacked. Good man. Bad demons.

Like sentient coils of smoke and flashing color, a pair of ilius wound like housecats around Dekkak's legs. "Seek your surrogates," she told them, and after one final rub against her shins, they headed straight for the house.

"Hey! Why are those two ilius going into my house?" I said, mostly for Bryce's benefit. He was sharp enough to get the hint that I wanted one of his people to keep tabs on the two demons.

Dekkak drew her lips back, revealing fangs that gleamed in the moonlight like ivory tusks. "Interfere, and you doom Krawkor and Makonite." An ominous growl backed her words.

I stared at her, utterly taken aback. She was talking about Corey Crawford and Marco Knight. What the ever-living *fuck*? "And those two demons are going to do what exactly?"

"Tend their brood," she said without further explanation. Still, it was the most direct response she'd made to me yet, so I decided to count it as a win.

"If by 'tend' you mean anything except 'care for,' call them back." I pretended to ignore her hiss and continued, "It's obvious you want something that only I can give, otherwise we wouldn't be having this nice little chat. I'll be a whole lot less likely to agree if, er, Krawkor and Makonite are harmed."

To my everlasting relief, Dekkak settled her wings and eased back. "Untended, they will never hatch." She tucked her first three fingers under her thumb, leaving only her wickedly clawed little finger extended, like giving me the bird except with her pinky. "On my honor, Kara Gillian."

Her eyes, her stance, and her very aura told me she would never say that frivolously. She definitely wanted something. And wanted it badly. A faint flicker of hope stirred from deep beneath the ol' fear of dying. If we were about to negotiate a trade, maybe I could shove the rescue of Elinor back onto the bargaining table?

I had no idea if I was supposed to throw any demon gang signs in response to Dekkak's pinky swear, so I opted for neutral territory and sought something vaguely flattering. "Your honor is . . . impeccable, imperator." I winced mentally at the unintended echo, then again as my stupid stressed brain tried to make a rap out of it. *Impeccable imperator, insides indigestible . . .*

I gave my brain a mental kick in the ass and focused on the impeccable imperator.

Dekkak withdrew her hand, but when she made no move to

kill me, I decided I must have made an acceptable response. "Seretis," she said in demon. "To me."

Seretis staggered to his feet and approached, the leash of potency still trailing into the rift. Behind him, said rift flared magenta then belched a nightmare creature that looked like an elephant-sized slug with several monster octopuses fused together where a head might be. Its hide and tentacles shifted colors in lazy splodges of midnight blue and neon pink, while in the midst of the tentacles, eerie blue light issued from its cavernous maw illuminating pale shapes of—

I recoiled as my eyes resolved the pale shapes into the human skulls that they were. Mouth dry, I forced myself to confirm that the creature was indeed wearing at least a dozen human skulls and severed heads on its smaller tentacles like ornaments. A few were fresh, as if either newly killed or arcanely preserved, and I suddenly found myself looking into the dead eyes of Sergeant Ted Palmer of the Dirty Thirty.

Cold sweat broke out beneath my shirt. I wrenched my gaze away, silently screaming at myself to hold it together, to swallow back the puke, set aside the horror, and keep a goddamn brave face on because too much was riding on me not fucking this up.

Seretis collapsed to his knees beside Dekkak, but my gaze went to his leash. Only now did it register that Slugthing held the other end within a wrap of tentacle. His keeper.

A deep and dark calm descended upon me. I wouldn't lose focus. Not now. This was *it*. Whatever *it* was.

Chapter 38

With a deft twitch of her claws, Dekkak shaped rakkuhr into a knot-like sigil and set it spinning overhead. I didn't need to understand rakkuhr to know the ward was for privacy, especially when my earpiece crackled and went dead.

In a foreboding gesture, Slugthing shot a tentacle around my blood bowl and knife and pulled them to a spot between Dekkak and me. A slurred, wet voice issued from its maw, saying in demon, "This frail hu-beast female has not the wit nor resources to procure the trinity."

What the hell was the trinity? And why did it need procuring? I had to assume this was part of the mysterious bargain, but I was already sick of the games and shows of dominance. Time to cut the crap.

I locked eyes with the imperator and—also in demon—said, "Your underling doubts your decision to negotiate with this *hu-beast*. Is such insolence rife in your domain?"

Dekkak shot an I'll-deal-with-you-later glance at Slugthing then huffed out a breath between her teeth. "Gurgaz merely echoes what I have already voiced," she replied, sticking to her own language since it was clear I understood it. "Doubt yet lingers within me regarding the merit of the defiler's claim." She gestured toward Seretis. "Though, as you have mastered our tongue, I concede you are more than a witless hu-beast."

Hey, I'd made it past Witless. Achievement unlocked. Or rather, achievement faked. The nexus gave me the demon tongue, but I wasn't about to let her in on the secret.

I inclined my head a bare inch. "I await your proposal, honored imperator."

"You sought to summon and bind me to your will," she growled. "Such will never come to pass, but listen well. The *kiraknikahl* Xharbek expects me to return with your severed head and the Elinor essence."

Bonus points to her for calling Xharbek an oathbreaker. And points to me as well for having guessed correctly that the ass-hole had engaged her to do his dirty work and get me dead. The essence thing was a surprise, though. And she'd so far failed to make a proclamation in the vein of, "Oh, and I decided not to kill you because fuck Xharbek." So that threat was still on the table.

But so was what she wanted. "Yet you haven't taken my head or the essence," I pointed out. "What did Xharbek offer in return?"

"Earth," she said, as if bartering *planets* was an everyday occurrence.

"Ah." I gave a knowing nod, as if I possessed vast experience in trade negotiations involving planetary real estate. Meanwhile, Inside-My-Head Kara was running in circles with her hands in her hair while shrieking *are you shitting me!?*

However, Slugthing's insulting comment had contained a nugget of useful info. Whatever the trinity was, it needed procuring. "But you want the trinity more than you want Earth," I said serenely. No way was I going to reveal that I knew nothing about this trinity. However, an unpleasant suspicion was beginning to form.

"And you want the shell of Elinor Bayliss," Dekkak said with an accompanying hiss.

I acknowledged her statement with a nod. "It seems we have the foundation of a mutually beneficial agreement."

"Seretis claims you are the zharkat of Mzatal." She snarled the last three words as if they were poison in her mouth.

"He spoke the truth."

Red sparkled in the depths of her eyes. "Will you betray your zharkat?"

That was quite the loaded question, and one I needed to consider very carefully before giving my answer. A "yes" would be a mark of dishonor. But a "no" could not only put an end to the negotiation, I might as well hand over my head so she could give it to Xharbek.

"Tell me why you want the trinity," I said instead. Her question had all but confirmed my suspicion about the trinity. It had to be the three essence blades. Mzatal's creations. To procure them, I would have to betray him—at least from her perspective.

Her eyes bored into me as if measuring my worth and potential, and it took everything I had to stand my ground before that ancient gaze. And I mean *ancient*. I'd often thought that the lords were "ancient," but now I was going to have to downgrade them to merely "really really old." Dekkak was older than the rivers and the mountains. Countless civilizations on Earth had risen and faded to dust in her lifetime, and a good number of them would have worshipped her. She'd have given even badass goddesses like Hel and Tiamat a run for their money.

Her nostrils flared, and the intense scrutiny eased. "The Ekiri changed our world," she said in a voice that resonated through me. "We, the Jontari, changed with it. There are outsiders who wish for us to return to our former way of being, before the change. Before rakkuhr." She spread her wings a few feet and leaned toward me. "We. Will. Not." Her wings snapped closed with a sharp report.

Her explanation was a little light on the specifics, but I got the drift. The Ekiri had "fixed up" the planet, and in the process—whether intentionally or not—they'd given the demons a big ol' leg up. Then the Ekiri, who had something to do with the rakkuhr, left. Now, several thousands of years later, there was a push to put everything back the way it was—wiping out every bit of the demons' evolution, improvements, and advancements.

I couldn't blame Dekkak for being pissed. It would be like trying to force modern society to live without electricity or indoor plumbing—and with all knowledge of it removed.

No, it would be like the gods asking modern society to give back the gift of fire and everything that came of it.

Beside Dekkak, Seretis caught my gaze and mouthed "Bryce"—quick but clear—before going quiescent again. He was telling me he'd communicated more to Bryce, which made my wild curiosity happy.

"How does the trinity fit in?" I asked.

Her low growl warned me that this was a touchy subject. "Last question. Last answer," she hissed. "The defiler Mzatal enslaved our Jontari elders: Vsuhl, Khatur, and Xhan. The gatekeepers of the rakkuhr. The first students of the Ekiri. He bound their essences between blade and gimkrah to hold dominion over the Jontari. We have recovered the three gimkrah. Now it is time for our elders to come home."

Well.

Fuck.

Okay then. *Back straight. Head up. Stand strong.* So what if Dekkak had just added a couple of tons to the weight already on my shoulders. It wasn't as if any of it was super critical like, say, the fate of two worlds, or a deep and personal relationship with the lord who'd enslaved a trio of demigod demons.

Didn't matter. I already knew what my answer would be, even without the threat of death hanging over me. I would agree for the sake of the Jontari, because the trinity was an abomination, no matter what sort of dire events had driven Mzatal to that length. And I'd agree for the sake of the lords, because the blades held a terrible and insidious sway over them, all the more dangerous for not being obvious. It wasn't a betrayal of my beloved. It was his salvation.

Later, after this crap was done and over with, I'd let myself think about the ramifications.

"You want the trinity," I said. "I want Elinor Bayliss. There are terms to be laid out."

"Agreement before blooding. Yes." A forked tongue darted out to lick her fangs. "My terms are simple. The trinity to me before your next spring equinox. Because I will complete my terms before you complete yours, my six warlords will remain unfettered on Earth, and two of your minions will abide with me. If you fail to deliver the trinity within the allotted time, your minions become mine, and I will hunt you as kiraknikahl." She paused. "Along with the trinity, you will deliver Mzatal, bound in makkas."

Yeah . . . no. Not in a million years, you demonic bitch. I'd maintained an impassive expression while she spoke, seasoned with a teensy dash of mild boredom. Now I offered a smile as far from friendly as, well, a Jontari was from Mzatal. "*My* terms. You will bring Elinor to me within the hour, alive and unharmed in any way by you or your demons. During this task, no other humans will be harmed. Demon incursions are to cease as of this moment. You will immediately surrender to me all human body parts collected by your minions since the beginning of the incursions. And you will release Seretis. *Now*." I paused. "As for your terms. The time frame for the trinity is agreed. *One* warlord is to remain on Earth, and only until the trinity is delivered to you. None of my people will accompany you to your realm. The matter of Mzatal as part of your lord collection is removed from this negotiation."

She growled. "Seretis is *mine*. The matter of Seretis is removed from this negotiation."

Crap. At this stage in the game, I didn't dare ask her to clarify what she meant by *mine*. Yet no way could I accept his dismissal from the terms without knowing more. "I would speak to Seretis," I said. "Alone."

Dekkak clicked her claws together in a complex staccato. I had zero doubt she was working out a way to deny me and still get what she wanted. "Fifty heartbeats," she finally said. "Unveiled."

"One hundred." I decided not to push the privacy issue and risk losing the opportunity altogether. "*Human* heartbeats," I quickly added since I didn't want to risk losing out because some weird demon had a pulse rate of three thousand beats per minute.

"Agreed."

Seretis stood as I approached. Barely a foot behind him, Slugthing towered like a wall of writhing tentacles and grisly human remains.

Since we had no privacy, this needed to be a show for Dekkak's benefit. I kept my face impassive. "What bargain did you make?"

"A selfish one," Seretis replied. "Is it wrong that I feel safer in the tender care of my mortal enemy than in the heart of my own realm?"

His words confirmed what Bryce had relayed about treachery at home but, dramatics aside, there had to be a deeper motivation at work than saving his skin. He couldn't speak openly with said mortal enemy in range of hearing, but perhaps he'd drop enough clues to let me figure it out on my own.

"Right or wrong, it is done," I said. "What was the bargain?"

He let out a soft breath, eyes on mine. "The honored Dekkak agreed to assess you before fulfilling her unblooded agreement with Xharbek. In exchange, I am hers."

Holy fuck. I wrenched my focus to an unruly twist of hair above his right temple, knowing too well that my uber-tough attitude would crumble if I looked into his eyes. Seretis had made an unbelievable end run around Xharbek and absolutely, hands down, saved my ass. If Dekkak had come through the rift with the intent to kill me rather than to talk, I'd be dead, along with everyone else in the compound, leaving Xharbek free to fuck up both worlds. This dude had balls. Gigantic and brass. And apparently well-hidden, with the rather hairy pair in plain sight a mere façade.

Tough-as-nails mien intact again, I dropped my eyes to his.

He'd sensed my brief struggle for control and waited a beat, but now his mouth curved in a sad smile. "I gave a blood oath that you will deliver the essence blades to her. If you do not . . ." He offered a barely perceptible shrug.

If I did not, his life would be at an end—or not worth living. I forced my mouth into a sneer. "Why would you do that?"

"Because acquiring the blades is near impossible, and she would agree to no less." His uninjured eye fixed on me. "And though I would give my life a hundred times over to rid the worlds of the anathema of the blades, I had not the direct means. But you, zharkat of Mzatal, you are my tool. Through you, I make my mark."

He'd couched his words in lordly eloquence, yet the meaning rang through, loud and clear: Seretis was willing to live and die as a captive if it meant getting the knives out of the hands of Szerain and Mzatal. More astonishing—to me at least—was his clear and unswerving belief that I was up to this incredibly difficult task. This really holy crap crazy what-the-hell unspeakably nigh near impossible task.

I stiffened my spine and bared my teeth at Seretis in the necessary show of disdain. "Through *my* actions I will make *my* mark," I snarled in my best potency-backed imperious voice.

A dark tentacle snaked around his waist and dragged him back against Slugthing. Fear shimmered briefly over his face before he regained his composure. "Then make your mark, Kara Gillian," he murmured.

Chapter 39

I turned my back on Seretis and reimmersed in the comfort and security of the super-shikvihr. Though his current situation tore at my heart, my estimation of him rocketed to infinite heights. Seretis had more strength of will and character than the rest of the lords combined—including, I had to admit, Mzatal. I loved my zharkat deeply, and he was a serious badass, but I couldn't deny that the blades and their origin and influence were a cancer in his essence.

Calm determination filled me. Though I was by myself on the nexus, I wasn't alone. With me was the gentle support of Rho and the strength of Seretis. Rhyzkahl watched me steadily from where he sat beneath the tree, while my friends and comrades stood firm and resolute around me. And, as always, the touch and resonance of Mzatal surrounded me in the super-shikvihr.

With my confidence bolstered, I instructed Pellini to have the DIRT teams wait outside the gate upon arrival, then I settled into the negotiations. Dekkak and I laid out terms, specified points and clarified details, while I also ruthlessly hunted down loopholes. The imperator would lunge at any opportunity to interpret wording to her advantage—like a genie who grants a man's wish to never be sick again by promptly killing him.

After at least a dozen exchanges, we reached a point where neither of us would concede the slightest detail and finally agreed upon acceptable compromises.

Dekkak would rescue Elinor and bring her to me, which was, of course, my primary concern. To my dismay, she refused to agree to my "no harm to humans" addendum and stated only that she and her demons would show restraint. Mzatal or Rhyzkahl could have driven a harder bargain, but I'd reached the limits of my powers of persuasion. Yet deep down I understood that for a mission such as the one I'd outlined, where her forces would be facing armed resistance, she simply couldn't swear to do no harm.

Didn't mean I had to like it, though.

Incursions by her clans would cease until the spring equinox. She advised me that she had no control over the actions of other clans, but with her demons out of the picture, rift activity would drop by seventy-percent or more.

Also, any viable pods left at Fed Central, including David Hawkins from Grounds for Arrest, would get the ilius support needed to successfully complete the pod process.

Lastly, before this full moon had waned to half, she would surrender the remains of the Dirty Thirty via the rift by the nexus.

In return for these concessions, I would deliver the blades to her no later than the spring equinox. Rather than the six warlords she'd originally demanded, four would remain on my property until I turned over the blades. Two reyza, a kehza, and the zhurn, all responsible for hunting game animals on their own for food. No humans, pets, or livestock. The warlords were also forbidden from attacking or deliberately causing harm to any resident or guest on my property—whether human, demon, animal, or lord—except in self-defense. At the same time, all sentient creatures under my authority would similarly refrain from attacking or deliberately causing harm to the "visiting" warlords.

The rift by the nexus would remain open until I fulfilled my end of the bargain.

And, finally, Dekkak would return to the demon realm with one human "guest"—a.k.a. hostage—who would be condemned to slavery and/or death should I fail or break my oath. Though I'd managed to negotiate her down to just the one hostage, sick heartache remained that anyone would have to go at all.

We repeated the terms one last time. The whole thing sucked from top to bottom, but my head and heart told me this was as good as I could possibly get under the circumstances.

"I agree to the terms and give my oath that I will abide by them," I pronounced.

Dekkak inhaled, as if drawing in my words. "My honor and my blood bind me to this covenant," she intoned, then with a claw the length of my forearm, gestured toward where my knife lay on the slab.

I picked it up, abruptly aware that I hadn't the faintest idea what the protocol was for blood oaths. For summonings, I'd always made cuts in my forearm, just deep enough to nick the surface veins. But that felt insufficient for an oath of this magnitude.

A twitch of movement from Seretis caught my eye. Face carefully blank, he made a fist with his right hand then relaxed it, palm up. Grateful, I gave a small nod, as if merely psyching myself up. He'd seen my befuddlement and offered a hint, reminding me of how Mzatal always cut across his palm for ritual work.

The palm it was then.

I adjusted my grip on the knife, casually shifting a few inches to my left to keep Seretis within my line of sight. I had faith that he'd give me a sign if it looked as if I was about to make a fatal faux pas.

Dekkak snapped her wings in the universal demon sign of impatience. Pretending to ignore her, I placed the edge of the knife against the meat of my palm then closed my hand around the blade like I'd seen Mzatal do.

Then again, the lords don't have to worry about permanently severing tendons, I thought sourly. I steeled myself and silently counted to three then pulled the knife through my grip as if drawing it from a sheath.

Fuckingshitgoddamn ow that hurt! Breathing through clenched teeth, I opened my hand to reveal the long gash then looked up at Dekkak expectantly.

She drew a claw across her own palm, opening a wound that dripped blood in a steady stream onto the black slab and its silvery inlay.

Without any warning, the nexus vortex reversed, sucking the arcane downward. My legs nearly buckled as my body abruptly felt impossibly heavy, as if gravity had quadrupled in strength.

Dekkak bellowed as her wings drooped under the arcane pressure, but quickly recovered from her surprise and peered intently down, making no move to stop the flow of blood. Her eyes narrowed with avid curiosity, as if trying to discern the reason for the shift in the vortex.

Crap! I didn't know what was going on, but I didn't want her to break my nexus by continuing to bleed all over it and gum up the works. Nor did I want to give away any nexus-y secrets to an imperator.

"Dekkak! Off my nexus with the blood. Now!" I spoke with as much force as I could muster while weighing five hundred pounds.

She utterly ignored me and spattered more blood, scrutinizing the slab.

The bindings and protections around the nexus dimmed briefly, like a brownout. Whatever this reaction to her blood was, it sucked a shitload of power. Power I needed. If I couldn't find a way to make her stop—

The sigil from the notebook. The one Szerain had told me to memorize.

Use it if—when—you want Dekkak to pay close attention to what you're saying.

I certainly needed that superpower now. Fighting against the steady downdraft, I traced the little sigil before me then spoke into it.

"Imperator Dekkak. Stop bleeding onto my nexus, or I *will* withdraw agreement." I could only hope that we weren't already done with the oath-swearing.

Her gaze lifted from the black surface, and for the barest moment she seemed . . . confused. Then she growled low and wove rakkuhr over the wound as if she hadn't been intentionally painting my slab red a moment earlier. The instant the blood stopped striking the nexus, the vortex returned to its normal updraft.

Hot damn. It worked.

"The agreement is made," she said, giving zero indication that she remembered my ordering her around. "The oath is in the making." She extended her wounded hand then waited, eyeing me.

Seretis turned his hand palm up, shifted it forward an inch then flicked his eyes at Dekkak.

Got it. I held out my injured hand.

"Now we seal our blood oath on this pact," she rumbled then seized my arm and swiped her thick, rough tongue over the slice.

I choked back a squeak of surprise and did my best to look as if that hadn't been really weird and kind of gross. Dekkak released me, still holding her own gashed hand out.

Oh. Eeeeeeew! She'd peeled off the rakkuhr bandaid, and the bleeding had pretty much stopped, but that didn't change the fact that I was clearly expected to lick an open wound on a big demon hand with a palm the size of my torso.

But if I hesitated any longer, I'd look weak. Steeling myself, I grabbed her massive wrist with both hands then glommed my tongue right smack onto the squishy middle of the gash and gave it the kind of girl-on-girl action this deal deserved.

I released her wrist and stepped back, keeping a confident smile in place and an iron hold on the urge to scrub my face and mouth.

"Bound by blood and oath, it is done," Dekkak proclaimed, dissipating the privacy ward. "I go for the shell of Elinor Bayliss."

Before I could ask if she needed directions, she spread her wings and let out a roar that shook the air. Slugthing, moving faster than a creature that big or that ugly had a right to move, wrapped Seretis in tentacles and tossed him bodily into the rift. Dekkak bounded up and over, landing twenty feet beyond Rhyzkahl's orbit. Slugthing followed.

The rift crackled with magenta flame, and a horde of creatures the size of large cats boiled forth. Flyers and walkers and slitherers. All colors and all forms. Moving in unison like a flock of birds, they converged to swarm around Dekkak. Potency coalesced around her as her deft hands bound and anchored rakkuhr.

Bryce's orders to the security personnel crackled in my ear. Assemble by the nexus. Keep clear of the demons.

Yulz thrashed in the net as the arcane bindings weakened. Cursing, I dragged my attention from Dekkak then unanchored the bindings and speed-chanted the dismissal. With a flash of blinding light and a ripping *crack*, Yulz was gone.

A circle of magenta and orange light the size of a manhole appeared on the ground before Dekkak. I twitched in shock. It was a rift. A perfectly circular *rift* that was expanding by the second. She wasn't flying to get Elinor like I'd assumed she would do. She was taking a shortcut through an arcane sinkhole.

I yanked my phone off my belt, found the number I needed and hit the call button.

A cool female voice answered. "DIRT HQ. How may I—"

"This is A.C. Kara Gillian," I interrupted, then rattled off my security code. "A rift is about to open in Beaulac, Louisiana. Best estimate is near the Post Office on Harper street. All non-essential personnel in a one mile radius need to be evacuated, on my authority, and yes, I'm aware that radius includes Fed Central. This is a confirmed event. Do *not* waste time sending this up and down channels."

"Yes, ma'am," she replied, completely unruffled. In the background I heard lightning fast typing. "Your security code has been accepted. I'm transmitting the order for an evacuation of all non-essential personnel within a one-mile radius of the Harper Street Post Office in Beaulac, Louisiana, including the Federal Joint Agency Command Center. Do you also wish to order a patient evacuation from the medical facility there?"

"No, there's not enough time," I said, concentrating on keeping my voice even. "They'll be safer and more secure where they are." I mentally crossed fingers and toes that everyone else would feel the same way.

"Of course, ma'am. Are you able to provide an estimated time frame and/or intensity of the predicted rift?"

I cast a worried glance at Dekkak and the widening sinkhole-rift. The original version of my plan had Dekkak flying to Fed Central, giving me a cushion of at least twenty minutes for people to evacuate. "Time frame is very soon. Within the next couple of minutes." How many people would be able to get out in such a short amount of time? "Estimated rift size is less than fifty feet with moderate intensity." I held off specifying that was the diameter, since I had no idea what it would be like at the other end.

"Thank you, ma'am. I'm forwarding that now. Do you have any further information?"

I rubbed my eyes. "No, that's all I could get."

Dekkak bellowed and dove into the sinkhole-rift with Slugthing and the swarm right behind her.

"Yes, ma'am. Is there anything else I can do for you at this time?"

Find a way for me to protect everyone? "No, you've been very helpful."

I half expected her to wish me a nice day, but she merely thanked me again and disconnected.

Gut twisting, I shoved the phone back into its holder. People were going to get hurt or killed, and it would be on my head. I could stand here and justify it until the cows came home, but it wouldn't change a thing.

"I need to see the DIRT crisis feed," I said. My voice sounded

weird and hoarse to my ears. "I need to know what's going on."
I need the casualty reports.

"I'll get the tablet," Tandon said and sprinted for the house.

Medic Nils Engen ran up and expertly bound my cut palm in
a pressure wrap of gauze, instructing me to keep my fingers
closed over the bandage until I could get stitches.

As soon as Engen finished, Pellini put a hand on my arm. I
let out a shaky breath. "I know what you're going to say," I said.
"You'll tell me it had to be done, that we exhausted all other
options. Maybe even something about how this will save far
more lives in the long run."

"Yeah, but my version would've been a lot more eloquent
and heartwarming," Pellini said then surprised me by pulling me
into a hug.

"I'm going to start crying," I choked out even as I clung to
him. "I can't start crying during a summoning and with all these
demons watching."

"Would you please shut the fuck up," he murmured then held
me close while I bawled. Thankfully, my uncontrollable sobbing
subsided within half a minute—like lancing a boil and getting
that first big spurt of pus, leaving the rest free to drain more
gradually. I went still and let him hold me, let him be tough for
me in this brief moment.

Because it was about to get a lot worse. I pulled away from
him then stepped to the center of the nexus. "I need everyone to
listen to me," I said, voice quavering. Damn it. I took a deep
breath. "Only a few people here know just how vital this summoning was, or why we all risked our lives in a bid to rescue one
woman. Yet even without knowing the details, every single one
of you performed so far above and beyond the call of duty it
defies measurement." I paused, tightening my hands to keep the
trembling at bay. "I can tell you now that if we'd failed to get
Elinor away from the one who held her, Earth would face certain
obliteration." Fuck. Fuck. Fuckfuckfuckfuckfuck. "Dekkak is
getting her right now. For a price. I'm paying part of it . . . but
for the rest, she wants a hostage: one human to return with her
to the demon realm until I fulfill my part of the bargain." I held
up a hand as everyone drew breath to speak. "I have her vow that
the hostage will be treated as a guest and won't be subject to the
kind of treatment Seretis endures. But . . . that's all I know, and
that still leaves a lot of room for a less than pleasant stay." I

swallowed. "However, if I don't uphold my end of the bargain, Dekkak will effectively own the hostage. Needless to say, I absolutely will not order anyone to do this."

"I volunteer," Bryce said instantly, chin up and expression fierce. "I'll go be Dekkak's hostage."

My shoulders slumped. Of course Bryce would volunteer. That was the kind of guy he was. "No," I said, wincing as he tensed. "I'm sorry, Bryce, but you're needed here." He drew breath to protest, and I added, "Seretis needs you here."

"Goddammit, Kara," he growled. "You don't get to decide what's best for him. I should be there—" He broke off, staggering from Suarez's friendly slap on the back.

Suarez grabbed his shoulder to steady him. "Beggin' your pardon, sir, but you're kinda full of shit." As Bryce goggled at him, Suarez gave him a nice, affable smile. "Your buddy Sarytess needs you safe and sound so he don't have t'worry 'bout you. And this place needs you to stay here 'cause you take care of everything and everyone. And Miss Kara needs you so she don't have to fret 'bout security." He paused. An instant later Bryce's face went white as Suarez's hand tightened on his shoulder. "But most of all, Miss Jill needs you." His face remained congenial, but his eyes held reproach. "Which means you can't be runnin' off havin' all the fun." He released his grip then turned to me. "I volunteer, Miss Kara. I ain't got no family to miss me other than everyone here, and it'd be an honor to represent y'all in the demon world."

It took me a few seconds to find my voice. "Are you absolutely sure?"

"More than I ever been in my whole life, ma'am. And I know in my heart that you got what it takes to get your part done. I'll be home afore you know it."

My throat tightened, but I managed a nod.

The air vibrated in a now-familiar resonance. Suarez and Bryce stepped back as Dekkak emerged from the sinkhole-rift with a person-shaped object gripped in one clawed hand, and the horde swarming around her. Slugthing followed, its color shifting in rapid patterns of deep blue and near fluorescent pink.

Cold dismay swept over me. Instead of Elinor, Dekkak held the broken body of a tactical-geared agent. The imperator hissed through her teeth and tossed the body to land on the nexus, crumpled against the trunk of the grove tree.

Sickened, I forced my gaze away. I'd grieve and cry and wallow later. For now I scanned the demons, anxiety rising as the arcane sinkhole snapped shut with no sign of Elinor. *No no no no no!* If Dekkak hadn't retrieved Elinor, I'd caused a lot of people to get hurt or killed for nothing.

A heartbeat before I freaked completely the fuck out, Slugthing opened its maw and barfed a slime-covered Elinor out to flop bonelessly on the grass just beyond Rhyzkahl's orbit.

I raced to her and cleared her nose and mouth with shaking hands. An instant later Giovanni was at my side, damn near tearing her away from me to cradle her close.

"Elinor." Tears streamed down his face as he held her to him. "God is in his heaven, and I have my Elinor back."

She was breathing, but I wasn't surprised that she remained unconscious. My aunt Tessa had stayed in a coma for weeks after she lost her essence to the Symbol Man's ritual.

Unfortunately, I hadn't warned Giovanni. His distress rose as Elinor's eyes failed to flutter open to see the face of her beloved.

"Why won't she wake up?" Giovanni demanded of Dekkak.

Her lips curled back as she hissed at the puny human who dared address her.

I cleared my throat. "Elinor is okay. Trust me?"

Giovanni didn't seem the least bit convinced, but he gave me the barest of nods.

Dekkak flicked her wing and, as one, her mutant demons bounded, flew, and slithered into the rift. "I have fulfilled my end of the bargain, summoner," she growled, deep and malevolent.

I expected her to add *Now it's your turn* or something along those lines, but apparently she didn't feel I needed the reminder. She was right, too. No way would I forget an onus of that magnitude, but at the moment I was happy to see the ugly ass end of those demons.

Dekkak turned her attention to Suarez. "Divest yourself of clothing and weapons."

Suarez obligingly unholstered both of his handguns and set them on the grass then pulled a backup piece from his right ankle and a knife from his left. His body armor followed, then he stripped off his shirt, surprising me with the unbelievable amount of hair that covered his body, a bizarre contrast to his egg-smooth bald head. The only spot that wasn't covered in fur was an eight inch wide shaved circle on his back where yet another pistol and holster were duct-taped between his shoulder blades.

I smothered a laugh that I knew would be incredibly inappropriate considering the horrendous circumstances, but Suarez merely caught my eye and gave me a broad wink. He unlaced his boots and tossed them aside, but when he dropped his pants to reveal the knives strapped to each thigh, I wasn't the only one who gave in to laughter.

"For the love of god, Suarez," Bryce said, a ghost of a smile rippling his stoic mask. "If you're carrying more armament up your ass, fucking wait until you're in the rift to pull it out."

Suarez stepped out of his pants then grabbed Bryce in a fierce hug. Terror flashed across Suarez's face, almost too quickly to see before he buried it under a wide, though shaky, grin. "Only weapon I got up there is from them burritos Tandon cooked up for lunch, and I'm savin' it 'til we get there."

"That's my man," Bryce said, though his voice cracked on the last word.

Suarez stepped back and turned to me. "It's been a real honor to work for you, Miss Kara."

"You still work for me, Suarez," I said fiercely then spoiled it by sniffling. "I expect a full report when I see you again."

"Will do, ma'am," he said with an echo of my sniffle. He took one last look at everybody, dropped his boxers to reveal an ass with more hair than I thought was humanly possible, then walked head high to the imperator.

"Reporting as ordered, Miss Dekkak."

The imperator gestured to the rift as if inviting Suarez to take a dip in a pool.

Comprehension broke over his face. He shot Bryce an I'm-so-fucked-but-fuck-if-they'll-beat-me smile, shrugged fatalistically, then sauntered to the lip of the rift. He stood there a moment, staring down into the shifting magenta light, then called out, "Later, y'all!" and took a step forward and tumbled out of sight.

Dekkak bellowed and leaped after him then was gone.

"Bryce, any casualty reports yet?" I kept my voice nice and even, but my stomach was doing pretzel imitations.

"Still coming in," Bryce said, tablet in hand and eyes on the screen. "So far they're reporting fourteen injured, four seriously." He looked up at me. "No fatalities reported, but a handful of personnel haven't been accounted for yet." His eyes didn't so much as twitch toward the body on the nexus, but it didn't matter. I knew it was there.

"Thanks." One dead for certain. But not the dozens I'd feared. I closed my eyes and gave myself a count of ten to savor the victories, however small, before I had to deal with the rest.

"You okay with me telling the DIRT squads to stand down?" Pellini asked.

"Yeah," I said, rubbing my gritty eyes. "In fact, you can dismiss them. They won't be needed here." I turned to Giovanni. "All right, let's—"

"She does not wake!" Distress shone in his eyes. "Why does she not wake?"

"Elinor is . . . incomplete." I sighed. "Her essence is still glued to mine, so she can't be, er, switched on."

He gazed down at his beloved and gently wiped the goop from her face.

But something was wrong apart from the missing essence. She wasn't awake, yet there was an awareness. Just like when she'd been aware of the people in her room and the ticking clock. I was no mind reader, but Elinor and I had an intimate connection. I took her hand then flinched as her fear ripped through me like an primal scream. Why?

With the physical contact, I *knew*.

Because she doesn't know she's here and safe. The majority of her perception had been through me, but whatever Xharbek had done to her in these last hours left her too freaked to pay attention to what I was doing.

I sat in the grass across from Giovanni. "Talk to her," I said. "Reassure her, and tell her that you're with her, that she's safe." I paused. "But you need to say it to *me*."

He stared at me as if I was insane. "To you?"

"To me. Trust me. Look right into my eyes and go for it."

Giovanni gave Elinor an uncertain look then squared his shoulders and drilled his gaze into mine. "My beloved Elinor. My heart fills with joy to have you safe in my arms." He continued to shower words of adoration at her through me, with impressive eloquence and uninhibited passion.

Yeah, this was fucking weird. But I had to hand it to him, the dude was giving it his all. I focused on taking in everything about him—not only his words, but his accent, the way his mouth moved, the way the light breeze ruffled his hair.

Elinor's body didn't so much as twitch, but around the time Giovanni was raving about the radiance of her skin, the scream eased off to distressed moans and whimpers. I waited to see if it would subside more, but no. Before Giovanni could launch into the perfection of her breasts, I held up my hand to stop him. "You did good. She's a little calmer now."

A hand touched my shoulder. I glanced up to give Pellini a smile of reassurance, then scrambled to my feet, heart thundering. Bryce and Pellini gave matching shouts of alarm and surprise, as both had been focused on the occupying Jontari demons.

Rhyzkahl. Out.

We were at the perimeter of his orbit, but he was *outside* it. Purple lightning bursts flickered over him, and writhing chains of potency trailed back to the rift-breach of his orbit, as if he'd emerged from viscous slime—Mzatal's protections clinging to him but diminished by the disruption. Sweat plastered Rhyzkahl's shirt to his chest, and his face spasmed from the pain of the wards.

Giovanni pulled Elinor close, his expression defiant though he shrank back from the threat of the lord. I reached for potency from the nexus even as Pellini and Bryce drew weapons a dozen feet away. The arcane answered my call in a sluggish flow, depleted by the drain of the summoning and disrupted by the straying of its Rhyzkahl-battery. Yet answer it did, though I wasn't at all certain it would be enough to take him down. "Return to your orbit, Rhyzkahl," I commanded.

"No, Kara Gillian," he said through gritted teeth.

I sent the potency into my hand to coalesce into a shimmering azure globe. "You know I'll win this challenge," I said, hoping it to be true. "Save yourself the pain and retreat."

"You can use that potency to smite me," he said, voice strained, "or you can use it to aid Elinor. Can you not feel her anguish?"

I blinked. Elinor. The one he had named zharkat. He hadn't fought through Mzatal's wards to deal with me, or even to escape. He'd fought through them for *her*.

He met my eyes. "Trust me in this, if in nothing else."

Giovanni glared. "We will not succumb to your trickery."

"When have I *ever* harmed her, Giovanni Racchelli?" Rhyzkahl winced as Elinor's mental whimpers twisted into a scream again. He seemed to hear them as clearly as I did. "It is *you* who prolong her suffering by denying me."

"Rhyzkahl is right, Giovanni," I said quietly. "In this one matter, I do trust him." He had loved Elinor—and still loved her—as much as he could love anyone after being manipulated, suppressed, and emotionally crippled by the demahnk. "You need to allow this. Elinor is suffering."

The last bit seemed to get through to Giovanni. He eased his death grip on her and gave an oh-so-reluctant nod.

"What do you need?" I asked Rhyzkahl.

"To hold her."

I wondered just how much of that was his personal need versus a requirement to help her, but decided it really didn't matter at the moment. With care, I tapped into the nexus and did my best to temper the wards so they weren't quite so painful, though I didn't dare ease them too much. "We can take her into your orbit."

"Your adjustments were sufficient. I am here now." Rhyzkahl dropped to one knee beside Giovanni and Elinor, then lifted her from her lover's arms. He cradled her close and murmured softly in demon.

I took her hand again to better monitor her condition—and Rhyzkahl's actions.

Giovanni looked on, his expression a mix of distress and worry.

Rhyzkahl traced three pygahs on her forehead—potent sigils, not thready and pale like they'd been for the past two months. "Kara, simple support," he said. "Please."

I dragged my thoughts from the implications of a fully arcane-functional Rhyzkahl and quickly sketched a half dozen glowing sigils that I set spinning beside him.

He bent to rest his forehead against hers, his hair curtaining their faces.

A gentle serenity welled in me, despite all that had transpired, and despite this surreal tableau of Giovanni, Elinor, and Rhyzkahl. Familiar and comforting. The grove. Rho. I released a soft breath and placed my free hand on Rhyzkahl's shoulder.

Warmth shimmered through me like a summer breeze and flowed to Rhyzkahl. He tensed beneath my hand, then eased. For a time, neither of us moved and nothing changed, then Elinor's mental cry softened and stilled, leaving me in strange silence.

Rhyzkahl lifted his head. "I have not the reserves nor the means to restore her," he said, his voice laden with exhaustion and regret.

"You've done enough," I said, hand still on him.

He kissed her forehead then transferred her back to Giovanni's arms. "I failed to do enough when it mattered," he said as he staggered to his feet.

Without another word, Rhyzkahl retreated to the breach, feet dragging as if he barely had the energy to move. The lightning wards slithered from him as he crossed the perimeter, and he collapsed into the remains of trampled purple irises.

Turek padded silently to Rhyzkahl, scooped him into his arms then returned to the tree to settle again at its base. Only a few feet away lay the federal agent's body. With the immediate crisis past, it felt revolting to leave him there like a pile of garbage.

"Roper. Engen." A knot built up in my throat. "Please get a sheet from my linen closet and wrap the agent's body." His death was on my head. The least I could do was treat him with as much respect as possible. "But leave him by the tree."

Both men nodded gravely and moved to comply. The moonlight on the nexus shifted, and I looked up to see that the tree had extended its branches back over the slab, as if to shelter the deceased agent.

Giovanni dropped his gaze to Elinor and gave her a soft smile. I pushed to my feet and stepped to where Bryce monitored the DIRT feeds on the tablet.

"Anything?"

"Still no fatalities reported. Seven in critical condition and another dozen hospitalized. Fifteen to twenty are being treated and released for minor to moderate injuries." His eyes echoed my own mix of sorrow and relief at the toll. "Everyone has been accounted for except one patient." His gaze flicked to Elinor then slid to the body on the nexus. "And one agent. Richard Knox."

"I need to set Szerain's bunker diagrams and get those two secured within them." I nudged my head toward Giovanni and his gooey girlfriend. "I'll . . . take care of other matters once Szerain, Zack, Ashava, and Sonny are here and safe."

He gave me a grim nod. "Pellini and I will mop up the rest."

"Thank you. For everything."

A gentle smile came over Bryce's face. "You make it easy to care."

Lovely warmth unfolded within me at the unexpected note of approval and support. "Would you mind calling Jill to give her a status update?" I asked. "I'm sure she's chewing nails by now."

His smile kicked up a few degrees. "I'll take care of it." He gave my arm a light squeeze then moved off to make the call.

Feeling oddly restored, I returned to the nexus and got down to business.

Chapter 40

Pellini and Roper removed the linen-wrapped body of Agent Knox to the grass beneath the tree, and within a dozen heartbeats white roots emerged from the ground to cradle him. A small measure of the weight on my essence lifted at the sight. Rho would keep the remains safe for now, allowing me to give my full focus to the task at hand.

By the time I had the residual potency cleaned up, the bunker diagrams constructed, and Giovanni and Elinor protected within them, fatigue had begun to infiltrate my defenses. However, there was still half an hour to go before the appointed time to bring our AWOL four home, and long experience told me that if I paused to rest for even a moment I'd never get moving again. Focusing on the crap that needed to be done was the only workable tactic.

With that in mind, I headed inside to check on the Krawkor-Makonite-ilius pod situation. The pods were still the same smooth, shiny black with red veining, but now white potency drifted up from them like arcane steam. Bryce stood nearby, arms folded over his chest, and expression perplexed.

"Those demons are tough to see," he said. "More smoke than substance."

"Yeah, part of their illusion camouflage." I passed my hands through the steam, but sensed only a faint tingle. "What did they do?"

"Each one settled on top of a pod. Then they just . . . melted. I think they're inside."

"Huh." Baffled, I placed my hand firmly on the surface of

Cory's pod. It was warm, with an arcane pulse. I could only hope that was a good thing. "Seems okay, as far as I can tell."

Bryce flicked a glance at the surveillance camera mounted in the corner. "I need to get some air."

"I can go for that." I led the way out to the front porch and waited for him to close the door behind us. "What's up?"

"Turns out Seretis started picking up my thoughts because of this." He pulled out a gold disk—the one with Seretis's image. "And, yeah, Turek knows I have it. We scraped by on the weight without this disk. Short a few ounces, but the contact didn't bat an eye."

"I'm glad you have it," I said, absurdly relived that this one survived. "You're saying that Seretis could pick up your thoughts, but not the other way around until he got here?"

"Right. I guess the disk worked like a broadcast antennae. Once he came through the rift, we had our normal two-way bond contact."

"Good to know. That means we might be able to get a message to him, if needed."

Bryce sobered. "Kara, be straight with me. Is the deal he made worth it?"

"Yes," I said, utterly serious. "It really is. He saved our asses. I know it kills you to see him fucked up like that, but he's a real hero. Dekkak would have killed every single one of us and given Xharbek the means to destroy Earth." I paused. "But it's not just that. He made one hell of a gutsy move with his proposal, and we ended up with Elinor as well as an agreement that I think will pay off for us in the end. It's risky, but he made a good call. You can be really proud of him."

"Oh, I am," he said, voice cracking only a little. He squared his shoulders and shook off the brief sentimentality. "He also gave me info about the rakkuhr and the Jontari. He said it might be useful to you."

"Every shred of info is more than I currently have."

"Here goes." Bryce moved to the porch railing and drew a donut shape in the dust. "The arcane that you summoners use is the surface potency, while rakkuhr is the planetary core potency." He added a second donut six inches away. "For both planets—the demon realm *and* Earth." A corner of his mouth lifted as I twitched in surprise. "Yeah, that caught me off guard as well." He drew lines from the outer edges of each donut to their centers. "Core rakkuhr and surface potency are in dynamic equilibrium. If there's too much surface potency, some converts to rakkuhr and sinks to the core, and vice versa. The planets stay stable."

"Okay, I'm with you so far. Rakkuhr is supposed to stay below and balance out the surface potency." Obviously, everything was out of whack now.

Bryce nodded. "Seems like it would be a self-correcting system, but there's a glitch." He dragged his finger between the two donuts. "All this time, there's been an interdimensional connection between Earth and the demon realm, like an energy umbilicus. Through it, the demon realm siphons off potency from Earth, and over the ages, has depleted Earth and filled itself to overflowing."

I cursed under my breath as I grasped the scope of the problem. "Now there's so much potency in the demon realm, the core can't contain the rakkuhr."

"Exactly. From what I can tell, a few thousand years ago the excess rakkuhr broke through in three locations, sort of like geysers. The Jontari have held those places sacred ever since and have built an entire arcane technology around their use." His shoulders lifted in a shrug. "Seretis said that would be important to you."

"It fills in pieces of the puzzle." Three sacred rakkuhr places. Three Jontari elders who were gatekeepers of the rakkuhr, currently enslaved in essence blades. Radical instability in the demon realm threatening to break up the planet—due to the potency overload. A problem for everyone.

"Seretis told me the lords can't keep up with the planetary balancing anymore via their plexus work." His brow creased with worry. "It's unraveling too much, too fast. He said there has to be another way besides flooding the Earth with rakkuhr."

"There is," I said with utter conviction. "We just have to find it."

"Damn straight." He erased the donuts with a swipe of his hand then headed off toward the security office. I remained on the porch and allowed myself a few minutes to mull over this new information.

Dekkak blamed the Ekiri for changing her world. Maybe they started the siphoning to suit their own needs, and in the process changed the world? Seretis hadn't so much as hinted at an Ekiri connection, but he might have been manipulated to forget it. Or perhaps it simply happened before his time.

I turned to go inside but paused at the sight of Eilahn's decorations surrounding the door. Floodlights blazed around the house, setting the crystal figurines sparkling, and a pang of longing went through me as I realized how much I missed Eilahn. The demon garland was exquisite, but if she were here, we'd have giant pumpkins on the roof, witches in every tree, and cauldrons of apples. Hell, probably even a haunted corn maze.

My eyes narrowed on the slug-squid-octopus figurine Pellini had noted earlier. "Well, helloooo, Slugthing," I murmured. The other unknown-to-me figures were probably real creatures in the demon realm, too. Interesting. And more than a little unnerving.

My watch beeped. Five minutes until Operation Phone Home Szerain.

I made my way through the house to the back yard and marshalled everyone into their respective positions. Giovanni sat beside one of the bunker diagrams with Elinor in his lap. Pellini took up his usual spot outside the super-shikvihr while Turek crouched at the edge of the nexus closest to the rift. This would essentially be a replay of my first attempt to reach Szerain, though hopefully without the part where he pulled me into a dimensional pocket. This time—I hoped—Szerain would catch my line of potency, grab the others from the stronghold, and let us pull them all home.

Pellini's attention stayed glued to his watch, which he'd calibrated to International Atomic Time right before the summoning. By 2:22 a.m., I had the ball of potency-string ready in my hand and my arcane eye on the resonance that marked where I needed to cast it.

The resonance abruptly dimmed and vanished, obscured by an odd static-like potency. It had the "scent" of Szerain though, which told me it was probably an aspect of the protections. My only option at this point was to trust that he'd be ready at the appointed time.

"Thirty seconds," Pellini announced then took the end of the potency strand from me without lifting his eyes from the watch.

"Five."

Four. Three. Two. One.

The static cleared precisely as Pellini said *now*. I flung the ball along the channel to that spot of perfect resonance and waited for my fishy to bite. One heartbeat. Two.

The potency line went taut, and Pellini and I pulled as hard as if we were trying to land Ahab's white whale.

I yelped and tumbled backward as the tension on the line abruptly disappeared. Pellini landed on top of me, driving my breath out in a whoosh, except that Pellini was standing a couple of feet away, and it was Szerain who rolled off me and onto his back. No sign of Ashava, Zack, or Sonny, to my rising dismay.

A transparent iridescent shield like a tetrahedron-shaped bubble popped up with the bunker diagrams as the vertices. Turek hissed and moved in to help Szerain sit up. Dried blood caked his hair, and he looked battered and exhausted, as if he'd been rolled down a rocky hill after running a marathon.

"I couldn't reach the others," he said with undisguised frustration. "Xharbek's presence was too strong."

I kept a firm hold on my worry. "Are they okay?"

"For now," he murmured, leaning heavily against Turek as if he didn't have the strength to move. "Elinor? I can't sense her."

"She's right here on the nexus," I reassured him. "We did it."

Szerain closed his eyes, and it seemed as if a palpable layer of tension sloughed away. "Looks like you didn't do badly at all for your first Jontari summoning," he said.

"Are you kidding?" I shuddered. "It was a mess from top to bottom."

"Nah, it's like flying a plane. Any time you don't crash, you've won." He shifted to sit without Turek's support then went still, gazing down at the slab beneath us as if looking into the depths of a crystal clear ocean. "I could spend a decade examining what Mzatal created here and not understand a tenth of it," he said with naked awe. Yet a heartbeat later sadness filled his eyes as they traced the connection to Rhyzkahl, trapped in his orbit.

Rhyzkahl met his gaze, revealing nothing in his expression or stance. Szerain breathed out a weary sigh, then turned his attention to his daughter where she lay cradled in her beloved's lap. Giovanni glared at Szerain and clutched Elinor closer, only relaxing a trifle as Szerain looked at me. I didn't miss the flash of hurt in his eyes at the rebuff, though.

"You pulled off the summoning without a gimkrah, which is no small feat," Szerain said. "How did you lose it?"

I scowled. "You make it sound like I left it on the bus or something. We got ambushed and never had a chance."

"Perhaps I should catch up on your exploits," he said with a wry chuckle. He reached toward my head but stopped in surprise as I jerked back.

"Not that way," I said with a grimace of apology. I had zero clue how to shield specific information, and no good would come from him reading that I'd made a pact with a demon to take Szerain's essence blade from him. "It's for your own good. Trust me. Please."

He regarded me with a calculating, narrow-eyed expression, the most lordly I'd ever seen on him. "Of course." He gave me a smile. "Turek is offering his perspective." He gestured toward my bandaged hand. "Will you accept healing?"

"Yes, thanks," I said and allowed him to unwrap the bandage. We'd moved past the incident, but Szerain wouldn't forget I intentionally withheld info from him, for his own good or not. Turek would inform him of my privacy-veiled meeting with Dekkak, thus giving him plenty of fodder for speculation.

Warmth flowed into my hand from Szerain's. He hummed softly as he worked, eyes unfocused, likely communing with Turek. After a quiet minute, his face lit up. "You have Elinor's journal? Fantastic! I need it. Immediately."

"Yeah, sure thing." Maybe one of her bug drawings had a deeper meaning? "Hey, Tandon," I called out. "Could you bring the journal from my nightstand, please?"

"Yes, ma'am," she said, and was off like a friggin' gazelle, long legs chewing up the distance in the blink of an eye.

The warmth increased to heat as the healing intensified. Szerain glanced at Turek, then back to me. "The discs," he said.

My shoulders hunched. "I'm so sorry. They were beautiful, but—"

"Kara, stop," he said, voice weary. "I felt each as it died in the fire. Now, at least, I know it was for Elinor and not the machinations of an enemy."

His gold-green eyes seemed to dull, reflecting the depth of his loss. I couldn't help but wonder what the discs were for, but this wasn't anywhere near the right moment to ask.

He withdrew his hands, and I sighed in relief as the heat faded. I turned my hand over to see a perfectly unblemished palm. "Thank you," I said in complete sincerity just as Tandon sprinted up with the journal.

Szerain climbed to his feet with the help of Turek then accepted the journal. "Having this simplifies matters tremendously. Without it, I'd still be able to make the essence transfer, but it would be more risky and take far longer. Come, we have no time to waste." He stepped off the slab and staggered. Turek leaped to steady him before he toppled.

"Wait, where are you going?" I asked. "Aren't you going to use the nexus?"

"No, we can't do it here," Szerain said. "We need to go to the valve by your pond."

"But it's *thick* with rakkuhr there."

He flashed a grin, made more rakish by the blood on his face. "Exactly."

Giovanni clutched Elinor to him. "How can we trust Szerain to do what he promises?" His voice wavered between grief and anger. "He slew Elinor before my eyes!"

Szerain's grin dropped away as he faced Giovanni. "Yes, but only to save her. Does she not rest in your arms even now? I swear that I can and will explain all, but first we *must* get to the valve, else we risk Xharbek taking her from you forever."

Giovanni's anger gave way to sullen acceptance.

With Turek's help, Szerain made for the edge of the woods at a fast clip while Giovanni stayed right on his heels. I followed, but not before seeing Rhyzkahl standing tense and rigid with frustration at his exclusion.

Silvery moonlight pierced the canopy, casting ample illumination for us to follow the trail through the woods. The pathway opened up on the pond clearing, where rakkuhr undulated in foot-high coils of red and black, and a Jontari kehza basked in the water as if it was his personal spa.

Szerain headed straight for the arcane valve without giving the demon so much as a glance.

"Giovanni, sit here and hold Elinor," Szerain ordered, pointing at a grassy spot a couple of feet from the valve. "Kara, you sit facing them."

Rakkuhr floated toward me as I settled on the ground. I shoved it away in distaste. "Do I need to hold her hand or anything?"

"No, I'll take care of making the connections when it's time." He remained standing, the third vertex of a triangle. Turek crouched behind him, nearly invisible in the gloom.

The air pressure seemed to drop. The rakkuhr ceased its random undulations and began to flow toward Szerain, swirling around his legs and torso, more and more and increasing in speed until he stood at the center of a rakkuhr tornado that flashed red and black.

He thrust a hand up, and the rakkuhr shot skyward like a beacon. A dozen feet up it seemed to hit an invisible wall and spread downward, as if coating the inside of an unseen globe.

Gobsmacked, I watched as the rakkuhr resolved into an exquisite lacework, passing through the ground to form a sphere with us at the center.

The rakkuhr tornado died down to a slow whirlpool around Szerain's calves and feet. The lace-sphere began a slow vertical rotation. A measure of tension left Szerain.

"That buys us time," he said with a crooked smile.

"It's a shield?" I asked.

"Among other things," he replied. "The rakkuhr will keep any demahnk interference at bay until we're finished." All trace of humor left him as his gaze went to Giovanni. "I had mere heartbeats to make a decision and act to save her." Emotion rippled through his voice.

Around Szerain, the lazy whirl of rakkuhr began to pick up speed, though not as fierce a tornado as before. Once again he lifted a hand, and the rakkuhr spun up and out to form a second lace-sphere a hairsbreadth within the first. It flashed in dangerous beauty as he set it rotating, this time horizontally.

"Kara, read Elinor's last journal entry." Szerain began a third sphere, drawing rakkuhr from the valve like silk from a spider's butt.

I fumbled the journal open and flipped to the last page with writing, then peered at it in confusion. I'd skimmed all of her entries, but I had no memory of this one.

"It was her final entry," Szerain said, "and deeply personal. I protected it in memoriam to her." He paused. "But she needs to hear it now. Read."

I cleared my throat self-consciously. "I am not loath to admit that my skills with the arcane astound no one," I began. "I am competent enough, but my passion lies with my illustrations of the demon realm flora and fauna. Lord Szerain knows this, and therefore I will trust he has reasons and knowledge beyond my ken that justify his decision to partner with me for the ritual. I dare not be uncertain. My will must be resolute.

"Giovanni worries, and I love him all the more for it. Yet I am doing this for him, for us. I adore this world, but I dare not quicken here and risk the babe. Confined to Earth, Giovanni would pine without the Lord's company and friendship, and my art would surely suffer. If the ritual succeeds in raising the Earthgate then mayhap my love and I can build a home on Earth and begin a family. The gate will give us both worlds, allowing free return here during those times when I am not with child."

Though I wanted to stop and process the whole "risking the babe" thing, I kept going and read the last bit. "I am prepared. I will succeed with the ritual. I will grow old with Giovanni and sit by the fire with him while our grandchildren play around us." I barely got the last few words out as my throat clogged with emotion. I'd thought of her as weak, but here was a woman who not only had the strength to tell Rhyzkahl that she couldn't be his zharkat, but was ready and willing to *literally* move heaven and earth to start a family with the man she loved.

Giovanni wept openly, murmuring softly in Italian as he cradled Elinor close. I reverently closed the journal and placed it on the grass between us, then looked up at Szerain. To my surprise, a dozen or more rakkuhr lace-spheres now spun around us, all rotating in different directions and orientations, like a gyroscope gone mad. Red and black sparked and flashed throughout it all, and the dizzying effect made me slightly nauseous.

Szerain ceased pulling from the valve and released the rakkuhr around him, letting it drift to the ground. "And now the answers to many questions," he murmured and called Vsuhl to his hand.

My gaze fixed on the knife. Parasite and power source in one. The living prison for the entity Vsuhl.

The spheres spun faster and faster until we floated in a disorienting blur of red. I clutched at the ground for balance—

I was in a summoning chamber, one I knew all too well from seeing it through Elinor's eyes. Except this time Elinor was standing a few feet away.

Holy shit. This is Szerain's *perspective.* It wasn't a dream-vision—I didn't *become* Szerain—but it was darn close.

Giovanni let out a choked cry of surprise, and I realized we were both seeing and experiencing the event, like two people watching the same show on different TVs. No, three. I had the distinct sensation of Elinor's essence peering over my shoulder.

In the vision, Elinor, clad in a brilliant green robe, wove sigils and lay ritual anchors with no hesitation or uncertainty. She might have been "competent enough" in typical arcane ventures, but it was clear she'd worked hard to prepare for this ritual and knew it inside out and backward.

Szerain moved in concert with her, and I sensed his deep satisfaction with Elinor's work. The ritual progressed and built, all aspects in perfect harmony. Even though I knew what was coming, I found myself silently cheering her on. I carried this woman's essence, and now I felt strangely honored that I'd been allowed to do so.

Szerain assessed. All was stable, ready. Elinor invited the grove energy, and it came to her in a rush of power that filled her with palpable vitality. She smiled, radiant. Szerain wove delicate ropes of rakkuhr, enhancing the ritual. Triumphant, he called to the Earthgate, felt it answer—

With no warning or discernible cause, a tremor shattered the protections. Utterly inexplicable. The screaming whine of the ritual signaled that the exquisitely controlled event was about to cascade beyond control like a sea of falling dominos.

Szerain called Vsuhl to his hand, needing more potency to help Elinor release the ritual and disengage.

The power flared. Her mouth opened in a scream.

Time seemed to slow to a crawl. I felt Szerain's horrified awareness as the world began to unravel.

In that instant he knew that, to temper the impending cataclysm, he had no option but to slay Elinor. The surest way was to sate Vsuhl with her blood and her essence, destroying her utterly—and losing Elinor and her potential forever.

Or he could slay her to save her. More risk, less certainty, but she would have a chance to survive, and damage repair would be swifter once he recovered her.

The world shook and tilted. Szerain moved to Elinor as she burned from within, seized her from behind with an arm around her waist.

The door to the antechamber hung on its hinges. Giovanni stumbled in, face twisting in horror as he took in the sight of his beloved.

"Call her!" Szerain shouted through the din of clashing energies.

"Elinor!" Giovanni struggled to move against a howling wind.

Szerain plunged Vsuhl into Elinor's chest, fought the blade's will and ignored Giovanni's shout of horror. "Call her!" he yelled and pulled the knife free, he hoped in time. "Do not cease calling!" Her blood sizzled on the blade. Szerain trembled with focus.

"Elinor!" Grief twisted Giovanni's face, but rage drove him forward.

Szerain bore Elinor to the ground then battled through the gale to reach Giovanni.

"Call her!"

And he sliced Vsuhl across the throat of his dear friend.

I let out a cry of shock. Current-day Giovanni exclaimed what sounded like a seventeenth century Italian version of What The Fuck.

Vision-Giovanni crumpled, and blood spread across the floor. A thread shimmered between the dying man and the essence blade.

"Call her."

The scene vanished. The rakkuhr spheres slowed their frenzied pace to a more leisurely rotation.

My mouth felt like a desert, but I managed to work enough moisture back into it to speak. "You connected them."

"I wove a link," Szerain said wearily. "Giovanni was to maintain Elinor and help me keep her essence from being consumed by the blade. I knew it would take at least a week for them to tranverse the void and recorporeate on Earth, allowing me ample time to do what was needed to stabilize Elinor's essence and to avert catastrophe when I restored her from the blade."

I rubbed my gooseflesh-covered arms. "But then the ways between the worlds slammed shut, and both Elinor and Giovanni were stuck."

Giovanni clutched at his throat, eyes wide. "Y-you killed me to save her?"

Szerain offered a sad smile. "There wasn't time to ask if you were willing."

After a moment's hesitation, Giovanni gave a reluctant nod.

"And it gave you a connection to Kara as well," Szerain said. "Removing the essence and restoring it to Elinor will be much easier with your aid," Szerain said. "If you're willing, that is. I promise not to kill you this time."

Giovanni let out a strangled laugh. "Yes. Yes, of course I am willing, my friend."

Szerain smiled. It was clear he'd wanted Giovanni to know the truth for reasons that went far beyond getting his willing help. "Very well."

Drawing both rakkuhr and normal potency, Szerain wove strands like fiber optic micro-threads between Elinor, Giovanni, and me, until it felt as if every cell in my body was accounted for. The rakkuhr buzzed through me but wasn't as unpleasant as expected. Turek watched every move as if assessing for flaws.

At long last, Szerain stopped and scrutinized every millimeter of the intricate connections. "Alrighty, Kara," he said, apparently satisfied. "This will hurt a bit."

Oh, crap. "A bit" in lord-speak could range from eyebrow-plucking to mind-numbing agony.

Tensing, I braced myself for the worst. A tingling ripple began at my scalp and flowed down my body to my toes. Another followed it, warm and pleasant. Slowly, I began to relax as ripple after gentle ripple swept through me and sent light pulsing down the strands. Szerain had been messing with me about pain, the asstard. At the very edge of my senses, information streamed—an update for Elinor, much like when I'd used the flows to orient Giovanni to the modern world.

I jerked. "OW! Shit!" It felt like a whole-body bandage had been ripped off. I glared at Szerain.

He returned a mild look. "I did warn you."

I scratched the side of my nose with my middle finger.

The strands dissipated into a million floating sparks. Szerain crouched and laid his fingers against Elinor's temple, then cursed softly.

"Is she not restored?" Giovanni asked.

"Yes, but Xharbek has already primed her to be used as a weapon." He picked up the journal and opened it to the odd code inside the back cover. "Fortunately, easily un-primed, thanks to a bit of advance work. I developed a way for her to understand and control her potential, removing the ability for anyone to exploit her. In modern-speak, it's a firewall." He swiped his fingers over the code, and an intricate sigil shimmered into life above it. "And this is the installation script." Gently, he pulled the sigil onto his fingers then placed it on Elinor's forehead. The sigil sank into her skin, flashed a brilliant blue and purple over her entire body, then was gone.

Szerain touched her head lightly one more time. "Time to wake up, my dear." He eased back then straightened.

Four pairs of eyes stared at Elinor.

She breathed out a sigh.

"Elinor?" Giovanni croaked out.

Her eyes opened slowly. "Giovanni," she whispered then smiled. "You called to me."

"Always." His voice cracked. "And now you answer."

She pulled his head down to hers then gave him a sizzling kiss that had been three-hundred years in the waiting. When they finally came up for air, she climbed unsteadily to her feet then threw her arms around Szerain.

He held her close, head bowed over hers and face awash with emotion.

After a moment, he reluctantly let her go. "I am so very glad to see you," he said.

"And I, you." She wiped away tears and then, to everyone's surprise, smacked him on the arm and announced, "My good Lord Szerain, you should know, being stabbed is quite fucking painful!"

My jaw dropped, and Giovanni made a choking noise. Szerain burst out laughing. "I have no doubt it is," he said.

Smiling, she gave him another quick hug then turned and looped her arm through Giovanni's. He recovered from his shock enough to give Szerain a look of profound gratitude, then he and Elinor made their way up the trail.

I hooked my own arm through Szerain's, and together we followed the happy couple at a weary stroll while Turek brought up the rear.

"Was it just me or did Elinor drop an F-bomb?" I asked after a moment.

Szerain's smile widened. "Just as her essence influenced you, so did you influence it. Your awareness and mannerisms infused it and transferred to her upon its return."

"Oh, that poor Giovanni," I breathed, earning me a chuckle from Szerain and a low hiss of amusement from Turek. My eyes went to the shadowed forms of Giovanni and Elinor. "She doesn't know you're her father, does she."

He was quiet a moment before answering. "I didn't transfer that information. She has so much to integrate already."

More likely he wasn't ready to face it head on. I'd let it slide for now. "About the journal: I had a dream-vision where Mzatal took it away from Elinor—long before she did the ritual. She obviously got it back, but then how did it end up with Mzatal again?"

"Mzatal returned it to her before she left his realm," Szerain said then smiled. "He'd have to be a *complete* asshole to keep her diary. After I developed the firewall, I stored it in the journal. None would think that such a frivolous thing could hold anything of worth." He sobered. "When I knew I was to be exiled, I asked Mzatal to hold the journal for safekeeping. Mzatal understood the journal's importance and gave me his word to protect it and the knowledge within."

"'Cause he rocks," I said with a grin then lowered my voice. "What did Elinor mean about not wanting to get pregnant in the demon realm and risk her baby?"

"There were no issues with pregnancies in the early days, but that gradually changed. By Elinor's time, the demon realm's much higher potency had a known teratogenic effect on developing human embryos, and pregnant women would miscarry if they remained past the second month."

"Even if the father was a lord?"

"I don't know," he said quietly. "All I've discovered is that, from the very beginning, if one of our partners became pregnant, the demahnk returned her to Earth with no memory of the relationship. Our memories were then adjusted to believe she had departed for a benign reason."

"But why?" My eyes narrowed. "If it was like that from the beginning, it had nothing to do with the potency imbalance."

"I have theories, nothing more. Zakaar still can't speak freely."

Zack had risked himself too many times already in order to give me much-needed information. "Do you remember Elinor's mother?" I asked.

"Aphra. She was a summoner and, for a time, a companion and lover." A smile lit his weary face. "She loved the grove. I'm certain Elinor was conceived beneath its branches."

I let out a soft breath. "And Elinor ended up with an affinity for the grove that nearly ended the world."

"A beautiful gift despite the tragedy."

A pang of grief went through me. My loss of the Elinor essence surely meant the loss of my connection with the grove. I stopped and looked up into Szerain's face. "Why did you attach her essence to *me*?"

He took both my hands in his. "It wasn't my initial intention," he said. "Your grandmother had agreed to host it."

Gracie Pazhel. His sworn summoner and Tessa's mother. "But when Rhyzkahl killed her, he messed up your plan, and you ended up with me?"

"With you too young to give consent," he said with a note of regret. "Tessa was unavailable, and your mother lacked the summoning phenotype." His hands tightened briefly on mine. "Then you were born. The perfect vessel."

"Vessel," I said, voice acid. "Sounds awfully utilitarian." My eyes narrowed to slits. "Gracie, Tessa, me. It was all because of our bloodline. Well? Which lord had the honor?"

"Not a lord," Szerain said. "Not for the bloodline in question. It was Aphra."

"Elinor's *mom*? I'm confused."

"You're descended from Elinor's younger sister."

I eyed him warily. "Were you her—"

"No! Aphra married after she returned to Earth and had Rebecca—your ancestor—two years later."

My legs wobbled in relief. Having Szerain in my lineage would have been weeeeeeird. "That means Elinor is my great-times-a-million aunt." I slipped my arm through his again and resumed walking. "And since Elinor didn't have any kids, you needed to attach the essence to the closest relative—a descendant of Elinor's mom."

"Yes, though there's more to it. During the pregnancy, Elinor's presence subtly altered Aphra's DNA. The grove affinity and attunement to rakkuhr passed on to Aphra's descendants."

Yikes. Like carrying a radioactive magic fetus. "Wait." Hope flared. "Does that mean I still have the grove connection?" My hand flew to my leaf.

"You were born with it," he said, giving my arm a comforting squeeze even as I felt the reassuring touch of Rho.

I had a billion more questions, but we'd reached the back yard, and the fatigue I'd denied for so long permeated every fiber of my being. Szerain was no better off. His eyes were sunken caverns, and he'd begun to lean at a perilous angle. Fortunately, Pellini was waiting at the edge of the woods and steadied me while I gratefully let Turek take over the job of keeping Szerain upright.

"I'm going to plug in and recharge," Szerain announced with a drunken laugh. He lurched across Rhyzkahl's orbit to the inner circle of grass and the tree, flopped facedown with one hand on the pale bark, and went still. If not asleep, then darn close to it.

But Rhyzkahl had eyes only for Elinor. In fact, it didn't look as if he'd moved a millimeter during our time at the valve.

Elinor's steps slowed as she and Giovanni neared the nexus. I heard her murmur to him that she needed a moment, then she moved to stand before Rhyzkahl.

He gazed down at her, face impassive. "I am pleased to see you restored."

"So formal," she murmured with a teasing smile then lifted a hand to his cheek. "Thank you for helping me."

A barely perceptible shudder went through him. He covered her hand with his own. "And you are safe now, I see," he said, relief blazing through the cracks in his lordly armor. He could sense the protection of the firewall, I realized.

Rhyzkahl placed a kiss in the palm of her hand before releasing it. "May your life be long and blessed, my lady," he said quietly.

Elinor leaned up on her tiptoes to kiss his cheek, stepped back and returned to Giovanni. Rhyzkahl watched them walk to the house then stalked around his orbit to the tree.

"I need to find Elinor clothes and stuff," I said to Pellini. "Forgot to do that for Janice. And a bed. She needs a bed." Damn, a bed would be nice right now. What else did Elinor need? Socks? Yeah, socks. Socks were good. And a towel.

"That's enough, Kara."

"Huh?" I realized Pellini had been calling my name. I blinked since there were two of him, and they were fuzzy.

"That's enough world saving for now," he said with a gentle smile. "You need sleep."

"Sleep," I agreed, though it came out more like *shleeurp*. I took a step and wobbled, and the next thing I knew Pellini had me swept up in his arms and was carrying me toward the porch.

I wanted to respond with something clever, but when I blinked again my eyes stayed closed.

Chapter 41

"Kara." Pellini's baritone hammered through deep and dreamless sleep. "Kara, I know you're exhausted, but you need to wake up." A firm hand seized my shoulder and shook me.

"'mwake," I mumbled. I was in my bed, though I had zero memory of getting there.

"Uh huh. Sure. Idris just showed up. He brought a big-ass crate and is currently putting it in the middle of the gun range so it won't mess up any of our wards."

"Yass. Got th' makkas turtle." I managed a wobbly thumbs up. "Gun range pew pew."

"Uh huh. Well, Idris also said that as soon as he took care of the crate he was going to go say Hi to his dad."

That woke me up as effectively as a bucket of ice water. "Crap!" I lunged out of bed and grabbed a crumpled pair of fatigue pants off the floor, pulled them on in an awkward one-legged hop as I headed for the hallway. Pellini thrust a sweatshirt at me, and I stuffed it under one arm while I dashed for the back door and did up the last of the buttons. I'd known an Idris-Rhyzkahl confrontation was inevitable, but I was determined to keep it from escalating into a bloodbath.

Chilly air slapped my cheeks as I crossed the porch, and I hurried to yank the sweatshirt over my head. Szerain was nowhere to be seen. I had to assume he'd recharged sufficiently. He was the least of my worries at the moment. A decent-sized tent had been set up in Rhyzkahl's orbit a dozen or so feet from the tree. Since Rhyzkahl was out of sight, I suspected he was inside it.

Idris rounded the corner of the house and stalked toward the nexus, aggressive stance shattering any possible hope that he was here for a friendly chat. Cursing under my breath, I started toward him, reminding myself that Idris knew Rhyzkahl's prison protected the lord from outside attack. I couldn't imagine Idris being stupid enough to strike out at him.

The dew-covered grass blazed like a million diamonds in the early morning sun, yet the prismatic spectacle couldn't hide the destruction wrought by the night's events. A battle-scarred reyza atop the security office outbuilding bellowed a challenge, sending a flock of sparrows into panicked flight from the nearby woods.

Idris's face was a stone mask, but he took note of the charred grass, the rift belching magenta flames, and the unfamiliar demons. I knew damn well he was aware of my presence, but he didn't so much as glance my way.

As he approached the edge of Rhyzkahl's prison, he slowed. For a brief moment I wondered if Rhyzkahl would simply stay in his tent and refuse to entertain Idris's desire for a confrontation. The whisper of uncertainty that crossed Idris's face told me he wondered the same thing. Though a huge part of me hoped for a nice absence of drama, I knew Idris would only be moodier as a result.

Idris stopped half a dozen feet from the perimeter. As if on cue, the flap on the tent flipped open. I came to a halt, watching and waiting.

Rhyzkahl stepped out and straightened with feline grace. Making an entrance. He gifted Idris with the barest of nods then swept his gaze over the back yard as if surveying his sovereign domain. The message was crystal clear: Idris's presence had been duly noted, and it was Rhyzkahl's decision whether to grant him an audience. It was an infuriatingly lordly tactic, yet I had to silently applaud Rhyzkahl for leveling the playing field.

Idris twitched with tension, eyes glaring hatred. But Rhyzkahl wasn't toying with him or making him wait just for giggles. He was making a point, subtle though it was, and once he finished his calculated perusal of his surroundings, he made his way around the circle to stand before Idris.

Seeing them together like this, no one could ever doubt a strong familial connection. This was the first time the two had looked upon each other with the knowledge that they were father and son, and I watched as each took in the similarities, the echoes of features seen in the mirror.

"Let's get one thing straight right now," Idris said through bared teeth. "You *aren't* my father. Jerome Palatino, the man who raised me, has that honor."

Rhyzkahl inclined his head. "Truly he deserves it. He reared a fine young man. It pleases me to know that my blood courses through your veins."

Translation: Yeah, he raised you, but you still came from me, kiddo.

A flush swept up Idris's neck. "Your *blood*? You and the Mraztur have spilled *my* family's blood. My sister was tortured and murdered! I was forced to *watch*. Because of you. Fuck your blood!"

"I knew nothing of the plan to sacrifice your sister," Rhyzkahl said, unruffled. "I assure you, I would never have condoned or allowed it."

Idris shifted closer, like a tiger positioning to pounce. "Why?" he asked. A strange smile tightened his mouth. "Tell me *why* you wouldn't have condoned my sister's murder."

Rhyzkahl gave a slow nod, as if in acceptance. "I could tell you that I would not have condoned or allowed her death because it was needless torment. A waste of a beautiful life. A tragedy visited upon all who hold her dear." He met Idris's eyes. "But you already know that to be false. You asked this question, despite knowing my true answer, because you wish to hear it from my lips. You hunger for me to speak it aloud and thus stoke your hatred and fuel your rage in the hopes that they will burn fiercely enough to illuminate the void that is your grief."

Idris recoiled, face paling.

"Here is my true answer, then," Rhyzkahl continued with barely a pause. "My gift to you, to do with what you will. I did not condone your sister's murder—nor her torment, nor your own as you bore witness to it—because it was *messy*." He hissed the word, eyes flashing with anger he no longer deigned to hide. "It was gratuitous, and it was foolish. It accomplished nothing that could not be gained by far less tangled means, and it courted exposure of carefully laid plans before all was in place."

Face dark with rage, Idris stepped into Rhyzkahl's orbit, trampling irises. He cocked a fist, ready to strike. "If it hadn't been messy, if it *had* served your purposes, you would have tortured her yourself, just like you did Kara."

Rhyzkahl's gaze bore into Idris. "Given dire circumstances, yes."

Idris let out a feral cry and launched his punch at Rhyzkahl's face. In a move like a striking snake, Rhyzkahl caught and held Idris's fist. Potency crackled around them in white-hot lightning bursts as they faced each other, eye to eye, tense and immobile.

Shit! This was exactly what I'd feared would happen. Rhyzkahl couldn't attack Idris, but what if the "rules" of his prison said all bets were off if he was defending himself?

Muttering curses, I drew on the nexus and formed ropes of potency with the plan to drag the two apart. Yet when I tried to lasso them, the potency ropes stopped several feet short, as if a force field stood in the way. No matter how much power I drew, the result was the same.

But was it Mzatal's doing? Or Rhyzkahl's?

After an eternity, Rhyzkahl exhaled a soft breath that wasn't quite a sigh. "Idris Palatino, I regret that who and what I am has forever garnered the enmity of a gifted summoner. Of my son." The lightning died around them even as he released Idris's fist.

Idris stared at Rhyzkahl, stricken and wide-eyed. After several agonizing seconds, he wrenched his gaze free and staggered to the grass beyond the prison. He made it three steps before dropping to his knees with a barely audible sound of despair.

Shock held me motionless—which was fine since I currently had zero desire to draw anyone's attention during what was obviously an incredibly private moment. I'd rushed out here braced for an ugly conflict and nasty fallout, and instead had witnessed . . . Well, I wasn't sure what I'd witnessed.

Rhyzkahl silently regarded the kneeling Idris. If the tremors that shook his son's shoulders moved him in any way, he didn't show it.

This is the fallout, I realized with a pang. Forcing myself into motion, I stumbled toward Idris, yet before I'd made it halfway he took a deep breath and pulled himself to his feet. Relieved, I slowed to an amble to give him time to finish gathering himself.

The hard expression he'd worn these last months had eased, and he seemed lighter now. He'd given his pressure cooker of suppressed anger an outlet and, I hoped, come out the better for it. An air of vulnerability clung to him, but it was as if he'd accepted that everyone was vulnerable, and realized it had nothing to do with being weak.

His careful scrutiny of the ground told me he was still processing it all. I doubted he'd be ready to talk about it any time soon.

"Hey, cousin," I said lightly. "You missed all the fun last night. You planning on joining us for breakfast?"

He met my eyes almost reluctantly, but then he let out a tiny, breathless laugh. "Does Pellini still make those bacon maple roll things?"

I smiled. "Sure does, though since real maple syrup is pretty hard to come by nowadays, he uses heaps of brown sugar instead."

"I guess I'll choke them down somehow," he said with a tragic sigh. I pretended not to notice the exhaustion that bled through his words, but at least he wasn't vibrating with tension anymore. The ever-present anger had retreated as well. It was far from gone, but he no longer appeared driven—and consumed— by it. Rhyzkahl had faced Idris's anger then calmly reached in and ripped out its roots.

Tears sprang to my eyes, and I threw my arms around Idris. "I'm so glad you're back."

He held me close. "Glad to be back," he replied, voice rough. A faint shudder rippled through him then was gone.

Only a few minutes had passed since I'd dashed out here. Everything felt different now, but I had no idea why or how much. Or what to do about it.

Together, Idris and I headed to the house. When we reached the steps, I snuck a glance back at Rhyzkahl in time to see him pass a hand over his face. I quickly looked away, but the image was seared into my mind. Was he simply tired? Weeping? Brushing away a mosquito?

Pellini was slouched in a chair on the porch, kicked back with a book in his hand. He gave every appearance of being there simply to enjoy the morning, but I had no doubt he'd deliberately remained outside for the entire debacle, watching my back and ready to intervene as needed. "There's coffee if y'all want it," he said, as if Idris and I were simply returning from a pleasant stroll.

"You know I do," I said. "Thanks for taking care of me last night."

"Any time. You were a bit faded." He stood and dropped the book onto the side table then followed us inside.

Szerain was in the kitchen, leaning against the counter with a mug of coffee in one hand. I was *mostly* sure he hadn't been there during my frenzied dash to the back yard, but with my focus locked on the impending Idris-Rhyzkahl smackdown, pink bald eagles could've been roosting in the sink and I wouldn't have noticed.

Szerain looked a thousand times better than last night, though a faint sense of "meat-grinder survivor" still lingered about him. He lifted his mug to me in greeting then pushed off the counter and extended his hand to Idris. "It's good to finally meet the greatest living summoner on Earth or the demon realm."

Idris looked discomfited by the praise but took the proffered hand. "I suppose I should thank my . . . sire for that," he said with a flat, not-quite smile.

"Hardly." Szerain gave a derisive snort. "It's not as if he did a damn thing except ejaculate at the right moment. Everything else has been your own efforts."

Idris stared at the very un-lordlike lord. "Ejaculate at the . . ." A sound that was almost a laugh slipped from him. "That certainly puts things in a different perspective. Thank you, my lord."

Szerain gave a mock shudder. "Let's not do the 'my lord' crap." He plopped into a chair at the end of the table. "Besides, we're all on the same team. Hell, I was one of the original members of Kara's Posse." He grinned.

"You and Zack were the first," I confirmed as I hunted for a clean mug.

Pellini set a bowl of dough and a baking sheet on the table. "Special Agent Ryan Fucking Kristoff," he drawled. "Jesus, you were an arrogant shit."

"And you were an obnoxious asshole," Szerain shot back with humor in his voice.

"Still am," Pellini said proudly. "Only way to stay sane around Kara."

"Truer words were never spoken!"

I rolled my eyes as the two fist-bumped in solidarity. "Oh, give me a break. I'm the one who has to deal with you two pricks."

Szerain clucked his tongue. "And verbal abuse, too."

"Wimps," I said, though I couldn't help but smile. The verbal sparring felt *homey*, like good-natured family squabbling.

Pellini dragooned Idris into helping make the faux-maple biscuit things. After locating a clean mug in the dishwasher, I poured myself a cup of coffee then set about doctoring it properly.

Now that the crisis was past, I was increasingly aware of a

not-quite-rightness, as if I was forgetting something. Or that the room had changed subtly. The world felt slightly off, but I couldn't put my finger on precisely what it was.

Thud

I turned with a frown. "What was that?"

Thud thud thud thud

The others shared similar wary expressions as the noise continued in ominous rhythm. "It's coming from down the hallway," Idris said, eyes narrowed.

"The pods?" Pellini said, rising to his feet. "Could it be Corey and Knight hatching?"

"Maybe." But hatching as what? My memory of the tentacle-handed monster at Fed Central was all too clear. I reached for a steak knife but paused at the sound of a feminine cry.

Thud thud thud thud thud thudthudthudthud

Szerain began to snicker.

Comprehension finally dawned. "Is that . . . ?"

Szerain nodded. "Elinor and Giovanni making up for three hundred years of lost time."

thudthudthudTHUD THUD THUD

As one, we exploded into laughter.

Soon enough the thudding ceased, and I wiped away tears of mirth. "Wow. I'd better call in a structural engineer to make sure the house is still stable."

"Yeah, that wall took a real pounding," Szerain said, straight-faced.

"Let's hope they didn't break a stud," Idris added with a smile.

Pellini guffawed and high-fived him while relief coursed through me. I couldn't remember the last time Idris had cracked a joke. Certainly not since the death of his sister.

With the mystery of the thud-thuds solved, biscuit making resumed, and the conversation shifted to swapping DIRT-related tall tales. Idris recounted a hysterical story of villagers successfully fighting off a *kzak* with flaming cow manure and slingshots, and Pellini countered with the one where a pair of reyza hurled a porta-potty like a water balloon and all of us ended up stained blue and stinking. Unfortunately, that one was a hundred percent true.

The conversation flowed around me as I watched a spider build her web outside the window. Despite the laughter and jokes, the strange not-right feeling persisted. I sipped my coffee and maintained a serene exterior while I struggled to identify the source of the disquiet.

"You okay?" Szerain asked softly from beside me. At the table, Pellini and Idris launched into a spirited argument about firearms.

"Feeling a little off-balance," I said, unsurprised that Szerain had noticed my distraction. No mind-reading needed. Just perception sharpened over millennia, coupled with the intuition of a good friend. I shrugged. "It's probably because I'm not worrying about dying in a summoning ritual."

"I'm sure that's part of it," he said. "Another might be that you're adjusting to having only your own essence."

"Oh. Right. Duh." I smiled ruefully. "That explains it."

"You'll be you in no time." Szerain gave my shoulder a comforting squeeze then turned away to refill his coffee cup, giving me space to process it all.

My gaze drifted outside again in time to see a fly blunder into the web. That had to suck. Minding your own business then *bam*. Game changer.

Kind of like *bam,* the Elinor essence nugget I'd lived with for pretty much my entire life was gone. I contemplated the strangeness of the concept. What kind of person would I be now if her influence hadn't been there?

Probably not all that different, I decided. Elinor seemed mild, sweet, and more than a little timid. I was not.

The loss of Elinor's essence chunk certainly explained the something-isn't-right sensation. Most of it, at least. A bit remained, a quiet nagging. I let my gaze drift to Rhyzkahl as he sketched graceful sigils for the shikvihr. I'd watched him dance it a hundred times, easily. It was the same sigils, the same rings, the same movements as when Mzatal danced it, yet infused with a completely different feel and energy.

"I spoke with Rhyzkahl while you slept," Szerain said as he stirred a shake of cinnamon into black coffee. "He'll need some time to adjust."

"Huh? Adjust to—" My confusion vanished as Szerain's meaning sunk in. I lowered my voice. "Rhyzkahl knows the truth about his parentage?"

"He needed to know. We *all*—all of the hybrids—need to know of our origins from human mothers and demahnk fathers." His eyes flashed with the intensity of his conviction. "But not all are ready."

"What made Rhyzkahl ready?" I asked. "Was it Zakaar breaking their ptarl bond?"

"That was the most critical factor," Szerain said with a nod, "but this timeout here on Earth primed him for even more." His expression grew somber. "I helped him remember his early life on Earth. His mother. His wife and twins. Our later . . . enslavement."

I blew out a breath. "How'd he take it?"

"Like Rhyzkahl." Szerain shrugged. "Poker-faced but deeply affected."

Yep, that was Rhyzkahl. "What about the headaches, or the demahnk screwing with his mind?"

"I taught him a few mental tricks and some rudimentary shielding," he said. "It's a start." He seemed poised to say more, but instead joined the gun discussion at the table.

Would I see Rhyzkahl dance another hundred shikvihrs before Mzatal returned to free him? I was sick to death of being Rhyzkahl's jailer, but what if Mzatal was too diminished by Ilana to finish what he'd started here? Then again, it might not be long before Rhyzkahl escaped on his own. He certainly wasn't a helpless invalid any longer.

The rift belched a gout of shimmering potency. *Rhyzkahl could have escaped last night.* He could have escaped and still saved Elinor. He didn't because—why? Honor? That seemed a stretch. Or maybe escaping would have, in some twisted way, been a victory for me, implying that the only way for him to get free would be to escape my tyranny. Perhaps he was simply biding his time, waiting for the perfect moment to throw off his shackles and bring low the hated slavemaster, thus proving that he'd been the victor all along.

Then again, it was possible that none of this had a fucking thing to do with "winning" anything.

For the first time since the night I found Rhyzkahl shaken and stumbling around the nexus, it felt wrong to cage him. Not that he didn't deserve punishment for his actions, but justice required a consideration of time served, and retribution needed to take a back seat to pragmatism. Rhyzkahl was restored, and all the lords were needed.

Understanding dawned on me with the intensity of a supernova. Mzatal's multi-faceted purpose for creating the prison on my nexus was suddenly crystal clear.

Mzatal had unmatched focus and foresight, able to see thousands of moves ahead and predict far-reaching ripples. He hadn't chained Rhyzkahl to my nexus for revenge. He'd forcibly removed him from the demon realm because Rhyzkahl was broken, his mere presence causing instability in an already unstable world.

Yet Mzatal didn't go on to kill him or lock him in a dimensional pocket dungeon or even chain him in agony to the nexus. He brought Rhyzkahl to a place where he could recover, far removed from any number of damaging influences. Moreover, Rhyzkahl's presence as a battery for the nexus compensated for the loss of my arcane abilities and gave me the means to rehabilitate.

But that wasn't the end of Mzatal's brilliance. Rhyzkahl's imprisonment had served to rehab my inner *Self* as well, helping to heal the worst of the unseen wounds from his torture ritual and more. The prison forced me to face Rhyzkahl every single day, seeing him at his best and his worst—and thus made it harder for my psyche to see him as a nothing but a monster. Yes, he was a creature capable of horrible acts, but every time I wished him harm, every time I gloated over having my tormentor as my prisoner, I did nothing but bind myself tighter to our ugly past.

With the root cause identified, my disquiet settled. Wry amusement whispered through me. All those times that Rhyzkahl demanded release and I'd responded that it wasn't up to me. Mzatal had known this moment would come, once Rhyzkahl and I were sufficiently healed.

I poured out the rest of my coffee, grabbed the walkie-talkie from its charger on the counter, then headed toward the back door. In my periphery I saw Pellini start to rise as if to follow, but Szerain stopped him with a light touch on his arm and a murmured, "Let her go."

The back yard grass no longer sparkled, and the mist at the edge of the woods had burned away. As I walked toward the nexus, Rhyzkahl finished the eleventh ring and ignited the entire series. It was still dimmer than a full-strength construct but not by much.

He regarded the finished shikvihr for barely a heartbeat then flicked his fingers to dispel it and began anew.

I crossed his orbit and stepped onto the nexus then, as I'd done so often before, let the by-now-familiar power course through me.

For the last time.

The thought reverberated through me, bringing sudden doubt in its wake. If Rhyzkahl left, so would the lord-power. Sure, I had most of my abilities back, but it was the semi-demigodness that I relied upon to do, well, pretty much anything that mattered. Without it, I never could have summoned Dekkak, or rescued Szerain, or even given Giovanni the ability to understand the twenty-first century. And the need for that lordy power wouldn't end when it left. Maybe it was irresponsible of me to give this up while the war still raged.

"Bullshit," I spat and glared down at the silver and black slab. There would always be an oh-so-reasonable excuse to justify exploitation. History was pockmarked with similar rationalizations. Hell, the demahnk likely had reasons out the wazoo for their enslavement of the lords. Fuck that. Keeping Rhyzkahl here, when I knew in my essence that he could—and should—be freed, would be slavery, full stop. We would survive without resorting to anathema.

I tapped into the nexus and looked deep into the workings of the prison, like Szerain had done the day before. Intricate patterns within patterns, fractals of potency, interlaced in harmonious unity. Unlike Szerain, there was no way I'd ever come close to understanding the entirety of how it worked, but I didn't need to. I only needed to find the off switch.

And there it was, a quiet glow amidst the exquisite creation code, calling no attention to itself but findable by me when it was time.

And it was, indeed, time. The rightness of my decision sang through me. I reached to that softly glowing speck of a sigil and, using the Rhyzkahl-power for the very last time, dispelled it.

There was no fanfare or fireworks. The power simply flowed away from me like water sheeting off my body after a shower, no more unpleasant than the hundreds of times I'd left the nexus and ceased being a semi-demigod.

Rhyzkahl froze in place, for an instant reminding me of a rabbit going still as a hawk's shadow passed over it. *Or like someone who wants to be sure there are no landmines in a suddenly changed environment.*

After nearly half a minute, Rhyzkahl dissipated the partial shikvihr and faced me. If he felt surprise—or anything else—he didn't let it show.

Eyes on him, I lifted the walkie-talkie. "This is Kara. I've freed Rhyzkahl. All personnel are ordered to allow him to depart the compound. Absolutely no one is to interfere with him while he leaves."

Rhyzkahl traced the first sigil of the shikvihr. It hung in the air before him, brilliant and potent, no longer drained by the nature of the prison.

I smothered the reflex to flip the prison's switch back on. The ethical dilemma of keeping him prisoner hadn't changed. Moreover, Rhyzkahl was now armed with the truth from Szerain. That had to have changed him for the better. I hoped. "I know you're dying to stay and tend your garden, but I'm kicking you out." I shrugged. "Sorry-not-sorry."

One side of his mouth lifted in a smile. "Endlessly entertaining."

I inclined my head. "I do my best."

"Kara Gillian, you have yet to discover your best."

While I digested his surprising statement, Rhyzkahl retrieved a cell phone from a dimensional pocket and placed a call, as naturally as if it was an everyday occurrence. "I need transport, forthwith," he said then sent the phone away. He regarded me for a moment more then turned on his heel, stepped out of his orbit, and strode toward the driveway and freedom.

Chapter 42

Szerain was sitting on the porch steps, waiting for me. When I reached him, he stood and gave me a big, warm hug.

"You knew what I was going to do," I said, gratefully accepting the embrace. "But you weren't touching me, so you couldn't have heard my thoughts."

His laugh vibrated against my chest. "Didn't have to. I know you pretty well."

The sound of raised voices reached us from inside the house. No, only one raised voice and Pellini's calm rumble.

"Idris," I said with a wince. "I should go talk to him." I'd known in the back of my head that there'd be people who wouldn't agree with my decision, and now I had to face it.

Szerain nodded and released me. "For what it's worth, Pellini understands why you let Rhyzkahl go. And even if he didn't, he trusts your judgment." He angled his head. "He's a good partner for you. Isn't afraid to call you on your shit."

I laughed. "You're right about that."

Buoyed by that knowledge, I entered the kitchen to see Idris with hair askew and face flushed. Blood smeared the knuckles of his right hand, and I suspected he'd punched a wall, realizing too late that it wasn't sheetrock.

He rounded on me. "This is bullshit, Kara!"

"I'll talk to you once you've calmed down enough to listen." I moved to the security monitor and watched Rhyzkahl's trek down my driveway toward the front gate.

Idris made an incoherent noise then stormed down the hallway.

"If you try to go after him, I'll have you tasered and re-strained," I snapped out in my I'm-not-fucking-around voice.

He stopped, fists clenched, and stood motionless for several seconds before wheeling to return to the kitchen.

On the monitor, the guard opened the gate. Rhyzkahl walked through and to the edge of the highway. As his foot touched the asphalt, a syraza appeared beside him, touched his shoulder, and then both disappeared.

Well, that's done.

Though I hadn't been aware of Pellini leaving, Idris and I were alone in the kitchen.

"Kara, why the hell would you let him go?" A current of hurt ran beneath the angry words.

"It was time," I said and resisted the urge to sigh. "Not to mention, every lord is needed to stabilize the demon realm."

"They can manage without *him*," he said. "How could you forget what he did to you?"

"I'll never forget it," I replied, folding my arms over my chest. "But I don't have to let it keep eating at me. I chose to forgive him."

Idris narrowed his eyes. "Wait. He apologized?"

"No."

"So you just rolled over and gave up?" He stared at me as if I'd sprouted an eyeball on a stalk. "I don't get it. How could you let him off the hook?"

His words should have pissed me off, but instead they helped bring order to my tumbled thoughts. The last whispers of doubt melted away. "That's not how it works, Idris," I said gently. "Forgiveness doesn't mean the other person has to redeem themselves or apologize first. Or ever." I dropped my arms, nodding to myself as the core concept resolved. "Forgiveness doesn't absolve the other person of their sins, but that's *their* burden. It's about giving up your own resentment, letting go and moving on. Forgiveness is for yourself."

Idris took a step back. "No. Rhyzkahl has done terrible things."

"And may again," I said, "but so have *we*. Maybe not to the same extreme, but our hands aren't clean. Sure, it's nice to think we're the white knights who can do no wrong, crusading for the powers of Light and all that shit. But we've crossed the line more than once. We committed treason by stealing a Skeeter-Cheater that might have made a difference elsewhere. A lot of innocent people got hurt in the bid to rescue Elinor. Hell, we *executed* J.M. Farouche after the battle at his plantation. Sure, we had damn good reasons in those cases—and I still believe that taking Farouche out was the right move—but there's no way to spin it to where those weren't bad things that we did. Thinking your side's shit doesn't stink is a dangerous mind-set."

Idris gave a subdued nod, anger gone. "We're the good guys, aren't we?"

"I believe that with all my heart," I said. "But at the same time, I doubt the Mraztur think of themselves as the bad guys. Remember, a whole lot of wars have started because both sides were absolutely certain they were in the right."

He made a face. "I can't imagine *anything* they do is right."

"Then you'd better start trying," I said, tone sharp. "If you can only paint your enemies as monsters, then you've lost all hope of a peaceful resolution." With a well-placed finger on his sternum, I pushed him back until he folded into a chair. "Szerain believes you're the greatest summoner alive, and I agree with him. But it's time for you to start looking at the bigger picture." I gentled my voice. "Mzatal never intended to keep Rhyzkahl bound to the nexus forever. You know that. It was time."

He looked thoughtful now, which told me I'd gotten through to him, at least a little.

"You should go sit under the grove tree," I said. "It's a really good thinking spot."

He gave me a dubious look but pushed up and headed outside. Through the window, I watched as he crossed the yard then flopped to sit under the brilliant canopy.

Good. Rho would help him get straightened out.

I allowed myself a few precious seconds to savor the all too rare peace and quiet, then followed up with a luxuriously hot shower and bath soak that lasted a decadent twenty minutes. Dressed, clean, and ever so slightly more relaxed, I returned to the kitchen where I found biscuits and bacon ready, with Pellini partaking of both. While I stuffed my face and downed more coffee, Pellini informed me that he and Szerain had checked out the stone turtle.

"It's not as big as I expected," he said between bites of bacon. "Only about two feet long. But Szerain found a spot on its belly that was different and opened 'er up." He paused and took an overly long sip of coffee.

"Tell me what you found. *Now*, or you'll be sleeping in Rhyzkahl's tent."

Pellini grinned and wiped his mouth. "Nine rolls of makkas wire. About seventeen gauge or so and at least fifty meters each."

"Sweet!" I said, relieved. "That's a lot better than the raw lump I was envisioning."

"My guess is that whoever stuck it in the turtle meant for it to be easy to use in a pinch." Pellini took a bite of biscuit then washed it down with a slug of coffee. "Szerain's downstairs now. Said he wants to talk to you once you've shit, showered, and shaved."

I lifted an eyebrow. "Is that how he phrased it?"

"Pretty much," he said with a laugh.

Since I'd already accomplished all three, I made my way to the basement.

Ryan Kristoff had lived down here for several months, ensconced in his own little man-cave with the usual manly comforts: TV and DVD player, futon, small refrigerator, gaming console. Then Idris had moved in, and it was just a spare bedroom in a slightly unusual location.

Szerain had pulled my big armchair over by the futon—currently in couch-form. Spread out before him was a ten-foot diameter circle of floor filled with complex sigils that crawled with rakkuhr and defied identification, at least by me. Everything else was exactly as Idris had left it. But though I couldn't in a million years define why or how, Szerain had turned it back into a man-cave.

"Did you get Idris all sorted out?" he asked when I reached the bottom of the stairs.

"For now," I said. "He's a good guy. Can't say I blame him for reacting the way he did, considering everything he's been through."

"And he's young." A corner of his mouth quirked up. "It's easy to forget that when he's so skilled and has such focus."

My lips twitched. "Greatest summoner alive, right?"

"For now," he said with a sly grin.

I could tell I was expected to assume that I'd someday surpass Idris, but I wasn't going to fish for compliments. "What's all this?" I waggled my fingers at the circle o' sigils.

"Monitoring," he said. "The dimensional stronghold as well as general arcane activity for when Xharbek decides to step up his game."

"When? Not if?"

"He expected Dekkak to kill you and then bring him Elinor's essence. Not only did that plan fall through, but we succeeded in retrieving and restoring Elinor." Szerain's mouth tightened into a humorless line. "He's not a happy demahnk right now."

"If Xharbek is the least restricted of all the demahnk, does that make him the fearless leader of the rest of them?"

"It's a good working theory."

I made a face and flung myself onto the futon. I preferred a system where the demahnk all had an equal say, rather than him being in charge. "Any ideas what he'll do?"

"Plenty." He shook his head. "And that's the problem. There are a myriad of steps he could take next, and there's no possible way to defend against them all."

"Which means you have to wait for him to act. Ugh."

"It sucks." He slouched back in the big armchair, revealing a flash of brilliant green and purple at his collar.

"Dude!" I sat up straight. "You got a leaf, too?"

Reverently, Szerain pulled the leaf from beneath his shirt. Like mine, the stem of his leaf formed a loop, but his hung on a delicate silver chain.

"I spent hours out there communing with Rho," he said. "Far better rest than sleep." He glanced at me. "Xharbek isn't my sire."

"Uh huh. You mentioned that. Is it Helori?"

"No, he's Kadir's. Rho is mine."

"Wait. Rho as in grove Rho?" My confusion only increased at his solemn nod. "But I thought . . . how could it . . . ? Whoa. Is Rho *demahnk*?"

"He is."

I stared at him. His daddy was a *forest*? "Why is Rho the grove, but Helori and the others default to the elder syraza demon look?"

"More forbidden knowledge," Szerain said with a bitter edge to his words. "Initially, Rho was the same as the rest of the demahnk, and we were ptarl bound. But from what I'm able to understand, when a harmonic disturbance collapsed the Earthgates, he merged with the planet and helped hold it together. It was a permanent change, it seems, since it involved uniting with the rakkuhr core. Xharbek became my ptarl—my guess is that he didn't have a lord-child—and I was conditioned to forget it had ever been any other way."

"That *sucks*," I said, angry and horrified on his behalf. Bad enough that he got ripped away from his Earth family, but then to lose his real ptarl-daddy, too? "If Rho was able to become a planetary-wide grove system, that means the demahnk could be *anything*. Are they Ekiri, too?"

"I've speculated as much, but don't have confirmation."

I frowned. "Though if so, why wouldn't they still call themselves Ekiri? Maybe they're Ekiri kids, like the lords are demahnk kids. Of course then y'gotta wonder who the Ekiri would have mated with to make the demahnk."

"I don't know," Szerain said with a shrug. "The ones who called themselves Ekiri were different in form than the demahnk, for whatever that's worth."

Interesting. One of Lannist's visions had shown me a willowy, dual-pupiled creature atop an Ekiri pavilion.

"But I *am* ninety-nine percent sure the Ekiri are the ones who bind the demahnk," he added.

Ha! I was right. The enforcers were the Ekiri. "With the same constraints that destroyed Lannist," I said sourly.

Szerain straightened. "Even as dissociated as Zakaar is from the demahnk, he felt Lannist scatter. What do you know of it?"

I gave him the CliffsNotes version of the events in Lannist's dimensional pocket, including the warnings he'd offered about Trask and Ilana. Yet when I went into seeing the lords as children, Szerain started to get agitated. Though he was free of most of the demahnk manipulation, I had a feeling some lingered. "Speaking of parentage," I said, deftly sliding into a parallel topic, "you've yet to answer my question about my lordy lineage."

His agitation evaporated. "Huh. You're right." He gave me a bland look.

I glared.

"Fine, I'll tell you," he said, eyes sparkling. "But don't blame the messenger. Your grandmother's father was Jesral."

"Ew." I made a face. "Oh well. At least it wasn't you, Rhyzkahl, or Mzatal. Though it's really going to ruin Christmas when everyone finds out that Great Grandpappy tried to turn me into Rowan." I angled my head. "Since we're on the subject, who *is* Rowan? I mean, I was her for a few minutes, but I still don't get it."

"Not who. What." He leaned forward to make an adjustment to a sigil. "During the years after the cataclysm when the ways were closed, I not only made repairs, but I also worked on creating a 'potency robot' to—"

I slapped my hands over my ears. "Dude, if you're about to tell me that you made an arcane sex doll, I'll take back my question."

"You're a filthy minded perv," Szerain said, rolling his eyes heavenward. "I created it to mimic the potential I'd seen in Elinor—though the construct couldn't match it. And while I could infuse a semblance of life, she was basically an arcane AI, with a body made up of minute, intricately entwined sigils tucked away in a dimensional pocket. She could be called up for interaction, but without a real person as an underlay, she couldn't *act*." He sighed and kneaded the back of his neck. "Rowan was an experiment, a creation I could learn from. She was never intended to be used."

"But then you were exiled, and the Mraztur stole your never-to-be-used weapon."

"Rude bastards," he muttered.

"And they tried to make me the underlay, because I had Elinor's essence and the right genetics," I said.

Szerain tweaked the loop of a second sigil then sank back into the chair. "Rhyzkahl had no idea you carried it until that night he hijacked your portal to escape Peter Cerise's summoning."

"The night that changed *everything*," I breathed. I'd been trying to summon a luhrek named Rysehl to aid in my investigation of a murder thought to be the Symbol Man's work. But instead of a goat/dog/lion-looking creature, I got a breathtakingly beautiful but seriously pissed off demonic lord. "When he shredded my bindings like tissue paper, I thought I was a goner." I snorted. "Then he looked deep into my eyes, and it suddenly turned into a seduction. Now I finally know why."

Szerain fell silent for a moment. "I apologize for placing it on you without your consent," he said, voice remote. "As I said before, it was supposed to be your grandmother. Gracie was ready and willing, and I had the firewall to give her control. However, Xharbek opposed the plan, and when I proved to be unmalleable, he found an alternate way to stop it."

My breath caught. "Rhyzkahl."

He nodded. "There was already deep friction between us. Rhyzkahl blamed me for Elinor's death and felt I had no right to use her essence—without including him, that is." A weary smile pulled up. "He felt I was getting too big for my britches with my sworn summoners, and despised my arrogance in planning to make a pseudo-Elinor via Gracie."

"And all Xharbek had to do was dangle the bait for him," I said.

"He swallowed it whole." Szerain shook his head. "I *was* arrogant, which is why I didn't see it coming. My focus was on Peter Cerise's summoning, and I got blindsided. Rhyzkahl tried to get Vsuhl from me, but I managed—barely—to fend him off, keeping the blade and the essence it contained."

"Which must have pissed him right the fuck off." My leg jiggled with poorly suppressed excitement as the sequence of events became clear. "Except he saw a way to hurt you where it counted and took control of the summoning portal. Suddenly he's in a room full of your summoners. Your precious sworn summoners. Time to die."

"Precisely. Moreover, he sensed another of Elinor's blood-line in the room."

My eyes narrowed. "Tessa, who he left unharmed."

"Rhyzkahl devised a plan to acquire Vsuhl, along with Eli-nor's essence, then groom Tessa as a host who would be dedi-cated to him."

"Essentially taking your game away so he could play it him-self," I said. "Xharbek must have liked that."

Szerain grimaced. "Very much so. He'd have Elinor's poten-tial in a configuration he could completely control even though it would be years yet before Tessa came fully into her abilities."

The rest crystallized. "Then I was born—with the bloodline *and* the genetic ability to be a summoner."

Regret and guilt darkened his eyes. "I had to act quickly. When you were only a few hours old, with the help of Helori, I released the essence from the blade and attached it to you. You were too young for me to install the firewall, though. That couldn't happen until you came into your own as a summoner, and the mental pathways were formed."

My throat felt tight. "But by then, you were exiled."

"Things started falling apart long before that." He flung him-self out of the chair and began to pace. "Not long after the bloody summoning, Katashi died, and Xharbek didn't hesitate to replace him with a syraza doppelganger, to better control the new age of summoners. He then made absolutely sure that Tessa found her way to syraza-Katashi for training and, in due time, to the demon realm to be properly groomed as the Elinor-host by Rhyzkahl—after placing a temporary block in her memory so she wouldn't realize he was the one who killed her mother." His steps slowed. "But eventually Xharbek figured out that you held the essence. It delayed his plans by fifteen years or so, but he's nothing if not adaptable. He shifted his attention to making absolutely sure you received training as a summoner so that he could eventually use you."

My pulse grew unsteady. "That's why my father was killed. Xharbek had fake-Katashi pave the way for me to end up in Tessa's care so that I could be trained as a summoner. Had to get those mental pathways formed, right?"

For an instant Szerain looked as if he felt every one of his three thousand years. "I'm so sorry."

"Except, Xharbek didn't need a *good* summoner." My words sounded thin to my ears. "Didn't *want* a good summoner, 'cause that would be harder to control. That's why I got only the most basic of training."

"I intended to train you properly and to overlay the code from Elinor's journal as your firewall. You were thirteen when I started making surreptitious plans to bring you to the demon realm." His hands tightened into fists. "Xharbek disagreed and attempted to *tweak* my thinking."

The air seemed to thicken as his aura grew heavy. Out of instinct, I shrank back into the futon.

"I'd learned much during my time in the interdimensions making post-cataclysm repairs," Szerain continued, "including how to covertly shield my mind with rakkuhr. I wouldn't tolerate interference in my plans for you, and I pushed Xharbek out of my head, consequently revealing that I knew how to shield. My resistance drove him to assault me with greater and greater force until I finally lashed out with rakkuhr, bound him in ropes of it—and discovered it's like kryptonite to the demahnk. It weakened him, but he redoubled his efforts to control my mind. I had no recourse but to add more rakkuhr and tighten it until he . . . stopped."

He took a deep breath, and his aura retreated. "Long story short, I scattered his essence across the dimensions. His absence gave me the freedom to finally locate the control-focus in my mind. I ripped it out, effectively crippling myself while I struggled to assimilate all of the memories that flooded in." He snorted. "Crappy timing, though. The demahnk council freaked when Xharbek went poof, and contained me. I refused to tell them why I was unreadable or how I scattered him, and so they gave me three choices: Open to them and be reconditioned." A shudder went through him at the mere thought. "Go into submerged exile on Earth until Xharbek collected himself and returned. Or go into stasis—with zero awareness of the worlds, the flows, *anything*—until Xharbek gathered himself and returned."

"Fucking hell," I said. "You didn't really have much of a choice, did you?"

"I didn't think so at the time. But I also didn't think I'd be submerged for fifteen years. Or that it would be so horrific."

I was on my feet and had him in a hug before I realized it. His arms wrapped around me, holding me close.

"The public message to demons and lords was that I willfully attacked my ptarl," he said after a moment, maintaining the embrace. "They declared the matter to never be spoken of, so great was the anathema." He made a sour noise. "Mostly because they didn't want speculation about any of it."

A shiver went through me. "And Rhyzkahl—who was already pissed at you—did the submersion."

"Rhyzkahl was *furious* that I still wouldn't turn Vsuhl and Elinor's essence over to him, when Tessa was ripe and available." He breathed out a small laugh. "Xharbek hadn't yet told him that you had the essence. And I felt no desire to rectify the error."

"At least I know now why Katashi wouldn't train me," I said. "And Tessa happily screwed me over, too."

Szerain pulled back and frowned. "You don't know everything. There were a number of influences on Tessa, reasons why she limited your training—" He broke off and snapped his focus to the sigils. "Xharbek has made his move," he murmured even as a sensation of wrongness flowed over me.

Chapter 43

"What did he do? And where?" I peered at the sigils as if I had a chance in hell of gleaning any sort of useful information.

"He cranked open the valve at ground zero. Not world-breaking, but enough to disrupt life as we know it if it continues unchecked." Szerain's gaze swept over the mass of sigils. His forehead creased. "There's something else happening at ground zero, but I can't identify it."

"He's trying to draw us out," I said with a scowl. "He's got something waiting for us there, a way to get rid of us while he stays nice and cozy within his fucking constraints."

"I'm sure he does." Szerain's tone was mild, but I felt the anger that he held in check.

"Xharbek needs to be stopped," I said, pissed and unafraid to show it. "He wants to step up his game? Then it's time for us to take him out of the game completely, give him the equivalent of a career-ending knee injury. Scatter his ass again."

He met my eyes. "I caught him by surprise last time. Now, he'll expect it and will either retaliate with extreme prejudice or bolt."

"All right, so you'll need a distraction." I clasped my hands together atop my head as if that could aid my thinking. "A big fucking distraction that'll let you get rakkuhr on him before he can react."

"Even so, rakkuhr alone won't affect him quickly enough." A smile spread across his face. "But you have all that makkas wire. We'll twist three or four strands together to give it a bit more stability, and I'll infuse it with rakkuhr. The rakkuhr-makkas will be the one-two punch to take him out, fast and hard."

"Hang on," I said, frowning. "How can you infuse makkas with rakkuhr? I thought the stuff blocked the arcane."

"It blocks *use* of the arcane. Both by or upon the user. Not only can't he tolerate rakkuhr, but infusing the makkas with it will turbocharge the arcane-blocking feature. Once the rakkuhr-makkas is on him, he won't be able to attack or escape."

"Once it's on him," I echoed, folding my arms over my chest. "So we'll still need a distraction. Along with a way to lure him to us in the first place, but I think it's best that we only focus on one impossible thing at a time."

Szerain scraped a hand through his hair in annoyance. "Yes, yes, we still need a distraction. Problem is, he'll see it coming. He can't read me, but if I'm close enough to get rakkuhr on him, our ptarl bond will give him just enough awareness to know something's hinky . . ." He trailed off, face paling. His throat worked as he swallowed.

"Szerain?" I touched his arm. "You okay? What's going on?"

"I can break the bond," he whispered then exhaled a shuddering breath. "I can break the bond," he repeated with more force. "There's our distraction."

Whoa. I weighed my words before speaking. "All right. I'm *all* for you ditching Xharbek, but I need to play devil's advocate here and remind you that Rhyzkahl was a puking wreck when Zakaar broke their bond."

"Rhyzkahl had no way to prepare for it, had no idea what was coming. I will." He seemed energized, as if finally seeing daylight after eons in the dark. "Plus, I'll be in control of the breaking, which should make a difference." He caught my dubious look and gave me a reassuring smile. "Worst case scenario, I'll be a puking wreck. But so will Xharbek. And that's when you'll lasso him with the makkas."

I turned the plan over in my head in search of holes or weak spots, but it appeared to be as sound as we could realistically expect. Szerain's breaking the bond was the edge we'd been looking for.

"You won't be alone this time, either," I said. "Besides me, we'll have Pellini and Idris, plus my squad and anyone else I can scare up." A thought tickled at the edge of my mind—someone I needed to contact, but before I could tease it out into the open, my phone bleeped with Pellini's you-need-to-read-this-now tone. "Crap." The need-to-read-this-now texts were never fun. Why couldn't pictures of fluffy kittens ever be marked urgent?

<Just rcvd word of weird shit at GZ. Stuff mutating. Every-thing. Ground, rubble, living stuff. Like plague but no pods and lots worse. Bunch of demons too. Reyza and others. Sending pics.>

I angled the phone to let Szerain read the message, then skimmed through the pics. Weirdly deformed creatures. Flowers with claws for petals. Not a single fluffy kitten in the bunch.

Gut churning, I thumbed in a quick reply to Pellini. *<Got it. Xh opened valve. Sz and I planning right now best response. Stand by.>*

"Dekkak sent Ilius to the pods here to somehow control the mutation," I said. "But the stuff in those pics . . . What the hell is causing it?"

Szerain wheeled toward the sigils and began making alter-ations. "There's nothing controlled about the changes at ground zero," he said through closed teeth. "It's what I felt earlier but couldn't identify. Xharbek diverted the mutagen—a specialized rakkuhr—into the valve flow. Fuck!" He clenched his hands, but then he closed his eyes. A few heartbeats later his hands relaxed and the tension in his stance eased. He'd pygahed. Probably more than once.

He opened his eyes. "The dose makes the poison," he said in a more reasonable tone. "A carefully targeted burst of nuclear radiation can kill cancer, but too much will cause all of your cells to die. Caffeine turns Kara into a functioning human being, but fifty cups of coffee would make her heart leap out of her chest."

"But so worth it," I said to lighten the godawful mood.

A smile touched Szerain's mouth. "The plague victims were exposed to a cup or two of mutagen coffee—controlled and di-rected. Currently, everything at ground zero is getting doused with bathtubs full of the stuff."

My humor vanished. "In other words, if we go to ground zero to close the valve, we risk getting horribly mutated."

"Actually, no. Undirected, the mutagen has no effect on ar-cane users."

I frowned at him. "But Marco Knight is sitting in a pod in my living room."

"Podding results from demon-directed mutagen. Plus, Marco Knight isn't an arcane user," Szerain said then shrugged. "What he does is different."

Ooh, I wanted to poke into that subject, but it would have to wait. "All right, it won't affect summoners or Pellini, but it'll work on everyone else." I swore under my breath. "Which means no military backup."

Szerain gave a tight nod. "He's staying within the fucking constraints as he chips away at our support."

"Wait a minute. That mutagen stuff is arcane, right?" I gave him a hopeful look. "What if we issue makkas wire bracelets to anyone who might be vulnerable."

His focus turned inward, as if he was running the numbers in his head. "That will work," he finally said, to my delight. "Six feet of wire per person should give more than enough protection. You could double it twice and twist it to make a simple wrap around bracelet. Needs to be worn against the skin, preferably under a sleeve to keep it from getting snagged and torn off—"

He fell silent as the basement door creaked open. A few seconds later Elinor and Giovanni descended the stairs.

She gave Szerain a smile. "So this is where you've been hiding . . ." Her voice trailed off. "What's wrong?"

"Nothing we can't handle," Szerain said with a comforting smile. He flopped into the armchair. "You've no need to worry."

Elinor pursed her lips at him, clearly not buying into the there-there routine, then leveled an expectant look at me.

"Xharbek's pissed and acting out," I told her then glared at Szerain when he made a Be Quiet throat clearing. "She of all people deserves to be in the loop."

Szerain spoke to me in demon. "What in the eleven chasms are you thinking?"

I answered in kind. "She may not be one who *needs* to know, but she *is* deserving of knowing that which affects her so deeply. They will both remain here for the confrontation, sheltered, and well clear of Xharbek and his mindreading."

Elinor's chin lifted. "Lord Szerain, you cannot protect me by keeping me ignorant of danger."

Szerain glowered at the double-pronged argument then lifted his hands in surrender. "Elinor, my dear, you had a will of iron before, and now you have this one's attitude." He jerked his head at me. I returned an innocent look. "Very well. Have a seat and I'll fill you in."

While he did that, I stepped away and texted Pellini the info about the mutagen, the arcane user immunity, and the specs for the wire bracelets for everyone else, including people and ani-

mals remaining behind, both here and at Jill's house—just in
case. After a bit of mental math, I added a request for fifty feet
of triple-strand makkas cable.

<On it>, he replied a few seconds later.

Awesome. Pellini would make sure everything was taken
care of. I started to type in a thanks then paused as the thought
from earlier reappeared at the edge of my mind. This time I let
it creep further out.

Right. It was past time to deal with that anyway.

"Hey, Szerain, how much wire would be needed to protect a
horse at ground zero?"

He stopped mid-word and gave me a long look. "Twenty-five
feet," he said after a moment.

"Gotcha," I said then texted *<Also need 12 lengths of 25ft of
wire plus another 12 bracelets>* to Pellini.

<Good deal>, he replied. *<What about the dog?>*

Damn, Pellini was sharp. "How much wire for a two-hundred
pound dog?" I asked Szerain.

Bafflement and curiosity warred on his face, but he simply
replied, "Ten feet?"

"Thanks," I said and relayed the info to Pellini.

<On it.>

I rejoined the others just as Szerain finished his rundown of
Xharbek's antics and our plans thus far.

"That seems a clever trap," Elinor said, brow furrowed. "But
how will you get him to tamely walk into it?"

"We hadn't quite reached that point in the planning," I said.
"Xharbek isn't stupid, which rather limits the possible ways to
lure him in."

"Is there perhaps an object he desires?" Giovanni offered.

Szerain leaned back and crossed his feet. "His wish list is a
touch more abstract than most."

Elinor stood a bit straighter. "I know what he desires—me,"
she said. "Use me as your lure." Her voice held the barest whisper of fear—noticeable to me only because I'd *been* her.

My estimation of her climbed higher. Being fearless was
overrated.

"Don't be absurd," Szerain said at the same time as Giovanni's, "Absolutely not!"

She shifted to better narrow her eyes at both men. "Excuse me?"

Giovanni wilted under the fierce gaze, but Szerain inclined

his head in apology. "What I meant is that you are of no use to Xharbek now that you have the firewall."

"Xharbek doesn't know that, though," I pointed out. Elinor shot me a grateful look.

Szerain grew thoughtful. "You're right. And he wouldn't be able to resist making a try for her."

"Wait, no," I said, wincing. "He'd be able to read the truth from her before he got close enough to be trapped."

Szerain shook his head. "With the firewall, I can shield her well enough."

"Perfect. How close can he get before he realizes she's no good to him anymore?"

"Within a few feet," Szerain said.

Close enough.

Giovanni reached for Elinor's hand. "My love, please. You cannot put yourself in such danger."

"Yes, I can, and I will." She gave his hand a squeeze. "Dear Giovanni, don't you see that I must?"

He searched her face, then his distress softened to acceptance. "I do, though I am loath to admit it. My beloved. I will remain here and await your triumphant return."

She gave him a smile of heart-melting adoration then leaned in and kissed him. "My little snake," she murmured ever so softly. He chuckled and kissed her back.

Curiosity swelled about the little snake thing, but I forced my mind to more important matters and hit Szerain with my next thought. "To keep Xharbek from discerning our intention, I propose that only Elinor, you, and I know that she's a lure, or that we're hoping to confront him at all. *We* can't be read. Everyone else needs to believe that we're there to close the valve, and the extra forces with us are to keep the demons at bay."

Szerain considered for a moment then blew out a gusty breath. "That seems to cover the needed bases. And Elinor can wear a makkas bracelet. It will be arcane camouflage to muddle her signature so Xharbek won't notice her until we get into place."

"At which time, she'll remove the makkas and be like a beacon of come-and-get-me."

Szerain gave a firm nod. "He'll take the bait, I'll break the bond, we'll wrap him in makkas and zap him with rakkuhr. Wham. Bam."

"I just had a nasty thought," I said. "What's to keep Xharbek from scooping everyone into dimensional pockets and leaving them to rot?"

"Aside from demahnk constraints—which Xharbek is good at loopholing—the area around ground zero is too unstable to allow access to any dimensional pockets." He looked around. "Anything else? No? Good. Go do what you need to do."

I pulled Elinor aside as we neared the stairs, then waited for Giovanni to reach the top before I leaned close. "What's the 'little snake' about?" I whispered. "Eilahn called him that, and he blushed scarlet."

She grinned, bright and mischievous. "He is quite skilled with his tongue," she whispered back, eyes dancing with merriment as I clapped a hand over my mouth to hold back my chortle. "Eilahn once heard me say it to him, and she does so love to tease." She looped her arm through mine as we climbed the stairs. "Do you not have a term of endearment for your Lord Mzatal?"

"Yep. I call him Boss." I grinned. "Because we both know who the real boss is."

Upstairs, Pellini had conscripted everyone with a working pair of hands into an assembly line for measuring, cutting, twisting, and trimming makkas wire. I told him that we were going to ground zero to get the valve and the flow of mutagen under control, and said nothing about Xharbek. Pellini, as usual, accepted the info I gave him and didn't press for more, even though it was clear he knew there was more to it.

"We're bringing DIRT in on this?" he asked.

"Just our squads," I said. "We'll muster at the fairgrounds. That's far enough away from ground zero for everyone to stay safe while they get issued makkas and instructed in the whys and hows of wearing it."

"Which are?"

"Against the skin. Probably should be taped down and worn under sleeves so they don't accidentally get ripped off." I paused. "I'm also going to talk to Boudreaux." Not only could we use his help, but it was time.

Relief flowed over Pellini's face, as if he was finally letting go of a worry—one he'd been holding onto ever since he decided to approach me about the arcane. Boudreaux and Pellini had been partners at work and best friends the rest of the time, and I'd become the main obstacle between them.

But all he said was, "Good," and left it at that.

*   *   *

I made the call from the privacy of my bedroom.

"Boudreaux here."

"It's Kara Gillian."

He paused barely an instant before replying in an acid voice. "So, what can I do for Your Royal Witchiness?"

"It's time for me to tell you the truth." I didn't have to explain about what.

"The truth?" He let out a harsh laugh. "You mean your version of it."

"No. The *truth*. I'll tell you what really went down at the Farouche Plantation that night. I only want one thing in return."

"Fuck you, Kara," he shouted. "We're not trading favors here. I'm not giving you shit for doing what you should have done a long time ago when I asked you straight to your face!"

And more than once. He'd *known* I was lying about not being involved in the plantation raid that ended with his mentor Farouche dead and his stepfather Angus McDunn in hiding from the police. Even worse, he'd known I was withholding info about the whereabouts of his mother—whom I suspected had gone to ground with McDunn.

"My favor to you is that I'll finally answer straight to your face," I said. "I'm on a pretty tight timeline, so you'd have to meet me at St. Long Elementary in twenty minutes. But if I talk to you in person, you'll know—without any shred of doubt—that I'm telling you the whole truth and nothing but the truth." *Including why it had to happen*, I added silently.

I heard his intake of breath. "Yeah, well, I'm pretty good about knowing when people are full of shit," he said, blustering with the faintest trace of uncertainty, likely rattled that I knew about his little knack for getting people to tell the truth. "What do you want from me?"

"Round up volunteers from your squad for a mission that's going down in about forty-five minutes and have them assemble at the old fairgrounds," I said. "If you determine I'm lying, you're done, and they can go home. But if you determine I'm telling the truth—whether you like that truth or not—you and your team join the mission."

"What kind of mission?" I could practically see his eyes narrow.

"Incursion at Ground Zero."

"I didn't get notification of a new rift."

"It's not a rift. Look, are you in or out?"

"Yeah. Sure, what the fuck."

"Good. See you in twenty."

He was at the abandoned school, smoking under the portico, when I arrived. As I walked up, backpack in hand, he tossed the half-smoked cigarette down and crushed it out with the toe of his boot.

"Let's get this bullshit over with," he said with an ugly curl of his lip. "Some of us have real work to do."

I dropped the pack beside a nearby bench then sat, deliberately letting him have the advantage of height. Boudreaux's career as a cop had been far from stellar, but the one thing no one could knock him for was his ability to get information and confessions out of suspects. It wasn't coercion either. There'd been a number of times when he'd interviewed a suspect and then come out and said the guy didn't do it. Didn't always go over well with the brass, especially when they were looking to make a fast arrest and close the case, but Boudreaux was always right.

I'd felt the force of his little knack for myself a few months ago, when I was arrested for the murder of J.M. Farouche. I'd resisted Boudreaux's influence at the time, but it had been hard as hell to hold back the unfiltered truth.

It was going to be even harder for him to finally hear it. Boudreaux had been a skinny kid with an amazing way with horses and big dreams of being a jockey, and James Macklin Farouche had been his mentor and benefactor. After Boudreaux nearly died in a racing accident, Farouche had moved heaven and earth to make sure he recovered as fully as possible, and even built him a house right by the stables. He'd been Boudreaux's idol, and for good reason.

And now I opened up to Boudreaux's influence, embraced the urge to unburden myself and told Boudreaux that, just as he had a special *knack* for gleaning the truth, this man he worshipped had also possessed a knack—one that allowed him to instill paralyzing fear in others. I went on to describe how Farouche had wielded his talent to influence, coerce, and terrorize other knack-gifted people to do his bidding, including kidnap, torture, and murder. And then I explained how Angus McDunn, who'd served as Farouche's right-hand man, used his own talent to enhance those knacks. Or, in my case, diminish.

As I spoke, Boudreaux's cocky sneer flickered and faded. I

paused at intervals to give him a chance to stop me, but though his eyes filled with increasing anguish, he kept signaling me to continue.

I told him about the women Farouche had ordered kidnapped, and how I took the place of a targeted victim to infiltrate the plantation and rescue Idris Palatino.

I told him about the Mraztur using the valve node at the plantation to come to Earth, and of the resulting battle.

I told him how Kadir dragged Farouche from the mansion, looked deep into his mind, and declared his life forfeit.

I told him how Bryce, ex-hitman for Farouche, intervened and claimed the right of vengeance, and how Farouche tried to influence Bryce in that moment and bring him back under his control.

I told him how I watched and did nothing while Bryce shot Farouche in the head.

And, finally, I admitted that, when Boudreaux had been frantic with worry about his missing mother, I'd purposefully withheld my suspicion that she'd fled with her husband, McDunn. At this, triumph flashed through the pain in Boudreaux's eyes. Though it lasted only the merest fraction of an instant, it was enough to tell me that he knew something of the current whereabouts of McDunn and his mother.

I fell silent. The urge to speak was gone because there was nothing left to say. Boudreaux stood like a statue, looking at a spot on the wall behind me. The anguished expression was gone. Now he simply looked bleak.

"Boudreaux, I—"

"You'll have your volunteers," he said in a voice scraped raw.

I had to hand it to him—he didn't like the truth one bit, but he wasn't one to welch on a deal. "We're rolling out to ground zero in less than fifteen, but I know it'll take longer to get horses ready, especially with this." I shoved the backpack forward with my foot. "There's a . . . magic radiation at ground zero that'll mutate just about everything, but the stuff in here blocks its effects. You and your people need to wear the bracelets against the skin. I suggest you duct taping them down. There's some for the horses and the dog, too. It all needs to be securely in place before y'all head to ground zero."

He fished one of the crude wire bracelets from the bag and eyed it doubtfully. "I thought you said we were dealing with an incursion?"

"I lied. We're going there to save the world."

His gaze snapped up to mine. "Jesus," he muttered. "You're serious, aren't you?"

"I am." I pushed to my feet. "Get your people ready as soon as you can so you don't miss the fun."

Chapter 44

An eerie quiet enveloped downtown Beaulac, as it had since a week after the valve explosion, when demon incursions put an end to search and rescue operations. Though at least by that time there'd been no more hope of finding anyone alive.

Cleanup efforts had, of course, never begun. Rubble remained where it had fallen. Broken glass glittered in the sun, and cars remained where they'd been abandoned.

As our vehicles neared the quarter mile perimeter of the valve, I ordered a halt. The color and texture ahead was *wrong*. I scanned with my binoculars, suddenly very glad I'd stopped the convoy.

It was like gazing into an alien landscape. The twisted and broken concrete looked as if it was covered with an undulating snot-green mold, and crimson vines snaked over everything like capillaries. And everywhere, movement. Rats? Inky black shiny rats?

We'd stopped near what was left of the First Bank of Beaulac, a good fifty yards from the edge of the weirdness. Elinor and Turek remained in the vehicles while everyone else piled out. Alpha and Bravo squads hustled into formation on the cracked sidewalk.

"Don't engage unless you have to," I told them. "But if you do, hit 'em fast and hard. Your primary job is to keep the demons away from us. Except for this one." I signaled Turek to come out of the APC. He'd *very* reluctantly donned a bright red XXL "SuperSwole Gym" t-shirt—with the sides slit to accommodate his massive chest and multiple arms, and the neck widened for his big head. He'd acquiesced only after I explained that precious

few humans would be able to tell him apart from any other savik. Hell, there were still plenty who couldn't tell a kehza from
a reyza. "He's an ally," I continued, "and the only demon you'll
see out there wearing a red shirt. Do *not* shoot him." I paused to
let the message sink in before continuing. "Bravo squad will
approach the valve from the east with Idris and Pellini as arcane
support. Alpha will move straight in from here along with my
team. Once we reach ground zero, Idris and Pellini will close
down the valve and stop the mutagen flow. My team and I will
be working close by. I don't know what's going to happen when
we start adjusting the valve, so be prepared for anything." That
was the closest I could come to warning them that we were
walking into a trap set by an increasingly unscrupulous
demahnk.

As soon as Bravo squad moved out, Bryce ushered Elinor
from our vehicle, making sure she kept her face hidden within
the borrowed hoodie. We needed to keep her presence secret
until it was time to reveal her as Xharbek bait, and the makkas
bracelet she wore only blocked arcane sensing. Beneath the
hoodie, she had on a set of my combat fatigues along with a pair
of my boots—an outfit that had thrilled her to pieces but would
also hopefully fool any demonic watchers in the area.

Bryce had surprised me by volunteering to serve as Elinor's
bodyguard, merely saying that he felt like he needed to come
along. Since his *feelings* were usually right on the mark, and
since Elinor didn't have the slightest whiff of tactical training, I
gratefully accepted his offer.

Elinor and Bryce tucked into the unit's formation behind
Szerain, Turek, and me. Sergeant Roma snapped orders to Alpha
squad, and we cautiously advanced into the strange terrain.

Very strange. Rakkuhr crawled everywhere like foggy py-
thons. As we proceeded forward, the street became oddly pliant,
akin to a rubberized track surface. The grass that had been finding its way through cracks now shied away from our approach—
which was better than the neon purple daisies along what was
once the sidewalk. One lunged and sank thorn-teeth into
Ahmed's boot before he could jerk back, leaving several embedded in the leather.

Rat-roach creatures with shiny black carapaces and glowing
red eyes scurried away from us to hide in crevices. One sought
refuge among the Dastardly Daisies and suffered numerous bites
before it could scramble free. A perfectly normal-looking spar-

row regarded us from atop a tumble of moldy bricks then belched a tiny gout of flame that crisped a tendril of crimson vine.

Yet throughout it all, in odd contrast to the weirdness, the air was filled with a pleasant clean and citrusy scent.

We were halfway to the valve when a mass of at least a hundred rat-roaches swarmed from beneath a crushed bus and scuttled toward us. Kowal took them out with her flamethrower before they could get close, then dealt with a cluster of hedgehog-sized horseflies in the same fashion. An Irish setter poked its head out of a gap between chunks of concrete, but as it emerged, it revealed a grotesquely long, serpentine-yet-furry body supported by a few dozen normal dog legs—complete with a wagging tail at the hind end. It started toward us, expression eager, then slunk away as I brought my pistol up to bear.

"Jesus." Pellini's voice cracked on the word. I looked over to see him lowering his gun as the dog-ipede retreated. "Glad I didn't have to shoot it, but maybe I should've anyway."

"Right there with you, dude," I replied and fought down a shudder.

Elinor pivoted slowly, taking it all in. "Such havoc Xharbek has wreaked for no just cause," she murmured. "That *asshole*."

Bryce cast a sidelong glance at me along with a hint of a smile.

I grinned. "Indeed he is."

The road became squishier the farther we went, until it was like memory foam on a giant trampoline. Rakkuhr drifted fifty feet overhead in thick, low-hanging clouds shot through with streaks of black lightning. There'd been no sign of the rat-roaches since the flamethrower incident, though dozens of other oddities kept us on our toes.

We were less than a hundred feet from the valve when a reyza flew over. Weapons snapped up and stayed trained on the demon as it landed atop a partially crumbled building.

My eyes narrowed. No gold, and nowhere close to rating even a one on the Gestamar size scale. "That's not a Jontari."

"You're right," Szerain said. "That's Kajjon. One of Amkir's." His gaze traveled over the area, then he lifted his chin. "And the reyza perched in that caved in window is Rodian. Jesral's."

I caught a glimpse of a small kehza before it ducked around a corner. Good grief, these demons looked downright *puny* after dealing with the Jontari and a certain imperator.

Roma moved up beside me. "Did the demons put their younglings out for us to fight?"

"No, these are a different kind," I said. That was easier than trying to explain the difference between lord-allied and Jontari. "They may be smaller, but they're *smart*. Geniuses with teeth and claws. Don't underestimate them. And for every one we spot, there are probably two or three more out of sight."

"Good to know."

As we neared the ruined PD parking lot, Alpha squad deployed to provide cover and suppress demon interference, even as Bravo squad signaled that they were in a solid flanking position to our right. From that same direction, I spied Pellini and Idris picking their way around a cluster of Biting Begonias on their way to the valve.

With Turek and Bryce following, Szerain, Elinor, and I headed to a spot across the street from the valve and what had once been the Grounds For Arrest coffee shop.

Now it was grounds for a nest. A shop-sized nest riddled with tunnels, made of trash glued together with a glistening amber resin. An awful scritch-scratching noise came from within, and my brain helpfully supplied an image of thousands of the rat-roaches lurking in the darkness. Gee, thanks, brain.

Szerain drew crackling potency to his right hand, ready for a strike. In silent accord, we moved on to the vacant storefront next door. This was bad. Bad-bad-bad. If these various vermin could not only mutate, but set up house and multiply in less than a day, Earth would be overrun before the week was out. Ants. Earthworms. Birds. Fish. Tigers. *People*. If we failed to get the mutagen shut down, we'd be in deep shit.

Bursts of small arms fire clattered here and there—the squads dealing with threats. Szerain continued another dozen feet to a relatively clear spot then began to dance the shikvihr. He needed the solid potency boost for his part in this. While Elinor fidgeted in a broken doorway, I tugged gloves on—since I needed my arcane abilities intact—then prepped the makkas wire into lassos. I wanted it to be as simple as possible to wrap Xharbek up in the stuff .

By the time I had a lasso ready in each gloved hand, Szerain's shikvihr was complete and ignited. Elinor drew herself tall and stepped out into the street, hands in tight fists by her side, likely to keep them from shaking.

Within the spinning rings of the shikvihr, Szerain raised his hand and called Vsuhl to him. I cursed under my breath in dismay. That wasn't in the game plan. Surely he didn't need the damn demon knife in order to break the bond.

Or maybe he did. Breaking the ptarl bond wasn't going to be a walk in the park. It was hard to blame him for wanting all the arcane support he could muster. To him, the knife was a powerful and well-established tool in his potency toolbox, like the shikvihr.

How the hell am I ever going to get that blade away from him?

Elinor looked over at Szerain and received a small nod of encouragement, then shot her gaze to me. She was scared but appeared determined not to chicken out.

I hurried to a nearby spot by a pile of rubble then gave her a smile and a thumbs up. "You got this," I said. "Just remember—we're literally soul sisters."

She blinked in surprise then brightened. "So we are!" Resolute, she took a deep breath, shoved the hood back, then gripped the makkas bracelet that kept her from Xharbek's notice and pushed it up and over her sleeve.

Crouching, I watched and waited, lassos ready in my grasp.

A demon bellow sounded from around the corner, followed by shouts and three shotgun blasts. Rifle fire cracked in the opposite direction as a pair of kehza beat their wings in hard flight toward the cloud cover.

Xharbek's here, I thought yet still startled when he appeared only a few feet from Elinor. He was in Zack form, but his sneering smile was one the true Zack had never worn. Rakkuhr swirled around him though it stayed at least a foot away, as if he had an invisible rakkuhr-blocking shield. He stepped toward Elinor, but the triumph on his face only lasted a fraction of a heartbeat before it shifted to black fury. I didn't have to be a mindreader to know he'd sensed the firewall and realized she was ruined for his purposes.

Elinor backed away. He moved as if to pursue, then flinched, though nothing physical had touched him. *Szerain.* A second later, Xharbek staggered and gave an incoherent cry that echoed through me with a strangely familiar sense of chaos.

Szerain stood as pale as a corpse, hands raised above him, clenched on Vsuhl. A shudder passed over his body, and I could practically see the bond shredding.

Xharbek stumbled and went to one knee even as Szerain let

out a heartrending scream and crumpled. He wasn't unconscious, but it was clear he couldn't *do* anything. *So much for Szerain having the advantage by being the one to break the bond.*

Xharbek was affected though, which was all I needed. I lunged up from my crouch with the lasso ready to drop over his head. But before I'd covered half the distance, he shoved upright and flung out a hand, smacking me with a blast of arcane that sent me flying back a good twenty feet to land in the street.

The air whooshed from my lungs, but the rubbery concrete saved me from broken bones. I rolled to my side and struggled to get my breath back as Xharbek let out a shriek of pent up frustration and visceral hatred. His face twisted—literally— shifting from Zack to Carl to a rookie cop whose name I couldn't remember to a state representative to at least a dozen other faces, male and female, none of whom I recognized. Through each change his eyes stayed wild.

"No more," he shouted, voice hoarse and furious. "Fuck the lords! Fuck all of you! Be it known that the hybrid spawn have destroyed themselves and you human insects with them."

He vanished.

"Kara!" Bryce was there, helping me to my feet. "What the hell just happened? That wasn't Zack, was it?"

"Xharbek," I wheezed then staggered as Elinor threw her arms around me.

"He is vanquished!" she cried. "How brave you are!"

"No, he's not vanquished," I said. His *Fuck the lords* still reverberated through my mind. "He isn't done with us yet." I cast a wary look around even though I knew I wouldn't see him coming.

Elinor released me and cast her own worried glance around. "Is he not restricted from doing us direct harm?"

"Yeah, but he's also *crazy*." Would Xharbek even give a shit about the constraints anymore? Especially since he wasn't as restricted as the other demahnk. He'd already increased the rakkuhr flow from this valve and added enough mutagen to disrupt life as we knew it. If he cranked it open more, would we be able to stop it?

A faint ground tremor set the crimson vines quivering. Turek let out a croon of worry as he cradled Szerain in both sets of arms. My *This Is Really Bad* feeling climbed higher.

The street vibrated but not like the tremor. A car engine

revved, and I spun to see a military light utility vehicle racing our way, tires squealing oddly on the rubbery street surface as it careened around rubble.

That's Jill, I realized in shock and dread. There was no reason for her to be driving here like a bat out of hell unless something horrible had happened to the others.

She screeched to a stop less than a dozen feet away then flung herself out of the vehicle, breathing hard.

"What the fuck are you doing here?" Bryce demanded an instant before I could say the exact same thing. Worry twisted his face as he ran to her, easing only slightly when he noted the makkas taped onto her arm.

Jill gave him a quick, hard hug that seemed to surprise them both, then wheeled toward me. "It's Ashava," she gasped. "She's practically beating on the inside of my head. She needs to come here, but you have to help her. *Now.* It's really important."

My tongue stumbled over itself in astonishment for several seconds. "Help?" I finally managed. "How?"

"She says to reach for her?" Jill gave a confused shake of her head then seized my hand. "She told me you'd know what to do. So *do* it. Hurry!"

There was no nexus here to aid me, but I had mega-Mom power instead. Using everything Szerain's sketches had revealed of Ashava's spirit and personality, I fixed the sense of her in my mind then mentally *reached*, as if extending a hand to help someone out of a ditch.

I *felt* a hand seize mine, both physically and in a ghost-grip of the arcane. The next thing I knew, a lovely young girl with auburn hair and brilliant blue eyes stood before us.

"Mommy!" she cried out with unabashed joy, then she threw her arms around Jill's waist and pressed her head to her mother's chest.

Jill let out a choked sob and held her daughter close. After only a few seconds, they stepped apart, as if both remembered the urgency of the situation.

Keeping hold of her mother's hand, Ashava turned to me, eyes grave in a ten-year-old's face. "Xharbek is mad," she said, and I clearly felt the dual meaning of angry and crazy. "You killed the Katashi syraza, his key instrument on Earth. You stole his chance to use Elinor. And Szerain broke the bond."

One thing was for sure, Ashava was hands down the most

well-spoken two-month-old I'd ever met. And the tallest. "We might have twisted his panties kind of tight," I said with a snort.

"The lords have failed him," she continued. "They wouldn't or couldn't do what *he* decided was needed to stabilize the demon realm. I'm now his last chance to execute a plan that benefits him more than any other."

I scowled "Exploiting you against your will in the process."

She wrinkled her nose. "I wouldn't be crippled as the lords are, but I'd be enslaved nonetheless." Her little shoulders squared with determination. "Xharbek's approach isn't the only way," she announced fiercely, as if to make her proclamation known to all. "And he will *never* have me."

Her face paled an instant before a strong tremor shook the ground. Beyond her, Pellini and Idris scrambled to their feet and backed away from the valve.

Jill pulled Ashava close as if to shield her. "What's wrong?"

"Xharbek has washed his hands of the lords," Ashava whispered. She looked up at her mother then at me, eyes wide. "And of me."

Chapter 45

The earth shuddered then shrieked as the spongy asphalt by the valve pulled apart in a rift-crack barely ten feet long and no more than a pace across. But instead of the magenta flames I was so accustomed to, luminous red potency roiled from the rift and spread like ground fog in all directions.

My heart began to pound. "He's ripped the valve open." Xharbek had tried to accomplish the same thing via Katashi's arcane bomb, but now he'd given the plan his own crazypants rift-style upgrade. This would be a catastrophic flood of rakkuhr.

Pellini and Idris eased toward the valve-rift, already engaged in the monumental task of rakkuhr containment.

Elinor let out a cry of dismay. "I will assist them." She took off, with Bryce on her heels.

"It's too much for us to control!" Ashava said, lower lip quivering ever so briefly. "Xharbek will destroy *both* worlds."

Jill jerked her chin up. "Then we'd better stop him." She took hold of Ashava's shoulders and gave her a full-strength *Listen up, because I mean business* glare—one that I'd been on the receiving end of a few times. "Xharbek wanted to use you, but he forgot that you've defeated him once already. You saved Earth when you were only a few minutes old. You have *power*."

Ashava's eyes darted to the incapacitated Szerain, then she gulped as it hit her that *she* was the Big Lord On Campus at the moment.

"Stop that," Jill ordered, voice rippling with love and tender rebuke at Ashava's doubt. "You're more than a demonic lord. More than all of them combined. You are a *qaztehl*." She spoke the last word with an intensity that seemed to ripple out from the two of them like shock waves.

Inhuman stillness settled over Ashava. "Thank you, mother," she said with calm assurance. "I am Ashava, firstborn daughter of Zakaar and Jillian Lenora Faciane. Unfettered qaztehl."

Her aura rolled over me like a Louisiana afternoon thunderstorm, magnificent power with the promise of destruction or life-giving mercy.

Holy shit. Mzatal had a powerful and intense aura, but while he was the Sun, Ashava was a SuperGiant star, dazzling all within reach.

Then she smiled brilliantly, shifting from goddess to girl in the blink of an eye. "I'm so glad you're here!" she cried out and threw her arms around Jill's waist.

"Ditto that," Jill said, hugging Ashava close. "Though I shudder to think what kind of turmoil my house will be in when I get back." She grinned at my questioning look. "After Roper dropped off the makkas, Michael *immediately* fixated on makkas-collaring the kittens." She rolled her eyes, but they sparkled with genuine affection. "Unfortunately, Pellini's dog thought 'chase the kitty' was a great game. Michael managed to collar four of them, but by the time I dashed out, two were still in hiding, and Lilith was breaking out the tuna—"

"Incoming!" Bryce shouted, bringing his rifle to bear on a zhurn flying in our direction like a piece of night.

Jill didn't waste a single instant. Before the *ing* left Bryce's mouth, she clutched Ashava close and dropped to the ground, shielding her with arms and legs and body, even as Ashava threw a barrier of potency around them both. Mother and daughter, fiercely protecting each other. Utterly adorable.

The *crack-crack-crack* of Bravo Squad's weapons filled the air, but the zhurn made a tough target as it darted from shadow to shadow. Bryce and I drew down on it as it came within range, both of us waiting for a clear shot.

Yet instead of arrowing straight at us, it swooped and snagged the makkas lasso with a claw then hurled it into the rift with the finesse of a Frisbee pro.

Then it let out a screech like tearing metal as two hundred pounds of dog slammed into it. A growl and the snap of teeth, and the screech cut off.

"Yeeehaaaw! Git 'im!"

I stumbled back barely in time to avoid being trampled as a

horse galloped past, hooves muffled by the soft ground. The rider let out another whoop as the dog shook the zhurn like a terrier with a rat then flung it aside. The horse reared and came down hard with both hooves on the mangled zhurn. As the demon discorporeated, the horse sidled away, snorting as if satisfied.

Another half dozen horses and riders cantered to a stop in the parking lot, Boudreaux in the lead.

"You made it," I said stupidly, grinning like an idiot.

"Fuck if I'll let you have all the fun," Boudreaux said. His eyes widened as he saw Ashava and Jill scrambling to their feet. "Why is there a *kid* here?"

"Mascot."

"Real funny, I—" Boudreaux's face went sheet-white. "Oh fuck. Fuck! No! Kid, stop! You can't pet that dog! He'll bite . . ." He trailed off, staring in shock as the bear-sized demon-killing Caucasian Shepherd wiggled and bounced like a puppy around a delighted Ashava.

"Okay, she's a bit more than a mascot," I said.

Ashava sucked in a sharp breath and called glorious violet potency to her free hand. In the next heartbeat, Rhyzkahl and a syraza appeared not ten feet away from us. Immediately, the demon released Rhyzkahl's shoulder and vanished.

"Hold your fire!" I shouted as the horsemen brought their weapons to bear on the intruder.

Boudreaux lifted a hand. "Horsemen, stand down," he said, eyes on the demonic lord. "It's cool." He licked dry lips, then he dragged his gaze away and closed his hand into a fist. "Move out northeast to support Bravo Squad." With a nudge of his knees, he turned his horse and took off down the street, with his unit right behind him.

Boudreaux's reaction struck me as odd, but I had bigger worries.

Potency rippled around Rhyzkahl like the distortion waves of a mirage. "Peace, young one," he said to Ashava, keeping his hands open and at his sides. "I bring no enmity."

"Why are you here?" I demanded. "We're a little busy at the moment."

"The situation is dire and affects us all."

My eyes narrowed to slits. "Thanks but no thanks. We don't need the distraction of worrying that you'll stab us in the back the instant we take our eyes off you."

"In this matter, we are allied, Kara Gillian." He paused. "And I will give you the eighth ring of the shikvihr."

"Wait, what?" I stared at him in utter disbelief. "Are you insane? It doesn't work like that."

My surprise doubled as Ashava released the readied potency strike and inclined her head to Rhyzkahl. "Dak lahn," she said then gave her mother's hand a tug and started toward the valve-rift. Jill shot a hard look at Rhyzkahl but went with her daughter, apparently trusting that Ashava wouldn't leave me if there was any real danger.

Great. Now I was alone with a nonsense-spouting lord.

Rhyzkahl's gaze locked on me with unnerving intensity. "Each ring of the shikvihr conveys an exponential increase in focus, power, and ability. You need every possible advantage if Xharbek is to be thwarted."

"No shit, Sherlock," I said, voice acid. "But I haven't learned the sigils or had any training for the eighth."

"There is no need. The sigils are merely the components." He lowered his head, eyes on me. "When you summoned Dekkak, you held the entirety of the ritual within you. You understood the whole of it."

"Only because I had the nexus and *your* power," I retorted. "I'm back to being an ordinary summoner now."

"Never ordinary," he said, amusement flashing through his eyes before he grew serious again. "Your prolonged work with my power through the nexus has attuned you to a new arcane frequency. The ability to comprehend the omneity remains with you, though perhaps not as readily accessed. You *know* the purpose and meaning of the eighth ring. We have but to culminate it."

His words reverberated with truth that my own essence echoed. I *did* know and understand the ring. Not only had I watched him a million times, but I'd danced it with Paul in the demon realm. More importantly, I *felt* it hovering on the edge of my awareness, fully formed and waiting to be taken. I'd never experienced that with any other ring.

Rhyzkahl had absolutely zero reason to lead me astray in this moment—not with the fate of both worlds in the balance.

"You're right," I said with a firm nod. "Okay. Eighth ring. Let's do it." A lord's intervention was required to complete mastery of each ring of the shikvihr. Regret lanced through me that it wouldn't be Mzatal this time, but necessity trumped sentiment.

"Dance, Kara Gillian," he said.

Determined, I stepped a few feet away, pygahed for focus, and traced the first sigil of the first ring. Except I didn't. Where the glowing sigil should have been, there was only empty air. Realization hit me like a punch to the gut. "This isn't going to work," I said, voice quavering with disappointment despite every effort to control it. "Without the nexus, I can't do floating sigils on Earth until I have all eleven rings of the shikvihr."

"Then I have wasted my time."

Words leaped to my tongue to tell him where he could shove his sick, end-of-the-world petty revenge games, but I reined them back. Rhyzkahl hadn't agreed with me. He'd simply commented on my own assertions. My own beliefs. My momentary *can't do* attitude.

Besides, it was downright stupid to think that he'd come to this godawful spot just to fuck with me. Nor would he purposefully waste his time. With all that in mind, I settled in again and sought the resources that *must* be there.

And I found them via his aura. It provided the eerie reminder of the Rhyzkahl-powered nexus and, through it, the resonance of the super-shikvihr.

Once again, I traced the initial sigil, unsurprised as it hung in the air with a perfect golden glow. With methodical precision, I danced the first three rings of sigils, but by the fourth, method melted into pure flow. The whole of the shikvihr, all eleven rings, shimmered in my essence like a waiting blueprint.

Beeeeee the shikvihr.

I ignited the seventh ring and flowed right into the eighth. My mind no longer thought in terms of individual sigils, but of shaping potency to match the resonance of the internal blueprint. My arms curved through the air with my hands leading them in perfect trajectories, graceful and free as I circled and created. I felt every shift and nuance and flow with effortless perfection. For the first time ever, I truly *danced* the shikvihr.

With a flourish, I added the last loop to the final sigil of the eighth ring, then reluctantly disengaged from the process. Seven rings glowed brightly around me. The eighth was dim in comparison, still unignited. Hot damn.

I faced Rhyzkahl. "Okee dokee. I'm ready for the lordy mojo."

Without a word, Rhyzkahl eased through the sigil rings to stand behind me. As he wove the rings together, I absorbed every subtlety of my creation. My awareness of the shikvihr grew until a sudden mental flashpoint of *knowing* it to be simply an extension and amplification of *me*. That was why each person had to dance their own shikvihr, and why only a handful of summoners had ever mastered all eleven rings. To have even a chance, you had to not only recognize your own potential, but accept and embrace it as well.

Rhyzkahl didn't need to tell me when he was finished. I felt it in every cell of my body, then ignited the eighth ring in a flash of cerulean blue. The power infused me like a caffeine overdose without any of the jitters, and I did a fist pump of victory. It would have been easy to tell myself that the eighth ring was Rhyzkahl's way of offering an apology for his various sins against me, but I knew it wasn't. Nor did it need to be. We'd united against a common threat, and the rest didn't matter.

"Dak'nikahl lahn," I said. *Thank you very much.*

To my surprise he replied with, "Tahnk si-a kahlzeb." *It was my honor*, instead of the expected *sihn* for *You're welcome*.

A pressure wave hit like a fist, sending us staggering and causing my ears to pop painfully. Less than a heartbeat later, the ground heaved, flinging us off our feet.

When the world stopped bucking, I struggled up to my hands and knees. Through the ringing in my ears, I dimly heard shouts of alarm along with the chatter of automatic weapons. I blinked to clear my eyes, only to see rakkuhr blasting from the rift like ash from an erupting volcano.

Rhyzkahl hauled me to my feet. "Xharbek has blown the valve rift wide open," he said eyes blazing with fury—and a barely perceptible touch of fear. An angry scrape covered one side of his face from cheek to chin. He started toward the rift, support-dragging me along.

The crew working at the rift had been knocked to the ground and now clambered to their feet. Ashava was the first up and darted toward the spewing rift with a cry of dismay.

"Rhyzkahl!" she shouted, child-voice at odds with the power it held. "Help me seal the rift!" Sealing was like placing a patch. It wasn't the same as permanently closing, but it would drastically slow the erupting of rakkuhr.

He released me and strode forward. "We cannot seal it until we ease the flow."

Ashava narrowed her eyes. "We'll form a shield to block the potency. The others can hold it in place while you and I create the patch seal."

He swept an assessing gaze over the assembly as if checking his available tools then nodded. "It will require supreme effort from all to accomplish this. Let us begin."

Ashava and Rhyzkahl took up positions on opposite sides of the rift, and the rest of us arranged ourselves to fill in the gaps— Idris and Pellini beside Rhyzkahl, and Elinor and me by Ashava. Yet worry dug at me like a tag on a new shirt. There was a flaw to the plan, or something we'd failed to consider, though I couldn't pin it down.

The two lord-types wasted no time in weaving a tight mesh of potency that stretched at chest level across the rift. This would be the arcane shield to block the rakkuhr while they worked on the patch seal. The non-lords took hold of the shield's potency strands, like holding the four corners of a blanket, then nearly lost control of it when Ashava and Rhyzkahl released their grip.

"We got this!" I yelled in hopes of rallying our little team. "Let's take this sucker down."

It was like trying to hold back the water blast of a broken fire hydrant with a baby's blanket, but millimeter by millimeter we forced it downward until it was about hip height, low enough for the lords to work.

Rhyzkahl and Ashava began to create the patch seal out of layers of intricately interlocking potency. The rest of us hung on grimly to the shield strands, counting the seconds until we could release it. Supreme effort, indeed, but we were doing it. We were sealing off Xharbek's big bomb.

The flaw lit up like neon.

"We're forgetting the second bomb!" I blurted. Rhyzkahl and Ashava looked at me with confusion, but Bryce and Jill stiffened as comprehension hit.

"Son of a bitch," Pellini breathed.

"What second bomb?" Idris demanded.

"It's a classic terrorist move," I said in a rush, already scanning the area. "Set a bomb, wait for people to come in and help the injured, then detonate the second and take out a bunch more people. All Xharbek had to do was wait until we're all occupied and then do something bad—oh, fuck, that's it right there."

A half dozen yards away, red glowed from a rift barely a foot long. Tiny, but with unspeakable potential for havoc.

Rhyzkahl cursed in demon. "When it lengthens, it will bisect

this one and destroy all hope of containment. Even now it desta-
bilizes our efforts."

"Why did Xharbek make the second rift so small?" I asked
but immediately realized the answer. "Because he blew his wad
on this big one." We were in the middle of a sea of rakkuhr, the
bane of the demahnk. That tiny rift was all he could manage
after the energy drain of making the first—which was why he
hadn't made a dozen more.

Not to mention, the rakkuhr fountaining up from it would do
the job for him. In barely half a minute, the new rift had already
lengthened several inches—a rate that would only increase.
How long did we have? Ten minutes?

Another six inches of asphalt split. Five minutes. If we were
lucky.

I tore my gaze away, stomach churning. The shield strands
nearly ripped from my grasp as the rakkuhr from our rift roared
with augmented vigor. Ashava and Rhyzkahl would never be
able to seal this in time. Xharbek would win, and Earth would
be destroyed—for humans, demons, *and* demahnk. Insane.

But maybe I could buy our team the time they needed. I
wasn't a lord and thus couldn't seal a rift on my own, but I had
plenty of practice locking Jontari rifts to keep them from expanding. On the other hand, the mini-rift was demahnk-crafted,
meaning I'd not only have to work at mega-record speed, but
also adapt my techniques. Plus, I'd be a sitting duck for Xharbek
and his various minions.

No doubt about it. If I attempted this, he'd squish me, constraints be damned. However, if I could manage to lock that rift
before he turned me into Kara-flavored mincemeat, it would all
be worth it.

Hell, at least I could put "Saved the world" on my heavenly
resume.

A calm certainty filled me. "I'm going to go lock the little
rift," I stated. "Can y'all hold the shield without me?"

"We can hold it," Idris said with grim determination, echoed
by similar avowals from Elinor and Pellini. I hurried to distrib-
ute my shield strands to them then stepped back.

"Xharbek will not abide your interference," Rhyzkahl said.

"I'm well aware of that," I replied. As long as I could get the
thing locked, he could *not abide* all he wanted.

Pellini suddenly jerked and let out a sharp cry as if stung.

"Oh shit. Shit!" Wide-eyed, he shoved his strands at Idris, grabbed at his chest, then staggered back from the valve. "Kara! I'm—" He vanished.

Kadir just called in Pellini's debt. Fuck!

Idris clung to the shield strands, white-faced with the effort of holding them. Heart pounding, I dove to seize mine back from Elinor before the force of the potency ripped both the shield and the patch seal away. That was some seriously shitty timing on Kadir's part. I could only hope the weird lord was doing his own thing to save the worlds and not purposefully screwing us.

Except that it wouldn't matter. With Pellini gone, I'd lost the chance to go lock the mini-rift. No way could Elinor and Idris hold this on their own.

"Give them to me, Kara," Bryce said from beside me, holding a hand out.

"The hell?" I gave him a baffled look then saw a gold disk shining like a sun in his other hand.

Bryce offered me a Seretis smile. "Give me the strands. I will hold the shield secure while you attend the other rift."

Bryce was *channeling* Seretis. Holy shit. I passed him the strands, easing as the non-arcane Bryce handled the arcane power with deft ease.

"Kara Gillian." Rhyzkahl's eyes met mine. "Pay close heed to your *purpose*."

At least he wasn't trying to talk me out of it. I gave him a sober nod then raced to the smaller rift, now nearly five feet long.

Rakkuhr swirled around me as I crouched beside the rift. Well, the *purpose* of rift-locking was simple enough: Lock the damn thing and keep it from fucking up the efforts of my team. Easy. I readied the potency then froze at the sight of a rakkuhr-free, two-foot circle of ground barely ten feet away. Crimson coils eddied around it, as if something within repelled the rakkuhr.

Or was shielded against it. Like, say, a certain *invisible* asshole demahnk.

My *purpose* abruptly crystallized. It wasn't to lock the rift or save my friends or go out with a blaze of glory in heroic sacrifice. Those were merely components, sigils in a ring. No matter what else happened, my purpose was to kick some motherfucking Xharbek ass.

Straightening, I lifted my hands out to either side in a fuck-yeah dramatic pose. Thanks to Xharbek, I was surrounded by a shitload of the very component I needed to make that ass-kicking a reality. I'd never learned how to handle the rakkuhr potency, but then again I'd never learned the sigils for the eighth ring or the ritual for summoning an imperator.

Beeeeeee the rakkuhr, I thought with a snicker as I brought it to me. It raced eagerly into my control, spilled over my hands and danced at my feet to wreathe me in crimson and night. With a whisper of will, I locked the rift and halted its growth. A second nudge sent the rakkuhr coursing toward the main rift to form a shield around everyone there, and another around Turek and Szerain. My rakkuhr shields weren't as cool or pretty or sturdy as Szerain's lace-spheres, but they'd keep Xharbek the hell away. After all, that was their *purpose*.

Xharbek had dropped the invisibility—or maybe had simply recovered enough to take on a corporeal form—and now the face of Carl the morgue tech seethed with anger before me.

"This is not over," he snarled.

"Oh, but it will be soon," I said cheerfully and wrapped his shielded bubble in a sexy little rakkuhr tornado. The height of fashion for scheming demahnk this season. I couldn't hope to scatter him on my own, but I didn't have to. I'd contain him until the others finished with the rift, then *they* would be more than happy to do the honor.

I continued to feed rakkuhr into the cyclone, swirling it tight and fast in the hopes that it would not only prevent him from teleporting out, but also start to wear away at his shields, like water eroding rock. Xharbek was a mountain, but I had a river of the potency streaming from the rift.

Triumph swelled as the rakkuhr-free zone began to narrow. Even better, he was starting to look a little transparent.

His fury abruptly vanished to be replaced by a truly nasty Fuck You smile. Shit. I'd missed something, but whatever it was, I'd deal with it. No way was I going to let this sonofabitch slip away again.

Since I was expecting a tricky reveal, I didn't startle when Ilana appeared in her own rakkuhr-free circle a couple of yards from Xharbek.

No, my full shock was reserved for the sight of Mzatal at her side.

Chapter 46

Oh. Fuck.

Mzatal stood with a blade in each hand, hair flowing loose about him while rakkuhr swirled around his boots and crawled like flames up his legs. Though the demahnk couldn't abide rakkuhr, the non-Mraztur lords had merely been conditioned to avoid its use. Easy enough for Xharbek or Ilana to remove that conditioning from Mzatal—or simply allow the demons of the blades to suppress his aversion, as they had in Siberia.

Mzatal's silver-grey eyes fixed on me, piercing and powerful—yet haunted, as if he *knew* he'd lost a vital part of himself but was too controlled, too influenced to determine its exact nature, much less do anything about it.

He slashed the air with Khatur. The rakkuhr tornado around Xharbek fell away into formless mist.

"My deepest thanks, honored lord." Xharbek placed a hand on Mzatal's shoulder then angled his head my way. "Perhaps such a dire threat to our realm and our person should be eliminated. Permanently."

Great. Xharbek still couldn't say, "Kill that annoying bitch," flat out, but he had no trouble with a strong suggestion.

Ilana gave Xharbek a long look, which told me his suggestion trod perilously close to forbidden territory. For a brief shining moment I thought she might question his goals and withdraw her support.

No such luck. My stomach gave a sick lurch as she put her hand on Mzatal's other shoulder in a mirror of Xharbek's pose. Adding her own whammy to Xharbek's suggestion, I had no doubt.

She doesn't care that Xharbek is bugfuck crazy.

No. It wasn't that she didn't care. Ilana had zero idea that she *should* care. The demahnk lived with a communal telepathy, which meant that she would never in a million years expect a fellow demahnk to have secrets or hidden plots. Not to mention, it probably would never occur to her that one of her kind could go insane, much less that Xharbek had lost all perspective and reason through a human-style break.

In that same vein, she'd have no way to fathom why a demahnk would deliberately find a way around constraints—especially when they were either inherent or had been placed for what the demahnk would consider to be good reasons. To top it all off, Xharbek was the senior dude, the one in charge, and the one who had the big Plan. Of course, Ilana would go along with whatever he said.

Wonderful. I'd gained insight into the demahnk psyche. Didn't change the fact that by bringing Mzatal here, Xharbek had made a nasty, dirty, and hideously brilliant move.

Mzatal's aura swelled into a malevolent volcanic furnace—a thousand times worse than in Siberia, when he'd nearly succumbed to the bloodthirsty vehemence of Xhan and Khatur.

I pulled the rakkuhr in close, ready to do . . . what? I had no idea. This was pretty much the worst possible scenario. Take the most badass lord of all the lords, strip his aversion to rakkuhr, have him wield a pair of demon-possessed power-augmenting knives, and put him under the control of *two* demahnk.

Yet Mzatal was resisting. Though it didn't show in his appearance or stance or aura, I *knew*.

"Zharkat," I said. "Mzatal. It's me, Kara." I mentally reached for him and came up against his walls. But I knew they weren't completely impenetrable. He'd come to my nexus and created the super-shikvihr with me. He'd called me to Siberia. Most of all, he'd so far failed to turn me into a smoking pile of ash.

Meanwhile, the dastardly demahnk duo of Ilana and Xharbek remained focused on him, their perfect weapon against me. I didn't have to hear them to know they were pouring treacherous shit into his mind.

Mzatal lowered his head, eyes blazing, and grip tight on the blades. His hair whipped about him like a physical manifestation of his aura, tendrils coiling in serpentine gyrations like living things.

Zharkat. Mzatal. We are one.

His aura enveloped me, suffocating and oppressive, a reflection of his internal conflict. He fought Xharbek and Ilana's influence, but he wouldn't be able to resist them forever. Plus, Xharbek surely noticed that I remained in one piece, and would do his best to rectify that wee oversight. Somehow I *had* to tip the balance, bring my own influence into play, and give Mzatal the support he needed to tell his oppressors to fuck off. Somehow.

Mzatal took a step toward me, stiff and graceless, as if advancing through a sucking mire. Then another, blades rising.

At a loss, I drew on the rakkuhr, used it to reinforce my mental fists as I hammered at his walls. *Remember me. Remember our bond. Remember us.*

Nothing.

Thinking at him really hard wasn't working. I focused on Xhan and *reached* in the hopes of making contact through the blade as I'd managed once before. But I immediately recoiled from their remorseless savagery. Both blades were stoked to a berserker frenzy, unrestrained and vicious. That avenue of communication was closed.

Impotent rage swelled within my chest, sending black lightning crackling through the groundcover of rakkuhr. I couldn't get through to him. I couldn't breach that wall. My team was occupied and unavailable to help. I was going to die at the hands of my lover.

And it would destroy Mzatal to be the instrument of my demise.

I'm so sorry, my beloved.

Heat flared at the small of my back. The twelfth sigil. Ashava's. Her gentle touch brushed my mind, imparting encouragement and unwavering support. Gratitude swept through me at the gesture, and on its heels an idea sparked into being. I bore eleven other sigils—an intricate scar for each lord. Experience had demonstrated that the scars maintained a connection to the lord they represented—and the lords were the offspring of telepathic beings who engaged in communal thought as easily as breathing. Moreover, the lords had passed their legacy on to their descendants. Me, Idris, Elinor, and so many more. Having Ashava's support rocked, but why stop there? I needed backup, and lots of it.

I placed the back of my hand over Ashava's sigil, reinforced the connection and let her feel my intent. She responded with understanding, followed by the sense of Jill—fiercely protective of all whom she held dear. Elinor joined them, her presence as familiar as my own skin.

Yes! They were busy with the rift, but I wasn't alone. A pleasant tingle in the scar on my left side accompanied the arrival of Seretis and Bryce. An instant later my upper chest blossomed with warmth as Rhyzkahl's sigil flared into life, then he and Idris joined the crazy mind-meld.

There were no words, simply a sharing of knowing.

Of *purpose*.

Now that's how to have a kickass posse!

"Zharkat," I said. The power of the gestalt backed my word, sending it reverberating through the air. "*Mzatal*."

His aura flickered, but the walls remained. He advanced another step, right arm drawing back for a thrust that would end with me consumed by Khatur.

A single concept floated through the gestalt. *More.*

To my surprise, Elofir's sigil scar along my right abdomen began to prickle. His calm touch joined the mind-meld, and with it a soft brush of his lover, Michelle Cleland. An instant later, my surprise turned to outright shock as Jesral's warmed. His presence followed—cold and calculating and snarky—with the unequivocal sense that this was merely a momentary truce. Fine by me.

Within the span of three heartbeats, others ignited. Rayst, whose sigil-scar lay entwined with Seretis's. Vrizaar, sigil flaring on my left back, then Vahl's along the right, followed by a caustic burning at the very base of my spine that marked Amkir's. With each addition, the gestalt grew—enemies uniting against a common threat. Even Szerain's sigil held a weak flutter of presence, bolstered by Turek. Last was Kadir, heralded by a creepy wash of goosebumps on my right side, and carrying with him the whisper-touch of Paul and Pellini.

Only one sigil remained still and silent. Mzatal's, in the very center of my chest. Its partner—*my* sigil—lay over his heart. He'd carved it there as a reminder of what he'd walled off.

"All right, Kara," I murmured. "*Tear down this wall*."

Lifting my hands, I pulled rakkuhr and sent it racing through the sigil-scars. They'd been born of rakkuhr, and now I called to that spark at the heart of each one, setting them aglow until I blazed with power. The sigils' original purpose was to replace my Self with the Rowan entity in order to turn me into a weaponized summoner. But Rowan couldn't hold a candle to what this Self was about to do.

Zharkat. Mzatal. I am here. We are one.

I encapsulated the emotion and heart and promise and truth of those words, then hurled it at Mzatal's barriers. The gestalt roared with unified purpose and drove the capsule forward to smash against his walls like an extinction event meteor slamming into a planet.

A crack appeared. Thinner than a hair on a bumblebee's ass, but a crack nonetheless. Through it, I arrowed straight to his essence.

Mzatal gave no outward sign that I'd reached him, but his response resonated in the core of my being—a brief touch, an acknowledgement. *We are one.*

On my chest, his sigil went supernova, and his white-hot presence merged with our glorious gestalt. He turned on Xharbek and buried both blades in the motherfucker's heart.

Faster than the speed of thought, we channeled our unified strike through Mzatal and into the seething malice of the blades. Xharbek threw his head back and flung his arms wide, mouth stretched in a silent scream. Light webbed over him, searing hotter and tighter until he burst into a vortex of a billion prismatic sparks that spun around the blades. Yet rather than scattering, the sparks picked up speed and began to rise.

Without missing a beat, Mzatal brought the tips of the blades together in the midst of the vortex. The sparks froze in place for a fraction of a second then collapsed into a golf-ball-sized orb of darkness balanced on the blade points.

Mzatal gave an unearthly roar of anger and hatred that reverberated through the gestalt like a clap of thunder. In a brutal move, he jerked the blades apart. Rakkuhr crackled between them, taking on the form of a dragon's head that snapped its jaws closed around the orb. An ethereal scream of anguish rose and faded even as the rakkuhr-dragon head dissipated, leaving nothing but empty air in its wake.

The world shuddered. Ilana collapsed like a puppet with its strings cut, then vanished.

I put my arms out for balance until the earth stopped moving. "We did it," I breathed. Did something at least. Wasn't sure exactly what. Was Xharbek scattered or destroyed completely? Or had the blades consumed him?

Doesn't matter, I told myself. For now, he was out of our hair.

With its purpose fulfilled, the group mind dispersed like a cluster of balloons released in the wind. The sigils faded to their former quiescence, except for Ashava's.

And Mzatal's.

Ashava's had eased to a mellow warmth, but Mzatal's sigil felt like a sun-scorched rock scraping the flesh from my sternum.

His appearance did nothing to reassure me. The skin of his face stretched taut over the bones, and his hands gripped Xhan and Khatur so tightly it was a wonder they hadn't shattered. His aura retreated, but as if it was being sucked away rather than by his own will.

Horror filled me. It was Siberia all over again, but supercharged. The blades had been hard enough to control after Mzatal bladed Big Turd, and this time they'd defeated—possibly even consumed—a *demahnk*. With a portion of his mental energies devoted to resisting manipulation, Mzatal lacked the razor-sharp focus needed to withstand the blades' influence. Now they sought to consume him. His sigil continued to blaze upon my chest because it was his lifeline.

Still holding the blades at arm's length, Mzatal dropped heavily to his knees, as if unable to spare the resources to remain upright. He was like a man struggling to stay on his feet while hurricane winds lashed at him. Rakkuhr sparked between Khatur and Xhan, setting the air crackling with an ancient and inscrutable potency. Mzatal bared his teeth as he fought the will of the blades, every muscle straining. Yet despite his efforts, his right fist rotated to angle Xhan toward his heart.

Frantic, I sought to resurrect the gestalt. Rhyzkahl, Seretis, and Ashava answered, with Szerain a faint whisper, and through them exuded the presence of Jill, Bryce, and Elinor. I didn't expect a response from the others—not without a world-destroying threat to act as a beacon. But surely our local crew would be enough to help Mzatal subdue the blades.

The gestalt hurled its full force at Xhan and Khatur, but the ferocity of the unified blade energy drove it back and sent me staggering. We might as well have been trying to put out a forest fire with a water pistol filled with gasoline. Mzatal shook with effort, skin translucent, while Xhan's point edged closer to his chest.

I slapped my hand over his sigil, and the howls of triumph of both blades screeched through my essence. They knew Mzatal couldn't withstand their combined attack.

"Rhyzkahl!" I swung around, surprised to find him standing only a few feet away. Over by the rift, Bryce-Seretis struggled to control the seal potency Rhyzkahl had passed to him. "Take Xhan back. *Please.* Mzatal can't hold out against both."

"No," he said, voice uncompromising though regret shone in his eyes. "I will not accept that burden again."

Though my heart plummeted, I couldn't blame him. He was finally free of his blade. "Can you distract it or something?" I asked. Begged.

Rhyzkahl remained silent for a terrifyingly long moment, gaze on the struggling Mzatal. His eyes dropped to the thick scar on his right hand, then he gave a soft snort of not-quite amusement and strode toward Mzatal.

Cold dread speared through my heart. That scar came from Mzatal's attack via Xhan, when he rescued me from the Rowan torture ritual. Even worse, Mzatal wasn't reacting to Rhyzkahl's approach. His entire focus was on preventing Xhan from skewering his heart—which meant he was utterly defenseless against an outside attack. If Rhyzkahl chose to seek vengeance for the injury or his nexus imprisonment, Mzatal couldn't do a fucking thing about it. If he tried to defend himself, he'd fall to the blades.

If I intervened to stop Rhyzkahl, he'd fall to the blades.

I have to trust Rhyzkahl. Fuck.

Rhyzkahl stopped a foot from Mzatal, eyes locked on his former essence blade. Xhan. Spikes thrust from its hilt, curling around Mzatal's fingers to lock the knife in his grip. The dark blue jewel in the pommel sparkled and flashed as if it contained a thousand manic fireflies, while the oily sheen of the blade captured and warped the light, and sent it crawling along the wicked edge.

Rhyzkahl's lips pressed thin. Through the gestalt, he sent a single concept. *Be ready.*

Like a striking cobra, he shot his scarred hand out, clamped it tight around the foul blade, then jerked it along the razor-sharp edge and away.

Even with his warning, I flinched in shock. Droplets of blood arced through the air and sizzled on the blade. Xhan shrieked with terrible delight as it *lunged* for Rhyzkahl.

Which meant, for this instant, it wasn't fixated on Mzatal.

I hurled a focused blast at Xhan and coupled it with a shout, both mental and out loud: *"Send it away, zharkat! Now!"*

Mzatal gave a mutinous cry and yanked Xhan up above his head. The rakkuhr connection between the two blades flickered.

The thorns withdrew. Xhan vanished.

Mzatal dragged in a labored breath, then a deeper, more controlled one. The balance had shifted back to him, but it was too soon for me to feel relief.

"Now the other," I urged him. "Send it away as well."

Still on his knees, he lowered his hands and bowed his head, gazing down at Khatur.

"Mzatal, send it *away*." I wanted to run and throw my arms around him, but I didn't trust that fucking blade. Would suck to get this far and end up with a gut full of Khatur.

Seconds ticked by while my nerves wound tight. Mzatal finally exhaled a long breath, lifted his head, and straightened his spine. But to my dismay, he slid his blade into the sheath at his side.

That's not the same fucking thing as sending it away! I thought in frustration. Sure, it wasn't in his hand anymore, but its influence remained damn near as strong. A tidal wave of dejection threatened to suck me under. Even though the fucking knife had nearly destroyed him, he still couldn't—or wouldn't—send it away.

And here I was, oath-bound to take *both* blades from him. Even diminished as he was, I couldn't imagine wresting them away. How was I supposed to manage it when he returned to full strength?

I did my best to shake off the gloom. Nothing I could do about it right now. *We'll just stick a pin in that particular problem.*

With Khatur sheathed, it was safe—safer—for me to go to Mzatal. I broke into a run but skidded to a halt when Ilana appeared a few feet beyond him. She wavered as if a strong wind would topple her. Her hide was a dull grey rather than its usual pearlescent white, and her delicate wings folded in tight as the rakkuhr retreated to leave her in a clear zone.

Without hesitation, I raised a protective rakkuhr veil around Mzatal. "Fuck off, bitch!" I snarled. "You're not taking him."

Ilana regarded me coolly with her large violet eyes, reminding me of a parent waiting for a child to get a tantrum out of their system.

"I can hold this shit all day," I told her with a nod to the veil. Her head tilted. "Can you, Kara Gillian?"

Of course I couldn't, but that didn't matter. The veil was a temporary barrier to keep her away from him until the others finished sealing the rift.

And then what? We couldn't fight Ilana the way we'd fought Xharbek. Not only was I working with a reduced gestalt, but I sure as shit didn't want to give Mzatal any excuse to call Xhan back to him. Besides, Ilana was his ptarl. He wouldn't attack her without overwhelming provocation—especially manipulated as he was. And even if, by some miracle, the rest of us found a way to take her down, Mzatal would suffer terribly as a result.

I had to make a choice: Fight for Mzatal right here and now and almost certainly lose, or bide my time and take action later. I had to hope that with Xharbek gone, the lords and the worlds weren't in the same peril as before. Even though Ilana would most likely continue to follow the course he'd laid out, she wasn't *crazy*. If I was reading matters right, she wouldn't stoop to Xharbek's level of machinations to circumvent the constraints. Moreover, until she herself proclaimed, "Fuck the lords," I had zero reason to believe she'd do Mzatal permanent harm.

Allowing her to take him now was the right choice. And I fucking hated it. Nausea roiled my stomach at the hideous unfairness of it all. I wanted to shriek and stamp my feet and give Ilana a true temper-tantrum, but instead I simply dropped the rakkuhr veil away from Mzatal.

I'm so sorry, my beloved.

Ilana helped him to his feet with a tenderness that made me want to scream. Mzatal drew himself up straight, cast an assessing look around, and met my eyes.

It lasted for less than a hundredth of a heartbeat, but it might as well have been eons. The walls still stood as a formidable barrier around his essence, but that whisper-thin crack remained. Ilana couldn't read or sense the bond and had no idea the crack was there. Mzatal didn't dare widen it and risk drawing her attention, but he also wouldn't close it or repair it. He needed that crack, needed me more than the walls.

Through it his essence radiated, suffusing me with *him*. And, for that hundredth of a heartbeat, I had a glimpse of his perspective—how he foresaw events and actions, and planned thousands of moves in advance.

And, how he so often had to make terrible, heartbreaking

choices, like the one I'd just made, where the only solace was the hope that it would turn out all right, and that the other party would someday understand.

His gaze swept past me as if it had never stopped, eventually returning to Ilana. He offered her a slight smile. She placed a hand on his shoulder.

And then they were gone.

Chapter 47

"Auntie Kara!" Ashava called out.

Auntie Kara? Hey, that was me! I turned and ran to her. "What's up, kid?"

"The dimensional pocket is collapsing!" Worry twisted her delicate features. "You have to get Zakaar and Uncle Sonny. *Right now.*"

"Do I just reach for them like I did for you?"

Ashava gave a quick little nod as she wove a segment of the rift seal with Rhyzkahl. "I'll help." Her voice was a touch higher than usual, the only evidence she was flustered. "Mom! Put your hand on my back, then hold Auntie Kara's hand."

Jill hurried to comply. The instant she touched me, Zack's presence fluttered into my awareness, weak and unsteady.

"I got you, big guy," I murmured. Trusting Ashava's support to guide me, I reached and made instant contact, then braced as Zack used me like an anchor point to haul his way through the interdimensions.

A heartbeat later, Sonny and Zack tumbled onto the spongy asphalt. Frost crusted their skin, and Sonny's face had a disturbing blue cast to it. He rolled to his back and sucked air in desperate gasps. Zack lay still and staring, face twisted in a grimace of pain, and body semitransparent as if he were part ghost.

Jill ran and dropped to her knees beside him. "Zack!" She shot me a frantic look. "Kara, *do* something!"

"I'm working on it," I said, even though I had no idea how to cure a failing demahnk.

Zack croaked something I couldn't make out.

I crouched by his side. "Say again?"

"Ra . . . kkuhr." The word came out in a raspy whisper.

"Oh shit." We'd pulled him straight into a swirling fog of demahnk hell. "Hold on." I didn't have the resources left for anything flashy, but more than enough to nudge the rakkuhr out of the way. Seconds later, Zack lay on rakkuhr-free ground. He looked just as faded, but he breathed easier, and the agony left his face.

Sonny groaned, rolled to his side, and puked. But at least his color was close to normal. Jill shifted to cradle Zack's head in her lap. "You're going to be okay," she whispered.

Zack offered her a weak smile. "Better now." He groped for my hand and wrapped fingers with barely enough substance to be palpable around mine. "Szerain. What has he done?"

"He broke the ptarl bond with Xharbek then collapsed," I told him. "He's safe with Turek now."

"Not safe," he said, voice so thin a puff of breeze could have stolen the words. "Dying. Essence ruptured."

My smile vanished as the horrific realization hit me. "And left to bleed out," I said. It's what Xharbek would have done to me if he'd managed to rip Elinor's essence away. Szerain was dying. Zack was dying. It was *bullshit* to get this far only to lose them.

No way in hell would I let that happen without a fight. I leaned down close to Zack's ear. "Both of you are essence-wounded from having broken ptarl bonds. You volunteered to be Szerain's guard and guardian here on Earth. You kept him sane. Neither of you were free to bond then, but what's stopping you now?"

"An oath."

"Fuck the oath," I retorted. "How can it mean shit when it's used to perpetuate slavery and anathema?"

His fingers spasmed against mine. "You're right. It's meaningless in this new world. Better to have wholeness from two shattered halves."

"Exactly. It makes perfect sense," I said, though I knew a bond took place on a level that had little to do with logic. "A ptarl bond will strengthen you both and give y'all the resources to heal."

Eons of tension seemed to drain from him. "If he is amenable."

If he wasn't, I'd kick his ass until he was. "Turek! Bring Szerain, please."

Jill and I shifted Zack into a sitting position. Jill tucked in behind him and wrapped her arms around his chest, supporting. "Our daughter is so perfect," she told him, voice rough. Her eyes went to where Ashava worked to finish sealing the rift. "She saved us all. From now on, we'll be right by her side, watching over her. Everything's going to be okay now."

I hoped she was right.

Szerain's head lolled as Turek carried him over and settled beside Zack. Szerain rested against Turek's belly scales as if in a living demon-chair.

"Must touch him," Zack said. "Must ask."

I lifted his hand and placed it on Szerain's forearm, covered it with my own hand to keep it from slipping off.

Szerain's eyes flew open. "Zakaar."

Zack's hand tingled under mine, and I sensed communication happening at the speed of thought.

Szerain sat taller and placed his hand over Zack's heart. "So be it."

From beside the rift, Ashava began to sing a haunting melody that transcended language. It wound through me, familiar but not, and so mournful and joyous at the same time it hurt to experience it. She and Rhyzkahl wove the final segment of the seal, and ignited its protection.

Bryce's legs buckled as Seretis's presence left him. Idris threw an arm around Bryce and helped him sit without falling, then plopped down a couple of feet away. Bryce's eyes went to where Jill held Zack. The smallest of sighs escaped him, but then he gave an equally minute nod and looked away. Scanning for threats. Guarding.

My throat tightened. I knew exactly what had just gone through Bryce's mind, as clearly as if I had the mind-reading abilities of a lord. He loved Jill, and that little nod was him resolving to be the best friend he could be for her, to push everything else away—because to do otherwise would hurt her. He was a good, decent guy—one who'd been forced to be a bad one for far too long.

Rhyzkahl pulled a cell phone from a dimensional pocket. His demeanor revealed nothing of his feelings on seeing Zack—his parent and ex-ptarl—in this state.

Zack's face relaxed into an expression of wonder and bliss, as if an eternity of pain had suddenly lifted. He nuzzled Jill's cheek. "All is well now, precious one," he breathed.

Hot damn. He deserved this. After all he'd been through, it was time he—

In the blink of an eye, Zack went from semitransparent to barely corporeal—like a ghost with a faintly perceptible, though still solid, outline. Brilliant sparkles gathered beneath Szerain's hand and swirled like a pool of prismatic stars. Zack's demahnk essence.

"What's happening?" Jill asked with understandable worry.

"It's going to be okay," I said with a knowing nod, even though I had absolutely zero idea what was happening.

The sparkles began to travel up Szerain's arm. I gasped in awe as they flowed beneath my hand, each sparkle an unfathomable glimpse into a boundless universe. They swirled in Szerain's chest before fading as if absorbed. From their brief but profound touch, I understood just enough to . . . understand— though I had a feeling my brain was combing the impressions down to something that would make half-ass sense to a mere human.

The demahnk were *Ekiri*. Xharbek, Ilana, Helori, and the rest of the ptarls—the whole lot, including Rho. And the Ekiri were freaking *aliens*. Part of a big collective of telepathic noncorporeals who basically spent their immortal lives going from planet to planet, or dimension to dimension.

Their modus operandi was to take on the form of native species to observe, interact, and expand their awareness as a collective, with some remaining as non-corporeal "overseers" so the rest could roleplay to their heart's content.

Eventually, the collective would either move on or, if the world met enigmatic-to-me criteria, the overseers would take their corporeal form and "arrive" as otherworldly visitors. At this point, overseers and roleplayers alike would work toward their oh-so-noble mission of uplifting the native inhabitants.

They interfered because, why not? It was what they did and who they were. They made worlds *better*.

Until they didn't.

They broke the demon realm, and Earth right along with it. Not on purpose, but eight thousand years later, the end result was the same.

The Ekiri were like potency magnets. Their mere presence in the demon realm drew potency from Earth through the connecting interdimensional umbilicus, changing the balance on both worlds. Unfortunately, the phenomenon was beyond even their vast experience, and they were completely blind to their role in it.

In an early effort to reverse the flow, Zakaar rallied a team of nineteen intrepid Ekiri to explore, investigate, and assess Earth. It was a radical plan, considering the Ekiri had never split their collective between two worlds, but Zakaar sought a solution and would not be swayed.

The nineteen took human form and assimilated into Earth societies, all while actively fighting the outflow of potency. For two thousand years, the Earth team slowed the potency drain, but it was a losing battle, for they hadn't yet realized the true cause of the problem. Planetary instability of the demon realm increased, and the surface rakkuhr crept toward levels that were toxic to Ekiri.

During this time, Zakaar and the Earth-Ekiri immersed in the role of their chosen form. They interacted, entered into relationships, and even produced offspring who, as for eons past, were wholly of the native species—in this case, human.

Until they weren't.

To the utter shock of the Ekiri collective, after two millennia of human offspring, eleven true Ekiri-human hybrids were conceived, all of whom carried both human and Ekiri traits. Mzatal was the first, and Kadir the last, still in the womb when Zakaar and Helori discovered that not only were the Ekiri themselves the cause of the planet-disrupting imbalance, but the hybrids were beginning to cause instability on the potency depleted Earth.

Causing harm to worlds was anathema.

The Ekiri collective chose to abandon the demon realm before more damage was done—yet without intervention, both worlds were doomed. Faced with a moral dilemma, and unwilling to leave their sons to die with the planets, Zakaar and the other ten who had sired hybrids made a pact: They would remain behind in order to guide their offspring and stabilize the worlds—once again challenging Ekiri codes, though this time by separating from the collective.

Controlling strictures were overlaid, including living in the demahnk form—a close mimic of the syraza species, as they were particularly adept at potency manipulation.

Zakaar and Helori lightly manipulated the hybrids in order to suppress their resistance, then abducted them to the demon realm. The simple presence of the hybrids had an immediate though subtle stabilizing effect on the potency-overloaded planet.

But before leaving the demon realm, the collective assigned one other Ekiri to remain as an impartial overseer. Xharbek.

The sparkle-touch faded. I blinked then sighed. It had imparted far more, but the rest would take time for me to process.

Zack's ghostly form faded to nothing, leaving Jill with an armload of empty clothing.

"Where's Zack?" she demanded. "What the fuck just happened?"

Szerain's head dropped back against Turek's scales, and he released a long, slow breath. "He's with me for now," he said, voice utterly weary but equally calm. "He's safe. Doesn't want you to worry."

Jill stiffened, every possible emotion other than "not worried" passing over her face. Behind her, Sonny sat up, eyes on her. I felt his talent at work, a deeply calming influence that had helped Zack make it this far.

A measure of the stress melted from Jill. "What does that mean?" she asked, looking from Szerain to me.

"He couldn't hold a physical form any longer," I told her, drawing on the *understanding* that Zack had shared as he passed into Szerain. "But he couldn't simply go non-corporeal either because he's cut off from the other demahnk, and has been ever since he broke the bond with Rhyzkahl. He was dying."

A flicker of movement drew my attention. I glanced up in time to see Rhyzkahl travel away with a syraza.

Ashava came and sat by her mother, snuggling in as Jill draped an arm across her shoulders and pulled her close.

"So . . . what did Zack do?" Jill asked as if unsure she wanted to know.

Ashava spoke up first. "He needed to go dormant, and Szerain agreed to host him," she said with quiet reverence. "He couldn't survive in isolation."

Szerain climbed to his feet with Turek's help. "He's in stasis, under my protection. It's similar to how I preserved Elinor's essence by attaching it to Kara. Also, his presence gives the wound Xharbek ripped in my essence the resources to heal. This way, we both have a chance."

Though Jill didn't look at all happy about the situation, she seemed resigned to it. "All right. What happens now?"

"He'll conserve energy and regenerate," I said with as much

confidence as I could stuff into my voice. "When the conditions are right, he'll be able to separate from Szerain."

Her eyes narrowed. "What conditions?"

Ashava looked up at her. "When the demahnk reach out for him to rejoin them."

Jill's expression took on a fierce edge as she hugged Ashava close. "Then I guess we'd we better light a fire under their asses."

Ashava giggled and squeezed her mother's waist.

I'd picked up on other possible outcomes during Zack's sparkly essence transfer to Szerain, but I kept them to myself. I had no idea how much Ashava knew, plus Jill was already on overload. Though I had yet to fully process the "understanding," I now grasped what Zack meant when he'd said it was better to have wholeness from two shattered halves. Zack's chances were slim, while Szerain's were good. Zack was willing to sacrifice himself for Szerain to be whole if it came down to that.

Jill didn't need to know the odds. Not at the moment, at least. Besides, we'd beaten crappy odds too many times to let them get in the way now. All we needed was a chance, and we certainly had that.

"Kara." Bryce approached, phone in hand. "Text from the house. Both of the pods have changed from black to opalescent."

"Right," I said. "Because we haven't had enough weirdness yet."

"Well, you keep raising the max-weirdness bar," he said with a chuckle.

"It's a gift," I said. "All right. We've destroyed enough for one day. Go ahead and tell the crew at Jill's house they can return to the compound. We'll wrap up here and join them in time for afternoon coffee."

He cocked an eyebrow at me. "You mean afternoon tea?"

"Please. If I ever ask for tea, you'll know I'm being impersonated by a syraza."

Chapter 48

With Xharbek defeated, the valve-rift secured, and various entities rescued, it didn't take long to wrap things up. Szerain carried out much-needed lordly healing on Sonny, and Idris volunteered to remain with the squads at ground zero to help with general mop-up as well as survey the area for any missed rifts or dangerous aberrations. When I suggested we delay the debrief until morning, not a single soul argued.

That settled, we bundled our people, demons, and lords into our vehicles. Szerain chauffeured Jill, Ashava, Turek, and me in the APC while Bryce followed with Elinor and Sonny in Jill's truck.

Szerain and I spent the drive in companionable silence, each of us needing time to process everything. Jill and Ashava cuddled in the seats behind us, their quiet conversation a soothing background noise.

As we pulled up to the house, Giovanni bounded down the front steps. Before the truck even stopped moving, Elinor leaped out and into his arms. An enthusiastic greeting ensued, which Giovanni broke off right before it got R-rated, then he swept Elinor up in his arms and carried her inside.

Fortunately, everyone else seemed content to let the vehicles come to complete stops before unloading.

Turek bounded off toward his favorite sprinkler. Szerain swung Ashava down from the APC then gave Jill a hand. Bryce busied himself with helping Sonny out of the truck, and tried not to be obvious about his quick glances toward Jill and Ashava.

"Uncle Bryce!" Ashava dashed up to him. "Uncle Sonny told

me lots and lots about you, and he was right! You were soooooo amazing at the rift."

Bryce startled but recovered quickly and smiled down at her. "You can't trust a single thing Sonny says. He's kooky in the head." He twirled one finger at his temple.

Ashava giggled. "He said you were funny and nice, too!" She turned her blue eyes on me. "Auntie Kara? Is it okay if Mom and I cook dinner?"

I heaved a dramatic sigh. "Gee, I dunno. Everyone really loves my cooking, especially my macaroni and ketchup casserole."

Bryce shuddered. "As the security chief of this compound, and for everyone's gastrointestinal safety, I'm putting Ashava and Jill in charge of tonight's dinner."

She let out a delighted little girl squeal. "Hurray!" With eager exuberance, she hustled a smiling Jill toward the house.

Bryce watched the pair until they disappeared inside then turned to Sonny. "Wanna see the security setup we have here?"

Sonny's face lit up. "You know it!"

The two men headed toward the outbuildings, already chattering like magpies about rotations and training and equipment.

I watched them go, truly glad that Bryce had Sonny here with him. Bryce had been Sonny's rock of support during their murderous years with Farouche, and right now Bryce needed an old friend.

And all the chicks are back in the nest. Everyone was here and safe and slipping into comfortable routine. It all felt like a little piece of *normal*, something each of us craved after the trauma of the day. Didn't matter that we knew it was only temporary.

I glanced at Szerain. "You want to check out the pods with me?"

"I thought you'd never ask," he said with a smile.

Michael burst from the house, his face twisted in distress. "Two kitties are *gone*, Kara! There's Fuzzykins and Bumper and Cake and Granger and Dire but but but no Fillion no Squig *anywhere*!"

"You know how mischievous those two are," I said, keeping my tone light and comforting. "I bet they found a super secret hidey hole. Didn't Lilith stay behind to look for them? She'll bring them home when they get hungry and come out."

He didn't seem the least bit convinced. "But I already looked in and out and everywhere." He wrung his hands. "They're *gone* for real."

Bryce turned, already halfway to the security office. "Hey, Michael?" he called. "Could you help me with something over here?"

Michael frowned, reluctant to be distracted from his kitten quest, but headed his way. I shot Bryce a grateful smile. Always paying attention. Always taking care of the business at hand.

Szerain and I continued inside, where the pods dominated the front room. They definitely weren't black with red veins anymore. Like huge opal spheres, they shone milky white with gorgeous rainbow colors.

Szerain whistled low. "I didn't have time to check them out earlier." He crouched between the pods and placed a hand lightly against each. "They'll emerge very soon."

A nervous flutter of worry started up in my stomach. "Do you know what Marco and Cory will end up like? And what's going to happen to the two ilius that went in with them? Will they stay around?" I couldn't quite see Detective Marco Knight and his sidekick Li'l Ilius making a big splash with the New Orleans PD.

Szerain gave me the side eye. "If all has gone according to demon plan, there are no ilius anymore. I mean, not in that form. They're absorbed to guide the mutation."

I gulped. "Absorbed like used up? Or absorbed to be diabolical little masterminds in control?" I clearly remembered Earl Chris, the violent, tentacle-handed mutant I'd tangled with in Fed Central's medical wing.

"More like silent partners," he said. "Unless something went wrong, Marco and Cory will still be Marco and Cory. With a little added perspective."

"But they didn't choose that," I said, scowling.

"In a way, they did. Not on a conscious level, but back when they first made contact with the mutagen at ground zero, something in them attracted the attention of the guide-ilius. There has to be a compatibility match, or the ilius won't latch on."

I made a face. "That's still wrong," I grumbled, though the concept gave me hope for the two men. Before he mutated, Earl Chris had been a repeat offender criminal, with an existing tendency toward violence.

Szerain shrugged. "So much is."

"Speaking of wrong," I said conversationally, "I picked up some stuff from Zack when he merged with you."

"I did too. A little. Before he withdrew into stasis." He went quiet.

I dropped to sit cross-legged before him. "Are we going to talk about it, or shall we continue to ignore the elephant in the room?"

Szerain gave me a long look then sketched a privacy sigil and set it spinning above our heads. "I'm weary of secrets."

He knew I held at least one secret from him, since I hadn't allowed him to read me after the summoning. But this wasn't a good time for me to blurt out, *Oh, by the way, I need you to give up your essence blade.*

Instead I said, "You lords are the children of the demahnk—the Ekiri—and they fucking used you."

Grief and anger swam through his eyes. "Yes. They used and enslaved their own children. They were charged by the main body of the Ekiri to rebalance the worlds, and we were their fucking tools, able to manipulate the core potency that they couldn't tolerate. They stripped our memories and crippled our abilities to keep us from rebelling."

"I'm so sorry." Then, because that felt insufficient, I took his hand and added in demon, "Tah sesekur di lahn." *I hold sorrow for you.*

"Dak lahn," he murmured and didn't pull away. After a moment he took a deeper breath and managed a light smile. "There was something about Xharbek, too. Did you pick up on that?"

"Some," I said. "There's still a lot to unpack that I haven't processed yet. But I got that Zack thinks part of why Xharbek went off the deep end was because he didn't have a kid."

Szerain nodded. "He was picked to stay on as the overseer for that very reason, but it bit him in the ass. The Ekiri are all connected, and it's that parental link to the offspring that helps the other demahnk-Ekiri stay relatively sane, despite the rakkuhr poisoning."

"The bond Xharbek made with you after Rho did his planetary tree thing wasn't as effective for him as a true ptarl-parental bond."

"Yes, though he lasted a lot longer than he would have without it," he said.

We fell into an easy silence. Voices drifted down the hallway from the kitchen, over a background of soft classical music. Jill and Ashava. Happy.

It was lovely, yet I couldn't relax and enjoy it. Instead I struggled to grasp a concept that had been floating just beyond my reach this entire time. The more I focused on it, the more it evaded me.

Fine. I didn't want that stupid ol' concept anyway. There were plenty of other interesting things for me to waste brain space on. Opal pods. Missing kittens. A young girl's musical laugh. My desperate need for a shower.

The concept wandered into my head and made itself comfortable. Not all of it, and there was plenty I still couldn't get a handle on it, but it was enough.

"The Ekiri are returning," I said before it could slip away again.

"Ah. I've been trying to tease that out." Szerain's brows drew together. "That was the ticking clock that drove Xharbek to his final rash actions. They're coming back to reassess the situation."

"What does that mean for the rest of the demahnk?" I asked. "Or, for that matter, the lords, demons, and humanity?"

"It's an unknown that we have yet to face."

I offered him a crooked smile. "Around here, that's a typical Monday."

Szerain chuckled then quickly dispelled the privacy sigil as Giovanni rushed in, bearing a laptop and a worried expression.

"Kara, you must view this news clip of import." Giovanni placed the laptop on the coffee table and clicked play on the video.

The clip was a fairly mundane report that showed Senator Olson speaking to an elementary school auditorium full of parents and press about his education initiative.

I was about to ask Giovanni why he'd brought this to me when the camera panned over a cluster of smiling first and second graders sitting cross-legged on the stage.

"Holy shit," I breathed. The view was brief, but it was enough. Kadir crouched in the midst of the children, his hands on the shoulders of the boy and girl on either side of him. He leaned over and spoke in the girl's ear, eliciting a giggle from her. Behind the group stood Pellini, wearing a men-in-black suit and sunglasses. Right beside him was Paul Ortiz, fingers moving rapidly over a tablet screen.

I exchanged a telling look with Szerain. What the hell was Lord Creepy playing at?

Giovanni stopped the playback. "I recognized Lord Kadir and thought you needed to see."

"You're right. I did. Good catch." Kadir's hand on shoulder thing was an unpleasant echo of Xharbek and Ilana's position when influencing Mzatal. Or maybe I was reading too much into it. Surely Pellini and Paul wouldn't go along with anything potentially harmful to the kids. But *damn*. Time to add "Keep tabs on sneaky lord" to my to-do list. "Thanks, Giovanni. Could you please leave the laptop? I'd like to have another look at the video in a few."

Proud of his discovery, he headed back toward the war room with a spring in his step.

"Thoughts?" I asked Szerain.

He shook his head slowly. "Kadir has always been an enigma, impossible to predict apart from his fastidious potency management . . . and his sadistic predilections."

Knight's sphere rocked, putting a stop to my speculations. "Is it time?" I asked, scrambling to my feet.

Szerain placed a hand on the surface then pulled it away. "This one's ready."

"Can you read them? Do they know what's happened?"

"With the human-demon mix, I can only get impressions. But they seem to be aware of the circumstances."

I fidgeted, ridiculously nervous about the outcome.

Knight's pod shimmered then dissolved into a cloud of mist with a sound like a thousand tiny bells. He lay naked, curled in a fetal position, and covered with a thin layer of clear mucus stuff. Nothing about him seemed different from before, except for a very un-Knight-like tranquil smile.

"Marco?" I said as Szerain ducked out of the room.

"Yeah, Kara?" he replied, voice not at all muffled by the mucus.

"You . . . okay?"

"I think I just might be."

Szerain returned with a couple of sheets and a stack of towels. I breathed a thanks then grabbed a sheet and draped it over Knight. He pushed up to sit then scrubbed the gunk off his face with a towel. His irises were a shimmery amber color ringed with gold, and a hint of rakkuhr flickered deep in the pupils. But other than the unearthly and compelling eyes, he looked normal. Unchanged.

He lowered the towel, stunned surprise on his face. "I can't see anything," he breathed.

Sick dread flooded me. "You're *blind*?" I waved my hand in front of his eyes.

Grinning, he batted my hand away. "Not like that. I don't *see* . . . stuff."

Comprehension kicked in. He wasn't getting unwanted peeks into other people's lives anymore. He was finally free of that burden. "Dude, that's awesome!"

"The *sight* isn't gone," he said. "In fact, it's probably better than before. But I have an on-off switch for it now." He let out a long, relaxed sigh. "And I don't ever *have* to turn it on."

After the loner life he'd led because of his ability, it wouldn't surprise me if he never activated it again. I had no idea what the demons got out of the process, which worried me, but so far Knight seemed to be okay.

"Your eye color is a little odd," I told him. "I mean, it's really cool and all, but you'll need to wear colored contacts at work if you want to keep this to yourself."

He gave a genuine laugh. "Are you kidding? I've been the freak of the NOPD for no reason anyone could nail down. This would be a cake walk." He pulled at the gunk stuck in his hair. "But you're right. Best to play it cool."

"Good plan." I grinned. "You hungry?"

"Starving. But I could really use a shower first, if you don't mind."

I sent him off with a promise of a loaner t-shirt and fatigue pants, unspeakably relieved that he'd emerged oriented and accepting and calm.

As soon as he left, Cory's pod vibrated.

"He was waiting," Szerain said.

"I suppose I can understand wanting a little privacy for un-podding," I said with a shaky laugh. Marco had come through all right, but . . . yeah. Demons. Pods. Mutations. I grabbed a sheet.

The sphere dispersed to mist, but I stood gaping rather than draping. Like Knight, Cory lay in a fetal position, but unlike Knight, he was definitely . . . different.

No way would we be hiding this with a pair of contacts. Though Cory remained quite human-shaped, and his right leg still ended mid-thigh, the skin of his shoulders and upper arms was alive with slowly shifting colors, rich and bright like impossibly flawless tattooing. His hair hung to his shoulders in perfect waves, with each strand a vibrant hue—hysterically ironic considering that the man had always avoided anything brighter than brown.

But the clincher was the trio of tails that curled around him. Bright and furry tails as thick as Ashava's wrist and who-the-hell-knew how long.

Cory shifted, tails moving with sinuous grace to help him push up to a sit. I snapped out of my shock and thrust the sheet around him.

"Welcome back!" I grabbed a towel and held it out.

He took it with a smile and wiped off his face. "Glad to be back," he said. A bright blue tail snaked out to better arrange the sheet over his privates. Cory cocked his head at the tail and laughed. "Ain't that some shit?"

"Um. Yeah. That's one way to put it."

His mustache was gone, and the rest of his face held zero hint of stubble. When he ran his hand over his hair, it seemed to move of its own accord. Like Knight, his pupils held a flicker of rakkuhr, but Cory's irises gradually shifted from one rich color to another. Turquoise to amber to violet and more. Mesmerizing.

"I've been dying to try this!" Using the tails as support, he stood and got his balance on his one leg, then walked several steps—slowly, cautiously, and bit awkwardly—but most certainly attaining ambulation.

"Nice!" I said in genuine awe. "The basement shower is open if you think you can make it down the steps, or you can wait for Marco to finish up in the bathroom down the hall." This was surreal as hell, but at least the changes seemed to suit both men.

"I'll give the stairs a try." Cory retucked the sheet around his waist then pointed a tail at the laptop. "Someone's trying to get your attention."

"Huh?" The camera light was blinking erratically. "Oh. I'll get our tech to check it out."

"No. It's Morse code. It's repeating 'Kara' over and over."

"What the . . ." I had no reason to doubt Cory, considering his ham radio skills. And there was only one person I knew who could and would hack into our system—into *any* system.

"A new pattern started as soon as you looked over," Cory said then watched it closely until the light stopped blinking. "It says, 'Thought you would want to see this. Paul.'"

Not only was Paul watching us, he knew Cory was a ham

radio operator and would know Morse code. Damn, the kid was scary sharp—as tapped in to electronic "flows" as I was to the arcane ones back when I could get all lordy on the nexus.

The screen went dark, then a single picture appeared. Perhaps from the camera of a laptop, judging by the angle. Paul had eyes everywhere.

I leaned in close to get a better view. Tessa was seated, half-facing the camera. Rhyzkahl stood behind her, hands gripping her shoulders, and expression dark. She looked haggard and worn. Not at all like the Tessa I knew. Her typically wild and curly blond hair was cropped short, and her eyes were puffy and bloodshot. In the background, Angus McDunn stood in profile. His expression and raised fist led me to believe he was arguing with someone off camera.

Ten seconds later, the image vanished, and the screen returned to the paused Kadir video. I pushed down the powerful urge to slap duct tape over the camera—mostly because it would be pointless considering how easily he could spy on us through the many security cameras we had around the place.

"What was that all about?" Cory asked.

"Just a jokester friend," I said lightly. "He probably thought he'd have me stumped with the Morse code. Nothing to worry about." I gave a little laugh. No need to drag Cory any deeper without reason.

"Lucky I was here." He smiled, but the shrewd look in his eye reminded me that he'd been a cop for over fifteen years. He wasn't fooled. "Shower time," he said then tail-stumped off, balance and coordination improving with every odd step.

As soon as he was gone, Szerain shoved the lid of the laptop closed. "Shit."

"My sentiments, exactly."

"You have a plan?"

"Not right now, I don't. We'll come up with something after the debrief tomorrow." I gazed down at the crushed sofa-bed and the puddles of goo, the only remaining evidence of the two pods. "If Tessa needs help, we'll help her. If she's an enemy, we'll capture her. Either way, we need to root her out along with whatever crew she's hanging with." I tugged both hands through my hair. "I think Boudreaux may know more about McDunn's whereabouts than he's letting on. And maybe this overture from Paul means he'll be more accessible. But I need to eat and sleep before I can deal with any of it."

Michael shoved the front door open. "Hey, everyone!" he hollered. "Squig and Fillion were hiding in Jill's truck. You gotta see!" He dashed off and leaped down the steps.

Jill came down the hall, followed by Ashava. "What's going on?"

"It seems the missing catlets have been found," I said then gestured toward the goo-puddles. "And we have two more for dinner. Makonite and Krawkor, formerly known as Marco Knight and Cory Crawford, and who are both currently showering off pod-gook."

Jill muttered something under her breath then followed Szerain and me outside. Bryce leaned on the porch rail, a big grin plastered on his face. His gaze tracked something in the air. A bird?

Jill moved close to Bryce's side. "Is that a . . ."

Bryce gave a laugh. "Yes. Yes it is."

I stared. From high above the driveway, a metallic-silver furball streaked toward a bewildered, tongue-lolling Sammy.

"Fillion!" Michael called. "Be a good kitty."

The catlet spread big bat wings wide to slow his dive, then spat a weak bolt of arcane energy at Sammy's tail before climbing again. Sammy yelped but immediately bounded around, barking upward as if wanting more of the game.

"Bryce?" I managed to get out.

"Seems the kittens stowed away in the back of Jill's truck," he said, eyes dancing with amusement. "She drove them straight to the middle of the mutagen."

Jill smacked him on the arm, grinning. "Not on purpose!"

"Oh no," I groaned. "And they didn't have makkas, so they mutated." Holy shit, that was *fast*. If we hadn't shut down the flow, the world would have been unrecognizable in a matter of days.

"Are they still friendly?" I asked. "And where's the other one?"

"I'll show you!" Michael dashed down the steps and peered into the bushes. "C'mon out, Squig! Peoples here to see you."

Out of the bushes stalked a winged catlet covered with furry green scales, tail straight up in the air. A tail covered with needle spikes instead of fur. I had the awful suspicion that she just might be able to hurl them.

"Good girl, Squig." Michael scooped her up and cradled her close, the biggest grin ever plastered on his face. "See, Kara?"

I grinned right back, relieved that Squig had flattened the needle spikes to avoid injuring Michael. "I see."

Szerain draped his arm over my shoulders. "Just wait 'til they grow up."

"I almost feel sorry for Fuzzykins," I said, giving a mock-shudder.

Ashava tugged on Jill's hands. "Mom, can I play with Fillion? Pleeeeeease?"

"Sure, sweetie. Just be careful with . . ." She trailed off as Ashava ran and made a flying leap off the porch, transforming midair into a blue and silver dragonet about twice the size of Fillion. "Alrighty then," Jill choked out then laughed as Ashava and Fillion started a game of aerial tag.

Szerain's arm tightened around me. I looked over to see tears gleaming in his eyes as he watched the young qaztehl play.

"She's beautiful," he said in a cracked whisper. "So free."

The pain and envy in his voice tugged at my heart. He'd been crippled and enslaved for thousands of years. How could he dare to believe he might someday be truly free?

I pulled him close. "You'll join her up there soon. I promise you that."

He gave a shaky smile, hope flickering weakly behind the despair in his eyes.

Jill peered toward the sky. "Ashava, dinner in ten minutes! No wings or claws at the table!"

The dragonet bugled an acknowledgement then did a neat barrel roll around Fillion.

"Spaghetti and meatballs, with green beans from Rhyzkahl's garden," Jill announced to the rest of us as she pushed off the rail. "If y'all behave, Ashava and I will make chocolate donuts for dessert."

I sucked in a breath. "Real chocolate donuts?"

"Real chocolate donuts." Her eyes sparkled. "I made sure to get all the ingredients during my pre-summoning errands."

"Sounds like heaven," I said, sighing happily. I placed my hand over the leaf and Mzatal's ring, pressed both tight over his sigil, and willed an impression of this one perfect moment to him. Later, I'd tackle demon pacts, lordy machinations, alien antics, and the billion other issues that weighed on my heart and mind.

But for this little slice of now, I planned to enjoy the company of family, friends, and demonic battle kittens.

Glossary

Terms Related to the Demon Realm

Anomaly: A tear in the dimensional fabric. Various causes. Effects can be catastrophic. Repairs done by demahnk, demonic lords, and (for small anomalies) syraza.

Blade (verb): To stab a being with an essence blade. With rare exceptions, results in permanent death and a scattering or consumption of the target's essence. The body of one killed by an essence blade will not discorporeate.

Demon realm and demon language: The world of the demons and demonic lords. The demon language has never been fully mastered by a human because of the verbal complexity and telepathic component. The same sound may have a multitude of different meaning depending on the telepathic pattern behind it. The demon word for their world is heavily telepathic and seventeen syllables.

Demahnk: Non-corporeal beings who take on demon and human forms. Their demon form looks like a large syraza with ridges on the torso and skull. Sometimes called "Elder syraza." Each of the eleven is ptarl bound to a lord, with the exception of Zakaar. The lords are half demahnk, half human.

Demahnk Council/Demon Council: Comprised of the eleven demahnk ptarl/advisors of the lords. Holds power and influence that Kara is still discovering. Enforcers of Szerain's exile.

Demonic lord: Half human, half demahnk hybrid. Able to monitor, maintain, and influence the potency flows of the demon realm.

Earthgate: One of eleven gateways between the Earth and demon realm. Defunct for thousands of years.

Eleven: A significant number in the demon realm in rituals, architecture, and managing potency. Also, the number of demonic lords (before Ashava).

Discorporeate: The immediate dissolution and disappearance of the physical form after death when the death occurs on the non-home world. A demon that dies on Earth will discorporeate with a chance of resurrecting in the demon realm, and the same goes for a human who dies in the demon realm. Death by blading precludes discorporeation.

Essence blades: Three knives created by Mzatal as artifacts of power. *Khatur* (Mzatal), *Xhan* (Rhyzkahl's, but currently with Mzatal), *Vsuhl* (Szerain).

Lord headache: Excruciating head pain triggered by thoughts of topics deemed off limits by the demahnk council.

Manipulation: The altering of memories or controlling of actions through telepathic means. Utilized by demonic lords and demahnk.

Mutagen: Specialized rakkuhr that can cause mutations.

Mraztur: Derogatory demon word used by Kara and her allies to refer to the demonic lords unified against her personal interests and those of Earth. Rhyzkahl, Jesral, Amkir, and Kadir. Rough translation (per Seretis): motherfucking asshole dickwad defilers.

Nexus: A confluence of potency streams harnessed as a focal point of power in each lord's realm. Universally marked by a platform of stone, wood, or crystal surrounded by eleven columns. Foundation for the most powerful rituals. Mzatal and Kara created a basic nexus in Kara's back yard. Mzatal later amplified it by anchoring Rhyzkahl to it.

Plexus: The chamber in each lord's realm where the arcane potency flows of the planet can be monitored, manipulated, and adjusted by a demonic lord. Used daily, often for many hours at a time. Most are furnished for comfort during long work sessions. Kara's rough translation: *a demonic lord's man-cave.*

Ptarl: The demahnk counselor and advisor to a demonic lord.

Qaztahl: Demon word for demonic lord. Both singular and plural. The lords are human in general appearance, but have a palpable energy aura and are able to shape and wield potency. Mind readers. Fully responsible for maintaining the potency stability of the planet. It is the one matter they agree on without question.

Rowan: As yet enigmatic personality that Rhyzkahl intended to overlay on Kara. Demonstrated arrogance and sense of invulnerability. Seems to be familiar with Szerain.

The Cataclysm: Demon realm disaster that began in the 17th century and lasted nearly a century. Earthquakes, floods, fire rain, and rifts in the dimensional fabric. Started by a ritual performed by Szerain and Elinor.

The Conclave: An annual meeting of all qaztahl where global issues are addressed and plexus schedules for the upcoming year are confirmed. Outward hostility is frowned upon. Intrigue is rife.

The groves: Clusters of white-trunked trees that form a network of organic teleportation nodes, with one in each realm of the eleven qaztahl and a dozen or so more scattered across the planet. Animate and sentient. a.k.a. Rho. Kara has a unique relationship with the groves. Teleportation can only be activated by a lord, demahnk, or Kara. Each grove has a *mehnta* as its caretaker—a lifelong commitment.

The "others": The vague designation given by Zack for ones he cannot speak of who, along with the Demahnk Council, hold and enforce ancient oaths.

The Three: Mzatal, Rhyzkahl, and Szerain when they each bore their essence blades. Dominated the demon realm unchallenged and unchallengeable for centuries.

Valve: An arcane conduit between the demon realm and Earth that acts as a potency pressure valve to help stabilize the demon realm.

Terms Related to Earth

Arcane Investigations: FBI special task force in charge of demon and arcane-related action and investigation.

Bertha: Cory Crawford's 1976 Chevy Nova. Kitted out with ham radio equipment.

Bloodbath Summoning: An attempt over thirty years ago by Peter Cerise and five other summoners to summon Szerain. Rhyzkahl came through instead and slaughtered all the summoners but Cerise, (including Kara's grandmother, Gracie Pazhel). Tessa witnessed.

DIRT: Acronym for Demonic Incursion Retaliation and Tactics. Special units on the frontlines of rift formation and invading demon suppression.

DNN: Demon News Network. Television network devoted to coverage of rifts and demon activity.

Federal Command Center a.k.a. Fed Central: Beaulac Ground Zero headquarters for DHS, NSA, CIA, and other national agencies, with the FBI Arcane Investigations task force taking the lead. Located in what used to be the Southern Louisiana Heart Hospital, now converted into a secure compound.

Kara's Kompound: Nickname for Kara's house and property.

Ground Zero: The Beaulac PD parking lot and immediate surroundings. Relates to the valve explosion and its resulting destruction and arcane activity.

Rift: An opening in the dimensional fabric, often manifesting on Earth in the form of surface crevices that span anywhere from a few inches to hundreds of feet in length. Jontari can use them to travel between the demon realm and Earth.

Skeeter: Slang for "mosquito". DIRT code word for a winged demon.

SkeeterCheater: Graphene-enhanced netting capable of holding a demon physically. Relatively immune to their arcane attempts to break free. Used to cover or partially cover rifts to slow demon arrivals. Exorbitantly expensive to produce.

StarFire Security: Legitimate high-end security company owned by J.M. Farouche.

Symbol Man: Peter Cerise. Serial killer who used blood and death magic. Tried to summon and bind Rhyzkahl. Killed by Rhyzkahl.

The Child Find League: Non-profit organization founded by J.M. Farouche to help find missing children. Impressive track record.

The Demonic Lords – the Qaztahl

Amkir (AHM-keer) Ptarl: *Dima*. One of the Mraztur. Light olive complexion, short dark hair. Unsmiling. Known for his temper.

Ashava (Ah-SHA-vah) No ptarl. Two-month old daughter of Jill Faciane and the demankh Zakaar (Zack Garner). Kidnapped by Szerain and Zack. In hiding from Xharbek. The only free demonic lord (a *qaztehl*).

Elofir (EL-oh-fear) Ptarl: *Greeyer*. Short sandy-blond hair. Slim, athletic build. Calm, gentle, deeply caring. Enjoys the quiet of his wooded realm. Zharkat of Michelle Cleland. Pacifist by nature.

Jesral (JEZ-rahl) Ptarl: *Ssahr*. One of the Mraztur. Slim, brown hair, keen gaze, impeccably styled and graceful. Smiling, outwardly friendly. Slick, cold, and calculating.

Kadir (kuh-DEER) Ptarl: *Helori*, estranged. One of the Mraztur. Tall, slender, blond, androgynous. Cold, psychopathic, chaotic, vicious. Utterly brilliant. Lives slightly "out of phase" with the rest of the demon realm. Nicknamed "Creepshow" by Kara. Associated demons: *Sehkeril* (reyza), *Kuktok* (kzak).

Mzatal (muh-ZAH-tull) Ptarl: *Ilana*. Essence Blade: *Khatur*. Also holds Rhyzkahl's *Xhan*. Tall and elegant, keen silver-grey eyes, Asian features, very long jet black hair worn in a braid. Powerful and focused. Creator of the essence blades. Has a bond with Kara. Essence bond: *Gestamar* (reyza), *Dakdak* (ilius). Associated demons: *Safar, Juntihr* (reyza). *Jekki, Faruk* (faas). *Tata, Krum, Wuki* (ilius). *Lazul* (mehnta). *Juke* (kehza). *Anak* (zrila). *Steeev* (syraza)

Rayst (rayst) Ptarl: *Trask*. Partner of Seretis. Swarthy. Stocky build, but moves with grace. Considerate, but not a pushover. Pays attention to the dynamics between others.

Rhyzkahl (REEZ-call) Ptarl: *None* (formerly Zakaar/Zack). One of the Mraztur. Essence Blade: *Xhan* (currently in the possession of Mzatal). Long white-blond hair, ice-blue eyes, tall, muscled, utterly beautiful. Seductive and charming. Betrayed and tortured Kara in a failed ritual to create a weaponized summoner (Rowan) and raise an Earthgate. Exiled from the demon realm by Mzatal and imprisoned beside the nexus in Kara's back yard. Associated demons: *Eilahn, Olihr* (syraza). *Pyrenth* (deceased, reyza). *Kehlirik* (reyza). *Rega* (faas).

Seretis (SAIR-uh-tis) Ptarl: *Lannist*. Partner of Rayst. Chiseled cheekbones, and shoulder length dark, wavy hair, reminiscent of a Spanish soap opera star. Bisexual. Loves being around humans, and has gone to extreme lengths to protect humans in the demon realm from other lords. Essence bond: Bryce Taggart.

Szerain (szair-RAIN) Ptarl: *Xharbek* (in hiding/presumed dead by most). Essence Blade: *Vsuhl*. Brilliant artist. Smart and inquisitive and very patient when his plans call for it. Is called a kiraknikahl—oathbreaker. Diminished and exiled to Earth as Ryan Kristoff, but now free. In hiding from Xharbek. Essence bond: *Turek* (savik).

Vahl (pronounced like the first syllable of volume) Ptarl: *Korlis*. Tall, black, and just the right amount of muscle. Tends toward rash decisions that cause him to be indebted to other lords.

Vrizaar (vree-ZAR) Ptarl: *Fiar* Dark-skinned, bald, with a goatee and no mustache. Dresses like a biblical king, with gold and jewels just shy of gaudy. As cautious and prudent as Vahl isn't when it comes to dealings with the other lords, but not so staid that he doesn't enjoy the thrill of adventure. Loves to sail.

The Demahnk Ptarl

Dima (DEE-muh) Ptarl of Amkir.

Fiar (FEE-ar) Ptarl of Vrizaar.

Greeyer (gree-YEAR) Ptarl of Elofir.

Helori (heh-LOR-ee) Estranged ptarl of Kadir. Supported Kara after Rhyzkahl's torture. Spurned by Kadir. Prefers human form to the "elder syraza" form. Often associates with Mzatal.

Ilana (ih-LAH-nah) Ptarl of Mzatal. Quietly influential.

Korlis (CORE-liss) Ptarl of Vahl.

Lannist (LAN-ist) Ptarl of Seretis. Attempted to thwart the essence bond between Seretis and Bryce.

Ssahr (suh-SAR) Ptarl of Jesral. Essence bound to Xharbek.

Trask: Ptarl of Rayst.

Xharbek (ZAR-beck) Ptarl of Szerain. Considered missing or dead by most until he showed up in pursuit of Zack, Szerain, and

Ashava after the PD valve explosion. Masqueraded as Carl, the morgue tech. Essence bound to the demahnk Ssahr.

Zakaar (zah-CAR) Ex-ptarl of Rhyzkahl. a.k.a. FBI Agent Zack Garner. Broke ptarl bond with Rhyzkahl during the Farouche Plantation incident. Was the guard and guardian of Szerain during his submersion and imprisonment as Ryan Kristoff. Fading and diminished after breaking the bond. Sire of Ashava. In hiding from Xharbek.

Residents on Kara's Property

Bryce Taggart: (40ish) Ex-hitman for J.M. Farouche. Kara's head of security. Has essence bond with demonic lord Seretis. Was a veterinary student when he accidentally shot and killed his roommate. Recruited by J.M. Farouche shortly thereafter. Changed last name from Thatcher. Was once Paul Ortiz's bodyguard.

Bubba Suarez: (early 40s) Security team. Construction specialist. General handyman.

Chet Watson: (mid 50s) Security team. Gunsmith and firearms expert.

David Nguyen: (late 20s) Security team. Tree expert.

Dennis Roper: (early 40s) Security team. Skilled in logistics and planning.

Jill Faciane: (late 20s) Red hair, blue eyes, petite, athletic. Kara's best friend. Custodian of arcane library. Smart and sarcastic. Mother of Ashava. Former crime scene tech. Former gymnast who'd been favored to make the Olympic team before a bad fall.

Jordan Kellum: (mid 30s) Security team. 5'4". Former world-class powerlifter.

Lilith Cantrell: Security team. Tech expert.

Nils Engen: (early 20s) Security team. Medic.

Ronda Greitz: (mid 30s) Security team. Mechanic and engineering specialist.

Sharini Tandon: (late 30s) Security team. Military experience. Black belts in Krav Maga and Danzan Ryū.

Vincent Pellini: (early 40s) DIRT Arcane Specialist. Trained and mentored in the arcane by Kadir. Black hair, dark eyes, mustache, not as overweight as he used to be. Boudreaux's work partner. Works in tandem with Kara. Former detective for the Beaulac PD as a partner to Boudreaux.

Other Security Team Members: Four to eight, as needed.

DIRT– Demonic Incursion Retaliation and Tactics
Named Characters

Joseph Starr, General

Kara Gillian, Arcane Commander

1st Cavalry Unit
    Marcel Boudreaux Lieutenant, unit leader
    Griz Caucasian Shepherd Dog

Alpha Squad
    Debbie Roma Sergeant, squad leader
    Kara Gillian Arcane Specialist/Commander
    Scott Glassman, Corporal
    Aali Ahmed
    Brett Petrev
    Christie Blauser
    Deke Wohlreich
    Harold Chu
    James Abercrombie
    Jeff Hines
    Jude Landon
    Meg Kowal
    Tiffany Hurley

Bravo Squad
    Vince Pellini Arcane Specialist
    Nate Rushton Corporal (deceased)
    Edward Sykes

Incursion Zone 212 (a.k.a. IZ-212, the Spires)
    Herman Hornak Captain
    Lucas Garvey Lieutenant
    Gail White Sergeant
    Jeb Frazier Corporal

Summoners Known to Kara

Aaron Asher: (30s) Katashi's student and associate. Former student of Rasha Hassan Jalal Al-Khouri. Associated with J.M. Farouche and the Mraztur. Whereabouts unknown.

Anton Beck: (40s) Associated with Katashi and the Mraztur. Recruited Idris for Katashi. Whereabouts unknown.

Cherie and Keveen Bergeron: (deceased) Grandparents of Raymond Bergeron a.k.a. Tracy Gordon. Killed by Rhyzkahl in the Bloodbath Summoning.

DIRT Summoners: Eleven summoners from all over the world. Includes Kara and Idris.

Frank McCreary: (deceased) Killed by Rhyzkahl in the Bloodbath Summoning.

Gina Hallsworth: (30s) Associated with Katashi and the Mraztur. Whereabouts unknown.

Graciella "Gracie" Therese Pazhel: Tessa's mother. Kara's maternal grandmother. Sworn summoner of Szerain. Killed by Rhyzkahl in the Bloodbath Summoning.

Idris Palatino: (20) DIRT Arcane Specialist. Delta Squad. Student of Mzatal (and Katashi). Kara's cousin. Son of Tessa and Rhyzkahl. Gifted summoner. Adopted as a baby, and then again as a young teen after his first adoptive parents were killed. Innocence stripped by the Mraztur. Forced to watch his sister raped and ritually tortured and murdered. Killed Isumo Katashi.

Isumo Katashi: (deceased at 100+) Master summoner. Tessa's mentor. Conducted the very first summoning after the arcane ways reopened post-cataclysm. Was once a sworn summoner of Mzatal but betrayed him. Associated with the Mraztur and J.M. Farouche. Every living summoner has been trained by him or by one of his students. Killed by Idris Palatino. Discorporeated.

Peter Cerise/Chief Eddie Morse: (deceased in his 60s) Organized the summoning of Szerain three decades ago that ended in a bloodbath with his wife and five other summoners slain by Rhyzkahl (the Bloodbath Summoning). Sworn summoner of Szerain. Became the serial killer known as the Symbol Man. Killed by Rhyzkahl when he attempted to summon and bind the lord.

Rasha Hassan Jalal Al-Khouri: (80s) One of Katashi's first students. Came out of summoning retirement to work with Mzatal in the demon realm. Associated with J.M. Farouche. Antagonistic relationship with summoner Aaron Asher.

Robert Lamothe: (deceased) Killed by Rhyzkahl in the Bloodbath Summoning.

Tessa Pazhel: (late 40s) Kara's aunt and mentor. Student of Katashi. Mother of Idris Palatino. Frizzy blond hair and eclectic fashion sense. Raised Kara from age eleven. Worked closely with Katashi. Betrayed Kara to serve Katashi's interests. Whereabouts unknown.

Tracy Gordon/Raymond Bergeron: (deceased in his late 20s) Grandson of two of the summoners killed by Rhyzkahl in the Bloodbath Summoning of Szerain. Attempted to use Kara as the sacrificial focus for an ill-conceived attempt to make a permanent gateway from Earth to the demon realm.

Tsuneo Oshiro: (late 20s) Associated with Katashi and the Mraztur. Bears a tattoo of demonic lord Jesral's sigil. Associated with the Mraztur. Whereabouts unknown.

William Slavin: (50s) Associated with Katashi and the Mraztur. Whereabouts unknown.

Other Non-Summoner Humans

Aja Patel: Physician at the Federal Command Center. In charge of the Chrysalis Project.

Amaryllis Castlebrook: Targeted for abduction by Farouche. Kara took her place to infiltrate the Farouche plantation.

Amber Palatino Gavin: Ritually raped, tortured, and murdered by Asher, Katashi, and Steiner as a control measure for her brother Idris, and to set a trap for Kara. Body left in an eighteen wheeler in Beaulac.

Angus McDunn: (mid 50s) Broad-shouldered, big and stocky. Red and grey hair. Was J.M. Farouche's right hand man. Husband of Catherine McDunn and stepfather to Boudreaux. Lost a young son over twenty years ago to abduction and murder.

Aria Farouche: Amicably divorced J.M. Farouche after their five-year-old daughter Madelaine was abducted and Farouche became obsessed with finding her.

Ashava: (2 months old) Daughter of Jill Faciane and the demankh Zakaar (Zack Garner). Kidnapped by Szerain and Zack. In hiding from Xharbek.

Carl: (mid 40s) Ex-morgue tech. Quiet and unflappable with an unspeakably dry sense of humor. Tessa's ex-boyfriend. Actually the demahnk Xharbek.

Catherine McDunn: (early 50s) Ex-head trainer for Farouche's thoroughbreds. Wife of Angus McDunn and mother of Detective Marcel Boudreaux. Whereabouts unknown. Suspected to be with Angus.

Cory Crawford: (early 40s) Sergeant with Beaulac PD. Dyed brown hair and moustache, brown eyes, stout. Chooses drab brown clothing and wild-colored ties. Good leader. On medical leave due to losing his right leg while trying to clear jail cells during the PD valve explosion.

Clint Gallagher: FBI Agent on the Arcane Investigations task force.

David Hawkins: Owner of the Grounds for Arrest coffee shop across the street from the Beaulac PD.

Earl Chris: (late 40s) Beaulac repeat offender with a propensity for violence. Was in the jail during the PD valve explosion.

Elinor Bayliss: 17th century summoner. Trained in the demon realm with Mzatal, Rhyzkahl, and Szerain. Killed by Szerain during a ritual that precipitated the Cataclysm. A part of her essence is attached to Kara's. Giovanni's lover.

Giovanni Racchelli: 17th century associate and art student of Szerain. Named by Gestamar as one of Szerain's favorite humans. Elinor's lover. Died young. a.k.a. Little Snake.

James Macklin Farouche: (deceased late 50s) Businessman, philanthropist, and vigilante-gone-wrong. Became obsessed with finding missing children and punishing those responsible after his five-year-old daughter was abducted nearly twenty years ago. Involved with Rhyzkahl and human trafficking. Arcane talent of influencing people. Executed by Bryce Thatcher.

Jerry Steiner: (deceased, late 30s) Hitman who enjoys his work. Very nondescript appearance. Easily blends in. Rapist and sociopath. Was one of the men who participated in the rape, torture, and murder of Amber Palatino Gavin.

Jonathan Lanza (Doc): (mid 40s) St. Long Parish pathologist. Easy-going manner.

Jade: Rasha's granddaughter. Abandoned Rasha to be with Aaron Asher.

Leo Carter: (mid 50s) Black. Close-cropped hair. Farouche's head of security. Trained sniper—preferred weapon a Bergara tactical rifle with a Schmidt and Bender scope.

Lenny Brewster: (late 60s) Hale, sharp-minded, and soft-spoken. Lanky black man. Barn manager for Farouche's thoroughbred farm.

Lida Moran: (deceased, 19) Was the lead singer and guitar player for Ether Madhouse. Ruthless. Sister of Michael Moran. Coerced him into murdering people. Killed by Eilahn.

Marcel Boudreaux: (early 30s) Head of DIRT 1st Cavalry Unit. Ex-Beaulac PD detective, partnered with Vince Pellini. Former jockey for J.M Farouche. Has a house on Farouche's thoroughbred farm. Keeps that life separate from his law enforcement career. Antagonistic toward Kara. Small and wiry. Chain smoker. Nickname of "Boo" to those in the horse world.

Marco Knight: (mid 30s) Detective for the New Orleans PD. Clairvoyant or similarly gifted. Loner. Smoker.

Michael Moran: (early 20s) Brain damaged in an accident. Brilliant pianist. Has the ability to form golems out of dirt. Taken to the demon realm by Rhyzkahl and given to Amkir. Paid for in blood and pain by Seretis, and lives in the realm of Seretis and Rayst. Can sometimes clairvoyantly see the lords' locations.

Michelle Cleland: (24) Physics major turned drug addict and prostitute on Earth. Taken to the demon realm by Rhyzkahl after the Symbol Man ritual. Empath. Flourished with Vahl as she came to understand her gift. Willing courtesan of the lords. Beloved of Elofir and resides in his realm.

Paul Ortiz: (22) Computer genius. Former captive employee of J.M. Farouche. Uses potency flows in tandem with computer networks to find information and accomplish hacker tasks. Beaten nearly to death by his cop dad because of his sexual orientation. Hispanic. Like a brother to Bryce. Critically injured by Mzatal. Resides in the demon realm with Kadir.

Pete Nelson: Bryce Taggart's vet school housemate. Accidentally shot and killed by Bryce.

Rob O'Connor: (mid 30s) Detective for St. Long Sheriff's Department. Arrested Kara as a suspect in the murder of J.M. Farouche.

Richard Knox: Federal agent. Federal Command Center.

Robert Turnham: (50s) Beaulac Chief of Police. Tall, slender, black man. Meticulous, quiet, efficient. 25 years law enforcement experience.

Rupert Olson: (early 60s) Senator with an education agenda.

Scott Glassman: (late 30s) Corporal of DIRT Alpha Squad. Ex-Sergeant and patrol training officer for Beaulac PD. Acts like a hick, but savvy. Stout, bald, ruddy complexion.

Sonny Hernandez a.k.a. Jose Luis Hernandez: (mid 30s) Former coerced hitman and kidnapper for J.M. Farouche. Has an enhanced talent for calming people. Caretaker for Zakaar after the bond with Rhyzkahl was broken. In hiding from Xharbek.

Tim Daniels: (mid 20s) Beaulac PD Officer. Open, friendly, and helpful. Found a stray cat that Eilahn adopted as Fuzzykins. Remained on the force after the PD explosion.

Tommy Lochlan: (9) Kidnapped Beaulac 3rd-grader.

Earth Pets and Animals

Griz: Caucasian Shepherd Dog. Two hundred pound demon-killing dog of DIRT's First Cavalry Unit.

Copper to Gold a.k.a. Psycho: Thoroughbred stallion on J.M. Farouche's horse farm. Stellar career ended by a track accident with Boudreaux aboard.

Fuzzykins: Eilahn's calico manx cat. Mother of Bumper, Squig, Granger, Fillion, Dire, Cake.

Sammy: Pellini's chocolate Labrador retriever. Goofy and lovable.

The Kittens a.k.a. catlets: Approximately 3 months old. Female: Squig, Granger, and Dire. Male: Bumper, Fillion, and Cake.

Demon Types-Summonable
Demons named in the books are in italics..

Faas (faahz) 6th Level. Resembles a six-legged furry lizard with a body approximately three feet long and a sinuous tail at least twice that length. Bright blue jewel-colored iridescent fur, brilliant golden eyes slitted like a reptile's. *Jekki, Faruk, Zhergalet, Rega.*

Graa (grah-ah) 8th Level. Spider-like with wings like roaches and heads like crabs. Can have anywhere from four to eight multi-jointed legs that end in strange hands that consist of a thumb and two fingers, each tipped with curved claws.

Ilius (ILL-ee-us) 3rd Level. A coil of smoke and teeth and shifting colors. Feeds on animal essence. *Tata, Wuki, Dakdak, Krum.*

Kehza (KAY-za) 7th Level. Human-sized, winged, face like a Chinese dragon, skin of iridescent red and purple, and plenty of sharp teeth and claws. Can tell if a human has the ability to be a summoner. *Juke.*

Luhrek (LURE-eck) 4th Level. Resembling a cross between a goat and a dog with the hindquarters of a lion. Often a good source for unusual or esoteric information. *Rhysel.*

Mehnta (MEN-tah) 9th Level. Appearing like a human female with long flowing hair, segmented wings like a beetles, clawed hands and feet, and dozens of snake-like strands coming out of their mouths. *Lazul.*

Nyssor (NIGH-sore) 5th Level. Looks almost exactly like a human child, often beautiful with angelic faces. Features a little *too* perfect, and eyes a little too large and having sideways-slit pupils. Hundreds of sharp teeth. Many humans find them creepy as fuck. *Votevha.*

Reyza (RAY-za) 12th Level. Three meters tall, leathery wings, long sinuous tail, skin the color of burnished copper, horns, clawed hands, bestial face, and curved fangs. *Kehlirik, Gestamar, Juntihr, Pyrenth, Safar, Sehkeril.*

Savik (SAH-vick) 2nd Level. Immature savik: two foot long dog-lizard kind of thing with six legs. Mature savik: Over seven feet tall, reptilian with dark and smooth bellies, and translucent glittery scales elsewhere. Head like a cross between and wolf and a crocodile. *Turek.*

Syraza (sih-RAH-za) 11th Level. Slender, almost birdlike, long and graceful limbs. Pearlescent white skin, hairless. Large and slanted violet eyes in a delicate, almost human, face. Wings that look as fragile as tissue paper but most assuredly are not. Shapeshifter. *Eilahn, Steeev, Olihr, Marr.*

Zhurn (zurn) 10th Level. Black, oily, shifting darkness. Winged. Burning red eyes. Voice like a blast furnace. Sharp claws. *Skalz.*

Zrila (zRIL-uh) 1st Level. About the size of a bobcat, looks like a six-legged newt with skin that shifts in hues of red and blue. Head like a hairless koala. Brilliant artisans who make the majority of the clothing and textiles in the demon realm. *Anak.*

Demon Types–Not Summonable

Hriss (h'RIS, huh-RIS) Pixie-like essence eaters. "Mosquitos from hell."

Kzak (k'ZAK, kuh-ZAK) Vicious, black, and dog-like. Rows of teeth and sinuous movement. *Kuktok.*

Luhnk (lunk) Mammoth-like. Six-legged. Huge females. German shepherd-sized males.

Nehkil (neh-KILL) Akin to a flying basking shark or living dirigible. Feeds on stray potency in the form of "ethereal spores."

Skarl (SCAR-ul) Hyena-like in form, but friendly as a socialized house cat. Musky. Gives off a comforting vibe when sleeping in a pack.

Named Demons
and associated demonic lord

Anak *zrila*: Mzatal. Textile artisan. Made one of Mzatal's neckties.

Bikturk *reyza*: No lord. Jontari. Nicknamed "Big Turd" by Kara.

Cheytok *faas*: Seretis.

Dakdak *ilius*: Mzatal. Never far from Mzatal in his palace. Dubbed as a "Mzatal Early Warning System" by Idris because he often arrives in a room shortly before the lord.

Dekkak *reyza*: No lord. Jontari. Warlord and imperator. More then three thousand years old.

Eilahn *syraza*: Rhyzkahl. Multiethnic beautiful in human form. Assigned by Rhyzkahl as bodyguard for Kara. Takes her job seriously. Adores holiday decorations and her cat, Fuzzykins.

Faruk *faas*: Mzatal. Jekki's mate. Delights in styling hair. Maintains Mzatal's intricate braid.

Gestamar *reyza*: Mzatal (essence bound). One of the oldest reyza. Sense of humor and scary all at the same time.

Gurgaz *unique*: a.k.a. Slugthing. Jontari. Associated with Dekkak.

Jekki *faas*: Mzatal. Spry and energetic personal attendant of Mzatal. Loves to cook. Faruk's mate.

Juke *kehza*: Mzatal. Summoned by Kara to assess a human for summoning ability. Loves pistachios.

Kajjon *reyza*: Amkir.

Kehlirik *reyza*: Rhyzkahl. Often summoned by Kara. Skilled with wards. Loves popcorn and human books.

Krum *ilius*: Mzatal. Sometimes mistaken for Wuki.

Kuktok *kzak*: Kadir. One of Pellini's demon mentors. Status unknown.

Lazul *mehnta*: Mzatal. Keeper of Mzatal's grove.

Marr *syraza*: Seretis. First syraza Kara ever summoned.

Olihr *syraza*: Rhyzkahl. Struck down by an anomaly in Szerain's realm. Saved by Safar and Ilana.

Pyrenth *reyza*: Rhyzkahl. Killed by Kara using an essence blade.

Rysehl *luhrek*: Elofir. The demon Kara was trying to summon when Rhyzkahl came through instead.

Rega *faas*: Rhyzkahl. One of Rhyzkahl's personal attendants.

Rodian *reyza*: Jesral.

Safar *reyza*: Mzatal. Escorted Kara in Szerain's realm when she first arrived. Crashed into the grove while carrying her.

Sehkeril *reyza*: Kadir. A lanky demon with a cruel streak. Eviscerated Kara during the Symbol Man's final ritual. One of Pellini's demon mentors.

Skalz *zhurn*: Vahl. Prefers to communicate telepathically.

Steeev *syraza*: Mzatal. Recruited by Kara as a bodyguard during Jill's pregnancy. Killed (on Earth) by J.M. Farouche's sniper. In stasis in the demon realm.

Tata *ilius*: Mzatal. That other ilius.

Turek *savik*: Szerain (essence bound). Ancient demon. Has known Szerain for thousands of years.

Votevha *nyssor*: Unknown. Summoned by Kara to assess a human for summoning ability. Likes bacon. Creepy.

Wuki *ilius*: Mzatal. Sometimes mistaken for Krum.

Yulz *reyza*: No lord. Jontari warlord associated with Dekkak.

Zhergalet *faas*: Vrizaar. Expert with wards.

Demon Words

Chak (like chalk without the L) Hot beverage without an Earth equivalent.

Chekkunden (cheh-KUN-din) Derogatory. Rough translation: *honorless scum.*

Chikdah (CHICK-daa) Derogatory. Rough translation: *cunt.*

Dahn (dahn) No.

Ekiri (ih-KEER-ee) Race that lived amongst the demons long ago, but departed for a new realm thousands of years past. Taught the demons mastery of the arcane. Built stone pavilions the demons call "gateways."

Iliok (ILL-ee-ock) The three essence blades. Created by Mzatal.

Jhivral (j'HIV-rall) A true plea. Not the casually polite usage of "please" in English.

Jontari (zjon-TAR-ee, jon-TAR-ee) Demons who do not associate directly with the demonic lords. The vast majority of the demon population. Cities and enclaves are far from the palaces of the lords.

Kibit (KIH-bit) Little snake.

Kiraknikahl (keh-RAK-nee-call) Oathbreaker.

Kri (kree) Yes.

Ptarl (puhTAR-ul) Demahnk advisor and counselor to a qaztahl. Bound by ancient oaths.

Pygah (PIE-gah) An arcane sigil used for calm, focus, and centering. A foundational teaching for summoners (though Kara was not taught it until she met Mzatal). Most effective when traced as a floating sigil, but may be done mentally.

Qazlek: (KAHZ-lehk) Demons who closely associate with the lords. Despised by the Jontari.

Qaztahl (KAHZ-tall) A demonic lord or the demonic lords as a group.

Qaztehl (KAHZ-tell) An unfettered, unmanipulated demonic lord. Ashava is the only one.

Rakkuhr (rah-KOOR) A red potency said to be alien to the demon realm. Rhyzkahl, Jesral, and Szerain are known to use it. Mzatal and Kadir despise it.

Saarn (sarn) A human or other creature who feeds on essence. Does not apply to species like the ilius or hriss whose natural food is essence.

Shik-natahr (SHICK-nahTAR) Rough translation: *born of the eleven*. An honoring designation. Spoken to Kara by Kadir.

Shikvihr (SHICK-veer) Rough translation: *potency of the eleven.* An eleven-circle ritual that offers a power base to other rituals and enhances a summoner or lord's abilities. Completion of all eleven circles/rings gives a summoner the ability to trace floating sigils on Earth.

Syraza (sih-RAH-za) Shapechanger.

Tah sesekur dih lahn (tah seh-seh-KUR dee lon) Rough translation: *I understand and feel for/with you.*

Vdat koh akiri qaztehl (v-DOT ko ah-KEER-ee KAHZ-tell) *Infinite resources to the all-powerful demonic lord unfettered.* Words spoken by Szerain when he completed the twelfth sigil on Kara's lower back.

Yaghir tahn (YAH-gear tahn) Forgive me.

Zharkat (ZAR-cat) Beloved.